QUEEN OF FIRE

Ace Books by Anthony Ryan

BLOOD SONG
TOWER LORD
QUEEN OF FIRE

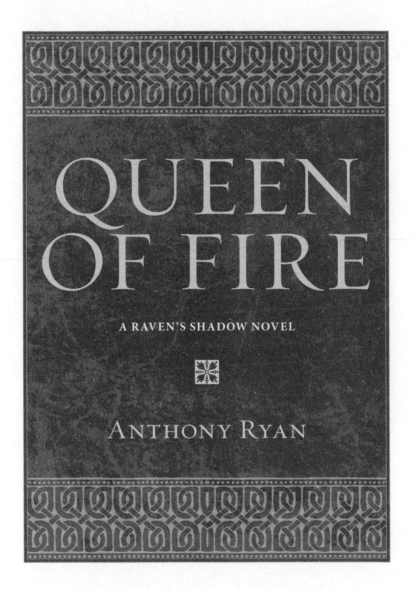

QUEEN OF FIRE

A RAVEN'S SHADOW NOVEL

ANTHONY RYAN

ACE BOOKS, NEW YORK

ACE

An imprint of Penguin Random House LLC
375 Hudson Street, New York, New York 10014

This book is an original publication of Penguin Random House LLC.

Library of Congress Cataloging-in-Publication Data

Ryan, Anthony.
Queen of fire / Anthony Ryan. — First edition.
pages ; cm. — (A raven's shadow novel ; 3)
ISBN 978-0-425-26564-2 (hardcover)
I. Title.
PR6118.Y3523Q44 2015
823'.92—dc23
2015002910

FIRST EDITION: July 2015

PRINTED IN THE UNITED STATES OF AMERICA

10 9 8 7 6 5 4 3 2 1

Cover illustration © Cliff Nielsen.
Cover photographs: abstract red background © Gile68/Shutterstock; red wine splash © Yeryomina Anastassiya / Shutterstock; fire frame © Mikhail Bakunovich / Shutterstock; flame © Mikhail Bakunovich / Shutterstock; metal texture © Waj/Shutterstock; sword © Olemac/Shutterstock.
Cover design by Judith Lagerman.
Interior text design by Tiffany Estreicher.
Main map by Steve Karp, based on an original by Anthony Ryan.
The Realm and the Empires map, Asrael and Cumbrael map, and the Northern Empire map by Anthony Ryan.

Penguin
Random
House

For Rod, Helen, Amber and Kyle

ACKNOWLEDGMENTS

Once again many thanks to my excellent editor at Ace, Susan Allison, who started this ball rolling three years ago with an e-mail to some guy in the UK who'd sold a few copies of his self-published fantasy book. Also, deep appreciation to my UK editor, James Long, for his support and commitment to this project. And finally, heartfelt thanks to my long-suffering second set of eyes, Paul Field.

PART I

The raven knows no rest
His shadow ceaseless
Upon the earth.

—SEORDAH POEM, AUTHOR UNKNOWN

Verniers' Account

He was waiting on the wharf when I arrived with my prisoner in tow. Standing tall as always, angular features turned towards the horizon, his cloak wrapped tight against the seaward chill. My initial puzzlement at finding him here faded as I caught sight of the ship leaving the harbour, a narrow-hulled vessel of Meldenean design, sent to the Northern Reaches with an important passenger, one I knew he would miss greatly.

He turned to regard my approach, a tight, wary smile on his lips, and I realised he had lingered to witness my own departure. Our interactions since the relief of Alltor had been brief, somewhat terse in truth, distracted as he was by the ceaseless tumult of war and whatever malady had plagued him in the aftermath of his already legendary charge. The fatigue that turned his once-strong features into a sagging mask of red-eyed lethargy and his strident if coarse voice into a droning rasp. It had faded now, I could see. Recent battle seemed to have restored him somehow, making me wonder if he found some form of sustenance in blood and horror.

"My lord," he greeted me with a sketch of a formal bow then nodded at my prisoner. "My lady."

Fornella returned the nod but gave no response, regarding him without expression as the salt-tinged wind tossed her hair, a single streak of grey visible amidst the reddish brown tumult.

"I have already received ample instruction . . ." I began but Al Sorna waved a hand.

"I come to offer no instruction, my lord," he said. "Merely a farewell and my best wishes for your endeavour."

I watched his expression as he waited for a response, the wary smile smaller now, his black eyes guarded. Can it be? I wondered. Is he seeking forgiveness?

"Thank you, my lord," I replied, hefting the heavy canvas bag to my shoulder. "But we have a ship to board before the morning tide."

"*Of course. I'll accompany you.*"

"*We don't need a guard,*" Fornella said, her tone harsh. "*I've given my word, tested by your truth-teller.*" It was true, we walked alone this morning without escort or formality. The reborn court of the Unified Realm had little time or inclination for ceremony.

"*Indeed, Honoured Citizen,*" Al Sorna replied in clumsy and heavily accented Volarian. "*But I have . . . words for this grey-clad.*"

"*Free man,*" I corrected before switching to Realm Tongue. "*Grey-clad denotes financial rather than social status.*"

"*Ah, quite so, my lord.*" He stepped aside and gestured for me to continue along the wharf to the quay where the ships waited, a long line of Meldenean war galleys and traders. Naturally, our vessel was moored at the farthest end of the line.

"*Brother Harlick's gift?*" he enquired, nodding at the bag I carried.

"*Yes,*" I said. "*Fifteen of the oldest books in the Great Library, those I could identify as useful in the small time allowed in his archives.*" In truth I had expected some argument from the brother librarian when I made my request, but the man had simply given an affable nod and barked an imperious order at one of his attendants to gather the requisite scrolls from the wagons that served as his movable library. I knew his apparent indifference to this theft was at least partly derived from his gift; he could always simply pen fresh copies, and openly since the need to keep such things hidden had disappeared. The Dark, as they called it, now revealed and discussed openly, the Gifted free to practice their talents without fear of swift torment and execution, at least in theory. I could see the lingering fear on the faces of those not so talented, and the envy, making me wonder if perhaps the wisest course would have been to keep the Gifted in the shadows. But could shadows ever linger in the fires of war?

"*You really think he's in there somewhere?*" Al Sorna asked as we walked towards the ship. "*The Ally?*"

"*An influence so malign and powerful is bound to leave traces,*" I said. "*A historian is a hunter, my lord. Seeking out signs in the undergrowth of correspondence and memoir, tracking prey via the spoor of memory. I don't expect to find a complete and unbiased history of this thing, be it beast or man or neither. But it will have left traces, and I intend to hunt it down.*"

"*Then you should have a care, for I suspect it will not be blind to your attentions.*"

"*Nor yours.*" I paused, glancing at his profile, seeing a troubled brow. *Where is your certainty?* I thought. It had been one of his most aggravating traits during our previous association; the implacable, unshakeable surety. Now there was just a grim and troubled man weighed down by the prospect of trials to come.

"Taking the capital will not be easy," I said. "The wisest course would be to wait here, gathering strength until the spring."

"Wisdom and war are rare bedfellows, my lord. And you're right, the Ally will most likely see it all."

"Then why . . . ?"

"We cannot simply linger here and wait for the next blow to fall. Any more than your Emperor can expect to remain immune from the Ally's attentions."

"I am fully aware of what message to deliver to the Emperor." The leather satchel bearing the sealed scroll was heavy about my neck, heavier even than my bag of books, though only a fraction of its weight. Just ink, paper and wax, I thought. Yet it could send millions to war.

We halted as we came to the ship, a broad-beamed Meldenean trader, her planking still scorched from the Battle of the Teeth, rails bearing the scars of blades and arrowheads, patches on the sails furled to the rigging. My eyes were also drawn to the serpentine figurehead which, despite having lost much of its lower jaw, retained a certain familiarity. My gaze found the captain at the head of the gangplank, thick arms crossed, his face set in a glower, a face I recalled all too well.

"Did you, perhaps, have a hand in choosing this vessel, my lord?" I asked Al Sorna.

There was a faint glimmer of amusement in his gaze as he shrugged. "Merely a coincidence, I assure you."

I sighed, finding I had scant room in my heart for yet more resentment, turning to Fornella and extending a hand to the ship. "Honoured Citizen. I'll join you in a moment."

I saw Al Sorna's eyes track her as she walked the plank to the ship, moving with her customary grace born of centuries-long practice. "Despite what the truth-teller said," he told me, "I caution you, don't trust her."

"I was her slave long enough to learn that lesson myself." I hefted my bag once again and nodded a farewell. "By your leave, my lord. I look forward to hearing the tale of your campaign . . ."

"You were right," he broke in, his wary smile returned once more. "The story I told you. There were some . . . omissions."

"I think you mean lies."

"Yes." His smile faded. "But I believe you have earned the truth. I have scant notion of how this war will end, or even if either of us will live to see its end. But if we do, find me again and I promise you'll have nothing but truth from me."

I should have been grateful, I know. For what scholar does not hunger for truth from one such as he? But there was no gratitude as I looked into his gaze, no thought save a name. Seliesen.

"I used to wonder," I said, "how a man who had taken so many lives could walk the earth unburdened by guilt. How does a killer bear the weight of killing and still call himself human? But we are both killers now, and I find it burdens my soul not at all. But then, I killed an evil man, and you a good one."

I turned away and strode up the gangplank without a backward glance.

CHAPTER ONE

Lyrna

She was woken by the snow. Soft, icy caresses on her skin, tingling and not unpleasant, calling her from the darkness. It took a moment for memory to return and when it did she found it a fractured thing, fear and confusion reigning amidst a welter of image and sensation. *Iltis roaring as he charged, sword bared . . . The ring of steel . . . A hard fist across her mouth . . . And the man . . . The man who burned her.*

She opened her mouth to scream but could issue no more than a whimper, her subsequent gasp dragging chilled air into her lungs. It seemed as if she would freeze from the inside out and she felt it strange she should die from cold after being burned so fiercely.

Iltis! The name was a sudden shout in her mind. *Iltis is wounded! Perhaps dead!*

She willed herself to move, to get up, call for a healer with all the power her queen's voice could muster. Instead she barely managed to groan and flutter her hands a little as the snow continued its frosty caress. Rage burned in her, banishing the chill from her lungs. *I need to move! I will not die in the snow like a forgotten dog!* Drawing jagged air into her lungs again she screamed, putting every ounce of strength and rage into the sound. A fierce scream, a queen's scream . . . but no more than a rattle of air through teeth when it reached her ears, along with something else.

". . . better be a good reason for this, Sergeant," a hard voice was saying, strong, clipped and precise. A soldier's voice, accompanied by the crunch of boots in snow.

"Tower Lord said he was to be minded well, Captain," another voice, coloured by a Nilsaelin accent, older and not quite so strong. "Treated with respect, he said. Like the other folk from the Point. And he seems fairly insistent, much as I can gather from a fellow that don't talk above two words at a time."

"Folk from the Point," the captain said in a softer tone. "To whom we have to thank for a snowfall at summer's end . . ." His voice faded and the crunch of boots became the tumult of running men.

"Highness!" Hands on her shoulders, soft but insistent. "Highness! Are you hurt? Do you hear me?"

Lyrna could only groan, feeling her hands flutter once more.

"Captain Adal," the sergeant's voice, choked and broken by fear. "Her face . . ."

"I have eyes, Sergeant! Fetch the Tower Lord to Brother Kehlan's tent! And bring men to carry his lordship. Say nothing of the queen. You understand me?"

More boots on the snow then she felt something warm and soft cover her from head to foot, her benumbed back and legs tingling as hands lifted her. She fell into darkness, untroubled by the jolting run of the captain as he bore her away.

◆ ◆ ◆

He was there when she awoke the second time, her eyes tracking over a canvas roof to find him sitting beside the cot where they had placed her. Although his eyes were tinged with the same red haze she had seen the day before, his gaze was brighter now, focused, the black eyes seeming to bore into the skin of her face as he leaned forward. *He burned me . . .* She closed her eyes and turned away from him, stilling the sob in her chest, swallowing and composing herself before she turned back, finding him kneeling beside the cot, head lowered.

"Highness," he said.

She swallowed and tried to speak, expecting only a faint croak to emerge but surprising herself with a somewhat strident response. "My lord Al Sorna. I trust the morning finds you well."

His head came up, the expression sharp, the black eyes still fierce. She wanted to tell him it was rude to stare, at a queen no less, but knew it would sound churlish. *Every word must be chosen,* her father had said once. *Each word spoken by the one who wears the crown will be remembered, often misremembered. So, my daughter, if ever you find this band of gold weighing upon your brow, never utter a single word that should not be heard from the mouth of a queen.*

"Quite . . . well, Highness," Vaelin responded, remaining on one knee as she stirred herself. To her surprise she found she could move easily. Someone had removed the dress and cloak she wore the night before, replacing the finery with a simple cotton shift that covered her from neck to ankle, the fabric pleasing on her skin as she sat and swung her legs off the cot to sit up. "Please rise," she told Vaelin. "I find ceremony tedious at the best of times, and of scant use when we're alone."

He stood, eyes never leaving her face. There was a hesitancy to his movements, a slight tremble to his hands as he reached for his chair, pulling it closer to sit opposite her, his face no more than an arm's length away, the closest they had been since that day at the Summertide Fair.

"Lord Iltis?" she asked.

"Wounded but alive," he said. "Also frostbitten in the small finger of his left hand. Brother Kehlan was obliged to take it off. He barely seemed to notice and it was quite the struggle to stop him charging forth to look for you."

"I was fortunate in the friends fate contrived to place in my path." She paused, drawing breath and courage for what she had to say next. "We had little chance to talk yesterday. I know you must have many questions."

"One in particular. There are many wild tales abroad regarding your . . . injuries. They say it happened when Malcius died."

"Malcius was murdered, by Brother Frentis of the Sixth Order. I killed him for it."

She saw the shock hit home as if she had slashed him with an ice-cold blade. His gaze became distant as he slumped forward, speaking in a whisper. "Wanna be a brother . . . Wanna be like you."

"There was a woman with him," Lyrna went on. "Like your brother, playing the role of an escaped slave, come all the way across the ocean with a grand tale of adventure. From her reaction when I killed him, I suspect their bond was close. Love can drive us to extremes."

He closed his eyes, controlling his grief with a shudder. "Killing him would not have been easy."

"My time with the Lonak left me skilled in certain areas. I saw him fall. After that . . ." *The fire raked across her skin like the claws of a wildcat, filling her throat with the stench of her own flesh burning . . .* "It seems my memory has some limits after all."

Vaelin sat in silence for what seemed an age, lost in thought, his face even more gaunt than before. "It told me he was coming back," he murmured finally. "But not for this."

"I had expected you to request a different explanation," she said, keen to draw him back from whatever memories clouded his mind. "For the way you were treated at Linesh."

"No, Highness." He shook his head. "I assure you I require no explanation at all."

"The war was a grievous error. They had Malcius . . . My father's judgement was . . . impaired."

"I doubt King Janus's judgement was capable of impairment, Highness. And as for the war, you did try to warn me, as I recall."

She nodded, pausing to quiet her racing heart. *I was so sure he would hate me.* "That man . . ." she said. "The man with the rope."

"His name is Weaver, Highness."

"Weaver," she repeated. "I assume he was an agent of whatever malignancy is behind our current difficulties. Hidden in your army, awaiting the time to strike."

Vaelin moved back a little, puzzlement replacing his grief. "Strike, Highness?"

"He saved me," she said. "From that *thing*. Then he burned me. I confess I find it curious. Though I'm learning these creatures have very strange ways." She faltered over a catch in her throat, recalling the fire that raged as the muscular young man pulled her close, the heat of it more intense even than that dreadful day in the throne room. She raised her head, forcing herself to meet his unwavering gaze. "Is it . . . Is it worse?"

A faint sigh escaped him and he reached across the divide to grasp her hands, rough callused palms against hers. She had expected some comforting clasp before he voiced the inevitable and terrible news, but instead he gripped her wrists and raised her hands, spreading the fingers to touch them to her face.

"Don't!" she said, trying to jerk away.

"Trust me, Lyrna," he breathed, pressing her fingers to the flesh . . . the smooth, undamaged flesh. Her fingers began to explore of their own volition as he took his hands away, touching every inch of skin, from her brow to her chin, her neck. *Where is it?* she thought wildly, finding no rough, mottled scarring, provoking none of the searing pain that had continued to plague her despite the healing balms her ladies applied to the burns every day. *Where is my face?*

"I knew Weaver had a great gift," Vaelin said. "But this . . ."

Lyrna sat clutching her face, caging the sobs in her breast. *Every word must be chosen.* "I . . ." she began, faltered then tried again. "I should . . . like you to convene a council of captains as soon . . . as soon as . . ."

Then there was only the tears and the feel of his arms around her shoulders as she rested her head on his chest and wept like a child.

◆ ◆ ◆

The woman in the mirror ran a hand over the pale stubble covering her head, a frown creasing her smooth brow. *It'll grow back,* she knew. *Maybe not keep it so long this time.* Lyrna turned her attention to the skin where the burns had been most severe, finding the healing hadn't left her completely unmarked after all. There were faint pale lines visible in the flesh around her eyes, thin and irregular tracks from her brow into her hairline. She recalled something the Mahlessa's poor, confused vessel had said that day beneath the mountain. *Not there yet . . . The marks of your greatness.*

Lyrna stood back from the mirror a little, angling her head to study how the marks looked in the light from the tent opening, finding they faded somewhat in direct sunlight. Something shifted in the mirror and she noticed Iltis over her shoulder, quickly averting his gaze, clutching the bandaged hand that protruded from the sleeve of his sling. He had shambled into the tent an hour ago, pushing Benten aside and collapsing to his knees before her. He had been stumbling through a plea for forgiveness when he glanced up and saw her face, falling to instant silence.

"You should be abed, my lord," she told him.

"I . . ." Iltis had blinked, tears shining in his eyes. "I will never leave your side, Highness. I gave my word."

Am I his new Faith? she wondered now, watching him in the mirror as he swayed a little, shaking his head and stiffening his back. *The old one proved a disappointment, so now he finds devotion in me.*

The tent opening parted and Vaelin entered with a bow. "The army stands ready, Highness."

"Thank you, my lord." She held out a hand to Orena, who stood holding the hooded fox-trimmed cloak she had chosen from the mountain of clothing Lady Reva had been overly pleased to provide. Orena came forward and draped the cloak over her shoulders whilst Murel knelt to proffer the impractical but elegant shoes for her royal feet. "Well," she said, stepping into the shoes and pulling the hood over her face. "Let's be about it."

Vaelin had placed a tall uncovered wagon outside the tent, moving to it and holding out a hand as she approached. She clasped the hand and climbed onto the wagon, the cloak bunched in her free hand so as to prevent her tripping over it. The prospect of falling flat on her face at such a moment provoked a girlish giggle, suppressed before it could reach her lips. *Every word must be chosen.*

She kept hold of Vaelin's hand as she stood surveying her new army. The plump brother from the Reaches had informed her, between stealing wide-eyed glances at her face, that the current complement of the Army of the North consisted of sixty thousand men and women, plus somewhere in the region of thirty thousand Seordah and Eorhil warriors. The regiments were arrayed in ranks, mostly untidy and lacking the polished cohesion displayed by the Realm Guard during those interminable parades in Varinshold. In truth the few Realm Guard present made a distinct contrast to their comrades, a tight, disciplined knot of denuded companies arrayed behind Brother Caenis in the centre of the line. But the majority of her new army consisted of Count Marven's Nilsaelins, the conscripts Vaelin had marched from the Reaches, and the recruits gathered along the way. She saw little uniformity in their ranks; mismatched armour and weapons, much of it looted from the copious Volarian dead, makeshift flags lacking the colour and clarity of the Realm Guard's regimental banners.

The Seordah had placed themselves on the right flank, a great throng of warriors standing in silence, curiosity the only apparent emotion. Behind them the Eorhil waited, most mounted on their fine tall horses, equally silent. Lady Reva had responded to Lyrna's polite request for attendance with the full complement of her House Guard, reduced to no more than thirty men, and seemingly all of her surviving archers. They stood in two long rows behind their Lady Governess, stocky hard-eyed men with longbows slung across their backs. Lady Reva herself was flanked by her Lady Counsellor, Lord Archer Antesh and the old bewhiskered guard commander, none of whom betrayed the slightest awe at Lyrna's presence. Off to the left, the Shield had brought the captains of the Meldenean Fleet, Ship Lord Ell-Nurin deliberately standing a few feet in front of the Shield, who stood with his arms crossed, inclining his head at her, habitual smile blazing as bright as ever. It was a pity, as she expected it to fade before long.

Behind them all the still-smoking city of Alltor rose from its island, the twin spires of the cathedral partly obscured by the dusty snow that continued to fall.

Lyrna paused atop the wagon, her eyes picking out the diminutive but distinct form of Lady Dahrena, standing in the front rank alongside Captain Adal and the North Guard. Unlike every other pair of eyes on this field, Lady

Dahrena's were fixed not on Lyrna, but Vaelin. Her gaze unblinking and unnerving in its intensity, making Lyrna conscious of the warmth of his hand in hers. She released it and faced the army, reaching up to draw back her hood.

It rippled through them like a cresting wave, a mingling of awed gasps, oaths, prayers, and outright shock, the already untidy ranks losing yet more cohesion as soldiers turned to their comrades in disbelief or amazement. However, she noted that the Seordah and the Eorhil remained silent, although their stance was now profoundly more alert. Lyrna allowed the army's babble to build into a cacophony before holding up her hand. For a moment it continued unabated and she worried she might have to ask Vaelin to quiet them, but Captain Adal barked a command to his men which was soon taken up by the officers and sergeants, silence descending on the ranks on swift wings.

Lyrna surveyed them, picking out faces, meeting their eyes, finding some unable to match her gaze, stirring in discomfort and lowering their heads, others staring back in blank astonishment.

"I have not yet had chance to address you," she called to them, her voice strong and carrying well in the cold air. "For those that may be ignorant of my name, my list of titles is long and I'll not bore you with it. Suffice to say that I am your queen, hailed as such by Tower Lord Al Sorna and Lady Governess Reva of Cumbrael. Many of you saw me yesterday, and you will have seen a woman with a burnt face. Now you see a woman healed. I make you this promise as your queen, I will never lie to you. And so I tell you honestly that my face was healed by use of the Dark. I claim no blessing from the Departed, no favour from any god. I stand before you restored by the hand of a man with a gift I do not pretend to understand. This was done without my bidding or contrivance. However, I see no cause to regret it or punish the man who did me this service. Many of you will no doubt be aware that there are others within the ranks of this army with similar abilities, good and brave people who, by the strictures of our laws, are condemned to death for the gifts bestowed upon them by nature alone. Accordingly, all laws prohibiting use of the gifts once known as the Dark are hereby rescinded under the Queen's Word."

She paused, expecting some upsurge of murmuring, some voices raised in discontent. Instead there was only silence, each and every face now rapt, those that had shunned her gaze seemingly unable to look away. *Something stirs here,* she realised. *Something . . . useful.*

"There are none here who have not suffered," she spoke on. "There are none here who cannot lay claim to a murdered wife, husband, child, friend, or parent. Many of you have tasted the whip, as I have. Many of you have suffered the mauling of filthy hands, as I have. Many of you have burned, as I have."

There was a growl building in the ranks now, a low rumble of stoked fury. She saw one woman in the middle of Captain Nortah's company of freed slaves, slight and small but festooned with multiple daggers, her teeth bared in a burgeoning grimace of rage. "This land was named in honour of its unity," Lyrna continued. "But only a fool would claim we have ever been truly united, always we have shed our own blood in senseless feud after senseless feud. As of now that ends. Our enemy came to these shores bringing slavery, torment, and death, but they also brought us a gift, one they'll regret for an eternity. They forged us into the unity that has eluded us for so long. They made us a single blade of unbreakable steel aimed straight for their black heart and with you at my side I'll see it bleed!"

The growl erupted into a fierce shout, faces distorted in hate and anger, fists, swords, and halberds raised, the tumult washing over her, intoxicating in its power . . . *Power. You have to hate it as much as you love it.*

She raised a hand and they fell quiet once more, though there remained the low hum of simmering heat. "I promise no easy victories," she told them. "Our enemy is fierce and full of cunning. They will not die easily. So I can promise only three things: toil, blood and justice. None who follow me on this path should imagine there will be any other reward."

It was the small woman with the daggers who began the chant, stabbing the air with a blade in each hand, head thrown back. "Toil, blood and justice!" It spread in an instant, the shout rising from one end of the army to the other. "Toil, blood and justice! Toil, blood and justice!"

"In five days we march for Varinshold!" Lyrna called as the chant continued, the pitch of its volume increasing yet further. She pointed towards the north. *Never be afraid of a little theatre,* the old schemer had said during one of the ceremonies where he handed out swords to ever-less-deserving recipients. *Royalty is always a performance, daughter.* The tumult doubled as she called again, her words lost in the rage-filled cheers. "TO VARINSHOLD!"

She stood for a few moments, arms spread wide in the centre of their adoring rage. *Did you ever have this, Father? Did they ever love you?*

The noise continued as she descended from the wagon, reaching for Vaelin's hand again, but pausing at the sight of the Shield. As expected his smile was gone, replaced by a sombre frown making her wonder if he still intended to follow her anywhere.

◆ ◆ ◆

"Varinshold lies over two hundred miles distant, Highness," Count Marven told her. "And we have barely enough grain to sustain the horses for fifty. Our Cumbraelin friends were most efficient in denuding this land of supplies."

"Better burnt than in the belly of our enemies," Lady Reva pointed out from across the table.

They were arrayed around a large map table in Vaelin's tent, all the principal captains of the army along with Lady Reva and the war chiefs from the Eorhil and Seordah. The Eorhil was a wiry rider somewhere past his fiftieth year by her reckoning. The Seordah was slightly younger, taller than most of his people, lean as a wolf with a hawk face. They seemed to understand every word spoken but said little themselves, and she noted how their gaze flitted constantly between her and Vaelin. *Is it suspicion?* she thought. *Or just wonder?*

Count Marven had spent the better part of an hour explaining their strategic situation. Never having had much use for the tedium of military history she was obliged to pick out the pertinent details from the morass of jargon. From what she could gather it seemed their position was not as favourable as a queen might expect after winning so great a victory.

"Quite so, my lady," the count told Reva. "But it does leave us perilously short of supplies, with winter only two months away into the bargain."

"Am I to understand, my lord," Lyrna said. "We have a mighty army but no means to move it anywhere?"

The count ran a hand over his shaven head, the stitched scar on his cheek seeming to glow a little more red as he sighed his frustration and sought to formulate the correct response.

"Yes," Vaelin told her from the opposite end of the table. "And it's not just a matter of moving it. If we don't find sufficient forage for the winter, this army could well starve."

"Surely we have captured Volarian supplies," Lyrna said.

"Indeed, Highness," plump Brother Hollun spoke up. Like most present he seemed to have difficulty in not staring at her face. "Twelve tons of grain, four of corn and six of beef."

"Without which my people will starve this winter," Lady Reva stated. "I've had to start rationing again already . . . Highness," she added, clearly still having trouble with etiquette.

Lyrna looked at the map, tracing the route to Varinshold, finding many towns and villages along the way but knowing most would now be little more than scorched ruins, devoid of any supplies. *Two hundred miles to Varinshold,* she mused, studying the map more closely. *Half that to the coast . . . and the sea.*

She looked up, finding the Shield standing outside the circle of captains towards the rear of the tent, his face half in shadow. "My lord Ell-Nestra," she said. "Your counsel please."

He came forward after a moment's hesitation, Fief Lord Dravus's twin grandsons making room for him with courteous bows he failed to acknowledge. "Highness," he said in a neutral tone.

"There are many ships in your fleet," she said. "Enough to carry an army to Varinshold?"

He shook his head. "Half the fleet was obliged to return to the Isles for repairs after the Teeth. We could perhaps carry a third of the number gathered here, and even then we would have to leave the horses behind."

"Varinshold won't fall to so few," Count Marven said. "Not if the Volarian woman is to be believed. They are well garrisoned and supplied from across the sea and from Renfael."

Lyrna switched her gaze to Varinshold. The capital and principal port of the entire realm, much of its wealth in fact drawn from trade with Volaria. She pointed to the sea-lanes off Varinshold and looked up at the Shield. "Ever take a ship in these waters, my lord?"

He considered the map for a moment then nodded. "A few. Not such easy pickings as in the southern trade routes. The King's fleet was always a watchful shepherd for Varinshold's trade."

"Now there is no fleet," Lyrna pointed out. "And the pickings are likely to be rich, are they not, given the enemy's losses at the Teeth?"

He nodded again. "Rich indeed, Highness."

"You gave me a ship yesterday. Today I give her back to you with a request you take your fleet and seize or burn any Volarian ship you find journeying to or from Varinshold. Will you do this for me?"

She felt the other captains stirring, hard gazes turning on the pirate. *Don't like to see a queen bargain,* she decided. *I'll speak to him in private in future.*

"My men may take some persuasion," he responded after a moment. "We sailed to defend the Isles. And that task is done."

Ship Lord Ell-Nurin stepped forward, bowing to her with accomplished grace. "I can't speak for the Shield's men, Highness. But my men are ready to follow you to Udonor's Halls if you ask. As I'm sure will many more. After the Battle of the Teeth and . . . your healing, many wouldn't dare refuse." He turned to the Shield with an expectant expression.

"As the Ship Lord says," the Shield grated after a moment. "How could we refuse?"

"Very well." Lyrna scanned the map once more. "Preparations must be complete within the week. Whereupon the army will march not north but east, to the coast. We will proceed to Varinshold via the coastal ports where our Meldenean allies will resupply us with whatever riches the Volarian Ruling Council deems fit to send its garrison. Also, ports mean fishing folk, who I'm sure will be glad of the custom."

"If there are any left," Reva said softly.

"I hereby make the following appointments," Lyrna went on, choosing to ignore the Lady Governess. "Please forgive the lack of ceremony but we have no time for such pettiness now. I name Lord Vaelin Al Sorna as Battle Lord of the Queen's Host. Count Marven is named Sword of the Realm and Adjutant General. Brother Hollun, I name you Keeper of the Queen's Purse. Captains Adal, Orven and Nortah are hereby made Swords of the Realm and elevated to the rank of Lord Marshal. Lord Atheran Ell-Nestra." She met the Shield's gaze once more. "I name you Fleet Lord of the Unified Realm and captain of its flagship." She cast her gaze around the assembly. "These appointments include all due rights and privileges set down by Realm Law with grants and lands to be allotted at the close of hostilities. I ask you formally, do you accept these honours?"

She noted Vaelin was the last to voice his assent, and then only after the Shield had taken a seeming age to bow in agreement, a ghost of his usual smile on his lips.

"Other business, Lords and good sirs?" she asked the Council.

"There is the matter of the prisoners, Highness," Lord Marshal Orven said. "Keeping them safe is proving a trial. Especially given the bow skills of our Cumbraelin hosts," he added with a glance in Reva's direction.

"They have been screened for useful intelligence, I assume?" Lyrna asked.

Harlick, the thin older brother, raised a bony hand. "That task was given to me, Highness. There are a few officers among them I've yet to question. Though, my experience to date indicates their usefulness is likely to be limited."

"They can work," Vaelin said, meeting her gaze with red-rimmed but steady eyes. "Rebuild what they destroyed."

"I can't have them in the city," Reva put in, shaking her head. "The people will tear them apart."

"Then we take them with us," Vaelin responded. "They can act as porters."

"And more mouths to feed," Lyrna said, turning to Brother Harlick. "Complete your questioning, brother. Lord Marshal Orven will hang them when you're done. My lords and sirs, to your duties if you please."

◆ ◆ ◆

She found him sitting by the river, seemingly no more than a well-built soldier plaiting rope with unusually nimble fingers. Vaelin had warned her not to expect much from him so it was a surprise when he scrambled to his feet as she approached, performing a bow of such perfection it would have shamed the most accomplished courtier.

"Cara said I should bow," he told her, his broad handsome face lit by an open smile. "Showed me how."

Lyrna glanced off to the right where the three other Gifted from the Reaches looked on. The girl, Cara, still pale and tired by her exertions the day before, regarded Lyrna with a suspicious frown, matched by the skinny young man who held her hand and the hulking fellow with copious hair who stood behind them both. *Do they think I come to punish?*

Benten put a hand on his sword as Weaver came closer, reaching out to touch her face. "It's all right, my lord," she told the former fisherman, standing still and allowing the healer's hand to play over her features. *It burned before, but now it's cold.*

"I came to offer my thanks, sir," she told Weaver. "I would name you a lord . . ."

"Your reward is already given," he said, withdrawing his hand. His face lost its smile, his brow creased with confusion as he tapped a finger to it. "Always the way, something comes back." His gaze widened a little as he stared into her eyes. "You gave more. More than any other."

Lyrna experienced a bout of the same near panic that had gripped her at the Mahlessa's mountain, the desire to run from something unknowable but undeniably dangerous. She exhaled slowly and forced herself to meet his gaze. "What did I give?"

He smiled again, turning away to sit once more, reaching for his rope. "Yourself," he said in a faint voice as his hands resumed their work.

"My Queen." She turned to find Iltis marching towards her, his face paler than she would have liked but he still refused to rest. Beyond him she could see Brother Caenis standing with four common folk, two young women from the city, a Nilsaelin soldier and one of Lord Nortah's free fighters. Lyrna saw the three Gifted from the Reaches stiffen at the sight of them, exchanging worried glances, the big one even hefting the quarterstaff he carried and stepping protectively in front of the girl.

"Lord Marshal Caenis requests a private audience, Highness," Iltis told her with a bow.

She nodded and beckoned Caenis forward, moving a short distance away from Weaver. She paused a moment to view the frozen waters of the Cold Iron, then glanced over at Cara, now glaring in naked animosity at Brother Caenis as he fell to one knee before her. *The power to freeze a river in summer, but she fears this man.*

"Highness, I crave your attention . . ."

"Yes, yes, brother." She waved him to his feet, gesturing at Cara and the other Gifted. "You seem to be making my subjects nervous."

Brother Caenis turned to the Gifted, grimacing a little. "They . . . fear what I have to tell you." He faced her, straightening his back. "My Queen, I come to offer the services of my Order in this conflict. We subject ourselves to your commands and shirk no duty in pursuit of victory."

"I have never doubted the loyalty of the Sixth Order, brother. Though I wish I had more of you . . ." Lyrna trailed off as she looked again at the group of common folk, seeing how they shifted under her scrutiny, every face tense and wary. "These folk do not strike me as likely recruits for the Sixth."

"No, Highness," he said and she had a sense of a man forcing himself to a long-feared duty. "We belong to another Order entirely."

CHAPTER TWO

Alucius

The Kuritai's name was Twenty-Seven, though Alucius had yet to hear him say it. In fact he had yet to hear the slave-elite say anything. He reacted to instruction with instant obedience and was the perfect servant, fetching, carrying and cleaning with no sign of fatigue or even the faintest expression of complaint.

"My gift to you," Lord Darnel had said that day they had dragged Alucius from the depths of the Blackhold, expecting death and gasping in astonishment when they removed his shackles and he found his own father's hands helping him to his feet. "A servant of peerless perfectitude," Darnel went on, gesturing at the Kuritai. "You know, I think I'm growing fond of your wordsmithing ways, little poet."

"Yes, I'm very well this fine morning," Alucius told Twenty-Seven as he laid out the breakfast. "How nice of you to ask."

They were on the veranda overlooking the harbour, the sun rising over the horizon to paint the ships a golden hue he knew would have sent Alornis scurrying to fetch her canvas and brushes. He had chosen the house for the view, a merchant's domicile no doubt, its owner presumably dead or enslaved along with his family. Varinshold was full of empty houses now, more to choose from should he grow tired of this one, but he found himself too fond of the view, especially as it covered the entirety of the harbour.

Fewer and fewer ships, he thought, counting the vessels with accustomed precision. *Ten slavers, five traders, four warships.* The slavers sat highest in the water, their copious holds empty, as they had been for weeks, ever since the great column of smoke had risen to blot the sun from the sky for days on end. Alucius had been trying to write something about it, but found the words failed to flow every time he put pen to paper. *How does one write a eulogy for a forest?*

Twenty-Seven placed the last plate on the table and stood back as Alucius reached for his cutlery, tasting the mushrooms first, finding them cooked to perfection with a little garlic and butter. "Excellent as always, my deadly friend."

Twenty-Seven stared out of the window and said nothing.

"Ah yes, it's visiting day," Alucius went on around a mouthful of bacon. "Thank you for reminding me. Pack the salve and the new books, if you would."

Twenty-Seven instantly turned away and went about his instructions, moving to the bookcase first. The house's owner had maintained a reasonable library, largely, Alucius assumed, for appearance's sake as few of the volumes showed much sign of having ever been read. They were mostly popular romances and a few of the more well-known histories, none suited to his purposes, which obliged him to spend hours ransacking the larger houses for more interesting material. There was much to choose from; the Volarians were boundlessly enthusiastic looters but had little interest in books, save as kindling. Yesterday had been particularly fruitful, netting a complete set of Marial's *Astronomical Observations* and an inscribed volume he hoped would arouse the interest of one of his charges in particular.

Ten slavers, five traders, four warships, he counted again, turning to the harbour. *Two less than yesterday . . .* He paused as another vessel came into view, a warship rounding the headland to the south. It seemed to be struggling to make headway through the water, only one sail raised and that, he saw as it came closer, was a ragged thing of soot-blackened canvas. The ship trailed sagging rope through the placid morning swell as it neared the harbour mouth, blocks and shattered beams hanging from her rigging, sparse crew moving about the deck with the stoop of exhausted men. As she weighed anchor Alucius's eyes picked out numerous scorch marks blackening her hull and many dark brown stains on her untidy deck.

Five warships, he corrected himself. *One with an interesting tale to tell, it seems.*

◆ ◆ ◆

They stopped off at the pigeon coop on the way, finding his sole remaining bird in typically hungry mood. "Don't bolt it," he cautioned Blue Feather with a wagging finger but she ignored him, head bobbing as she pecked at the seeds. The coop was situated atop the house of the Blocker's Guild, the roof spared the fires that had gutted the building thanks to its iron-beamed construction. The surrounding houses hadn't been so fortunate and the once-busy building where he had come to have his poems printed now rose from streets of rubble and ash. Seen from this vantage point the city resembled a grimy patchwork, islands of intact buildings in a sea of grey-black ruins.

"Sorry if you're finding it lonely these days," he told Blue Feather, stroking her fluffy breast. There had been ten of them to begin with, a year ago. Young birds each with a tiny wire clasp about their right leg, strong enough to hold a message.

This had been the first place he had hurried to on release from the Blackhold, finding only three birds still alive. He fed them and disposed of the corpses as Twenty-Seven looked on impassively. It had been a risk leading the slave here to witness his greatest secret, but there was little choice. In truth, he had expected the Kuritai to either cut him down on the spot or shackle him once more for immediate return to captivity. Instead he just stood and watched as Alucius scribbled the coded message on a tiny scrap of parchment before rolling it up and sliding it into the small metal cylinder that would fit onto the bird's leg clasp.

Varinshold fallen, he had written though he knew it was probably old news to the recipients. *Darnel rules. 500 knights & one V division.* Twenty-Seven didn't even turn to watch the bird fly away when Alucius cast it from the rooftop and the expected deathblow had never fallen, not then and not when he released the next bird the night the Volarian fleet set sail for the Meldenean Isles. Twenty-Seven, it appeared, was neither his gaoler nor Darnel's spy; he was simply his waiting executioner. In any case his worries over what the Kuritai saw had long since faded, along with the hope he might live to see this city liberated . . . and watch Alornis draw again.

He briefly considered sending Blue Feather with his final message—those he reported to would no doubt find the news of the ragged warship interesting—but decided against it. The ship portended a great deal, and it would be better to await discovery of the full story before expending his last link to the outside world.

They climbed down from the rooftop via the ladder on the back wall, making for the only building in Varinshold that seemed to have suffered no damage at all, the squat fortress of black stone sitting in the centre of the city. There had been a bloody battle here, he knew. The Blackhold's garrison of Fourth Order thugs putting up a surprisingly good fight as they beat back successive waves of Varitai, Aspect Tendris in the thick of the fight, spurring them on to ever-greater feats of courage with unwavering Faith. At least that's how the story went if you believed the mutterings of the Realm-born slaves. It had finally fallen when the Kuritai were sent in, Aspect Tendris cutting down four of the slave-elite before a dastardly knife in the back laid him low, something Alucius found extremely unlikely, though he did concede the mad bastard had probably gone down fighting.

The Varitai at the gate stepped aside as he approached, Twenty-Seven in tow with his books and various medicines in a sack over his broad shoulder. The interior of the Blackhold was even less edifying than its exterior, a narrow courtyard within grim black walls, Varitai archers posted on the parapet above. Alucius went to the door at the rear of the courtyard, the Varitai guard unlocking it and stepping aside. Inside he followed the damp winding steps down into the vaults. The smell provoked unwelcome memories of his time here, musty rot mingling with the sharp tang of rat piss. The steps ended some twenty feet down, opening out into a torchlit corridor lined by ten cells, each sealed with a heavy iron door. The cells had all been occupied when he was first brought here, now all but two stood empty.

"No," Alucius replied to Twenty-Seven's unvoiced question. "I can't say it is good to be back, my friend."

He went to the Free Sword seated on a stool at the end of the corridor. It was always the same man, a sour-faced fellow of brawny build who spoke Realm Tongue with all the finesse of a blind mason attempting to carve a masterpiece.

"Which 'un?" he grunted, getting to his feet and putting aside a wine-skin.

"Aspect Dendrish I think," Alucius replied. "Irksome duties first, I always say." He concealed a sigh of frustration at the Free Sword's baffled frown. "The fat man," he added slowly.

The Free Sword shrugged and moved to the door at the far end of the corridor, keys jangling as he worked the lock. Alucius thanked him with a bow and went inside.

Aspect Dendrish Hendrahl had lost perhaps half his famous weight during captivity, but that still made him considerably fatter than most men. He greeted Alucius with the customary scowl and lack of formality, small eyes narrowed and gleaming in the light from the single candle in the alcove above his bed. "I trust you've brought me something more interesting than last time."

"I believe so, Aspect." Alucius took the sack from Twenty-Seven and rummaged inside, coming out with a large volume, the title embossed in gold on the leather binding.

"'Fallacy and Belief,'" the Aspect read as he took the volume. "'The Nature of God Worship.' You bring me my own book?"

"Not quite, Aspect. I suggest you look inside."

Dendrish opened the book, his small eyes peering at the text scribbled on the title page which Alucius knew read: Or *"Pomposity and Arrogance— The Nature of Aspect Hendrahl's Scholarship."*

"What is this?" the Aspect demanded.

"I found it at Lord Al Avern's house," Alucius told him. "You remember him, no doubt. They called him the Lord of Ink and Scroll, on account of his scholarly accomplishments."

"Accomplishments? The man was an amateur, a mere copier of greater talents."

"Well, he has much to say on your talents, Aspect. His critique of your treatise on the origin of the Alpiran gods is particularly effusive, and quite elegantly phrased I must say."

Hendrahl's plump hands leafed through the book with expert precision, opening it out to reveal a chapter liberally adorned with the late Lord Al Avern's graceful script. "'Simply repeats Carvel'?" the Aspect read in a furious rasp. "This empty-brained *ape* accuses *me* of lacking originality."

"I thought you might find it amusing." Alucius bowed again and moved to the door.

"Wait!" Hendrahl cast a wary glance at the Free Sword standing outside and levered himself to his feet, not without difficulty. "You must have news, surely."

"Alas, things have not changed since my last visit, Aspect. Lord Darnel hunts for his son through the ashes of his great crime, we await news of General Tokrev's glorious victory at Alltor and Admiral Morok's equally glorious seizure of the Meldenean Isles."

Hendrahl moved closer, speaking in a barely heard whisper. "Master Grealin, still no word on him?"

It was the one question he always asked and Alucius had given up trying to extract the reason for this interest in the Sixth Order's store-minder. "None, Aspect. Just like last time." Oddly, this response always seemed to reassure the Aspect and he nodded, moving back to sit on his bed, his fingers resting on the book, not looking up as Alucius left the cell.

As ever, Aspect Elera proved a contrast to her brother in the Faith, smiling and standing as the door swung open, her slender hands extended in greeting. "Alucius!"

"Aspect." He always found he had to force the catch from his voice when he saw her, clad in her filthy grey robe they wouldn't let him replace, the flesh of her ankle red and raw from the shackle. But she always smiled and she was ever glad to see him.

"I brought more salve," he said, placing the sack on the bed. "For your leg. There's an apothecary shop on Drover's Way. Burnt-out, naturally, but it seems the owner had the foresight to hide some stock in his basement."

"Resourceful as ever, good sir. My thanks." She sat and rummaged through the sack for a moment, coming out with the small ceramic pot of salve, removing the lid to sniff the contents. "Corr tree oil and honey. Excellent. This will do very well." She rummaged further and found the books. "Marial!" she exclaimed in a delighted gasp. "I once had a full set. Must be near twenty years since my last reading. You are good to me, Alucius."

"I endeavour to do my best, Aspect."

She set the book aside and looked up at him, her face as clean as her meagre water ration allowed. Lord Darnel had been very particular in his instructions regarding her confinement, a consequence of her less-than-complimentary words during his first and only visit here. So, whilst Aspect Dendrish was treated to only the cruelty of indifference and a restricted diet, Aspect Elera was shackled to the wall with a length of chain that restricted her movements to no more than two square feet of her tiny cell. As yet, however, he had not heard her voice a single complaint.

"How goes the poem?" she asked him.

"Slowly, Aspect. I fear these tumultuous times deserve a better chronicler."

"A pity. I was looking forward to reading it. And your father?"

"Sends his regards," Alucius lied. "Though I see him rarely these days. Busy as he is with the Lord's work."

"Ah. Well, be sure to pass along my respects."

At least she won't call him traitor when this is done, he thought. *Though she may be the only one.*

"Tell me, Alucius," she went on. "Do your explorations ever take you to the southern quarter?"

"Rarely, Aspect. The pickings are hardly rich, and in any case there's little of it left to pick through."

"Pity. There was an inn there, the Black Boar I believe it was called. If you're in need of decent wine, I believe the owner kept a fine selection of Cumbraelin vintages in a secret place beneath the floorboards, so as not to trouble the King's excise men, you understand."

Decent wine. How long had it been since he'd tasted anything but the most acid vinegar? The Volarians may have had little interest in the city's books but had scraped every shelf clean of wine in the first week of occupation, forcing him into an unwelcome period of sobriety.

"Very kind, Aspect," he said. "Though I confess my surprise at your knowledge of such matters."

"You hear all manner of things as a healer. People will spill their deepest secrets to those they hope can take their pain away." She met his gaze and there was a new weight to her voice when she added, "I really wouldn't linger too long in seeking out the wine, good sir."

"I . . . shan't, Aspect."

The Free Sword rapped his keys against the door, voicing an impatient grunt. "I must go," he told her, taking the empty sack.

"A pleasure, as always, Alucius." She held out a hand and he knelt to kiss it, a courtly ritual they had adopted over the weeks. "Do you know," she said as he rose and went to the door. "I believe if Lord Darnel were truly a courageous man, he would have killed us by now."

"Raising his own fief against him in the process," Alucius replied. "Even he is not so foolish."

She nodded, smiling once again as the Free Sword closed the door, her final words faint but still audible, and insistent. "Be sure to enjoy the wine!"

◆ ◆ ◆

Lord Darnel sent for him in the afternoon, forestalling an exploration of the southern quarter. The Fief Lord had taken over the only surviving wing of the palace, a gleaming collection of marble walls and towers rising from the shattered ruin that surrounded it. The walls were partly covered in scaffolding as masons strove to remould the remnants into a convincingly self-contained building, as if it had always been this way. Darnel was keen to wipe away as much of the inconvenient past as possible. A small army of slaves laboured continually in pursuit of the new owner's vision, the ruined wings cleared to make room for an ornamental garden complete with looted statuary and as yet unblossomed flowerbeds.

Alucius was always surprised at his own lack of fear whenever he had the misfortune to find himself in the Fief Lord's presence; the man's temper was legendary and his fondness for the death warrant made old King Janus seem the model of indulgent rule. However, for all his evident scorn and contempt, Darnel needed him alive. *At least until Father wins his war for him.*

He was admitted to the new throne room by two of Darnel's burlier knights, fully armoured and smelling quite dreadful despite all the lavender oil with which they slathered themselves. As yet it seemed no blacksmith had solved the perennial problem of the foul odours arising from prolonged wearing of armour. Darnel sat on his new throne, a finely carved symphony of oak and velvet, featuring an ornately decorated back that reached fully seven feet high. Though yet to formally name himself king, Darnel had been quick to attire himself with as many royal trappings as possible, King Malcius's crown being chief among them, though Alucius fancied it sat a bit too loose on his head. It shifted on his brow now as the Fief Lord leaned forward to address the man standing before him, a wiry and somewhat bedraggled fellow in the garb of a Volarian sailor, a black cloak about his shoulders. Alucius's fear reasserted itself at the sight of man standing behind the sailor. Division Commander Mirvek stood tall and straight in his black enamel breastplate, heavy, scarred features impassive as always when in the Fief Lord's presence. Darnel might need him alive, but the Volarian certainly didn't. He took some heart from the sight of his father, standing with his arms crossed at Darnel's side.

"A shark?" Lord Darnel said to the sailor, his voice heavy with scorn. "You lost your fleet to a shark?"

The sailor stiffened, his face betraying a man suffering insult from one he considered little more than a favoured slave. "A red shark," the sailor replied in good but accented Realm Tongue. "Commanded by an *elverah*."

"Elverah?" Darnel asked. "I thought this fabled elverah was engaged in delaying General Tokrev at Alltor?"

"It is not a name, at least not these days," Mirvek explained. "It means witch or sorceress, born of an old legend . . ."

"I could give a whore's cunt hair for your legend!" Darnel snapped. "Why do you bring me this defeated dog with his wild tales of witches and sharks?"

"I am no liar!" the sailor retorted, face reddening. "I am witness to a thousand deaths or more at the hands of that bitch and her creature."

"Control your dog," Darnel told the Division Commander quietly. "Or he'll get a whipping as a lesson."

The sailor bridled again but said no more when Mirvek placed a restraining hand on his shoulder, murmuring something in his own language. Alucius's Volarian was poor but he was sure he detected the word "patience" in the commander's soothing tone.

"Ah, little poet," Darnel said, noticing Alucius. "Here's one worthy of a verse or two. The great Volarian fleet sunk by a Dark-blessed shark answering the whim of a witch."

"*Elverah*," the sailor said again before adding something in his own language.

"What did he say?" Darnel asked the Division Commander in a weary tone.

"Born of fire," the commander translated. "The sailors say the witch was born of fire, because of her burns."

"Burns?"

"Her face." The sailor played a hand over his own features. "Burned, vile to look upon. A creature not a woman."

"And I thought you people were absent all superstition," Darnel said before turning back to Alucius. "What do you imagine this means for our great enterprise, little poet?"

"It would seem the Meldenean Islands did not fall so easily after all, my lord," Alucius replied in a flat tone. He saw his father shift at Darnel's side, catching his eye with a warning glare, however Darnel seemed untroubled by the observation.

"Quite so. Despite the many promises made by our allies, they fail to secure me the Isles and instead bring dogs into my home barking nonsense." He pointed a steady finger at the sailor. "Get him out of here," he told Mirvek.

"Come forward, little poet." Darnel beckoned him with a languid wave when the Volarians had made their exit. "I'd have your views on another tall tale."

Alucius strode forward and went to one knee before the throne. He was continually tempted to abandon all pretence of respect but knew the Lord's tolerance had its limits, regardless of his usefulness.

"Here." Darnel picked up a spherical object lying at the foot of his throne and tossed it to Alucius. "Familiar, is it not?"

Alucius caught the item and turned it over in his hands. A Renfaelin knight's helmet, enamelled in blue with several dents and a broken visor. "Lord Wenders," he said, recalling that Darnel had made his chief lapdog a gift of an unwanted suit of armour.

"Indeed," Darnel said. "Found four days ago with a crossbow bolt through his eye. I assume you have little trouble guessing the origin of his demise."

"The Red Brother." Alucius concealed his grin. *Burned the Urlish to nothing and still you couldn't get him.*

"Yes," Darnel said. "Curious thing, they tended his wounds before they killed him. What's even more curious is the tale told by the only survivor of his company. He didn't last very long, I'm afraid, victim of a crushed and festered arm. But he swore to the Departed that the entire company had been buried in a rock-slide called forth by the Red Brother's fat master."

Grealin. Alucius kept all expression from his face as he asked, "Called forth, my lord?"

"Yes, with the Dark, if you can believe it. First the tale of the Dark-afflicted brother, now the ballad of the witch's shark. All very strange, wouldn't you agree?"

"I would, my lord. Most certainly."

Darnel reclined in his throne, regarding Alucius with arch scrutiny. "Tell me, in all your dealings with our cherished surviving Aspects, did they ever make mention of this fat master and his Dark gifts?"

"Aspect Dendrish asks for books, and food. Aspect Elera asks for nothing. They make no mention of this master . . ."

Darnel glanced at Alucius's father. "Grealin, my lord," Lakrhil Al Hestian said.

"Yes, Grealin." Darnel returned his gaze to Alucius. "Grealin."

"I recall the name, my lord. I believe Lord Al Sorna made mention of him during our time together in the Usurper's Revolt. He minded the Sixth Order's stores, I believe."

Darnel's face lost all expression, draining of colour, as it often did at mention of the name Al Sorna, something Alucius knew well and counted on to provide suitable distraction from further astute questioning. Today, however, the Fief Lord was not so easily diverted.

"Store-minder or no," he grated after a moment. "It now seems he's a pile of ash." He pulled something from the pocket of his silk robe and tossed it to Alucius; a medallion on a chain of plain metal, charred but intact. The Blind Warrior. "Your father's scouts found this amongst the ashes in a pyre near Wenders's body. It's either the fat master's or the Red Brother's, and I doubt we'd ever get that lucky."

No, Alucius agreed silently. You *never would.*

"Our Volarian allies are extremely interested in any whisper of the Dark," Darnel told him. "Paying huge sums for slaves rumoured to be afflicted with it. Imagine what they'll do to your friends in the Blackhold if they suspect they have knowledge of more. The next time you visit them show them this medallion, tell them this tall tale, and report back to me every word they say."

He got to his feet, walking towards Alucius with a slow gate, face quivering a little now, lips wet with spittle. They were roughly of equal height, but Darnel was considerably broader, and a seasoned killer. Somehow, though, Alucius still felt no fear as he loomed closer.

"This farce has dragged on long enough," the Fief Lord rasped. "I ride forth tonight with every knight in my command to hunt down the Red Brother and secure my son. Whilst I am gone you will make sure those sanctimonious shits know I'll happily hand them over to our allies to see them flayed skinless if it'll drag their secrets forth, Aspects or no."

CHAPTER THREE

Frentis

*S*he wakes, her eyes finding a dim yellow glow in a world of shadow. The glow resolves into the flame of a single candle, not so clear as it should be. For a moment she wonders if she has been reborn into a half-blind body, the Ally's joke, or further punishment. But then she recalls that her sight, her first body's sight, had always been unusually sharp. "Keener than any hawk," her father had said centuries ago, a rare compliment that had brought tears to her eyes then but brings nothing to these now. These weaker, stolen eyes.

She lies on hard stone, cold and rough on her naked skin. She sits and something moves in the gloom, a man stepping from the shadow into the meagre light. He wears the uniform of the Council Guard and the lean face of a veteran but she sees his true face in the leer of his shaded eyes. "How do you find it?" he asks her.

She raises her hands, flexing the fingers and wrists. Strong, good. Her arms are lean, well sculpted, similarly her legs, lithe and supple.

"A dancer?" she asks the Council Guard.

"No. She was found when young. The northern hill tribes, richer in Gifted than elsewhere in the empire. The gift is powerful, an uncanny way with the wind. Something I'm sure you'll find a use for. She was trained with knife, sword and bow from the age of six. Security against your inevitable fall."

She feels a faint anger at this. It was not inevitable. Any more than love is inevitable. She is tempted to let the anger build, fuel her new body with rage and test its abilities on the leering Messenger, but is given pause by another sensation . . . The music flows, the tune is fierce and strong. Her song is returned!

She finds a laugh bubbling in her breast and lets it out, her head thrown *back, the sound exultant as another thought comes to her, no less fierce in its joyful realisation:* I know you see me, beloved!

◆ ◆ ◆

He came awake with a start, raising a curious whine from Slasher who had been sleeping at his feet. Next to him Master Rensial slept on, an oddly serene smile on his face; a man content in slumber. Apart from battle it was the only time he appeared sane. Frentis sat up with a groan, shaking his head to clear the dream. *Dream? Do you really believe that's what it was?*

He pushed the thought away and pulled on his boots, hefting his sword and exiting the small tent he shared with the master. The sky was still dark and he judged it no more than two hours into the new day by the moon's height. Around him the company lay sleeping, the tents provided by Baron Banders a wondrous luxury after so many days of hardship. They were encamped on the southern slope of a tall hill, one of the downs that made the Renfaelin border country so distinct, campfires forbidden by the baron, who saw no reason to give Lord Darnel an indication of their numbers.

Six thousand men, Frentis thought, his eyes surveying the camp, recalling the intelligence provided by the unfortunate Lord Wenders. *Enough to take a city held by Darnel's knights and a full division of Volarians?*

A soft sound drew his attention back to the tents where his company slept, a soft giggle rising from the tent Arendil shared with Lady Illian. He heard faint but urgent whispers followed by more giggles. *I should stop this,* he decided, starting forward, then paused as the words Illian had spoken the day before came back to him. *I am not a child . . .*

They lost their youth in my bloody crusade, he thought. *With worse to come at Varinshold.* He sighed and moved away until the sounds grew faint.

It was a half-moon tonight, but the sky was clear, providing enough light for a good view of the low country beyond the downs, so far free of any enemy. *Will he wait?* Frentis wondered. *When Darnel hears that Banders has raised his fief against him and now harbours his son, will he come?* His hand ached as he gripped his sword hilt, the bloodlust surging again, calling her voice as it always did. *Not so free of its delights, after all, beloved?*

"Leave me be," he whispered in Volarian, teeth gritted, forcing his hand to release the sword.

"Learned a new language then, brother?"

Frentis turned to find a brother about his own age approaching from the shadows, tall with a narrow handsome face and a lopsided grin. It was the grin that stirred his memory. "Ivern," he said after a moment.

The young brother halted a few feet away, eyes tracking Frentis from head to foot in blank wonder. "I thought Brother Sollis was playing a joke when he told me," he said. "But when does he joke about anything?" He came forward, arms encircling Frentis in a warm embrace.

"The Order," Frentis began when Ivern moved back. "The House has fallen. There are no others . . ."

"I know. He told me your tale. Little over a hundred of us, all that remains of the Sixth Order."

"Aspect Arlyn lives. Darnel's lick-spittle confirmed it, though he couldn't tell us where in Varinshold they imprisoned him."

"A mystery to be solved when we get there." Ivern inclined his head at the cluster of tents nearby. "I've half a bottle of Brother's Friend left if you'd care to share."

Frentis had never been particularly partial to the Order's favourite tipple, disliking the way it dulled his senses, so he confined himself to a polite sip before handing the flask back to Ivern who seemed to have no such concerns. "I tell the unvarnished and complete truth," he insisted after a healthy gulp from the flask. "She kissed me, full on the lips."

"Princess Lyrna kissed you?" Frentis enquired with a raised eyebrow.

"Indeed she did. After a perilous, and dare I say, now legendary quest through the Lonak Dominion. I was halfway through writing it all down for inclusion in Brother Caenis's archive when news of the invasion came." His grin became rueful. "My finest hour as a brother, lost to history thanks to larger concerns." He met Frentis's gaze. "We heard a lot about you on the way south. The tale of the Red Brother flew fast and wide. There's even a version that says you saw her die."

The fire licked at her face as she screamed, her hair blackening as she beat the flames with her hands . . . "I didn't see her die," he said. *I just killed her brother.* He had given a full accounting to Brother Sollis the previous evening, whilst his company ate their first real meal in days, some so slumped in relief they couldn't raise the food to their mouths. Sollis had absorbed every word without comment, his pale-eyed gaze betraying nothing as the epic of murder and pain ran its course. When it was done, like Aspect Grealin, he gave strict instructions not to repeat the tale to anyone and maintain the same fiction believed by the people who followed him. *The same lie,* the woman's voice added in faint mockery.

"So there's a chance," Ivern pressed. "She could still be alive."

"I ask the Departed every day to make it so."

Ivern took another drink. "The Lonak didn't understand what a princess was, so called her a queen. Turns out they were right. If I were a Volarian I'd be praying for her death. I wouldn't want to be in the eye of that woman's vengeance."

Vengeance, Frentis thought, looking down at his hands, hands that had snapped the neck of a king. *Or justice?*

◆　◆　◆

He returned to his company in the morning, finding Davoka in conversation with Illian, the young highborn sitting rigid and pale of face as the Lonak spoke in instructional tones. "You must be careful," she cautioned, working a stone along her spear-blade. "Swollen belly no good in battle. Make sure he spends on your thigh."

When Illian caught sight of Frentis, her face turned an immediate shade of scarlet. She stood up, walking away with a stiff but rapid gait, managing only a faint squeak in response to his greeting.

"Such things are not discussed openly among the Merim Her," Frentis told a puzzled Davoka, sitting down beside her.

"Girl is foolish," she muttered with a shrug. "Too quick to anger, too quick to part her legs. My first husband had to give three ponies before I lay a hand on him."

Frentis was tempted to ask how many ponies Ermund would be required to hand over in due course, but decided it would be an unwise question. Bound as he was by his oath, the knight had been quickly reinstated at Baron Banders's side and they would sorely miss his sword. Davoka, however, seemed unperturbed by his sudden absence from their company and Frentis wondered if he hadn't been anything more than a welcome diversion during the infrequent quiet days in the Urlish.

"Things are different here," he said, more to himself than her. *Illian transformed from a pampered girl into a deadly huntress, Draker from an outlaw into a soldier, Grealin from a master to an Aspect. Everything is different. The Volarians have built us a new Realm.*

Brother Commander Sollis arrived as they were eating breakfast, favouring Davoka with a respectful nod, pausing only slightly at the sight of Thirty-Four, who smiled back with a gracious bow. "Baron Banders holds council," Sollis told Frentis. "Your words are wanted."

◆　◆　◆

"Five hundred knights and a piss-pot full of Volarians, eh?" Baron Banders raised a bushy eyebrow at Frentis, voicing a small laugh. "Hardly a mighty army, brother."

"If this Wenders spoke truly," Sollis commented.

The baron held his council in a field away from the main camp, the various captains and lords of his army standing in a circle with scant ceremony or formal introduction. It seemed Banders had little use for the often elaborate manners of the Renfaelin nobility.

"Wenders did not strike me as a man with enough wit for deception, brother," Frentis told Sollis before turning to Banders. "There are upwards of eight thousand men in a Volarian Division, my lord. Plus they have the Free Sword mercenaries who guard the slavers and contingents of Kuritai. I caution you not to underestimate them."

"Worse than the Alpirans are they?"

"In some ways."

The baron grunted and raised an eyebrow at Ermund who gave a solemn nod. "We killed many in the forest, my lord, but it cost us dear. If they have more, taking the city will be a bloody business."

"If Darnel is wise enough to stay behind his walls," Banders mused. "And wisdom is not one of his virtues."

"He has recruited wisdom," Frentis said. "Wenders told us Lakrhil Al Hestian has been pressed into service as Darnel's Battle Lord. He'll know full well the value of not taking to open field against us."

"Blood Rose," Banders said softly. "Couldn't abide the man, truth be told. But he never struck me as a traitor."

"Darnel holds Al Hestian's son as hostage to his loyalty. We should regard him an enemy, and not one given to misjudgements."

"Couldn't hold Marbellis though." Banders glanced at Sollis. "Could he, brother?"

There was a slight pause before Sollis replied and Frentis wondered what horrors crowded his memory. "No one could have held Marbellis, my lord," he said. "A pebble can't stand against an ocean."

Banders fell silent, his hand on his chin. "Was hoping the Urlish would mask our advance," he said in a reflective tone. "At least for a time, providing timber for ladders and engines into the bargain. Now even that is taken from us."

"There are other ways, Grandfather," Arendil spoke up. His mother, the Lady Ulice, stood at his side with a tight grip on his arm. Her relief at finding him alive the day before had been a spectacle of tearful kisses, though she had plainly been chagrined by her son's insistence on staying with Frentis's company.

"The good brother," Arendil said, gesturing to Frentis, "Davoka, and I made our escape via the city's sewers. If we can get out, surely we can get in the same way."

"The harbour pipe is too easily seen by their sailors," Frentis said. "But there are alternatives, and one in our company who knows the sewers near as well as I."

"I've four thousand knights who won't fit so easily in a dung pipe, brother," Banders pointed out. "Take their horses away and they're as much use as a gelding in a whorehouse. The rest are men-at-arms and a few hundred peasants with grudges to settle against Darnel and his dogs."

"I have over a hundred brothers," Sollis said. "Plus Brother Frentis's company. Surely sufficient strength to seize a gate and hold it long enough to allow your knights entry."

"And then what?" Banders asked. "Street fighting is hardly within their experience, brother."

"I'll fight in a bog," Ermund said, "if it'll bring Darnel within reach of my sword. Do not mistake the temper of your knights, my lord. Their course was not chosen lightly and they'll follow you to the Beyond and back if you command it."

"I don't doubt their temper, Ermund," Banders assured him. "But our fief lost enough wars to learn the lesson that a charging wall of steel cannot win every battle. And supposing we do manage to take the city, the bulk of the enemy's strength is still besieging Alltor. And when they're finished, where do you suppose they'll march next?"

"From what little intelligence we can gather," Sollis said, "Fief Lord Mustor has held out far longer than expected. Winter will be closing in by the time the Volarians take his capital and subdue his fief. Long enough for us to entrench, gather strength from Nilsael and the Reaches."

At mention of the Reaches Banders turned to one of his captains, a veteran knight in white-enamelled armour. "No word, I take it, Lord Furel?"

"It's a long ride to Meanshall," the knight replied. "And a longer voyage to the Reaches. Our messengers were sent only ten days ago."

"I had hoped he'd be on the move by now," Banders mused and Frentis had no need to hear the name in the forefront of his mind.

"He is," he said. "I know it." He looked at Brother Sollis who replied with a nod. "And having Varinshold in our hands by the time he arrives will make our task much easier."

"You ask me to risk much on the basis of faith alone, brother," Banders replied.

"Faith," Frentis replied, "is my business, my lord."

♦ ♦ ♦

The baron's army was well supplied with horses, most taken from the estates of knights who had sided with Darnel. They were all stallions, impressively tall at the shoulder with the restlessness of horses bred to the charge. Master Rensial wandered the temporary paddock where the horses were corralled, seemingly unaware of their snorts and whinnies as he played his hands over flanks and neck, his expression the concentrated stare of the expert.

"Not so . . ." Davoka fumbled for the right word as they watched the master go about his work. "*Ara-kahmin*. Head-sickness."

"Mad," Frentis said, seeing the surety with which Master Rensial moved. "Not so mad when he's with horses. I know."

"He looks on you and sees a son," Davoka said. "You know this too?"

"He sees many things. Most of which are not there."

The master chose a horse for each of them, leading a youthful grey to Frentis and a broad black charger to Davoka. "Too big," she said, moving back a little as the great horse sniffed her. "No ponies here?"

"No," Master Rensial told her simply and walked off to select more mounts.

"You'll get used to him," Frentis assured her, scratching the grey's nose. "Wonder what name you'll earn."

"Merim Her," Davoka muttered in derision. "People are named. Horses used and eaten."

They rode south at midday, Brother Sollis scouting ahead with his brothers, the knights and retainers following in a tight column. At the baron's order, every man was armoured and ready for battle. The peasant rebels followed behind on foot, mostly hardy-looking men with little armour but a rich variety of weapons. There was a grim uniformity to their expression that Frentis knew well, the faces of the wronged and the angry. From the stories Ivern had told him of the brother's journey from the Pass it was clear that, shorn of the Crown's authority, Darnel had lost little time in settling long-nurtured grievances, much of his ire falling on the common folk who worked the lands of his enemies. Frentis's company, few of whom could be called expert riders, made up the rear-guard, strung out in a loose formation many had difficulty maintaining for long.

"I . . . fucking . . . hate . . . horses!" Draker huffed as he bounced along on the back of the russet-coated stallion Rensial had chosen for him.

"It's easy!" Illian told him, spurring on ahead, moving in the saddle with accustomed ease. "Just raise yourself up a little at the right moment."

She laughed as Draker made a less-than-perfect attempt to comply, thumping himself onto the saddle with a hard grunt. "Oh, my unborn children."

Next to Frentis and Master Rensial, Arendil and Illian were easily his best riders. He sent Arendil west and Illian east with instructions to scout the flanks and strict orders to return on seeing any sign of friend or foe. Lady Ulice had betrayed a clear unhappiness at sending Arendil out of her sight once again but confined her objections to a stern scowl. She had joined them as they were forming up, offering few words beyond a statement that she would be travelling with her son by order of the baron, though she did seem heartened by the presence of Davoka.

"I know I owe you his life," she told the Lonak woman. "Whatever you require by way of thanks . . ."

"Arendil is *Gorin* to me," Davoka told her shortly, adding when the lady frowned in incomprehension, "Clan." Davoka held her arm out and swept it around their company, from Frentis to Thirty-Four and Draker still wincing with every jolt of his saddle. "My clan. Burnt Forest Clan." She barked a laugh. "Now yours."

"You could go home now," Ulice told her. "The north is clear all the way to the mountains."

Davoka's expression darkened as if she had been insulted, but softened when she saw the woman's honest curiosity. "Queen is not found," Davoka said. "No home for me until she is."

◆ ◆ ◆

They entered the rougher hill country by late evening, Banders acceding to Sollis's choice of campsite; the north-facing slope of a promontory offering clear views in all directions and shielded on the southern side by a deep ravine. Fires were permitted now, Banders knowing full well further attempts at concealing such a large force would be redundant this far into Asraelin territory.

Frentis's company were given the eastern flank to guard and he posted pickets in a tight line, pairs of fighters standing three-hour shifts. Illian returned as he was touring the perimeter. "You stayed out too long," he told her. "Arendil got in an hour ago. Be back before nightfall in future."

"Sorry, brother," she replied, avoiding his gaze and he realised her embarrassment from this morning still lingered.

"Anything to report?" he asked in a less severe tone.

"Not another soul for miles around," she replied, brightening a little. "Except for a wolf ten miles back. I've never seen one so big, I must say. Nor so bold, just sat there looking at me for what seemed an age."

Probably smelling the blood to come, Frentis thought. "Good. Get some rest, my lady."

He completed his tour of the pickets, finding the remaining fighters in a resilient mood. Now the terrors of their flight from the forest were over they were as combative as ever, many voicing an eagerness to get to Varinshold.

"The scales haven't shifted yet, brother," former City Guard Corporal Vinten told him, the slightly wild gleam in his eye provoking memories of Janril Norin. "Far too much blood weighing on our side. We'll balance them at Varinshold or die trying."

He returned to the main camp, sharing a meal with those still awake. Thirty-Four had taken on much of the cooking duties these days, producing a tasty stew of freshly caught partridge and wild mushrooms that put Arendil's amateur efforts to shame.

"They teached you cooking as well as torturin', then?" Draker asked him between mouthfuls, the grease beading his beard as he chewed.

"My last master's cook-slave fell ill during the voyage here," Thirty-Four replied in his now eerily accentless Realm Tongue. "He was required to teach me his skills before he died. I have always been able to learn quickly."

Lady Ulice accepted a bowl of stew from the former slave, her expression cautious. "Torturing?" she asked.

"I was a numbered slave," Thirty-Four replied in his precise, uncoloured tones. "A specialist. Schooled in the arts of torture from childhood." He continued to ladle out the stew as the lady stared at him, her gaze slowly tracking across the faces around the fire. Frentis knew she was seeing them truly for the first time, the brutality that had shaped them now plain in the hard set of Draker's eyes, Illian's frowning concentration as she tightened the string on her crossbow, and the preoccupied cast in Arendil's eyes as he stared into the fire, spooning stew into his mouth with automatic and unconscious regularity.

"It was a hard road, my lady," Frentis told her. "Hard choices had to be made."

She looked at her son, reaching over to smooth the hair back from his forehead, drawing a tired smile. "I'm not a lady," she said. "If we are to be clan-mates, you should know that. I am the unacknowledged bastard daughter to Baron Banders, nothing more. My name is just Ulice."

"No," Arendil stated, casting a hard glare around the fire. "My mother's name is Lady Ulice, and any calling her by a different name will answer to me."

"Quite so, my lord," Frentis told him. "Quite so."

◆ ◆ ◆

He busied himself with cleaning his weapons, long after the others had taken to their tents, the familiar drone of Draker's snores drifting across the camp. When his sword and knife were gleaming, he cleaned his boots, then his saddle, then unstrung his bow and checked the stave for cracks. After that he sat and sharpened every arrowhead in his quiver. *I do not need to sleep,* he told himself continually though his hands were beginning to tingle with exhaustion and his head constantly slumped unbidden to his chest.

Just dreams. He tried to force conviction into the thought, casting a reluctant gaze at his tent. *Just the stain of her company, the stink of her in my mind. Just dreams. She does not see me.* He finally surrendered when his fatigued hands left him with a bleeding thumb, returning the arrows to his quiver and walking to the tent on weak legs. *Just dreams.*

◆ ◆ ◆

She stands atop a tall tower, Volar spread out beneath her in all its ancient glory, street after street of tenements, marble mansions, gardens of wondrous construction and myriad towers rising from every quarter, though none so tall as this one: the Council Tower.

She raises her gaze to the sky seeking a target. The day is clear, the sky mostly unbroken blue, but she spies a small cloud some miles above, thin and wispy but sufficient for her purposes. She searches inside herself for the gift, finding she has to suppress her song to call it forth, but when it does the power of it staggers her, making her reach for the parapet as she sways. She feels a familiar trickle from her nose and understands the price for this one will be harder to bear even than the wonderful fire she stole from Revek, his words returning now with precise irony: Always the way with stolen gifts, don't you find?

What did he know? *she thinks, though the scorn is forced and hollow.* He knew enough not to be blinded by love.

She forces unwelcome thoughts from her head and focuses on the cloud, the gift surging, more blood flowing from her nose as she releases it, the small cloud swirling into a tight vortex before flying apart, tendrils fading in the clear blue sky.

"Impressive."

She turns to see a tall man in a red robe emerge from the stairway onto the tower roof. Two Kuritai follow him into the light, hands resting on their swords. She has yet to test the skill offered by this new shell and has to resist the urge to do so now. Hide an advantage and you double its value. *One of her father's axioms, though she suspects he may have stolen it from a long dead philosopher.*

"Arklev," she greets the tall man as he moves to her side. She can see a change in him, a new weariness around his eyes, an expression she knows well. He grieves.

"The Messenger did not linger," he tells her. "Save to say that the Ally's guidance will now be spoken only by you."

The Ally's guidance . . . As if he could comprehend the true meaning of those words, what it means to a soul in the Void to hear the Ally's voice. She almost laughs at the ignorance of this ancient little man. Centuries of life and still he knows nothing.

He is staring at her in expectation, a faint concern on his brow, and she realises it has been several moments since he spoke. How long had she been standing here? How long since she climbed the tower?

She breathes deeply and allows the confusion to fade. "You're grieving," she tells him. "Who did you lose?"

He draws back a little, concern deepening into fear, no doubt wondering how much she already knew. She was learning the appearance of omniscience could offer as much power as omniscience itself.

"My son," Arklev says. "His vessel never reached Varinshold. The scryers can no longer find a trace of him in times to come."

She nods and waits for him to say more but the Council-man fixes a mask on his face and stays silent. "The Ally wishes you to elevate me to Council," she tells him. "The Slaver's Seat."

"That is Council-man Lorvek's seat," he protests. "One he has discharged with care and diligence for near a century."

"Lining his pockets and failing to breed enough Gifted in the process. The Ally feels his guidance has not been fully appreciated. And with our new assets coming to maturity, he feels I would offer a more trustworthy overseer for this very particular enterprise. If Lorvek won't step down, I'm sure ample evidence

of corruption will be found to justify a charge of treason. Unless you prefer a quieter method."

He says more but she doesn't hear him, feeling time slip away once more. How long has she stood here? When the confusion fades she is alone again and the sky is a darker shade of blue. She turns her sight to the west, tracking the broad estuary to the coast and the ocean beyond. Please hurry to me, beloved. I am so very lonely.

CHAPTER FOUR

Reva

S he had seen enough corpses to know the dead rarely retained expression. The rictus smiles and fear-filled grimaces merely the tightening of sinew and muscle as the body's humours drained away. So it was a surprise to find the priest's face such a picture of serenity; but for the deep narrow cut in his throat he could easily have been mistaken for a slumbering man, his features betraying a soul content with the world.

Content, she thought, moving back from the corpse to rest on her haunches. *How fitting he should only find peace in death.*

"This is him?" Vaelin asked.

She nodded and rose as Alornis came to her side, touching her hand in reassurance. Vaelin held up his sister's sketch, eyes switching from the priest's face to the rendering on the parchment. "What a talent you have," he told her with a smile before turning to the hulking man standing near the tent wall. "And you, Master Marken. Quite the eye for detail."

Marken's beard constricted with a brief smile and Reva noted how tightly his hands were gripped together, and his staunch refusal even to look at the second corpse. It lay alongside the priest, the features more typical of Reva's experience, the skin a pale blue, the lips drawn back and the tongue protruding from the bared teeth, part severed by his death rattle. However, as with the priest his features were sufficiently recognisable to match Alornis's sketch.

"Uncle Sentes said his name was Lord Brahdor," she told Vaelin. "Lady Veliss tells me he owned land a little east of here, good vines. More renowned for white than red."

"That's all?" Vaelin asked. "No suspicions? Tall tales of strange powers or unexplained events?"

"That's all. Just a minor noble with a few hundred acres of grapes . . . and a barn."

Vaelin looked expectantly at Marken. The big man gritted his teeth for a moment then pointed a thick finger at Lord Brahdor's corpse, still refusing to look at it. "This one I'll not touch, my lord. I can feel it, seeping out of him like poison. Forgive my cowardice. But . . ." He shook his shaggy head. "I can't. I . . ."

"It's all right, Marken," Vaelin assured him, nodding at the priest. "And him?"

Marken huffed a relieved sigh and turned to crouch beside the priest, rolling up his sleeve and placing a meaty hand on the corpse's forehead. After a moment he winced as if in pain, his mouth twisting in disgust as it seemed he was about to draw his hand away, but she saw him stiffen his resolve, closing his eyes and maintaining a statuelike stillness for several minutes. Eventually he exhaled a long slow breath, sweat shining through the mass of hair that hung over his heavy brow. He rose, his gaze resting on Reva, warm with sympathy and sorrow. "My lady . . ." he began.

"I know," she told him. "I was there. Master Marken, please tell Lord Al Sorna all you saw."

"His early years are confused," Marken said to Vaelin. "It appears he was raised in the Church of the World Father. There are no images of his parents so I judge him an orphan, apprenticed to a priest, a common fate for Cumbraelin orphans I believe. The priest who raised him was kind, a former soldier in the Lord's guard, called to the church in later life, keen for his charges to acquire both his martial abilities and the fierceness of his devotion. The boy spent long years steeped both in study of the Ten Books and training for war. In manhood he endured long years of shame when he looked at women. The younger the woman, the greater the shame, and the more he looked. I sensed a compulsion to hide in the Ten Books, to find refuge from his desires in the church's teachings.

"Alltor and the cathedral loom large in his memory and I believe he was sent there in preparation for priesthood. I saw him meet the Reader and receive his priestly name. They never met in public and I sensed the priest had been chosen for a secret role. I saw a journey away from Alltor halting when he finds a man with a scar, here." Marken paused to touch his cheek. "The man is speaking before a large crowd and the young priest burns with new passion on hearing his voice. He returns to the Reader and is sent forth again. Then there are many months of meetings in dark rooms and secluded hollows, men clustering together and fearful of discovery as they pass letters and gather weapons in hidden caches. He never sees the scarred man again but the memory comes to him often. Then at another hidden meeting he finds this thing." Marken nodded at the second body, grimacing as his gaze touched Brahdor's dead face. "It talks, the words are lost to me as you know, my lord. But they make his passion burn even brighter. The thing leads him to a farmhouse at night, inside an old couple sit before a fire fussing over a little girl." He looked again at Reva and swallows. "The priest's shame is deeper than ever when he looks at her."

"They killed my grandparents, didn't they?" Reva asked. "They killed them and they stole me."

He nodded. "They waited until you had been put to bed. The old couple were killed, the girl stolen from her bed, the farmhouse burned."

"And then many happy years in a barn," Reva muttered as Marken fumbled for the right words to say.

"Any names?" Vaelin asked the Gifted.

"A few, my lord. The priest would write them down to memorise. He would burn the paper but the memories remain."

"Make a list and give it to Lady Reva."

She moved back to the priest's corpse, feeling a great temptation to smash her boot into his contented face, spoil his slumber forever. "Reva," Alornis said, tugging at her sleeve. "There's nothing more to learn here."

"I . . ." Marken stammered. "I do have his name, my lady. The Reader wrote it down when he gave it to him."

"No," she said, turning to walk to the tent flap. "Burn it if you're done," she told Vaelin. "No words are to be spoken for him."

"My lord," Marken continued as they made to the leave. "If I may. About Brother Caenis . . ."

"I'm aware of the matter, Master Marken," Vaelin told him.

"We didn't follow you here to become servants of the Faith . . ."

"We'll discuss it tonight," Vaelin told him in a level voice. "With Lord Nortah. Your concerns are fully noted."

They walked in silence back to the causeway, Reva preoccupied with the Gifted's tale, Vaelin no doubt pondering Brother Caenis's revelation to the queen. Alornis followed at a discreet distance, eyes scanning the city walls and her ever-present leather-bound bundle of sketches clutched to her chest, already filling up with renderings of the destruction behind the walls. She had cried the day she found Reva standing amidst the corpse-littered streets. Upon seeing her, Alornis had thrown her arms around Reva, convulsing with relief, provoking an old ache that Reva found didn't pain her in quite the same way.

"The Seventh Order," she said to Vaelin as they halted before the causeway. "Not a legend after all. But, I suppose you've known that a while."

"Yes." His face was sombre, not quite so fatigued as it had been recently, but still he seemed to have aged much in a few days. "Though there was something I should have known, but didn't."

"Brother Caenis?"

He nodded and changed the subject. "What will you do with the names Marken gives you?"

"Hunt them down and subject them to trial. If they are proved to be Sons, I'll hang them."

"My Lady Governess favours harsh justice."

"They plotted the death of my uncle, with the full contrivance of the church that has compelled the people of this fief to servile respect for centuries. They conspired with foul creatures of the Dark to subject me to a lifetime of abuse before sending me after you in the hope I would die. And let's not forget their attempt to kill our queen. Must I go on?"

He studied her face for a moment and she felt the harshness of her expression soften under the scrutiny. "I'm sorry for everything that happened to you here, Reva. If I had had any inkling . . ."

"I know." She forced a smile. "Join us tonight. Veliss found a new cook, though we can offer only two courses, and no wine."

"I can't. There is much to do." He glanced back at the camp where soldiers were busy packing gear and supplies in preparation for tomorrow's march and the commencement of what was fast becoming known as the Queen's Crusade.

"She wanted me to ask," he said, turning back, "how many men you will send with us."

"I'll not be sending any. I'll be leading them, the full House Guard plus five hundred archers."

"Reva, you have done enough . . ."

Arken's slack, lifeless face, the sword in his back . . . The archers flailing in the river as the arrows lashed down . . . Uncle Sentes dying on the cathedral steps . . . "No," she said. "No I haven't."

◆ ◆ ◆

Veliss came to her somewhere past midnight. They had reverted to keeping separate rooms in the aftermath of the siege, more at the Lady Counsellor's insistence than hers. Their numerous indiscretions might have been overlooked in the storm of daily battle, but the city had begun to resume a strange normality now the corpses and the worst of the rubble had been cleared away, and the cathedral reopened.

"Are you sure you want to meet them alone?" Veliss asked. They lay side by side, covered in a faint sheen of sweat, Reva enjoying the feel of the Lady Counsellor's unbound hair clinging to her skin.

"They need to know I speak with my own mind," she replied. "Given what I have to tell them."

"They won't like it . . ."

"I should hope so." She pulled Veliss closer, pressing a kiss to her lips to forestall further discussion.

"Lady Alornis," Veliss said, a while later. "You care for her."

"She is a friend to me, like her brother."

"No more than that?"

"Jealous, Honoured Counsellor?"

"Trust me, you don't want to see me jealous." She raised herself up, hugging her knees. "I was always going to leave, you know. When the war was done, if your uncle had lived. Take the gold he offered and go. Never cared about all the names they called me, or the Reader's sneering condescension. But I was getting tired of it all, the lies and the intrigue. Even for a former spy, it can grow wearisome."

Reva reached out to stroke her naked back. "And now?"

"Now I can't imagine being anywhere else." Reva felt her tense in anticipation of her next words. "The Queen's Crusade . . ."

"Is my crusade. And not a topic for discussion."

"Do you think she would be so welcoming if she knew your true nature? If she knew about us?"

"Unless it proved an impediment to liberating this Realm, I doubt she would care one whit." She recalled her first meeting with the queen, the fierce intelligence shining through the seared mask of her face, and the implacable determination, the singularity of purpose Reva recognised from infrequent youthful glances at her own reflection. *But I was sent in search of a myth*, she thought. *Her quarry is all too real, and I doubt she'll be satisfied with however many we find at Varinshold.* "In truth," she confessed to Veliss, "that woman scares me more than the Volarians ever did."

"Then why follow her?"

"Because *he* does. He tells me this is necessary. I once failed to heed his words, I'll not make the same mistake again."

"He's just a man," Veliss murmured, although Reva could hear the uncertainty in her voice. The tale was on every set of lips, Cumbraelins as enraptured by it as all the others, flying far and wide with every telling. One man, cutting his way through an army to save a city, and living to tell the tale.

Living? Reva remembered how his features had sagged that day, her tears and the pounding rain washing the blood away as she screamed at him to stay with her. But he hadn't, she had seen it plainly. For those few seconds, he had not been in his body.

"I'll need you to take care of things while I'm gone," she said. "Rebuild as best you can. I'll leave Lord Arentes here as surety of my word, though no doubt he'll hate me for it. How about a new title? Vice-Governess, maybe? I'm sure you can come up with something better."

Veliss hugged her legs tighter. "I don't want titles, I just want you."

◆ ◆ ◆

Lords Arentes and Antesh preceded her into the cathedral, striding through the cavernous interior towards the Reader's chambers as she followed with twenty of the House Guard at her back. The two priests standing guard at the chamber door were subdued without particular difficulty, Lord Arentes thrusting the doors open and standing aside to allow her entry. Reva paused at the sight of the priest held to the wall by Lord Antesh, a sallow-faced man with a heavily bandaged hand and misshapen nose.

"I never learned your name," she said.

The priest scowled and said nothing until Antesh gave him a none-too-gentle shake. "My name is for the Father alone."

"And I believe he wants you to share it." She beckoned two guards forward. "Take this one to Lady Veliss. Tell her I think he would benefit from some herbal medicine."

She turned back to the open door as they hustled the priest away, entering at a sedate pace and offering a brisk greeting to the seven old men she found seated at a circular table. "Good bishops!" There were supposed to be ten but three had perished in the siege, not, she suspected, by virtue of any courageous act.

One of the bishops struggled to his feet as she walked to the only empty chair at the table, a wizened and bird-like man she recalled had objected when she gave the cathedral over to the care of the wounded. "This is the holy conclave of the ten bishops," he sputtered. "You are not permitted . . ."

He fell silent as Lord Arentes brought a gauntleted fist down hard on the table. "The correct form of address for the Lady Governess," he told the quailing cleric, "is 'my lady.' And no door in this city is barred to her."

Reva paused at the empty chair, naturally the most ornate in the room with an ample cushion for the old bastard's bony behind. She sighed and pushed it out of her way. *Can't kill him twice, more's the pity.*

"Now, now, my Lord Commander," she told Arentes. "We should respect the good bishops' privacy. Leave us, for we have much to discuss."

They sat in dumb silence as the doors closed with an echoing boom. She waited for it to fade before speaking, all vestige of respect stripped from her tone. "So, have you chosen?"

Only one spoke up, a slight man with a prominent nose, a little younger than his colleagues. "We had not yet counted the ballots, my lady." He indicated a plain wooden box in the centre of the table.

"Then do so now."

Reva studied him closely as he reached for the box, finding she remembered his face from the day the Reader died, one who smiled when she charged the old man. *A possible ally?* She steeled her thoughts against the suggestion; Marken's revelations left no room for accommodation. *I have no friends in this room.*

"The Bishop of the Southern Parish," the thin bishop reported after counting the ballots. "By unanimous assent."

Reva scanned the faces around the table, finding six scared old men and one sleeping ancient who hadn't raised his head since her entry. "Who is?" she enquired.

The thin bishop cleared his throat in discomfort. "I am, my lady."

She gave a short laugh and turned her back on him, her gaze drawn to a candlelit alcove at the rear of the chamber where ten large tomes sat on lecterns. The books were ancient, the bindings flaking and cracked with age. *The first to be bound in the land of Cumbrael,* she knew, finding it odd that she felt no upswelling of awe at the sight. *Just a collection of old books in a room of old men.*

"I have in my possession," she said, turning back to the table, "what I believe to be a complete list of adherents to the heretical sect known as the Sons of the Trueblade. In due course each and every name on this list will be captured and put to the question. I am sure you will join me in rejoicing at this news, given the wealth of intelligence they are sure to provide."

She scanned each face in turn, finding confusion on most, but fear on others. *They knew,* she realised. *Not all, but some.* She saw how the Bishop of the Southern Parish avoided her gaze, a few beads of sweat forming on his wrinkled brow. *Him in particular.* She was right; there were no allies here.

She walked slowly around the table, watching each stooped back flinch as she passed by. She wore no weapons today, having returned her grandfather's sword to its place in the library, but had little doubt she could snap every neck in this room should she choose. She halted behind the chair occupied by the Reader-elect and pointed at the ballots neatly piled at his side. "Give me those." His spotted, bony hands trembled as he complied, dropping the ballots and scrambling to retrieve them before managing to fumble them into her palm.

"'Deception is both sin and blessing,'" she quoted as she took the ballots from him, the Fifth Book, the Book of Reason, fast becoming her favourite. She turned and walked slowly back to the alcove, ballots in hand. "'The paths set for us by the Father are many and their course is ever winding. At every turn the Loved find themselves presented with a plethora of choices as their paths fork, split by war or famine, love and betrayal. To walk the varied paths of life without deception is impossible.'" She stopped before the alcove, holding the ballots to one of the candles, letting the flame consume half their length before tossing them onto the stone floor where they continued to burn, soon no more than a swirl of black cinders.

"'But,'" she told the bishops with a smile, now staring in outrage or horror, "'the Father forgives the lie spoken in kindness, or service to a greater purpose.'"

She stood, the smile fading from her lips, waiting for a single voice to be raised in dissent. But they all just sat and stared, stoking her anger with their dumb inaction. *This venal church collaborated with murderers,* she knew. *Allied themselves with the servants of an enemy that brought slaughter and slavery to this land. The people of this city would hang you all from the towers of this cathedral if I wished it. I won their love, whilst you cowered here and prayed for miracles that never came. With sword and bow I won their love.*

One word to Arentes and it would be done, the bishops dragged outside, charges read as the people looked on and she fired their rage with a few well-chosen truths. They were all killers now, save the children and even they were hardened to the sight of death. There would be no protest, no hand raised to stop her, and she would have what the priest once made her lust for, a new church to be moulded into her father's vision.

My mad father's vision. The thought dispelled her anger, replacing it with a weary realisation. They had lost so much, but the church had endured for centuries and this land would not heal if she ripped open yet more wounds.

The sleeping ancient stirred, snuffling awake with a bleary-eyed glance around the room. "Lunch!" he demanded, thumping his walking stick on the table.

Reva moved to the ancient, smiling down at his reproving scowl. "And who might you be, good bishop?"

"I," he began, drawing himself up, "am the Holy Bishop of . . ." He frowned in confusion, his shoulders slumping a little, licking his lips. "The Bishop of . . ."

"The Riverland Parish," the bishop at his side supplied in a tense whisper.

"Yes!" The ancient bishop brightened, fixing Reva with an imperious glare. "I am the Bishop of the Riverland Parish and I demand my lunch."

"You shall have it," Reva assured him with a bow. "And more besides." She moved to the door, pausing to cast an expansive gesture at the other bishops. "For your colleagues have voted you Holy Reader to the Church of the World Father. Please accept my heartfelt congratulations, Reader, and be assured of House Mustor's most pious loyalty. I await your first sermon with the keenest interest."

◆ ◆ ◆

The sword room was mostly bare now, the once-full racks empty of blades save a few too highly set on the wall to be easily reached. She spent an hour in practice with her grandfather's sword, dancing her dance with the heavy blade whirling and slicing, her muscles straining.

"I could watch you do that for hours."

Reva stopped in mid-pirouette, finding Alornis standing in the doorway, charcoal-stained fingers still clutching her leather case. "I doubt you'd have liked the view a few days ago," Reva said, massaging her back.

Alornis's gaze became sombre. "It was bad, I know. So much of the city destroyed. On the march here I saw things . . . Things I felt I had to draw." She tapped her case. "I thought putting them on paper might get them out of my head. But still they linger."

The severed heads raining down . . . The Volarian's defiant glare as he was led to the block . . . "They should," Reva told her. "Will you be coming to Varinshold? There are rooms aplenty here if you wish to stay. And I'm sure Lady Veliss would like the company."

Alornis smiled but shook her head. "Alucius and Master Benril. I have to find them." She hesitated then came into the room, eyes widening in appreciation at the paintings on the upper walls, the swordsmen in their various poses. "This was done by a skilled hand."

"At the cost of my great-grandfather's coin, no doubt. He seems to have been a little too free with it, according to Veliss's records. Perhaps why he lost so many wars to the Asraelins. I find governing a fief to be mostly a matter of coin."

Alornis's brow creased as she looked at Reva, shaking her head in faint wonder. "So changed in such a short time."

Reva found her scrutiny hard to bear and turned away, hefting the sword. "You," she told it, "are just too heavy."

"What happened to your old one?" Alornis asked. "That was a thing of beauty."

Standing over Arken's body, her arm moving in a ceaseless, deadly arc, the rage spilling from her lips in a meaningless torrent . . . "I broke it." She raised her gaze to the few remaining blades on the higher racks, picking out an Asraelin sword somehow missed by the servants sent to ransack the place for arms. "You can help me find another."

She cupped her hands to create a stirrup and Alornis placed a foot in it, reaching up as Reva hoisted her, snatching the sword from the rack before slipping from her grip and falling. Reva caught her, holding her tight as she laughed, drawing back to meet her gaze.

"My brother says Lady Veliss was once a spy in King Janus's service," Alornis told her.

"I know. She has been many things."

"Well, I think she's lovely." She stood on tiptoe to press a kiss to Reva's forehead. "I'm happy for you."

She turned, retrieved her case of sketches and left. Reva closed her eyes, feeling the warmth of the kiss fade from her skin. *Her gaze was always far too keen. Foolish to imagine she wouldn't know.*

She hefted the sword, drawing the blade free of the scabbard, finding it old but not rusted, the edge notched but not so bad it couldn't be sharpened keen. "So," she said, putting the scabbard aside and assuming a fighting stance. "Let's see if you're a better fit. We have much work to do."

CHAPTER FIVE

Lyrna

The horse was a gift from the Eorhil, fourteen hands at the shoulder and white from nose to tail save for a tuft of black hair between her ears. Lyrna had found the Eorhil woman they called Wisdom waiting with the horse when she emerged from her tent that morning. She proffered the reins with a surprisingly well-executed formal bow.

"She has a name?" Lyrna asked her.

"It translates as 'An Unseen Arrow as She Runs through Snow and Wind,' Highness," Wisdom replied in her perfect Realm Tongue. "My people are not known for their brevity."

"Arrow it is," Lyrna said, scratching the mare's nose and drawing forth a faint snort.

"She misses her rider," Wisdom said. "He fell before the city. I feel you may be able to mend her heart."

"My thanks." Lyrna returned her bow. "Will you ride with me today? I greatly wish to know more of your people."

There was a somewhat sardonic lilt to the woman's voice as she replied, "Have you not already read every book in your library concerning the Eorhil, Highness?"

"I am increasingly aware that the sagacity of books is limited in comparison to experience."

"As you wish." Wisdom turned and vaulted onto the back of her own horse, looking down at Lyrna in expectation. "My people ride now."

Iltis and Benten were obliged to scramble onto their own horses as Lyrna mounted up and trotted off with Wisdom. They rode to the eastern edge of the camp where the Eorhil host was already in motion, the various war bands galloping off seemingly at random. No neatly ordered ranks and columns here, although every rider seemed to move with a purpose and she noticed how the host took on a definite if loose formation as they crested the eastern hills and entered the low-lying fields beyond.

"Good country for horses," Lyrna commented to Wisdom an hour or so shy of midday. The ride had been hard but not exhausting, her journey through the Lonak Dominion having left her well adapted to long hours in the saddle. Plus she found her new mount something of a delight, faster than poor old Sable and less fractious than Surefoot.

"Still too many hills for my people's liking," Wisdom replied, taking a long pull from her waterskin. "And not an elk to be had since we came here. Some of the young ones are chafing at it, for true adulthood only comes when you take your first elk."

Lyrna looked at the riders around them, noting how their eyes strayed constantly to her face but displayed none of the awe shown by the Realm folk. If anything she detected a discomfort in finding themselves in such proximity.

"You call it the Dark," Wisdom said, somehow sensing the question she was about to ask. "We call it simply *Exilla*, 'power' in your tongue."

"Not one I possess," Lyrna pointed out.

"It doesn't matter. We know of it but few of us are visited with such gifts."

"Those that are find themselves shunned, I assume."

Wisdom voiced a faint laugh. "Do not judge us by the standards of your people, Highness. Those with gifts are not shunned, but they are respected. The greater the power, the greater the respect, and respect can grow into fear if the power is great enough. As yet, there is not a story or a song in our history that tells of a power greater than that used to heal you. They worry what it might mean."

"Do you?"

Wisdom's age-cracked lips formed into a smile, small but rich in sympathy. "No, great and terrible queen, I know full well what it means."

Sanesh Poltar came trotting up on his tall piebald stallion, offering Lyrna a cautious nod. "Scouts say many men to the south," the war chief told Wisdom. "The queen stays here while we go look."

"I think not," Lyrna said, fixing the Eorhil with a bright smile.

"Tower Lord says to keep you safe above all others," Sanesh Poltar replied. "And we are bound to him, not you."

"And I am bound to neither." She tugged on Arrow's reins, pointing her nose southward and kicking her into a gallop.

◆ ◆ ◆

The Eorhil soon overtook her, of course, though she was gratified by the hard glare Sanesh Poltar shot at her as he galloped past. Iltis and Benten closed in on either side as they trailed in the riders' wake, Lyrna finding herself blinking away dust as the sun rose to dry the earth. They crested a low rise a half hour later, reining to a halt beside the war chief as he surveyed the shallow vale beyond. To the east and west his outriders galloped forth in a perfectly coordinated envelopment whilst the bulk of his riders stayed put on the low ridge. She noted most had notched an arrow to their horn bows.

Sanesh Poltar sat in silence, scanning the vale with a hawkish intent. Lyrna followed his gaze, seeing nothing beyond empty country. "How many men were seen?" she asked the war chief.

"Less than were at the city," he replied without turning. "More than we have."

Another Volarian force sent by Tokrev to raid the south? she wondered. Master Marken had searched through the dead general's mind revealing what he described as a swamp of vain ambition and petty jealousy but no inkling of another large force nearby. *Could they have landed early?* she wondered. *Tokrev sending for the second wave to speed the conquest.*

Sanesh Poltar straightened in his saddle and pointed. It was another few seconds before Lyrna saw them, a small band of cavalry galloping into the vale then drawing up short at the sight of so many horsemen on the skyline ahead. They fanned out, still too distant to make out any details, one of their number galloping off to disappear over the lip of the valley. Next to Lyrna, Wisdom unhooked her bow from the saddle and notched an arrow. *Old as she is,* Lyrna thought, *and she's still expected to fight.*

The horsemen in the valley sat waiting for several minutes, Lyrna thinking it odd that none had yet drawn a sword. Sanesh Poltar's gaze shifted once more as a tall banner appeared over the rim of the valley, bobbing at the head of a column of infantry led by a man on horseback. They marched into the valley in close ranks, making no move to assume battle formation, Lyrna realising why as the motif on the banner became clear: a tower rising from a wave-tossed ocean.

She laughed and kicked Arrow forward, ignoring Iltis's appalled protest as he galloped along behind. The marching column came to a halt as she approached, sergeants barking commands unheeded by men who stared at her in open wonder. She made for the rider at the head of the column, raising a hand and smiling warmly. He climbed down from his saddle, not without some difficulty, and slowly lowered himself to one knee.

"What a welcome sight you make, my lord!" Lyrna told him.

Tower Lord Al Bera looked up at her with a pale but intent expression, raising himself with effort as she leapt down from her saddle, coming to him with hands outstretched. "Highness," he said, his voice hoarse and back stiff as he lowered his lips to her hands, eyes hardly leaving her face as he straightened. "We heard so many terrible stories. I'm greatly pleased to find one at least to be false." He turned, raising an arm towards the men at his back as more came marching into sight. "I present the Army of the Southern Shore. Twenty thousand horse and foot ready to march and die at the Queen's Word."

◆ ◆ ◆

"They sent about five thousand men into the southern counties," the Tower Lord reported to the council of captains that evening. Lyrna had been obliged to order him to sit as the man's exhaustion and evident pain threatened to tip him over at any moment. He sat on a camp-stool, both arms cradled in his lap, the left heavily bandaged and the right hanging loose from a drooping shoulder. Lyrna had offered to take him to Weaver but the Tower Lord's shocked expression was enough for her to let the matter drop.

"The slave soldiers mostly," Al Bera went on. Lyrna knew this to be a man promoted through merit rather than blood and his voice held the broad vowels singular to the common folk of southern Asrael. "Plus about a thousand cavalry. And slavers, of course. Laid waste to several villages before word reached the Tower. I marched out with the South Guard and what men I could levy from the coast, caught them as they were finishing up a slaughter at Draver's Wharf on the lower reaches of the Cold Iron. Had a sense they were expecting a less speedy response. Unsurprising, since I should be dead by rights." Al Bera paused to give a wan smile. "Made 'em pay for it. The numbers were about even so it was a bloody business, but we made 'em pay."

"Prisoners?" Vaelin asked.

"The slave soldiers don't surrender, but we took a few cavalry and slavers. I gave them to the people we freed. Probably should've just hung them, but blood pays for blood."

"Quite so, my lord," Lyrna told him. "Please continue."

"Been gathering men and training 'em best I could since then. Word came two weeks ago telling of the Meldenean fleet sailing up the Cold Iron so I judged it time to move north."

"You judged correctly," Lyrna said. "However, you find us short of supplies."

"Supplies I've got, Highness. My lady wife has family connections on both sides of the Erinean. Seems some Alpiran merchants were willing to trade with us. The terms were hardly favourable and the South Tower treasury stands just about empty, but since the Emperor lifted the embargo I s'pose they couldn't pass up a chance at profit."

Lyrna saw Lord Verniers raise his head at that. He was a deliberately obscure presence in the army, keen to avoid conversation with any save herself and Vaelin, though she made it plain he was welcome at all meetings and free to record all words spoken. The Shield had made something of a fuss of him in the aftermath of the battle, proclaiming him "The scribe who killed a general!" with a hearty laugh echoed by his crew. Verniers, however, seemed to shun any rewards his heroism might offer, though he had persisted in requests for a private interview.

"Your Emperor seems better disposed to our Realm, my lord," she told him.

The chronicler squirmed a little as the captains turned to regard him, voicing only a short response. "So it seems, Highness."

"Do you think he knows of the Volarians' great scheme? Could that be the reason for this change of heart?"

"The Emperor's mind is never easily gauged, Highness. But anything that might injure the Volarian Empire is likely to please him greatly. They have been our enemy far longer than yours."

"We should send an ambassador," Vaelin said. "Forge an alliance, if possible."

"All in good time, my lord," Lyrna said, turning again to Al Bera. "I'll pen a letter for Lady Al Bera giving assurance that any debts incurred in purchasing more supplies will be settled in full at the close of hostilities, she is free to agree suitable terms of interest with any and all merchants. In the meantime, half her available supplies will be shipped to Alltor to succour the Cumbraelin people through the winter. The other half will come to us"—her finger traced across the map to a town on the Renfaelin coast—"at Warnsclave, where we rendezvous with our Meldenean allies in fifteen days. As for now, my lord, *please* get some rest."

◆　◆　◆

She spent the journey to Warnsclave travelling with a different contingent each day. One with Lady Reva's Cumbraelins, the next with a regiment of miners from the Reaches, the third with the South Guard. Every face displayed either awe, fascination or, in the case of Lord Nortah's Free Company, a fierce and unhesitant loyalty.

"The Departed have blessed you, my Queen!" one man called out to her as she drew up alongside Lord Nortah, the shout soon taken up by his fellow fighters.

"Silence in the ranks!" the company sergeant barked, an athletic young man with long hair and a sword strapped across his back in the manner of the Sixth Order.

"Apologies, Highness," Lord Nortah offered as they set off. "They're not easy to control at the best of times. And it's not like I can flog any."

"No, my lord," Lyrna replied. "You certainly cannot." She found it strange that they rode in silence for much of the morning; the boy she remembered as the son of her father's First Minister had rarely been quiet, a braggart and sometimes a bully, quick to taunt and even quicker to cry when his taunts were returned. She saw none of that boy in the bearded warrior at her side, a small smile playing on his lips as he watched his great cat bounding alongside.

"I intended to offer you restoration of your father's lands and titles," she told him when the silence became trying. "However, Lord Vaelin advised you had no interest in such honours."

"Never did my father much good, did they, Highness?" he replied, affably enough but with a slight edge to his tone.

"I was not privy to the King's decision in that matter," she said. "I believe it to have been . . . regrettable."

"I harbour no bitterness, Highness. Time has dimmed my memory of a man I recall I loved almost as much as I hated. In any case, without his death I would not have been set on the course that led me to my wife, my children and the home I hunger for. And the Faith teaches us to accept the gifts brought by fate."

"You still hold to the Faith?"

"I left the Order, Highness, not the Faith. My brother may have lost his in the desert somewhere but mine still lingers on. Though my wife longs for me to abandon it in favour of the sun and the moon." He gave a soft laugh and she could hear his homesickness in it. "The only thing we ever quarrel about, in truth."

They rested at midday, Lyrna climbing down from Arrow's back and drawing up in alarm as a woman rushed from the ranks of the Free Company with a dagger in both hands. Iltis's sword came free of its scabbard in a blur but, rather than launching herself at Lyrna, the woman sank to her knees, head bowed with her twin daggers raised high.

"My Queen!" she said in a tremulous gasp. "I beg you to bless these blades so they might do your work."

The rest of the freed fighters immediately dropped to their knees, all drawing weapons and holding them aloft. This was clearly a ceremony planned on the march, one she judged Lord Nortah knew nothing of from his weary and slightly disgusted expression.

Never be afraid of a little theatre. Lyrna took a breath and placed a kindly smile on her lips as she moved to the kneeling woman, recognising her as the slight figure who had been first to take up the cry at Alltor. "What is your name?" she asked her.

"F-Furelah, my Queen," the woman stammered, not looking up.

Lyrna gently took hold of the woman's trembling hands. "Lower your blades, sister," she told her. "Stand up, look at me."

Furelah slowly looked up, eyes wide as they drank in the sight of her face, coming to her feet as Lyrna kept hold of her hands. "Who did you lose?" she asked her.

"M-my daughter," the slight woman breathed, tears flowing from her eyes. "Born out of wedlock, shunned and called a bastard her whole life, but always so sweet. They d-dashed her brains out with a rock." She sagged as the sobs took her, sinking to her knees. Lyrna pulled her close as she wept, her daggers still gripped tight.

"I cannot bless this woman's blades," she told the fighters, many now weeping openly. "For she blesses me. You all do. I am your blade, and you are mine." She raised the still-sobbing Furelah to her feet, leading her back to the company's ranks. "Accordingly I hereby name you as the Realm Guard's Sixtieth Regiment of Foot, to be known hereafter as the Queen's Daggers." They parted before her as she released Furelah, the woman instantly falling to her knees once more, her comrades all reaching out to touch tentative hands to Lyrna's gown as she moved among them, fierce devotion on every face. *I cannot become drunk on this,* she thought, smiling and touching her hands to heads lowered in supplication. *The lure of it is too great.*

"Toil, blood and justice!" the cry began unbidden, a spontaneous shout from a faceless voice in the kneeling ranks, repeated over and over as they stabbed the air with their assorted weapons. "Toil! Blood! And justice!"

Lyrna felt the seduction of it sweep through her, the power of it, the knowledge that these few hundred wounded souls would die for her in an instant. She was on the verge of surrendering to it completely when something gave her pause, a single face not stricken in adoration. Lord Nortah stood beside his horse, running a hand over the head of the great cat crouched at his side, his faint look of disgust now replaced with one of deep and obvious disapproval.

◆ ◆ ◆

She met with Brother Caenis in the evening, alone since Vaelin seemed keen to avoid his former brother, an attitude shared by many in the army's ranks. Even Orena, who struck Lyrna as a woman of great practicality, had begged leave for an early night rather than remain to greet the brother's arrival. *Fear of the Dark does not fade in an instant,* Lyrna concluded.

The newly revealed brother of the Seventh Order sat at stiff attention on a camp-stool, refusing the offer of refreshment with a polite shake of his head. For all his evident hardiness and renown as a warrior there was a definite timidity to this compact, war-hardened man, a shift in his eyes as if wary of attack at any moment. *So long living in the shadows,* she thought. *The light of day can be as frightening as the Dark.*

"My brothers and sisters ask me to offer thanks, Highness," he said. "For your consideration."

"A queen has care for all her subjects, my lord."

"If it please you, Highness. My preference is to be addressed as 'brother.' I am a man of the Faith in all things."

"As you wish." Lyrna reached for the scroll he had handed her on arrival, a complete list of his Order's members and their various gifts. "You have a brother who can see the past?"

"Brother Lucin's gift is limited, Highness. His vision confined only to whatever location he finds himself in."

Lyrna nodded, frowning at the next description on the list. "And this Sister Merial can truly pull lightning from the air?"

"Not exactly, Highness. She can exude a power, an energy from her hands. In darkness or shadow it can seem like lightning. The gift is very draining, fatal if over-used."

"Can she kill with it?"

He hesitated then gave a short nod.

"Then she and her gift are greatly welcome in this army." Lyrna read through the rest of the list, glancing up at him with a raised eyebrow. "I find there is one name missing, brother."

His discomfort visibly deepened but his gaze remained steady and his tone held no note of compromise. "My gift cannot be revealed, Highness. By strict order of my Aspect."

She was tempted to remind him the Faith was subject to the Crown, but decided against it. *There is too much of use in what he brings me. And this is not a good time for conflict with the Faith, especially when they continue to hide so much.*

"I spent so many years in search of your kind," she said, putting the list aside. "Even risking death in the mountains to seek evidence of your existence. And yet it seems all I had to do was await the tide of history and I would be deluged with more evidence than I could ever wish."

Brother Caenis confined his reply to a cautious nod, his gaze averted as she continued, "It must have been difficult, living in concealment for so long. Lying to your brothers for years on end."

"The Faith required it, Highness. I had no choice in the matter. But yes, it was a hard duty."

"Lord Vaelin tells me you were the most loyal subject my father could ever wish for. That your enthusiasm for the desert war was great. So much so he thought your heart broken when it all came to naught."

"Aspect Grealin was very precise in the role he wished me to play. My devotion to the Faith was so strong he felt it best masked as devotion to the King. But my brother was right, my enthusiasm for the war was true, inflamed by my Aspect who told me it was the key to securing the future of the Faith. For reasons of his own, he didn't tell me how that security would be achieved, or my brother's fate. I always thought Aspect Grealin's reasoning to be infallible, he never steered me to the wrong course, he never made mistakes."

"Have you heard from him, since the capital fell?"

"Sadly no, Highness." Caenis lowered his head, his voice dulling with sorrow. "Brother Lernial has a facility for hearing the thoughts of those he has met, even over great distances. We know the Aspect had taken refuge in the Urlish with a band of free fighters, the details are vague since Lernial's gift is limited. At Alltor he took a wound to the head, waking two days later with a great scream. I hoped his words no more than a symptom of a damaged mind, but he has healed much since and his gift tells him there are no more thoughts to be heard from Aspect Grealin."

Seeing the brother's evident grief, she reached out to clasp his hand. "My commiserations, brother."

He stirred in discomfort, forcing a smile. *Does he fear me?* One of the names on his list apparently had some facility for peering into the future and she wondered what revelations Caenis might be privy to, recalling Lord Nortah's grim visage and Wisdom's words from the first day on the march. *I know full well what it means.*

"During Brother Harlick's questioning," she said, moving back. "The Volarian woman we took at Alltor spoke of an Ally. Lord Vaelin seems to think you may be able to elaborate on her meaning."

"Brother Harlick has already told you all we know, Highness. It resides in the Beyond and plots our destruction. We know not why."

"If it exists in the place beyond death, does not that suppose it was once alive? It was once a man, or a woman?"

"It does, Highness. But as yet no member of any Order has divined how it came to be what it is, nor what malign agency could have twisted it into such evil."

"There must be records, ancient texts describing its origin."

"The Third Order has spent centuries gathering the oldest words written by human hand, paying considerable sums for scraps of parchment or shards of clay. The Ally is there, but only ever as a shadow, unexplained catastrophe or murder committed at the behest of a dark and vengeful spirit. Sorting truth from myth is often a fruitless task."

His words stirred her faultless memory, calling forth a line from Lord Verniers' *Cantos of Gold and Dust*: *Truth is the scholar's greatest weapon, but often also his doom.* She decided a private audience with the Alpiran chronicler was overdue.

"Am I to assume," she said to Caenis, "that your Order now requires a new Aspect?"

"There are formalities to the choosing, as you know, Highness. Until such time as a conclave can be convened, my Order remains without an Aspect. However, my brothers and sisters have affirmed their willingness to accede to my leadership in the interim." His gaze became steady again. "Which brings me to another matter."

"The people from the Reaches."

"Indeed, Highness. My Order has lost many brothers and sisters in this war. Our ranks grow thin."

"And you would take these others into the Order, against their loud objections? Lord Vaelin has been very clear on their thoughts in this regard. They follow him, not you."

"My Order is the shield of the Gifted. Without us they would all have perished generations ago."

"And yet, you continued to hide yourselves for decades whilst they faced discovery and death at the hands of the Fourth Order."

"A necessary subterfuge. Most of us are discovered at an early age, Gifted children born to Gifted parents and long-time members of the Order. Not all are so fortunate, or grow to be kind of heart or immune to greed. For all our power, we have human souls like any other. Before Aspect Tendris's ascension those Gifted found by the Fourth Order would be judged to see if they were suitable for inclusion within our ranks. Whether they joined us or not was their choice."

"Not, I assume, if they stood outside the Faith?"

"The Seventh Order is of the Faith, Highness. That cannot change."

Do I have another Tendris here? she pondered, seeing the implacable belief in his gaze. She had often wondered why her father didn't have the ever-troublesome Aspect of the Fourth Order quietly poisoned by one of his many hidden agents. But even the old schemer hadn't been immune to the Faith, or ignorant of the power it wielded.

"This is a free Realm," she told Caenis. "That also cannot change. You may speak to the Gifted from the Reaches and offer them a place in your Order. However, if they refuse, you will let the matter drop and I will not hear it raised again during my reign, which I expect to be of considerable duration. Unless your Sister"—she consulted the list again, for show since she had memorised the contents at the first glance—"Verlia scries a different future, of course."

"My sister's visions are . . . infrequent," he replied. "And require considerable interpretation. When it comes to Your Highness, so far she sees little."

"And what little does she see?"

He straightened, once more seemingly a warrior rather than an Aspect in waiting, face set in the knowledge of coming battle. "Fire," he said. "She sees only fire."

◆　◆　◆

She travelled with the Seordah the next day, choosing to walk as they did. Lady Dahrena accompanied her to act as interpreter, a somewhat redundant role since few of the forest folk seemed inclined to speak to them, most in fact keen to avoid looking in their direction. She could see the lady's grief at this, the way her smile faltered as the hawk-faced warriors looked away or grunted clipped responses to her approaches. In contrast, their attitude to Lyrna seemed more one of curious bafflement rather than fear.

"Healing touch very rare in the forest," Hera Drakil told her, the only one of his people to stay at Dahrena's side for more than a few steps, and even then she sensed a tense reluctance in the war chief, as if every step was a test of courage. "Not known for many generations."

"Do your people have books?" Lyrna asked, her thoughts straying to the Mahlessa's vast library under the Mountain. "Records of the time before the Marelim Sil?"

"Books?" the war chief frowned.

"*Virosra san elosra dural,*" Dahrena told him. Lyrna's Seordah was markedly less accomplished than her Lonak, but she had enough for a rough translation. *The words that cage the spirit.*

"No," the Seordah told Lyrna. "No books for the Seordah. Not now, not in the before times. All is spoken and remembered. Only the spoken word is true."

Lyrna saw Dahrena hesitate then say something in the Seordah tongue, too fast to easily translate and rich in words beyond Lyrna's knowledge. Whatever their meaning, the words were enough to darken Hera Drakil's expression and he turned away, striding off through the disordered ranks of his people.

"Is he offended?" Lyrna asked Dahrena.

The lady's face was drawn in sadness as she watched the war chief walk away. "Only the spoken word is true," she said. "I told him the truth. He didn't like it."

◆ ◆ ◆

The army swelled as it moved east, hidden bands of fugitives and escaped slaves emerging from forest and cave to join them or beg food. Lyrna made sure all were provided for, even those reluctant to join their ranks, though these were few in number. There were numerous Realm Guard stragglers among the new recruits, eager for a return to regiments that were now mostly extinct. At her request Brother Caenis had stepped down as Lord Marshal of the Realm Guard contingent, though his decision had caused some discord in the ranks. Regardless of any Dark affliction, many still saw him as a saviour, the fearless commander who led them to deliverance after calamitous defeat. Others were less accepting, mainly the men who had served under Lady Reva at Cumbrael and the fugitives found on the march, leading to a fair amount of loud quarrelling and even a few fist-fights. A formal delegation of sergeants had gone to Vaelin requesting Caenis's reinstatement and the Battle Lord had been obliged to calm their anger by elevating one of their own in the brother's place, a veteran sergeant of stocky build with a face like scarred leather.

"Sergeant Travick, Highness," he said, going to one knee before her the day she joined them on the march. "Late of the Sixteenth Regiment of Foot."

"Ah, the Black Bears as I recall," Lyrna said, gesturing for Benten to bring her the item he had procured from Brother Hollun's travelling armoury.

Travick blinked at her in surprise. "Yes, Highness. Your memory does you credit."

"Thank you. However, I must advise you that your etiquette, by contrast, is sadly lacking."

The veteran lowered his head, frowning in embarrassment. "Forgive me, Highness. Not used to such things."

"Hardly an excuse," Lyrna said, holding out her hand as Benten handed her the sword, an Asraelin blade, as befit the occasion. "For a Sword of the Realm to refer to himself as a sergeant. I profess myself shocked."

His head snapped up in alarm, eyes widening at the sight of the sword. "Lord Marshal Al Travick," she said, reversing the weapon to lay it across her forearm, handle first, "do you accept this sword offered by your queen?"

Behind Travick the Realm Guard were stirring in their ranks, less neat and well shaved as she remembered, but all uniformly hardened and possessed of the air of dangerous men. *Dangerous I can use,* she decided. *Let them fight each other if they must, as long as they fight harder against the Volarians.*

"I-I do, Highness," Travick stammered.

"Then take it, my lord, and do get up." His meaty, scarred hand closed on the sword-handle and he rose, holding it up with an expression of blank astonishment.

"It is my wish that the Realm Guard be reordered, Lord Marshal," she went on, recapturing his attention and making him snap back into a soldierly posture, spine straight and eyes averted.

"Whatever my Queen commands."

"A respect for the past is a good thing, but we cannot allow it to obstruct our purpose. Many proud regiments now retain mere fragments of their former complement or were wiped out completely. If I calculate correctly, there are little over six thousand Realm Guard under your command, many of them holding to regimental ties that no longer have meaning. Of those regiments still remaining only three can truly be called such, and even they are greatly reduced in number. You will bring these up to full complement and divide the remaining men into three new regiments, their names and banners to be determined by the men, subject to my approval. Also you will add Lord Nortah's company to the Realm Guard roster as the Sixtieth Regiment of Foot."

She turned her gaze on the ranks of the Realm Guard. The regimental loyalty of the Realm's soldiery was legendary and she saw open dismay on many faces. "When this war is won," she told them, raising her voice, "I give you my word the Realm Guard will be rebuilt and any wishing to rejoin their former regiments will be granted leave to do so. For now, we have a war to win and sentiment will not aid us in that endeavour."

Lord Travick barked a command, his sergeant's voice a thunderclap, sending every soldier to one knee, heads bowed. "The Realm Guard is yours, Highness," he said. "To forge as you will, and," he added, his voice loud and carrying to every soldier in his command, "if I hear any man say differently, I'll flog him down to the bone."

◆　◆　◆

The walls of Warnsclave had been neglected for many years, the long period of peace heralded by her father's ascension making them an expensive irrelevance to successive town factors. Vaelin opined they had been strong enough to repel one Volarian assault, but ultimately proved too weak to withstand another. They were rent in several places, great gashes torn into the stone from ground to parapet, offering an all-too-clear view of what lay beyond as Arrow brought Lyrna closer.

"Nothing remains, Highness," Lord Adal had reported that morning, having returned from reconnaissance. "Not a house, and not a soul."

Her faint hope the North Guard had exaggerated dwindled with every tread of Arrow's hooves, the ash and rubble visible through the breaches told of utter destruction. She found Vaelin waiting at the ruined gate, expression grim. "The harbour, Highness," he said.

The harbour waters were cloudy with silt and scummed by oil leaking from the scuttled boats of the town's fishing fleet, but she could see them clearly enough, a great cluster of pale ovals, tinged green by the algae in the water so they resembled a mound of grapes after the harvest.

Lyrna swept her gaze around the remnants of what she recalled as a lively if somewhat smelly town, grimy in fact, the people speaking in a coarse accent, more ready to meet her gaze than in Varinshold, and less ready to bow. But they had been happy to see her, she remembered, cheering as she rode through, offering babies to kiss and tossing flower petals in her path. She had come to open an alms-house, paid for by the Crown and staffed by the Fifth Order. She had found no trace of it in the journey to the harbour, just street after street of piled brick and scorched timber.

"They chained them together," Vaelin said. "Pushed the first in and the rest followed. Perhaps four hundred, the only survivors from when they took the town, I assume."

"Didn't want to be burdened with slaves on the march north," Lord Adal commented. His voice had the clipped tones of well-controlled emotion, but Lyrna saw how the muscles of his jaw bunched as he stared down at the water.

"March north, my lord?" she asked him.

Lady Dahrena stepped forward with a bow, her face showing the kind of paleness that only came from the deepest chill. "I believe I may have useful intelligence, Highness."

"It's gone?" Lyrna asked her a short while later. She had ordered Murel to fetch the lady a hot beverage and she sat in her tent now, small hands clutching a bowl of warm milk. Vaelin stood by regarding Dahrena with evident concern, already having voiced his disquiet at her using her gift.

"Alltor cost you much," he said. "Flying free again so soon was unwise."

"I am a soldier in this army," the lady replied with a shrug. "Like any other, and my gift is my weapon."

Lyrna forced herself to stillness as the air seemed to thicken between them, knowing much was being left unsaid, but still they knew each other's mind as if the words had been shouted. *Whilst I know so little of what lies behind his eyes.*

"Burnt to ash from end to end," Dahrena confirmed. "The Urlish is dead, Highness."

Lyrna remembered the day Lord Al Telnar had come begging her father to lift the strictures on harvesting timber from the Urlish, how he had been sent scurrying from the council chamber, face red with humiliation. "The Urlish is the birthplace of this Realm," Janus had told a cringing Al Telnar as he signed another decree reallocating yet more land formerly owned by the Minister of Royal Works. "The cradle of my rule, not to be grubbed over by the likes of you."

Al Telnar and the Urlish, she reflected. *Now both nothing but ash. Strange he should sacrifice himself for me after so many years of Father's torments.* "And this army moving across the Renfaelin border towards Varinshold?" she asked Dahrena. "Could you gauge their number?"

"Somewhere over five thousand, Highness. Mostly on horseback."

"Darnel calls his knights," Lyrna mused. "He'll certainly need them before long."

"I don't think so, Highness," Dahrena said. "There's a soul among them, burning bright but red. I've seen it before, when I flew over the Urlish. I'm certain it was fighting the Volarians there."

Lyrna nodded, recalling a night spent in a Renfaelin holdfast, only months ago but it seemed like years now. *There are many*, Banders had said, *who find the prospect of being ruled by that man a stain on their honour.*

"And the filth who slaughtered the people in the harbour?" she asked. "Any trace of them in your flight, my lady?"

She sensed a certain resignation in Dahrena's response, a grim acceptance of the consequences of the intelligence she provided. "Four thousand or so, Highness. Twenty miles north-west. Most on foot."

Lyrna turned to Vaelin. "My lord, please ask Sanesh Poltar for the fastest horse the Eorhil can provide and an escort for a royal messenger. They will seek out this Renfaelin army and divine their identity and intentions."

He gave a shallow bow. "Yes, Highness."

"I will see to the recovery of the bodies from the harbour and ensure they are given to the fire with all due ceremony, whilst you will take every rider we have and hunt down their murderers. And I expect to hear no more word of prisoners."

CHAPTER SIX

Vaelin

We will make an ending, you and I.

"My lord?"

Vaelin snapped back to the present at Adal's words, finding the North Guard commander mounted alongside, his eyes narrowed in shrewd appraisal. "My men found some stragglers two miles north," Adal said. "Close to exhaustion and not having eaten for days. Seems likely the rest won't be in much better shape."

Vaelin nodded, turning away from the man's scrutiny, looking to the west where the Eorhil were galloping off to perform the encircling manoeuvre he had ordered that morning. He experienced a moment's disorientation as the plainsmen crested a rise and disappeared from view, an increasingly familiar sensation mingling frustration with disappointment. There was no song to accompany the ride of the Eorhil, as there had been no song to guide him when Lyrna was found healed in body if not, apparently, in spirit. Nor had there been any song to accompany Orven's hanging of the Volarian prisoners at her command, nor any music now as he turned back to Adal and ordered him to take his men to cover the east.

He saw no reluctance in Adal's demeanour before he turned his mount about and rode off, but there was uncertainty there, even a faint concern. He wondered if the North Guard's animosity had worn thinner since Alltor, that if there wasn't some actual regard for his Tower Lord these days. But, where once such things were so easily divined, now there was only continual uncertainty. *Is this what it is to live without a gift?*

He recalled those brief years when his song had fallen silent, his refusal to heed it leaving him bereft, without guidance. It had been hard to be so rudderless in a sea of chaos and war. This, however, was much worse, because now there was the chill, the bone-deep cold that had seeped into him in the Ally's domain and lingered on here in this world of myriad paths, all seemingly so dark. And the words, of course, those words that hounded him from the Beyond.

We will make an ending, you and I.

Nortah trotted up beside him, Snowdance bounding on ahead, as ever enlivened by the prospect of blood.

"You belong with your regiment," Vaelin told him.

"Davern has them well in hand," his brother replied. "Truth be told, I'd be grateful if you'd ask the queen to promote him in my stead. Boundless hatred and bloodlust are not easily tolerated for long."

"They'll need firm leadership, and a restraining hand."

Nortah raised an eyebrow. "Is that sentiment shared by the queen, brother? If so, I'd be greatly surprised."

Vaelin didn't respond, recalling his joy on seeing her that day at Alltor as the boat carried her across the river, the blossoming relief as she stepped ashore. The song's absence was a physical pain and she seemed to offer an antidote, a single point of certainty, burned but glorious. *How could I ever have imagined she might have fallen?* he had thought, sinking to his knees before her.

But as the days passed, and the army's evident love for their queen swelled by the mile, he had felt the song's absence ever more keenly. *She raises so many questions. And yet seems to ask none herself.* He saw great differences from the girl he had met in that palace corridor so many years ago, the unbridled ambition forged into something new, and more troubling. *She hungered for power, now what does she hunger for?*

"My people met with our brother," Nortah said. He always referred to the Gifted from Nehrin's Point in this way, as if they were a nation unto themselves. "As per the queen's request. They told him no, as expected." He paused. "Have you spoken to him? Since his little revelation?"

Vaelin shook his head, keen to avoid discussion on this topic. The questions it raised were even more troubling than those surrounding the queen.

"Seventh Order or not," Nortah went on. "Faith or not. He's still our brother."

He always knew more, Vaelin thought. *More than he ever said. Knowledge that might have been useful, saved many, perhaps even Frentis . . . or Mikehl.*

"I'll talk to him," he promised Nortah. *For we have much to discuss.*

"You're not going to do anything . . . foolish today, are you?" Nortah asked.

"Foolish, brother?"

"Yes, brother." Nortah's face was stern. "Such as throwing yourself at an entire army. They can compose all the songs they like, it was still bloody silly. We have a home to return to, if you recall. The Order is behind us. There is something to live for now, *someone* to live for."

There was an additional weight in his voice and Vaelin knew his meaning well enough. Dahrena had been at his side for most of the journey, except today as he begged her to rest after her efforts to find their quarry. It was strange but, for all the time spent together, they spoke little, conversation seemingly unnecessary. He knew she could feel the absence of his song and feared it would create a barrier between them, but she was more at ease with him now than ever before, and the reason was not hard to guess. *Two souls meeting in the Beyond, not a bond to be easily broken.*

For all the discomfort the realisation brought, he remained grateful for her company, for it was only in her presence that the chill seemed to abate. It lurched anew now, a sudden ache deep inside, often making itself known when he rode for a long while, or engaged in any serious exertion.

"No foolishness, brother," he told Nortah, pulling his cloak tighter about his chest. "My word on it."

◆ ◆ ◆

His horse had belonged to a North Guard and, like most mounts bred in the Reaches, was of Eorhil stock: tall, fleet, and of placid nature when not called to battle. Captain Adal said his former owner had been a man of great practicality and little sentiment, referring to the animal simply as "Horse" and Vaelin had yet to think of anything better. He felt the beast tense as they neared a hilltop in late afternoon, his nostrils flaring as they caught a scent too faint for Vaelin's nose, though he could guess its meaning: the sweat of many fearful men.

They came into view as he crested the rise, the Nilsaelin cavalry falling in on either side of him, spreading out as they reordered their ranks in preparation for the charge. Nilsaelin cavalry were lightly armoured and their horses bred for speed rather than strength, most riders armed with a seven-foot lance. They eyed the Volarians with set faces, devoid of mercy or fear. Word of the atrocity at Warnsclave had been quick to spread and these men had already witnessed horrors aplenty on the march to Alltor.

The Volarians had formed battalions arranged into a square, ragged and twitching on the left where Vaelin judged the Free Swords were placed, solid on the right where the Varitai stood awaiting their fate with rigid indifference. Beyond them the Eorhil had cut off their line of retreat and were drawn up on flat ground, clustered into their war bands and moving forward at a slow walk. Off to the east he could see the North Guard riding into position to seal any escape route whilst Orven's mounted guard drew up on the western flank.

"At your command, my lord," the Nilsaelin cavalry commander said, a wiry man with the typically villainous appearance of his fief's soldiery, shaven-headed and sporting fresh scars no doubt earned at Alltor. In common with his men Vaelin could see the man's eagerness to get at the enemy, the way his gloved hand clasped and unclasped the haft of his lance.

"Wait for the Eorhil," Vaelin told him. He reached over his shoulder and drew his sword, finding it strange that there was no comfort to be found in the feel of the handle. Where once it had felt like holding a living thing, now it was just a length of steel and wood, heavier than he recalled.

A familiar hissing sound drew his attention back to the field, finding the air above the Volarians dark with arrows at the apogee of flight, the Eorhil now boiling across the flat ground at full pelt. Vaelin raised his sword as the Nilsaelin buglers sounded the signal to prepare for a charge, slashing down as the Eorhil volley struck home. He kicked at his horse's flanks and they spurred to the gallop in unison, thunder rising from the earth.

◆　◆　◆

The shock of impact left him reeling in the saddle, his horse's manic whinny lost in the instant cacophony of rage and the clashing of metal and flesh. He hung on to the saddle by the pommel, feeling something hard scrape along the chain mail covering his back. A Volarian lunged at him from the throng, eyes wide and desperate though his short sword remained level and true. Vaelin released the pommel and tumbled to the earth, rolling into the Volarian with enough force to send him flying. Vaelin struggled to his knees, sword coming up to parry a thrust from a well-built Free Sword, a veteran judging by his age and the ease with which he danced out of reach as Vaelin replied with a slash at his legs, marvelling at his own sluggishness. The Free Sword brought his blade down on Vaelin's with a practised efficiency, just above the hilt, jarring it from his grasp.

He stared at his empty hand, a thought repeating itself with a strange, calm detachment. *I dropped my sword.*

The Free Sword stepped closer, sword drawn back for a hard thrust to Vaelin's neck, then twisting in an oddly elegant pirouette, blood gushing from his part-severed neck as Nortah dragged his horse to a halt a few feet away, Snowdance following in his wake, teeth and claws already bloody.

Vaelin stood, taking stock of their surroundings. The charge had carried them almost to the centre of the Volarian ranks, combat raging on all sides as the Nilsaelins stabbed with their lances and Orven's guardsmen hacked with their swords. A fresh arrow storm was falling somewhere to the west, indicating the Eorhil had found a stubborn pocket of Varitai resistance.

Lord Orven's voice sounded nearby and Vaelin saw him rallying his men for a charge at a dense knot of Free Swords, fighting with all the desperation of doomed men. A loud whinny sounded and he saw his riderless horse plough into the Volarians, rearing and stamping, teeth bared as he screamed. The Volarian knot soon broke apart as Orven's men charged home, Nilsaelins spurring in to join the slaughter.

"No foolishness?" Nortah asked, looming above with a reproachful glare.

Vaelin looked down at his empty hand, flexing the fingers and feeling the chill rise again. Something nuzzled his shoulder and he turned to find his horse, snorting loudly and tossing his head, a fresh cut on his nose. "Scar," Vaelin said, running a hand over his snout. "Your name is Scar."

◆ ◆ ◆

"Hold still," Dahrena admonished as he winced from the sting of the ointment she applied to his back. His tumble from the saddle had left him with a spectacular bruise from hip to shoulder, not to mention the constantly repeated words that plagued him on the journey back to Warnsclave. *I dropped my sword.*

"Hasn't your legend grown enough already?" Dahrena went on, working the ointment into his skin, her fingers moving in hard tense circles. "You have to charge into every army you find? Now, apparently, with a Dark-commanded horse."

"Hardly," he groaned, sighing in relief as she rose from his side, going to the small chest holding the various pots and boxes containing her curatives. "I suspect my new horse just likes to fight."

He had taken a basement room in the one structure left standing in Warnsclave, the harbour-master's fortresslike house rising from the base of the mole, entirely built of granite and too substantial to be easily torn down. The queen and her retinue occupied the upper floors whilst the army made camp amidst the ruins, the ranks swelling yet again as more people trailed in from the surrounding countryside.

"Like his master," Dahrena muttered, making him wince again. This was the first cross word between them since Alltor, stirring fears their bond might not be so immune to injury after all. The battle had been brief, hardly surprising given the odds, the Volarians running after no more than a quarter hour of combat, the time it took to cut down the Varitai. The surviving Free Swords fled in all directions, soon hunted down by the Eorhil whilst the Nilsaelins finished off the wounded and engaged in the time-honoured soldier's treat of looting the dead. To his surprise Vaelin was greeted with grave respect as he walked the field, soldiers offering bows and raised lances in salute. *Do they choose not to see?* he wondered. *Preferring to believe in a man of foolish courage and a Dark-led horse rather than a weakened fool who can't stay in the saddle and drops his sword.*

"I came close to dying today," he told her, his tone flat, reflective. She didn't turn but her back stiffened. "You know I lost my song," he went on. "When you brought me back. Without it . . . I dropped my sword, Dahrena."

She turned, a frown of anger on her face. "Is that self-pity I hear, my lord?"

"No." He shook his head. "Just honest words . . ."

"Well, I have some honest words for you." She came to him, kneeling to clasp his hands, small slender fingers working to clasp his own. "I once saw a boy fight like a savage to win a banner in some dreadful game. I thought it cruel then, in truth I still do. But the boy I saw that day did not hear a note from his song, otherwise I would have felt it. You were always more than your gift." She took a firmer grip on his hands. "A gift is not muscle, or bone, or a skill learned since boyhood, a skill I cannot believe has dulled in but a few weeks."

She raised her gaze, the anger faded now as she stood, releasing his hands to enfold his head, pulling him close. "We both have much still to do, Vaelin. And I believe our queen's purpose would be better served with you at her side." She moved back, smiling down at him, her smooth, warm hand tracing from his brow to his chin before placing a kiss on his lips. "Did you happen to find a key for this door?"

Later she lay with her head resting on his chest, her small and perfect form pressed against him, dispelling any vestige of the chill. It had begun at Alltor with scarcely any word spoken that first night. There had been no preamble, just silent and unabashed need as they coiled together in the dark, drawn together by something neither felt any inclination to resist.

"The queen hates me," she whispered now, her breath ruffling the hairs on his chest. "She strives to hide it, but I can feel it."

Whereas I can only suspect it, he thought. "We break no law and offer no insult," he said. "And even a queen is allowed her own feelings."

"You and her, when you were young, did you . . . ?"

He gave a faint chuckle. "No, such a thing could never have happened." His smile faded as Linden Al Hestian's face came to mind, so many years on and still the guilt of it cut him.

"She loves you," Dahrena went on. "You must see it."

"I see only the queen I am bound to follow." *Best for all if I see nothing more.* "What do the Seordah say of her?"

He felt her tense, her head shifting on his chest. "Nothing, to me that is. What they say to each other, however, I cannot say."

He knew the Seordah's attitude to them both had undergone a severe transformation since Alltor, a deep wariness replacing the affection they held for her and the reluctant respect they had begun to show him. "What is it?" he asked her. "Why do they fear us so?"

She remained silent for a long time, eventually raising herself up to rest her chin on her hands, her face hidden in the dark but her eyes catching the light from the small opening in the basement wall. "Like the Faithful, the Seordah do not see death as a curse. But they believe when a soul takes leave of the body it goes not to a world beyond this, but to a hidden place, a world that exists in every shadow and dark corner, unseen and unknowable by living eyes. In this world you take every lesson learned when alive, every hunter's trick or warrior's skill, every scrap of lore, and you embark upon the great and endless hunt, but free of fear or uncertainty, every burden carried in life gone, leaving only the hunt. You may have seen them in the forest sometimes, reaching a hand into the shadowed hollow of a tree or the shade cast by a rock, hoping for a whispered message from a loved soul lost to the hunt."

"When you brought me back," he said. "You deprived me of a gift."

"The greatest gift."

"You should talk to them, tell them the truth of it."

"I did. It didn't help. In their eyes I am a transgressor and you should no longer be walking this earth. They are lost to me now."

He held her as she lowered her gaze once more, playing his hands over her shoulders and feeling her sorrow. "Then why do they stay?" he asked.

Her reply was soft, sighed through tears, "They do what we do: heed the wolf's call."

◆ ◆ ◆

Reva's sword thumped against his bruised side drawing a pain-filled grunt. She hopped nimbly backwards as he answered with a clumsy upward slash, then lunged forward in a crouch, jabbing a thrust at his chest. He dodged away, flicking her wooden blade up and aiming a cut at her legs which struck home as she waited too long to form the parry.

"Better," she said. "Don't you think?"

Vaelin moved to the nearby tree stump where his canteen sat, drinking deep. The sky was overcast today and the air chilled, heralding the onset of autumn and the prospect of a less-than-easy march to Varinshold. They had lingered at Warnsclave for three days now as they waited for the Meldenean fleet to appear. The supply situation had been alleviated by Lord Al Bera's provisions but they still lacked sufficient stocks to sustain the northward advance, especially in light of their ever-growing number of recruits. Over a thousand people had made their way to the ruined city since their arrival, forcing the addition of yet more companies to Nortah's regiment. The Volarians, it seemed, hadn't been quite so efficient as they imagined in gathering slaves, though scouts brought daily evidence of their proficiency in slaughter, telling tales of one ruined village after another, each well stocked with rotting corpses.

"No," he told Reva. "If anything I'm worse today." He tossed his canteen aside and charged at her, delivering a rapid series of thrusts and slashes, his wooden sword moving in a blur. She dodged and parried with a fluency that put her early lessons to shame; battle-honed skill always counted for more, he knew. He also knew she was going easy on him, allowing him to land strokes she could have easily blocked, making her replies just fractionally slower than they should have been.

"This won't do," he muttered, pulling up short from another lunge.

"Oh come now," she mocked. "Not giving up, are you?"

You love me too much, he thought with an inward sigh. *Scared to watch me die again.* He cast his gaze at the field below the hill where they practised, the army labouring under the instruction of officers and sergeants, new recruits and old being honed into their queen's deadly instrument of justice. He could see her cantering along on her white horse, black cloak trailing in the wind, raising salutes and exhortations wherever she rode.

"Do you . . . ?" Reva had come to stand beside him, speaking in hesitant tones.

"What?" he prompted.

"The queen." Reva's eyes tracked Lyrna's horse as she trotted towards Nortah's new companies, people falling to the knees as she came to a halt. "What was done to her. Do you ever wonder what it might mean?"

"Her healing?"

"No. Not her healing. What was done before. To suffer what she suffered, healed or not the scars run deep."

"As deep as yours, sister?"

"Perhaps deeper, that's what worries me. My hands are red, as are yours. We have no claim to innocence and I'll answer to the Father when my time comes. But she . . . Sometimes I think she would burn the whole world if it meant the death of the last Volarian. And even then she wouldn't be sated."

"Don't you hunger for justice?"

"Justice, yes. And to make my people secure once more. To do that I'll fight her war and free her city. But that won't be enough will it? What will you tell her when she orders you to follow her across the ocean?"

No song. No guidance. Just ever-more-silent uncertainty.

"Thank you for the practice, my lady," he said, turning to offer a bow. "But I think I need a less caring tutor."

◆ ◆ ◆

Davern's ash sword batted Vaelin's parry aside and cracked against his unarmoured ribs, leaving him winded and doubled over. Davern stepped back as Vaelin gasped for air, glaring up at him. "Who told you to stop, sergeant?"

The former shipwright gave a momentary frown, which quickly transformed into a bright-toothed grin, lunging forward to deliver a jab at Vaelin's nose. He twisted, the ash blade missing by a whisker, grabbing the sergeant's arm and throwing him over his shoulder. Davern was quick to recover, leaping to his feet and whirling to deliver a round-house slash at Vaelin's legs. Wood cracked as Vaelin blocked the blow then replied with a series of two-handed strokes aimed at chest and head, the sergeant backing away and blocking every blow, deaf to the calls of the onlookers.

Three days now and Vaelin had yet to land a blow, drawing a larger crowd with each repeated bout of practice. Davern, as expected, had needed little persuasion to fight with the Battle Lord, his evident delight increasing further when Vaelin's reduced skills became apparent. It would have been easy to do this away from the eyes of the army but Vaelin resisted the temptation, finding the scrutiny of so many critical eyes a useful impetus to greater effort.

He was improving, he could feel it, the chill not so deep now. But still the sword felt strange in his hand, the once-sublime artistry replaced with workmanlike efficiency. *How much was the song?* he wondered continually. *How much do I need it?*

Davern ducked under another stroke, jerking to the side then delivering a precise thrust that found its way past Vaelin's guard to jab into his upper lip, drawing blood and making him reel backwards.

"Apologies, my lord," Davern said, his sword smacking into Vaelin's right leg and sending him to the ground, slapping his feeble counterstroke away and raising his weapon for a no-doubt-painful final blow. "But you did say to display no restraint."

"That's enough!" Alornis was striding forward, face red with fury. She shoved a smirking Davern aside and knelt by Vaelin, pressing a clean rag to his bleeding lip. "This is over," she told the sergeant. "Go back to your regiment."

"Does your lady sister command here now, my lord?" Davern asked Vaelin. "Perhaps she should."

"Sergeant." The voice was soft but Davern's smirk disappeared in an instant. Nortah stood nearby, casting his eye about the onlooking soldiers, mostly free fighters from his own regiment, all quickly finding somewhere else to be. Snowdance moved from Nortah's side to nudge at Vaelin's shoulder, purring insistently until he got to his feet.

"Your man is a brute," Alornis told Nortah, continuing to staunch the blood flowing from Vaelin's lip.

"Merely following his lordship's order, Teacher," Davern said to Nortah. Whereas he showed a complete absence of fear in regard to Vaelin, his attitude to Nortah was always markedly more respectful.

"Indeed he was," Vaelin said, pausing to hawk a red glob onto the ground. "And very well too, I might add."

Nortah spared Davern a brief glance. "See to the pickets," he ordered quietly.

The sergeant bowed and hurried off.

"A thousand things can happen in a battle," Nortah said to Vaelin. "You put too much stock in one dropped sword."

"Wars aren't won with dropped swords, brother." Vaelin took the rag from Alornis and walked towards the tree where he had tethered Scar.

"Brother Kehlan should see to that," she called after him but he just waved and climbed into the saddle.

◆　◆　◆

Finding Caenis wasn't difficult. The Seventh Order contingent, now grown to some four brothers and two sisters, were housed in a canvas roofed ruin near the harbour, somewhat removed from the rest of the army, who continued to eye them with unabashed suspicion. Caenis sat with the others, talking in low but earnest tones, each of them listening with keen attention. They were all younger than his brother. The gift of youth provided a greater chance of surviving the Volarian onslaught, the young being better suited to the rigours of battle or more likely to catch the slavers' eye. One young man had clearly endured some harsh treatment, sitting shirtless as he listened to Caenis, his back striped with recent whip-strokes, raw and red in the evening light.

"The province of war is no longer confined to the Sixth Order," Caenis was saying. "Now all the Faithful are called to join this struggle. Now we are all warriors. Concealment is a luxury we can no longer afford."

He fell silent as Vaelin stepped from the shadows, the others turning to regard him with a mixture of customary awe and grave respect.

"Brother," Vaelin said. "I would speak with you."

They walked the length of the mole as darkness fell, a three-quarters moon showing through intermittent cloud. Caenis said nothing, waiting for him to speak, perhaps fully aware of the first word he would say.

"Mikehl," Vaelin said when they had come to the end of the mole. The evening tide had drawn the sea back from the mole so it seemed they stood atop a great height, assailed by a strong breeze, the gently lapping waves barely visible below. He searched Caenis's face as his brother gave no response, seeing what he had expected to see. Guilt.

"Before I sailed to the Reaches Aspect Grealin assured me he had no part in it," Vaelin went on. "Placing the blame squarely on Brother Harlick, who in truth has admitted his part, though not in the most fulsome terms. Is there perhaps something you would like to add to the story, brother?"

Caenis's expression didn't change and his voice was toneless as he replied, "My Aspect instructed me to keep you safe. I did as I was instructed."

"The men who killed Mikehl told of another, someone I fancy they met in the forest that night. Someone they feared."

"They were expecting a brother of Harlick's acquaintance, someone complicit in his scheme. I found him, killed him, and took his place. The assassins hired by Nortah's father were not so easily killed, so I sent them in the wrong direction, a direction I expected would lead them clear of any brothers. Mikehl, however, was always so slow, and so easily lost."

Vaelin turned away from him, staring out to sea. The wind was rising and the wave-tops shone white in the dim moonlight. Farther out he could see a black shape on the horizon, soon joined by several more. "Our Fleet Lord makes good his promise," he observed.

Caenis glanced at the approaching ships. "This war has garnered some strange allies."

"And revealed much in the process."

"That day you found us . . . My words were unfair. I had lost so many men, so much unforeseen death. It seemed the Departed had abandoned us, as if your Faithlessness had drawn their judgement. It was a foolish notion, brother."

"Brother," Vaelin repeated softly. "We've called each other that for so long I wonder if it still holds meaning. So much has been concealed, so many lies spoken. That first day, in the vaults, Grealin patted you on the shoulder and you flinched. I thought you feared his imaginary rats, but he was greeting you. You weren't joining the Sixth Order, you were reporting to your Aspect."

"It is how we persist, how we continue to serve the Faith. At least until now. With Aspect Grealin gone the burden of rebuilding this Order falls to me. It would sit easier with your help."

"The Gifted from the Reaches want no part of your Order. Cara and Marken aren't even of the Faith and I doubt Lorkan could summon the will to believe in anything."

"Much like you, brother." Caenis's words were softly spoken but Vaelin heard the judgement in them clearly.

"I did not lose my faith," he told Caenis. "It shrivelled and died in the face of truth."

"And will this great truth win this war, brother? Look around you and see how many have suffered. Will your *truth* sustain them in the months and years ahead?"

"Will your gift? I've yet to learn what manner of power you hold, and if I am to command this army, I should greatly like to know."

Caenis stood regarding him in silence, eyes intent and unblinking. Vaelin's hand went to the hunting knife at his belt, gripping the handle tight, ready to draw it forth, stab it into his brother's eye . . . He breathed out slowly, releasing the knife and finding his hand trembling.

"So now you know, brother," Caenis said before turning and walking away.

CHAPTER SEVEN

Alucius

Aspect Dendrish sagged on hearing the news, seeming to shrink as his bulk subsided onto his too-narrow bed. His jowls shimmered as he worked his slug-like lips, brow drawn in a frown of despair. "There . . ." He paused and swallowed, gazing up at Alucius with wide-eyed desperation. "There could be some error in this. Some misunderstanding . . ."

"I doubt that, Aspect," Alucius said. "It seems Master Grealin has truly met his end, though in rather strange circumstances." He went on to relate the tale Darnel had told him, complete with the Dark powers attributed to the fallen Master of the Sixth Order.

Dendrish's response was swift, immediate and far too practised to be anything but a lie. "Utter nonsense. In fact I am appalled a man of learning could lend any credence to such lurid piffle."

"Quite so, Aspect." Alucius fished inside his sack and brought out a fresh volume, tossing it onto the bed. One of his more prized finds, Brother Killern's *The Voyage of the Swift Wing*. He had intended to annoy the Aspect with an annotated copy of Lord Al Avern's *Complete and Unbiased History of the Church of the World Father*, but felt the plump scholar's spirits might be in need of a lift. Dendrish, however, didn't even glance at the book, sitting and staring at nothing as Alucius begged leave and departed the cell.

Aspect Elera was more careful in her response, commenting briefly about her scant acquaintance with the late master before expressing her deep appreciation for the fresh medicine and new books. Her tone, however, became markedly more intent when she asked him, "And the wine, Alucius?"

"I have yet to seek it out, Aspect."

She met his gaze, speaking in a surprisingly harsh whisper. "Then be sure to slake your thirst *soon*, good sir."

◆　◆　◆

With Darnel and much of the Renfaelin knights gone off to hunt down the elusive Red Brother, Varinshold was even more quiet than usual. Most of the Volarian garrison were Varitai, never particularly talkative, and the smaller contingent of Free Swords kept to themselves in the northern quarter mansion houses they had transformed into barracks. The streets, such as they were, remained unpatrolled for the most part since there was hardly a soul left to police. Most slaves had been shipped across the ocean weeks ago and those that remained were fully occupied fulfilling Darnel's vision of his great palace, one in particular providing the most valued labour, so valued in fact that Darnel had threatened to sever the hand of any overseer who touched him with the slightest kiss of a whip.

Visiting Master Benril was not one of Alucius's favourite obligations, a task to be undertaken as infrequently as his conscience allowed, usually when images of Alornis loomed largest in his mind. He found the old master hard at work on the western wall, a ragged and burnt eyesore in the aftermath of the city's fall, marking the apex of the palace's destruction, now covered in fresh marble from end to end. Benril was accompanied by a portly, balding slave, older than most but spared execution by virtue of his skill with stone, and his expert knowledge of where to find more. He rarely spoke more than a few words, the overseers having been given no injunction about applying the whip to his back, but revealed a highborn's cultured vowels when he did. Alucius had yet to learn the man's name, and in truth avoided doing so. Slaves could never be relied upon to live long enough to make any association worthwhile.

"Coming along rather nicely, Master," he greeted Benril, calling up to the second tier of the scaffolding where the sculptor laboured to craft the great relief depicting Darnel's glorious victory over the Realm Guard.

Benril left off hammering to glance over his shoulder. He offered no greeting but gave an irritated flick of his hand, granting leave for Alucius to ascend the ladder. Alucius always marvelled at the speed with which they worked, the portly slave guiding a rasp over recently completed carvings as Benril continued to birth more from virgin stone. Only one month into Darnel's vainglorious project and it was a quarter complete, the finely carved figures emerging from the stone in accordance with the vast cartoon Benril had unrolled before the Fief Lord's approving eye.

Perhaps his greatest work, Alucius mused, watching Benril chisel away at the heroic profile of a Renfaelin knight in combat with a cringing Realm Guard. *And it's all a lie.*

"What is it?" Benril asked, leaving off from his carving for a moment, reaching for a nearby earthenware bottle.

"Merely my regular assurance that both Aspects remain alive and unmolested," Alucius replied. It had been the master's price that day they dragged him before the Fief Lord, merely raising an eyebrow at Darnel's promises of torture or swift execution, only becoming compliant when his threats turned to the Aspects. For all his disdain for custom and propriety, Benril remained a man of the Faith.

The master nodded, drinking from the bottle and passing it to the slave. The man cast a cautious eye at Twenty-Seven before taking a swift drink, returning to his work with determined haste. Alucius retrieved the bottle, removing the stopper and sniffing the contents. *Just water.*

"I hear tell of a hidden stock of wine," he told Benril. "If you would care for some."

"Wine dulls the senses and makes the mediocre artist imagine himself a great one." Benril spared him a hard glance before returning to his work. "A truism with which you are intimately acquainted, I believe."

"It has been, as ever, a great pleasure, Master." Alucius gave an unheeded bow and returned to the ladder, pausing to cast an eye over Benril's bony but still-strong back, his rope-thin, muscle-knotted arms moving in expert rhythm as they worked the stone. "There was one other thing," he added. "It seems Master Grealin had taken up with a band of fighters in the forest. You recall Master Grealin? Great, fat fellow who minded the Sixth Order's stores."

"What of it?" Benril asked, continuing to chisel away.

Alucius kept his eyes on Benril's hands. "He died."

It was barely a slip, merely the slightest irregularity left in a carving of wondrous execution. But it was too deep to sand away, a timeless testament to a brief lapse of concentration.

"Many have died," Benril said, not turning. "With many more to come when Lord Al Sorna gets here."

The portly slave dropped his rasp, casting a fearful glance at Twenty-Seven before quickly retrieving it. Nearby, one of the overseers turned towards them, his hand going to the coiled whip at his side.

"Please have a care, Master Benril," Alucius told him. "I take no pleasure in the prospect of describing your death to the woman I love."

Benril still refused to turn, his hands once again moving with the same effortless precision. "Don't you have some wine to find?"

◆ ◆ ◆

It took several attempts before he identified the correct ruin, unearthing a blackened wooden sign from beneath a pile of tumbled brick, the lettering burnt to nothing but the crudely rendered image of a boar visible through the scorching. "Yes," he agreed with Twenty-Seven. "I am fully aware this is probably a fool's errand, thank you. Help me shift this stone."

They worked for over an hour before he found it, clearing rubble away from the floorboards to reveal only a faint outline under the dust; a rectangle about a yard square. "A bottle or two of Wolf's Blood would indeed be very welcome," he told Twenty-Seven, wiping the dust away to reveal the hidden entrance, his fingers probing the edges. "Too tight a fit. Use your sword to prize it open."

Twenty-Seven went about the task with his usual unhesitant obedience, jamming his short sword into the edge of the door and levering it up, the strain of the effort plain in the bulge of muscle on his arms, though his face remained as impassive as ever. Alucius took hold of the edge of the door as it came free, hauling it open all the way, revealing a horizontal drop into blank darkness.

He had had the foresight to bring a lamp and lit it now, then lay flat to lower it into the opening, the yellow glow illuminating only a tunnel of rough stone, free of any telltale gleam of glass.

"No," he said, shaking his head. "I don't fancy it much either, my friend. But a man must follow his passions, don't you think?" He moved back from the hole and waved at the slave. "You first."

Twenty-Seven stared back and said nothing.

"Faith!" Alucius muttered, handing him the lamp. "If I die down there, they'll whip you to death. You know that, I trust."

He took hold of the edge of the hole and lowered himself in, hanging from his fingertips then dropping into the blackness below, finding the air musty and stale. Twenty-Seven landed nimbly at his side a second later, the lamplight illuminating a tunnel of uninviting length.

"There best be some Cumbraelin red at the end of this," Alucius said. "Otherwise I shall be forced to say some very harsh words to Aspect Elera. Some very harsh words indeed."

They followed the tunnel for no more than the span of a few minutes, though the echoing footfalls and absolute dark beyond the limit of the lamp's meagre glow made it seem considerably longer, as did Alucius's growing conviction that there was no wine to be found here. "I don't care what you insist upon," he hissed at Twenty-Seven. "I will not simply turn back now."

Finally the tunnel opened out into a broad circular chamber, Alucius drawing up short at the fine brickwork contrasting with the rough stone walls of the tunnel. The chamber was ringed by seven stone pillars and shallow steps descending to a flat base in the centre of which stood a long table. Alucius went to the table, playing the lamp over the surface and finding it free of dust.

"On second thoughts," he said. "Perhaps you have a p—"

A sudden whisper of disturbed air and the lamp shattered in his hand, flaming oil scattering onto the stone before blinking out, darkness descending with dreadful speed. Alucius heard Twenty-Seven's sword scrape free of its scabbard then nothing, no clash of steel or grunt of pain. Just the darkness and the silence.

"I . . ." he began, swallowed and tried again. "I don't suppose you have any wine."

Something cold and hard pressed against his neck, positioned precisely above the vein he knew would see him dead in a few heartbeats should it suffer even a small puncture. "Aspect Elera!" Alucius said in a rapid exhalation. "She sent me."

A pause then the blade disappeared from his neck. "Sister," a female voice said, smooth and cultured but also hard and clipped. "Light the torches. Brother, don't kill the other one just yet."

◆ ◆ ◆

"Alucius Al Hestian." The young woman regarded him from across the table with a steady and not especially welcoming expression. "I've read your poems. My master thought them the finest works of modern Asraelin verse."

"Clearly a man of some taste and education," Alucius replied, casting a furtive glance at Twenty-Seven, crouched into a fighting stance, his sword moving back and forth in a slow parody of combat. On either side of him stood a man and a woman, both young like the woman seated at the table. The woman was plump and short with a large rat perched on her shoulder. The man was taller, well-built and wearing a heavily besmirched City Guard uniform. The plump woman regarded Alucius with a faint smile whilst the guardsman ignored him, staring fixedly at Twenty-Seven and his slothful sword play.

"Actually," the young woman at the table said, "I found them cloyingly sentimental and overly florid."

"Must have been my early work," Alucius said, turning back to her. Her face was finely featured, a narrow aquiline nose and a softly pointed chin, her hair a pleasing shade of honey blond, and her eyes set in a cold stare of hostile appraisal.

"Your father's a traitor, poet," she stated.

"My father is forced to hateful duty by his love for me," he returned. "Kill me if you would have him abandon it."

"How noble." The young woman spread her fingers on the table where a line of small steel darts were arranged in a neat arc. "And a wish easily granted, should I find you less than honest."

The plump woman came forward, her rat running the length of her arm to jump onto the tabletop, scurrying over to Alucius, snout raised to sniff at his sleeve. "Don't smell a lie on his sweat," she advised the young woman in coarse, street-born tones.

"My sweat?" Alucius asked, feeling a fresh trickle of it trace down his back.

"Liar's sweat's gotta sting to it," the plump woman advised. "Beyond us but Blacknose here smells it well enough."

She extended her hand and the rat trotted over to her, jumping into her arms and settling into a contented huddle.

The Dark, Alucius thought. *How delighted Lyrna would have been to see this.* He forced the thought away; remembrance of Lyrna was painful and likely to provoke distracting grief at a time when he should be focused on continued survival. "Who are you people?" he asked the young woman.

She stared back in silence for a moment then raised her left hand, the fingers flat and level. She blinked and one of the darts rose from the table, hovering no more than an inch from her index finger. "Ask another question," she said. "And this goes in your eye."

"Can we move this along, sister?" the guardsman said in a strained voice. "This one's mind is easily clouded but I can't do it forever."

The young woman blinked again and the dart slowly descended to the table. She clasped her hands together, her eyes unwavering from Alucius. "Aspect Elera sent you?"

"Yes."

"What is her condition?"

"She resides in the Blackhold. Unharmed, save a raw ankle and sore need of a bath."

"What did she tell you of us?"

"That you had wine." Alucius risked a glance around the chamber. "I'm guessing she lied about that."

"She did," the young woman replied. "We also have scant food or water remaining and our forays into the city above yield us nothing."

"I can bring food. Medicine too, should you need it. I assume that was her true purpose in sending me . . ." He paused to draw breath. "In sending me to the Seventh Order."

The young woman angled her head, mouth twisting in a sardonic smile. "You speak of legends, poet."

"Oh, what difference do it make now?" the plump woman said, moving to stand behind her sister. "You've got the right of it, y'lordship. I'm Sister Inehla, she's Sister Cresia, and that over there is Brother Rhelkin. All that remains of the Seventh Order in this fair city."

Alucius gestured at their surroundings. "And this place?"

"Once a temple to the Orders," Sister Cresia replied. "Built before such frippery was expunged from the Faith. Our brothers in the Sixth Order found it some years ago, a hide for criminals, subsequently put to better purpose."

Alucius turned to obtain a better view of Twenty-Seven and Brother Rhelkin, noting the strain on the guardsman's face as the slave continued to move his sword as if through treacle. "What is he doing to him?"

"Making him see what he needs him to see," Cresia said. "We've found it's their principal weakness, those like him and his less deadly cousins. Minds so empty are easily clouded. He thinks he's fighting a horde of assassins, come to spill your blood. Brother Rhelkin can also control the speed of the vision, making it last an hour or a second."

"But not," Rhelkin added through gritted teeth, "forever."

Alucius turned back to Cresia. "Food and water," he said. "What else do you need?"

"News of the war would be welcome."

"The Volarian fleet sent to the Meldenean Isles suffered some form of calamitous defeat. Tokrev is poised to take Alltor and Darnel has ridden out with his knights to hunt down the Red Brother."

"Lord Al Sorna?"

Alucius shook his head. "No word as yet."

Cresia sighed and rose from the table. "When will you return?"

"Two days, if you can wait that long. Gathering extra provisions without raising suspicion takes time."

She nodded at Twenty-Seven. "Should we kill this one?"

"His only task is to protect me or kill me should I step outside the city. In all other regards he is blind and dumb."

She nodded. "I'm trusting you because Aspect Elera would not have sent you without reason." She opened a pouch at her belt and the darts on the table rose to balance on their blunt ends before arching into the pouch in a precise sequence, making Alucius smile at the elegant impossibility of it.

"The night the city fell," Cresia added. "I lost count of the men I killed with these, and other things besides. I bled myself white with killing and would have died if my sister hadn't found me and brought me here. Know well, poet, if you abuse our trust, I'll drain every drop of blood in my body to kill you."

◆ ◆ ◆

He found his father at the gate to the North Road, deep in counsel with the Volarian Division Commander as a battalion of Free Swords laboured to dig a deep ditch behind the wall.

"Lamp oil?" the Volarian was asking as Alucius approached, halting at a respectful distance, though still close enough to hear their discussion.

"As much as you can gather," Lakrhil Al Hestian replied. "Enough to fill this ditch from end to end."

The Volarian looked at the map spread out before them, scanning the lines depicting the walls and the country beyond. Alucius indulged some faint hope the man had enough arrogance to disregard his father's counsel, but sadly, he again proved himself no fool. "Very well," he said. "Have you chosen where to site the engines?"

Alucius's father pointed to several points on the map as the Volarian nodded approval. "However," Lakrhil said, "I will of course need engines to site."

"They will be here in thirty days," the Division Commander assured him. "Together with a thousand Varitai and three hundred more Kuritai. The Council has not abandoned us."

If Lakrhil Al Hestian took any comfort from the man's words, he failed to show it. "An army can travel far in thirty days," he said. "Especially an army fuelled by love of a resurrected queen."

Alucius stifled his gasp lest it draw the Volarian's anger, his heart hammering worse than in the darkness below the ruined inn. *She lives?*

Mirvek straightened, fixing his father with a hard glare. "A lie told by cowards seeking to excuse failure," he stated in unequivocal tones. "And that's what you'll tell your king when he returns. Whoever leads this rabble is not your queen."

His father replied only with the slightest of nods. Alucius had yet to see him bow to any Volarian. The Division Commander gave him a final glare and turned to march away, his aides scurrying to keep up. Alucius approached his father with his heart still pounding. "Queen?" he asked.

"So it's said." Al Hestian didn't look up from the map. "Restored to life, and apparently beauty by Dark means. If it's really her. I'd not put it past Al Sorna to find a double somewhere and make her a figurehead."

Vaelin too? And if he comes, then so too does Alornis. "What of Tokrev? Alltor?"

"Killed and saved. A messenger arrived from Warnsclave this morning. It seems every man in Tokrev's army lies slaughtered and a great army marches north at the word of a Dark-blessed queen. My son, it seems you are shortly to be provided an ending to your poem."

Alucius took a breath, turning from the map to look at the Free Swords labouring in the ditch. "Aren't ditches normally dug outside the walls?"

"They are," his father replied. "And if time allows, I'll dig one there too, for the sake of appearances. The real defence is here." He tapped the map with the barbed spike protruding from his right sleeve and Alucius saw an intricate web of black lines tracing through the maze of streets, streets that no longer existed. "A series of barriers, choke points, fire traps and so on. Al Sorna's cunning enough, but he can't work miracles. This city will be his army's grave."

"My lord," Alucius spoke softly, moving to his father's side. "I beg you . . ."

"We have spoken on this matter already." His father's tone was absolute, implacable. "I lost one son, I'll not lose another."

Alucius recalled the night the city fell, the screams and the flames waking him from drunken slumber, stumbling downstairs to find his father in the main hall, surrounded by Kuritai, slashing madly with his sword as they circled, one already dead but they made no move to kill him. Alucius had stood frozen in shock as a meaty arm closed over his neck and the short sword pressed into his temple. A Free Sword officer shouted to his father, pointing to Alucius. The expression on his face as he straightened from the fight was hard to forget, not shame, not despair, just honest and desperate fear for a loved son.

"Thirty days," Alucius said softly, moving away, hugging himself tight. "Winterfall Eve is in thirty days, is it not?"

"Yes," Al Hestian said after a moment's thought. "Yes, I suppose it is." Alucius felt his father's eyes on him, knowing they were heavy with concern. "Do you need anything, Alucius?"

"Some more food," he said. "Aspect Dendrish threatens to hang himself if we don't feed him more. Though I doubt the bedsheets will hold him."

"I'll see to it."

Alucius turned back, his smile bright, heartbeat steady now the weight of indecision had lifted. "Thank you, my lord."

He was walking away when a commotion rose at the gate, the Varitai guards parting to allow entry to a lone rider. Alucius judged him as one of Darnel's hunters, in truth a bunch of rogues and cutthroats recruited from the dregs of Renfael to hunt down the Red Brother. The man sagged in his saddle as he rode towards Alucius's father, foam on his horse's flanks and mouth. He nearly collapsed on dismounting, sketching a bow and speaking words too faint for Alucius to hear, though from the way his father straightened on hearing them, clearly of some import. Al Hestian strode off, barking orders, his two Kuritai guards in tow, Alucius hearing the word "cavalry" before he disappeared from view.

"First a risen queen and now a need for cavalry," Alucius mused aloud to Twenty-Seven. "I believe it's time to say good-bye to an old friend."

◆ ◆ ◆

Blue Feather delivered a painful nip at his thumb as he lifted her clear of the coop, the message dangling from her leg. *So much weight on such a fragile thing,* Alucius thought, eyeing the thin wire clasp.

"Do you want to say good-bye to her?" he asked Twenty-Seven who, as ever, said nothing.

"Oh, ignore him," he told Blue Feather. "*I'm* going to miss you." He held her up and opened his hands. She sat there for a moment, seemingly uncertain, then leapt free, her wings a blur as she ascended, then flattened out to catch the wind and fly away south.

Winterfall Eve, Alucius thought as he lost sight of the bird. *When it's said all grievances are forgiven, for who wants to bear a grudge through the hardships of winter?*

CHAPTER EIGHT

Frentis

A stiff autumn wind played over the remnants of the Urlish, raising swirling columns of ash to sting eyes and choke throats. It stretched away on either side of them, a dirty grey blanket covering the earth, broken only by the occasional black spike of a once-mighty tree.

"Would've thought some of it might have survived," Ermund said, hawking and spitting before tying a scarf about his face.

"Darnel was certainly thorough," Banders said. "Marching across this will not be pleasant."

"We could skirt it," Arendil suggested. "Head to the coast."

"The coast road is too narrow," Sollis said. "Too many choke points, and Al Hestian is bound to know them all."

"And if we maintain this course," Banders replied, "the dust trail we raise will give him ample signal of our approach. Not to mention filling our lungs with this stuff."

"The country to the west is more open," Sollis admitted. "But will add another week to our march."

Frentis stifled a groan at the prospect of more days spent dreading dream-filled nights. Varinshold had become a focus for his desire for an ending, an ever-growing hope that whatever the outcome of their assault he would at least be assured release from *her*.

"Can't be helped, brother." Banders turned his horse about, nodding to Ermund. "Spread the word, we turn west until we clear the ash."

◆ ◆ ◆

"It was there again," Illian said at breakfast, smiling thanks at Thirty-Four as he handed her a bowl of his honey-sweetened porridge.

"What was there?" Arendil asked.

"The wolf. I've seen it every day for a week now."

"Throw stones," Davoka suggested. "Wolf will run from stones."

"Not this one. He's so big I doubt he'd feel them. Anyway, he's not scary. Doesn't chase after me, or growl or anything. Just sits and watches."

Frentis saw discomfort in Davoka's expression as she watched the girl eat her porridge. "I come with you today," she said. "See if he watches me."

Illian scowled, speaking a laboured but precise Lonak phrase he knew translated as, "The coddled cub never hunts."

Davoka gave a soft laugh and returned to her own meal, though Frentis saw her lingering disquiet. "I'll come too," he said, keen to seek out any distraction from the persistent stain of last night's dream. It had been stranger than usual, a confused jumble of images, mostly violent, often full of pain and sorrow, but not always. *She whimpers as she lies abed, staring at her bedroom door . . . She laughs as she strangles a woman beneath a desert sky . . . She shudders in pleasure as he moves in her, heart swelling with feelings she had thought long dead . . .*

On waking, sweating and striving to quell a torrent of sensation, he realised he had not seen her waking hours, but her dreams. *I dream her dreams. What does she dream of me?*

◆ ◆ ◆

They rode west until midday, finding nothing save empty fields and the occasional cluster of slaughtered cattle or sheep, mostly older animals, the younger ones no doubt having been herded off to Varinshold. Another mile's ride brought them to an empty farmhouse, the roof gone and walls blackened by fire, no sign of any life within. "Why do they destroy so much?" Illian asked. "They take slaves, which is evil but at least comprehensible. But to tear down everything whilst doing so. It's beyond reason."

"They think they're cleansing the land," Frentis told her. "Wiping it clean so their own people can start anew. Build another province to the empire in its image."

Illian pulled her horse to a halt an hour later, turning to Davoka and pointing to a nearby rise, her smile bright. "There. Isn't he beautiful?"

Frentis found it quickly, a shadowed outline on the skyline, taller than any wolf he had seen before. It sat regarding them with impassive scrutiny as they trotted closer, Davoka resting her spear on her shoulder for a quick throw. They stopped some thirty yards short of the beast, close enough for Frentis to see its eyes, blinking as it looked at each of them in turn, fur ruffling in the wind. He saw the plain truth in Illian's words; it was beautiful.

The wolf rose and turned, moving off towards the north at a brisk trot for a hundred paces or so then stopping once more, sitting and watching as they exchanged glances.

"It didn't do this before," Illian said after a moment.

Davoka muttered something in her own language, face dark with foreboding, but Frentis noticed she had lowered her spear. He turned back to the wolf, seeing how its gaze was fixed entirely on him. He kicked his horse forward and the wolf rose again to follow its northward course. After a second he heard Illian and Davoka spurring to follow.

The wolf started to run after a half mile or so, its long, loping stride covering the distance with deceptive speed. Frentis lost sight of it several times as they galloped after, tracking it over low hills of long grass. Finally they reined in as it came to a halt on one of the taller hills and a familiar scent came to Frentis's nostrils. He raised a questioning eyebrow at Davoka who nodded and climbed down from the saddle. Frentis joined her and they handed their reins to Illian. She pouted in annoyance as he pointed an emphatic finger at the ground to fix her in place.

They ascended the hill at the crouch, dropping to a crawl at the summit. The wolf had sunk to its haunches, waiting no more than a few feet away, still regarding Frentis with the same blank scrutiny.

"What a fool the man must be," Frentis breathed, staring at the scene before them. The camp sat in open ground, the rear flank covered by a shallow stream, pickets patrolling the perimeter but not far enough out. The scent of smoke and horse sweat was richer now, campfires threw dozens of grey columns into the air, only partly obscuring the banner that rose from the centre of the camp: an eagle on a red-and-white-cheque background.

Five hundred men at most, Frentis mused, eyes scanning the camp. *And Banders's army stands unnoticed between him and Varinshold.* "Take Illian," he told Davoka. "Tell Banders I'll lead them to Lirkan's Spur. Master Sollis knows the way."

"She can go," Davoka said. "You shouldn't do this alone."

He shook his head, grinning as he nodded at the wolf. "Seems I'm not alone. Ride fast."

◆ ◆ ◆

He waited a good hour after their departure, watching the camp as scouts came and went, small groups of men with hunting dogs reporting in or galloping off in a fresh direction. *He thought we'd make for Nilsael,* Frentis decided, seeing how most of the scouts rode off to the north or the west. *Didn't consider we'd try for Renfael, his own land, the people so fiercely loyal.* He shook his head, wondering if Darnel's mind was truly that of a fool or if the man wasn't in fact just a barking loon.

It took the best part of another hour before a scouting party came their way, two riders and a clutch of dogs making directly for their hill. The wolf rose when they had begun to climb the slope, the riders immediately dragging their mounts to a halt whilst the hounds milled about, whining in fear as their masters whipped at them, uttering curses and threats.

And the wolf howled.

Frentis shrank from the vastness of the sound, sinking to the earth, eyes clamped tight shut and hands over his ears as it soared across the fields and hills, the force of it cutting through him like a ragged saw-blade. Not since the long years of the binding had he felt so helpless, so small.

He opened his eyes as the howl faded, finding the wolf staring down at him, green eyes meeting his and birthing a realisation that it knew him, knew his every secret, every hidden scrap of guilt. It dipped its head, a rough tongue scraping over Frentis's forehead, drawing a whimper and leaving something new. A message. It wasn't a voice, more a certainty, a clear and bright surety shining in his mind: *you must forgive yourself.*

Frentis felt a laugh escape him as the wolf drew back, blinked again, then turned to lope away. Frentis stood to watch it run, a silver streak through the twisting grass, disappearing in a heartbeat.

The whinny of a panicked horse brought him back to his senses, turning to find the two riders staring at him in shock, their dogs a good distance away, yelping in fear as they raced for the camp. Frentis chose the rider on the left, palmed a throwing knife and sent it into his throat. He fell from his horse, blood frothing from his mouth as he clutched at his neck. His companion's wide-eyed gaze shifted to Frentis and back again, hands twitching on his reins, his sword untouched at his side.

"You have a report to make," Frentis told him. "Give Lord Darnel the Red Brother's regards."

◆　◆　◆

He remounted and guided his horse to the crest of the hill, sitting and watching as the huntsman galloped back to camp. It took no longer than the space of a few heartbeats before it convulsed, knights struggling into armour and running to their horses, tents falling as squires packed up, and a single rider emerged from the burgeoning dust cloud, blue armour gleaming in the late-afternoon sun. Frentis raised a hand in a friendly wave, lingering long enough to ensure Darnel had seen it, then turned and galloped towards the east.

He led them on a winding course, buying time for Banders to get his people moving. He would gallop east for a time, halt, and watch Darnel's pursuit for a few moments, then strike out towards the south. Darnel edged closer with every pause, but his horse and those of his knights were too burdened by their riders' armour to mount an effective pursuit. Frentis would wave every time he stopped, the last time leaving it long enough to ensure Darnel saw his mocking bow.

He came to Lirkan's Spur some two hours into the chase, a narrow thumb-shaped spit of grassland jutting into the broad waters of the Brinewash. The river was shallow here, fordable even this late in the year with open country to the north and a tall, rocky hill some three hundred paces south, shielding the eastern bank from view. He pulled his horse to a halt and scanned the surroundings, finding no evidence of any ally.

He turned his horse about, calming him with a stroke to the flank as he waited. The wolf's message still sang in his breast, his newborn spirit leaving him with a faint smile that refused to budge from his lips, even as Darnel's five hundred knights thundered towards the spur.

Come, my lord, he urged Darnel silently. *Just a little closer.*

His risen spirits took a slight tumble at the sight of Darnel raising a hand, his entire command coming to a halt some two hundred paces short. Frentis reached over his shoulder and drew his sword, raising it high before pointing it directly at Darnel in a clear and unambiguous challenge. *Be true to yourself, my lord,* Frentis implored him. *Be the fool.*

Darnel's horse reared as its rider drew his own sword, one of his retainers trotting forward, perhaps keen to offer a cautionary word, but Darnel dismissed him with a furious wave before spurring his horse to a gallop. Frentis made ready to begin his own charge, then paused as a new sound came to his ears; horns sounding a high pealing note to the east, too high for a Renfaelin knight and the Sixth Order had no use for horns. He paused to glance over his shoulder, his smile fading completely at the sight of at least two battalions of Volarian cavalry charging towards the eastern bank of the Brinewash.

Al Hestian! he cursed. Another tumult drew his attention to the south, the great churning roaring of many horses charging through shallow water. Banders led his knights around the rocky hill and straight for Darnel's company, Frentis spying the dim figures of his brothers atop the hill, bows drawn. He switched his gaze back to Darnel, finding the Fief Lord now halted, his men milling in confusion behind him. Frentis cast a final look at the onrushing Volarian cavalry, now fording the river, but prevented from galloping by the water's height.

He fixed his gaze on Darnel once more and kicked his horse into motion, sword held out straight and level as he charged, covering the distance in barely a few seconds. He could see the black streaks of his brothers' arrows arcing into Darnel's host, horses rearing and knights falling as they struck home. One of Darnel's retainers took hold of the Fief Lord's reins and tried to drag him towards the Volarians, falling dead as Darnel hacked his long sword into the man's neck, wheeling about and meeting Frentis's charge head-on.

Their horses collided with bone-shattering force, Frentis's sword rebounding from Darnel's blade as the Fief Lord slashed at him before the animals reeled back. Frentis's horse staggered, snorting foam and blood, sinking to its knees as he leapt clear, crouching as Darnel leaned low in the saddle to try for a decapitating blow with his long sword. Frentis let it whisper past then dived to catch hold of Darnel's armoured forearm, hooking both arms around the steel-clad limb and hauling him from the saddle. He landed with a crash of rending metal but recovered quickly, lunging to butt his helmeted head into Frentis's side, sending him sprawling, then bringing his long sword up in a two-handed grip. Frentis could see his eyes behind the visor, wide and full of unreasoning hate.

He rolled as the blade came down, cleaving into the earth, springing to his feet and slashing at Darnel's visor. The Fief Lord dodged the blow and brought his sword around in a great arc, Frentis grunting with the effort as he parried the blow, Darnel's steel biting deep into his Order blade. He reached out to catch Darnel's gauntleted wrist before he could draw the blade back, stepping in close, angling his sword to thrust up through the visor. Darnel jerked his head back as the blade sank home, the tip emerging bloodied, the Fief Lord roaring in fury and pain.

Frentis spun, bringing the blade round to slash into Darnel's legs, not piercing the armour but with enough force to send him to the ground. The Fief Lord howled and hacked at him again but Frentis blocked the blow and delivered a kick to his sword hand, the blade flying free. He smashed his sword guard into Darnel's visor, stunning him before planting a boot on his neck, laying the tip of his blade on the opening, meeting the eyes behind it, smiling fiercely at the fear he saw.

"BROTHER!"

It was Arendil, charging towards them, men locked in combat on either side, his sword pointed at something over Frentis's shoulder. He didn't waste time with a glance, diving to the left as a Volarian cavalry sword left a shallow cut on his cheek. The Volarian dragged his horse around for another blow then tumbled from the saddle as Arendil's sword lanced through his shoulder.

Frentis turned, finding himself faced with four more Volarians charging at full gallop. He heard the thunder of hooves behind him and threw himself flat, feeling hot breath wash over his neck as a horse leapt him. He looked up to see Master Rensial deliver a precise upward stroke to one of the onrushing Volarians, the man's breastplate parting with the force of the blow. Rensial ducked under a wild slash of the Volarian to his right and replied with a backward stroke as he rode past, the cavalryman arching his back as the blade cut him to the spine.

The remaining two Volarians came for Frentis, close together and blades levelled, then tumbling to the ground as a cloud of arrows arched down from the hilltop to claim both riders and horses.

Frentis whirled, searching for Darnel amidst the raging chaos. Banders's knights had shattered the Fief Lord's command but were now fully engaged with the Volarians, men and horses wheeling in a mass of steel and rending flesh. Frentis caught a flash of blue armour through the heaving confusion to the right, a hunched figure on a horse being led away by two Volarians. Horns sounded and the cavalry began to withdraw, riders delivering a final slash before turning about and galloping back to the river.

Frentis saw a riderless horse a dozen feet away and vaulted onto its back, spurring in the direction of Darnel's flight, hacking at any unfortunate Volarians in his way. He spied Master Rensial nearby, cutting down an unhorsed Volarian, and yelled to get his attention. The master's eyes found him quickly, as ever in battle, focused, calm, and seemingly free of madness. Frentis pointed at the blue-armoured figure now nearing the river and the master spurred his horse in pursuit, Frentis riding hard on his heels.

Darnel was already labouring through the water when Rensial and Frentis caught up with his escort. Both men turning at the water's edge to face them, manoeuvring their mounts with uncanny precision, Frentis grunting in annoyance at the sight of the twin swords on their backs. *Kuritai.*

Rensial attempted to skirt them, hanging half-out of his saddle to avoid a Kuritai's blade, but the slave-elite leapt from his horse, landing nimbly on Rensial's saddle and stabbing down with his twin blades. Rensial unhooked his foot from the stirrup and swung himself around his horse's head, delivering a double kick to the Kuritai's chest as they ploughed into the river, the slave flying free of the horse and the master regaining the saddle.

Frentis tried to dispatch the second Kuritai with a throwing knife, waiting until he was near level with the slave before sending it into his eye. The man barely seemed to notice the injury, hacking at Frentis as he rode by, the blade missing by inches, turning his horse to follow but falling dead as Davoka's spear erupted from his chest. She hauled it free of the corpse and spurred her own horse onward, following Frentis into the river.

He could see Darnel ahead, flogging his horse bloody as it laboured onto the far bank, galloping east as an escort of Volarians closed around him and a rear-guard stood firm at the water's edge. Rensial charged straight into them, his sword a blur as men fell around him, spurring after the fast-retreating Darnel then rearing as a Volarian blade cleaved into his horse's neck. Another Volarian rushed towards the master, sword poised to strike at his back. Frentis's horse ploughed into the Volarian's mount before he could strike, his head transfixed by the Order blade a second later.

Davoka screamed in frustration as she fought her way through the remaining Volarians, spear whirling, blood trailing from the blade, leaving only two remaining cavalrymen, who vainly attempted to follow their comrades' retreat, falling dead to arrows launched from behind. Frentis turned to see Sollis and Ivern fording the river at speed, bows in hand. Behind them the western bank was calm in the aftermath of battle, knights and free fighters wandering among the dead.

Frentis cast his gaze back at the dust cloud rising in Darnel's wake, knowing they wouldn't catch him now. Davoka uttered a Lonak curse and threw her spear into the ground. Nearby, Rensial knelt at his horse's side, smoothing a hand along its neck and whispering softly as it breathed its last.

"That was reckless, brother." Sollis's pale eyes regarded him with stern disapproval, deepening further as Frentis laughed, long and loud.

"Yes, brother," he replied as the mirth faded, knowing the expression on Sollis's face to be a mirror of his own when he looked at Rensial. "Very reckless. My most profound apologies."

◆ ◆ ◆

"We had him!" Ermund fumed, hands on his sword hilt, stabbing the scabbard into the earth. "I was less than two yards away in the melee. We had him and still he lives. He's laughing at us, I can hear it."

"His knights lie dead or captured and he runs for Varinshold like a whipped dog," Banders replied. "I doubt he'll be laughing."

"Though he does now have full knowledge of our number and whereabouts," Sollis pointed out.

"But not the strength to do much about it," the baron returned.

They were atop the rocky hill overlooking the spur. Below, Frentis's fighters were moving amongst the dead, looting weapons or valuables. Near the riverbank a small cluster of Darnel's knights waited under guard. They made a curiously pathetic sight when shorn of armour, just tired defeated men, eyes wide with fear and nerves frayed by the instant death meted out to those Volarians who had attempted to surrender.

"What's these poxed whoresons doing alive, brother?" Draker had demanded of Frentis earlier, the prisoners within earshot and moving in a restless shudder. "Traitors to the Realm, ain't they?"

"They yielded according to custom," Ermund told him, not without a note of regret. "The baron will decide their fate."

"Best keep 'em away from us on the march," Draker muttered darkly before stomping off to do some more looting.

Banders had extracted enough information from the captured knights to reveal the depth of Darnel's current delusions. "Rebuilding the palace, making himself a king," he said, shaking his head. "I'm given to wonder if the Volarians haven't put some Dark spell on him, stripping away all reason."

"It was always there, Father," Lady Ulice said quietly. "This madness. I remember it well enough. As a girl I mistook it for passion, love even. And it may well have been, but love for himself, bound only by his father's will. With Fief Lord Theros gone he feels himself free, able to fly at last."

"We'll have to hope his unreason leaves him deaf to Al Hestian's counsel," Banders said. "Taking Varinshold by stealth may well be impossible now and all he need do is wait behind its walls whilst his allies conclude their business in Cumbrael."

"I should still like to attempt the sewers, my lord," Frentis said. "Alone if necessary."

This drew some odd glances from the assembled captains, Sollis's gaze particularly grave in its intensity. Frentis knew his freshly lightened soul showed on his face but the wolf's gift was a cherished thing and he saw little reason to hide it. *You must forgive yourself.*

"I'll . . . be sure to bear that in mind, brother," Banders assured him with the kind of tight smile Frentis recognised. *The smile you offer to one you think mad.*

"We stand barely a few miles from the Nilsaelin border," Lord Furel said. "A pause here to rest and await word from my messengers might be the best course. Reinforcements could well be marching to our side as we speak. At the very least some word will be coming from the Reaches."

Banders looked at Sollis with a questioning eye. "I'll send my brothers out in all directions," the Brother Commander said. "If there's word to be had within fifty miles of here, we'll have it within two days."

Banders nodded. "Very well. We camp here. Brother Frentis, you come under your brother's word, not mine, but I think we are of like mind in saying your visit to Varinshold will have to wait."

Frentis shrugged, bowing with an affable grin. "As my lord wishes." His smile lingered as he made his way back to his tent, the unease he had felt at the very sight of his bedroll now vanished. *A dreamless sleep,* he thought, pulling off his boots and lying back on the blanket. *I wonder how it'll feel.*

◆　◆　◆

She watches them fight with cold detachment, assessing skill and speed as they dance in the pit below. Steely echoes rebound from the walls that surround her, the stone roof above coarse and free of decoration, for these are new pits, chiselled out far below the streets of Volar, the birthplace of long-gestated children.

Do you like them, beloved? *she asks him, knowing he sees them, keen to engage his interest, hungry in fact to hear a single word from across the gulf that divides them.* We learned so much from you.

The men in the pit below fight without restraint and die without screams. But their faces are not those of Kuritai, no blank automata here. These men grimace in pain and snarl in fury, register grim satisfaction at bloody victory. There are at least a hundred in the pit, moving with all the fluency of those bred to the fight.

Give a dog too tight a leash, *she thinks,* and it chokes. And however much you whip it, it will always be a dog. But these, beloved. *She smiles down at the men in the pit.* These are lions.

She turns away, moving along a stone walkway to a narrow door. The sounds of combat follow her as she walks; the tunnel is long and dark but she has walked here before and has no need of torches. The chamber she comes to is broad and high, tiered walkways rising on both sides allowing access to rows of cells, each sealed with bars of iron. She pauses and lets her song wander, feeling the dulled fears emanating from each of the cells. Drugs are widely employed by the over-seers who service these cells, but still the fear always lingers. Her song alights on a cell on the middle tier to the left. The note is harsh, sombre, stirring a hunger.

She is momentarily troubled by this. Usually the song chooses an innocent, some pale-faced youth stolen from a slaughtered hill tribe or identified by the overseers in the training dens. She had liked to play the benefactor, the kindly mistress come to offer them deliverance from this place of endless fear, enjoy-ing the desperate hope in their eyes, even granting them the mercy of a swift death by way of reward.

Now it is different. The song speaks of a loathsome soul and it's this that stirs her hunger. Was this you, beloved? *she asks him.* Did you change me so much? *Despite her unease she knows this shell must be sustained, the Messen-ger having related how quickly a stolen shell can sicken, the demands of mul-tiple gifts drain them so. She starts for the nearby stairwell but pauses as two Kuritai approach, dragging a red-clad figure between them and providing a welcome distraction.*

"Council-man Lorvek," she greets the red-clad. "It's been so very long. I'm glad to see the years have not withered you one bit."

The red-clad appears to be a man in his mid-thirties, though she first met him some eighty years ago when he first rose to Council, in this very chamber in fact. He had been triumphant then, she recalls, preening with satisfaction at having secured fabled immortality. Now he just seems to be what he is, a scared man, cowed by torture and expectant of death.

"I . . ." he begins, swallows, a faint trickle of blood coming from the corner of his mouth. "I . . . humbly regret any offence caused to the Ally or his ser-vants . . ."

"Oh, there you go again, Lorvek," she says, shaking her head with a sad smile. "Always saying the wrong thing. What was it you called me that day in Council, oh, twenty years ago? You remember, the day I came back from my excursion to the realm of the slant-eyed pig?"

Lorvek hangs his head, summoning the will to plead further. "I . . . I said . . . unwise words . . ."

"Murderous whore to a pestilent phantom." She takes hold of his hair and pulls his head up. "Yes, that was unwise. And now you call me a servant. I do wonder how you ever rose so high with such poor judgement. After everything the Ally has given you."

A wave of weariness sweeps through him and his eyes grow dim for a sec-

ond. She assumes he has exhausted his ability to beg, but then he draws breath, a light coming back into his eyes as he spits blood into her face. "The Council will not stand for this, you vile bitch!" he hisses.

"Evidence of corruption is hard to ignore," she tells him, finding a glimmer of admiration for this final flare of courage. "I'm afraid the vote was unanimous. Besides . . ." She moves closer, whispering, "Just between the two of us, the Council won't have to stand for anything soon." She presses a kiss to his cheek and steps back.

"Back there," she tells the Kuritai, jerking her head at the tunnel leading to the pits. "Give him a sword and throw him in. Tell the overseer I want to know how long he lasts."

He screams as they drag him away, more defiance, dwindling again into contrite pleas as they enter the tunnel and his voice fades. She summons the song once more, seeking out the cell with the dark note and making for the stairs.

◆　◆　◆

Frentis came awake with a shout, despair and grief doubling him over. He felt tears flowing and covered his face with his hands, sobs tearing from his throat.

"Boy?" Master Rensial reached out to touch him, hand tentative on his shoulder, bafflement in his voice. "Boy?"

Frentis continued to weep as the mad master patted his shoulder, aware that the others had stirred from their tents, that they stood outside looking on in amazement, but he found he couldn't stop. Not until the morning sun rose and all chance of sleep had safely faded.

◆　◆　◆

"My blood grandmother had many dreams." Davoka's eyes were intent on his face as she rode alongside, though her tone was light, her usual growl absent this morning.

Frentis gave a tired nod and didn't reply. Breakfast had been a mostly silent affair, Thirty-Four passing him a bowl of porridge with a troubled frown, Illian and Arendil unable to meet his gaze, and Draker staring, bushy brows narrowed in concern.

Tears from the Red Brother, Frentis thought. *They forgot I was a just a man . . . Perhaps I did too.*

"She saw stars falling from the sky to shatter the land," Davoka went on. "And floods high enough to drown the mountains. One day she gave away her pony and all her goods because a dream told her the sun would explode at twilight. It didn't and people saw just a mad old woman with dreams, and dreams mean nothing."

They are not dreams, he wanted to tell her, closing his eyes and rubbing at his temples as fatigue swept through him. "You think I am not fit to lead?"

"Our clan would follow you into the Mouth of Nishak if you asked. They fear for you, that is all."

He opened his eyes and forced himself to scan the horizon. West of the Spur the ground was mostly pasture, though now devoid of cattle, the grass grown long through lack of grazing. Master Sollis had acceded to his request to scout the southern approach, though his pale eyes spoke of harsher judgement than that offered by the people who had followed him from the Urlish. *He thinks me damaged,* Frentis knew. *Destroyed by the burden of so much guilt.* He hadn't told Sollis of the wolf's blessing, the liberation from guilt it had brought, for it seemed empty now. What use was there in being freed from guilt if he was condemned to see through *her* eyes every night?

Davoka stiffened at his side and pointed. Frentis shook away the doubts clouding his head and followed her finger, finding two figures on the horizon, both mounted and moving at a steady canter through the long grass. He knew they couldn't be Volarian—they never patrolled in small numbers—and he doubted Darnel had many more hunters to send forth, especially without dogs. Besides, it was plain they had already seen the two riders to the north and came on regardless. Not the actions of an enemy. Nevertheless he unhitched his bow and notched an arrow as the riders came closer, Davoka edging her horse away and angling it so her spear was concealed, held low on its right flank.

Frentis frowned as the riders' features came into view, finding one a woman and the other a man. The woman had long hair tied back in a tight braid, mounted on a tall piebald mare. Her clothes were unfamiliar, a mix of leather and Volarian gear, including a short sword tied to her saddle though she also carried a lance adorned with feathers and what seemed to be talismans of carved bone.

He heard Davoka give a surprised grunt. "Eorhil."

The man was dressed in the garb of Realm Guard infantry, his somewhat gaunt features set in a permanent frown, somewhere between bafflement and pain, his mouth open and lips free of expression. They reined to a halt some ten yards away, the woman's gaze shifting between them, faintly amused by Frentis and his bow, stern and guarded when she turned to Davoka, the Realm Guard at her side sparing them only a tired glance.

Davoka said something in an unfamiliar tongue, the words hesitant and formed with difficulty. The Eorhil woman barked a laugh before speaking in heavily accented Realm Tongue, "Lonakhim sound like a birthing ape."

Davoka bridled, taking a firm grip on her reins and hefting her spear though the Eorhil woman just grinned, turning to Frentis. "My . . . husband teach me . . . you tongue. You a . . . brother?"

"Yes," he said. "Brother Frentis of the Sixth Order. This is Lady Davoka, Lonak Ambassadress to the Unified Realm."

The Eorhil blinked in bafflement at the unfamiliar words and shook her head, patting her chest. "Insha ka Forna, I am Eorhil."

"We know," Davoka said evenly. "What do you do here?"

"This Brother Lernial." The Eorhil gestured at the Realm Guard who was now staring silently at the ground. "Kwin sent us."

"Kwin?" Frentis asked.

Insha ka Forna grunted in frustration and turned, pointing towards the south, speaking with slow deliberation. "Queen."

CHAPTER NINE

Lyrna

The name was halfway down today's list, clearly legible in Brother Hollun's neat script. It had become her daily habit to read the list after breakfast, the brother waiting patiently as she scanned every name. She had been gratified to find that he had already compiled a complete list of every subject in her army, apart from the Seordah and Eorhil, who reacted to his approaches with baffled disdain. Since arriving at Warnsclave she had asked him to expand it to include the refugees who continued to trail into the wasted city. The portly brother undertook the task with his usual diligent care, though he had been obliged to expand his staff of scribes to over thirty, mostly older folk skilled in letters and poorly suited to soldiering.

"These people all arrived yesterday?" she asked.

"Yes, Highness. We put them in the western quarter, shelter is sparse but Captain Ultin's miners have been busy, bringing in timber to repair roofs and such. They've even begun raising some stone houses from the rubble."

"Good. Assign more men to help them." She looked again at the name on the list, recalling the final words of a drowning man. *Don't forget your promise, Highness.*

She put the list aside and smiled at Hollun. She had taken to receiving her subjects in a large room on the second floor of the harbour-master's house, a comfortable but somewhat scorched chair standing in for a throne, Iltis and her ladies at her back with a dutiful stillness she found quite irksome even though she recognised the necessity for it. *A queen must have a court.*

"This takes us up to some thirty thousand new mouths to feed, does it not, brother?" she asked her Lord of the Queen's Purse.

"Thirty-one thousand, six hundred and twenty," the brother replied with customary alacrity. "Thank the Departed for Lord Al Bera, or they'd all be starving."

"Quite." Lyrna decided not to add that, but for her newly acquired subjects, her army would have been on the march by now. Instead they were obliged to loiter in this ruin, ensuring the people were fed and training new recruits, fierce in their desire to get at the Volarians but lacking the strength to march more than a mile. The pickings provided by the Meldenean fleet had been less copious than she had hoped for, barely a ton of grain so far, though the pirates who came and went from the harbour seemed fairly well attired in silks and jewellery. The Shield had yet to make an appearance, though Ship Lord Ell-Nurin had arrived the previous day, the deck of the *Red Falcon* laden with captured arrows once destined for Varinshold.

There was a loud rap on the door and Orena went to open it, revealing Benten lowered to one knee. "Lord Al Sorna and Lady Al Myrna, my queen."

She nodded, smiling again at Brother Hollun. "I look forward to tomorrow's report, brother."

He bowed and moved to the door, standing aside as Vaelin and the Lady Dahrena entered. "I would talk to the lord and lady in private," Lyrna told her court, who duly bowed and withdrew, Iltis with obvious reluctance as he rarely let her out of his sight these days, but knowing better than to argue the point. Lyrna watched Vaelin and Dahrena rise in unison, their movements almost as synchronised as those empty-headed Nilsaelin twins. Looking at their matched, neutral expressions she wondered if they were aware of it, of how unnerving it was to see, or how painful.

A queen is above jealousy, she reminded herself. *Though after today, they may be forgiven for thinking otherwise.*

"Lady Dahrena," she said, keeping her tone as light and brisk as she could. "I have been pondering your report on the rich gold deposits to be found in the Reaches. From what I can surmise from Brother Hollun's estimates, the mines hold enough gold to pay our current and future debts to the Meldenean merchant class several times over."

Dahrena gave a short nod. "I believe so, Highness."

"Strange that I can recall no instance when King Malcius expressed an awareness of such riches within his Realm."

The lady's answer was swift and, Lyrna judged, well rehearsed. "The full survey of the deposits was not yet complete at the time of the King's tragic demise, Highness. In truth, I suspect there are more seams yet to be found."

"I am glad, my lady. Such wealth may well serve as the saviour of this Realm in years to come, for we have much work still to do. And yet, it is of scant use to us lying in the ground, hundreds of miles away, whilst the men with the skill to mine it are here, along with one best placed to organise their efforts."

She saw them stiffen, once again with the same unnerving uniformity. "My queen?" Vaelin asked in a hard voice.

Lyrna took a breath, summoning her regretful smile. She had spent a while at the mirror practising this morning, for it had never been one of her best. "Lady Dahrena, it is my hard duty to order your immediate return to the Northern Reaches where you will exercise the Queen's Word until such time as Lord Vaelin can resume his duties. Ship Lord Ell-Nurin's vessel waits in the harbour to carry you there. With kindly weather you should reach the North Tower in three weeks, his ship being so uncommonly swift. I will also order sufficient vessels gathered to transport Captain Ultin's miners home as soon as possible."

"They want to fight," Vaelin stated, Dahrena standing expressionless at his side. "Sending them away will cause trouble . . ."

"I'll speak to them," Lyrna told him. "Explain that every swing of a pick is worth a hundred strokes of a sword. Besides, they've done enough fighting to justify any claim to honour, wouldn't you say?"

"I would, Highness," Dahrena said before Vaelin could speak. "I . . . regret the necessity of your order." She glanced briefly at Vaelin before lowering her gaze. "However, I can find no argument against it."

How fortunate, since I will hear no argument from you. Lyrna chained the words behind another smile, rising and coming forward to clasp the small woman's hands. "Your service in this war has been great and wondrous. It will never be forgotten, nor is it over. Bring me riches, my lady, so that I might buy justice."

She released Dahrena's hands and stepped back, forcing herself to meet Vaelin's gaze, the glint in his narrow gaze hard to bear. *This is not jealousy,* she wanted to say. *You know me better than that.*

"You will wish to say your farewells," she told them. "I have business with our new arrivals."

◆ ◆ ◆

The newcomers were unusual in that, unlike most of the other groups to make their way to Warnsclave over the past week, they were rich in children. One of the most frequent and difficult sights on the march had been the plethora of small corpses, often herded into houses and burnt to tiny remnants, others just slaughtered like unwanted livestock and left to rot in the open. Seeing so many still living gave a lift to Lyrna's spirits, though they were mostly gaunt and silent, staring at her as she moved among their mean accommodations.

"Brother Innis," Brother Hollun introduced a thin man in a grey robe. "Master of the Orphanage at Rhansmill. He hid his charges in the woods for weeks."

"Brother." Lyrna returned the man's bow with grave respect. "I thank you, with all my heart. Your deeds credit the Faith."

Brother Innis, clearly unused to royalty and ill from lack of food, staggered a little but managed to remain upright. The children clustered around him, clutching at his robe, some glaring at Lyrna as if she had done him harm. "I had a great deal of help, Highness," the brother said, gesturing at the comparatively few adults in the group. "These people starved so the children could eat, led the Volarians away so that they might remain undiscovered. Some paid dearly for their courage."

"They will receive full justice for their sacrifice," she assured him. "If you require anything, speak to Brother Hollun and it will be provided."

He gave another unsteady bow. "Thank you, Highness."

"Now. I seek a woman named Trella Al Oren."

Innis blanched at the name, shooting a guarded glance at a shelter nearby, a roof of thin planking over what had been a woodshed. "She . . . gave much to keep these children warm," he stammered. "Forgive me, Highness. But I beg that no punishment be visited upon her."

"Punishment?" Lyrna asked.

"How may I serve, Highness?"

Lyrna turned to find a tall woman standing outside the shelter, arms crossed. She was somewhere past her fiftieth year, handsome features set in a wary frown and white streaking her black hair. "My lady"—Lyrna bowed to her—"I bring news of your son."

Lady Al Oren had contrived to preserve a china tea-set throughout her ordeal, two small cups and a spherical pot, finely decorated with an orchid motif inlaid with gold. "Alpiran," she said, pouring the tea as they sat outside her shelter. "A gift from my aunt on the occasion of my wedding."

Lyrna sipped her tea, finding the taste surprisingly rich. "My lady is resourceful," she offered, hoping to ease the woman's obvious tension. "To keep such treasures safe, and procure tea of such quality."

"We found a merchant's cart a few weeks ago. The owner killed, of course.

They took everything but the tea, though a single sack of grain would have been more welcome." She sipped her own tea and sighed, steeling herself to ask the obvious question. "How did he die?"

"Saving my life, and the lives of those who now make up my court."

"But not his own."

"My lady, if there had been any way . . ."

Lady Trella shook her head, eyes closed and face downcast. "I kept hold of my hopes, throughout it all, during the flight from Varinshold, the long days on the road, finding Brother Innis and the children . . . I held to my hope. Fermin was always so clever, if never wise. If there was a way to survive the city's fall and escape the dungeons, he would have found it."

Lyrna thought of the shark and the battle, wondering if she should share her suspicions, her belief that Fermin had found at least some form of escape, and vengeance. But the words were beyond her, the enigma of it all so great. *Was he a man living in a shark? Or a shark with a memory of once being a man?* In either case, she felt sure this brave woman had no need to be burdened by further mystery.

"It is my wish," she said, "to make Fermin a posthumous Sword of the Realm. In honour of his sacrifice."

Lady Trella's lips formed the faintest smile. "Thank you. I think he would have found the notion . . . amusing."

Lyrna glanced around at the onlooking people, the adults busying themselves with the chores of cooking or building, but Brother Innis and his clutch of children continuing to view their meeting with deep concern. "Brother Innis said you kept them warm," she said.

Lady Trella shrugged. "Anyone can light a fire."

"Also, to survive the assault on the city, and the flight southward. Quite an achievement."

"I don't know how much Fermin told you of our circumstances, Highness, but despite our name, we did not live a noble existence. Poverty makes one resourceful."

"I'm sure. But still, a woman alone, surviving war and hunger for so long." She watched Lady Trella sip more tea, seeing how she forced herself to swallow. "You may have heard," she went on, "that I have lifted all strictures on use of the Dark in this Realm. The Gifted now occupy an honoured place in my army, and upon speaking to them, I have noticed that they share a common trait. In each case their mother also had a gift, but not always their father. Curious, don't you think?"

Lady Trella met her gaze then slowly raised her hand, splaying the fingers. "A Volarian soldier kicked my door in that night, found me hiding in my bedroom closet, laughed as he took hold of my hair and made ready to cut my throat." A small blue flame appeared on the tip of her index finger, dancing prettily. "He didn't laugh for long." The flame turned yellow and flared, engulfing Trella's hand from fingers to wrist.

"Highness!" Iltis appeared at her side, sword half-drawn. Lyrna realised she had risen and backed away, staring at the flames.

"I know of your edict, Highness," Trella said. "But mere words do not dispel centuries of fear. My mother made certain I knew well the danger of revealing my nature, the terror it aroused, and the unwelcome attention it drew from the Faithful." She closed her hand and the flames died. Lyrna took a breath, forcing the tremble from her limbs. She gave a nod of reassurance to Iltis and resumed her seat, sipping some more tea until the memories faded. *The smell of her own skin as the flames licked over it . . .*

"The Seventh Order is bound by my word," she said after a moment, when she was sure there would be no quaver to her voice. "I will not allow them to compel any subject to join it. There is a small company of Gifted from the Northern Reaches who stand apart from them, answering only to Lord Vaelin and myself. You would be welcome to join them."

"I am an old woman, Highness."

"Not so old, I think. And I feel your son's soul would smile on your service, don't you?"

Trella's eyes went to the children standing nearby. "I have obligations here, Highness."

"These children will be well cared for, you have my word on it. They have no more need of your fire, but I do."

Something must have coloured her voice then because the wariness on Trella's face deepened, her eyes taking on the guarded cast Lyrna was seeing more often on a few select faces. *Nortah, Dahrena, Reva . . . Vaelin. Those not in awe see more clearly.* "I make no command," Lyrna added with a smile. "Merely a queen's request. Think on it a while. Meet with Aspect Caenis or the folk from the Reaches. I am sure either would welcome you."

"I will, Highness." Trella bowed as Lyrna rose. "One more thing, if I may crave a boon."

"Of course."

"My son's sigil." The lady's eyes were bright with tears now, the children coming to her side as they sensed her distress. "I should like it to be a weasel. Of all the little beasts that followed him home, they were his favourite."

"As my lady wishes," Lyrna assured her with a bow. *Better a weasel than a shark.*

◆ ◆ ◆

Although much of Warnsclave had been destroyed down to its cobbled streets, the infrastructure below the town remained largely intact, numerous cellars providing useful additional shelter, and places of confinement. The Volarian woman had been secured in the coal cellar of what had once been a black-smith's shop, judging by the soot-covered anvil sitting amidst the rubble. Two Realm Guard stood outside the steps leading down to the cellar whilst Lord Verniers waited, resting on the anvil as she approached, scribbling away in a small notebook. He rose on seeing her, bowing with his usual fluency and greeting her in Realm Tongue uncoloured by even the trace of an accent. "Highness. My thanks on granting my request."

"Not at all, my lord," she replied. "However, I feel I have brought you here on a false premise."

"Highness?"

Lyrna gestured for the guards to open the door to the cellar. "Yes, my lord. I know you are keen for my knowledge to add to your history, but I regret scholarship will have to wait upon the needs of diplomacy."

She bade him follow her down the steps, Iltis preceding her into the darkness. Fornella Av Entril Av Tokrev sat at a small table, reading by the light of a single candle. She wore no chains and her face and hair were clean, Lyrna having allowed her a bowl of water each morning for ablutions. She had also been provided with parchment and ink, the table before her covered with a scroll inscribed from end to end in neat Volarian.

Fornella rose and bowed as Lyrna entered, her face impassive until she saw Lord Verniers whereupon she favoured him with a cautious smile. "Highness, my lord," she said in her basic Realm Tongue. "Two visitors. I am honoured."

"We'll speak in your own tongue," Lyrna told her, dropping into Volarian. "It is important there be no misunderstanding between us." She told Iltis to wait outside and gestured for Fornella to sit, moving to the table and scanning the scroll she had written, finding it a list of names, places and goods, each name marked with a circular symbol Lyrna recognised. "A writ of manumission," she said. "These are your slaves, I take it."

"Yes, Highness. Though the document is in fact a will. The slaves are to be freed upon my death."

"My understanding of Volarian law is limited," Lyrna lied. "But I believe a slave, regardless of owner or importance, can only be freed by special edict of the Ruling Council."

"Quite so, but my brother sits on the Council. I have little doubt he will accede to my wishes in this."

By the time he hears of your death, Lyrna thought, *I expect he'll be too preoccupied with the imminence of his own demise to care about your final wish.* "Am I to take it," she asked instead, "that your liking for your empire's principal institution has waned recently?"

Fornella glanced at Verniers, the scholar standing rigidly against the cellar wall and refusing to meet her gaze. "We have made many mistakes," the Volarian woman said. "Slavery is perhaps the worst, only surpassed by our bargain with the Ally."

"A bargain that, if Lord Verniers' account is to be believed, has provided you with several centuries of life."

"Not life, Highness. Merely existence."

"And how is it achieved, all these additional years?"

Fornella lowered her gaze and for the first time Lyrna had a sense of her true age in the faint lines now visible around her shrouded eyes. "Blood," Fornella said after a moment, her voice no more than a murmur. "The blood of the Gifted."

Lyrna's memory flashed to the ship, the overseer prowling the slave deck, whip coiled. *All here, trade for one with magic.* She moved closer to the table, her fists resting on the surface as she leaned towards Fornella, the Volarian woman's face still lowered. "You drink the blood of the Gifted," she grated. "That is where your years come from."

"There is a place," Fornella said in a whisper. "A great chamber beneath Volar, hundreds of cells filled with Gifted. Those who are party to the bargain go there once a year . . . to drink. And every year, there are more empty cells, and always more red-clads clamouring to share in the Ally's blessing."

"And so you need more, and the Ally promised you would find them in this Realm. That is why you came here."

"And to secure a northern front for the Alpiran invasion, as I said. But yes, the Ally promised this land would be rich in Gifted blood."

"And when that was all gone, and the Alpiran lands also stripped, what then? Send your armies forth to rape the whole world?"

Fornella's head rose, her eyes steady though her voice was uneven, the voice of a woman facing her final moments. "Yes. In time, he promised the world would be ours."

Is it shame I see in your eyes? Lyrna wondered. *Or just disappointment?*

"I assume it was the promise of endless life that seduced Lord Darnel to your cause?" she asked.

Fornella gave a rueful shrug. "The lure of immortality is hard to resist, especially for a man in love with himself."

Lyrna moved back from the table, turning to Verniers. "My lord, do you find this woman's words to be truthful?"

Verniers forced himself to look at Fornella in reluctant but close appraisal. "I doubt she has lied, Highness," he said. "Even as her slave, I found honesty to be her only interesting quality."

"And do you think your Emperor would find her believable?"

"The Emperor is wiser than I in all respects. If she speaks truly, he will hear it."

"And, I hope, understand the value of forgetting past differences."

Verniers' face was grave as he met her gaze. "There is much to forget, Highness."

"And a world to fall if we cannot forge common purpose." She turned back to Fornella. "There is a man in Brother Caenis's Order who can hear lies. You will state to him your willingness to travel to Alpira with Lord Verniers where you will tell the Emperor all you have told me. If he hears a lie, Honoured Citizen . . ."

"He will not, Highness." Fornella's relief was palpable, her years showing again in the sag of her mouth. "I will do as you ask."

"Very well." Lyrna looked at Verniers, summoning her regretful smile. "And you my lord? Will you do this for me?"

"No, Highness," he replied, the even tone of his voice and narrowness of his gaze making it clear her smile was a wasted effort. *This one sees far too much.*

"I will do it," Verniers went on, "for my Emperor, who is great in his wisdom and benevolence."

◆ ◆ ◆

She stood on the roof of the harbour-master's house to watch the ships leave, seeing Vaelin's farewell to Dahrena, finding herself unable to look away even though she felt like an intruder. *He held her for such a long time.* The small woman moved back from him, exchanged farewells with Lady Alornis, Lord

Adal, Brother Kehlan and Sanesh Poltar, then turned and walked the gang-plank to the *Red Falcon*, Ship Lord Ell-Nurin greeting her with a bow. As the ship made for the harbour mouth, Lyrna wondered if there was any signifi-cance in the fact that not a single Seordah had come to see her off.

Vaelin stayed to watch the ship sail away, responding to his sister's embrace with a slight shake of the head before she and the others drifted away. After a while Lord Verniers and the Volarian woman arrived and she saw him escort them to the ship. She was still puzzled over the interest he had shown in choosing the vessel to carry them to the empire, but he was ever a man of secrets.

She turned as Orena climbed onto the roof bearing a fur-trimmed cloak. "The wind is harsh today, Highness."

Lyrna nodded her thanks as the lady placed the cloak over her shoulders, still watching him as he stared after the departing scholar. "Murel says he's the most frightening man she's ever met," Orena mused softly.

"Then there is wisdom in the young," Lyrna said. "Does he frighten you, my lady?"

Orena shrugged; of all her attendants, she was the least given to formal-ity when they were alone, something Lyrna found sufficiently refreshing to forgive her often-wayward tongue. "Some men are brutes, some are kind. Every once in a while you meet one who's both." She straightened then gave a formal bow. "Lord Marshal Travick craves an audience, Highness. It seems his new recruits are squabbling over what to name their regiments."

"I'll be there directly, my lady."

Alone again, she waited and watched as he turned back from the har-bour, walking away with a purposeful gait. *It wasn't jealousy,* she thought. *I can permit you no distractions, my lord.*

◆ ◆ ◆

She was awoken in the small hours by Murel's soft but insistent hand. There had been no dreams tonight and wrenching herself from an untroubled sleep birthed a foul mood. "What is it?" she snapped.

"Lord Vaelin is downstairs, Highness. With Captain Belorath. It seems he bears an important message from the Isles."

Lyrna ordered her to fetch a bowl of cold water and plunged her face into it, gasping at the instant headache as the lingering tiredness vanished. She dressed in her simplest robe and managed to summon a welcoming visage by the time she descended the steps to her makeshift throne room.

Captain Belorath matched Vaelin's bow though his face betrayed his discomfort at finding himself in a servile position to a woman once his captive, a captive he had come close to killing. After the Shield took over the monstrous Volarian flagship, Belorath had resumed command of the *Sea Sabre*, sailing back to the Isles for repairs and to impart news of the great victory at Alltor. Also, Lyrna had hoped, to fetch more ships for the fleet.

"My lord, Captain," she greeted them, settling onto her throne. "I trust the news is grave enough to justify the lateness of the hour."

"Indeed, Highness," Vaelin said, nodding to Belorath.

The captain's face betrayed a certain reluctance as he spoke, the tone clipped and careful. "As Your Highness knows, the Ship Lords have been keen to ensure the security of the Isles through . . . certain discreet measures . . ."

"You've had spies planted in this Realm for years, Captain," Lyrna broke in. "A fact not unknown to the late King or myself."

"Yes, Highness. Most have fallen silent since the invasion; however, we have continued to receive occasional intelligence from one in Varinshold."

"The one who warned the Volarian fleet had sailed," Lyrna recalled.

"Quite so. Upon returning to the Isles I found another message had arrived from the same source." Belorath pulled a scroll from his belt and came forward to hand it to her. "It's addressed to you, Highness."

Lyrna unfurled the scroll, finding the words scant, but enough to make her wonder if, for all her vaunted intelligence, she wasn't just a fool after all.

Lyrna—

Attack on Winterfall Eve. Avoid the walls if you can. Aspects E & D in Blackhold. I'm sorry.

—Alucius

Chapter Ten

Alucius

"Don't lie to me, little poet!" Darnel glowered at him, his voice low and filled with dire promise, the recently stitched cut below his eye threatening to split as he snarled. "They must have told you something."

Alucius spread his hands in a helpless gesture. "No more than regret at the passing of a brother in the Faith, my lord. Though I did sense a certain satisfaction from Aspect Dendrish at finally becoming the fattest man in Asrael."

Darnel rose from his throne, his hand going to his sword, face red with fury. He halted when Division Commander Mirvek gave a warning cough and Alucius's father stiffened, stepping closer to his son's side. Darnel's gaze swept around them all, his hand quivering on his sword-handle. His recent flight from the Red Brother and the news that his fief was now raised in rebellion had done little to improve his temperament. Also Mirvek's increasing disregard and deference to his Battle Lord provided ample evidence of Darnel's burgeoning irrelevance. Only a handful of his knights remained and there were no more to be had in his fief. Alucius wondered why the Volarian didn't simply have Darnel killed and assume command himself, but the man was clearly a soldier to his core and would continue to follow orders until contrary word came from the Council. Darnel was their appointed vassal and Mirvek lacked the authority to depose him, however useless he had become.

"They know of more Gifted," Darnel told the Volarian, failing to keep a desperate note from his voice. "I'm sure of it."

Not so much a fool he doesn't know his stock has fallen, Alucius realised, watching Darnel fidget. *Seeking to buy security with the Aspects' knowledge.*

"The Aspects are precious to all those still free in these lands," Alucius's father said. "Harming them in any way invites further rebellion."

"His people rebel in any case," Mirvek pointed out in a reflective tone. "These Aspects of yours are intriguing. The warrior Aspect intriguing enough the Council ordered him shipped back to the empire the day he was captured. Questioning them could prove fruitful."

Alucius didn't like the weight the Volarian placed on the word "questioning." "If you'll allow me more time," he said. "I'm sure they will prove more accommodating. Aspect Dendrish in particular would probably spill every secret in his head for a full dinner."

Mirvek failed to laugh, regarding him with a narrow gaze. Up until now his attitude to his slave general's son had been one of vague contempt, but now Alucius knew he was seeing him with uncomfortable clarity. "My most able questioner was taken by your Red Brother," the Volarian said. "He could have had them talking in seconds. I have sent for a replacement, arriving with our reinforcements by the week's end. You have until their arrival."

Alucius replied with a grateful bow, backing away as the Volarian dismissed him with a flick of his hand. He could feel Darnel's eyes on him as he made his way from the throne room and once again wondered at his complete absence of fear.

◆　◆　◆

"Well," Alucius said as Sister Cresia panted in his ear, her naked form atop him, trembling a little. "That was unexpected."

She levered herself off him, turning her back and reaching for her blouse. "I haven't spent my entire life skulking here," she said. "I was bored. Don't fall in love with me, poet."

He forced away an image of Alornis's face, hiding guilt in a laugh. "Trust me, sister, I need no such instruction."

Sister Cresia shot him a sharp glance and rose from the pile of furs where she made her bed. She had said nothing when he made his way down here once again, inclining her head at a side passage and leading him to her chamber, shrugging her clothes off and standing naked with a questioning look. Alucius had glanced at Twenty-Seven standing in the passage outside, his blank gaze seemingly fixed on the fine brickwork. Cresia's brother and sister were off somewhere in the nighttime streets above, gathering knowledge and supplies she said, though he had brought sufficient to last them until Winterfall Eve, after that a lack of provisions was likely to be the least of their concerns.

"Who was she?" Cresia asked, her tone lightly curious.

"Who was who?"

"The woman you were thinking of a few moments ago." She fastened the belt to her trews and sat to pull on her boots.

Is that her design? he wondered. *Seeking to garner knowledge through intimacy. She's as much a spy as I am.*

"How could any man think of another when in your arms, my lady?" he replied, sitting up. He felt her flinch at his caustic tone and felt a pang of regret. *I always hurt them,* he recalled, thinking back over the years, the girls drawn to the handsome poet with the sad smile, the sweet embraces and the inevitable tears. Alornis was the only woman he had never contrived to disappoint, and he had never even kissed her.

"If you require intelligence from me," he told Cresia, "it might be simpler, and less time-consuming, to just ask."

She rose and tossed him his shirt. "Very well. When my brother and sister return. And I'll expect a full account if we're to help in this escapade of yours."

They ate a sparse meal of dried beef and bread washed down with water, since his father hadn't seen fit to provide wine with the extra provisions. If Inehla and Rhelkin sensed any tension between them, they failed to show it, though he fancied there was a faint glint of amusement in the glance Inehla gave her sister.

"How can you be certain the queen's army will attack on Winterfall Eve?" Rhelkin asked when the meal was done.

"I can't," Alucius admitted. "The only surety I can give is that I sent word for them to do so."

"How?" Cresia asked.

"By pigeon. My last, in fact. So please don't ask me to send any more."

"How does a poet come to keep pigeons?"

"Because he's also a spy in service to the Meldenean Ship Lords." Alucius sipped his water, sighing in fond remembrance of his last taste of decent wine as the others stared in silence. It had been a bottle from his father's cellar, one of his oldest, Cumbraelin naturally, a deep and richly flavoured red from the southern vineyards. The bottle had been pleasant but not enough to see him to the sleep he craved, plagued as he was by the ache left by Alornis's departure to the Reaches. So he had sought out a bottle of brandy from the kitchens, falling into bed only to be roused some hours later by a Volarian army.

"Then you," Sister Cresia said, breaking through his reminiscence, "are a traitor to this Realm." Alucius noted her hand had moved to the leather pouch on her belt whilst Brother Rhelkin was now turned towards Twenty-Seven, poised no doubt to employ his gift.

"I suppose so," Alucius said. He looked at his cup of water and grimaced, putting it aside.

Cresia continued to glare as the silence thickened. "Why?" she asked eventually.

"That is not your concern," Alucius stated. "What matters is that we have a common interest in ensuring this city is recovered for the Realm with a minimum of bloodshed. And, at present, I stand best placed to achieve this outcome."

"A spy deserves no trust."

"Trust? You speak of trust?" Alucius laughed. "You who have lived a lifetime of lies. What service have you done in the name of the Faith, I wonder? How much blood spilled in the shadows over the years?"

Inehla's rat scurried along the table, sniffing his hand then baring its teeth with a loud squeak. "Does he smell a lie?" Cresia asked her.

The plump sister shook her head, her expression dark. "No, only this one's contempt for us."

Cresia's face registered a scowl of fury before she forced it to a neutral frown, her hand retreating from her pouch. Inehla's rat gave a final squeak then ran back to its mistress as Brother Rehlkin turned away from Twenty-Seven.

"How is it to be done?" Cresia asked Alucius.

"The Volarian reinforcements are due to arrive on Winterfall Eve," he said. "To be greeted at the docks by Commander Mirvek, Lord Darnel, and my father. I doubt any will object, or notice if I'm there. I shall require your sister's skill to create sufficient diversion."

"Diversion from what?"

"This city will stand or fall on my father's judgement. Without it, Darnel and his allies are doomed."

"A hard thing for a son to kill a father," Rehlkin observed.

"If you doubt my ability to do this," Alucius replied, "you should kill me now and keep skulking here until Queen Lyrna arrives." He saw the man's dislike in his cold glare and found himself beyond caring. "I'll need you and Sister Cresia to secure the Aspects."

"Breaking into the Blackhold is no easy task," Cresia said.

"But within your abilities, I'm sure. I've little doubt their guards have orders to kill them should the city fall, and it's better to risk death than blindly accept it."

He saw them exchanging glances, reaching agreement in silent nods, Cresia's the most reluctant. "We'll do this," she said. "But when it's done, poet, you will not be spared an accounting."

"No." He got up and turned away, walking back to the tunnel with Twenty-Seven falling in behind. "I don't imagine I will."

◆ ◆ ◆

"I must say, Aspect," he said, sitting on the bunk beside her. "I found the wine rather bitter."

"But you did find it?" she asked, her gaze intent.

"Indeed I did. Only three bottles, though."

Her mouth twitched in suppressed disappointment. "Pity."

"Disappointment was ever my lot, Aspect. I do, however, have news. It seems we have a new queen."

"Lyrna? She lives?"

"Hale, whole and leading an army to our salvation as we speak, an army commanded by Lord Al Sorna himself, having crushed General Tokrev at Alltor."

Aspect Elera sat straight, closing her eyes, her shoulders pulled back as she breathed a series of controlled breaths. He had seen her do this before, when her usual composure slipped and the faint sheen of tears glimmered in her eyes. After a few seconds she reopened her eyes and smiled, the same calm, open smile he knew he would miss a great deal.

"Excellent news, Alucius," she said. "Thank you for telling me. And when can we expect our queen's arrival?"

Alucius flicked his eyes at the Free Sword outside. The man might appear dumb as a stump and capable of no more than a few words of Realm Tongue, but Alucius's short spying career had taught him the value of seeing beyond appearances. "Such intelligence is far beyond my reach, Aspect." He folded his arms and extended three fingers towards his elbow, seeing understanding in her gaze as she resisted the impulse to nod.

"It is my belief you should not save the wine," she said in a brisk tone. "These are troubled times, and wine always offers an *escape* from worry, don't you think?"

"You are kind to think of my comfort, Aspect. But, if ever a man has drunk his fill, it's me."

The Free Sword gave an impatient jangle of his keys and Alucius stood.

"Though, I am able to share two bottles with you," Alucius told her. "Your own comfort being of paramount importance to me."

Her smile faltered a little, a stern glint appearing in her gaze. "Wine should not be wasted, Alucius."

"And it won't be." He knelt, meeting her eyes, seeing how she fought tears. Instead of raising her hand for him to kiss, as was their habit, she leaned forward and pressed her lips to his forehead, whispering, "I beg you, go."

He clasped her hands and kissed them, standing and moving from the cell. He was careful in his scrutiny of the Free Sword as he locked the door, seeing only the dull eyes of a brutal fool. Nevertheless, he was glad he had told Cresia to kill him the instant she entered this chamber.

◆ ◆ ◆

It was the one house he had never visited since the city's fall, a part-tumbled-down, once-impressive mansion near Watcher's Bend, shaded by the branches of a great old oak. The roof was even more threadbare than he remembered and the windows were all gone, stirring memories of how hard Alornis had worked to keep them clean and intact. The house had been spared burning by some happy chance, perhaps because of its size or the barren rooms within, void of any useful loot, at least to those unskilled in spotting concealment.

The door was half-off its hinges, the hallway beyond all peeling paint and bare floorboards. He remembered his first visit here, the falsely confident knock she took so long to answer. "Alucius Al Hestian, my lady," he had greeted her, bowing low. "Former comrade to your noble brother."

"I know who you are," she replied with a puzzled frown, opening the door only wide enough to look him up and down. "What do you want?"

It had taken several visits before she let him in, and only then because it had been raining, pointing him to a stool in the kitchen with a stern warning against dripping on her drawings. It had been duty that made him persist, the appearance of adherence to a royal command, but it was the drawings that made him come back the next night, suffering her puzzled indifference and occasional barbs. He had never seen anything like them, the clarity and feeling rendered with such economy, as irresistible as he came to find their creator.

He made his way to the kitchen where she had spent most of her time, the floor tiles liberally adorned with broken crockery, the table where she prepared the meagre meals they shared tipped over and lacking a leg.

"Protect me?" she had laughed when he explained his reason for coming here every night. Her eyes went to the short sword at his belt, twinkling a little. "I'm sorry, but that really doesn't suit you."

"No," he admitted. "It never did. But, thanks to your brother, I do know how to use it."

In truth, he always knew she needed little protection. Those few Faithful sufficiently deluded to imagine her some kind of substitute for her brother were sent away with implacable and waspish refusal, whilst the King never had reason to suspect her loyalty. She worked every day under Master Benril's less-than-pleasant tutelage and spent her nights in this empty house, her charcoal and silverpoint crafting wonders from the parchment she starved herself to buy. It was parchment that bought her toleration, for he always had an ample supply and would bring some when he came, content to sit and watch as she worked, a bottle of Wolf's Blood never far away despite her obvious disapproval.

"Every word she speaks regarding her brother and her father is to be recorded," Malcius had told him that day he had been called to the palace, ostensibly to receive the queen's endorsement of his latest collection of poems, but in reality to press him to a new duty. Malcius's face had been grave as they walked together in the gardens, a king forced to reluctant necessity. "The identity of any and all visitors also. Lord Vaelin's shadow was ever far too long, Alucius. Best if she's not caught in it, don't you think?"

He thought he was making me a spy, Alucius mused, glancing at the wall where she had pinned her sketches, bare now, save for the outline of parchment on whitewash. *Little knowing the Meldeneans had got there first. Poor old Malcius, Janus would have known in an instant.*

He climbed the creaking and partly missing stairs to the upper floor, Twenty-Seven following, hopping the gaps with nimble swiftness. He paused only a little at the door to Alornis's room, as he had done at the end of many a drunken night, just to catch the soft whisper of her breath as she slept. *Why did I never tell her?* he wondered. *Words spoken so easily to so many others, but I could never say them to her, the one time they would have been true.*

The room where he had slept was mostly intact, his narrow bed still sitting against the wall complete with mattress, though the sheets were gone. He pulled it away from the wall and knelt, dislodging a fragment of plaster to reveal a small hiding place, missed by the Volarians who had come looting. He sighed in relief at finding the narrow leather bundle intact.

"Doesn't seem much does it?" he said to Twenty-Seven, placing the bundle on the bed and undoing the ties, revealing a small dagger. The handle was undecorated whalebone and the sheath plain leather. He drew it, baring a well-made blade six inches long. "But," he went on, "the man who gave it to me said the barest touch is enough to kill. Not instantly, but the poison on the blade will ensure a swift death." He met the slave's eyes, something he rarely did since there was nothing there to see. "What would you do if I tried to stab you with this? Kill me? I doubt it. Disarm me more likely, break my wrist perhaps. Or would you, I wonder, simply stand there and die, sure in the knowledge that I'll find another just like you at my side before the day's out?"

Twenty-Seven stared at him and said nothing.

"Don't worry, my good friend." Alucius returned the dagger to its sheath and pushed it into his belt. "It's not for you. Besides, I find I've grown too fond of your company. Your conversation being such a delight."

He pushed the bed against the wall and settled onto it, lying back with his hands behind his head. "How many battles have you seen? Ten, twenty, a hundred? I was in a battle once, well three times if you count the Bloody Hill and Marbellis, though my part was hardly worthy of note. No, my one true battle was in the Usurper's Revolt, the High Keep. The first great victory in the illustrious career of our soon-to-be deliverer. There are songs about it, awful and dreadfully inaccurate, but I'm in them, most of them anyway. Alucius the poet-warrior, come to avenge his brother, 'his sword like lightning from a righteous storm.'"

He fell silent for a moment, remembering. It was always the smell and the sound he recalled best, much more vivid in his mind than the images, which were just a red-tinged jumble. No, it was the sound of horses screaming, the stink of sweat, the odd crunch steel makes when it pierces flesh, voices begging their god for deliverance, and shit . . . the acrid, stinging perfume of his own shit.

"I made him teach me," he told Twenty-Seven. "On the march. Every night we'd practice. I got better, good enough to fool myself I had some kind of chance, some hope of surviving what was coming. I knew I was wrong when Malcius ordered the charge. Knew in an instant I was no warrior, no avenging soul, just a scared boy with shit in his trews. I remember screaming, I suppose the others thought it a war cry, but it was just fear. When we charged the gate they sought to bar our entry with their bodies, linking arms, shouting prayers to their god. When we struck home the force of it sent me flying. I tried to get up but there were so many bodies pressing me down, I screamed and I begged but no one pulled me free, then something hard came down on my head."

He remembered the kindly sister who had nursed him back to health, later destined to find herself in the Blackhold for heresy and treason, all because she spoke against the war. He remembered his father's face the day he returned to the mansion, the sigh of relief followed by a curt order: "You will not venture again from this house without my consent." He had nodded meekly, handed back Linden's sword, and gone to his room where he had stayed for the best part of a year.

"I have always been a coward, you see," he said. "And the more I learn of this world I find it the only sensible course in life, for the most part. At Marbellis I stood and watched a city burn, then watched my father hang a hundred men for burning it. I stayed at his side throughout the siege, even when he led a charge to seal a breach in the defences. Didn't shit myself that time, though I was very drunk. When the walls fell I ran when he ran. Darnel was there, oddly enough, just as terrified as the rest of us. I remember he had to fight his own men to get to the ship that took us to safety, and when we sailed away I looked at his face and knew him to be every bit the coward I am."

He turned to Twenty-Seven, beckoning him closer and speaking softly. "I need you to remember something."

He spoke for a short time, the words unrehearsed but flowing well. When he was finished he ordered Twenty-Seven to repeat them, the slave doing so in a disconcertingly precise imitation of Alucius's voice. *Is my accent really that mannered?* he wondered when the slave fell silent.

"Very good," he said, then gave careful instruction regarding when and to whom his words were to be repeated. "I'll sleep now," he told Twenty-Seven. "Wake me by the eighth bell, if you would."

◆ ◆ ◆

He was gratified to find Darnel on horseback at the docks, his few remaining knights clustered about him on foot. The Fief Lord was ever keen to tower above those around him and insisted on riding whenever he ventured from the palace. A full battalion of Free Swords was lined up along the wharf behind Mirvek, waiting to greet whatever luminaries approached on the huge warship now cresting the horizon. Alucius knew from his father the Volarian supply convoys had been subject to frequent attack in recent weeks, the Meldeneans no doubt happy to find piracy as profitable an endeavour in war as in peace. However, a ship possessing the size and power of the monster sailing towards them could surely expect to remain immune from their attentions.

Alucius had spent the morning in expectation of some great commotion, men rushing to man his father's carefully laid positions as Lyrna's army appeared on the southern plain. But there had been no alarm, no warning trumpets to pierce the morning air and no armies to besmirch the surrounding country.

If she could have come, she would, he knew. *If only to hang me.* He had been keen to avoid her since the war, her scrutiny being ever so acute, their meetings limited to the occasional palace function. There had been times when she sent messengers requesting his attendance at luncheon but he had always demurred, fearing what her insight might tell her. *I know what you did, Lyrna.*

It had begun the day he returned from Marbellis and she came to the docks to greet the feeble remnants of her father's once-great army. Her smile perfect; grave, encouraging, free of judgement or reproach. But he saw it, just for an instant as she watched a Realm Guard with a missing leg being carried from the ship. *Guilt.*

It had all tumbled into place later, an instantaneous realisation when he learned their new king was safely returned to the Realm and Vaelin taken by the Alpirans. He had been at the palace when Malcius, pale-eyed and gaunt beneath his beard, placed the crown upon his head and the assembled nobles bowed . . . and Lyrna's face betrayed the same flicker of expression he had seen that day at the docks.

I know what you did.

He had always marvelled at how quickly the Meldeneans found him. Drink, women and the occasional flurry of poetry had been his chief distractions in the two years since Marbellis, liquor making him somewhat incautious with his words, words that some might take as sedition. The Meldenean had sat down next to him one night in his favourite wineshop, so favoured because the first cup was always free for veterans, a small expense since they were so few in number. The Meldenean wore the garb of a sailor, as befitted his nationality, speaking initially in coarse, uncultured tones. He bought wine for Alucius, professing himself ignorant of letters upon hearing his occupation, but asked many questions about the war. He came back the following night, buying less wine but asking more questions, and the night after that. With every meeting Alucius noted his accent was not so coarse as before, and his questions more searching, especially regarding the King and his sister.

"They're traitors," Alucius had said, a little too loud from the way the man winced and gestured for him to speak softer. "The whole family," he went on, knowing he was far too drunk and not caring. "Janus sent my brother to die in the Martishe, had my father slaughter thousands for nothing. Abandoned my friend to the Alpirans. She did that, not Janus. It was *her*."

The Meldenean gave a slow nod. "We know," he said. "But we'd like to know more."

They offered him money, which he refused, proud of himself for being sober when he did so. "Just tell me what you want."

Spying, he discovered, was an absurdly easy occupation. *Few people ever see more than they wish to,* he decided, having accepted an invitation to read poetry to a gaggle of merchants' wives, rich in gossip and fat with information regarding the new trade routes their husbands had been obliged to forge since the war. They saw a handsome young poet, tragic hero of a tragic war, wilted obligingly at his verse and proved very helpful when he asked for likely investment opportunities. "For my father, you understand. He needs something to occupy him these days. Peacetime is such a trial for a military man."

He would go to inns frequented by the Realm Guard, finding welcome among the veterans who had been at Linesh with Vaelin, embittered cynics to a man and talkative when sufficiently full of ale. He made it known he was available for commissions, penning love poems for smitten young nobles and eulogies for the funerals of rich men, gaining access to the wealthy and the powerful in the process. His Meldenean contact was happy with his work and provided the pigeons to speed delivery of his intelligence, and the dagger should he ever face discovery.

"I'm not an assassin," Alucius told him, eyeing the dagger with distaste.

"It's for you," the Meldenean told him with a grin before walking from the wineshop. Alucius never saw him again. The following week came the summons from the King and his order to spy on Alornis, after which he found his enthusiasm for his new occupation began to wane. Being with her dimmed his anger, made the sting of betrayal less acute. He continued to gather information, mostly trade gossip of little value, sending the birds off and knowing, should he include his notice of retirement among the messages, the Meldeneans were more likely to offer a blade than a pension. As it turned out, the Volarians made such worries redundant.

Alucius stood with Twenty-Seven some ten yards behind his father, who had positioned himself outside Darnel's coterie of sycophant knights. "Impressive beast, isn't it?" he asked, moving to stand on his father's left.

Lakrhil Al Hestian nodded as the ship came closer, Alucius seeing two smaller vessels following in its broad wake. "Apparently it's the sister ship to their *Stormspite*," his father said. "I forget the name. Mirvek thinks it a sign of the Ruling Council's continued faith in his command, bringing more reinforcements than expected."

Alucius remembered the *Stormspite* as a brooding monster that had sat in the harbour for days until General Tokrev sailed it off to Alltor, never to return. Picking out details as its sister came closer, he was struck by the similarity between them; even for ships built to the same pattern the resemblance was striking, though the Volarians were a people greatly fond of uniformity.

"Are your preparations complete?" he asked. "All made ready to bleed Lord Vaelin's army white?"

"Hardly," his father grunted. "The Free Swords are lazy when not set to pillaging, and the Varitai little use in labour. Give them a shovel and they just stare at it. Still, it seems we'll shortly have more hands to complete the task."

"Could you have held Marbellis? If you had had this much to work with?"

Lakrhil turned to him with a quizzical expression; it was an unspoken understanding that Marbellis was a subject neither of them wanted to discuss. "No," he said. There must have been something in Alucius's expression, some vestige of his intent, for he leaned closer, speaking softly. "You don't need to be here, Alucius. And you've yet to produce a single useful word from the Aspects." His eyes flicked to Darnel. "I can't protect you forever."

Alucius's gaze went to his stolen house, finding the balcony where he ate breakfast and counted the ships every morning. She was there as requested, a small, plump figure leaning on the balustrade, her gaze fixed on Darnel, or rather Darnel's horse. "It's all right," Alucius told his father. "You won't have to."

Darnel's horse gave a loud snort, jerking and shaking its head. "Easy now," the Fief Lord said, smoothing his hand over its neck. Alucius was relieved to see Darnel wore no armour today, just finely tailored silks and a long cloak. He reached for the dagger at the small of his back, concealed beneath his coat, his eyes intent on Darnel's horse. It snorted again, giving a loud whinny, eyes widening into panicked mania as it reared, too sudden for Darnel to grab a tighter hold of the reins, pitching him from the saddle. Free of its rider the great warhorse wheeled around, lashing out with its hooves at the nearest of Darnel's knights, the iron shoes ringing loud on the man's breastplate as they sent him sprawling. The animal pivoted on its forelegs, vicious hind hooves scattering the remaining knights as Darnel back-pedalled on the ground, eyes wide in panic. The horse stopped its assault on the knights and turned again, wild eyes fixing on Twenty-Seven before charging with a shrill scream. The slave-elite's expression remained as calm as ever as he attempted to dive clear of the horse's path, proving fractionally too slow as the animal's flank collided with his shoulder, spinning him to the ground, slack and senseless.

Alucius drew the dagger from its sheath and sprinted towards Darnel, now climbing to his feet, well clear of any protection. *Only use the shortest possible thrust,* Vaelin had told him, all those years ago when he fancied himself a hero. *It's the fast blade that draws blood.*

Some battle-won instinct must have sounded in Darnel's mind, for he turned just as Alucius thrust towards his back, the blade piercing his cloak and becoming entangled in the folds. Darnel snarled, bringing his fist around to smash at Alucius's face. He ducked under it, tearing the dagger free of the cloak and lunging for Darnel's arm, knowing even the slightest cut would be enough. The Fief Lord sidestepped, his sword coming free of its scabbard in a blur. Alucius felt a great stinging burn flare across his chest, the shock of it sending him to his knees, Darnel looming above him, sword drawn back. His expression was fiercely triumphant, smile broad in anticipation of the kill. "*You* think to kill *me*, little poet?" he laughed.

"No," Alucius replied, feeling blood bathing his chest as he glanced over Darnel's shoulder. "But I expect *he* will."

Darnel whirled but too late. Lakrhil Al Hestian speared the Fief Lord through the neck with the spike protruding from his right sleeve. Darnel took some seconds to die, spitting blood and weeping as he hung from the spike, eyes bulging and lips babbling gibberish before he finally slumped to the wharf. Alucius still thought it hadn't taken long enough.

A cold hand seemed to enfold him on all sides as he collapsed, feeling his father catch him, smiling up at his ice-white face. "The Aspects," he said. "Get to the Blackhold . . ."

"Alucius!" His father shook him, his voice a rage-filled scream. "ALUCIUS!"

Alucius was aware of a great clamour somewhere, though his vision was too dim to make out the source, men yelling in alarm and summoning memories of the High Keep. He found it strange that the sky above his father's head seemed to be filled with black streaks, like the arrows at the Bloody Hill, another unwelcome memory. He closed his eyes, pushing it all away and filling his mind with Alornis's face as the last of his blood seeped away.

CHAPTER ELEVEN

Frentis

"Winterfall Eve," Brother Lernial said in his perennially dull voice. He had said almost nothing since arriving with the Eorhil woman the day before, slumping in front of a fire and staring at the flames for hours. Insha ka Forna stayed at his side, her gaze continually drawn in expectation.

"The Seventh Order," Ivern said, watching with Frentis from the fringes of the gathered captains, his face a mix of confusion and suspicion. "Hiding in the Realm Guard. And where else, one wonders."

"Aspect Grealin gave the impression they had many guises," Frentis said.

"Grealin." Ivern shook his head. "Just how many lies did they tell us, do you think?"

"Enough to keep us safe." Frentis straightened as Brother Lernial said something and Insha ka Forna raised a hand to beckon him over.

"What happens on Winterfall Eve?" Banders asked the brother.

"Varinshold." Lernial frowned in concentration, a vein pulsing in his temple and sweat beading his brow. "Lord Al Sorna attacks Varinshold. Something . . . something will happen."

"Al Sorna's army is in Warnsclave," Banders said. "How could he make such an attack?"

Lernial gave a pained grunt, arching his back and exhaling slowly, then slumping forward, features slack with exhaustion. "That's all," he muttered.

"There must be more," Banders persisted, drawing a glower from Insha ka Forna.

"Leave him!" she said. "This . . . hurts him, much."

"You can hear Lord Vaelin's thoughts?" Frentis asked Lernial in a gentler tone.

The brother shook his head. "Brother Caenis only. It's . . . easier that way." He gave a wan smile. "But to wade through even the most disciplined mind is a tiring task."

Frentis nodded his thanks and rose from the man's side, moving away to confer with Banders and Sollis. "Three days until Winterfall Eve," the baron said. "Scant time for planning. I've had my lot fell the few trees around here for ladders and engines, but none are ready yet."

"Which makes the sewers our only option," Frentis said. "We know from Darnel's knights that Aspects Elera and Dendrish are in the Blackhold, perhaps Aspect Arlyn too. I don't give much for their chances if the city is attacked. I can secure them if you'll allow me."

"Securing a gate is more important," Sollis said.

"The Aspects . . ."

"Are aware that the Faith occasionally requires sacrifice. We will secure a gate to allow Baron Banders's knights into the city, then make for the Blackhold."

"We, brother?"

Sollis's pale gaze was steady, yielding no room for argument. "Brother, you have led your company well, and they are loyal to you. But your loyalty is to me. Or are you no longer willing to call yourself a brother?"

"I will never call myself anything else," Frentis returned, anger rising to colour his face.

Sollis merely blinked and turned to the baron. "We'll set out at dawn, which should enable us to approach the city under dark in three nights." He looked at Frentis. "Choose your people and be ready."

◆ ◆ ◆

They followed the Brinewash towards Varinshold, moving in single file along the bank, which was damp enough to prevent any betraying dust cloud. Frentis chose Davoka, Draker and Thirty-Four to accompany him through the sewers, provoking Arendil and Illian to loud protests at being excluded. Davoka sternly rebuked the lady for her petulance, and Banders refused to even countenance the thought of Arendil leaving his sight. "You'll stay by me at all times," he told his grandson. "If this goes right, the fief will have need of a new lord by the week's end."

They stopped after a two-day trek, occupying a shallow dip in the ground just south of the Brinewash, Varinshold out of sight just over the horizon.

Sollis's brothers scouted the surrounding country, mostly grass and expanses of ash left by the demise of the Urlish. They returned at nightfall reporting the Volarians seemed to have abandoned patrolling. "Could be they've no cavalry left for such duty," Ermund suggested. "We killed hundreds back at the Spur."

They settled down to rest as night set in, huddling in cloaks against the chill as fires could not be risked. Frentis sat watching the others sleep, determined to stay awake, as he had for the past two nights, fighting exhaustion with every step. At one point he had snapped awake finding himself held in the saddle by Davoka, shaking his head at her stern entreaties to rest come the night. *She waits for me there,* he knew with a cold certainty.

"Will it end tomorrow, brother?" It was Illian, sitting a few feet away, swaddled in a cloak taken from a dead Volarian at the Spur. It covered her easily, leaving only the pale oval of her face peering out from the hood.

So young, Frentis thought. *So small. You would never know, as no one knew when they looked at* her. Annoyed by the comparison, he looked away. "Will what end?" he asked, keeping his voice low.

"The war," she said, shuffling closer. "Draker said it'll all be over come the new day." She gave a rueful smile. "Then he said he'd buy a whorehouse with his spoils."

"I doubt there are any left to buy, my lady."

"But we'll be done? The war will end?"

"I hope so."

She seemed oddly deflated by this, a flicker of her increasingly rare pout on her lips. "No more *Gorin,*" she murmured. "No more Davoka. Arendil will go off and rule his fief, Draker to his whorehouse, you to the Order."

"And you, my lady?"

"I don't know. I have no idea if my father lives, if his house still stands."

"And your mother?"

Illian's expression soured a little. "Father used to tell me she died when I was little. One day I heard two of the maids gossiping, seems my darling mother took off with a sea captain when I was no more than a year old. Father had every scrap of clothing she owned stripped from the house, along with every image of her. I don't even know what she looked like."

"Not all are suited to parentage," Frentis said, thinking of his own family, if they could be called that. "Whatever your father's fate, his lands and assets are now yours by right. I feel sure the queen will see to proper restitution in due course."

"Restitution." She looked around at the surrounding fields of ash, rendered silver-blue in the moonlight. "Is that even possible now? So much has been broken. Besides, I'm not sure I want to regain ownership of an empty ruin."

"Arendil . . ." Frentis began in a cautious tone, "You seem . . . fond of him."

She gave a soft sigh of embarrassed exasperation. "I am. He's very sweet, and one day I expect Lady Ulice will find him a wife suited to fine dresses and balls and empty talk with privileged fools. I am not. Not now, if I ever was." She wriggled in the folds of her cloak, hefting her crossbow, her hands tight on the stock. "I'm made for this. I'm made for the Order, brother."

He could only stare at her completely serious expression. "There are no sisters of the Sixth Order," he said, lost for any other response.

"Why not?"

"There just aren't. There never have been."

"Because only men fight wars?" She nodded at Davoka. "What about her? What about me?"

He shifted uncomfortably, lowering his gaze. "The composition of the Orders is set down by the tenets of the Faith. They can't simply be cast aside . . ."

"They could if you were to vouch for me. Especially if Brother Sollis were to add his voice. Everything has changed, I've heard you say so yourself."

"This is a foolish notion, Illian . . ."

"Why is it foolish?"

"Do you want to be like me?" He leaned forward, eyes locked on hers, suddenly angered by her naïvety. "Do you have any notion of what I have done?"

"You're a great warrior, and the man who saved my life."

Seeing her mystified, wide-eyed gaze, he sighed, his anger evaporating as he slumped back. "I have killed my way across half the world to return to this Realm, and when the queen comes to claim her throne she'll make sure I face a reckoning."

"For what? Winning the war?"

He just shook his head. "I was once just like you, lost, seeking a home, begging the same favour from someone who came to hate himself for saying yes. And I find myself with a surfeit of hate, my lady. Approach Brother Sollis if you wish, he will say the same thing."

"We'll see," she muttered, falling into a sullen silence.

He watched her put the crossbow aside and pluck a bolt from her quiver, working the iron-headed barb on a small whetstone. *No,* he conceded. *No longer made for dresses and balls.* "Did you know," he said, "in the southern jungles of the Volarian Empire, there lives a beast, fully twelve feet tall and covered all over with fur, that looks just like a man on stilts?"

She angled her head at him, raising an eyebrow. "You're making it up."

"No, it's true. I swear on the Faith. And in the oceans to the east are great sharks, as big as a whale and striped red from end to end."

"I've heard of those," she admitted. "My tutor showed me a picture once."

"Well, I've seen them. There is more than war to find in this world, Illian. There is as much beauty as there is ugliness, as long as you have the eyes to see it."

She gave a small laugh. "Perhaps I'll find a sea captain of my own one day, go looking for it." The words were empty, he knew, the humour forced. Her mind was set on but one course.

"I hope so too."

He saw her frown as she scanned his face, youthful beauty marred by concern. "You *must* sleep, brother. Please. I'll watch you. If you start to get . . . upset, I'll wake you."

There are some dreams you can't wake from. But he was so tired now, and a battle waited no more than three hours hence. "Don't neglect your own rest," he told her, settling onto his side, breathing deep, then closing his eyes.

◆ ◆ ◆

She sits alone in a spacious chamber of marble floors and fine furnishings; it is midafternoon and a gentle breeze sways the lace curtains hanging over the arches leading to the balcony. The chamber belonged to Council-man Lorvek and is filled with artifacts bought or stolen from all corners of the world; Alpiran statuary of bronze and marble, fine paintings from the Unified Realm, exquisite ceramics from the Far West, garish war masks from the southern tribe lands. A priceless collection, the fruit of several lifetimes' labour. It is how they persist, these select few red-clad, filling their endless days with successive obsession, for art, wealth, flesh . . . or murder.

She casts a glance around Lorvek's collection and decides to have it all destroyed the following morning. The feeding two days ago has left her invigorated but with a sour edginess. The Gifted had been foul indeed, a nondescript man of middle years with the ability to hold a person in place, frozen, immobile, but awake. He had spent over two decades wandering the empire killing women, freezing them so they could only suffer in silence as he visited all manner of torments upon their flesh. He would have been a useful recruit for the Ally, given enough time, but his mind was far too fractured to justify the effort needed. He had tried to resist her, somehow sensing the threat despite the drugs, casting his gift at her like the flailing invisible hand of an addled drunk. She would have laughed at him once, even retreated for a while to allow the drug haze to fade before returning to enjoy his impotent rage as she made it last. But she hadn't, the stumbling wretch deserved little regard and certainly no pity, but the blood had tasted foul as she slashed his throat, fighting a reflexive gag as she forced herself to drink deep, wondering if all the death she had wrought would also taint her blood.

She forces the memory away and slows her breathing, calming her mind, focusing her thoughts. I feel you, beloved, *she tells him.* I know you feel me too.

She waits, mind open to a response, knowing he is there, but feeling only the depth of his enmity. Will you not talk to me? *she implores.* Are you not lonely too? And we have shared so much.

Anger swells, reaching across the great divide to lash at her, making her wince. I fear for you, *she persists.* We know she lives, beloved. We know she comes to take the city, and you know what she will do when she finds you.

The anger dims, replaced by grim acceptance and a great depth of guilt.

Forget all the nonsense they instilled in you, *she begs.* All the lies they told you. The Faith is a child's illusion, nobility a coward's mask. They are not for such as us, my love. You felt it, when we were killing together. I know you did. We soared above them all, and we can do so again. Leave now. Run. Come back to me.

The sensation changes, emotion fading to be replaced by an image, a darkly beautiful young woman, half her face bathed in firelight, her brow creased in confusion and regret. Her lips move but the sound is lost to her, although she knows the words with absolute clarity. I made my bargain, beloved. I cannot make another.

I had no choice, *she tells him now.*

The image fades, swirling in her mind until it transforms into a voice, hard and cold but blessedly familiar. Neither do I.

◆ ◆ ◆

They mustered two hours shy of dawn, gathering around Sollis as he unfurled a recently drawn map of the city, pointing to the north-east gate. "I suggest an attack in two directions, my lord," he said to Banders. "Your knights to press a charge along Gate Lane, it's wide enough for ten men abreast and leads directly to the harbour. If successful, you'll cut the city in two and sow confusion in the enemy's ranks. My brothers, Brother Frentis's company and the Renfaelin common folk will make for the Blackhold. It's a stout fortress and will provide a place of retreat should the day go against us."

Banders nodded his agreement and turned to address his assembled captains. "The odds do not favour us, as you know. But we are told Lord Vaelin comes to take this city and I intend to aid him in doing so. Tell every knight and man at arms that come the morning there will be no turning from the charge, no restraint is to be shown, and no mercy. The city stands infested, and we will cleanse it." He glanced at Arendil, adding in a sombre tone, "Lord Darnel is not to be taken alive, regardless of any entreaties to knightly custom. He has forfeited life and knighthood long since."

◆　◆　◆

The four of them made their way to the city on foot, heading for the northern stretch of wall where the Brinewash emerged from the city through a great sluice gate. They crawled slowly for the final half mile, Draker grunting along behind and drawing an irritated kick from Davoka. The outlaw had become much stealthier over the months but often had need of a reminder. As expected, the sluice gate was too well guarded to allow entry, even if it had been possible to navigate the frothing current that slid over the barrier in a constant rush. Instead Frentis led them into the river and followed the wall north. They wore thin clothing of light fabric, boots having been abandoned before entering the chill waters, their weapons confined to daggers and swords.

The pipe emerged from the wall three feet above the water where the river began to arc away from the city and commence its long winding journey into the heart of the Realm. A continual stream of effluent flowed from the pipe, leaving a foul-smelling stain on the river that had Draker gagging as they swam through it. Frentis hugged the wall, eyes fixed on the parapet above, finding it empty though there was the faint murmur of Volarian voices nearby. He had discounted this exit when they escaped the city during the invasion given the ease with which archers would have picked them off as soon as they emerged. Now he gambled on its vulnerability, doubting even a soul as cautious as Blood Rose would see much threat in so exposed an entry point.

He moved along the wall, hands exploring for holds, but finding nothing.

"It's too slippy, brother," Draker whispered next to his ear, his large hand scraping moss from the stone.

Frentis turned as Thirty-Four tapped his shoulder. The former slave patted his chest and pointed to the mouth of the pipe, then made an upward-pushing motion with both arms. Frentis took another look at the moss-covered wall and gave a reluctant nod. The splash of disturbed water would have to be risked if they were to continue.

He and Davoka moved to either side of Thirty-Four, drawing breath then sinking under the water. Frentis took hold of the man's slim leg and placed the foot on his shoulder, counted to three to ensure Davoka was similarly prepared, reached out to slap her arm, and they both kicked upwards in unison, boosting Thirty-Four out of the water to clamp his hands on the rim of the pipe. He hung there for a few seconds as they scanned the wall above, waiting for any sign of discovery. Nothing. Even the murmur of voices seemed to have gone.

Thirty-Four levered himself onto the top of the pipe and caught the coiled rope Frentis threw him, looping it over the great iron tube and tying it tight with his usual facility for knots. Draker hauled himself up first, squirming into the pipe and biting down curses at the filth now piling up in front of him. It took several anxious moments before his head finally disappeared into the pipe. Davoka followed him, grunting as she heaved herself into the opening, pushing Draker's bulk ahead of her. Frentis gestured for Thirty-Four to follow then climbed up, casting a final glance at the walls as he undid the rope from the pipe, dragging it behind as he squirmed through.

"Nothing beats the smell of home, eh, brother?" Draker asked as he emerged into the sewers. The big outlaw stood in the channel of rushing filth, casting his gaze right and left. "Reckon it's this way," he said, pointing right. "Channel loops back around towards the gate, as I recall."

"Lead on," Frentis told him.

It took over an hour of sloshing through the polluted water, and a couple of wrong turns before they came to the requisite drain. It was an iron grate twenty feet from the north gate with a narrow opening where the inner wall met the road. Frentis remembered slipping through the opening with relative ease one time, many years ago when he had run from a vengeful shop owner. Now, however, even Thirty-Four found the opening too narrow.

"There's a wider one on Firestone Way," Draker recalled.

"Too far," Frentis said. He peered through the opening at the wasted streets beyond, finding a series of jagged silhouettes, collapsed walls, and burnt-out buildings, devoid of good cover, the sky above now a grey-blue signifying a fast-approaching sunrise. "They'll see our approach."

He pulled a dagger from his belt and started chipping at the mortar around the bricks forming the opening, the others soon joining in. "Softly," he cautioned Draker as the big man jabbed his short sword hard into the mortar.

Sunrise had come on by the time they loosened enough brick to allow egress, long shadows stretching from the ruins as they hauled themselves free. Frentis led them from shadow to shadow towards the gate, finding it manned by a dozen Varitai.

"We should've taken Illian with us," Draker grumbled in a whisper. "She'd pick off a few in short order."

Frentis beckoned to Thirty-Four. "We need a distraction."

The former slave nodded, sheathing his short sword and rising to run towards the gate, gesticulating wildly. "The general!" he called in Volarian as the Varitai stirred, moving to confront him with swords drawn. "He calls for you!" Thirty-Four went on, pointing towards the southern quarter. "Slaves are in revolt! You must come!"

As expected, they just stood regarding him in silence. Varitai were conditioned to respond only to orders given by their officers and there was no chance they would follow his commands. However, they were still compelled to look in his direction as he scurried away, halting and beckoning madly. "Come! Come! Or I'll be flayed!"

A tired-looking Free Sword sergeant emerged from the gatehouse, rubbing bleary eyes and buckling on his sword as he took in the sight of the desperate slave. "What the fuck do you want?"

Frentis nodded to the others and slipped from their shadow, crawling closer under concealment of a low pile of blackened bricks, no more than fifteen feet from the gate.

"A revolt, Honoured Citizen!" Thirty-Four said to the sergeant, an impressively convincing whine colouring his voice. "Please! Oh please!"

"Shut up," the sergeant said wearily, moving towards Thirty-Four, clearly puzzled by his clothing, mean even for a slave, and the sight of his sword. "Who gave you that? Give it here!"

"Certainly, honoured sir," Thirty-Four said as the sergeant reached for his sword, drawing it in a single fluid motion and flicking the blade across the man's eyes. Thirty-Four stepped nimbly past him as he collapsed to his knees, screaming and clutching at his face, killing a Varitai with a thrust to the neck then turning and running. Six Varitai took off in pursuit, one falling dead with Frentis's throwing knife in his throat, two more quickly hacked down by Davoka and Draker.

Frentis hefted a spear dropped by the Varitai he had killed, hurling it at his onrushing comrade with enough force to pierce his breastplate. Thirty-Four skidded to a halt, pivoted and delivered a precise cut to the leg of the Varitai chasing him, Draker's blow nearly decapitating the slave soldier as he fell.

"Stay close!" Frentis ordered, scooping up a fallen blade and charging for the gate, a sword in each hand. The five remaining Varitai formed a tidy defensive knot, impassive faces behind levelled spears. Frentis threw his left-hand sword at the one in the centre, the blade sinking into his face just beneath his helmet. Frentis leapt through the gap, slashing left and right, the others moving in to finish those he wounded. A pain-filled yell drew his gaze and he found Draker on his back, parrying thrusts from a Varitai's spear, a newly earned gash on his forehead. Davoka moved to help him but the outlaw proved his hard-won skills by rolling under the Varitai's guard to stab at his groin, spoiling the accomplishment somewhat by proceeding to bring the slave soldier down with a series of frenzied blows, obscenities flowing from his snarling lips in a torrent.

"Raise the gate," Frentis told Davoka, making for the steps leading to the parapet. He found two Free Swords there, youthful faces aghast at the carnage they had witnessed below, pointing their swords at him with trembling hands.

"Fight or run," Frentis told them in Volarian. "You'll die today in either case."

They ran, sprinting away across the parapet without a backward glance. "Tell your comrades the Red Brother's here!" Frentis yelled after them before turning to pull a torch from a stanchion. He hopped onto the battlement and waved the torch back and forth, peering into the misted fields beyond the walls. A few heartbeats later he saw it, a single torch flaring to life, burning brighter as the bearer came closer, and two thousand Renfaelin knights resolved out of the mist at full gallop. Banders was clearly visible at the head of the tight column, his faux-rusted armour catching the rising sun, Arendil and Ermund on either side of him. They thundered through the gate without pause, the clatter of steel-shod hooves on cobbles rising to a deafening pitch as they charged along Gate Lane. A few Varitai came running from the western quarter to oppose them, a single company managing to form ranks across the lane before being smashed aside by the tide of horse and steel.

"Brother!" Frentis looked down from the gatehouse, finding a grinning Ivern there, mounted, with Frentis's horse at his side. "The Blackhold awaits!"

◆ ◆ ◆

The squat fortress was already in uproar when they got there, two Varitai lying dead at the main gate and several more inside. They were obliged to fight their way into the courtyard as more guards came rushing from a maze of shadowed doorways, mostly Varitai with a few Free Swords showing none of the cowardice of their comrades on the wall. Sollis took his brothers up the stairs and into the upper levels, clearing the archers from the parapet and sending their own arrows down on the defenders below.

Frentis led his company from doorway to doorway, Draker breaking them open as they searched for the Aspects, finding only more Volarians, most willing to fight, others cowering, but all destined to die. He was emerging from a storeroom when a Kuritai appeared out of the shadows, twin short swords flashing. Frentis parried his first blow but slipped on a patch of blood, tumbling to the flagstones, the Kuritai looming above . . . then falling dead when a crossbow bolt punched through his breastplate.

"Not like you to be so clumsy, brother," Illian observed from across the courtyard, words garbled somewhat by the bolt held between her teeth as she braced the crossbow against her midriff to draw the string back.

He was about to tell her to join Brother Sollis on the parapet but found his attention drawn to a commotion rising from a half-open door at the rear of the courtyard. He went to it, finding a set of steps leading into the bowels of the Blackhold. He called to Davoka to follow and took the stairs at a run. At the base of the steps he found a dead Free Sword with what appeared to be steel darts embedded in both eyes; beside him lay the body of a man in a bedraggled City Guard uniform, bloodied sword in hand and belly rent open.

In the chamber beyond the stairwell lay three Varitai, steel darts jutting from their necks; beyond them a young woman was grappling with a burly Free Sword, blood streaming from her nose and eyes as he forced her to her knees, short sword inching towards her throat. Frentis drew his sword back for a throw but Illian was faster, sending a bolt into the Volarian's temple before he could bring his blade to bear.

The woman slumped beneath the collapsing Free Sword, blood bubbling on her lips as she issued a groan of near-complete exhaustion. Frentis hauled the corpse away and helped her upright, finding her eyes still bright despite the paleness of her skin. "My brother . . ." she whispered.

"Brother?"

"Rhelkin . . . City Guard."

Frentis shook his head and the woman moaned in sorrow, blinking red tears before speaking again. "Aspects . . . are they safe?"

He cast his gaze around the chamber, taking in the sight of the cells. From one of them he could hear an implacable thumping noise, a voice within shouting something unintelligible but with an odd note of authority. "Search the bodies," he told Illian. "Find the keys."

Aspect Dendrish stood still and straight-backed as the door swung open, face rigid and composed though his rapidly blinking eyes told of a man expectant of a swift death. "Aspect," Frentis greeted him with a bow. "Brother Frentis. I doubt you remember, but we met at my Test of Knowledge . . ."

The Aspect seemed to deflate, issuing an explosive sigh of relief and doubling over, as much as his bulk would allow. "Where is Aspect Elera?" he demanded after a moment, raising a haggard face that somehow managed to retain a vestige of the imperious self-regard Frentis recalled.

"Brother Frentis," she said as the door opened, sitting on her bed, smiling in welcome, her hands clasped in her lap. "How you've grown. Is Alucius with you?"

There was a pounding of running feet and Ivern appeared at the door to the cell, his grin even wider than usual. "Brother Sollis sends his regards, Aspects," he said, nodding briefly at them in turn before addressing Frentis. "He says to gather your people and forget about holding this place. We need to get to the docks."

CHAPTER TWELVE

Vaelin

"Have I ever told you," Nortah began, his pallor somewhat grey in the dim light of the hold, "how much I detest sea travel?"

Behind him one of his fighters gave a grunt of agreement before heaving into his helmet. "Do it in the bilges," Nortah rebuked him. "You'll have to wear that before long."

Vaelin gave his brother a soft pat on the arm and moved deeper into the hold, passing ranks of free fighters dressed in Volarian armour, taking the steps to the lower deck where the Seordah sat in equal misery. He found Hera Drakil sitting next to a half-open porthole, eyes closed and mouth open to suck in the sweet outside air.

"We're five miles from the harbour," Vaelin told him, drawing a puzzled frown. "We'll be there soon," he clarified. "Make your people ready."

"They have been ready to get off this horrible thing since they stepped on it," the war chief returned with a baleful glint in his eye. Without Dahrena's guidance, persuading them to this stratagem had not been an easy thing. He had explained it all in detail to Hera Drakil, the queen adding her voice with promises of great rewards and everlasting gratitude should they consent to take ship to Varinshold. The Seordah listened to it all in silence then walked back to his people's encampment. Vaelin and Lyrna lingered on the periphery watching the argument unfold. The Seordah were not a demonstrative people, rarely given to raised voices or gesticulation, so there had been a certain ominous quality to the increasing stillness and quietude evident in the various war chiefs as they sat in a circle and debated the merits of Vaelin's plan. Eventually, after several hours and with night coming on, Hera Drakil returned, his face rigid with reluctance as he said, "We go on the big water."

"Salt staining every breath," the Seordah said now. "No earth beneath your feet. How can such a thing be borne for any time?"

"Greed or necessity," Vaelin replied. "You recall your part in this?"

"Kill all the two-swords we find and make for the big black building." The Seordah stirred as Vaelin rose, leaning forward, fixing him with the same questing gaze he had shown him since Alltor. *What is he looking for? Vaelin wondered again as the war chief's eyes met his. Does he ponder if there is another soul behind these eyes? Or is it more what I may have brought back?*

"You . . ." The Seordah paused, searching for the right words. "You are more . . . you now, *Beral Shak Ur.*"

Vaelin replied with a cautious nod. In truth he felt stronger, the chill having lifted from his bones, for the most part. Also his final practice with Davern had actually seen him defeat the shipwright, much to his sister's delight. She had taken to watching the daily contests and gave a squeal of triumph as Vaelin's wooden sword found a gap in Davern's defences, jabbing into his midriff with enough force to provoke an obscenity-laden shout of pain. His dark-faced fury at Alornis's taunts had been something of a guilty pleasure, though Vaelin was careful to hide it as he thanked the sergeant for his service and released him from future obligations.

"I am," Davern grated, "*always* at your disposal, my lord."

He made his way to the top deck and joined Reva at the helm, dressed in her light mail shirt, sword on her back, and bow in hand, laughing at something the Shield had said. The man's humour faded at sight of Vaelin and he beckoned his helmsman forward to take the wheel, offering a cursory bow. "My Lord of Battle."

"Fleet Lord Ell-Nestra," Vaelin replied, bowing lower. The Shield's resentment was more carefully hidden than Davern's, though, he suspected, no less deeply felt.

"Our pet savages are prepared, I take it?" Ell-Nestra asked.

"Don't call them that," Vaelin told him, annoyed at the ease with which the Shield provoked him. *Defeat and humiliation are poor tutors, it seems.*

"Your pardon, my lord. Though you must agree they make poor sailors."

"Who can blame them?" Reva said, her face only slightly less grey than Nortah's. "I'd fight half the world to get off this tub."

"Tub?" The Shield rounded on her in mock fury. "My lady insults the finest vessel ever taken by a Meldenean sabre. Why, I would challenge you, if you were not merely but a feeble woman."

He took the lightning slap she gave him with good grace, making her laugh again with a florid bow before striding off to order his first mate to muster a fighting party. *I thought at least she'd be immune to his charms,* Vaelin thought sourly.

"Your people are ready?" he asked her.

She jerked her head at the rigging above, Vaelin seeing the densely packed archers on the platforms at the top of the great ship's two towering masts. A figure leaned over the side of the foremost platform to wave at them, Vaelin recognising Bren Antesh's silhouette. He sensed a certain impatience in the archer's movements. "I think your Lord of Archers is keen for you to join him aloft," he advised.

"In which case he'll be disappointed," she replied with a level gaze.

He let the matter drop; cautioning her seemed irrelevant given their mission. *A wasteful gamble,* Count Marven had called it, not without justification. Vaelin looked at the two ships following in their wake, the only Volarian vessels captured by the Meldeneans during their brief campaign, each crammed with more Seordah. Beyond the horizon waited all the ships they could commandeer on short notice, thirty vessels laden with more forest folk and three regiments of Realm Guard, including the Wolfrunners. The cream of this new army, gambled on an expectation of Volarian arrogance.

The Shield had sailed into Warnsclave a day after Belorath's arrival, his great flagship laden with stolen supplies, relating his dismay at failing to seize a ship of equal size and design to his own newly acquired monster. "It was like fighting a mirror image," he told Lyrna, his usual ebullience muted somewhat, and unlike most, less inclined to stare at her face. "Except one captained by a fool," he went on. "Sadly, the fires we birthed in her were too great and she went down, along with a few hundred Free Swords, judging by the screams."

The idea had been birthed then, triggering instincts Vaelin had thought lost with his song. *They expect the* Stormspite's *twin at Varinshold.* He had pondered it for a day and a night before seeking the queen's approval. "We don't have ships enough for the whole army," she reminded him.

"But enough to seize the docks, and Varinshold will stand or fall on who holds them. Plus, Brother Caenis will relate the need to attack on Winterfall Eve to the Renfaelin host via Brother Lernial."

"The odds." She shook her head. "Even if these Renfaelins, whoever they are, do ride to our aid, the odds still do not favour us. Marven is right, the risk is too great."

"Not for the Seordah," he said. "Not if they make the first attack, aided by Lady Reva's archers. The docks will be taken within an hour."

"Their prowess impresses you that much?"

He recalled the Kuritai that day as the rain beat down, swift and deadly but seeming like slow children as the forest folk broke their line. "You didn't see them at Alltor, Highness." He straightened, addressing her formally. "My queen, as Battle Lord I tell you this is the only way Varinshold will be in our hands before the year's end."

"By the Father," Reva's whisper brought him back to the present. She stood at the rail as they rounded the southern headland and Varinshold came into view. For a moment Vaelin felt certain they had sailed to liberate nothing more than a ruin, the entire southern quarter seemingly just a mass of piled brick and blackened wood. As they drew closer however, he began to pick out familiar buildings still standing amidst the rubble: the merchants' houses overlooking the harbour, the northern wing of the palace just visible through the fading morning mist, and in the centre, the dark stump of the Blackhold, where he hoped the Aspects still drew breath.

Reva turned back from the view, her face grim, waving at the archers above, who promptly crouched, disappearing from view. The Shield donned a shirt of broad-ringed mail and buckled on his sabre. "Best if you stay by me, my lady," he told Reva with a wink. "I'll protect you."

This time she failed to laugh, the sight of the city seemingly robbing her of humour. "It's they who need protection," she muttered, jerking her head at the Volarians now visible on the quay. Her face had taken on a tense aspect, her brow furrowed and gaze focused. On any other woman her age it might be taken for sullenness but Vaelin knew it was the face she wore throughout the siege, the face so many Volarians had seen in their final seconds of life.

He reached out to place a hand on her shoulder and she clasped it before he moved away, going to the prow. Nortah's chosen men were coming up on deck, dressed in their Volarian gear, his brother making a convincing Free Sword Battalion Commander as he arrayed them in good order. He would be first down the gangplank to exchange salutes with whatever senior Volarian came to greet their arrival, before striking them dead and leading the charge against their escort, the Cumbraelin archers raining death on all others.

The sails were trimmed as they approached the harbour mouth, all in silence to prevent those ashore wondering why Meldenean voices could be heard on a Volarian ship. Vaelin could see their reception more clearly now, neatly arrayed rows of Free Swords standing to the rear of a single officer, hopefully the senior Volarian commander in the city. A cheering sight since the man would probably be the one to greet Nortah, or if not, would be almost certain to die in the arrow storm. Off to the left stood a tall figure on a warhorse, long dark hair tied back from his handsome face. Lyrna had given orders for Darnel to be taken alive if possible, keen to extract whatever intelligence he held regarding Volarian plans, but Vaelin gave little for the man's chances once the Realm Guard came ashore. He would have to get the Shield to spirit him away . . .

He straightened as Darnel's horse abruptly began to rear, tipping its master from the saddle and lashing about with its hooves. For a second all was confusion as the horse went wild, trampling men and charging away, then he saw a slender young man rushing towards Darnel, a faint gleam of steel in his hand. *Alucius!*

He saw it all, standing helpless as the ship inched closer to the shore, saw Darnel's sword cut through Alucius's chest, saw a tall familiar figure impale Darnel with the spike he wore in place of a hand, saw the Volarian commander marshal his men in response.

"Antesh!" Vaelin called, cupping his hands and casting his voice at the platforms. The Lord Archer's head appeared above the platform edge and Vaelin pointed to the wharf. "Kill them all!"

Reva appeared at his side. "What is it?"

"Forget the plan," he told her, reaching over his shoulder to draw his sword, the quay no more than ten feet away now. "Tell Nortah to get his people ashore and start killing."

He hoisted himself onto the rail, watching the arrows streak down from above, Volarians falling by the dozen, Al Hestian visible through the milling confusion, crouched protectively over his son's body. Vaelin took a final judging glance at the quay and leapt from the rail, landing hard and rolling to absorb the shock. He sprinted towards Al Hestian, finding his way blocked by a knot of Free Swords, using their comrades' bodies as shields as they backed away under the orders of a veteran sergeant. Vaelin hacked his way into their midst, laying about with his sword in a two-handed grip, two falling in quick succession, the veteran sergeant skewered through chest and neck by multiple arrows, the others attempting to flee but soon tumbling to the stones under the deadly rain.

Vaelin ran on, cutting down any Volarian who contrived to block his path. The sword flashed with all the effortless, terrible grace he had thought lost, parrying and killing as he moved without conscious decision. *Perhaps it was never the song,* he thought grimly, sidestepping a thrust from a Free Sword and moving behind him to lay open the back of his neck. *You don't need a song to be a killer.*

He saw Al Hestian ahead, still crouched over Alucius, a group of Volarians rushing towards him. Something thrummed past Vaelin's ear and the lead Volarian fell dead with an arrow protruding from his breastplate. Vaelin glanced behind to see Reva notching and loosing arrows from her finely carved bow with a speed and precision he knew he would never match. He sped on towards Al Hestian, seeing two more Free Swords fall to Reva's arrows. Another came close enough to hack down at the former Battle Lord. Vaelin leapt, extending his blade to block the blow, hammering a fist into the man's face. The man staggered, drawing his short sword back for a riposte, then snapped his head back and collapsed as one of Reva's arrows found his eye.

"Alucius!" Vaelin shoved Al Hestian aside and crouched next to the poet, his eyes tracking over the terrible wound in his chest to his face, the features bleached white, eyes half-closed. Reva crouched at his side, touching a hand to Alucius's face, sighing in sorrow.

"Drunken sot," she muttered.

"Weaver!" Vaelin said, standing to cast his gaze out to sea. "He's on the third ship with the other Gifted . . ."

"Vaelin," she said, reaching out to grasp his arm. "He's gone."

He stood, dragging his gaze from Alucius's body as the Seordah swept past them on either side, tearing through the hastily assembled ranks of Free Swords, cutting their line apart. Some fought, hacking and stabbing with their short swords at the too-swift, silent phantoms that assailed them, their blades finding only air as they fell by the dozen. Others fled, sprinting away through the ruins or throwing themselves into the harbour, willing to risk drowning rather than face such an onslaught. Here and there Kuritai could be seen, managing to strike a blow or two before they were clubbed down. Beyond the slaughter Vaelin could see a dense formation of Volarians building in the more open ground near the warehouse district, neat ranks of Varitai falling into place with their uncanny precision.

"They'll fall back to the palace."

Vaelin turned to find Lakrhil Al Hestian regarding him with a vacant frown, his voice dull, listless. "There are fire-traps surrounding it. They could hold out for days."

He looked down at Alucius once more, bent to retrieve the dagger still clutched in the poet's hand, and raised it towards his own throat. Vaelin's punch jabbed into the nerve cluster below Al Hestian's nose, leaving him unconscious on the stones.

"Muster your archers on the quay," he told Reva, nodding towards the dense ranks of Varitai, now attempting a fighting withdrawal into the city, the Seordah continually harrying them with volleys of arrows from their flat bows. Despite their retreat he knew this was far from over; he could see more Volarian formations moving through the ruins, battalions forming in the northern quarter with more to the west. He saw Nortah a short distance away, mustering his fighters amidst the remnants of a Free Sword company, sword bloody from end to end.

"Move towards the north gate!" he called to him. "Stop them joining up. I'll send the Realm Guard to join you when they dock."

Nortah nodded, then drew up short at the sight of something towards the east, laughing and pointing his reddened blade. "Perhaps that won't be necessary, brother."

Vaelin heard them before they came into view, a great, cacophonous clatter of steel on stone. Clearly the Volarian commander heard it too as he attempted to switch companies to his left flank, all too late. The knights tore into the Volarian ranks, longswords and maces rising and falling as they hacked their way through the Varitai, cutting the formation in two. The Seordah charged in to complete the destruction, a fine red mist of mingled blood, breath, and steaming horse sweat rising to cover the raging carnage. The Varitai, unlike the Free Swords, didn't know how to flee and fought to the last.

Vaelin ordered Nortah to join up with Reva's archers and sweep towards the palace. "There's still half a division to kill," he told them. "Take no chances, keep them divided and let the archers do their work."

He waited for the Realm Guard to come ashore, the Wolfrunners the first Regiment to arrive, now commanded by a former corporal Vaelin vaguely remembered from the Alpiran war. "Set guards on this man," Vaelin ordered, pointing to Al Hestian's unconscious form. He took a final glance at Alucius, knowing he would have to be the one to tell Alornis and feeling like a coward for hating the duty. "And secure this man's body," he said. "The queen will wish to say words when we give him to the fire."

He walked through the scene of the Varitai's defeat, a dense carpet of bodies breasting the wharf from end to end. A broad-chested knight on a tall charger trotted up to him, trampling bodies and breaking bones under hoof. He pushed back the red-painted visor covering his face, greeting Vaelin with a forced laugh. "Quite the spectacle, eh, my lord?"

"Baron." Vaelin bowed. "I had hoped it would be you."

A young, bare-headed knight guided his horse to Banders's side, his bright gaze alighting on Vaelin for a moment before scanning the quayside with intense scrutiny. "Where is he?" he demanded, hefting a gore-covered long-sword.

"Arendil, my grandson," Banders explained to Vaelin. "He's keen to meet Lord Darnel."

"Back there, young sir." Vaelin pointed over his shoulder. "Quite dead, I'm afraid."

The young knight slumped in his saddle, sword arm sagging. His face betrayed as much relief as disappointment. "Well, at least it's over." He brightened at the sight of a group of people approaching along Gate Lane at the run, raising his hand in a welcoming wave. Vaelin initially took them for some of Nortah's fighters but soon realised they were an even more unusual mix, varying greatly in age and garb, including a girl of no more than sixteen, a Lonak woman of impressive stature . . . and a muscular young man with an Order blade.

Frentis stared at him as he approached, a faint smile on his lips. Vaelin halted a few feet away, taking in the sight of a man who was both brother and stranger. His frame was even more impressive now, powerful and, Vaelin noted, free of scars judging by the skin visible through his torn shirt. His face also had lost the youthful smoothness he remembered, hard lines forming around the mouth and eyes. For once, Vaelin was grateful for the song's absence as he found himself uncertain he wanted to know what those eyes had seen.

"I heard you died," he said.

Frentis's smile widened. "Whilst I knew you couldn't have."

Seeing his evident and genuine warmth, Vaelin felt his sorrow deepen yet further. "I require your sword, brother," he said, holding out his hand.

Frentis's smile slowly faded and he glanced at the people flanking him before nodding, coming forward to proffer his blade hilt first. Vaelin took it and beckoned the Wolfrunners' new commander forward. "This man," he said, "is bound by the Queen's Word to answer for the murder of King Malcius. He is to be shackled and confined pending her judgement."

PART II

It is a singular mistake to think of the slave as fully human. Freedom is a privilege afforded by the excellence of our lineage as true Volarian citizens. By contrast the slave's station, earned through birth to enslaved parents, just defeat in war or a demonstrated lack of industry and intelligence, is not merely the artificial construct of society, it is the accurate reflection of a natural order. It therefore follows that attempts to upset this order, through misguided policy or even outright rebellion, are always doomed to failure.

—COUNCIL-MAN LORVEK IRLAV,
VOLARIA: THE APEX OF CIVILISATION,
GREAT LIBRARY OF THE UNIFIED REALM
(LIBRARIAN'S NOTE: TEXT INCOMPLETE DUE TO PARTIAL BURNING)

Verniers' Account

In contrast to my first voyage aboard this ship I found myself provided with a cabin, once occupied by the first mate who had perished at the Battle of the Teeth. Our captain stated loudly to his threadbare crew that he had yet to find a worthy replacement and I might as well have it since none of these dogs deserved the honour. The welcoming prospect of ship-borne comfort, however, was diminished by his insistence that I share the space with my former owner.

"She's your prisoner, scribe," he stated. "You guard her."

"To what end?" I enquired, gesturing at the surrounding ocean. "To where is she likely to escape, pray tell?"

"Might damage the ship," he replied with a shrug. "Might throw herself to a passing shark. Either way, she's your responsibility and I've no hands spare to watch her."

"It's a small bed," she observed as the cabin door slammed shut behind us. "Still, I don't mind sharing."

I pointed to a corner of the cabin. "Your place is there, mistress. If you're quiet, I might spare you a blanket."

"Or what?" she asked, pointedly sitting on the narrow bunk. "Will you flog me? Bend me to your will with cruel torment?"

She smiled and I turned away, going to a small map table set into the woodwork below the porthole. "There are a dozen men on this ship who will happily mete out all the correction you require," I said, reaching into my bag and extracting the first scroll to hand.

"I've no doubt," she agreed. "Will you watch? My dear husband liked to watch when the slave girls were whipped. He'd often pleasure himself at the sight. Will you do the same, my lord?"

I sighed, biting down a response and unfurling the scroll. An Illustrated Catalogue of Volarian Ceramics, Brother Harlick's precise but overly florid letters provoking me to an amused grunt. Even the man's script is pompous.

Although I couldn't pretend any liking for the brother, I had to concede Harlick's draughtsmanship was excellent, the illustrations possessed of a flawless exactitude, the first depicting a hunting scene from a vase dating back some fifteen hundred years, naked spearmen pursuing a stag through pine forest.

"Ceramics," Fornella said, peering over my shoulder. "You think the Ally's origins lurk in pots, my lord?"

I didn't look up from the scroll. "When studying an age often bereft of writing, decorative illustration can be highly informative. If you can enlighten me as to another course, I would be grateful."

"How grateful?" she asked, leaning close, breath soft on my ear.

I merely shook my head and returned to the scroll as she laughed and moved away. "You really have no interest in women at all, do you?"

"My interest in women varies according to the woman in question." I unfurled the scroll further, finding more hunting scenes, some images of ritual worship, various gods, and creatures of bizarre design.

"I can help," she said. "I . . . would like to."

I turned, finding her expression cautious but earnest. "Why?"

"We have a long voyage ahead. And whatever you may suspect of my motives, I am keen to see this mission succeed."

I looked again at the image on the scroll, naked revellers frolicking before a great ape-like creature, mouth agape and vomiting fire. Kethian jug fragment, *read the inscription below the image.* Pre-Imperial.

"When exactly," I asked her, "did the Volarians give up their gods?"

◆ ◆ ◆

"It was all long before my birth," she said, "long before my mother's birth in fact. But she was ever a studious woman and keen for me to learn the history of our most glorious empire."

We had repaired to the deck, sitting near the prow as she spoke and I scribbled my notes. The captain had growled something at our appearance but made no protest and the crew seemed happy to ignore us, bar a few hostile glances at Fornella.

"The empire may speak with one tongue now," she went on, "and follow the Council's edicts be they denizens of the greatest city or the foulest swamp. But it was not always so."

"I know your empire was forged in war," I said. "Many wars in fact, lasting some three centuries."

"Quite so, but whilst the Forging Age left us with an empire, true unity eluded us for centuries to come. There were too many different coins with too

many different values. Too many languages spoken by too many tongues. And far too many gods. My mother used to say that men would fight and kill for money, but they would only die for their gods. For the empire to endure we required that kind of loyalty, untainted by any divine distraction. And so there were more wars, called the Wars of Persecution by some, but Imperial historians refer to the entire period as the Great Cleansing, a sixty-year trial of blood and torture. Whole provinces were laid waste and entire peoples took flight, some to the northern hills, others across the sea to found new nations free of Volarian persecution. But, for all we lost, it was this that truly birthed the empire, for this is when we became a nation of slavers.

"There had always been slaves, of course, mostly in the Volarian heartland, but now there were more, conquered for refusing to give up their gods, beaten, cowed and bred so successive generations forgot them altogether. To marshal such a resource requires two things: great organisation and vast cruelty. I often think it was these particular traits the Ally found so alluring. After all, we must have been chosen for a reason."

"Do you know when he made himself known?"

"I know not whether the Ally is male, or even truly human. My mother told of a time, near four centuries' years ago, when the empire was strong in its unity. War with the Alpirans was nothing new but it took on a new intensity, the battles grew in size, the campaigns lasted years instead of months, though victory still eluded us. Eventually the Alpirans became tired of our endless attacks and launched one of their own, overrunning the southern provinces in a matter of months. Crisis has a tendency to reveal noteworthy talent and thus it was that a young general from the southern city of Mirtesk rose to prominence, a general with a revolutionary notion, and the means to make it happen. If our slaves could build our cities and work our fields, why not also fight our wars? And so, via his new-found knowledge, we created the Varitai and Kuritai. Through tactical genius and prodigious use of his slave soldiers, our new general won eternal fame by driving the Alpirans back. He was lauded the length and breadth of the empire, statues were raised in his honour, epics composed by our finest scholars to document his wondrous life."

Fornella paused, her lips forming a wry smile, though her eyes betrayed a sadness I hadn't seen before. "But it was not a normal life. For our young general stayed young, whilst his fellow officers grew old and withered around him, he stayed young."

"He was the first," I said.

"Indeed. The first Volarian blessed by the Ally's voice, or, I assume, the first

he sent one of his creatures to seduce. But his gifts didn't end with the secret of binding slaves so completely they would fight and die at their masters' command. No, he had more to offer, the greatest gift of all. It was from him the Council learned the secret of endless life, at the Ally's behest of course. And, over time, they all made themselves its creatures. The general became the Ally's voice on the Council, speaking softly at first, guiding rather than commanding, hinting at the great task it had chosen for the empire. Although, as the years passed, the general's behaviour became ever more erratic.

"My mother said she met him once, at a feast held in his honour. My family is, as you may understand, vastly wealthy and has held a Council Seat since the empire's earliest days. I asked my mother what he was like and she laughed, 'Quite dreadfully mad,' she said, 'though I hear his daughter is worse.'"

"His daughter?" I asked.

Fornella pulled her woollen shawl tighter about her shoulders, the sadness fading into fearful remembrance. "Yes, a daughter. I met her too, once. One meeting was more than sufficient."

"Are they like you? The general and his daughter, do they still live?"

"The general's madness grew with the centuries, his hunger for victory over the Alpirans becoming a madman's obsession, birthing a calamitous defeat. The Council, by now all recipients of the Blessing and advised by the Ally's other lieutenants that the general's glorious career should reach a conclusion, employed their chief assassin to provide one. If what the queen says is true, however, she may well have met her end alongside King Malcius."

"The general's daughter? She killed her own father?"

"She's taken countless lives the breadth of this world, my lord. If we're fortunate, she'll plague us no more. But I increasingly find fortune to be a rare commodity."

"Does your mother still live? Did she also take the Ally's Blessing?"

She shook her head, raising her gaze to meet mine, smiling fondly. "No. She grew old and she died, though I begged her to join me in this new age of limitless life. She alone knew the true nature of the bargain we had struck, though none would listen to her. She knew what drew the Ally, if not what had birthed it."

"And what is it? What draws it?"

"Power. That's how the first were chosen, not those with the greatest wealth, but those with the most influence, the greatest sway in Council. Because it happened over decades rather than years, only one being chosen to receive his bounteous gift in every dozen years, it seemed the choosing was random, the

whim of a being as close to a god as any could be. But my mother lived long enough to see the pattern. Every bargain struck increased its hold on us, every gift bestowed made us more its servants.

"She said just one word the last time I was permitted near her, before she ordered me barred from her house. She was nearly ninety years in age, just a tiny collection of bone and skin in a very large bed. But her mind had never faded and her eyes were so very bright, and though she could only speak in whispers, I heard it, clear and true, though at the time I thought it just the final croak of a bitter old woman."

She fell silent, gazing off towards the southern horizon where a heavy cloud bank could be seen, signalling an uncomfortable night, not that I expected to sleep much lying by her side. There was more grey in her hair now, I saw, watching it swirl in the wind.

"Just one word," she said in a faint voice. "'Slave.'"

◆ ◆ ◆

As I had predicted, sleep proved elusive. The sea grew turbulent come nightfall, the wind rising to lash the clouded glass of the porthole with rain and howl through the myriad channels in the fabric of this ship. Fornella lay on her back, breathing slow and regular. I lay on my side, turned towards the hull. I had removed my shoes but was otherwise fully clad whilst she was naked, sloughing off her clothes without the slightest flicker of embarrassment, slipping into the bed beside me as I turned my back. We lay in silence for the better part of an hour, robbed of rest by the wind and the sheer oddness of our circumstance.

Finally, she said, "Do you hate me, my lord?"

"Hatred requires passion," I replied.

"Ah, The Cantos of Gold and Dust, verse twenty. Don't you think it a trifle conceited to constantly quote your own work?"

"The verse was drawn from an ancient ode sung by the tribes of the western mountains. As noted in my introduction."

She gave a soft laugh. "So I do not stir your passion? Hardly surprising, given your preferences. Still, a woman accustomed to male admiration can't help but feel somewhat slighted." I felt her shift behind me, moving to lie on her side. "Who was he? The man you said you loved?"

"I will not discuss that with you."

Something in my tone must have held sufficient warning because she gave a sigh of amused frustration before persisting. "I may have something to stir your passion, at least as far as it relates to your lust for knowledge. A small nugget of information concerning the Ally."

I gritted my teeth, hard, wondering if I didn't in fact hate her after all. I sat up, turning to find her regarding me with head tilted on her pillow, the gloom sufficient to hide all but the gleam of her eyes. "Then tell me," I said.

"The name," she insisted.

I rose, turning my back to swing my legs off the bed. "Seliesen Maxtor Aluran," I said.

I had expected laughter, cruel and mocking, but instead her tone was calmly reflective. "The Hope of the Alpiran Empire, slain by the very man who destroyed my darling husband's army. My people do not hold to notions of fate, the concept of invisible forces moving to shape our destiny is anathema to a people cleansed of superstition. But there are times when I wonder . . ."

I felt her shift again, her warm nakedness pressing against my back, resting her head against my shoulder. There was no desire in the way she held to me, at least none I could sense, just a need for closeness. "My sorrow for your loss, honoured sir," she said in formal Alpiran. "My brother is the longest serving member of the Volarian High Council, so he knows the Ally's schemes better than most, and even he is blind to their true nature, their ultimate purpose. However, its servants have often spoken of a man, endless in years like us, but not in thrall to the blood of the Gifted. A man who has lived many lifetimes and walked around the world more than once. The Ally is drawn to power, as I said, and what greater power is there, than the defeat of death itself?"

"It seeks him?"

"Indeed, but never has it found him."

"And he has a name, this endless man?"

"A thousand, changed with every lifetime as he passes from nation to nation. One of the Ally's creatures, the one they call the Messenger, caught his scent some fifteen years ago in the Unified Realm. He was calling himself Erlin."

CHAPTER ONE

Lyrna

It took some time to find her garden, the ruins having been cleared by Darnel's slaves to make way for his architectural ambitions, leaving only an outline of stunted brick and bare earth where flowers had once grown. Strangely, her bench was still intact, if somewhat blackened. She sat surveying the wasted remnants of the vanished refuge she had cherished. It was here she had led Vaelin that night, winning his enmity with her clumsy intrigues but learning a lesson in the process; some eyes will always see through a mask. Here also she had spent those delightful hours with Sister Sherin after securing her release from the Blackhold, the healer's innate kindness and sparkling intellect dispelling jealousy, for the most part. Lyrna remembered finding friendship an enjoyable if brief novelty and, when Sherin sailed away to Linesh, she had stopped coming here. The secluded courtyard no longer felt like a welcoming haven, just an empty corner of a palace where a lonely woman nursed flowers and schemes whilst she waited for her father to die.

"Ler-nah!"

She raised her gaze in time to catch a glimpse of a tall figure striding towards her before Davoka's embrace forced the air from her lungs and pulled her from the bench, her feet coming free of the ground as she was crushed into the Lonak woman's chest. Lyrna heard the pounding of boots accompanied by swords scraping free of scabbards. "Unhand our Queen, savage!" Iltis snarled.

Davoka ignored him, releasing Lyrna after a final crushing squeeze, clasping her head in both hands. She was smiling, something Lyrna found she couldn't remember her doing before. "I thought I had lost you, sister," she said in Lonak, fingers tracing over her face, from her brow to the rapidly growing red-gold locks beyond. "He said you burned."

"I did." Lyrna clasped her hands and kissed them, nodding reassurance at Iltis and Benten, who sheathed their swords, retreating with bows and bemused expressions. "I still do, sister."

Davoka stepped back, a certain tense reluctance showing in her gaze before she spoke again, slipping into Realm Tongue with practised ease. "Brother Frentis . . ."

Lyrna turned away from her, Davoka falling silent at the sudden sharpness in her expression. Mention of the famed Red Brother had been frequent since her arrival the previous evening, amongst the first words spoken by her Battle Lord on disembarking at the docks, as well as a heartfelt entreaty from Aspect Elera and a clipped request for mercy from Brother Sollis. She had given the same answer to each of them, the same answer she gave Davoka now. "Judgement will be rendered in due course."

"We fought together in the forest before it burned," Davoka went on. "We are *gorin*. He is my brother as you are my sister."

The Volarian woman's red tears, the searing pain as her hair caught alight . . . Lyrna closed her eyes against the memories, feeling the breeze on her skin, her healed, unmarred skin. *Healed?* she asked herself. *Is that what I am?*

The night before she had watched Alucius on the fire. She had spoken briefly beforehand, formally naming him Sword of the Realm, his sigil to be a pen and a wine cup, for she knew it would have made him laugh. Lady Alornis stepped forward to add her voice, face pale and expressionless but with tears streaming from her eyes as her brother laid comforting hands on her shoulders.

"Alucius Al Hestian . . ." she began, faltered then continued in a broken voice, ". . . will be called a . . . hero by many. A poet by others, and . . ." she paused to form a faint smile, "overfond of wine by some. I will always call him . . . simply, my friend."

Lakrhil Al Hestian had been permitted to attend, standing by, hollow-eyed and silent in his chains. He made no speech and stared at the rising flames with dry eyes. Lyrna allowed him to remain until the fire burned down to embers then ordered him returned to the dungeons, now crowded with other traitors awaiting the queen's justice.

Justice. She had watched the smoke blossom on the pyre, concealing Alucius's face and sparing her the sight of the flames consuming his flesh. *What justice would I have shown you, old friend? Spy, traitor to the Realm, and now hero of Varinshold's liberation. My father would have made show of forgiveness, lauded you with titles and gold, then, after a decent interval, had one of his hidden talents ensure a suitably accidental end. I would have been far crueler, Alucius. I would have made you follow me, stand witness as I administered full justice to our enemies, and for that, I know you would have hated me.*

The clouds above must have parted for she felt a blush of warmth on her head, her new-grown hair no doubt making a fine sight as it shimmered, the sensation pleasant and free of the tear-inducing agony she recalled from her days on the *Sea Sabre*. *Healed?* she wondered again. *You can remake a mask but the face beneath still lingers.*

She opened her eyes and her gaze lit on something, a small yellow flower emerging from between two shattered flagstones. Lyrna crouched, reaching out to touch a finger to the petals. "Winter-bloom," she said. "Always the clearest signal of changing seasons. Ice and snow come, sister, bringing hardship but also respite, for no fleet will sail the ocean whilst winter storms rage."

"You think they will come again?" Davoka asked. "When the ocean calms?"

"I'm certain of it. This war is far from over."

"Then you will need every sword, every ally."

Lyrna looked at the winter-bloom again, resisting the urge to pluck it and resolving to plant a new garden here in time, one without walls. She rose, meeting Davoka's gaze and speaking in formal Lonak. "Servant of the Mountain, I have need of your spear. Will you wield it in service to my purpose? Think well before you answer for our road is long and I offer no promise of a return to the Mountain."

Davoka's reply betrayed no hint of hesitation. "My spear is yours, sister. For now and always."

Lyrna nodded her thanks, beckoning to Iltis and Benten. "Then you had best meet your brothers. Try not to kill Lord Iltis, his manner can be somewhat provoking."

◆ ◆ ◆

Karlin Al Jervin stood as straight as his somewhat bent back would allow. Lyrna remembered him as a cheerful, pot-bellied fellow with a shiny bald head, less inclined to obsequiousness than many of his fellow nobles and not one to linger at court longer than his business required. Slavery and hard labour, however, seemed to have robbed him of humour and belly alike. His cheeks were hollowed and his eyes sunken, though he met Lyrna's gaze with admirable composure. His daughter, however, was less well attuned to royalty and fidgeted as she stood before the throne, an appreciable gap between her and her father. Lady Illian wore a hunter's garb, buckskin trews, and a light cotton blouse, stained brown and green to hide her in the forest, her hair cropped so it wouldn't encumber her eyes. A dagger sat in a sheath strapped to her ankle with another at her wrist. Despite her martial accoutrements she still seemed very young as she squirmed under the scrutiny of those present and avoided her father's glares. Behind her stood Brother Commander Sollis and Davoka, whilst Lord Al Jervin stood alone.

Lyrna had been quick to discard the garish monstrosity Darnel called a throne in favour of a comfortable straight-backed chair retrieved from one of the abandoned merchants' houses, and found herself grateful for the depth of the cushion beneath the royal posterior. She had been hearing petitions for some four hours now and could only marvel at the lingering pettiness of people fortunate enough to survive such a savage occupation. They came with complaints of theft against vanished neighbours, claims of inheritance for property now naught but ash, appeals for restitution of lordly status, and a plethora of other trivia that shortened her patience by the hour. However, not all claims were petty, or easily resolved.

"Brother Sollis," Lyrna said. "You must admit, Lord Al Jervin makes several valid points. This is all very unusual."

"Forgive me, Highness," the Brother Commander replied in his customary rasp, "but I doubt anything in this Realm could now be termed as 'usual.'"

"My knowledge of your Order's history is hardly copious, but I believe there has never been a sister of the Sixth Order. And are not recruits normally inducted at a much younger age? Circumstance may have forced us to forget some custom in the face of necessity, but this is a radical step indeed."

"There is provision in the Order's tenets to allow for older recruits, Highness. Master Rensial, for example, came to us as a former captain in the Realm Guard cavalry. As for Lady Illian's gender, war has provided ample evidence that our custom in this regard may require modification."

"Are our laws to be cast aside now, Highness?" Al Jervin spoke up, once again glaring at Illian. "The Sixth Order cannot just take a man's daughter."

"They aren't taking me!" Illian responded hotly, then flushed and lowered her gaze as Lyrna turned to her. "Your pardon, Highness."

"Lady Illian," Lyrna said, "is it truly your wish to join the Sixth Order?"

The girl drew breath and raised her head, speaking in a clear and certain tone. "It is, Highness."

"Despite your father's objections? His well-founded fears for your safety?"

Illian glanced at Al Jervin, her expression sorrowful and her voice low. "I love my father, Highness. I thought him dead for so long, finding him alive when the city fell was wondrous. But I am not the daughter he lost, nor can I be. I am fashioned by war into something else, a role I believe ordained for me by the Departed."

"*She* is a child!" Al Jervin stated, his face reddening. "By the laws of this Realm her status and condition are mine to decide until her majority." He quailed a little as Lyrna met his gaze, refusing to look away but adding "Highness," in a strained whisper.

"Lady Davoka has told me much of your daughter, my lord," Lyrna said. "By all accounts she has served with great distinction in the struggle to free this Realm. She stands before me now the author of many well-deserved ends suffered by our enemies. According to the Sixth Order's tenets she is vouched for by a subject of good character and Brother Sollis is willing to accept her, setting aside ancient custom and the usual tests in recognition of her evident skill and courage. As a Sister she will no doubt provide even greater service to the Realm and the Faith. Whilst you, my lord, apparently spent the entire war carving fatuous art for the traitor Darnel."

Al Jervin flinched but managed to control his tone as he responded, "I hear rumour Your Highness was also made a slave by our enemies. If so, I'm sure you know well the shame of performing a hated act in pursuit of survival."

Iltis bridled, stepping forward and speaking in ominous tones. "Caution your tongue, my lord."

Al Jervin gritted his teeth, pausing before speaking on, his voice coarse and fighting a choke. "Highness, I have no house, no wealth, no pride left. My daughter is all that remains to me. I ask you to cleave to our laws and prevent her taking this mad course."

This is not injured pride, Lyrna decided. *He simply wants to keep her alive. A good man, and a builder with skills much needed when peace comes.* She looked again at Illian, watching her reveal a set of perfect white teeth as she smiled at an encouraging nod from Davoka. *Beautiful, but so is a hawk, and for now I have more need of hawks than builders.*

"Lady Illian," she said, gesturing for one of the three scribes present to formally record a Royal Pronouncement, "Under the Queen's Word I hereby strip you of all rank and set aside your father's authority. As a free subject of this Realm you may choose any path open to you by law."

◆ ◆ ◆

She had been surprised to find the council chamber mostly intact, though there was a sizeable gap in the west-facing wall, the tapestry that covered it flapping in the breeze. In a break with custom Lyrna had requested the two surviving Aspects attend the Council, formally appointing Aspect Elera as Minister of Royal Works and Dendrish as Minister of Justice. Neither her father nor her brother had ever appointed an Aspect to an official position and there had been some notable apprehension among the other council members.

Never give them an inch more than you have to, her father had once said of the Faith. *I tied the Crown to them to win the Realm, but if I could, I'd sever them from me like a diseased limb.* Lyrna however, felt time had taught a different lesson. Aspect Tendris's diatribes against her brother's toleration of Denier beliefs had done much to weaken the Realm, but his power had been limited by the closeness of the other Orders to the Crown. *Your mistake wasn't in binding to them, Father. It was in not binding them tight enough.*

"As in Warnsclave, more people arrive by the day," Brother Hollun reported, seated on Lyrna's left. "The civil population of Varinshold now stands at over fifty thousand. We can expect the figure to double within the month."

"Can we feed so many?" Vaelin asked him.

"With careful rationing," Brother Hollun said. "And continued supply from our Alpiran friends and Fief Lord Darvus's provision of Nilsaelin produce. The winter months will be hard but none should starve."

"How stands the army, my lord?" Lyrna asked Vaelin.

"With our new recruits, Baron Banders's knights and common folk, we will have eighty thousand men and women under arms before the year's end."

"We need more." Lyrna turned to Lord Marshal Travick. "Tomorrow I will draft an edict of conscription, all Realm subjects of fighting age will be inducted into the Realm Guard. Train them hard, my lord." She switched her gaze to Lady Reva. "The edict will extend to all fiefs, my lady. I trust you have no objection."

The Lady Governess maintained a neutral expression but Lyrna saw she was carefully phrasing her response. "For myself Highness, no," she replied after a moment. "And for many of my people who suffered at Volarian hands. However, there are some corners of Cumbrael untouched by war where old resentments will linger."

"To be dispelled by the Blessed Lady's words, I should hope," Lyrna told her. "Perhaps you should return home for a time, Lady Reva. Let your people see you, hear the tale of your deeds, for they are so inspiring."

Reva's nod of assent was immediate and her tone free of any rancour. "As Your Highness commands." *Never the slightest glimmer of disloyalty from this one,* Lyrna mused. *So why does she cause me such unease?*

She set the question aside for further consideration and turned to the Shield. "Fleet Lord Ell-Nestra, please advise on the strength of your command."

As was his wont these days, the Shield's perpetual half grin disappeared as he addressed her, his eyes only briefly meeting hers. "Just over eight hundred ships of varying draughts, Highness. We've captured quite a few Volarian traders but the seas grow ever more empty as the winter storms descend."

"A decent-sized force to repel any invasion," Count Marven commented. "Crewed by the best sailors in the world. Plus, this time we are forewarned."

"How many soldiers could your eight hundred ships carry?" Lyrna asked Ell-Nestra.

The Shield frowned in puzzlement, his tone cautious as he responded. "If we make full use of the Volarian vessels, perhaps forty thousand, Highness. And certainly not in any comfort."

"Comfort is a long-forgotten luxury, my lord." She calculated for a moment, feeling the silence thicken. *They know what you're about. And they fear it.* "Your man is here?" she asked Vaelin who nodded and ordered the Realm Guard on the door to bring in the shipwright. Sergeant Davern marched to the centre of the chamber, giving a smart salute and a formal bow, seemingly completely untroubled by his august audience.

"My Battle Lord tells me you build ships, sergeant," Lyrna said.

"Indeed, Highness." He favoured her with a smile that would have shamed the Shield for its innate confidence. "I was inducted into the Shipwrights Guild at sixteen. The youngest ever, so I'm told."

"Very impressive. I require a ship capable of carrying five hundred soldiers across the ocean to Volaria. You will design and build it in such a manner so as to be easily duplicated and constructed by unskilled hands."

Davern blanched as the other captains at the table stirred in discomfort, apart, she noted, from Vaelin, who betrayed no surprise at all. "Such a task is . . . a mighty one, Highness," the sergeant began. "Requiring much labour, not to say timber . . ."

"Brother Hollun has compiled a list of surviving subjects with suitable skills and experience," she told him. "They will be placed at your disposal.

As for timber, rest assured it will be provided. I name you . . ." She pondered for a moment. "Davern Al Jurahl, Master of the Queen's Yard. Congratulations, my lord. I shall expect your designs on the morrow."

Davern stood in dumb silence for a moment longer then gave a hesitant bow and walked from the chamber.

"I believe that concludes today's business," Lyrna said, rising.

As expected it was Count Marven who spoke; the Nilsaelin commander was brave by all accounts, but also unabashed in counselling caution. "Highness, if I may?"

She paused, raising an eyebrow as he faltered then forced himself to continue. "So there is no misunderstanding, it is Your Highness's intention to invade the Volarian Empire?"

"It is my intention to win this war, my lord. By the most expeditious means."

"To sail across the ocean with so many. I must voice my doubts as to the practicality of such a thing."

"Why? The Volarians managed it."

"With years of preparation," the Shield pointed out. "And not borne from a Realm so damaged as this one."

"A Realm that has already performed wonders." She scanned their faces, finding doubt on most though once again Vaelin alone gave no sign of unease. "My lords, this council is not a debating chamber. I ask for counsel as I see fit and issue commands accordingly. And I command a fleet be built to carry our justice to the Volarian Empire, for when our business there is complete they will never again dream of returning to this land save in their nightmares."

She paused, awaiting further dissent, but finding only wary acceptance. "I thank you for your counsel and set you to your duties."

◆ ◆ ◆

Lakrhil Al Hestian failed to rise when she entered his cell, merely glancing up at her with dull eyes, slumped in a corner on bare stone, shackles on his wrists and ankles. Iltis gave an angry grunt at the discourtesy but Lyrna restrained him with a wave. "Guard the door, my lord, if you would."

Iltis bared his teeth at Al Hestian in a disgusted snarl before exiting the cell, leaving the heavy door ajar and standing with his back turned.

"They call this the Traitor's Nook," Lyrna told Al Hestian, moving to the only window, a narrow gap in the thick stone wall through which a patch of sky could be glimpsed. There were faint marks on the stone, some ancient inscription scratched by desperate hands long ago.

"Last occupied by Artis Al Sendahl on the eve of his execution," she went on, turning back to Al Hestian. "It speaks much for our enemies that, for all the destruction wrought on this city, they left our dungeons intact."

Al Hestian gave the faintest of shrugs, his shackles sounding a dull clink. "Artis Al Sendahl was given no trial," she continued. "Simply waking one morning to find a brace of guards at his door holding a King's Warrant. A week later he was dead."

"Whilst I am afforded only two days," Al Hestian said, his voice a toneless croak. "And also no trial."

"Then let this be your trial, my lord." She raised her hands, gesturing at the surrounding walls. "And I witness and judge both, eager for your testimony."

"My testimony is redundant. My reasons plain." He turned his gaze from her, resting his head against the wall. "I make no defence or appeal for clemency, save that the matter be settled with all dispatch."

She had known this man since childhood and never with any fondness, finding perhaps too clear a reflection in his naked ambition. But the sons with whom she had played as a child had never faltered in loving him, for all his flaws. "Alucius will be honoured for all time in this Realm," she said. "Your house is partially cleansed of dishonour by his sacrifice."

"A dead son has no need of honour. And I have two to face in the Beyond if you would do me the favour of sending me there."

Her gaze went back to the scratches on the wall, finding two words legible in the scrawl sufficient to divine the meaning of the rest. *Death is but gateway to the Beyond* . . . The Catechism of Faith, upon which so much had been built, and also destroyed. To her it had always been empty words, devoid of interest when there was so much genuine wisdom to be read.

"I have no mercy for you, my lord," she told him. "Only more punishment. Lord Iltis!"

The Lord Protector returned, standing at stiff readiness as she pointed to the shackles on Al Hestian's ankles. "Remove those and bring him."

Darnel's former knights and huntsmen stood blinking in the courtyard outside the cavernous vaults that served as the city's dungeons. They numbered perhaps three dozen men, stripped of all armour and possessions save for threadbare clothing, surrounded on all sides by Lord Adal's North Guard, chosen for the strength of their discipline; the Realm Guard were likely to commit massacre when faced with those who had betrayed them at the first fateful clash with the Volarians. Lyrna led Al Hestian to a walkway looking down on the assembled prisoners, finding most too cowed to meet her gaze, though some stared up in silent entreaty.

"You know these men, I believe?" Lyrna asked him.

Al Hestian looked down at the captives, his impassive mask unchanged. "Not well enough to grieve their passing, if it is Your Highness's intention to have me witness their murder."

She moved away from him and stepped closer to the edge of the walkway, raising her voice. "You all stand guilty of treason and worthy of immediate execution. Many of you will no doubt make a defence of loyalty, service to an oath binding for life. I tell you now this is no defence, an oath sworn to a traitorous madman is worthless, to be set aside by men of reason or true knightly honour. You have shown yourselves possessed of neither." She paused to glance at Al Hestian, finding him meeting her gaze with grim understanding.

"However," she spoke on, "the Faith teaches us the value of forgiveness for acts truly regretted. And this Realm stands in need of all hands fit to hold a sword. For these reasons alone I offer you the chance to swear another oath, an oath to your queen. Swear your service to me and I will spare your lives. But know that your sentence is not commuted, condemned you stand and condemned you remain until the day battle claims you. You will be the Dead Company. Any who do not wish to swear this oath, speak now."

She waited, watching them tremble and sag in relief. One man, a great broad-chested fellow of knightly bearing, wept openly whilst beside him a scrawny man, probably a hunter, stood shuddering, with urine flowing down both legs. She waited for a full minute but no voices were raised.

"My lord," she turned to Al Hestian, gesturing at the men below. "Your new command awaits, if you'll accept it."

Lakrhil Al Hestian stood expressionless for some time before replying with the smallest of bows.

"Very well," she said. "In addition to these wretches, our patrols find the country to be depressingly rich in outlaws, scum preying on those fleeing the Volarians. Rapists and murderers will be executed of course, but the remainder I'll send to you." She moved to his side, speaking softly. "You have your sons to thank for your life. And know well, I will not prove as kind as my father should you betray this Realm once more."

◆ ◆ ◆

She returned to the palace in the evening having spent the day amongst the newly arrived refugees, finding the usual mix of beggared nobles and dispossessed commoners each with their own epic of woe and survival. As in Warnsclave, however, there were precious few children and those mostly orphans. She had them gathered and conveyed to the palace rooms set aside for Brother Innis's charges where she spent the rest of the evening.

It was amazing to see how quickly the children's spirits returned as they raced around her, loud with laughter and play, though there were a few who sat apart from the others, eyes haunted by lingering horrors. She spent most time with the silent ones, speaking in soft tones and trying to draw them out, usually with only marginal success though one little boy climbed into her lap and fell into an immediate sleep the moment she opened her arms to him. She stayed and sat with him as night fell and the others went to their beds, waking somewhere past midnight at Murel's gentle nudge.

"Lady Davoka begs your attendance in the courtyard, Highness."

Lyrna gently laid the boy in one of the many empty beds. "Where is Orena?" she asked as they made their way through the corridors.

"She craves pardon, Highness. The sight of the children always upsets her so I took her duty."

Gentle hearts are often well hidden, Lyrna thought.

In the courtyard she found Davoka embracing a slight figure beside a stout, bare-backed pony flanked by two Eorhil warriors looking on with obvious suspicion. "Lerhnah!" Davoka called to her. "My other sister comes with the Mahlessa's word."

Kiral displayed none of the confusion left by the Mahlessa's healing beneath the Mountain, smiling shyly as Lyrna approached. Her scar had healed well but still made a grim sight, a deep line from chin to brow provoking unpleasant memories of the night Lyrna had given it to her. "Servant of the Mountain," Lyrna greeted her in Lonak.

"Queen." Kiral surprised her with a warm embrace. "And sister, also."

"What word from the Mahlessa?"

"She sends no word, Queen, save two gifts." She held up a small glass vial containing a dark viscous liquid. "She believes you will have use of this, and has provided me the knowledge of crafting more."

Lyrna hesitated before taking the vial, recalling the screams of the thing that had possessed this girl as a single drop touched her flesh. "How is it to be used?" she asked.

"She said it is a key to unseen chains and you would know best how to use it."

Lyrna handed the vial to Murel with stern instructions to keep it safe and on no account open it. "And the other gift?" she asked Kiral.

"Only myself." She cast a questing gaze around the courtyard. "I seek one who lost his song, so that he might hear mine."

CHAPTER TWO

Vaelin

The conclave was held in the House of the Sixth Order, the only intact building remaining to the Faith in the vicinity of Varinshold. The place had been abandoned in the aftermath of Frentis's visit, the courtyard, halls and corridors shouting their silence at Vaelin as he toured them, awash in memory as his eyes lit on the landmarks of his childhood. The corner of the yard where they used to play toss-board, the chipped cornice near the Aspect's chamber where Barkus had made an over-enthusiastic swipe with his sword. He spent a few moments staring at the steep stairwell in the north tower, his eyes picking out the copious dark stains on the stone where an unfortunate brother or Volarian had met his end, but made no move to ascend to the room above. *Some memories are best left to wither.*

He had only agreed to come thanks to Aspect Elera's insistent note and purposely delayed his arrival, having no wish to be drawn into discussion or decision regarding the Faith's many challenges. However, as the brothers on the door permitted him entry to the dining hall, he found them still engaged in fervent argument. There were perhaps twenty people in attendance, all that remained of the senior servants of the Faith. A quick survey revealed more blue cloaks than others, though the Seventh, represented by Caenis and a handful of his more mature subordinates, wore no formal robes. Aspect Dendrish was accompanied only by Master Benril, apparently the sole surviving members of the Third Order in the city. The Aspect was holding forth in typically loud voice, the words "mad enterprise," fading from his lips as Vaelin entered.

"Do I interrupt, Aspect?" Vaelin enquired. "Please continue."

"Vaelin." Aspect Elera rose to greet him with hands outstretched, limping a little as she approached. Her touch was as warm as ever though he detected a faint tremble in it and found himself disconcerted by the paleness of her complexion.

"Aspect," he said. "You are well?"

"Quite well. Come." She turned, leading him forward. "Your counsel is welcome here."

Aspect Dendrish gave a conspicuous snort whilst he noticed Caenis stiffen a little in his seat, his expression more grimly accepting than welcoming. "I confess I know not what counsel I can offer," Vaelin said. "This proceeding being of the Faith, whilst I am not."

"The Faith still holds to you, brother," Sollis said. He was flanked by Brother Commander Artin from Cardurin and Master Rensial, who sat with his wide-eyed gaze fixed on the floor, arms tight across his chest. "Regardless of whether you hold to it."

"We believe your insight will be valuable," Aspect Elera went on. "Especially as regards the queen's intent."

Vaelin nodded at Brother Hollun, the only representative of the Fourth Order in attendance. "Brother Hollun is at the queen's side every morning. I'm sure he can provide ample clarity as to her intent."

"She wants to invade the Volarian Empire," Aspect Dendrish said, his voice coloured by an unhealthy rasp. "With this Realm in ruins, she intends to spend our remaining strength on a . . ." He paused, jowls quivering a little as he struggled to formulate the least offensive phrase. "A questionable course."

"The queen's course is not yours to question," Vaelin told him.

"You surely understand our concerns, Vaelin," Elera said. "We are charged with protecting the Faithful."

"Forgive me, Aspect, but the current state of this Realm is ample evidence of your failure in that regard." He moved away from her, his gaze roaming over them, the remnants of something he once thought immutable, eternal. "You kept secrets for centuries, and spilled blood in the keeping. Knowledge, strength and wisdom that might have aided us when the Ally's blow fell. All in the name of preserving a Faith built on a lie."

"One man's lie is another man's truth." The voice was frail, tremulous, but strong in conviction, spoken by an old man in a stained white robe. He sat alone, kept erect by a gnarled staff formed from an old tree branch, regarding Vaelin with a single bright blue eye, his other milky white.

"Aspect Korvan," Elera said. "Last of the First Order."

"The Departed are captured souls," Vaelin told the old man. "Gifted ensnared in the Beyond by a being of vile purpose. Is that a lie?"

Aspect Korvan sighed, lowering his head in momentary weariness. "For five decades I was Master of Insight at the House of the First Order," he said. "Today I find myself an Aspect, a title derived from the varied character of our Faith. And the Faith is but a reflection of what awaits us in the Beyond."

"I've been to the Beyond," Vaelin returned. "Have you?"

The old man's hand twitched on his stick and he took a moment to answer. "Once, long ago. You are not the first to taste death and return, young man. The Beyond is a place that is not a place, both form and mist, endless and yet finite. It is a crystal formed of many facets and you have seen only one."

"Perhaps," Vaelin conceded. "And perhaps the Faith is but a fumbling attempt to understand a thing beyond understanding. But I saw enough to know that our enemy is not done, he wishes our end and will not stop. The queen sees the key to his defeat in striking at the heart of the empire he built to crush us. Be assured that the queen's intent is also mine."

"Though it may lead us to ruin?" Dendrish asked.

"Ruin has already befallen us," Vaelin replied. "Queen Lyrna offers a chance to avoid utter destruction." He turned to Caenis with a questioning glance. "Are there no signs and portents to guide us, brother? No messages divined from the swirling mists of time?"

"Brother Caenis is now Aspect Caenis," Elera said, somehow contriving to retain her smile.

"Congratulations," Vaelin told him.

Caenis's lips formed a small smile and he got to his feet. "My brother knows well scrying is not an exact art," he said. "And there are few left in our ranks with gifts capable of aiding us in this decision. I can only speak for my own Order, and I have already sworn us in service to the queen's purpose, regardless of where it might lead us."

Vaelin turned at the scrape of a chair, finding Master Rensial on his feet. He stood casting his gaze around them for a few seconds, frowning in concentration. When he spoke his voice was free of any shrillness or quivering uncertainty. "They tortured me first," he said. "But stopped when it became clear I could tell them nothing. They chained me to a wall and for four days I listened to my brothers' torment. The same question was asked, over and over, 'Where are the Gifted?' Through it all I heard no answers given." His gaze lost focus again and he hugged himself tighter, sitting down once more, adding in a whisper, "Where is the boy? The forest is burning and the boy is gone."

Sollis rose, placing a hand on the mad master's shoulder as he continued to mutter to himself. "By assent of this conclave," Sollis said. "I speak for my Order until Aspect Arlyn is recovered or proved dead. We will follow the queen's course."

"As will the Fourth Order," Brother Hollun stated.

Aspect Dendrish slumped into his seat, waving a plump hand in either dismissal or assent. It was Master Benril who spoke, standing to regard them with a grim visage. "War is ever the folly of the ignorant. But I have seen much to convince me some wars must be fought, to the bitterest end if need be. Our Order, such as it is, will support this endeavour."

The Second Order was represented by a pair of sisters from their mission in Andurin, both tired from the journey and clearly overawed by the occasion. They apparently had no knowledge of their Aspect's fate though rumours told of all their brothers and sisters perishing when their House burned to rubble. They conferred for a second before the older of the two confirmed their agreement in a strained voice.

"Aspect?" Sollis asked Elera.

Her smile had faded completely now, her face, always so open and bright as to defy signs of age, now told of a tired woman of middling years with eyes that had seen too much. She stood in silence for some time, hands clasped together and face downcast. "So much has changed so quickly," she said eventually. "So many certainties overthrown in the space of a few months. Lord Vaelin is right to speak of our past crimes, for we are guilty of grievous errors. I myself said nothing when my brightest pupil was taken to the Blackhold for speaking against the desert war. There is blood on our hands. But I fear what crimes await us should we take this course. Every day people come to my Order for healing but burning with a hatred I have not seen in all the troubled years to beset this Realm. When the queen takes them across the ocean, what manner of justice will she ordain?"

"I am Battle Lord of the Queen's Host," Vaelin said. "And will allow no violence to be visited on those who do not raise arms to oppose us."

She raised her gaze, smiling at him once more, but with something behind her eyes she hadn't shown him before: regret. *I delivered you*, she had told him once. *Perhaps she wonders what she pulled into the world?* "I will trust your word, Vaelin, as I always have." She turned to the others, speaking formally. "The Fifth Order pledges to support the queen's course."

◆ ◆ ◆

He said farewell to Reva at the south gate, pulling her close to plant a kiss on the top of her head, finding himself both surprised and heartened when she returned the embrace. "No doubts?" he asked her as she drew back. "No hesitation in following the queen's orders?"

"Doubts I have aplenty," she replied. "But that's nothing new. At Alltor I saw enough to convince me this fight is to the death. They won't stop, so neither can we."

"And will your people see it that way?"

Her expression grew sombre, her tone soft with reluctant admission. "They will when they hear the Blessed Lady speak with the Father's voice."

She mounted up and rode off with an escort of House Guards. Watching her go, he was struck by a sudden sense of loss, a knowledge he might never see her again.

"My lord." He turned to find himself confronted with one of Lyrna's ladies, the taller one with dark eyes, though her name escaped him. "The queen requests your presence at the palace."

Her eyes flicked to the left, a slight frown of unease on her brow. He followed her gaze to where the Gifted folk from the Reaches had established themselves in a half-ruined wineshop. A couple of passing Realm Guard were recovering their composure, clearly victims of Lorkan's love of surprising the non-Gifted, the young man bowing in apparently sincere apology as Cara smothered a laugh in the background. Lorkan caught Vaelin's eye and gave a weak smile before turning and walking to a shadowed corner where he seemingly blinked out of existence.

He turned back to the lady, finding her narrow gaze still fixed on the shadow where Lorkan had disappeared. "Forgive me, my lady," he said, recapturing her attention. "I don't believe I know your name."

"Orena, my lord." She bowed again. "In truth, Lady Orena Al Vardrian, by the queen's good graces."

"Vardrian? From south of Haeversvale?"

"My grandmother was from Haeversvale, my lord."

He was about to inform her that they most likely shared some blood but the evident discomfort in the woman's face gave him pause. She clearly didn't relish the prospect of remaining so close to the Gifted and there was a tenseness to her demeanour that discouraged further conversation. "These people are our allies," he said, nodding to the wineshop. "They offer no threat."

Her face took on a bland neutrality and she bowed. "The queen waits upon your attendance, my lord."

She was in the palace grounds surveying the part-completed marble relief carved by Master Benril. A short way off the Lady Davoka stood alongside another Lonak woman, younger and considerably less tall. The younger woman straightened at sight of Vaelin, her face curious, as if voicing an unspoken question.

"My lord," Lyrna greeted him brightly. "How went the conclave?"

He was unsurprised by her knowledge. She had all of her father's gift for accruing intelligence and more subtle ways of exploiting it. "The Faith seeks to rebuild itself," he said. "And will, of course, support your endeavour with all their remaining strength."

"And Lady Reva?"

"Also unrelenting in pursuit of your purpose, Highness."

She nodded, her gaze still fixed on the marble relief. Although it was unfinished Vaelin found the carvings remarkably lifelike, the expressions and poses of the figures possessed of a precision and verisimilitude surpassing even Benril's other work. The faces of the Volarian soldiery and Realm folk alike were riven with all the fear, rage and confusion of people truly faced with the horrors of war.

"Remarkable isn't it?" Lyrna observed. "And yet Master Benril has formally petitioned me to have it destroyed."

"No doubt it serves as a painful reminder of his enslavement."

"But in years to come, perhaps we will all require something to remind us of what provoked our course. I think I'm minded to leave it as it is. If the master's temper cools in time, he may be persuaded to finish it, to his own design of course."

Lyrna raised a hand to call Davoka and the other Lonak woman forward. "This is Kiral of the Black River Clan. She has a message for you."

◆ ◆ ◆

"You speak my tongue very well." He had taken her to his father's house where he and his sister made a home of sorts amongst the less damaged rooms. Alornis was absent, gone to the docks on some errand, probably keen to paint the panorama of ships crowding the harbour. They sat together under the sheltering oak in the yard, its mighty branches bare of leaves as winter's chill grew deeper by the day.

"*She* knew your tongue," Kiral said. "So I know it."

He had heard the story from Lyrna and could scarcely credit it: a soul possessed by one of the Ally's creatures and now freed. And a singer with a message. Yet somehow he knew the truth of it, just by looking into her face he knew she heard a song and found himself shamed by the jealousy it stirred.

"She remembered you," the Lonak girl went on. "You barred her from a kill. Her hatred was great."

He remembered Sister Henna's enraged, hissing face as he held her to the wall. "You possess her memories?"

"Some. She was very old, though not so old as her brother and sister, nor so deadly. She feared them and hated them in equal measure. I have the healing arts she learned in the Fifth Order, the rites performed by a priestess somewhere in the far south of the Alpiran Empire, the knife skills of a Volarian slave girl sent to die in their spectacles."

"Do you know when she was first taken?"

"Her early memories are a mist of confusion and fear, chief among them the sight of mud huts burning under a broad night sky." Kiral paused to give an involuntary shudder. "The vision fades and she hears *his* voice."

"What does he say?"

She shook her head. "She always shrank from the memory, preferring to dwell on her many lifetimes' worth of murder and deceit."

"I'm sorry for you. It must . . . hurt."

Kiral shrugged her slender shoulders. "When I dream, mostly." She looked up at the branches of the great oak above her head, a small smile coming to her lips. "There," she said, pointing to a wide fork near the main trunk. "You would sit there, watching your father groom his horses." Her smile faded. "He was afraid of you, though you never knew it."

He stared up at the oak for a time. His memories of playing in its arms had always been happy, but now he wondered if his child's eyes had seen more than he recalled. "Your song is strong," he told her.

"Yours was stronger. I can hear its echo. To lose such strength must be hard."

"As a younger man I feared it, but in time I knew it as a gift. And yes, I miss it greatly."

"So now I will be your song, as the Mahlessa commands."

"And what does she command?"

"I hear a voice calling to me from a great distance, far to the east. It's a very old tune, and very lonely, sung by a man who cannot die, a man you have met."

"His name?"

"I know not, but the music carries an image of a boy who once offered him shelter from a storm, and risked his life to save him and his charge."

Erlin. It all tumbled into place in a rush, the rage Erlin had been shouting into the storm that night, his world-spanning travels, and his unchanged face when he came to share the truth about Davern's father. *Erlin, Rellis, Hetril, he's got a hundred names,* Makril had said, though Vaelin now knew he had begun with only one. *That day at the fair as he stared at the puppet show . . .* "Kerlis," he said in a whisper. "Kerlis the Faithless. Cursed to the ever death for denying the Departed."

"A legend," Kiral said. "My people have another story. They tell of a man who offended Mirshak, God of the Black Lands, and was cursed to craft a story without ending."

"You know where to find him?"

She nodded. "And I know he is important. The song is bright with purpose when it touches him, and the Mahlessa believes he is key to defeating whatever commands the thing that stole my body."

"Where?"

Her scar twisted as she gave an apologetic grimace. "Across the ice."

CHAPTER THREE

Frentis

S he pauses to survey the Council before taking her seat, twenty men in fine red robes seated around a perfectly circular table. The council chamber sits halfway up the tower, each member having been hauled to this height by the strength of a hundred slaves working the intricate pulleys that trace the length of this monolith. Blessed by endless life though they are, no Council-man relishes the prospect of climbing so many stairs.

She sits through the tedium of the opening formalities as Arklev intones the formal commencement of the fourth and final council meeting of this, the eight hundred and twenty-fifth year of the empire, the slave scribes scribbling away with their unnatural speed as he drones on, introducing each member in turn, until finally he comes to her.

"... and newly ascended to the Slaver's Seat, Council, ah, Woman ..."

"I am to be recorded as simply the Ally's Voice," she tells him, casting a meaningful glance at the scribes.

Arklev falters for a moment but recovers with admirable fortitude. "As you wish. Now, to our first order of business ..."

"The only order of business," she interrupts. "The war. This council has no other business until it is concluded."

Another Council-man stirs, a silver-haired dullard whose name she can't trouble herself to recall. "But, there are pressing matters from the south, reports of famine ..."

"There was a drought," she says. "Crops fail and people starve. Have any surplus slaves killed to husband supplies until it abates. All very sad but survivable, our current military situation may not be."

"Admittedly," Arklev begins, "the invasion has not progressed according to plan . . ."

"It's been a miserable failure, Arklev," she breaks in, smiling. "That preening dolt Tokrev orchestrated his own death and defeat with more efficiency than any of his victories. Sorry about your sister by the way."

"My sister yet lives and I have no doubt as to her facility for continued survival. And we still hold their capital . . ."

"No." She reaches out to pluck a grape from the bowl nearby, popping it into her mouth, savouring the sweetness. Although not entirely to her liking, this shell does possess an impressively sensitive palate. "As of three days ago, we don't. Mirvek lies dead along with his command. The Unified Realm is lost to us."

She enjoys the shocked silence almost as much as the grape. "A tragedy," one of them says in cautious tone, a handsome fellow of misleadingly youthful appearance. She remembers killing a man at his request forty years ago, husband to some slattern he wanted to wed. She never thought to ask if the marriage was a success.

"But," the handsome Council-man continues, "whilst the disgrace of defeat is hard to bear, surely this means the war is at an end. For now at least. We must gather strength, await a suitable opportunity to launch another attempt."

"Whilst an entire nation with every reason to hate us gathers its own strength."

"They are weakened by our invasion," Arklev points out. "And an ocean stands between us."

"I imagine King Malcius entertained the very same delusion up until the moment he felt his neck snap." She gets to her feet, all humour vanishing from her face as she looks at each of them in turn. "Know, Honoured Council-men, that the Ally does not indulge in conjecture. I speak unalloyed fact. The Unified Realm now has itself a queen and she sees no more obstacle in an ocean than she would a shallow stream. When the seas calm she will be coming, whilst we have spent our best forces on an invasion commanded by a fool, one chosen by your vote, as I recall."

"General Tokrev was a veteran of many campaigns," the silver-haired Council-man begins, falling quiet at her glare. She lets the silence linger, feeling a familiar lust build in her breast as her song senses the burgeoning fear, clenching fists to keep it at bay. Not yet.

"It is the Ally's wish," she says, "that reserves be mustered to meet the threat. Former Free Swords will be recalled to their battalions and the con-

scription quotas for new recruits are to be tripled. The garrisons in Volar are to be reinforced by troops drawn from the provinces."

She waits for dissent, but they all just sit and stare, these men who own millions, ancient cowards for the first time realising the depth of their folly. She considers leaving with a final veiled threat or humiliating barb, but finds herself possessed of a great desire to be away from them.

Was this how it was for you? *she asks the uncaring ghost of her father as she turns and walks wordlessly from the chamber.* Did they see how sickened you were by their stench? Is that why they had me kill you?

◆　◆　◆

He was woken by the harsh clatter of the lock in his cell door. His principal gaoler, like all his guards, was drawn from the Queen's Mounted Guard, a veteran sergeant with a distinct disinclination to conversation who glared at Frentis with unabashed detestation every time he opened the door. The queen had been punctilious in choosing guards unlikely to be swayed by the legend of the Red Brother. Today, however, the man's hatred was slightly muted as he pulled the heavy door ajar and motioned for him to come out. To his continued surprise, Frentis had not been shackled, or in fact subject to any mistreatment. He was fed twice a day and provided with a fresh jug of water each morning when the sergeant came to fetch his waste bucket. Otherwise he was left to sit in darkness, absent any company or conversation . . . save *her* of course, waiting every time he succumbed to sleep.

The sergeant stood well back as he exited the cell, finding the queen standing in the chamber beyond flanked by Davoka and her two ennobled guards. "Highness," Frentis said, dropping to one knee.

The queen gave no response, turning to the sergeant. "Leave us please. Give your keys to Lord Iltis."

She waited until he had gone before speaking again. "The Blackhold has not been so empty since the day of its construction." Frentis remained on one knee as she surveyed the chamber, eyes tracking over dark stone lit by meagre torchlight. "I find I prefer it that way. I intend to have it torn down at the conclusion of our current difficulties."

Frentis lowered his head and took a breath, speaking in formal tones, "My Queen, I most humbly offer my life . . ."

"Be silent!" Her voice lashed like a whip as she advanced towards him, coming close enough to touch as she loomed over him, her breath harsh and ragged. "I killed you once before. So I already have your life."

Her breathing slowed after a moment and she moved away. "Rise," she ordered with an irritated wave and he stood, waiting as her flawless face regarded him, anger replaced by an icy calm. "Brother Sollis has related your account to me in full. Your actions were not your own, you are no more to blame for the King's death than a sword is to blame for the blood it spills. I know this, brother. And yet I find I have no forgiveness for you. Do you understand?"

"I do, Highness."

"Lord Vaelin also tells me you claim that Lord Al Telnar was complicit in the Volarian invasion."

"He was, Highness, on the promise of power and . . . other rewards."

"And what might they be?"

"He was at pains to extract promises that no harm should come to you during the attack."

She sighed, giving a faint shake of her head. "And I thought he died a hero."

Frentis drew breath, steeling himself before uttering his next words. "Might I crave a moment to speak in private, Highness? I have a message to convey."

"Lady Davoka and these lords have seen me at my lowest state and still judge me deserving of their loyalty. Any words you say to me are worthy of their ears."

"I speak for a Lord Marshal of the Mounted Guard, a man I saw slain when the palace fell. His name was Smolen."

The queen's face betrayed no emotion as she stared at him, but he saw how her hands shifted as if itching to reach for a hidden weapon. "Relate your message," she ordered.

"He said it was a great thing to travel so far with the woman he loved."

Her hands clenched, forming tight fists as she advanced towards him. He heard two swords scraping free of scabbards as her lords came to her side, steel poised to take his life. "How did he die?" she demanded.

"Bravely. He fought well but the Kuritai are skillful, as you know."

He found himself unable to meet her gaze, the impassive perfection of her face a terrible contrast to the burnt screaming woman who had fled the throne room. "I make no plea for mercy," he said, lowering his head. "And await your judgement."

"Do you hunger for death then? Do you imagine the Departed will make a welcome for one such as you?"

"I doubt it, Highness. But hope is at the heart of the Faith."

"Then your hope is to be dashed, for now at least." She gestured Iltis towards a locked cell, the Lord Protector working the keys and hauling the door wide, he and his fellow lord going inside to retrieve the occupant. Unlike Frentis this man had been festooned with chains, ankles, knees, wrists and neck all secured with newly forged shackles, forcing him to move in an inching shuffle as the two lords dragged him into the light. Despite his obvious discomfort his face was absent of any sign of distress, the features the familiar immobile mask of the slave-elite. His chest was bare and thick with well-honed muscle, a patchwork of scars covering the flesh from waist to neck.

"Kuritai," Frentis murmured.

"The only one we have managed to capture in this entire war," the queen said. "Found senseless at the docks the day the city fell. According to Lord Al Hestian he was set to guard Alucius, assurance of his father's compliance. His name is Twenty-Seven."

She moved closer to the slave-elite, her eyes scanning him from head to toe in critical appraisal. "Brother Harlick tells me these creatures have no will of their own, it's driven from them through torment, drugs and, according to Aspect Caenis, various Dark means that stink of the Ally's influence. Much as your will was driven from you, I imagine. What would he do if we were to free him, I wonder?"

"I would strongly advise against it, Highness," Frentis said.

She turned to him with the same look of examination still in place, her eyes going to a particular spot on his chest. "Lady Davoka tells me the wound I gave you festered, that you have her to thank for your life."

Frentis glanced at Davoka, finding her more ill at ease than he could remember, her forehead beaded with sweat. He saw she held a small glass bottle, the contents seeming to shimmer a little and he noted her hand was actually trembling. "That is correct, Highness," he said, his unease deepening. *What's in there that could scare her so?* "Though I believe it was your knife that truly saved me. Somehow it . . . freed me."

"Yes." Her gaze returned to the prisoner and she held out her hand to Davoka, speaking in Lonak. The queen accepted the bottle from her and held it up to the dim light, the dark liquid inside producing a foul odour as she removed the stopper. "The blade that freed you was coated with this," she told Frentis. "A gift from our Lonak friends. One I suspect may prove highly useful to our purpose." She moved closer to the Kuritai, speaking to him softly in Volarian, "I take no pleasure in this."

She lifted the bottle to a spot at the top of his chest, tipping it to allow a single drop of the liquid to fall onto the slave's scars. The result was immediate, the scream that erupted from the Kuritai's throat enough to pain the ears as he convulsed, collapsing in his chains to writhe on the stones. The queen stepped back from him, her face grim, eyes bright as she stoppered the bottle. Frentis saw how she stiffened her back and forced herself to watch the slave's torment. After a few seconds his screams abated to agonised whimpers, his back-straining writhes diminishing to gasping shudders. Finally, he lay still, panting and bathed in sweat.

Lyrna took a cautious step forward but Frentis raised a hand. "If I may, Highness?" She gave a nod of assent and he went to the Kuritai's side, crouching to peer into his face, finding life returning to pain-dulled eyes.

"Can you talk?" he asked in Volarian.

The eyes blinked, finding focus, the response a croaking cough from a throat unused to speech. "Yesss."

"What is your name?"

The eyes narrowed a fraction, the answer coming in rough, harshly accented Volarian. "I . . . began as Five Hundred. Now . . . I am Twenty . . . Seven."

"No." Frentis leaned closer. "Your real name. Do you know it?"

The eyes wandered a little, his brow creasing at a rush of memory. "Lekran," he said, his voice faint then turning to a snarl. "Lekran . . . My father . . . was Hirkran, of the red axe."

"You are far from home, my friend."

Lekran jerked, his chains snapping tight. "Then . . . get this fucking metal off me . . . so I can go back there. For time on this earth is short, and I have many men to kill."

◆   ◆   ◆

"It truly prevents dreams?" Frentis gave the contents of the flask a dubious sniff, finding the scent less than inviting, like mildew mixed with stewed tea.

"It renders a sleep deep enough to prevent them," Brother Kehlan replied. "I first concocted it in the aftermath of the Ice Horde. There were many in the Reaches troubled by nightmares when the killing was done, myself included. It will stop your dreams, brother. Though the aching head you'll have come the morning may make you pine for the dreams."

They aren't dreams, Frentis knew. *But it might at least guard against wayward thoughts when she touches my mind.* The Fifth Order had established itself in the merchants' houses near the docks, the many rooms and deep cellars providing space enough for most of the wounded and storage for their growing supply of bandages and curatives. It seemed Lady Al Bera had managed to persuade a few Alpiran merchants to risk a final supply run across the wintry Meldenean, bringing much needed medicines along with the food.

He thanked the healer and made his way outside, walking along the wharf to where Vaelin stood regarding the huge Volarian warship. He was aware of the many glances he drew as he walked, and more than a few openly hostile glares, but mostly just fear or surprise. He might still be the Red Brother to some, but to most he was now the King's Assassin, freed by virtue of their queen's endless grace. She stirred no fear in them, only adulation, and they laboured tirelessly at her command. Everywhere he looked people were at work, rebuilding fallen walls, hammers ringing in makeshift forges and new recruits being drilled to unaccustomed discipline. He saw fatigue on many faces but no idleness, all moving to their allotted tasks with a singular determination. *Her captains might fear her course, but these people would sail every ocean in the world at her word.*

He heard raised voices on the ship as he neared, his eyes picking out two figures on the deck, one short, the other tall. The shorter of the two seemed to have the loudest voice. "Your sister has a surprisingly waspish tongue, brother," Frentis observed to Vaelin.

"Our new Lord of the Queen's Yard brings out the worst in her," he replied, watching Alornis angrily bunch up a sheaf of parchment and throw it in Davern's face before stomping off the gangplank. "He asked her to make drawings of the ship. Something I suspect he now regrets."

"Arrogant numb-head!" Alornis fumed, having made her way to the quay, her stern visage unmoved by her brother's comforting hug.

"He didn't like the drawings?" Vaelin asked.

"It wasn't the drawings." She raised her voice, casting it back at the ship. "It's his pigheaded refusal to listen to reasonable advice!"

"I'm sure he knows his business," Vaelin said, earning a reproving scowl.

"This monstrosity," she said pointing at the *Queen Lyrna*'s hull. "Is massively over-engineered, yet he wants to copy it, expending vast amounts of labour and timber in the process."

"Your own design being more elegant, no doubt?"

"Actually, yes, dear brother, it is." She drew herself up, clutching her satchel to her chest. "I shall take this to the queen." She gave Frentis a stiff bow and walked off with a determined gait.

"When last I met her," Frentis said, "she was more softly spoken."

"We are all much changed, brother." Vaelin turned away from the ship, walking towards the mole with Frentis falling in alongside. "The queen's design for you," he said, halting a good distance from other ears. "You can refuse."

"Hardly, brother. Nor would I wish to."

Vaelin gazed out to sea, grey waters chopped by the wind under a turbulent sky. "The woman who haunts your dreams, do you think she will sense your coming?"

"Possibly. Though I'm hoping Brother Kehlan's physic will mask my thoughts. In any case, her interest in me might work to our advantage, my mission being diversionary."

"It seems we both have hard roads ahead of us."

"It would be best if you don't share your course with me. If she found me and somehow took me alive, I . . . doubt I could keep secrets from her should she bind me again."

Vaelin nodded, turning back from the sea, sorrow plain on his brow. "I searched for you for such a long time, casting my song out far and wide, but I never caught more than the vaguest glimpse. Now, it seems I am bound to send you away again and have no song to find you in any case."

"I have much to balance, brother. And an assassin shouldn't linger in sight of his victim's sister." He extended his hand and Vaelin gripped it tight. "We'll find each other in Volar, of that I've no doubt."

◆　◆　◆

The headache was everything Brother Kehlan promised, the pain alleviated somewhat by the welcome realisation that the concoction worked. His sleep had been free of dreams, absent any further horrors or entreaties to surrender to her will. He had continued to sleep at the Blackhold in the days since his release, he and Lekran now more comfortably accommodated in the guard room. It was a strange feeling to reside in such a large building now stripped of all but two occupants, the queen having quickly redeployed her guardsmen to training duties. He found the former Kuritai at practice in the courtyard, moving with all the speed and precision instilled by years of conditioning and battle. Instead of the usual twin swords today he wielded an axe, whirling as he fought an army of imaginary opponents.

"Redbrother," he greeted Frentis, coming to a halt, panting a little from the exertion. He had forsaken the razor since his liberation and a dark stubble had formed on his face and head. "Your chief-woman sent a slave with this. She makes a mighty gift." He hefted the axe, grinning broadly. It was a double-bladed weapon of Renfaelin design, the flat steel of the inner blades inlaid with an intricate pattern of gilded gold. *Probably one of Darnel's toys,* Frentis decided, once again feeling a pang of regret that he hadn't been the one to kill the Fief Lord.

"There are no slaves here," Frentis told him, a fact he had been obliged to repeat several times. Lekran seemed to have difficulty conceiving of a land free of slavery. He was fulsome in his description of his homelands, apparently lying somewhere among the wild mountain country beyond the northern provinces, his tribe's principal occupations seemingly digging for ore and waging constant war on their neighbours.

"Good stuff." Lekran said after a hearty gulp of wine. "You have any more?"

Frentis gestured to a stack of bottles nearby, found beneath the bed of the Free Sword officer who had command of this place. The city had turned out to be rich in hidden stashes of wine and assorted loot. The Volarian army permitted looting on a formalised basis, as long as all booty was declared and subject to a one-tenth tax, but clearly many had felt disinclined to abide by this policy.

"Your chief-woman," Lekran said, sitting down again with bottle in hand. "She has a man?"

"She's called a queen, and no."

"Good. I'll claim her." He took a long drink and burped extravagantly. "How many heads will it take, do you think?"

Apparently it was the custom of Lekran's tribe to offer the heads of fallen enemies to prospective brides as proof of husbandly worthiness. "A thousand should do," Frentis advised.

Lekran frowned and gave an annoyed huff. "So many?"

"She's a queen. They're expensive." He watched the former slave exhaust the bottle in a few gulps and knew, for all his bluster, this was a man attempting to drown the many horrors in his head. "How long were you Kuritai?" he asked him.

"I had nineteen years when they took me. Now I see my father's face when I look in the mirror. Time is lost to the binding." Lekran grimaced at the empty bottle and threw it against the flagstones.

"You don't remember it?" Frentis pressed. "I recall every instance of mine."

"Then you are greatly unfortunate." Lekran sat fidgeting for a moment, muscular arms bulging as he clasped his hands together, casting a hungry glance at the wine. "I remember . . . enough."

"Alucius Al Hestian, you remember you were set to guard him?"

A very faint smile played over Lekran's lips. "Yes. He wanted a drink too."

"He died a hero, trying to kill a much-hated enemy of mine."

"That fuck-brain on the big chair?" Lekran gave an amused grunt. "Well, good for him. Let's drink to his memory." He rose to fetch another bottle.

"You know our course?" Frentis asked him as he rummaged through the wine, unstoppering a bottle to sniff the contents before grimacing and tossing it aside. "You are content to follow me?"

"My father was the only man I ever followed willingly." Lekran sniffed another bottle, raising his eyebrows in appreciation. "But I'll lend my axe to your cause on the way home." He sat back down, grinning as he took another drink. "Your queen is owed a thousand heads, after all."

◆ ◆ ◆

"Belorath," the captain introduced himself, regarding Frentis with obvious suspicion, deepening even further at the sight of Lekran stepping off the gangplank complete with twin swords on his back and axe in hand. "Welcome to the *Sea Sabre*. Your comrades are here already."

The morning air was bracing, the sea-borne wind adding a cutting edge as they came aboard, the cluster of familiar figures on the deck huddling in their cloaks as Frentis advanced on them, his chill banished by a sudden anger. "What is this?" he demanded.

"Come to follow the queen's command, brother," Draker said, getting to his feet, the others rising at his back. "In truth, brother. She was kind enough to grant our request, since none of us relished the thought of life in the Realm Guard."

Frentis's gaze swept over the thirty survivors of his company from the Urlish, hard-faced men and women garbed in muted colours and bristling with a variety of favoured weapons. Although there was one exception. Illian made a striking figure in her dark blue cloak, seeming to have grown somewhat in the few days since their last meeting. On either side of her sat Blacktooth and Slasher, both gazing up at him with wide eyes and heads lowered as they licked their lips; pups greeting the pack leader. Frentis knelt to run a hand over their heads, provoking a welcoming whine.

"Brother Sollis has a message, I assume," Frentis asked Illian, unable to keep the disappointment from his voice.

She replied with a tight smile, her tone formal. "Only that you allow me to join this mission, brother. And to ensure my training doesn't slacken during the voyage."

Frentis forced down the impulse to order her from the ship as she continued, "Davoka wasn't happy about it either, if that's any comfort."

"It isn't . . . sister. She stays by the queen's side, I take it?"

Illian nodded. "Not without regret. She did give me this." She held up a sack containing a number of leather flasks. "Mixed by Brother Kehlan according to the Lonak recipe."

Frentis nodded. "Keep it safe, and don't be tempted to open a single flask." He rose from the dogs as Thirty-Four came forward to grip his hand. "You are a free man now," he reminded the former slave. "Returning to the land of your bondage. And our success is far from certain."

"I've yet to find my name," Thirty-Four replied with a shrug, dropping his voice a little and slipping into Volarian. "And I find your queen . . . troubling."

Frentis released his hand and turned to Master Rensial, standing apart from the others, expression more vacant than usual. "I had hoped you would return to the stables, Master," Frentis told him. "The Order will have need of your talents."

"The boy isn't there," Rensial muttered. "Or the girl, or the tall woman." He glanced around suspiciously and moved closer, speaking in a whisper. "Where are the horses?"

"We go to find them, Master." Frentis gripped his arm in reassurance. "Far across the sea is a whole empire of horses."

Rensial replied with a grave nod then wandered off towards the prow. Frentis decided to warn Captain Belorath to make sure his men gave the horse master as much space as possible. His gaze was drawn to the rail where an unfamiliar figure stood staring out to sea, a young well-built man with a thick head of curly blond hair.

"His name's Weaver," Draker said. "Doesn't talk much."

Frentis knew the name of course. *The Gifted who healed the queen.* "He also comes at the queen's command?"

"Not really sure, brother. He was already aboard when we arrived."

Frentis nodded, turning back to meet the weight of their collected gaze. "I thank you all," he said. "But you offer me too much. Please go ashore and leave me to this mission." They stared back in silence, expressions expectant rather than angry. None made a single step towards the gangplank. "This mission holds no return journey . . ." he began then stopped as Draker gave a broad grin.

"I think our captain is eager to be off, brother," he said.

Chapter Four

Reva

Lord Brahdor's house must have been a grand place once. Formerly a minor stronghold, successive generations had seen it moulded into a sprawling three-storey mansion, grown beyond the walls that once enclosed it, the defensive ditch long since filled in. The surrounding fields were dotted with stables, storehouses, and, Reva well knew, a large barn over the crest of a nearby hill. She had called there earlier, halting her horse a good distance short of the dilapidated pile of leaning timber, the roof now vanished and the doors lying on the weed-rich ground.

She was alone, having ordered her guards to proceed to Alltor without her some miles back. She found Kernmill ravaged and burnt as expected, all the people she had once spied on dead, taken by slavers or fled. The house of Lord Brahdor lay some two miles north and was in only marginally better repair. It seemed to have escaped the attentions of the Volarians, possibly because its evident ruin had been wrought before their arrival, the various rooftops stripped of slate, either by the elements or greedy villagers, the walls streaked with dirt and peeling daub, every door seemingly vanished.

What do you expect to find here? she asked herself with an inward sigh before dismounting and tethering her mount to a fence-post. It was a placid mare, much more amenable than poor old Snorter, who had been lost to the stewpot during the early days of the siege. She left her to nibble at the long grass as she approached the house, peering through glassless windows at the musty darkness within. *Did they meet here?* she wondered. *Was this the seat of their plots? The Sons coming to huddle in front of the godly lord who spoke such wondrous truth, never knowing the true nature of the thing that lied to them, probably laughing to itself the whole while.*

She went to a doorway and stepped into the chilled shadows inside. Despite the gloom she was impressed by the grandeur of the lobby, an elegant staircase sweeping down from the upper storey to a chequerboard floor of fine marble, a ringing echo rising from her boots. She scanned the walls seeking paintings or sigils, finding only bare plaster and no sign as to the character of the late occupant. A brief exploration of the other rooms on the ground floor was no more fruitful so she tentatively mounted the staircase, finding it surprisingly firm underfoot, sounding only the faintest creak as she went aloft.

The upper floor was colder, wind gusting through the ruined windows, stirring rags that had once been drapes. She went from room to room, finding only dust, shards of pottery and the sticks of ruined furniture. In one room she paused at the sight of a large stain on the floor, part obscured by a moulded carpet, a cobweb-shrouded bed standing against the wall. She knew the stain of blood well enough to make closer inspection unnecessary; someone had died here, but not recently.

She was turning away when she caught it, a slight acrid tint reaching her nostrils, the scent of a recently snuffed candle. She paused, closing her eyes, nose and ears alive to further clues. It was just the smallest creak to the beams above her head, only a few ounces too heavy for a rat. She opened her eyes, raising her gaze to the ceiling, picking out a hole no bigger than a copper coin, flickering light then dark as something covered it.

She went to the hallway and sought out the steps to the third storey, finding them much less well preserved than the grand staircase. The balustrade was gone and several steps were missing, forcing her to leap and grab her way up. This final level consisted of four attic rooms, only one of which held a door. She tried the handle and, finding it locked, kicked it open, drawing her sword before going inside. There was a small but neat pile of blankets near the window, the room shielded from the elements by a few planks of wood, tied in place with twine. The stub of a candle sat next to the blankets, a thin tendril of smoke rising from the wick.

Reva surveyed the rest of the room, finding a small stack of books and a pile of assorted vegetables in the corner, carrots and potatoes, mouldy and sprouting roots, small bite marks in some. It was the intake of breath that warned her, a sharp gasp just above her head.

Reva took a step forward and something landed behind her. She whirled, the sword coming round in a precise slash, connecting with a small knife, the blade skittering away into the shadows. Its owner stared up at her with wide eyes in a dirt-smeared face framed by a mass of matted curls.

"Who are you?" Reva demanded.

The girl's face held the same astonished gape for a second then transformed into a snarl. She hissed, launching herself at Reva, her hands like claws, long nails seeking to tear at the intruder's face. Reva dropped her sword, sidestepped the charge and caught the girl about the waist, pinning her arms as she thrashed, snarling and spitting. She held her in place as she continued to struggle, feeling the bone-thin form beneath her ragged clothes and wondering at the ferocity of one so near starvation. The girl subsided after a full two minutes' thrashing, slumping exhausted in Reva's arms, voicing a whimper of helpless rage.

"Forgive the intrusion," Reva told her. "My name is Reva. Who might you be?"

◆　◆　◆

"Did Ihlsa send you?"

Reva added more fuel to the fire and checked the contents of the pot, an old iron vessel found amidst the shattered remnants of the mansion's kitchen. The girl had followed her readily enough after Reva released her, although she had maintained a sullen silence until now, sitting opposite her in front of the fireplace as Reva stacked broken furniture for fuel. She had filled the pot with the oats from her saddlebags flavoured with a little honey and cinnamon, bought from a Nilsaelin soldier back in Varinshold for the price of a Volarian officer's short sword and dagger. Long weeks marching with the Queen's Crusade had told her much about the character of the Realm's various subjects, and Nilsaelins could usually be relied upon to supply a few luxuries for the right price.

"Who's Ihlsa?" she asked, stirring the porridge.

The girl drew herself up a little, chin jutting as she attempted a dignified air. "My maid."

"Making you the lady of this house?"

"Yes." The girl's face clouded somewhat. "Since Mother died."

"You are daughter to Lord Brahdor?"

The girl's expression abruptly switched from sadness to outright fear. "You know my father? Is he coming back?"

Reva sat down, meeting the girl's fearful eyes. "What is your name, girl?"

She took a few attempts before managing to form a reply, the word a hesitant whisper. "E-Ellese."

"Ellese, I must tell you, your father is dead. Slain at Alltor, along with many others."

There was no grief in the girl's face, just sagging relief. She hugged herself, head lowered to her knees, the soft sound of weeping emerging from behind her mask of matted hair. Reva hadn't appreciated just how young she was before, but now saw she couldn't be more than ten, and so thin.

Reva scooped some porridge into a wooden bowl and held it out to the weeping girl. "Here. You need to eat."

The sobs stopped after a moment, the smell of the porridge raising an audible groan from Ellese's belly as she raised her head and reached for the bowl. "Thank you," she said in a faint voice before commencing to attack the porridge with unladylike gusto.

"Slowly," Reva cautioned. "Eat too quick on an empty belly and you'll sicken."

The girl's gulps slowed a little and she nodded. "Did the Fief Lord kill him?" she asked when the bowl was almost empty.

"What makes you ask that?"

"Ihlsa said the Fief Lord would visit the Father's justice upon one who was . . . cursed."

"How was he cursed?"

"It happened when I was little. Before he was kind, as much as I can recall. But he fell ill, a brain-fever Mother said. I remember she took me into their room to say good-bye. He had fallen to a deep sleep and she said he would never wake up." She looked down at her porridge, scraped the last few dregs from the bowl, and put it aside. "But he did."

"And he was different?"

"Father wasn't Father anymore. He . . . hurt Mother. Every night. I could hear . . . Through the walls. For years he hurt her." Her face bunched and she began to weep again, tears streaking through the grime on her face.

"Did he ever . . . hurt you too?"

The girl's head sagged again, her continued sobs all the answer Reva needed. After a while she spoke again, forcing the words out. "He would keep us locked up when he was away, the house going to ruin around us. The day before he left he . . . He killed her. He tried to kill me too but Ihlsa took my hand and we ran. We ran to the woods and hid, for such a long time. When we came back the house was empty . . . apart from Mother. We went to the village but there were soldiers there, not the Realm Guard or the Fief Lord's men. They were doing terrible things. We ran back to the house and hid in the rafters. They came in and stole things, breaking what they didn't want, but they didn't find us. Ihlsa would go out and find food for us every few days. One day she didn't come back."

Reva watched her weep, head filled with images of a girl shivering in the dark as she huddled in a corner of a barn, clutching the carrot she had stolen the day before. She wouldn't eat it right away because there might be none tomorrow.

"He wasn't killed by the Fief Lord," she told Ellese. "He was killed by a soldier in service to the queen. If it's any comfort, his death was far from quick." She reached for her pack and extracted the scroll-case containing Alornis's sketch of the priest. "Did you ever see this man here?" she asked, holding it out to Ellese.

The girl's head rose and she wiped a threadbare sleeve across her face before reaching for the parchment, nodding as she glanced at the image. "Sometimes. Father called him his holy friend. I didn't like the way he looked at me. Neither did Mother, she would take me upstairs whenever he came. But one time I heard them arguing and went to the top of the stairs to listen. Father's voice was too soft to hear but I could tell it was different, not like him at all. The other man was louder, angry, he said something about years of wasted effort." Her eyes darted to Reva's face for a second. "He kept saying things about a girl, a girl of some importance I think."

"What did he say?"

"That her mar . . ." Ellese trailed off, fumbling over the word.

"Martyrdom?" Reva suggested.

"Yes. Martyrdom. He said the girl's martyrdom should wait upon her uncle's hand, when there were more eyes to see it."

Her uncle's hand. Reva grunted in grim amusement. *They thought Uncle Sentes would kill me. Vaelin's arrival made the Ally's creature change his plans. How much do they fear him?*

"Thank you." She took the sketch from the girl's hand and returned it to its case then rose, gathering up her things and strapping on her sword. "If there's anything you want to take, fetch it now."

The girl's head came up, eyes wide and fearful once more. "Where are you taking me?"

"To Alltor. Unless you'd rather stay here."

◆ ◆ ◆

"What happened to the walls?" Ellese asked three days later as they crested the hill east of Alltor. She sat atop the mare's back, Reva leading her by the reins. The girl's legs were too weak to allow her to walk any distance and the mare not strong enough to bear the weight of two. However, regular meals had done much to brighten her spirits, and provoke an unending torrent of questions.

"They were broken," Reva told her.

"By what?"

"Big stones launched by great engines."

"Where are they now?"

"They were burned."

"By who?"

"One by me, the other two by a load of pirates."

"Why?"

"They were very angry." Reva's eyes went to the river, swelled by winter rains, the dark waters concealing the boats that bore the dread engines along with the Father knew how many corpses. "And the queen asked them to."

"Is she very beautiful? Mother went to Varinshold once. She said Princess Lyrna was the most beautiful woman she ever saw."

At Warnsclave she had seen the queen with the orphans, the smile she showed them so different to the one she showed all others, a smile of real warmth and depthless compassion. Later the same day she received word of a band of outlaws preying on refugees to the west and ordered Lord Adal to hunt them down, sparing one in every three captured and these were to be flogged before being pressed into service as porters. She sent the North Guard commander off with a smile that day too.

"Yes," she told Ellese. "She is very beautiful."

She saw scaffolding on the walls as they progressed along the causeway to the main gate, clustered around the breaches where men could be seen at work hauling stone.

"Blessed Lady Reva!" the House Guard sergeant on the gate fell to one knee before her, his men following suit. "Thank the Father for your safe return."

"Just Lady will do," Reva told him, her eyes taking in the sight of the city. *Rubble all gone but still so many ruined houses.* "Or just Reva if it suits you."

The sergeant gave an appalled laugh as he backed away, head still lowered.

Ellese leaned forward in the saddle, speaking in a covert whisper, "Who are you?"

"I told you who I am." Reva's eyes lit on a burgeoning cluster of people in the streets beyond the gate, downing tools and starting in her direction, voices already raised in joyous welcome. "Sergeant, I believe I will require escort to the mansion."

◆ ◆ ◆

Veliss greeted her with a formal bow and a chaste embrace. "I've been away too long," Reva murmured, feeling the flush build on her cheeks.

"I heartily agree, my lady." Veliss turned to Ellese standing nearby and squirming a little under the scrutiny. The crowd beyond the mansion gate was large and loud with acclaim. News of Varinshold's liberation and the extinction of the Volarian army had spread swiftly to all corners of the Realm and Reva's arrival seemed to serve as a spark for a general victory celebration.

"This is Lady Ellese," Reva said, beckoning the girl forward. "Heir to Lord Brahdor's estate and now Ward of the Lady Governess. Find suitable rooms for her, if you would."

"Of course." Veliss extended a hand to Ellese, who came forward to take it after a moment's hesitation.

"I thought Lord Sentes ruled here," the girl said.

"He died." Reva glanced back at the still-cheering crowd. "Declare a holiday," she told Veliss. "Forever more this will be the Day of Victory. And hand out that hidden stock of wine you think I didn't know about."

◆　◆　◆

"The walls," she said later when they were alone in the library and Ellese tucked into a voluminous bed upstairs.

"To be repaired first by virtue of popular demand," Veliss explained. "The people don't feel safe without them. I've seen to the reconstruction of the larger dwellings when I can, but they wanted the walls repaired and who am I to deny them?"

"The treasury?"

"Surprisingly healthy. Volarian soldiers were rich in loot and I had Arentes set his men to gather up as much as they could before the Nilsaelins or sundry outlaws got to it. Even so, rebuilding a city is a costly business, and when that's done we have a half-ravaged fief to see to."

"The queen has made firm promises regarding the costs of reconstruction. Apparently the Northern Reaches now yields more gold than it does bluestone. It may take some months to arrive, however."

"Well, we shouldn't starve thanks to Lady Al Bera and Lord Darvus. It'll be a hard winter though." She sat next to Reva on the couch beside the fire, taking her hand, their fingers entwining with automatic intimacy.

"The Reader?" Reva asked, resting her head on her shoulder.

"Sends a messenger every week with stern advice on how best to govern the fief in accordance with the tenets of the Ten Books. Sometimes it's addressed to your grandfather, sometimes your great grandfather, and it rarely makes much sense. Last week he fell asleep during his own sermon, not that it matters since the cathedral was mostly empty."

"A good choice then."

"So it seems."

"Where is Arentes?"

"Off chasing down the last of the Sons and hopefully subduing a band of outlaws in the western dales. They're becoming a bit of a problem. War tends to succour only the vilest hearts."

"The Book of Reason, verse six." Reva smiled and pressed a kiss to her neck. "Are you becoming seduced by the love of the Father, Honoured Lady Counsel?"

"No." Veliss stroked a hand through her hair, even longer now as Reva couldn't recall the last time she had cut it. "I've only ever been seduced once. And I find it more than enough."

Reva tensed in anticipation of the response to her next words, feeling a great temptation to leave it until the next morning but knowing the reaction would be even worse if she did. "Tomorrow I will call a general assembly in the square, where I will read out the queen's Edict of Conscription."

Veliss's hand withdrew from her hair, her eyes wary. "Conscription?"

"The queen builds an even greater army, and a fleet to carry it to Volarian shores."

Veliss rose from the couch, moving to the fireplace, her hand gripping the mantel. "This war is won."

"No, it is not."

"Am I to take it, my Lady Governess, that you will sail with the queen and her mighty fleet?"

Reva resisted the urge to reach out to her, seeing the whiteness of her knuckles on the mantel. "Yes."

Veliss shook her head. "This is madness. Her father, for all his myriad schemes, would never have dreamt of such folly."

"We need to stop them coming back. This is the only way."

"Lord Al Sorna's words, or yours?"

"We are of the same mind."

"Or are you just hungry for another war? I *can* see it, you know. The way you chafe with impatience to be gone when you're here, how bored you are by this place, by me."

Though the words were softly spoken they held enough truth to make

Reva flinch. "I will never be bored by you. If I seem impatient it's because I'm not made for governance. And believe me or no, I have seen enough of war. But this has to be done, and I require your help to see it done right."

"What's conscription?"

Reva turned to find Ellese standing at the library door, wrapped in a blanket and rubbing her eyes. "Couldn't sleep?"

The girl nodded and Reva patted the couch next to her, Ellese trotting over to sit beside her. "I had a dream," she said. "Father was alive again, looking for me in our house."

"Just a dream," Reva told her, smoothing back the now-unmatted hair from her forehead. "Dreams can't hurt you."

Ellese's gaze moved to Veliss, still standing at the fireplace, back stiff and eyes averted. "What's conscription?"

Veliss's shoulders slumped and she gave the girl a weary smile. "The worst of things, love. A hard sell."

◆　◆　◆

"All men of sound health between the ages of seventeen and forty-five are to report to Alltor by the last day of the month of Interlasur, bringing with them any bows or other weapons in their possession. Any childless woman of the same age may also volunteer her service. All who serve will be paid at the same rate as the Realm Guard and will receive a pension for the rest of their lives at the conclusion of the war, this pension to be paid to the widow or surviving children of any who sacrifice their lives in this cause."

Reva fell silent, handing the scroll to Veliss and trying not to make her scrutiny of the crowd too obvious. Veliss had placed a wooden crate on the topmost of the Cathedral steps, giving her a complete view of the throng, some five thousand people in the square itself with more crowding the ruins beyond. There was some murmuring, clear surprise showing amidst the sea of faces before her, but for the most part they were silent, the predominant expression one of expectation. *They await the Blessed Lady's word,* she thought, keeping the sour grimace from her face.

"We have suffered much," she told them. "Our trials have been many and our struggle long. I wish I came before you with news of peace, I wish I came to tell you our battles are over and we can at last rest, but that would make me a liar. You trusted my word when the enemy was at our walls and I beg you to trust me again now." She paused, gathering strength, her own words loud in her head . . . *that would make me a liar . . .*

"And trust that I have heard the Father's voice." She put all the force she could muster into the words, hearing them echo from the walls of this wasted city. "And he will permit no turning from this path. Many of you will have heard of the so-called Eleventh Book. I tell you now that book is a lie, worthy only of your scorn. But the Father has ordained there will be a new book, the Book of Justice, written by the Father's own hand with us as his mighty instrument!"

It wasn't a cheer, more a roar, instant and savage, rising from the throat of every soul present. There was hate on their faces now, every head no doubt filled with ugly memories of fallen loved ones and burning homes, a hatred permitted free rein by the Blessed Lady who spoke with the Father's voice. *We drowned in their blood,* Reva thought as the sound washed over her. *And still it wasn't enough.*

She stepped down from the crate, pausing at the sight of Ellese burying her head in Veliss's skirts, small face tensed with fearful tears as she tried to hide from the crowd's roar. Reva knelt beside her and wiped the wetness from her face. "It's all right," she said. "They're just happy to see me."

◆ ◆ ◆

She waited two days for Arentes to return, greeting the old guard commander at the gates with a warm embrace. "Forgiven me yet, my lord?"

"My lady commands and I follow," he replied, his tone a little stiff though she could detect the vestiges of a smile behind his moustache. "Besides," he went on, gesturing at the line of shackled men arrayed on the causeway, "securing your enemies is my sacred charge, and not one I'll shirk for any glory."

"There was no glory to earn. Just more blood." Her eyes tracked over the captives, about twenty emaciated men in varying states of raggedness, some fearful and sagging with exhaustion, others glaring at her in sullen defiance. "The Sons."

"Plus a few outlaws. Thought it best to hang them in front of the people, make an example."

"Unless they've raped or murdered I'll send them to the queen. She's keen to make use of all men, even those of meanest worth."

"Word of the edict flew far and wide. Not all were glad to hear it."

"They will when they've heard the Father's word. I'm afraid I'll need you and your men on the morrow, it's time I saw my fief in full."

He gave a precise bow. "Of course, my lady." He turned a baleful eye on the prisoners. "What do you want done with the Sons?"

"Lady Veliss will question them. When I return we'll see justice done."

◆ ◆ ◆

Ellese had clung to her and cried again, begging to be allowed to come. Reva had been firm in ordering her to remain with Veliss, firmer than necessary judging by the increased pitch of the girl's wails. "Motherhood has a price," Veliss told her, holding Ellese to her bodice.

I'm not her mother, Reva had stopped herself saying, crouching to push the hair back from Ellese's eyes. "Mind Lady Veliss well and stay at your lessons. I'll be back soon enough."

She let Arentes choose their route, acceding to his greater knowledge of the fief. "West then south I think, my lady," he advised. "Westerners are the least godly folk in Cumbrael so we may as well get the hardest task done first."

There was plenty of evidence of Volarian activity to the west, a procession of ruined villages and the occasional pile of rotting corpses amidst the vineyards. In each instance Reva ordered a halt to have them buried, the words spoken by the only priest to accompany them, a spindly fellow of middling years chosen for his renowned courage during the siege and taciturn nature. She found herself greatly disinclined towards sermons these days. *The quiet priest is the good priest,* she quipped to herself, wondering if she should write it down.

The devastation abated the farther west they went, disappearing altogether in the hill country on the Nilsaelin border. She knew from Veliss this was one of Cumbrael's more prosperous regions, the wine being of the finest quality and the people noted for gay celebrations and lax adherence to the Ten Books. Arentes guided her to the largest town in the region, essentially a sprawling hill-fort ringed by impressive walls that traced the line of the surrounding vine-covered slopes in an uninterrupted ribbon of stone.

"Easy to see why the Volarians left it alone," Arentes commented as they rode up to the gates.

"They'd have gotten to it in time," Reva said. She expected some difficulty at the gates—it was quite possible these people had no notion as to who she was after all—however she found the town guard already drawn up in ranks and the gates standing open. A stout man in a long robe was on both knees beneath the gate arch, arms spread in supplication.

"Lord Mentari, the town factor," Arentes explained. "Owns most of the vineyards for miles around. He had great regard for your grandfather."

"But not so my uncle?" Reva asked.

"Your uncle was much more punctilious when it came to the collection of taxes, and less inclined to favouring old friends."

"Lucky it is then, that I only have new friends."

"Blessed Lady!" Lord Mentari clasped his hands together as she approached, dismounting to cast her gaze around the city, finding it strange to see so many intact buildings after weeks of viewing ruins. "You bring the Father's word to our unworthy ears."

Reva frowned down at the man's wide-eyed countenance, expecting to see some glimmer of calculation there but instead his awe appeared completely genuine. "All ears are worthy of the Father's word," she told him. "But he doesn't require you to kneel, and neither do I."

The stout lord got to his feet, though his back remained at a servile stoop. "The tale of your victory is already legend," he gushed. "The gratitude of our humble home knows no bounds."

"I'm glad to hear it, my lord." She hefted the scroll-case containing the queen's edict. "For I bring word of how it can be expressed."

It took two days to gather the people from the surrounding country to hear the Blessed Lady's words, two days suffering through the feast Mentari organised in her honour and a round of petitions, by far her least favourite occupation. She gave judgement in only the most clear-cut cases and had Arentes note the others for dispatch to Veliss. Despite the apparent comfort and security enjoyed by these people the petitions did give an insight into the fact that war didn't have to visit your doorstep to cause ill. Complaints abounded of refugees from the east stealing produce and livestock or occupying land they didn't own, and whilst Tokrev's armies might not have marched here, his slavers certainly had; weeping mothers telling of sons and daughters stolen in raids. For all their sorrow, Reva took a grim comfort from these tales, her task made easier by the Volarians' talent for birthing hate in every soul they touched.

She read the edict on the evening of the second day, standing on the porch of Mentari's house as people crowded the space below, a broad avenue surrounding an elegant fountain of bronze. This time the murmuring was louder when she finished, and the expressions of the crowd not so rapt. However, despite the evident discomfort, there was no open dissent or shouts of disapproval and plenty of godly souls to voice their approval as the Blessed Lady told her lie.

"An eleventh book," Lord Mentari breathed as she stepped down, the crowd still cheering. "To think I would live to see such a thing."

"We live in changing times, my lord." Reva accepted the book Arentes handed to her and checked the notes Veliss had provided on this region. "My honoured advisor calculates your quota as a minimum of two thousand men of fighting age, accounting for recent troubles and the census compiled five years ago. I'm sure the Father will smile upon you should it be exceeded."

◆ ◆ ◆

Touring the entire fief took the best part of a month, town after town, village after village, some swollen with refugees, others nearly empty as many of the occupants had fled in advance of the expected Volarian onslaught. She found her lie most readily welcomed in those places rich in the dispossessed, many of whom had firsthand experience of the enemy's nature. Even in places where none had been scathed by the war, there were still plenty of willing ears keen to hear the Blessed Lady's words, though not all were so open to the Father's message.

"Got four sons and the queen wants three of them," said a burly woman in a village in the south-western riverlands. People here were renowned for their hardiness, scratching a living from the eel-pots with which they harvested the myriad waterways surrounding their homes, settlements often limited to no more than a few houses and rarely accompanied by a church. The woman glared at Reva as the assembled villagers gave a murmur of agreement, though some were clearly intimidated by Arentes and his fifty guardsmen. The glaring woman, however, paid them no heed at all. "How's a family s'posed to feed itself with no hands to work the boats and haul the pots?"

"No one will go hungry," Reva assured her. "Any additional food required will be provided by House Mustor and the queen at no charge."

"Heard promises from your house before," the woman replied. "When my husband got dragged off to get his throat cut by those Asraelin bastards. Now you want us to fight for them."

"This fief was saved by Asraelin hands," Reva said. "And Nilsaelins, folk from the Northern Reaches, the Seordah and the Eorhil. At Varinshold I fought alongside Meldeneans and Renfaelins. The old age is dead, now we fight for each other."

The woman pointed a finger at Reva, her voice rising to an angry growl. "You fight for them, girl. I don't know them, never seen these . . . Volarans you talk of, and any liar can claim to talk with the Father's voice."

The guardsmen immediately snapped to attention, their sergeant stepping forward with sword half-drawn before Reva barked at him to halt. "She speaks blasphemy and treason, my lady," the sergeant said, face rigid with fury as he glared at the woman in the crowd, now standing alone as her fellow villagers moved back, any former sympathy abruptly forgotten. Despite the lack of support the woman stood her ground, glaring at Reva with no sign of fear or regret on her weathered features as the sergeant spoke on, "You were not at Alltor. You did not see what the Blessed Lady did for us. But for her, you, your sons and this village would now be nothing but ash and bone. You owe her everything, as do we all."

The woman's gaze didn't shift from Reva. "Then you'd best hang me, lady. For my sons aren't yours to take, Father's word or no."

Reva's eyes scanned the crowd, picking out three young men near the back, two of them clearly cowed by the circumstance, heads lowered and no doubt praying for the confrontation to end, but the tallest stood regarding the burly woman with a grim resentment.

"Can your sons not speak for themselves?" Reva asked he woman. "Both the Ten Books and Fief Law decree manhood at age seventeen. If your sons are of age, let them make the choice."

"My sons know their duty . . ." the woman began but trailed off as the taller of the three young men held up his hand and pushed his way through the crowd.

"Allern Varesh, my lady," he said with a bow. "I offer my service in accordance with the Queen's Edict."

"Stop that!" the woman growled, stepping forward to aim a cuff at the young man's head before glowering at Reva once again. "He's not yours to take!"

Reva was about to simply ignore her and thank the young man for his loyalty but paused as she saw the wetness in the woman's eyes, how she moved protectively in front of her son. Reva stepped down from the cart, coming forward to stand in front of the woman. "Your name?"

The woman clenched her teeth and wiped her eyes with thick fingers. "Realla Varesh."

"You have lost much, Realla Varesh. And it pains me to ask for more." She pointed at the still-kneeling Allern. "Therefore, in recognition of your sacrifice the quota for this village will be considered fully met by this man's service."

The woman sagged, hands going to her face. From the shocked reaction of her son and the crowd Reva surmised it was probably the first time any living soul had seen her weep. "Lord Arentes," Reva said.

"My lady!"

"This young man has sufficient height for a guardsman, wouldn't you say?"

Arentes gave Allern a brief look of appraisal. "Just about, my lady."

"Very well. Allern Varesh, you are hereby inducted into the House Guard of Lady Governess Reva Mustor." She glanced again at the man's sobbing mother. "You have an hour to say your farewells. Lord Arentes will find you a horse."

◆ ◆ ◆

She returned to Alltor with five hundred men and fifty women in tow, all volunteers willing to march at the Blessed Lady's command. There could have been a thousand of them but they had neither the provisions or packhorses to supply so many. The lands south of Alltor had been richest in recruits and willing ears for her lie, having suffered much at the hands of Volarian raiding parties. They had fought a minor war of their own among the Cold Iron's forested banks and tributaries and were rich in captured weapons. According to Arentes the region had always been the heartland of Cumbraelin archery, the first longbows being hewn from the yews that proliferated in the thick forest. In the face of the Volarian threat long-defunct companies, once the backbone of Cumbraelin military strength, had re-formed under veteran captains, fighting a deadly game of chase among the trees for months until Alltor's relief.

Reva ordered the companies to stay in formation and gather more strength before mustering at Alltor in the spring. For all the fierceness of their commitment she found them a disconcerting lot, hard-eyed and grim of aspect, the many rotting bodies of captured Volarians hanging in the forest evidence of a lust for vengeance far from sated. *What will they wreak when we sail the ocean?* she wondered, searching her memory in vain for a passage in any of the Ten Books that gave succour to vengeful thoughts.

Ellese greeted her with a fierce joy, thin arms tight around her waist as she complained of Veliss's endless lessons. "She makes me read every morning and every night. And write too."

"Skills of great importance," Reva told her, gently undoing her arms. "Still, I have a few to teach you too, in time."

Ellese's small face frowned up at her, the gauntness now gone though she retained a slightly sunken look to her eyes. "What skills?"

"The bow and the knife. The sword too when you get older. Only if you want to."

"I want to." She gave an excited jump, taking Reva's hand and dragging her towards the mansion. "Teach me now!"

Reva caught the grave expression on Veliss's face and hauled the girl to a halt. "Tomorrow," she said. "I have another task today."

◆ ◆ ◆

"Still no name for me?"

The broken-nosed priest cast a single, tired glance at her and shook his head. They were lined up on the causeway, twelve men in threadbare clothing, besmirched from their captivity in the mansion's cellars, some swaying a little as the effects of Veliss's various herbal concoctions could linger for days. The notes she had accrued during the interrogations were fulsome, near five hundred pages of names, dates, meetings, murders, enough to see the Church of the World Father revealed as a nest of traitors from Reader to Bishop, perhaps enough to shatter it completely.

"He really thought he could do it?" Reva asked the nameless priest. "Bring down House Mustor and rule the fief in the Father's name?"

The priest raised his head, swallowing as he mustered his courage. "A holy endeavour, blessed by the Father."

"Blessings spoken by a wretch in service to a creature of the Dark." Reva stepped back, raising her voice and casting her gaze across each face. "You are fools, so steeped in the Ten Books you can't even see the truth they hold. The Father does not bless deception and murder, the Father does not offer succour to those who would torment children to vile ends."

She fell silent, feeling it build again, the same rage that had seized her during the siege, the fury that had seen her slit the throats of slavers and cut the heads from prisoners. The nameless priest shuddered, swallowing again as he fought down terror-born vomit. Arentes stood behind the shackled line with a full company of House Guard, swords drawn, each of them glaring at the traitors with an expression of grim hunger.

We are all killers now, she remembered. *Bathed in blood with more to come.* Her gaze lit upon a familiar figure at the end of the line, a wiry man, unlike the others in his willingness to meet her gaze, his visage oddly reverent. *Shindall,* she recalled. The innkeeper who had set her on the road to the High Keep. *Seeing your face is the only thanks I'll ever need.*

Reva took the scroll tucked into her belt, holding it up so they could see the seal and the somewhat unsteady signature. "By order of the Holy Reader you are all named as ex-communicants from the Church of the World Father. You are forbidden from reading or reciting any of the Ten Books as you have proved yourselves unworthy of the Father's love." She looked once again at the broken-nosed priest. "And I know your name since the Father doesn't want it, Master Jorent."

She watched them close their eyes, heads bowing, some whispering prayers, one or two weeping with stains on their trews, much like the Volarian prisoners before being led to the block, though they hadn't prayed, only begged.

"Lord Arentes," Reva said. "Remove the shackles. Let them go."

◆   ◆   ◆

Veliss hadn't voiced any rebuke, only puzzlement. "They plotted against your house once, what's to stop them doing so again?"

"A plot requires concealment, hidden names, hidden faces. Now they are denied the shadows."

"And you have denied yourself justice."

"No, only revenge. The Father has ever been clear they are not the same thing."

The various contingents of conscripts began arriving a month later, even though the rapidly descending winter did much to discourage marching. With the ever-deepening cold Reva ordered work on the walls stopped and all hands put to repairing the city proper, tents and oilskins to be replaced with walls and tiled roofs. Rationing was resumed as the snows blocked the passes through the mountains to Nilsael and halted further supply from the southern shore.

Reva began each day with Ellese's lessons, starting with the knife, finding a long-bladed dirk that suited the girl's small grip. For all her enthusiasm she was a clumsy student, given to frequent falls and scraped knees, though, unlike every other chore she was put to, her lessons with Reva never provoked tears, but her passion for questions remained unabated.

"Were you my age when you learned to do this?"

"I started younger. Don't jump when you thrust, it'll leave you unbalanced."

"Who taught you?"

"A very bad man."

"Why was he bad?"

"He wanted me to do bad things."

"What bad things?"

"Too many to list. Watch me, not your feet."

She left her to practice on the lawn and joined Veliss on the veranda, wrapped in furs against the frosty air and holding a sealed scroll. "It's come then?"

Veliss nodded, handing her the scroll, though her gaze was still on Ellese, dancing her clumsy dance on the lawn. "She's not really suited to this."

"She'll learn, from both of us."

"Why did you take her in? You could have found a decent home for her elsewhere. Cumbrael is rich in bereaved mothers hungry for children."

Reva glanced back at Ellese as she parried a thrust from an invisible enemy. "She didn't run. When I went into her house she tried to stab me, and when I took her knife away she still didn't run." She turned back to Veliss. "I would appreciate it if you would see to the articles of adoption."

"You're sure? She's so young."

"She's of noble birth and keen mind, with you to guide her she'll do very well. And we need to secure the future."

Veliss's eyes went to the scroll, lingering on the queen's seal. "I have never asked you for a promise. But I ask one now. Whatever awaits you across the ocean, promise you will stay alive and come back to me."

Reva unfurled the scroll, finding it penned in the queen's own hand, rich in warm regard and appreciation for her diligent enforcement of the edict, ending with a politely phrased order to bring her forces to South Tower by the last day of Illnasur. *When winter will not have ended,* Reva realised. *She intends to sail before the onset of spring.*

"Reva," Veliss said in a choked whisper.

Reva took her hand and pressed a kiss to her cheek, voicing another lie. "I promise."

CHAPTER FIVE

Vaelin

Vaelin had once spent a winter at the Skellan Pass attempting to combat an upsurge in Lonak raids. Then it had been busy with brothers and Wolfrunners, a stark contrast to the silent walls and turrets he saw now, bereft of brothers to greet them as they approached the squat tower at the mouth of the pass. He knew Sollis had abandoned it with good reason, the Lonak having agreed peace and the invasion requiring every hand he could muster, but still the emptiness of the Realm's great northern shield was disconcerting, a measure of how much had changed in so short a time.

"My people would have rejoiced at such a sight once," Kiral said, no doubt sensing his feelings. "Now even they find it a grim omen."

Vaelin turned as Lord Marshal Orven reined to a halt at his side, his fifty men all that remained of the Queen's Mounted Guard. "Post guards. We'll rest here tonight."

He spent the night in the tower with Kiral and the Gifted from Nehrin's Point, all of whom had opted to accompany him rather than join the queen's impending voyage across the Boraelin. The queen herself had blessed their endeavour with well-chosen words and a fine smile, both of which belied her reaction when he had related his intention in private.

"You want to go trekking across the northern ice floes in the middle of winter?" She had called him to her rooms at the palace and the hour was late. Although, judging by the laughter seeping through the door, some of the children were still awake. They had grown steadily in number since the city's liberation until there were near two hundred orphans crowding this wing of the palace, all formally recognised as Wards of the Crown under the Queen's

Word. Lyrna's rooms were mostly bare of finery, filled with books and a selection of Brother Harlick's scrolls, her desk holding several neat piles of notes in her precise script. The space was dimly lit by a single lamp and the glow from the fire, leaving half her features in shadow as she fixed him with a frown of wary bemusement, as if waiting for him to conclude a poor joke.

"Kiral's song will be our guide," he replied. "She speaks with the Mahlessa's blessing, I know you trust her word."

"I trust the Mahlessa to act only in the interests of the Lonak. If it suited her purpose to set us on a fool's errand, I've no doubt she would do so." Her frown softened and she reached for a piece of parchment on the desk, holding it up to the light. He recognised it as Alornis's work—the lines were too precise and perfect for another hand—but the subject was new, a semicircular design of some sort, the shape formed from an intricate pattern of straight lines.

"Your sister proposes a radical departure from traditional methods of ship construction," Lyrna said. "An inner hull formed of interconnected short beams describing a curve, essentially a practical application of Lervial's concept of tangential arcs, though she claims never to have read it. If we adopt her approach, unskilled hands can be put to work crafting thousands of straight beams, saving months of skilled labour."

"Then why not do so?"

"Because it's never been done before. No ship has ever been built along such lines. Just as, insofar as I can recall from any history I have ever read, no explorer has successfully journeyed across the ice floes, not even in the height of summer."

"Kiral trusts her song, and I trust her."

"This man Erlin is so important?"

"I believe so. One so long-lived will possess knowledge far more valuable than anything in Harlick's scrolls. And the legend says he was denied the Beyond, which may mean he has glimpsed it, as I have. But perhaps he saw more than I did."

Lyrna's brow furrowed once more in remembrance. "Arendil once told me a story about Kerlis, claiming his uncle had met him years ago. He said he had been cursed to live forever for refusing to join with the Departed. So he spent his endless days circling the earth in search of one who has the means to kill him, one who would be born to the Gifted of this land." She sighed a weary laugh. "All just tales, Vaelin. You can't expect me to sanction this course, to send my Battle Lord to die in the frozen wastes, on the basis of legend."

"To our cost, we have both learned not all legends are bereft of truth." He straightened, drawing breath to speak in formal tones but she held up a hand to stop him.

"Spare me the offer of resignation, please. I may command every other soul in this Realm, but I'll not pretend to do so with you."

"My thanks, Highness. I propose Count Marven be appointed Battle Lord in my place."

"Very well. How many troops will you take?"

"None. Just myself and Kiral."

She shook her head. "That is unacceptable. The Gifted from the Reaches and Lord Orven's company will escort you."

"Orven's wife is with child. I'll not ask him to follow such a hazardous course . . ."

"But I will, my lord. Orven is a soldier and knows his duty, happy news or no."

He saw the implacable set of her face and nodded. "As you wish, Highness. The other matter we discussed?"

Her hands twitched on the desk as her face hardened yet further. "You ask much of me, Vaelin."

"He was not responsible . . ."

"I know. But the sight of my brother's murder does not easily fade."

"If it's punishment you desire, it seems the course I have proposed should provide it in ample measure."

She met his gaze, the pale lines on her forehead standing out in the firelight, her voice flat with certainty. "I desire but one thing, my lord; a secure future for this Realm. I'll send your brother across the ocean to be the harbinger of my coming, but do not ask me to forgive. I find such sentiment no longer within my grasp."

Had Janus had his way, we would be married now, Vaelin reflected. He had taken leave of the others and climbed to the top of the tower, cloak wrapped tight and breath misting as he stared at the pregnant darkness beyond the pass. *Would our children have been beautiful or terrible? Or both, like her.*

There was a faint shift in the wind gusting across the tower, carrying a slight scent: mingled woodsmoke and sweat. "I know you're there," Vaelin said, not turning from the view.

Lorkan gave a wry laugh as he appeared at his side, unruly hair tumbling across his frost-pale face. "My lord's gift has returned then?"

"There are other senses than sight." He let Lorkan's hesitant fidgeting continue for several moments before speaking again. "I assume you come with a request?"

"Indeed, my lord." Lorkan rubbed his hands together, eyes averted, attempting a jovial tone. "It, ah, seems to me, my lord, this grand crusade of ours has provided all the excitement I could wish for. Proud as I am of my service, which I think you would agree, has been valuable, the time has come for me to seek adventure in warmer climes."

"You wish to be released."

Lorkan inclined his head with a smile. "I do."

"Very well. Given your gift I could hardly compel you to come in any case."

"My thanks, my lord." He lingered, fidgeting some more.

"What is it?" Vaelin demanded in a weary sigh.

"Cara, my lord."

"She also wishes to be released?"

"No, she is firm in her determination to follow you. However, if you were to order her to leave . . ."

Vaelin turned away from him. "No."

Lorkan's tone grew harder. "She is little more than a child . . ."

"With a woman's heart and a great gift. She is welcome in my company and I am proud to have her loyalty." He went to the stairwell in the centre of the roof. "You can keep your horse, weapons, and any booty gathered during the campaign, but please be gone before sunrise."

"I can't!" Lorkan was glaring at him now, his shout ringing through the pass. "You know I can't leave without her."

Vaelin cast a glance back at the young Gifted, face tense with anger and a little fear, his stance poised as he no doubt prepared to blink out of sight. "I know that sometimes life gives us nothing but hard choices," Vaelin told him before starting down the stairs. "If you're not here come the morning, I'll be sure to explain your absence to Cara."

◆ ◆ ◆

They were five miles beyond the pass the next day when Kiral abruptly reined her pony to a halt, her eyes turning towards the west, features drawn in sharp scrutiny. "Trouble?" Vaelin asked her.

She narrowed her eyes, frowning in confusion. "Something . . . Some-one new."

"Another song?"

She shook her head. "Not a singer, and my song holds no warning. But he calls to me."

"From where?"

Her face took on a sudden wariness, the first sign of fear he had seen her exhibit. "The Fallen City."

Vaelin nodded, turning and beckoning to Orven. "I require five men, my lord. Make camp in the valley ahead and await our return." He raised his voice, addressing a somewhat sullen figure farther back along the column. "Master Lorkan! Please join us."

It was a two-day trek to the city, the journey shortened by Kiral's intimate knowledge of the mountains. The ruins were much as he remembered, though now he felt none of the oppressive weight that had plagued him during his last visit here, although both Kiral and Lorkan enjoyed no such immunity.

"Faith, this is worse than the forest." Lorkan grimaced and sagged in his saddle, his complexion taking on a pale hue.

"Never have I come so close before," Kiral said, her unease clear in the rigid set of her shoulders. "This is no place for the living."

"Master Lorkan?" Vaelin said, favouring the youth with an expectant smile and nodding at the ruins. After a long moment's hesitation Lorkan inclined his head and climbed down from his horse. He took a deep breath and started for the city at a steady walk, slipping into the air after a few steps and drawing a murmur of disquiet from the guardsmen.

"Whoever waits in there will see him," Kiral advised.

"I know," Vaelin replied.

"Then why send him?"

"What is life without an occasional amusement?"

They sat surveying the silent ruins for only a few more moments before the shout came, a shrill exclamation of alarm echoing from the tumbled stones. Kiral unlimbered her bow and the guardsmen fanned out, swords at the ready as Lorkan burst into view at the city's edge, cloak trailing behind him as he pelted in their direction, eyes wide with unabashed terror. The reason for his flight soon became apparent, a large brown shape lumbering in pursuit, mouth wide and teeth bared in a challenging roar.

"Didn't know they grew so large," Vaelin commented. The bear must have stood perhaps five feet tall at the shoulder, meaning its full height would be nearer ten. Although its pursuit of Lorkan appeared laboured, it covered the ground with deceptive speed thanks to the length of its stride.

"Kill it, for Faith's sake!" Lorkan yelled, sprinting towards them, the bear now only a few strides behind.

"Don't!" Vaelin said to Kiral as she raised her bow, his eyes picking out a figure among the ruins, small and familiar with another at its side, only slightly taller and holding aloft a long stick of some kind. The bear skidded to an abrupt halt, scattering gravel, a mournful growl issuing from its snout. It bounced on its forelegs, claws digging into the rocky ground, continuing to stare in challenge at Lorkan who was now on all fours behind one of the guardsmen, panting and clearly on the verge of losing his breakfast.

Scar, like the other horses, had begun to rear at the sight of the bear and was now on the verge of outright panic, tossing his head in protest as Vaelin hauled on the reins. "It's all right," he said, dismounting to smooth a hand along the animal's flank. "He won't hurt you."

The bear snorted again, shaking its great head from side to side as if gathering strength for another charge, but then stiffened, became near as still as a statue. "He still young." A small, fur-clad man holding a bone as long as a staff appeared at the bear's side, his voice holding a note of apology. "Friend and enemy smell same."

"Wise Bear!" Vaelin came forward to clasp hands with the shaman, heartened by the strength of his grip. "You are far from the Reaches."

"You go on the ice," Wise Bear replied with a shrug. "I show you how."

"He was very insistent." Dahrena stood a short distance away, smiling tightly. "Could hardly let him come alone."

Vaelin went to her, pulling her close, the realisation of how much he had missed her provoking a harsh ache. *I will send her back,* he thought, knowing himself a liar. *In the morning I will send her back.*

◆ ◆ ◆

They shared a meal of spitted goat, apparently the victim of the great brown bear's hunting skill judging by the deep rents in the carcass. "Iron Claw brings good meat," Wise Bear said. "Only keeps insides for himself."

When the meal was done Vaelin followed the old shaman as he toured the ruins, peering at the shattered statuary and occasionally jabbing his bone-staff at weed-covered rubble. The bear roamed nearby, displaying equal scrutiny as he poked his large snout into the various nooks and crannies, sometimes using his dagger-like claws to pull the stones apart.

"Iron Claw wants bugs," Wise Bear explained. "Bear belly never full."

"How did you know to come here?" Vaelin asked him.

Wise Bear gave him a quizzical look, as if the answer were obvious, raising his eyebrows when Vaelin failed to discern his meaning. "Big . . ." He frowned, fumbling for the right words. "Big power, big . . ." He made a wide, flailing gesture with his arms, blowing air through his lips.

"Disturbance?" Vaelin asked, adding, "Storm?" at the shaman's blank gaze.

"Storm, yes, big storm in the . . . sea. Power sea."

Power sea. He sees the Dark as a sea of power. "You can see the power sea?"

Wise Bear barked a laugh. "None can see it all. Just feel storms, feel those touching it, hear songs if they sing. Felt the storm brewing, heard the girl's song, followed it here with Flies High Woman." His frown returned as they came to the great stone head Vaelin recalled from his first visit here, the bearded man with a troubled brow.

"The storm is coming here?" Vaelin asked, watching him tentatively touch the tip of his staff to the stone face.

"Storm came here before." Wise Bear lowered his staff to place a hand on the bearded man's forehead, closing his eyes. "Now just echo."

"Of what?"

"What was, what will be." The shaman removed his hand from the stone head, sadness dominating his wrinkled face.

"I thought he might be a king, a chief," Vaelin said but Wise Bear shook his head.

"No, wise man, keeper of many stories."

"But not wise enough to stop the city falling?"

"Some things nothing can stop. He build this place, shamans filled stone with power to sing its song."

Filled stone with power? Vaelin recalled Wisdom's tale of how she had gained her name, the stone given to her by the shade of Nersus Sil Nin, and she but a memory preserved in the stones in the Martishe and the Great Northern Forest. "They could place their memories in stone?" he asked.

Wise Bear nodded. "More than . . . memory. Feeling." He raised his staff and swept it slowly around, tracking over the remnants of a city that must once have been wondrous. "This place, filled with power."

He moved on, eyes bright with scrutiny, scanning the ruins with a near-predatory intensity. Vaelin followed him through the maze of rubble, past the rare intact building Brother Harlick had fancied a library and onto what appeared to have been some kind of raised platform. Vaelin judged it might have stood ten feet high when intact, but the supporting pillars were shattered and the stone surface had tumbled to be cracked from end to end. Wise Bear paused, his limbs betraying a spasm of discomfort before he stepped onto the platform, moving to the centre where he touched his staff to the bare stone.

"Something here," he said. "Something . . . black."

Vaelin found he didn't like the confusion he saw on the shaman's face, his features sagging a little, making him seem even more aged. "Something black?" he prompted as the old man crouched to touch a tentative hand to the stone. "You mean Dark? Something that had the power?"

"Black," Wise Bear stated in an emphatic tone before straightening. "Gone now, far away. Taken."

"By who?"

Wise Bear turned, meeting Vaelin's gaze. "You know," he said. "We go across ice to find him."

◆　◆　◆

"I left Ultin in charge," Dahrena said, settling next to him and pulling the furs across them both. "I doubt he relished the honour but there wasn't anyone else halfway capable."

"The gold?" Vaelin enquired.

"The first shipload should dock in Frostport within the month, much to Lord Darvus's delight I'm sure."

"He won't be the first or the last to profit from war." He paused, enjoying the feel of her pressed against him, regretting the necessity for his next words. However, she evidently read his intent and spoke first.

"I'm not leaving." She raised her head to press a kiss to his lips then settled back. "How is Alornis?"

He recalled Alornis's rigid face the morning he left, her valiant attempt at holding back the tears, falling to ruin as she collapsed against him, only drawing back at Lyrna's gentle but insistent tug. His final glimpse of her lingered like a guilty stain, her head on Lyrna's shoulder as she turned her face, refusing to watch him ride away. "She does good service in the queen's cause," he told Dahrena. "Her talents are even greater than we knew."

She shifted a little, turning her gaze to the sky, clear of cloud and offering a fine view of the stars. "It's faded," she murmured. He knew the star she spoke of; Avenshura, from which Sanesh Poltar had taken his Eorhil name. *It's said no wars can be fought under the light it brings.* Now it was just a small pinprick of light amongst many others.

"We'll see it shine again," he told her. "We just have to live a very long time."

She turned back to him, her voice sombre. "I do not like this place."

"Terrible things were done here once. Wise Bear says the stone carries the memory."

"Not the city. The mountains, the home of the people who birthed me . . ." She trailed off but he knew the words she left unsaid.

"And killed your husband."

Her head moved in a faint nod.

"What was his name?"

"His people named him Leordah Nil Usril, Lives in Dreams. I just called him Usril. The Seordah thought him a quiet soul, seldom given to speech and often lost in thought. He rarely joined war parties against the Lonak though in the battle with the Horde he had proved himself brave and skillful. One summer the Lonak came in larger numbers than usual, raiding deeper than they had before. I was visiting with my father when word came of the raid. I flew to the forest, finding his body amongst many others, a dead Lonak lay atop him. I remember how peaceful they looked, as if they had fallen asleep together. I searched far and wide for his soul, but he was at least a day gone."

She fell silent, her breath soft on his chest as he held her even tighter. When she spoke again her voice was barely above a whisper and coloured with suppressed fear, "I did my best to die that day, Vaelin. I hung above the forest and watched over his body, knowing my own would soon lose its warmth, hoping I could join his endless hunt in the shadows . . . Father brought me back, somehow I heard his voice pleading with me to return. I barely felt the chill when I slipped back into my body, in truth for weeks I barely felt anything. Then I went to the stone and sought counsel with Nersus Sil Nin. She told me something, something I didn't want to believe."

She rose, bringing her face level with his, staring into his eyes. "She told me I had much still to do. That great trials lay ahead and a lifetime of grief was not a luxury I would be permitted. And she said she had once gifted a Seordah name to a man, a man I would come to love." She gave a laugh, her breath soft on his lips. "I thought she was mad. I was wrong."

◆ ◆ ◆

They returned to Orven's company two days later, finding them all mounted and drawn up in battle formation. The reason was easily found, at least a hundred Lonak on their stout ponies plainly visible on the crest of a hill a quarter mile to the north.

"They appeared this morning, my lord," Orven reported as Vaelin rode up, greeting Dahrena with a surprised bow. "Very good to see you again, my lady."

"My lord. I hear congratulations are in order."

Orven gave a small grin before casting a wary glance at the Lonak. "I fear they'll have to wait."

Vaelin raised an eyebrow at Kiral who looked upon her fellow Lonak with steady gaze. "They come at the Mahlessa's bidding, though not without misgivings."

"Then we'd best say hello." He told Dahrena and the others to wait with Orven's men and rode forward with Kiral. They approached to within a few yards of the base of the hill, halting when one of the Lonak spurred his pony down the slope, a hulking man with a bearskin vest and a mazelike tattoo covering his shaven head. His face provoked a rush of recognition as he halted his pony a few yards away, regarding Vaelin with a baleful glare and greeting Kiral in terse Lonak.

"This is Alturk," she told Vaelin. "Tahlessa of the Mahlessa Sentar."

"We've met," Vaelin said, nodding at the big man. "Your son is well?"

Alturk's face spasmed with anger and Vaelin resisted the urge to reach for his sword as Kiral tensed beside him.

"My son was varnish," Alturk said in harsh Realm Tongue. "A worthless life well ended."

Vaelin wondered if he should voice some word of sympathy but guessed it would only be taken as further insult. "The Mahlessa has granted us passage," he said. "What is your purpose here?"

Alturk gritted his teeth, speaking in slow controlled tones as if worried his anger might choke him. "The Mahlessa commands one hundred of the Sentar follow you. The finest blood of the Lonakhim, to be spilled at your word."

"You know our course? We travel across the ice to the lands of our enemy. The dangers are many."

"Word from the Mountain is not questioned." Alturk tugged on his reins, turning the pony. "Follow our track, do not stray from it. There are few here who welcome your coming and I give no promise of safety."

◆ ◆ ◆

They covered thirty miles by nightfall, the Sentar setting a punishing pace through myriad canyons and valleys. Vaelin noted they rode with weapons ready, many holding bows with arrows notched, eyes constantly scanning the surrounding hilltops. His eyes also picked out a few riderless ponies among them and noted some warriors sported recently bound wounds.

"The Mahlessa asks much of our people in allowing your passage," Kiral explained, following his gaze. "The False Mahlessa may have fallen but her words still linger in many ears."

"But you are . . . were the False Mahlessa," Vaelin said. "Won't your presence among us discourage them?"

Kiral smiled sadly. "When the Mahlessa freed me I went forth from the Mountain with my sisters, telling my story at the fires of every clan. It's a story welcome at any fire, being so rich in incident. Most believed it, some didn't, thinking me somehow turned from my true course by the Mahlessa. The thing that held me had a way with words, an ability to plant the seeds of doubt in the hearts of those already versed in malice and cruelty. It's easier to hate when given a reason, and she had many."

They encamped amidst the crags of a low plateau some hours later, Alturk posting a heavy guard on all approaches. Most of the Sentar seemed content to stay away from the Merim Her but not all were so wary, one stocky woman approaching to peer at Dahrena as she unsaddled her horse, speaking in rapid Lonak.

"I don't know your language," Dahrena said, clearly discomforted by the scrutiny.

"She asks if you belong to the Arrow Glass Clan," Kiral explained. "Your face reminds her of a cousin she lost years ago."

Dahrena offered the stern-faced Lonak woman a cautious frown. "Lost how?"

"A raid," Kiral related. "An entire village was wiped out, her cousin died along with her sisters and their children. They thought it the Seordah but the tracks were wrong, and the Seordah never kill children."

Dahrena's expression became more intent and she laid down her saddle, stepping closer to the Lonak woman. "Did her cousin have a name?"

"Mileka," Kiral translated. "It means Owl." She paused as the Lonak woman spoke on. "She asks if you have a story for the fire."

"Yes." Dahrena gave a reluctant nod. "I have a story."

The Lonak woman brought a dozen or so more Sentar to hear the story, squatting around the fire as Kiral translated Dahrena's tale. The presence of Wise Bear and Iron Claw was an obvious source of discomfort but apparently not sufficient to assuage the desire for a new tale. They sat, clearly fascinated as she related her dim memory of the destruction of her village. Some became agitated when she mentioned the wolf that had borne her through the forest, but they all stayed until she finished, relating how Lord Al Myrna had found her and made her his daughter, nodding and grunting in appreciation as she fell silent.

"They liked it," Kiral said, a note of relief in her voice. "A good story means much to my people." She tensed somewhat as Alturk stepped from the shadow of a nearby crag, arms crossed and gaze fixed on Dahrena.

"You lived as Merim Her," he said. "But your arms are adorned with Seordah trinkets."

"I am both Merim Her and Seordah," she replied evenly. "In soul if not in blood."

Alturk grunted something that might have been a laugh. "Lonak blood doesn't weaken so easily. You may feel it swell again before this tale is done." He growled something at the onlooking Sentar and they quickly scrambled to their feet before disappearing into the shadows. "Be sure to wake before dawn," he told Vaelin, stalking back into the night.

◆ ◆ ◆

The first attack came the following day as they traversed a deep canyon half a day's march from the plateau. A group of some two dozen Lonak appeared out of a cave mouth to launch a volley of arrows before hurling themselves at the Sentar, clearly intent on fighting their way through to the hated Merim Her. Only one managed to breach the cordon, the others being clubbed down or speared in short order, seemingly without any loss to the Sentar. The lone warrior ran directly for Vaelin, screaming madly with war club raised, then skidding to a halt as Iron Claw lumbered into his path. The Lonak stared, eyes wide in horror as the bear bellowed his challenge, rising to his full height. The warrior dropped his club, apparently now unreasoned by terror and numb to the arrow that punched through his chest a second later. Kiral walked to the corpse, bow in hand, kicking his legs to make sure before kneeling to reclaim her arrow.

They were attacked again three nights later, though this time their assailants were content to linger in the shadows and loose arrows at the campfires, claiming the life of a Sentar who had stepped in front of the glow at the wrong moment. Alturk gathered together twenty warriors and led them into the darkness, returning a little while later with bloodied clubs and lance points. Their efforts seemed to have been enough to ensure an untroubled night and a group of Sentar soon appeared at their fire in search of a story in what was becoming a nightly ritual.

"I'll take a turn," Orven said. "The Tale of Lord Vaelin's Charge at the Battle of Alltor."

Vaelin got to his feet with a groan. "Spare me."

"But they want a story, my lord," Orven said with a small grin.

"I, however, do not." He walked away from the fire as Orven began the tale, moving through the camp where the other Sentar greeted him with cautious eyes or studied indifference. He found Alturk sitting alone, wiping a buckskin rag over his war club, a recently sharpened knife placed close to his side.

"I come to ask more of your son," Vaelin said. "I hope my actions had no part in his death."

Alturk didn't look up, grunting, "Your hope is wasted."

"You killed him for disobeying the Mahlessa?"

The Lonak's eyes rose from his work, bright with warning. "My clan killed him. His death was right and just. And I'll speak no more of it."

Vaelin moved to the fire, squatting down to extend his hands to the warmth. The nights grew ever colder, the northerly winds stiff with ample warning of what lay ahead. "My queen told me men are forbidden the company of your Mahlessa," he said. "You have never met her, yet you follow her word without question."

"Do you question your queen?"

Vaelin grinned a little. "Not openly." Alturk failed to respond, putting his war club aside and settling his gaze on the fire. Vaelin saw that the years had aged his face if not his body, lines etched deep into the ink around his eyes.

"You should know," he told the Lonak, "I believe few of us will return from this journey. Those not claimed by the ice may well fall in battle."

Alturk sat in silence for several minutes, watching the fire with his aged eyes. Finally, as Vaelin made to leave, he said, "A man already dead need fear nothing."

◆ ◆ ◆

Two more weeks brought them in sight of the ice, a ribbon of white on the eastern horizon beyond a curving shoreline fringing grey ocean waters. The mountains had begun to diminish in size in recent days until now they were but foothills, mostly bare of greenery and affording little cover to their enemies. The attacks had become more sporadic the farther north they travelled, possibly through simple weariness, though Vaelin suspected the constant attrition exacted by the Sentar to be the main reason. For all their lack of uniformity or soldierly custom they were every bit as disciplined as any company from the Sixth Order, and perhaps nearly as skilled; only two more had been lost since the night raid.

"Faith, that bites!" Lorkan said, wincing at the cutting wind and casting a questioning glance at Cara. "Can't you do something?"

She confined her response to a disgusted glance and dismounted as Wise Bear arrived with Iron Claw. The horses had grown only partially accustomed to the bear's presence and the shaman usually travelled at a short remove from the main body of the company, bouncing along on the beast's back. There was an odd wariness in the Lonak's attitude to Wise Bear, moving around him with a cautious silence, and he was the only one of the outsiders not required to share a story at the fire.

"Hello you!" Cara said, scratching at Iron Claw's mighty head, the animal snorting in pleasure and hunkering down at her feet, though his shoulder still reached as high as her chest.

"Need hunt more," Wise Bear told Vaelin. "More meat."

"We have meat," Alturk said. "Enough for a month's travel at least."

"Not on ice," the shaman insisted. "Need more and more."

"From where?" Alturk gestured at the barren country around them. "There's nothing to hunt here."

Wise Bear stared at him for a moment then gave one of his cackling laughs, pointing towards the shoreline. "Sea brings gifts, Painted Man."

◆ ◆ ◆

Wise Bear disappeared with Iron Claw for several hours before returning to lead them to a cliff overlooking the bay where the beasts made their home. There were perhaps forty of them crowding the rocky shore, plump, fur-covered bodies flopping around as they squabbled and barked at each other, impressive tusks bared. "What are they?" Lorkan asked, his voice kept to a whisper although they were a considerable distance from the creatures.

"Fur seals," Dahrena replied. "We have them on the northern shores of the Reaches, though I don't recall seeing any so big."

"Big," Wise Bear agreed with a happy nod. "Big meat to take on ice."

"It'll spoil," Alturk stated. "And we have not the salt to preserve so much."

Wise Bear replied with a baffled frown and it took some time for Vaelin to translate the meaning. "Spoil, hah. Meat not spoil on ice. Too cold. Just smoke over fire. Keep many many days." He beckoned to Kiral and started for a narrow track leading to the shore. "We hunt, you build fires."

They toiled on the shoreline for the best part of another week, building fires and butchering the unfortunate seals at Wise Bear's instruction. He skinned the first victim with an unconscious and rapid skill, harvesting a complete hide with seemingly only a few strokes of his knife, a feat none of them managed to match despite continued labour. The meat was cut into strips and hung over the fires to smoke whilst the hides were set aside to be cured, the shaman making it clear they would be needed later, his eyes constantly returning to the white line on the horizon.

"Have we made the journey too late?" Vaelin asked him on the last night. They sat together on a rocky outcrop near the shingle beach where the bloody work had been done, Iron Claw happily munching on a pile of entrails nearby.

"Still time." Wise Bear raised a hand, the thumb and forefinger forming a narrow gap. "Small time." He glanced over his shoulder at the camp where a crowd of Sentar were listening as Kiral translated Lorkan's somewhat ribald version of the Woodsman's Daughter, a cautionary tale of unrequited love involving murder and adultery, though not usually in such quantity or detail.

"Not all make the islands," Wise Bear went on. "Way of things on the ice. Always takes some, even Bear People."

"The islands?" Vaelin asked.

"Where we go. Other side of ice. Home of Bear People once."

"I thought your people lived on the ice?"

Wise Bear shook his head, eyes moving to the ice once more. It seemed to glow, lit by a pale green luminescence in the night sky the Lonak called Grishak's Breath in honour of their wind god. "Only small times," Wise Bear said. "Our travel to your land the most time ever on ice for Bear People."

Vaelin recalled the emaciated, hollow-eyed folk clustered at Steel Water Creek, a nation raised to survive the harshest climes and yet still brought to their knees by the ice. "I would not ask this of any soul," he said, "if I didn't know in my heart it must be done."

CHAPTER SIX

Lyrna

"**A**re there no words I can speak to dissuade you from this course?" They had requested the audience early that morning and stood before her now in the throne room, Hera Drakil's hawk face betraying no emotion whilst Sanesh Poltar at least managed a regretful grimace. "War is won," he said with a shrug. "The elk herds grow with no one to hunt them, eat all the grass. We are needed on the plains."

Lyrna turned to the Seordah war chief, speaking in her barely adequate Seordah. "And you, forest brother?"

"We heeded the wolf's call," he replied. "Now it fades. The forest calls us home."

The finest light infantry and cavalry in the world, Vaelin had called them, not assets to be easily lost. "Our enemies will return if we cannot defeat them," she told them. "And when they do I may not be able to shield you from their savagery."

"We fought for this land," Hera Drakil insisted. "We are glad to have done so. The land across the great water is not ours to fight for."

She knew there was something more behind his words, a faint flicker in his eyes she knew all too well. She recalled the forest people's discomfort in Lady Dahrena's presence, their inherent revulsion at what she had done for Vaelin and their intense dislike of the sea. *The Seordah saw much when they left the forest,* she surmised. *And came to know fear.*

"You swore no oath to me," she said. "So I cannot compel your loyalty. And I would be a fool and a liar to claim this Realm would now be free without your help. Please journey home safely, with my thanks, and rest assured the Seordah and Eorhil will enjoy the friendship and protection of the Unified Realm for all the ages."

They surprised her by bowing, something she had seen neither do before. "If the dark-hearts come back," Hera Drakil said as he straightened, "we will fight with you again."

They left at noon, Lyrna watching from the walls as the great mass of Eorhil galloped away north, the Seordah following in their loose tribal formations, some adorned with various trinkets gathered during their sojourn.

"A grievous loss, Highness," Count Marven commented at her side. "They would have done fine work across the ocean."

"The Realm Guard is already three times their number," Lyrna said, striving to ensure her confidence didn't sound forced. "And not all have left." She nodded at the Seordah and Eorhil encamped near the gatehouse, perhaps three hundred warriors who had opted to stay. Some had formed close bonds with the Realm folk they had met on the march, even a few marriages; she could see Lord Orven's rapidly blossoming wife moving among the elk-hide shelters. Others had elected to join her crusade in pursuit of justice for the many outrages witnessed during the campaign, the remainder possessed of nothing more than basic curiosity, a desire to see what lay beyond the great water. The Eorhil elder, Wisdom, was chief among the latter. "I find there is always room in my head for more knowledge, Highness," she had said in answer to Lyrna's query.

"At least we won't have to find room for so many horses," her new Battle Lord continued. "Burdened as we are with the Renfaelin knights and our own cavalry." He paused, no doubt mustering the nerve to voice unwelcome advice. "Highness, the fleet grows daily but also slowly. Consequently, I believe it may be necessary to send the army in two waves. The first carrying the elite of the Realm Guard and Lady Reva's archers. They will secure a defensible port whilst the fleet returns for the remainder."

Lyrna watched the last of the Seordah disappear over a distant rise. She fancied there was a single figure who lingered a moment. Hera Drakil perhaps, or just a warrior looking on a place he never hoped to see again. "Is there a Countess Marven?" she asked. "A family waiting for you in Nilsael?"

"In Frostport, yes. My wife and two sons."

"You should bring them here. They will be very welcome at court."

"I doubt that, Highness. My wife is . . . possessed of a difficult temper. Within a day of her arrival she would be demanding her own palace."

"Ah." She turned from the view as the lone Seordah disappeared from sight. "Attacking in small numbers will avail us nothing, my lord. The Volarians have lost many soldiers but their empire is rich in more. We will descend upon them in but one wave, washing their filth from the land in the process."

"Forgive me, Highness. But we do not possess even half the number of ships required."

"No," she agreed. "A state of affairs I expect to see rectified shortly."

◆ ◆ ◆

Davoka waited with the horses in the palace courtyard. "It's done?" Lyrna asked her in Lonak, climbing onto Arrow's back.

"It was as you foretold," Davoka replied, her bland expression at odds with her tone.

"Pity." Lyrna turned Arrow towards the palace gate. "Let us find a welcome distraction."

Varinshold thrummed with activity as they rode through the streets flanked by Benten and Iltis, people pausing to bow or call out a loyal greeting before hurrying to their tasks. For all its bustle the fabric of the city was scarcely healed, a few newly completed buildings rising from the devastation, and these only plain, functional barracks devoid of aesthetic value. *Malcius would have wept,* she knew, surveying her capital, now a city of canvas and wood rather than stone. *He did so love to build.*

The activity was even more intense at the docks. Varinshold was a port city but had traditionally built few ships, most of the Realm's vessels being the product of the South Tower and Warnsclave yards where thousands now laboured at a frantic pitch to give her the fleet she demanded, though never fast enough. Winter was upon them and no more than a dozen new ships were ready, and these only warships of traditional design. An exasperated Lord Davern had advised that building a vessel on the dimensions she required would demand the construction of a completely new yard. "Then build it, my lord," she told him simply.

The Queen's Forge, as it had come to be called, occupied much of the wharf previously taken up by the city's warehouses, a sprawling collection of smithies and workshops where skilled artisans laboured day and night in ten-hour shifts. They were former apprentices mostly, young enough to run from the slavers who had claimed their masters, many having to be extracted from the ranks of the Realm Guard, often at great protest. As per her strict orders they gave no pause to bow as she entered the Forge, though there were many quick glances of awe or admiration to greet her.

She proceeded through the cacophony of pounding metal and ceaseless saws to the cavernous space where Alornis waited with Lord Davern, and rising behind them the hull of a vessel fully thirty feet high. Lyrna's gaze tracked over the scaffolding that covered her sides and the wrights working caulking and pitch into the upper seams. "I was given to believe she stood ready to launch, my lord," she said to Davern.

"Finishing touches only, Highness," he assured her with a weary bow, turning and extending a hand to the new-born ship. "I give you the *Realm's Pride*, one hundred and sixty feet long, forty-five at the beam, a draught of twenty-three and capable of carrying five hundred fully armed Realm Guard the breadth of any ocean."

"And," Alornis added in a prim voice, "constructed in only twenty days by less than a hundred men."

"So," Lyrna said to Davern. "It worked."

"Indeed, Highness." He inclined his head at Alornis. "My initial skepticism seems to have been unfounded."

Lyrna moved closer to the ship, pausing to take Alornis's hand, squeezing it tight. "Thank you, my lady. I hereby name you the Queen's Artificer. Now the ship is done I would ask you turn your mind to the prosecution of the war. We will face great numbers in Volaria, I should be grateful for any devices you can conceive that might even the odds somewhat."

She felt Alornis's hand twitch in her grip. "I . . . know little of weapons, Highness."

"You knew little of ships yet that seemed to be of scant matter. I await your designs with interest." She released her hand and turned to Davern. "When does she launch?"

"The evening-tide, Highness. The masts should be fitted within two days."

"Have copies of the plans sent to the yards in Warnsclave and South Tower. No other design is to be followed from this day on."

"Yes, Highness."

Her eyes picked out the lettering on the hull. *The Realm's Pride. Fitting but hardly inspiring.* "And change the name," she added, turning to go. "She's to be called the *King Malcius*. I shall provide a list of titles for her sisters."

◆　◆　◆

The Dead Company was obliged to encamp beyond the city walls. Count Marven had given them a watchtower on the northern headland to guard, a decent remove from many veteran Realm Guard and former slaves keen to settle old scores. She found Al Hestian training his men with customary gentility.

"Get up you worthless shit-eater!" he growled at a prostrate youth, clutching his belly where the Lord Marshal had delivered a blow with the butt of his halberd. "Guts enough to steal but not enough to fight, eh? Let yourself be beaten down by a crippled old man." He delivered a vicious kick at the boy's legs as he continued to cower. "Up! Or it's a flogging!"

Al Hestian straightened as Lyrna guided Arrow closer, ignoring his bow and looking down at the cringing youth. He stared up at her with bright appeal, tears swelling in his eyes. *Little more than a boy,* she realised. "Your Lord Marshal gave you an order," she told him quietly, returning his stare and knowing he saw no kindness in her gaze.

The boy got to his feet, fighting tears and sketching a bow. "Sergeant!" Al Hestian barked and a broad-shouldered man came running to his side, saluting smartly. Lyrna recognised him as the knight from the dungeons, the one who had cried when she gave them their lives. "Run this coward until he drops," Al Hestian told him. "No rum for a week."

"This one would do well among the Lonakhim," Davoka commented at Lyrna's side.

Al Hestian came forward to hold Lyrna's reins as she dismounted. She could see a new vitality in him, the defeated man from the Traitor's Nook seemingly replaced by the epitome of a Realm Guard Lord Marshal, which, she reminded herself, he once had been. However, his straightened back and perfect uniform couldn't mask his eyes; they still told of a man in the midst of grief.

"My lord," she said, gesturing at the bluffs where Orena and Murel were laying out a table and chairs. "I come to watch my new ship's first voyage. Would you care to join me?"

He had his men light lanterns and hang them from poles along the cliff-top, sitting stiffly opposite her as the sun faded and a harsh seaward breeze drew a whisper from the grass. "How do you find your new command, my lord?" Lyrna asked him, accepting a cup of wine from Orena.

"A mixed bag, Highness. Knights seeking to reclaim their honour serving alongside the scum of the Realm. My Blackhawks could have slaughtered them all in a day."

"Yes, had they not been wiped out of course." She looked at the wine in her cup, a dark Cumbraelin red, the scent sweet, holding a tinge of mint and blackberry. "Any desertions?"

"Two, Highness. They were recent recruits, witless outlaws in truth, with little notion of how to evade capture. They were easily returned."

"And flogged, I presume?"

"Hanged, Highness, in front of the whole regiment." He nodded his thanks at Orena as she poured his wine. "Examples must be set."

"Quite so. I would prefer not to drink with you," she added as he made to sip the wine. He hesitated a moment then laid down his cup, his face betraying no sign of offence.

Benten turned back from the cliff-top, pointing towards the harbour. "My Queen."

Lyrna rose, beckoning Al Hestian to join her. The headland offered an excellent view of the docks where many torches glimmered as people crowded the wharf to watch the birth of the queen's mighty ship. The Forge had been built with a slipway jutting out into the harbour, the interior glowing bright and bathing the waters in a yellow glow. Even from this distance she could hear the sound of multiple mallets pounding the blocks that held the vessel in place, fading abruptly to be replaced by a huge cheer from the wharf as the great hull slid down the slipway and into the water, her wake shimmering like gold in the torchlight.

"She makes a fine sight, don't you think?" Lyrna asked Al Hestian, gesturing for Orena to bring more wine.

He watched the ship for a moment, his sunken eyes brightening only a fraction. "An impressive vessel, Highness."

"Yes. I must confess I have misled you somewhat, Lord Marshal. My mission here tonight was not to show you my ship."

She saw him tense, glancing at Iltis and Benten who stood a little way off on either side, eyes hard and hands resting on their sword hilts. "It was not, Highness?"

"No." Lyrna turned as Orena approached, meeting her gaze and tipping her wine onto the grass. "It was to show you the face of our enemy."

Orena froze, all expression draining from her features, but her eyes flicked across them all with an unnatural speed.

"Lord Vaelin noticed," Lyrna told her. "You saw the boy who can't be seen, unless by another Gifted. That was foolish."

Orena didn't move, her eyes settling on Lyrna as Benten and Iltis closed in on either side, swords drawn and levelled, Davoka moving behind her with spear poised.

"Orena Vardrian," Lyrna continued. "Family names follow the female line among the farming folk of Asrael. Brother Harlick has memorised every census ever taken in this Realm so it was an easy task to discern that you and Lord Vaelin are cousins, sharing a grandmother, one who no doubt passed her Gifted blood to both daughters. Maternal blood carries the Dark but the nature of the gifts can vary between generations. What is hers?"

Orena's features spasmed, a variety of expression marring her mask-like visage, malice, fear and amusement all flickering across her face before settling on the most unexpected; sadness, her brow softening and mouth forming a slight grimace. When she spoke her voice was flat, though Lyrna found the cadence horribly familiar. "She can place her thoughts in the heads of others. A difficult gift to master and one she rarely used, being so terrified of discovery, knowing her own people would deliver her to the Fourth Order should it become known. Little wonder she determined to escape the farm and marry a rich husband, she made great use of her gift during the courtship."

"And to tell your fellow creature and his pet priest where to find me that night at Alltor."

Iltis bared his teeth, sword quivering a little as he fought his rage, though she was gratified by the discipline he displayed in not surrendering to it.

"A task I was forced to," Orena said. "Like countless others."

"More than once, no doubt. I assume our enemies are fully aware of our preparations."

"They know all I know."

"So why risk discovery tonight? Lady Davoka has kept careful watch on you since Lord Vaelin imparted his suspicions. Why choose tonight to poison my wine?"

Orena said nothing though Lyrna saw her eyes flick in Al Hestian's direction.

"It seems our enemy fears you also, my lord," Lyrna told the Lord Marshal. "I find myself suddenly glad I didn't execute you." She levelled her gaze at Orena once more. "Why does the Ally want his death?"

"He has a genius for command. One that will be of great use when you reach Volaria."

"We have met before, have we not? In the mountains."

"It matters not." The woman's voice grew yet more devoid of emotion, her gaze losing focus, shoulders slumping in defeat. "Nothing matters. Build your fleet, gather your army, sail them to their deaths. We are all but pieces on his board and if the game goes awry, he'll start another. I have died a hundred times and woken in shell after shell, each time praying that this time he will leave me be. When I first awoke in this one I heard no whisper of his voice and I thought . . ." She fell silent, head lowering as she hugged herself.

"You had ample opportunity to kill me on the *Sea Sabre*," Lyrna said.

"During the battle, it would have been an easy matter with so many arrows flying, so much smoke to conceal the deed. Why didn't you?"

Orena issued a wistful laugh, soft and soon lost to the wind. "You made me a lady. You were . . . my queen. And . . ." She paused to smile. "And there was Harvin. To live so long without ever touching another heart is a terrible thing. To think I should find it with him, a common outlaw with no more wit than a scavenging fox."

"You expect me to believe this?" Lyrna felt her anger quicken and fought to keep it in check. This thing's attempt to manipulate her was dangerous, provoking her to hasty revenge. "A creature such as you is immune to love."

"You think yourself so wise, my queen, but you are still a child. I have seen much done in the name of love, the wondrous and the horrifying, always finding it so amusing. There is a corner of my soul that wishes you were right, that I had remained immune to its touch, for then my grief would not have been so great. I think that's how he found me again, hearing my despair as it seeped into the void, calling me back to his service."

"A call you could have refused."

"He bound me to him long ago, welded my soul to his, cutting away any will to resist. It's how he chooses us, those souls best suited to his purpose, those with malice sufficient to match his own and weakness enough to be moulded."

She sank to her knees, glancing over her shoulder where Davoka now stood, a small glass bottle in hand. "You should know," Orena said, turning back to Lyrna, "that the mind of this shell is fractured. Broken by rape and near strangulation the night the city fell, saved only by her gift, which shattered the mind of her assailant, but left her spent and easily claimed."

"She will have the best care," Lyrna said. "And I promised Lord Vaelin I would return his cousin."

Orena nodded and drew back her sleeve, raising her hand, palm extended. "This time there will be no forgiveness, my failures become too frequent, my soul too sullied by feeling. This time he will rend me to nothing, stripping away even the memory I was once alive. A fate I believe will suit me very well." Her face was set, determined, her fear well controlled, a stark contrast to the girl who had begged and wailed beneath the Mountain. "I am ready, my queen."

In later years there would be few among the Dead Company left alive to recall the scream that pealed across the headland that night. But those that did, although calloused by many horrors, would still manage a shudder at the memory of the sound, recalling it as an omen of what lay ahead.

◆ ◆ ◆

The full fury of winter came early that year, heavy rain giving way to snow with unwelcome speed, the tent roofs of Varinshold sagging under its weight. Lyrna had ordered fuel stockpiled but the depth of the cold took many by surprise and there were some who perished in its grasp, mainly the old and the sick. Others were found outside the city walls, shorn of warm clothing, their frozen faces often serene, accepting. The invasion had left many bereft of all family and vulnerable to despair, precious hands lost to grief that wouldn't heal.

Despite the cold and the privation the work continued, the Forge produced weapons at a furious rate and Davern's wrights had given her three more ships in less than a month, the pace of construction quickening as they grew accustomed to the new techniques. "You should forget the gold from the Reaches, Highness," Davern advised one day with his customary grin. "When the war's won this land will be made rich on shipbuilding alone."

In truth she often wished she could forget the gold. Acting Tower Lord Ultin was a frequent correspondent with his demands for more miners and Fief Lord Darvus's scribes were scrupulous in counting and weighing every ingot to reach Frostport, even to the point of delaying onward shipment to the Alpiran merchants. *If Your Highness were to send more scribes,* the old man had written in response to her gently worded rebuke, *I feel sure the flow of gold would resume with all alacrity.* She had resisted the urge to dispatch Lord Adal with a formal edict dissolving Darvus's agreement with Vaelin and placing the gold trade under Crown control. However, as her Minister of Justice was ever keen to remind her, she had already exercised the Queen's Word with a frequency that made her father appear the paragon of light-handed rule and was loath to earn a reputation for setting aside inconvenient laws.

Aspect Dendrish had taken on the unenviable task of hearing petitions, troubling her with only the cases of greatest import or complexity. He also had been obliged to reconstitute a system of courts in a land now severely denuded of lawyers or magistrates, obtaining her permission for a complete reorganisation of the Realm's machinery of justice.

"Three Senior Judges?" she asked him on reading his plan. "Should the role of highest judge not fall to you, Aspect?"

"Too much power vested in a single office is often a recipe for corruption, Highness."

She gave him an amused frown. Although possibly the least personable man she had met besides the blessedly deceased Darnel, the Aspect had quickly earned a reputation for sound judgement and rigid impartiality, reporting every attempted bribe and decreeing swift punishment on the transgressor. "You feel corrupted by your duties?" she asked.

"I will not hold this office forever." There was a weight to his words that gave her pause, taking in the paleness of his skin and rapidly disappearing girth. She had noticed before how his words were often coloured by a faint wheeze and he would pause to cough with a disconcerting frequency.

"Three judges," she said, turning back to the document. "To ensure their decisions are not deadlocked, I assume?"

"Indeed, Highness. All rulings to be subject to your approval, naturally."

"Also, I note there is no mention of the Faith in your amended code of criminal transgressions."

"The Faith pertains to the soul and the Beyond. The law pertains only to the Realm and its subjects."

"Very well. I shall need time to fully consider this."

"My thanks, Highness." He hunched over, trying to suppress a cough and failing, a lace handkerchief held to his mouth, coming away spotted with red. "Forgive me."

"I will. I'll also order you to see Brother Kehlan immediately and abide by whatever instruction he gives you."

He gave a reluctant nod as she set down the document, musing, "Neither my brother nor father ever attempted such radical change to the Realm's laws."

Aspect Dendrish drew a wheezing breath, his eyes slightly moist as he replied, "All in this Realm is changed, more than I would ever wish it to be. But wishes do not make a land fit to live in."

◆ ◆ ◆

"It's based on a Volarian engine," Alornis said, her slender arm working the windlass at the rear of the contraption, gears clanking and diagonally crossed arms drawing back. It did indeed resemble one of the ballistae with which the Volarians festooned their ships, but was substantially larger with a heavy iron box fixed over the central body. It stood on a wide base also of iron, but with a bowl-shaped aperture through which a supporting rod was thrust, allowing the entire engine to be swivelled about with surprising swiftness despite its size.

Lyrna had joined her Battle Lord on the Realm Guard's main practice ground to witness the trial of her Lady Artificer's first invention. The broad plain that played host to the Summertide Fair was mostly covered in snow now, troops of conscripts labouring through the drifts a good way beyond the row of targets placed at varying distances from the device. Each target consisted of four Volarian breastplates arranged in a square, Alornis having assured them the device had enough power to pierce their armour.

"The range, my lady?" Count Marven enquired.

"A Volarian ballista can manage about two hundred yards," Alornis replied, locking the engine's thick string in place and stepping back. "I'm hopeful we'll better it. They use wood for their bow staves, we have used steel." She took a moment to align the contraption then thumped her palm onto a lever. The bow arms snapped forward in a blur, the bolt flying free too fast for Lyrna to track its flight, though the tinny clunk from one of the farthest targets indicated it had found its mark.

"Close to three hundred yards," Count Marven said with a laugh, bowing to Alornis. "Well done, my lady. A remarkable feat."

"Thank you, my lord. But I am not yet done. The original Volarian design was slow to load, taking over a minute to loose two bolts. However, I recalled seeing a grain seeder, which gave me an odd notion." She reached for the windlass again and began to work it, the arms drawing back as the gears rattled anew. "It's all a matter of aligning the cogs," she explained, grunting a little with the effort. "The gears draw the string back to a certain point whereupon the box on the top releases a new bolt." A faint clatter came from the engine as she continued to work the windlass. "And the next gear releases the string."

The bow arms snapped again, scoring another hit on the farthest target. "All one need do is continue to turn the windlass," Alornis went on, adjusting the engine's aim so the next bolt flew towards a different target. "Until the bolts are exhausted, whereupon a new box can be hauled up to replace it."

She continued to work the engine, loosing bolts at varying trajectories until all targets had sustained a hit. When the last bolt had flown she stood back, perspiring a little despite the cold. "Still some details to work out," she said, chest heaving a little. "It tends to seize up if it's not oiled frequently, and I think I can improve on the design of the bolt-heads."

"Give me a hundred of those, Highness," Count Marven said, his tone now entirely serious. "And I'll match us against any army the Volarians can field."

Lyrna went forward to favour Alornis with a soft embrace, planting a kiss on her forehead. "What else can you show me, my lady?"

CHAPTER SEVEN

Frentis

Illian ducked under the arc of his wooden blade and countered with a jab at his eyes, easily turned before stepping close to trap her arm under his shoulder, pulling her close. "Now what will you do, sister?" he asked in a light tone.

He saw her bite back a retort, features red with frustration, detecting the decision in her eyes a fraction of a second too late. Her forehead connected painfully with his nose, leaving him stunned for the brief moment it took her to wrestle free, her ash sword coming round in a clumsy but fast swipe at his midriff. His wooden blade connected with hers an inch from his chest, deflecting it with a loud crack, then sweeping it aside to thrust into her belly. She grunted from the blow and lowered her sword, chest heaving and eyes dark with resentment.

"Anger is your enemy," he reminded her, wiping blood from his nose. "A little better this time, but still not fast enough. Practice your scales until midday then feed the dogs."

She took a deep calming breath before nodding, her tone carefully modulated. "Yes, brother."

He left her to it and strode across the deck where his company were engaged in their own practice, Draker teaching a trio of their younger members the basics of cutting a man's throat. "Gotta get it done in one stroke," he advised, a beefy arm around the chest of a lanky youth named Dallin, a Renfaelin farmhand rescued from slavers shortly before their time in the Urlish reached its disastrous conclusion. "Forget about finding the veins." Draker demonstrated the technique with a sheathed dagger. "Just cut deep and draw it all the way around. Then get hold of his hair and pull the head back to open the cut as wide as you can."

Frentis passed Weaver on the way to the stern, Slasher and Blacktooth at his side as they often were these days, seemingly fascinated by his work. Halfway through the voyage he had abruptly stopped plaiting rope and begun working strips of leather into a tight arrangement fixed onto a circular frame, replying with only a vague smile when asked what he was about. The creation had initially resembled a shallow basket but its purpose had gradually become clear as Weaver fixed straps to the concave side and borrowed pitch from the crew to cover the curving outer surface.

"A fine shield, sir," Frentis offered, pausing at his side and raising a hand for Slasher to lick.

"A Lonak design," Weaver replied, an oddly familiar cadence to his voice as he used a large bone needle to thread twine along the edge of the shield. "Though rarely used, since their martial culture is essentially aggressive in nature."

He continued to work, not looking up as Frentis moved on. Captain Belorath was at the stern, standing as still as the shifting deck would allow, his sextant trained on the horizon. Frentis had no notion of how the device worked or the meaning of the numbers the captain paused to scribble on parchment, but knew it was how he fixed their position on this ocean.

"Seas are calmer today," he offered. In fact it was the first calm day for over a week; the stories he had heard of the Boraelin's tempestuous wintry nature had not been exaggerated.

Belorath replied with a customary grunt, raising his sextant once more. "But the clouds aren't. Promises another storm by tomorrow." He squinted, keeping the sextant level, his eyes tracking to a brief glimpse of the sun through the cloud. "I believe, brother," he said, consulting the numbers on his parchment. "We are less than two weeks from Volarian shores. It's time a decision was made."

◆　◆　◆

"Eskethia." Thirty-Four's finger tapped the chart where a two-hundred-mile-long stretch of Volarian coastline traced from north to south. "One of the last provinces to fall to Volarian rule. The free people there may be less inclined to fight for the empire. Also, New Kethia is home to the largest slave market in the western provinces. Many of the slaves seized in your homeland will still be there, awaiting the winter auctions."

"Well garrisoned?" Frentis asked him, although it was Lekran who replied.

"At least a division," he said. "As our friend says, Eskethians are ever resentful at the loss of their sovereignty, though it happened centuries ago."

Frentis eyed the chart closely, gauging the distance from Eskethia to Volar. *Close enough to threaten the capital, but sufficiently distant to ensure any forces sent against us won't have time to return when the queen lands.* He raised his gaze to Belorath. "Captain?"

"It's not a shore I'm familiar with, may take a while to find a suitable landing site. Luckily the coming storm should mask our approach from their patrol ships."

Frentis nodded. "Eskethia then," he said, hating himself for the dread that clutched at his chest, knowing the decision meant his weeks of dreamless sleep would soon have to be abandoned. *Just one night,* he told himself. *What can she do in just one night?*

◆ ◆ ◆

There was a time she would have made them watch, delighting in their impotence as they squirmed in their bonds, helpless witnesses to the slaughter of their families. But for reasons she can't fathom such diversions hold no interest for her now and she has been content to gather them atop the Council Tower, standing at the parapet with the tip of a sword pricking every back, watching smoke and flames rise from the wealthier districts of the city as their estates are laid waste. It is close to midnight and the flames are bright, though they are at too great a height to hear the screams. For all their unnatural vitality these greats of the empire are now revealed as old men, sagging in grief, weeping or choking out desperate pleas for mercy, kept upright only by the promise of instant death should they falter.

"I realise this may be a redundant statement, Honoured Council-men," she tells them. "But the Ally is less than impressed by your efforts to fulfil his great design."

She moves to the grey-haired dullard, the one whose name she still can't recall although she is almost certain he must have known her father as a youth. He wears the formal robes of a Council-man, red from head to toe, though a telltale stain is spreading across the fabric around his legs. "Barely a tenth of the forces required have been gathered," she tells the somewhat pungent greyhead, "whilst you present me with an endless parade of ever-more-pathetic excuses. The Ally has ordained a great destiny for this empire whilst you wallow in your comforts and blind yourselves to the threat growing across the sea."

He attempts to beg, but his words emerge in a stumbling incoherent babble of spit and tears. She lets him burble on and turns an appraising glance on the man standing at his back, dressed in light armour like the Kuritai, but armed with but one sword, the blade longer and more slender than the Volarian standard, reminiscent in fact of the Asraelin pattern. Also, unlike the Kuritai, his armour is enamelled in red rather than black. He is of average height but his body is toned to near perfection, the product of decades of breeding and years of conditioning. It had always been a persistent delusion among these long-lived clods that the Kuritai were the ultimate slave soldiers, incapable of improvement, and now here they were, once again proved fatally wrong.

The swordsman is aware of her scrutiny, returning her gaze with a respectful nod, a grin of anticipation on his lips. They had been the Ally's most cherished project for centuries, a slave soldier capable of thought as well as obedience, but successive generations had proved a disappointment, either too difficult to control or too easy. It was her beloved who had provided the clue; during his time in the pits they had studied him closely, finding him most deadly when the binding was loosened, when his rage added precious speed to his blows. And so they had begun to change their diet of drugs, subtly alter their training regimen, weeding out those lacking the required spirit. In a few short years the results achieved had been . . . impressive.

"Step forward," she tells the swordsman and his grin widens as he complies, his sword digging into the Council-man's back. The scream is long as he plummets to the ground. She doesn't bother herself to view the result, waving a hand at each of the swordsmen in turn, the Council-men forced over the edge with varying degrees of panic and terror, some begging as they fall, as if their pleas will conquer gravity. In a few moments only one remains. He stands with his back straight, staring fixedly at the northern suburbs where his villa burns, the ornamental lake that surrounds it providing a fine reflection as the air is still tonight.

"Nothing to say, Arklev?" she asks him.

He doesn't react, not even to turn his head. She moves closer, finding his posture oddly noble, stoic in the face of death, refusing to acknowledge his enemy. A classic Volarian pose, worthy of any statue. "I've always wondered," she says, resting her arms on the parapet beside him. "Was it you who proposed the Council employ me to assassinate my father?"

The question is pointless, she knows. He will not speak to her. She is an unworthy enemy, bereft of consideration, deserving of no more respect than the tiger that eats the unwary traveller.

Instead, he chooses to surprise her. "It was not a proposal," *he says, face still composed and voice free of any quaver.* "It was an order, conveyed by the creature you call the Messenger."

She stares at him for a moment then laughs. Was it reward or enticement? *she wonders.* "I ordered your wife and most recently spawned brats be killed quickly," *she says.* "I felt I owed you that much."

He says nothing, his composure still fully in place. She toys with the idea of letting him stand there for a full day, curious to see how long it will take before his legs buckle, but yet again finds her appetite for indulgence diminished this night. "Take him to the vault," *she tells the swordsman standing at his back.*

Arklev casts an appalled gaze at her then lurches forward, trying to launch himself from the parapet, but his guard is too swift, catching him by the legs and dragging him back. "Kill me!" *Arklev rages at her.* "Kill me you pestilent bitch!"

"You have too much yet to do, Arklev," *she replies with an apologetic smile. He continues to rage as his guard drags him to the stairs, his cries echoing all the way down.*

She lingers for a while, watching the fires, wondering how many living in the city below had any notion of what they portended, of the different world that would greet them on the dawn, a now-familiar fugue of confusion settling over her mind.

The fires are smaller when she comes back to herself, the confusion fading. How long has she stood here? She turns to one of the swordsmen, the one who had killed the greyhead, finding him viewing her with open admiration, his eyes lingering where the slit in her gown reveals a length of thigh. "Do you know what you are?" *she asks him.*

"Arisai," *he replies, meeting her gaze with a grin.* "A servant of the Ally."

"No." *She turns back to the city.* "You are a slave. In the morning I will be an empress, but also a slave. For we are all slaves now."

She is moving to the stairs when it strikes her, the sensation of his return falling like a hammerblow. She staggers, falling to her knees. Beloved! *Her song swells in welcome and foreboding, the same notes it has always sung in his presence. He is close, she can feel it, the ocean no longer between them.* Beloved, do you come to me?

The song shifts as it touches his hatred, his sweet hatred, a vision coming to her mind, foggy but clear enough to discern a stretch of coastline, tall waves breaking on a rocky shore, a single word in his voice, his wonderful hate-filled voice: Eskethia.

◆ ◆ ◆

"Reminds me of southern Cumbrael," Draker said, shielding his eyes from the sun as he surveyed the landscape. "Did some smuggling there in my youth."

Eskethia did indeed bear some resemblance to the Realm's driest region, and seemed similarly rich in vineyards, rows of neatly ordered vines stretching away across the rolling hills, interspersed with an occasional villa or farm building. Frentis glanced back at the *Sea Sabre*, wallowing in the morning tide. Belorath had been obliged to land them when the shore was clear of waves to avoid smashing them onto the rocks, resting the hull on the sands before they disembarked. "I'll ask the gods to favour your mission," the captain had called down to Frentis from the stern, casting a wary eye at the shore, his final words a barely heard mutter, "though I doubt even they could preserve you here."

"I put us fifty miles south of New Kethia," Thirty-Four advised, examining an unfurled map. "If the captain's reckoning is to be trusted."

"Good navigation is about the only thing I'd trust a Meldenean with." Frentis's gaze tracked to the nearest villa, perhaps a quarter mile off with outbuildings large enough to be stables.

"It'll be home to a black-clad," Thirty-Four said, following his gaze. "Too grand for anything else. They are likely to have guards; house Varitai. An estate this large will keep perhaps a dozen."

"All to the good." Frentis gave the sign for the company to adopt the loose skirmish formation he had taught them in the Urlish. "We need to start somewhere."

They managed to take a Varitai alive, a guard posted on the villa's western side, roped and beaten down by Draker with Thirty-Four's assistance. His comrades were not so fortunate, running to confront them with weapons drawn when a panicked slave gave the alarm, screaming shrilly of bandits as she fled back to the house. Frentis had ordered no chances taken and the fight was short, half the Varitai cut down by their arrows and Illian's crossbow before the company closed in with drawn swords to finish the others.

How much they have learned, Frentis thought, finding a grim satisfaction at the efficiency with which his people dealt with the Varitai, lanky Dallin ducking under a short sword to jab his own into a slave soldier's eyes then moving behind him to finish it with Draker's trick. Beyond them Illian deflected an overhead slash and delivered a deadly counter-thrust, finding a gap in the Varitai's armour just above the breastbone. It was over in a few moments, the company kneeling beside fresh corpses to claim weapons and trinkets, a ritual born in the forest.

"Leave that," Frentis barked. "Search the villa. If he hasn't fled, the owner will be in the upper rooms. Draker, take Thirty-Four and gather the slaves."

"Redbrother." Lekran stood at the arched entrance to the villa's courtyard, wiping blood from his axe, his expression dark. "Something you should see."

The man had been strong, the muscle on his arms and back clearly revealed as he hung from two posts, dried blood streaking his wrists where the shackles held him upright. His head hung forward, still and lifeless, the length of his broad back striped with two-day-old whip strokes. Frentis noted his left foot was stunted, the front half having been hacked off at some point, the standard punishment for slaves who run from their masters, death being the fate of any who run twice.

Opposite the dead man a young woman had been chained to another post, arms drawn back and legs tied in place so she couldn't turn, a leather gag secured about her mouth. She was partially naked, breasts and shoulders showing the signs of repeated beatings. She collapsed in Illian's arms as Lekran smashed the chains with his axe and the sister cut away her bonds. She choked on the water from Illian's canteen, an expression of utter confusion on her face fading slowly as she took in the sight of Frentis, her eyes tracking over his garb, the blue cloak and the sword on his back. "Brother?" she asked in Realm Tongue, her accent unmistakably Asraelin.

"Yes, Brother Frentis." He knelt at her side. "This is Sister Illian."

The woman's head lolled, her gaze losing focus. "Then I am finally dead," she said with a shrill laugh.

"No." Illian took her hand, squeezing it gently. "No. We are here. Come to save you at our queen's orders."

The woman stared at her, apparently unable to comprehend the reality of her survival. "Jerrin," she said after a moment, raising herself up, gazing around with a wild animation. "Jerrin. Did you save him too?" She stopped as her gaze found the man hanging from the posts. She sagged in Illian's arms and voicing a despairing wail. "I told him we shouldn't run," she whispered. "But he couldn't stand the thought of him touching me again."

Frentis turned at the sound of a fearful whimper. A plump little man in loose robes of black silk stood trembling beside the ornate fountain in the centre of the courtyard, his chins bulging somewhat as Master Rensial pressed his sword blade harder, forcing him to stand on tiptoe. "Where are the horses?" he demanded.

The plump man raised a shaking hand, pointing to an arched doorway off to the left. Rensial raised a questioning eyebrow at Frentis. He turned back to the woman they had freed, seeing the depth of hatred in the stare with which she fixed the plump black-clad. "Not just yet, Master," Frentis told him. "If you don't mind."

◆ ◆ ◆

They found another six Realm folk among the slaves, none more than forty years in age, all possessing skills of some kind. "Jerrin was a wheelwright," his wife explained. Her name was Lissel, a chandler from Rhansmill come to live in Varinshold at her husband's insistence. "Money grew tight after the desert war. Varinshold would be our fortune, he said." She began to voice another of her shrill laughs but mastered the impulse with a visible effort, her gaze moving to the villa's owner, now stripped naked and chained to the posts where her husband had died. Thirty-Four had questioned him for a short time, his skills unnecessary as the black-clad had been all too eager to cooperate.

"He tells of a larger estate twelve miles to the east," Thirty-Four reported. "The master there is a renowned breeder of horses and has also purchased many slaves from the recent influx."

"The nearest garrison?" Frentis enquired.

"Ten miles north of here, a single battalion of Varitai, though fewer in number than they should be. It seems the Council has been concentrating forces on the capital recently."

"Not for much longer." Frentis took the whip they had found on the overseer's body. He had tried to run, displaying an impressive turn of speed for such a large man, but Slasher and Blacktooth were faster. Frentis placed the whip in Lissel's lap. "I leave this matter in your hands, mistress."

He went outside where Draker had gathered the slaves, the Realm folk standing apart from the others, some already holding weapons taken from the Varitai and greeting Frentis with bows and expressions of grave intent. The others numbered over forty people and displayed only fear. A clutch of girls, the youngest no more than thirteen, clustered together in a protective huddle, casting tearful glances at the men surrounding them. Only one slave was prepared to meet Frentis's gaze, a trim man of middle years dressed in a clean dun-coloured tunic. He winced a little as the first scream came from the courtyard, the crack of the whip an indication that Lissel was a quick learner.

"You are One here?" Frentis asked the trim man.

He winced again as another scream sounded, then bowed low. "I am, Master."

"I am not a master and you are not a slave. What is your name?"

"Tekrav, m— Honoured Citizen."

Frentis studied the man's face, seeing the keen intelligence he tried to hide with a servile stoop. "You were not always a slave. Those born to slavery have no names. What was your crime?"

"An overfondness for dice." Another scream pealed forth, longer and louder, followed by a babble of desperate entreaties and promises. Tekrav swallowed and forced a smile. "And a dislike of resultant debt."

"Your skill?"

"I am scribe and bookkeeper here. Should you require my talent, Honoured Citizen, I am at your disposal."

"I'll have need of it in time. Whether you choose to offer it is a matter for you." Frentis stepped back, raising his voice to address them all. "By order of Queen Lyrna these lands are hereby seized for the Unified Realm and all who reside here afforded the rights and privileges due free subjects of the Crown."

There was little reaction beyond bafflement, most remaining immobile, eyes fixed on the ground, the clutch of girls huddling even closer together.

"You're free," Frentis went on. "You may go and do as you please. However, any who wish to join with me and free your brothers and sisters are welcome."

More silence; even Tekrav just stared at him in incomprehension.

"You're wasting your time, brother," one of the Realm folk said, a short but broad man with the teardrop scars of the forge visible on his forearms. "You'll find more spirit in a whipped dog than this lot."

Frentis gave them a final glance, seeing the truth of his words plainly enough and suppressing a sigh of frustration. *Slavery is more than just chains,* he knew. *It binds the soul as much as the body.*

"We leave in an hour," he told the slaves, turning away. "You may take what you like from the villa, but I advise you not to linger."

◆ ◆ ◆

The Varitai exhibited no fear, kneeling with his arms bound behind his back, stripped of armour and undershirt to reveal the pattern of scars. They were less elaborate than the matrix that once covered Frentis's chest, similar to Lekran's markings but plainly administered with scant regard to artistry or the discomfort of their wearer.

"How much?" Illian asked, removing the cap from the flask.

"No more than a teardrop," Frentis said, watching the Varitai keenly as she stepped closer, pouring a small amount of the liquid into the cap.

"Varitai are not as strong as Kuritai," Lekran advised in a wary tone. He stood at the rear of the bound slave soldier, axe at the ready. "Could kill him."

"Then we'll try a smaller dose on the next one." Frentis nodded at Illian and she upended the cap, allowing the contents to fall onto the scars on the Varitai's chest.

Unlike Lekran there was no scream, the Varitai's head snapping up, the veins in his neck bulging, teeth gritted so tight it was a wonder they didn't break. His eyes widened, the pupils shrinking to dots as spit began to drool from his mouth. A second later he collapsed, convulsing on the ground with white foam covering his lips, his jerks gradually slowing to twitches, then nothing.

Frentis crouched down to feel for the pulse in his neck, finding it weak, and slowing. "He's dying," he said with a sigh. He looked up as a shadow fell across him, finding Weaver staring down at the scene with naked disgust. Frentis began to rise when Weaver's fist came down in a blur, connecting with his jaw and sending him sprawling.

Frentis lay stunned, hearing Illian's sword scrape free of its scabbard. After a moment his vision cleared and he found Weaver on his knees, both hands placed on the dying Varitai's chest, paying no heed to Illian, who had touched her sword point to the nape of his neck. "Leave it," Frentis ordered, getting to his feet and waving her back.

Weaver kept his hands on the Varitai's chest for some time, his expression one of deep concentration, eyes half-closed and lips moving in a silent whisper. Frentis heard Illian stifle a gasp as the slave soldier's scars began to fade from his chest, shrinking to faint pale lines in a matter of minutes. Finally Weaver removed his hands and rose, stepping back as the slave soldier issued a weary groan.

"He'll sleep a while," Weaver said, turning to Frentis with a stern expression. "Freedom will not be won with cruelty."

Frentis rubbed his jaw, feeling the bruise already beginning to form and the iron tang of blood on his tongue. "I'll leave it in your hands next time."

◆ ◆ ◆

They built a pyre for Lissel's husband in the courtyard, liberally dousing the stacked wood with oil before doing the same to the villa. She had left the owner alive, though he was barely conscious, hanging bloodied and ruined from the posts. She had borrowed a knife from Illian and a small red lump was visible in the large pool of blood beneath his splayed legs. Frentis assumed he would probably find the flames a mercy.

They moved east as the sky dimmed, the burning villa casting a tall column of smoke into the air at their backs. The stables had yielded half a dozen carts but only enough horses for ten riders. Frentis sent Master Rensial and Lekran to scout their route and set the others on either side of their small column. The freed Varitai sat in the back of one of the carts, head lolling and features drawn in a perpetual frown of deep confusion. They had managed to elicit only a few words from him; naming himself only as Eight before voicing a keenly expressed desire to know when he would receive his next dose of karn.

"It's a mix of various drugs," Thirty-Four explained. "Subdues the spirit, dulls the memory and captures the will. He will feel its absence tonight."

Frentis recalled the nights Thirty-Four had spent writhing and moaning in the forest after he had discarded his own vial. His recovery had been swift but he was a man of considerable inner strength and had at least the memory of freedom, whilst this Eight had clearly been a slave since birth.

"Have we freed this man or cursed him?" he wondered aloud.

"Freedom is never a curse, brother," Thirty-Four insisted. "But it is often a hard road."

Frentis turned as a shout came from the rear, finding a small group of figures running from the burning villa. He tugged his horse to a halt and waited as they came into view, Tekrav followed by the clutch of girls plus a few of the younger male slaves, all burdened with various bundles of clothing and valuables.

Tekrav came to a halt a few yards away, chest heaving and staring up at Frentis with a desperate appeal. Behind him the girls and the men huddled together, not so fearful as before, but still wary.

"Honoured Citizen . . ." Tekrav began, falling silent as Frentis held up a hand.

"My name is Brother Frentis of the Sixth Order," he said. "If you join us, you will be free but you will also be soldiers. I offer no protection and promise no victory."

Tekrav hesitated, glancing back at his companions in search of guidance. They shuffled uncomfortably until one spoke up, a dark-skinned girl no more than twenty, her voice coloured by a faint Alpiran accent. "Your men will not touch us?"

"Not unless you want them to," Draker said, quickly lowering his gaze at Frentis's glare.

"You will not be mistreated in any way," Frentis promised the girl.

She exchanged glances with the others then stepped forward with a nod. "We will join you."

Frentis briefly scanned the bundles they carried, picking out the telltale gleam of gold and silver amongst the rolled blankets and clothing. "Keep hold of any weapons," he said. "But we cannot be burdened with loot. Discard it."

He sat and waited until they complied, tossing away their shiny cups and plates with varying degrees of reluctance, Tekrav wincing as he gently laid a small, gold-embroidered tapestry on the ground.

"Sister Illian," Frentis called her over. "These people are in your care. Commence their training on the morrow."

◆　◆　◆

They came upon the horse breeder's villa the next day, finding it far richer in spoils but also much better protected, boasting a complement of over thirty house Varitai. It sat atop a wide hill surrounded by enclosed fields where horses were set to grazing and mounted Varitai moved in well-organised patrols.

"Not an easy prospect, brother," Draker said. They had crawled to the top of a rise a half mile away. "If I was looking for a likely place to steal, I'd pass this by."

"We fight our way in," Lekran said with a shrug.

"It'll cost us," Draker warned. "And we've scant swords to lose."

Frentis suppressed a groan. He had resumed taking Brother Kehlan's sleeping draught the night before and the resultant headache left him impatient to get on and tempted to accede to Lekran's desire for a fight. He was about to order them to their mounts when Illian dropped down beside him, the Alpiran girl from the villa crouching at her side. "Brother," Illian said. "I believe our new recruit has some intelligence to impart, but my Volarian is too poor to discern her meaning."

The girl blanched a little as Frentis and the two men turned to her, looking down and stumbling over her first words. "What is your name?" Frentis asked her in his broken Alpiran.

She lifted her gaze, a faint smile playing over her lips and making him wonder how long it had been since she heard her own language. "Lemera."

"Your words have value, Lemera," he told her, switching back to Volarian. "Speak on."

"I have been to this place." She pointed at the villa. "The master sent me and two others. We were . . . amusements for the owner's son on his birthday. That was almost a year ago."

Frentis turned to Lekran who grinned and nodded. "We kept the Varitai's armour."

◆ ◆ ◆

In the event they suffered but one casualty, one of the newly freed Realm folk displaying an over-abundance of courage when Illian led them over the wall that shielded the villa's southern side. The main house had already fallen and the remaining Varitai were being forced back into the central courtyard, formed in a tight ring around their master and his family. He had made the mistake of coming to greet them at the main entrance, his broad grin disappearing as Tekrav's black silk mask fell away from his face and Lekran's axe hacked down the nearest Varitai. Despite his shock, the master's wits were quick enough to organise a hasty defence as he fled back inside, though not quick enough to organise an escape, which should have been his first priority.

Frentis had pulled his fighters back from the dense knot of Varitai and set the archers to work when Illian's recruits came over the wall. The young man had run at the Varitai unarmoured and armed with only a small wood-axe, his face betraying a depth of hatred nurtured over the months of his captivity. He managed to bury the axe in the skull of a Varitai before a dozen rapid sword strokes cut him down. However, he had disordered their ranks sufficiently for the following recruits to pile in and break their formation apart, the men hacking away with clubs and axes and the girls stabbing with the daggers Illian had distributed. Cursing, Frentis raised his sword and led his fighters into the fray, Lekran voicing a joyful whoop as he leapt and bore a Varitai to the ground, both feet planted on his breastplate and axe sweeping down.

It was over in a few moments, all the Varitai slain along with the master and his family. The master lay across the bodies of his wife and son, a boy who couldn't have been more than fifteen, his father's black silks rent in a dozen places and soaked with blood.

"I tried to hold them, brother," Illian said, face lowered in contrition. "But the Realm folk are full of rage and the others can't understand a word I say."

His rebuke died on his lips in the face of her evident dismay. "Gather the weapons and armour," he told her. "Then search the villa. Take any documents you find to Thirty-Four."

Draker called to him from atop the west-facing wall, waving his club. "Riders coming in, brother."

Frentis ran outside where Rensial waited, mounted with sword drawn. Frentis mounted his own horse and unhitched his bow from the saddle. "Master," he said, trotting his mount to Rensial's side. "Shall we?"

◆ ◆ ◆

They managed to take two of the riders alive, both knocked senseless when they tumbled from their mounts as Rensial's sword neatly severed the ties of their saddles. Frentis accounted for the remainder with his bow, none of the Varitai coming close enough to press a charge and displaying a typical failure to realise the hopelessness of their cause.

As promised he gave the captives over to Weaver. Vaelin had intimated the man was possessed of a confused mind, and his behaviour during the voyage had done much to confirm it, so it was strange to witness the grim understanding on his face as he surveyed the two unconscious Varitai. "Great pain," he said softly.

"Pain can bring freedom." Frentis held up the satchel containing their supply of the Lonak elixir. "It freed me. It will free them, with your help."

The screams were terrible, rising high into the night sky as they gathered in the courtyard to eat a meal of looted spoils. The freed slaves had proved even less welcoming of liberation than at the first villa, several weeping at the sight of their master's body. "He was sparing with the whip," Lemera explained. "Allowed the children he fathered on the pleasure slaves to live. Usually they are exposed and left to die. He would keep them until they were old enough to sell. A generous man."

"These people are fucking disgusting," Draker said when Thirty-Four translated, casting a dark glower at the slaves keening over the master's body. "Shut up you simpering dogs!" They scattered as he threw a half-eaten chicken leg at them, fleeing into the darkness or retreating to their quarters, too fearful to even ask about their fate.

The Varitai's screams ended abruptly, heralding a silence that seemed to last an age. Frentis scanned the faces of his veterans at the fire, for the first time seeing a grim understanding of the magnitude of their task. *A handful against an empire was always a hopeless cause.* He had known it from the day they sailed, but had they?

"Should we go after the runners?" Illian asked, breaking the silence. "They'll no doubt spread warning of our arrival."

"Good," Frentis said. "We are here to cause as much fear and confusion as possible."

"We need more fighters," Lekran stated. "The cowards we keep finding won't make an army."

"Then we may be in luck." Thirty-Four produced a large ledger, opening it to reveal row after row of neatly inscribed figures. "The master's scribe kept excellent records. It seems he did much business with a Varikum to the south."

"Varikum?" Frentis asked. "I don't know this word."

"Training school," Lekran translated. "For the Garisai, those chosen to partake in the spectacles."

"Slaves?"

He nodded. "But not like Varitai or Kuritai. No binding for them. Captured in war and chosen for strength, or savagery. Nearly got sent to one myself but the Kuritai quota was light that year."

"It will be well defended," Thirty-Four advised. "Inside and out."

Frentis turned to Lemera, noticing for the first time the perfection of her profile, skin smooth and flawless. A few hours ago he had seen her stabbing at the master's body, teeth bared and voicing a joyful laugh every time the knife came down. "It's a rare man who can guard against beauty," he said.

CHAPTER EIGHT

Vaelin

W ise Bear called it The Long Night, the time when the sun vanished from the ice for a full month, its coming heralded by the
shortened days and the increased brightness of Grishak's
Breath. "Must reach islands before it comes," he had warned the first day
they set foot on the ice. "Long Night kills all."

The first week had been easier than expected, the novelty of traversing
such a vast and stark environment doing much to dispel their discomfort at
the ever-deepening cold. Wise Bear led the way, moving with short econom-
ical strides with Iron Claw lumbering along behind. The great bear would
sometimes disappear for a day, returning with dried blood on his snout
though Vaelin was baffled as to what prey it had managed to find. To him
the ice seemed as barren as the Alpiran desert, a place void of life for all its
beauty, fully revealed at twilight when the green-tinged fire danced in the
sky and the ice became a mirror to its majesty. The Lonak would fall into a
reverent hush when the sun fell, whispering thanks for Grishak's blessing.

Wise Bear seemed to hold a similar reverence for the dancing sky lights,
greeting their appearance by sinking to his knees and holding his bone-
staff aloft, a lilting song rising from his throat. Vaelin had yet to hear the
shaman speak of any god but it was clear the sky-fire held considerable significance.

"He's not praying," Kiral said one evening as Vaelin's gaze went to the old
man, her face sombre as her song related the meaning of Wise Bear's lilting
ode. "He offers greetings to his wife and the children they lost on the ice."

Vaelin looked up at the swirling green fire, watching it coalesce and
break apart in an unending dance. It might resemble flame but there was no

fury to it, the constant swirl conveying a strange sense of serenity. "He thinks she's up there?" he asked.

"He knows it. Every soul that ever lived is there, looking down on us until the world's end."

The Beyond made real, Vaelin mused, watching Wise Bear finish his song and lever himself upright with his staff. *At least he can see the object of his faith.*

They moved only in daylight at first, horses and ponies laden with supplies and dragging the sleds Wise Bear had them make before leaving the shore, simple frames of twisted gorse branches skidding along on runners fashioned from seal-bone. Scar, like all the horses, had shied the first time his hoof touched the ice, eyes widening in alarm at the unfamiliar sensation, only consenting to venture further at Vaelin's gentle insistence. Even after several days the animal still displayed a wariness of his new surroundings, as if understanding the grim warning Wise Bear imparted when they set off: "Horses won't last. Have to eat them before the end."

As the days grew shorter the shaman kept them moving into the night, until the last vestige of luminescence lit the horizon, leaving only enough light to see by as they made their camp. The nightly fires were small, their supply of wood quickly diminishing and augmented by horse dung which burned well but birthed a foul stench, cloying at clothes and hair.

"What a grand adventure you lead us on, my lord," Lorkan said one evening, his red-nosed face scarcely visible amidst the swaddle of seal fur, his misting breath leaving icicles on the hem of his hood. "Cold that cuts to the bone and the stink of shit from morn to night. If I have failed to say so before, please accept my humble gratitude for the opportunity to partake of such momentous history."

"Shut up," Cara told him wearily. She sat as close to the fire as she could, her face a worrying shade of white. The past days had been harder on her than any other in their company, seeing her stumble on at the tail end of their narrow line, shaking her head at Dahrena's entreaties that she ride her pony for a while. *I should have sent her back to the Reaches,* Vaelin thought, a pang of guilt prickling his chest as Cara held her mittened hands to the fire, her eyes a dull gleam in dark hollows. *She gave enough at Alltor.*

Wise Bear appeared at Cara's side, stooping to peer into her face with a critical frown before straightening, his expression one of hard reproach as he looked from Dahrena to Marken. "Why you not share?" he demanded.

Marken frowned at him, heavy brows bunching in bafflement. "Share what? She is welcome to my rations."

"Cah!" Wise Bear pointed his bone-staff at the large Gifted, sweeping it round to point at Lorkan, Dahrena and Kiral in turn. "Not meat. Share power." He laid a gentle hand on Cara's head, his voice softening with a faint tone of regret. "She is needed."

Dahrena leaned forward, her expression intent. "How? How do we share?"

Wise Bear stared at her for a moment then uttered a cackle of realisation. "Know so little," he said, shaking his head. He bent down to guide Cara to her feet and took her hand, holding his other out to Dahrena. "All share."

Dahrena rose to take his hand, soon joined by a cautious but clearly intrigued Kiral. Marken hesitated then went to take the huntress's outstretched hand. Lorkan, however, sat still and stared at them with sullen reluctance until Vaelin gave him an insistent prod with the tip of his scabbard. He got slowly to his feet but kept his arms crossed, his gaze lingering on Cara as she swayed a little from fatigue. "How do we know it won't hurt her?" he asked.

"No hurting," Wise Bear assured him. "Only need small power from each."

"It's all right, Lorkan," Cara said, smiling a little as she held out her hand. "If I trust him, so should you."

Vaelin stood as Lorkan completed the circle, casting a careful eye over the Lonak, sensing their sudden unease. Some murmured softly and turned their backs to walk away. A few lingered, shuffling in discomfort but seemingly unable to resist the sight of the Gifted, or the palpable change in the air around them; a new warmth that prickled the skin and drew a thin mist from the ice beneath their feet. They stood in utter stillness, hands clasped and silent, their features placid, even content, a small smile appearing on Cara's lips as the warmth deepened and they became wreathed in mist, a thin pool of melt-water playing about their fur-wrapped feet.

Vaelin found himself shamed by a sudden surge of envy, an unwelcome knowledge that such things were lost to him now. At Alltor he had thought himself the master of his song, finding a sense of completion amongst all the blood and carnage. *I was still just a child,* he realised, fighting a burgeoning sense of resentful despair, his gaze fixing on Wise Bear. *How much could he have told me?*

Cara gave an abrupt gasp, opening her hands to break the circle, her smile turning into a delighted laugh, cheeks flushed with a healthy pinkness. The others seemed similarly enlivened, Marken pulling the girl into an embrace and lifting her with a happy bellow, the others all exchanging glances rich in shared joy. Dahrena touched hands with Kiral, their faces bright with an identical expression of understanding. She caught sight of Vaelin and laughed, rushing to wrap her arms around him, her breath hot on his face as she raised herself to plant a kiss on his lips. Looking down at her wide-eyed, honest exuberance, he pulled her close, his resentment withering away.

Wise Bear gave a grunt of satisfaction and thumped his staff on the ice. "Sharing," he said then turned his gaze to the north, his wizened features hardening as he scanned the jagged horizon. "Needed soon."

◆ ◆ ◆

The storm hit the following day, a gale-driven blizzard swallowing the sun and turning the world into a howling white morass. The air became so thick with snow every breath drew jagged ice into Vaelin's throat and the wind seemed to cut through his furs as if they were no more than paper. He soon found himself fully occupied with holding fast to Scar's reins as the horse stumbled through the piling drifts, head lowered and eyes tight against the wind, his mane frozen and stiff on his neck.

This is madness, he knew with an awful certainty, a gust of wind driving into his side like a hammerblow. *I have doomed us.*

He turned as a shout reached him through the storm, catching a glimpse of two small figures, no more than the vaguest shadows in the ceaseless white. It seemed as if one of the figures raised something and the shadows instantly resolved into full clarity; Wise Bear holding his bone-staff aloft, his other hand clasped tight to Cara's as she knelt at his side, her face bleached and drawn from the cold but also set in a determined frown. The snow seemed to swirl around them, leaving them in a bubble of calm air, growing larger as they shared their power. The bubble expanded steadily, the calm air sweeping over Vaelin and Scar, the horse huffing a relieved sigh as the wind abated. Vaelin cast around until he found Dahrena, huddled against her pony's flank.

"And I thought the Black Wind the harshest in this world," she said, forcing a smile as he hurried to her side, lifting her clear of the snow that had collected around her and the pony.

Vaelin surveyed the company, finding them all now nearly enveloped in the bubble, the blizzard still raging beyond its confines. Orven's guardsmen were the last to receive its shelter, many stumbling to their knees in shock as they struggled free of the storm's fury. He saw Alturk moving amongst the

Sentar, dealing out cuffs and harsh rebukes as they stood staring in wonder and fear, forcing them back into motion. Vaelin went to Wise Bear and Cara, the shaman still holding her hand whilst she stood in serene indifference, her gaze distant, face free of any sign of fatigue. "How long can you do this?" he asked.

"As long as there is power to share," the shaman replied, pointing his staff at the other Gifted. "Hope storm ends first."

It took another day and a night for the storm to fade, the Gifted taking turns to share their strength with Cara. She was kept in the centre of the group, now tightly bunched to stay within the limits of the bubble she had crafted, moving east at a slow but steady pace. Whilst Cara showed no sign of weariness the sharing took an evident toll on the others, Marken sinking to his knees when his two-hour shift was done, wiping a trickle of blood from his beard before stumbling on as Vaelin hauled him up, providing a shoulder to lean on until he recovered sufficiently to walk unaided. Dahrena and Kiral were even more drained, rendered unable to walk and sagging pale and listless on the backs of their ponies. For some reason Lorkan proved the most durable of the Gifted, lasting a full three hours at Cara's side and only consenting to release her hand at Wise Bear's harsh insistence.

The storm ended as quickly as it had begun, the wind dying and the last flurries of snow falling to reveal a bright midday sun. Cara swayed a little when Wise Bear released her hand but otherwise seemed unharmed by her exertions, though her initial triumph at the feat dimmed at the sight of her companions. "I . . . didn't know I had taken so much," she offered to a pale-faced Lorkan.

He just smiled and shook his head. "Take all you want."

She shifted a little in discomfort at the directness of his gaze and turned to Wise Bear. "We should be cautious. There will be a price. There always is."

He nodded and thrust his staff through the snow to touch the ice beneath, angling his head as if straining to hear a distant sound. He stood unmoving for some time then straightened and turned to Vaelin with an urgent light in his eyes. "Need move fast," he said. "Much fast."

◆　◆　◆

They covered another six miles by nightfall but Wise Bear permitted no rest, hounding them on with impatient wafts of his bone-staff and tirades in his own language, unintelligible clicks and grunts that nevertheless conveyed the clear message that to linger meant death. Although cold enough to freeze misted breath, the air was calm now, barely touched by a breeze, the sky clear and bright with stars and the occasional flurry of Grishak's Breath. The atmosphere took on such a depth of silence that, when it came, the sound was enough to make Vaelin lift his hands to his already covered ears.

It was more a boom than a crack, a tremor thrumming the ice beneath his feet and making Scar rear in alarm. The entire company was forced to halt as the other horses gave shrill whinnies and sought to break free of their masters' grip. The booming crack went on unabated, the sound at first seeming to surround them on all sides but soon becoming concentrated on the westward floe they had just traversed, Vaelin's eyes picking out a curtain of shattered ice rising from the surface and moving from north to south so fast his eye couldn't track its course.

The sound ended without warning, leaving a vast but brief silence soon filled by a great grinding, almost beastlike in its intensity; as if the ice itself were groaning in pain. Another tremor shook the ice, this time with enough force to tip many from their feet, the surface beneath rising and falling in a great heave as the grinding faded. About a half mile to the west a fog of displaced snow and ice had risen, lingering for long enough to make Vaelin wonder if what he looked upon might be some trick of the eye; could the ice really be moving?

As the fog faded, the truth of it became clear; a huge expanse of ice was adrift, snow trailing from its jagged flanks as it detached from the main body and began a southward voyage. It must have measured at least five miles across, a newborn island where they would have undoubtedly perished as it bore them away.

◆　◆　◆

Kiral woke him whilst the sky was still dark, shaking him from Dahrena's slumbering embrace with insistent shoves. "My song is dark," she said. "Something to the north."

He followed her to the northern flank of the camp where they found Alturk kneeling amidst a broad patch of red-stained ice, gloved hands tracing the marks left by a brief but furious struggle. Vaelin had enough tracking skill to discern the meaning of the surrounding marks, the amount of blood and the furrows leading away into the blackness beyond the firelight. "How many were taken?" he asked.

"One, and his pony." Alturk, rose to his full height, heavy brows knitted in mingled anger and puzzlement. "These marks I do not know."

Vaelin looked down at the impressions left in the snow: a paw print, large enough for a black bear but not a brown.

"Not a bear," Kiral said, tracing an outline around one of the marks with the tip of her hunting knife. She rose to unsling her bow. "My song will find it soon enough."

"No." She turned at the sound of Wise Bear's voice, the shaman striding closer to prod at the bloodied prints with his staff. "Sent to leave a trail so you would follow."

"Something hunts us," Alturk said.

Wise Bear said something in his own language, mouth twisting in disgust as if the words stained his tongue. He caught Vaelin's enquiring gaze and provided a terse translation, "Cat People."

◆ ◆ ◆

"I hoped they had all perished." Dahrena sat close to the fire, extra furs heaped on her shoulders, clasping hands with Cara and Lorkan. "They were so few in number after the battle."

Vaelin resisted the impulse to ask her to forget this; shared strength or not, her gift always exacted a heavy toll and the prospect of once again confronting the Ice Horde no doubt stirred ugly memories. She saw his concern and gave a reassuring smile. "A short flight only. Wise Bear assures me they can't be far."

She closed her eyes, body stiffening and her face taking on the expressionless mask that indicated she had flown free, Cara and Kiral both issuing a gasp at the sensation. "She takes much," Kiral said with a grimace.

"What is this?"

Vaelin glanced up to find Alturk at his side, gazing at Dahrena with deep suspicion. Like all the Lonak his distrust of the Dark was obvious, but so far he was the only one who dared enquire as to its nature.

"She seeks our hunter," Vaelin told him.

The Tahlessa paced back and forth as Dahrena continued to sit immobile, his face betraying the only sign of fear Vaelin had yet seen in him. "There are Gifted among your people," he said, nodding at Kiral. "She serves the Mahlessa, as you do."

"As she should, for such things are only for the Mahlessa to know. Children like her are taken to the Mountain. If not they grow to be varnish, or worse."

"What happens to them at the Mountain?"

Alturk shrugged. "Some come back, some do not."

Vaelin returned his gaze to Dahrena, recalling her tale of the wolf and the men who had come to lay waste to her village. *It took her away, before she could journey to the Mountain. Was it saving her from death or from something worse?*

Dahrena's face spasmed and she uttered a harsh groan, slumping forward, prevented from falling into the fire by Kiral and Cara who gently guided her onto her back. She shuddered for a while as her body returned to warmth, finally getting to her feet, a deep frown betraying barely controlled pain. "A rock," she said. "Jutting from the ice five miles to the north-west. Only one man, but many cats. I think he sensed me. And I don't think he liked it."

Wise Bear's staff thumped hard onto the ice, his ancient face twisting as he voiced a name in his own language. Iron Claw seemed to sense his master's fury and lumbered to his side with an inquisitive growl.

"You know who we face?" Vaelin asked him.

"Cat People shaman," Wise Bear said. "The one who set them to war. Cat People named him Shadowed Path. Bear People called him No Eyes."

◆ ◆ ◆

The Sentar adopted a battle formation as they moved towards the north-west, stringing out in a loose but cohesive skirmish line for a hundred paces on either side of the company, the Gifted in the centre leading the horses and ponies. Orven's company brought up the rear, marching with swords drawn under orders to keep a constant watch on all approaches. Vaelin took the lead alongside Alturk and Wise Bear, Kiral trailing a little behind with an arrow notched to her bow. Iron Claw was out ahead, moving at a sedate run with an occasional pause to sniff the air.

Vaelin was struck by the abrupt change in Wise Bear; but for his creased face, all signs of age seemed to have vanished and he moved with a steady, unfaltering stride, bone-staff gripped tight and eyes locked on Iron Claw. He knew the expression well, a man intent on revenge.

Iron Claw halted and Wise Bear raised his staff bringing the company to a stop. The bear swayed from side to side, voicing a low rumble of disquiet as it eyed the ice ahead. It was different from the usual flat expanse, the surface raised in places to form jagged abstract shapes wreathed in a low-hanging mist. In the distance Vaelin could see the dim grey spike of the rock Dahrena had described, stabbing at the clear sky like a misshapen dagger.

"Good place for ambush," Alturk commented, eyes tracking over the fractured ice-scape.

Wise Bear strode to Iron Claw's side and took a two-handed hold of his staff, raising it above his head and standing immobile. He uttered no sound but Kiral's sudden gasp indicated he had sent a message by different means. Vaelin saw the huntress's gaze darken somewhat as she stared at the old man, her eyes betraying an even greater depth of awe, along with a clear sense of dread that caused Vaelin to wonder what grim notes rose from her song.

Wise Bear lowered his staff, expression unchanged as he stood, waiting.

It was only the space of a few seconds before an answer rose from the jagged ice, a cacophony of hissing, feral howls, a sound he had only heard from one beast before, but now there were many. He unslung his own bow as Kiral moved quickly to Wise Bear's side. Vaelin shrugged free of his heaviest furs and moved to the shaman's left, arrow notched, eyes scanning for the slightest movement.

"There!" Kiral shouted, her bow coming up but Vaelin was faster, his shaft flying free in an instant, streaking towards a silver-grey shape that had leapt into sight from behind a jagged ice pillar. It bounded on for a few strides then tumbled to the snow, lying still.

Wise Bear gave a harsh grunt and started forward, Iron Claw loping in his path. "We should wait," Vaelin told him. "There are more."

Wise Bear ignored him and kept on, betraying no reaction at all when a dozen more war-cats appeared out of the ice and charged towards him at full pelt. Vaelin judged them as roughly the same size as Snowdance but of much leaner appearance, their fur patchy and far more ragged, and their eyes . . . Snowdance was fearsome but he had never seen her eyes shine with such malevolent intent.

He put an arrow into the cat directly to his front as Kiral claimed two more in quick succession. The Sentar's bows also thrummed into life, more cats falling to the swarm of arrows, but leaving six still charging at Wise Bear, too fast for any archer to claim.

The lead cat, larger and even more ragged in appearance than its companions, leapt at Iron Claw, fangs bared and eyes blazing with an unnervingly knowing hatred. The great bear's claw caught it in midair before it could land a bite, sending it sprawling. It scrabbled on the ice, gathering itself then leaping once more, its wailing hiss enough to pain the ears. This time Iron Claw made sure of the kill, both arms closing on the cat as it sought to latch its fangs onto his throat, ribs breaking with audible cracks as it was borne to the ice and the bear stamped down, his shoulders rising and falling in rapid hammerblows until the beast lay in a broken and bloody ruin.

Vaelin notched a second arrow and took a bead on the other cats, finding to his horror that Wise Bear now stood before them, arms open and offering no resistance as they closed. Vaelin drew back his bowstring, aiming for the nearest cat's flank.

"Don't!" Kiral laid a hand on his arm. "Wait!"

Alturk barked a command at the Sentar and they lowered their bows, standing in appalled amazement as Wise Bear extended a hand to one of the beasts . . . and it shrank back, the snarl fading from its face, eyes suddenly freed of hate. The shaman's eyes roamed over the each of the cats producing an identical result, every one becoming instantly cowed under his gaze, lowering themselves in supplication, eyes averted, some even trembling.

Wise Bear turned to Vaelin, his expression no less implacable than before. "You come. Others stay."

◆ ◆ ◆

They proceeded through the maze of jagged ice alone save for Iron Claw, who was obliged to clamber over much of the disrupted surface as their way became ever more narrow. "How did you do that?" Vaelin asked, unsure whether he wanted, or would even understand the answer. The more he learned of Wise Bear the more mysterious, and more worrying his power.

"No Eyes grows weak," the shaman replied, a grim note of satisfaction in his voice. "Hold slackens. Cats are mine now."

"So there was no need for us to kill the others?"

Wise Bear paused as they came to an opening in the ice ahead, little more than a narrow crack in the blue-white wall. Beyond it Vaelin could see a patch of granite, the spike of the huge rock now looming above them, its flanks gleaming like poorly polished metal where ice had found purchase. "Not enough meat for all," Wise Bear said. His gaze locked onto Vaelin's, fierce and certain. "Say nothing. Do nothing. Listen only."

The ice beyond the crack was flat, forming a wide frozen moat around the great rock. Wise Bear led Vaelin to the right, a burgeoning stench of something rotten birthing a nausea in his gut, deepening at the sight of a large brownish black stain spreading out from the rock's eastern face. Moving closer Vaelin saw the stain was littered with bones; seal vertebrae and ribs mostly but here and there the unmistakable shape of a human skull, picked clean of flesh. The source of the stench became clear a moment later, a freshly dismembered pony carcass lying beside a shallow grotto in the face of the rock. From the crude but regular shape of it Vaelin deduced it as a man-made feature, providing some measure of shelter from these terrible climes.

A man sat at the base of the grotto, clad in moulded furs and seated on

QUEEN OF FIRE · 257

what appeared to be a chair fashioned from lashed-together bone. He was old, though not as old as Wise Bear, his skin leathery and discoloured, red sores visible on his bald head and cadaverous cheeks, and his eyes were two dark patches of old scar tissue. He sat so still Vaelin initially assumed him a corpse but then saw his nostrils flaring as he caught their scent and a thin smile curved his cracked lips.

"We'll speak in my brother's tongue, old friend," he said to Wise Bear. "It's only polite, don't you think?"

Vaelin knew him then, the awful familiarity of his voice, the same mocking smile. Wise Bear raised a hand and he realised he had unconsciously taken hold of his sword and started forward, intent on this thing's immediate murder. *The Witch's Bastard. How long has he been waiting?*

He released his grip and stepped back as Wise Bear stood regarding the thing in silence.

"Nothing to say?" the thing enquired, hairless brows raised above its scar eyes. "No final curses or long-prepared speeches? I've heard many over the years. Sadly, most are rather forgettable."

Wise Bear kept silent, shifting his gaze to the bones littering the surrounding ice, using his staff to prod at a skull lying amidst a shattered rib cage. It was small, little larger than an apple, but clearly human.

"Last of the Cat People," the thing said, hearing the sound of bone on bone. "They died happy, you know. Worshipping me, content to surrender their flesh in sustenance of my divine light."

His grin widened, revealing blackened and half-rotted teeth, his eyeless face turning to Vaelin. "They were a remarkable people, brother. Centuries spent living apart from all vestige of what we term civilisation, yet they had laws, art and wisdom enough to survive in the harshest place on earth. But they had no notion of a god, until I taught it to them, and how quickly they succumbed to the idea. After all, what else would you call a man who comes back to life after a spear-hawk rips the eyes from his skull?"

The cracked lips lost their smile, the face turning to Wise Bear once more. "It could all have been avoided, old friend. If you had but opened your heart to my message, my great mission for the ice people. The southern lands would have fallen to us, and the great forest beyond. Now your people are a wasted remnant and mine nothing but bones."

The sound of breaking ice heralded Iron Claw's arrival as he clambered over the surrounding wall, moving to Wise Bear's side, nostrils flaring at the scent of flesh. The eyeless man stiffened at the sound of the bear's approach but his voice remained free of fear. "You cannot threaten me, little man. Your beast holds no horrors for me. Ask my brother, he killed me once before and yet here I am. As I am elsewhere. I have waited here these long years for you to come. Pity my cats proved unequal to the task, but I am patient and I suspect you still have far to go."

"So you wait," Wise Bear said, moving forward in a rush, his hand flashing out to clamp onto the eyeless man's bald scalp. "Wait longer."

The eyeless man's mouth gaped, foul air rushing forth as he voiced a soundless scream, jerking spasmodically on his bone chair. He tried to claw at Wise Bear's arm but his fingers lacked any strength, fluttering like feathers over his sleeve as he convulsed.

Finally the shaman released him, stepping back as the eyeless man sagged, his face a mask of confusion and pain. "What did you do?" he asked in a faint rasp, his hands flailing at his own chest and face, the nails leaving shallow scars on his flesh.

"You wait," Wise Bear said again, turning his back. "Then you die. Forever."

"This is . . ." The thing tried to rise from the bone chair, reaching out to Wise Bear as he began to walk away. "This is impossible."

Wise Bear didn't turn, striding towards the crack in the ice wall with Iron Claw lumbering along behind.

"Brother!" It slid from the bone chair, reaching out to Vaelin as it crawled towards him, imploring. "Brother! Make him free me!"

Vaelin watched the thing crawl, seeing how little strength remained in its limbs, a twisted collection of skin and bone destined to perish when night brought a deadly chill. He gave no reply, turning to follow Wise Bear.

"You loved Barkus!" the thing called, voice cracking. "I *am* Barkus! I am your brother!"

Vaelin kept walking.

"I have knowledge! I know the Ally's design."

Vaelin stopped.

"I know . . ." The thing's voice faltered as he dragged air into ruined lungs. "I know what he wants."

"So do I," Vaelin said, glancing over his shoulder, seeing a dying man flailing amidst rotting flesh. "He wants to make an end. And we will."

◆　◆　◆

"Did you kill all of it?"

Wise Bear gave a regretful smile and shook his head. They had encamped in the shadow of the great rock amidst the shelter offered by the jagged ice, the Lonak raising their shelters at an even greater remove than usual, disconcerted by the five war-cats that sat around the shaman in unnerving silence. Vaelin turned to watch as Cara cautiously held a morsel of seal meat out to one of the cats, the beast ignoring her until Wise Bear glanced in its direction whereupon it snapped the treat from her fingers in a lightning bob of its head.

"Only part," he said turning back and extending his hand, splaying the stubby fingers. "Take one, can still use," he went on, miming the amputation of his thumb and making a fist. "But weaker now."

"If we find other parts of it," Vaelin said, "can you do the same to them?"

Wise Bear nodded. "If we find."

Vaelin looked at the looming rock spike wondering if the Witch's Bastard still somehow clung to life. *I suspect you still have far to go,* it had said. *It knew we were coming, but not why.* "Oh, I've little doubt they'll find us."

CHAPTER NINE

Lyrna

T ower Lord Al Bera's health had improved greatly since the liberation
of Varinshold, his skin notably less pale and his hands free of any
tremors. However, he still had difficulty standing for long periods
and Lyrna had been quick to usher him into a chair. She had summoned him
to her father's old rooms adjoining the council chamber. Once richly adorned
with various treasures it was now, of course, stripped of all but a few paintings and tapestries, former possessions of the late Lord Darnel no doubt
looted from murdered nobility. She had been scrupulous in cataloguing
every item found in the palace, distributing the list so that their true owners
could reclaim them, but no more than a handful of beggared lords and merchants had so far come forward.

"I recall my father naming you the Smuggler's Scourge, my lord," she told
Al Bera. "A hard-won title, no doubt."

Al Bera gave a stiff nod. She had noted before his discomfort in her presence, a wariness presumably born of the low station from which he had been
raised. "The smuggling gangs were greater in number in my youth, Highness," he replied. "I was a captain in the Realm Guard before King Janus
ordered me to take charge of his excisemen, a slovenly lot, given to graft and
drunkenness. Forging them into an effective arm of the Crown took time,
and more than a little blood."

"And yet you did it, breaking the strangle-hold the smugglers had on the
southern shore and doubling the port revenue in the process."

Al Bera gave a cautious smile. "With a little help from the Sixth Order."

"Nevertheless, the sword my father gave you was well earned." She
reached for the small wooden chest on the desk. "Sadly, I do not have another

to give you. As you might expect, the Volarians stole the entire royal collection. But I did find an old trinket of mine in the ruin of what was once my own rooms." She extracted the item from the box. The chain was new, fashioned from finely crafted silver but attached to an ancient amulet, a plain disc of bronze inlaid with a single bluestone.

"It's said this was worn by the mother of King Nahris," she continued. "The first to claim overlordship of all four fiefs of the Realm. Sadly, he was prone to bouts of madness and so the business of ruling his dominion fell to his formidable mother, Bellaris, the first to be named Chamberlain and Regent of the Unified Realm. A title I myself held briefly towards the end of the Alpiran war, and this"—she placed the amulet on the desk and slid it towards him—"was my badge of office."

The right choice, she decided, seeing the way he eyed the amulet, like a child regarding a snake for the first time.

"I . . ." he began, face reddening a little. "I am to be left behind, Highness?"

"You are to serve this Realm as ordered by your queen."

"If it is a question of my fitness for battle . . ."

"It is a question as to whom I can safely entrust governance of these lands in my absence. Nothing more. Lord Chamberlain Al Bera, please put on your badge of office."

He fingered the silver chain for a moment, jaws clenched and striving to conceal a faint tremble in his hand. "Did King Janus ever tell you why I was so good at catching smugglers, Highness?"

She smiled blandly and shook her head.

"Because my father was a smuggler. A man of great kindness at home but vicious temperament in business, a business that would have been mine had I not fled to join the Realm Guard at thirteen. By then I had come to understand what manner of man he was, how he was steeped in deceit and murder, and I wanted no part of it." He removed his hand from the chain. "And I want no part of this."

She maintained her smile, taking the chain and amulet from the desk and standing to move behind him. She felt him sag as she lifted the chain over his head and laid it on his shoulders, although it weighed no more than a few ounces. "Exactly, my lord." She leaned down and planted a soft kiss on his cheek, choosing to ignore his flinch as she moved back and he rose unsteadily to his feet.

"I will leave you twenty thousand Realm Guard," she told him. "They are to crush every remaining vestige of criminality within Asraelin borders, all miscreants to be executed without exception under the Queen's Word. I feel we have been too lenient of late. You will, however, steer clear of Cumbraelin lands unless in dire emergency or called upon by Lady Veliss. I will provide a list of other priorities, Aspect Dendrish's legal reforms and the reconstruction of this city being the most pressing."

She angled her head, studying the way the amulet hung around his neck, finding that his stoop had worsened a trifle. "It suits you very well, my lord."

He gave the most shallow of bows, his reply tense and clipped to remove all expression. "Thank you, Highness."

◆ ◆ ◆

Orena liked to dance in the afternoons, moving among the barren palace gardens with a joyful grace, sometimes catching hold of Murel's hands and pulling her into a whirl, laughing her girlish laugh. Today she wore winter-blooms in her hair, pale petals shining like stars in the dark mass as she spun and spun.

"Sit with me," Lyrna said as her dance finally came to a halt, Orena's skirts blossoming as she whirled to the ground with an exhausted but happy giggle. "I have cakes."

They were in the remnants of her former hidden garden, Lyrna arranging cakes alongside a porcelain tea-set on the bench next to her. Orena was very fond of cakes but continually lacking in manners, cramming one into her mouth the moment she sat down, fingers sticky with icing and cream. "Yum," she said, one of the few words she consented to speak these days, although it transpired this new Orena had little need of speech. Lyrna's head momentarily flooded with the sensation of enjoyment, the texture of the cake on her tongue, the softness of the cream. She had to concentrate to clear the images, a skill learned from Aspect Caenis, who advised repeating a numerical sequence as the best means of blocking Orena's wayward thoughts.

"Brother Innis tells me you have not been attentive at lessons recently," Lyrna told her.

Orena's thoughts took on a bored weariness, swallowing the last of the cake and rolling her eyes.

"Learning is important," Lyrna persisted. "Don't you want to read again?"

Orena shrugged and her thoughts shifted: joy and sunshine, the whirl of the dance.

"You can't dance forever, my lady." Lyrna reached out to take her hand. "I have to tell you something."

A sudden wariness at the gravity in her voice, a swelling fear.

"I have to go away for a time."

The fear surged and Orena's gaze went to Murel, standing nearby, hands clasped tight and forcing a comforting smile. She found being in Orena's company a painful trial, the weight of her unconstrained gift hard to bear, especially when it chose to share memories dreadfully reminiscent of those Murel fought to suppress.

"Yes," Lyrna said. "Murel too. And Iltis and Benten."

More fear, bordering on terror, a jarring sense of abandonment. Orena's hands clutched at Lyrna's, a desperate plea filling her gaze.

"No." Lyrna forced a note of command into her tone. "No, you cannot come with us."

Anger mingled with churlish reproach as Orena snatched her hands away, averting her gaze, her face a mirror of her thoughts.

"It is my hope," Lyrna said, voice soft as she traced her fingers through Orena's dark curls, "to return with a man who I think can heal you. I was selfish to let him go, but when he looked at me, looked at this face, I knew he saw that his gift had failed. I am beyond healing, but I think you are not, for your soul is so bright."

Orena's features softened, her face suddenly losing all vestige of the woman-sized child she appeared to be. She met Lyrna's gaze, brow furrowing . . . and the memories flooded forth.

Lyrna tried to summon a calculation to suppress the inrush of image and sensation, but the torrent was too great, overwhelming the trickle of numbers with an ease that told her Orena had been exercising much more control over her gift than they knew. The smell came first, brine, sweat and excrement. Then the sounds, the clink of chains, the muffled sobs of despairing souls. Vision and pain arrived together, the shackles chafing wrist and ankle, the dim outline of huddled captives. She was back in the hold, a slave once more. Her panic flared then receded as she saw the view differed from her own memory, the steps leading to the upper deck now seen from a less acute angle, and chained next to them a young woman in a blue dress, her face shadowed but the play of light on her hairless scalp revealing dreadful burns. Nevertheless, she knew this profile, she had seen it outlined against a campfire on a distant mountainside a few months before. Exhilaration mixed with malicious satisfaction in her breast . . . along with heady anticipation of the Ally's reward.

The memory blurred, fracturing and re-forming into a scene of terror, the hull splintered by the shark's ramming, screaming desperation on all sides. She saw the burnt woman standing next to the steps, key dangling from her grasp. The moment of hesitation was brief, barely noticeable but these eyes had centuries of practice in discerning weakness and she knew in a rush of grim understanding that this newly risen queen was about to abandon her subjects to their fate.

It had been a long time since she felt anything close to wonder, but the sensation that gripped her as she watched the burnt woman return to free first the brutish brother, then the outlaw, and then, incredibly, herself, was the closest she had come for many lifetimes. The babble of thanks she offered the burnt woman as she struggled towards the steps surprised her further, for it was completely genuine.

The images blurred into another memory, Harvin's scarred face poised above hers, breath mingling as their lips touched. "I'll never hurt you," he whispered. "And nor will anyone else."

"You can't promise that," she whispered back. "No one can."

His fingers played over the bruises on her neck, faded but still dark enough to spoil the pleasing smoothness of this shell's skin. "I promise I'll visit bloody murder on every Volarian shit we find, just on the off-chance he was the one who did this."

She felt something then, something more than familiar lust, and it irked her. "Enough talking," she said, pushing him onto his back and straddling his waist. "And try to keep quiet this time."

The final shift was more abrupt, as if Orena sensed her discomfort. The deck of the *Sea Sabre* pitched continually that day, the seas around the Wensel Isle were rarely calm. She looked up at the burnt woman and the ring she offered, wondering why the tears came so easily. Normally she had to force them, but that day they streamed unbidden from her eyes. "I think such trivia is beyond us now, my lady," the burnt woman said and a thing that had long forgotten its own name knew then she had found a queen.

Lyrna gasped as the final memory slipped away, finding herself staring into Orena's apologetic eyes, an uncertain smile on her lips.

"Highness?" Murel hovered at her side, touching a tentative hand to her shoulder.

Lyrna stood and pulled them both into an embrace, Orena clutching her waist as Murel rested her head on her shoulder. "I only ever had ladies," Lyrna told them. "Never friends."

Orena's thoughts gave a final pulse, heavy with a sense of regretful necessity; a lesson she barely understood but needed to share: *they can change.*

◆ ◆ ◆

They thronged the docks to watch her go, drowning her in a tumult of cheers and exhortations as she ascended the gangplank to the deck of the *Queen Lyrna*, all those not chosen to sail the ocean and finish her great crusade; the old, the young and the skilled. Many were weeping, some openly decrying their shame and begging to be allowed to join her. A cordon of Realm Guard kept them back, preventing the more ardent from jumping into the harbour and attempting to swim for the ship.

"Fleet Lord Ell-Nestra," she greeted the Shield as he performed a precisely formal bow.

"Highness," he said in the neutral tone she found ever more grating. "The ships from South Tower and Warnsclave approach. We will rendezvous ten miles from shore, weather permitting."

She ignored the final jibe, softly spoken though it had been. He and several of his captains had voiced objections to her decision to sail so early in the year, advising the winter storms would still be raging on the high seas. He was unmoved by Brother Harlick's carefully prepared tables of historical weather patterns, indicating the northern Boraelin underwent a five-week period of relative calm during the months of Illnasur and Onasur. "Just marks on paper, Highness," the Shield had said, casting a dismissive eye over the librarian's papers. "Udonor doesn't read."

"He may not, but I do," Lyrna replied. "Our enemies do not expect us until the spring and I will not pass up an opportunity to surprise them. Our fleet will be complete within the month whereupon we will sail, with or without you."

Her gaze went to the *King Malcius*, unfurling sail as she cleared the mole. Beyond her a long line of equally huge vessels ploughed towards the horizon. At the end of the mole she could see a figure seated before a vast canvas perched precariously on an easel. Master Benril, come to capture the scene, though the slate-grey sky and misted horizon made for a gloomy spectacle.

The Shield bowed again and began calling out the orders that would see them away from the docks, the crew running to detach lines and heave the beams into place to push them from the wharf.

"Wait!" Lyrna ordered as her gaze found a diminutive figure at the prow. Alornis didn't look up from the contraption as Lyrna approached, gently tapping a small hammer to some piping on its underside. "My lady," Lyrna said.

"Highness." Alornis gave the pipe a final tap, smiling in satisfaction at the sound it produced.

"If your work here is complete," Lyrna went on, "I would ask that you go ashore."

"Sadly this new device requires more work." Alornis gave a transparently forced laugh and crouched to inspect the machine's supporting legs. "I can't possibly let it sail in such condition, Highness."

Lyrna went to her side, speaking in soft tones. "I gave your brother the most solemn promise that I would keep you safe. Now, remove yourself to the shore or I'll have Lord Iltis do it for you . . ."

"They killed Alucius!" Alornis whirled towards her, the hammer flying across the deck as she tossed it aside, face livid, her shout heralding a frigid stillness on the deck. "You promise justice." Alornis's voice had taken on a strangled tone though she forced the words out, her gaze tearful but unwavering. "I have travelled the length of this Realm recording murder and destruction with every mile, and laboured without sleep for months to provide you these deadly instruments. All without request for reward or expectation of favour, because you promised justice, and I want mine."

He will never forgive this, Lyrna knew. *Even if she lives.*

"Fleet Lord Ell-Nestra," she said, turning away. "Please get us under way."

◆　◆　◆

The first few days were hard, the seas high enough to rob the fleet of any appearance of cohesion, many of the ships lost to sight in the near-constant rain. At the Shield's orders, every vessel had experienced navigators on board, most of them Meldeneans who could be trusted to keep an eastward bearing regardless of the weather. Even so there were times when Lyrna looked out on the shifting grey wall that surrounded them and had to suppress the feeling they were sailing alone.

Belowdecks Lord Nortah's regiment suffered continually with sea-sickness and the confines of shipboard life. They had to be ferried to the top deck in relays for fresh air and exercise, most stumbling through their drills, moving with perfunctory lethargy, though Lyrna's presence seemed to provide some stimulus to extra effort. The slight woman with the daggers she remembered from Alltor greeted her with a grave bow upon ascending into the daylight the third morning out from Varinshold, proceeding to throw herself into a series of sword drills with zealous energy before collapsing in a sudden convulsion. Her bleached white face looked up at Lyrna stricken with mortification as she strode forward to help her up.

"I beg forgiveness, Highness," she stammered. "Though my wretched weakness deserves no pardon . . ."

She fell silent when Lyrna pressed a hand to her forehead, finding it far too chilled and clammy. "Guardswoman Furelah," she said, "you are unwell."

Furelah blinked in surprise at being addressed by name then drew herself up to her not-considerable full height. "No more than anyone else, Highness." She staggered as the ship's hull crested another steep wave, Lyrna feeling how she trembled as she reached out to steady her by the arm.

"What did you do?" she asked. "Before the war."

"My father owned a mill, Highness. I worked it with him."

"Then you are familiar with gears and machinery?"

"Had to be, Highness. After that worthless fu— . . . My daughter's father was not a dutiful man, forcing us to seek refuge with my father. After a while his hands got too gnarled for fixing things."

"Come with me."

She led her to the stern where Alornis was rigging a tarpaulin over one of the ship's four ballistae. The constant rain and spume were a source of great consternation as she sought to keep her precious engines free of rust and the salt that played havoc with her various mechanical novelties. "Lady Alornis," Lyrna called to her, gesturing at Furelah. "I am appointing this guardswoman as your assistant. Please instruct her in the operation of your engine."

Alornis greeted Furelah with a bemused smile. "Thank you, Highness, but I need no assistance."

"Battle will be upon us soon, my lady," Lyrna replied. "And it plays no favourites. Should you fall it is important your knowledge not perish with you."

Alornis winced a little at the harshness of her tone then offered her hand to Furelah who, despite her evident nausea, stood regarding the ballista with deep fascination. "You built this, my lady?"

"I had help." Alornis took her hand and led her towards the contraption. "Come, best if we start with the gearing."

◆　◆　◆

The evening of the tenth day brought the first storm, a howling northerly gale slamming a series of ever-taller waves against the *Queen Lyrna*'s port side, eventually forcing the Shield to order a turn to the south. Lyrna had expected some expression of reproach as she watched him take the tiller, his hands moving with expert efficiency to steady the great vessel, but instead he seemed oddly content, casting occasional glances at the sky and frowning in apparent satisfaction.

"It seems my calculations may have been optimistic," Lyrna offered, having to shout above the wind as she moved to his side.

"You mean this?" A spectre of his once-continual grin played over his lips as he jerked his head at the roiling sky overhead. "This is a gentle breeze compared to the Boraelin's usual winter fury. It'll have blown itself out come the morning."

She lingered, seeing his reluctance to look at her, the stiffness of his shoulders. "Why did you stay?" she asked. "I know you wanted no part of this."

"Despite my misgivings I can't deny the wisdom in your words. If we don't finish them, they'll come again. Better one long war than a dozen short ones, bleeding the Isles white with every generation called to fight them. Besides, I made a commitment, as you may recall."

She remembered that night after the Teeth, his offer of another life and the promise made beneath the stars. "If it's any comfort," she told him, "we would never have sailed the western ocean together. Regardless of any other . . . developments."

He didn't turn but she saw his shoulders slump a little. "No," he replied, his tone sombre rather than bitter. "That day at Alltor, the way you looked at Al Sorna . . . And I thought there was nothing else he could take from me. And your face. The face of a stranger."

"I had hoped you might see the face of a friend."

She heard him utter a faint laugh above the wind. "Is that what you imagine the future holds for us? Friendship? When this war is won you think I'll still command your fleet? Stay at your side for all the long years of your reign? Your faithful former pirate? Your muzzled dog?" He glanced over his shoulder at her, rain coursing down his face, all vestige of his smile gone. "I let you put me in a cage, Lyrna. Don't ask me to live in it forever."

Lyrna turned as Murel tugged insistently on her arm, gesturing at the door to her cabin where Iltis stood, drenched from head to toe and wearing an expression of pointed impatience.

"I strongly suggest you take shelter, Highness," the Shield said, hauling on the tiller anew as another wave lifted the prow towards the sky. "Storms have no respect for rank."

◆ ◆ ◆

As he had predicted the weather calmed over the succeeding days, allowing Lady Alornis an opportunity to demonstrate her new device. "Brother Harlick was kind enough to provide a few inspiring examples from history," she said, fitting a large set of bellows onto a copper tube protruding from the contraption's underside. The engine had been placed on the *Queen Lyrna*'s port bow and was even odder in appearance than the ballista; a brass-and-iron tube some twelve feet long, bulbous at one end tapering to a narrow spout. A large barrel sat atop it halfway along its length and it rested on an identical base to the ballista, meaning even someone of Alornis's diminutive proportions had little difficulty adjusting its angle. Furelah stood at the thing's narrow end, fixing what appeared to be an elongated oil lamp to the spout. From the way she stood, working with arms fully extended and eyes continually straying to the barrel fixed to the device, Lyrna divined her Lady Artificer's latest novelty harboured considerable potential.

"There were no images to work from," Alornis went on, running a cloth over some kind of circular lever on the contraption's bulbous end. "But an Alpiran text from some six hundred years ago did provide a fulsome description of the machinery. The greatest difficulty was in establishing the correct mix for the fuel."

"This is an Alpiran device?" Lyrna asked her.

"Indeed, Highness. Used in a sea battle during one of their civil wars. It seems the emperor of the day witnessed its first use and promptly outlawed it, fearing the gods might judge him needlessly cruel. They called it Rhevena's Lance."

Rhevena, Lyrna knew, was a principal goddess in the Alpiran pantheon, guardian of the dark paths that must be traversed by every soul upon death. But Rhevena was a kindly goddess and lit the paths with fire so that no good souls lost their way. However, the fire was a living thing, possessed of wisdom and insight, and would flare to engulf an unworthy soul. Lyrna's heart began to beat faster as she noted the way Furelah completed her task and moved back from the engine with ill-concealed haste, the lamp she had fitted to the spout now lit with a bright yellow flame.

"Lamp oil is too thin," Alornis continued, working a spigot on the side of the barrel, "and burns away too quickly. So I was obliged to use base oil. Even then it required thickening with pine resin." She stood back, giving her invention a final look of appraisal before turning to Iltis and Benten. "My lords, the bellows if you would."

The two lords moved to the bellows, standing side by side to grip the large iron rod fixed to it, both raising a questioning glance at Lyrna. She tried to still the rising pitch of her heartbeat and inclined her head to set them to work. It took several heaves before anything happened but when it did Lyrna was grateful for the shout of alarm that sounded the length of the ship as it concealed her own fearful gasp. A stream of bright yellow fire erupted from the machine's spout, arcing fully thirty feet from the ship to cascade into the sea amidst a cloud of steam. The becalmed seas had allowed much of the fleet to resume their formation and a chorus of excited shouting could be heard from the nearby ships as the arc of fire continued to flow.

"Aiming is fairly straightforward," Alornis said, manoeuvring the lance about so the arc wafted the air like a flaming fan. She signalled for Benten and Iltis to stop and turned to Lyrna, the last dregs of burning oil falling behind her, smiling in expectation of royal praise.

Lyrna resisted the urge to wipe the sweat from her brow and kept her hands clasped together beneath her cloak, fearing so many eyes witnessing how badly they trembled. *The smell of her hair burning . . . The searing lick of the flames as they ate her flesh . . .* The tremble in her hands increased, threatening to spread to her arms as she continued to stare at Alornis's prideful visage. *What have I made in you?*

She felt a gentle touch on her arm and turned to find the Shield at her side, favouring Alornis with his broadest grin. "A remarkable feat, my lady," he said. "A weapon to win a war if ever I saw one. Wouldn't you agree, Highness?"

Lyrna took a breath, feeling the tremble abate as the warmth spread from his touch. "My Lady Artificer exceeds all expectations," she said to Alornis. "Do you have more of these?"

"I brought sufficient components for only another two, Highness. Perhaps, when we reach our destination I can fashion more if the right materials could be found."

More? I'm not sure I want one. "Please proceed with construction. Fleet Lord Ell-Nestra will decide which vessels will benefit from your mighty gift."

◆　◆　◆

She tried to sleep but found herself unable to settle, squirming in her bunk and trying to force the image of the flaming arc from her mind. Finally she abandoned the attempt and went to seek out Alornis, Iltis rousing himself and following without need of any instruction. The Queen's Artificer was hard at work in the corner of the hold given over to her various novelties. Furelah lay in a hammock nearby, her sleep untroubled by the gentle sway of the ship. "Her stomach seems to have adjusted to ship life," Alornis said, looking up from a length of copper tubing. "Sleep comes easier to her now."

"She is fortunate," Lyrna replied. "You find her work satisfactory, I trust?"

"She's very deft and clever, Highness. Given enough time I'm sure she'll craft some devices of her own."

Lyrna sat on the bench opposite Alornis, watching her work, nimble hands shaping the copper tube as she held it over a flame to soften the metal. "You should get some rest yourself," Lyrna told her.

A faint tic of discomfort passed across Alornis's brow, though she remained intent on her task. "I find sleep often eludes me these days, Highness."

"You miss your brother, and Alucius."

She saw Alornis smother a sigh and put the tube aside. "Is there something you require, Highness?"

"Don't you wonder what he would have made of this? If he would have been as fierce in his devotion to this cause as you are?"

"Alucius was a peaceful man. It didn't save him."

"He was also a spy in service to a foreign power. Did you know that?"

"Not until recently. The slave soldier, the one set to guard him, came to me before he left with Brother Frentis. Alucius gave him a message for me before he died. So yes, I know all about his . . . unfortunate allegiances, and I find it does not lessen my opinion of him one whit."

"What else did the message say?"

"Words for my ears alone, Highness."

Lyrna felt she could discern the contents of the freed Kuritai's message clearly enough from the guarded look in Alornis's eyes. *Did you love him back?* she wanted to ask, but stopped herself. "War has changed us all," she said instead. "And I know Alucius would not have relished seeing the change in you."

Alornis's gaze became a hard glower. "Or in you, Highness."

"You have a choice, I was robbed of such luxury the day they took my face and came to ruin our nation. But you can still turn away. How do you imagine you'll feel when that monstrous device of yours turns men into living torches? The cries of a burning man are not an easy thing to hear."

"You have asked all of us to bear many burdens. I'll not shirk mine."

I will send you back the moment we land, Lyrna decided as Alornis returned to her work. *I should never have brought you, the Realm has no need of one more twisted soul, however skilled.*

She raised her head as a shout sounded through the decking above, soon followed by a tumult of booted feet and the rapid pounding of the bosun's drum calling all hands to arms.

"What is it?" Alornis asked.

"An enemy ship." Lyrna rose and made for the steps to the upper deck. "Perhaps we'll have an early opportunity to see your novelties at work."

◆ ◆ ◆

Crewmen ran to their stations, weapons in hand, whilst archers climbed the rigging with bows on their backs. The deck below her feet thrummed with the din of Lord Nortah's regiment readying itself for battle. She found the Shield at the starboard rail, eyeglass trained on something to the south.

"How many?" Lyrna asked, moving to his side and peering into the gloom, finding only the faintest smudge some miles distant. The sky had brightened somewhat, still dim and thick with cloud but there was enough light to reveal the horizon.

"One," he replied and pointed to a smaller Meldenean vessel a half mile away, sails full and wake bright about her hull as she ploughed towards the newcomer. "I've signalled the *Orca* to investigate."

Lyrna glanced at the prow where Alornis and Furelah were busy readying the ballista and resisted the urge to order her below. "A patrol ship?" she asked Ell-Nestra.

"Most probably, though they're too far out for this time of year."

It took perhaps a half hour's tense waiting as the *Orca* faded into the misted horizon before the Shield gave a satisfied grunt and lowered his spyglass. "The *Orca* hoists the signal for a captured prize and requests we come alongside."

"Then do so."

The Shield's orders sent men hurrying to haul sail and it wasn't long before the *Orca* came into sight, her sails lowered as she wallowed next to a dark hulled Volarian freighter, held close by numerous lines and boarding ladders. Lyrna could see several Meldeneans on the Volarian's deck, standing over a short line of kneeling captives, all grey-clad with one exception. *A red-clad,* Lyrna wondered as the captive's appearance became clearer. *In the middle of the ocean with no escort.*

"Have that one brought aboard," she told the Shield, pointing to the red-clad who she now saw was of somewhat ragged appearance, his robes dishevelled and face grey with stubble and fatigue. Peering closer she found a familiarity to his features, a resemblance to another red-clad who had the misfortune to find himself in Meldenean hands. "And signal the ship carrying Aspect Caenis," she added. "I have need of one of his brothers."

◆ ◆ ◆

"How old are you?"

The red-clad stared back at her with dull eyes, features slack with fatigue.

She had ordered him taken to her cabin where he sat slumped in a chair with Iltis standing at his back. Brother Verin of the Seventh Order stood near the door, a thin young man with a nervous smile who had only managed the barest mumble of acknowledgment at Lyrna's greeting before bowing with such haste he nearly fell over. She could only hope his awe didn't affect his gift.

As the red-clad continued to stare silently Iltis put a large hand on his shoulder, leaning down to speak softly in his ear. "Answer the queen or I'll skin your hide before the pirates throw you to the sharks."

From the red-clad's spasm of anger Lyrna deduced his understanding of Realm Tongue to be more than adequate, though he spoke in Volarian. "Older than you can imagine," he said, his voice the cultured vowels of the Volarian ruling class.

"Oh I think not," Lyrna replied in Realm Tongue. "And speak in my language, if you please. As to your age, from what your sister told me, I estimate you to be somewhere over three hundred years old."

His gaze regained some spark of life at the mention of his sister, though he gave no reply.

"Honoured Citizen Fornella Av Entril Av Tokrev," Lyrna went on. "She is your sister is she not? And you are Council-man Arklev Entril." *Whose son I had the pleasure to kill some months ago,* she added silently.

"You hold my sister?" he asked, dropping into heavily accented but understandable Realm Tongue.

"Not at present. Though she was well when last I saw her, if slightly aged."

"Where is she?"

"You seem to misunderstand the purpose of this meeting, Council-man. We are not here so I can answer your questions, quite the opposite in fact. And our first order of business is to establish why a member of the Volarian Ruling Council comes to be so easily captured on the high seas."

Arklev slumped further, weariness and defeat plain in the sigh that escaped him. "There is no Ruling Council now, just the Ally and the elverah he chooses to name Empress."

Lyrna glanced at Brother Verin. He had been carefully instructed in his role though his hands shook a little as he touched a single finger to his wrist.

"Elverah means witch or sorceress, as I recall," Lyrna said.

"The name began with her, she earned it well." A faint glimmer of defiance crept into his eyes as he raised his head. "You met her the day she had her creature kill your brother."

Lyrna fought down the anger and the instant flood of horror-filled memories. *Anger is dangerous here,* she knew. *Provoking unwise action when so much can be learned.* "Brother Frentis killed her," she said.

"Merely the destruction of an old shell. Now she has a new one."

"And this creature alone has seized your empire?"

"She does the Ally's bidding. It seems he has decided the Council was superfluous to his needs."

"They were killed?"

He lowered his gaze and nodded.

"And yet you survive."

"I was delayed on a business matter the day she struck. Her Kuritai were everywhere in Volar, killing all who served the Council, every servant, slave and family member. Thousands purged in a single day. I managed to flee to the docks. My family owns many ships, though there was only one in the harbour and we were obliged to sail with scant supplies. The ship was half-wrecked by a storm three days ago."

Lyrna saw Brother Verin stiffen and gave him a questioning glance. His nerves clearly hadn't abated but there was a certainty in his movements as he touched his wrist, this time with two fingers.

"I assume," she said, turning back to Arklev, "this new Empress is fully aware of our intentions?"

"Your invasion was expected in the summer. She gathers forces at the capital and calls the remaining fleet there. It was the Ally's plan to sail out to meet you with a thousand ships and all the troops we could muster. It seems he becomes impatient and keen to see an end to any more frustrations."

Lyrna's gaze flicked to Verin's hands, finding he was once again touching his wrist with two fingers instead of one.

"I realise I have been remiss," she said to Arklev, gesturing at the young brother, "in not introducing Brother Verin of the Seventh Order, a young man with a very useful ability. Brother, please relate what lies this man has told me."

Verin coughed, flushing a little and speaking in slightly tremulous tones. "I . . . I believe he was present when the Council fell. He lied about running to the docks and taking ship. He lied about the plan to counter the invasion."

"Thank you, brother." She looked down at Arklev, finding him now tense with fear but also a determined defiance, glaring back at her, jaw set and mouth firmly closed. "Lord Iltis," Lyrna said. "Remove this man's robe."

Arklev tried to fight, flailing at Iltis with his manacled wrists only to be cuffed to the deck and pinned with a knee pressed into his back. The Lord Protector ripped the robes from his back in a few seconds, revealing an intricate pattern of fresh scars covering his torso from waist to chest.

Lyrna turned to a white-faced Brother Verin who blanched a little under her gaze, edging away a little. "Please fetch Lady Davoka," she told him. "She will know what to bring."

CHAPTER TEN

Frentis

T he Varikum sat on a low hill, a squat stone fortress of five interconnected circular bastions. They had been obliged to wait for three
days in the hills to the south for a caravan to appear, twenty wagons
bearing supplies and fresh slaves for training. It was well protected with a
mix of mounted Varitai and Free Sword mercenaries. Fortunately it appeared
news of the Red Brother's favoured tactics hadn't made it across the ocean
because they reacted with all predictability to the sight of a cluster of terrified slave girls stumbling along the road. Whoever had command of the convoy's guard promptly sent his Free Swords galloping to investigate without
bothering to properly secure the column's flanks. Frentis waited until the
Free Swords surrounded the girls, watching as Lemera tearfully related the
tale of her poor murdered master, collapsing to her knees from the terror of
it all. The Free Sword leading the riders made the mistake of dismounting to
pull her upright, taking hold of her head and turning it side to side in
appraisal, then staggering back as her hidden knife came free to slash his
neck open.

The archers accounted for the remaining Free Swords, a cloud of arrows
arcing down from the surrounding rocks to claim them, the girls falling on
those still living as they lay in the road, daggers rising and falling in a frenzy.
Frentis led Illian's group of freed slaves on foot against the convoy's flank,
Slasher and Blacktooth bounding on ahead to each drag a Varitai from the
saddle. The column's fate was sealed when Master Rensial and their dozen
mounted fighters charged against its rear, quickly dispatching the remaining
defenders. The convoy's overseer was the last to fall, a typically hulking figure, standing atop the lead wagon, his whip cracking viciously as he lashed

at the circling riders with no apparent sign of fear. Illian ducked under his whip to leap up onto the wagon, slashing his feet from under him and deftly tugging the whip from his hand as he fell. In the Martishe they had always endeavoured to take any overseers alive; newly liberated slaves tended to appreciate it.

The slaves numbered over thirty people, mostly men, sitting shackled in caged wagons in the centre of the column. There were also half a dozen women, chosen for youth and strength. "The spectacles are more popular when they offer a certain variety," Lekran explained. "It's a tradition to match women against beasts in honour of ancient myths. The Volarians discarded their gods but kept much of their stories, especially the bloody tales."

Frentis was gratified to find most of the slaves were Realm folk, with some dark-skinned Alpirans from the southern empire. From the treatment meted out to the overseer it was also clear they would make willing recruits.

"You did well," Frentis told Lemera, crouched over the body of a Free Sword as she divested it of any useful or shiny items. She replied with a shy smile which faded into a wince at the overseer's scream. "Freedom is a hard road," Frentis told her before going to find Thirty-Four.

◆ ◆ ◆

"You are content with your part in this?"

Eight glanced at his two fellow former Varitai and nodded. The days since their liberation had seen them suffer through many hours of sleepless pain as the absence of karn took its toll. However it had also brought a new light to their eyes, plus a tendency to stare at the sky or the landscape, as if seeing them for the first time. They spoke little and Frentis had begun to wonder if they truly understood their situation, but now saw an awareness in their gaze, as well as a sense of certainty.

"We will free as many Varitai as we can," Frentis went on, "but we cannot free all. You understand this?"

Eight nodded again, speaking slowly, his voice raspy and the words formed with deliberate care, "We were . . . dead. Now . . . we are alive. We will make others . . . live."

"Yes." Frentis lifted the sword taken from a fallen Varitai and handed it to Eight. "Many others."

Thirty-Four's brief discussion with the overseer revealed the Varikum to be protected by no less than sixty Varitai supplemented by a dozen overseers. Fortunately they were largely devoted to internal defence with no more than a handful set to guarding against an incursion. "Garisai are notoriously difficult to keep," Thirty-Four advised. "They are never given drugs and are not bound like Kuritai."

"How many can we expect to free?" Frentis asked.

"The overseer estimated over a hundred. But you should not expect all to be willing recruits, brother, or easy to command. Life in the Varikum is brutal and short, many perish in training and fewer still survive their first experience of the spectacles. It is not uncommon for Garisai to be driven mad by their trials."

Frentis glanced at Master Rensial, sitting on the ground nearby with the vacant expression that always seemed to grip him in the aftermath of a battle. *Then they'll be in good company.*

He had Lekran play the role of the overseer, clothed in black with whip in hand. Frentis and Master Rensial had donned the garb of Free Sword mercenaries and rode alongside the lead wagon as it ascended the slope to the Varikum's main gate. The establishment's lack of preparedness was evident in the fact it was already open, a large man striding forth to greet them with a harsh glower.

"You fuckers are late!" he snarled at Lekran, then paused with a suspicious frown. "Where's Mastorek?"

"If the old women in my village are to be believed," the former Kuritai said, standing to unsling his axe from where it was hidden beneath his jerkin, "suffering a thousand years torment beyond the endless sea. You can greet him there."

The overseer was still wearing a baffled expression as the axe swept down to cleave his skull.

Frentis spurred his horse forward, sword drawn as he galloped through the gate, cutting down another overseer trying desperately to haul it closed. Two Varitai rushed forward from a shadowed doorway, short swords drawn back, then rolled under the hooves of Master Rensial's horse as he rode them down. Frentis dismounted, falling in beside Lekran as he came charging past, axe in hand, the three former Varitai close behind along with all the fighters in their small army, Frentis having seen little point in moderation now.

According to a prearranged plan, their force divided as it reached the inner keep, Lekran taking half the force right whilst Frentis went left. Resistance was sporadic but fierce, three or four Varitai at a time attempting to block their path but soon overwhelmed by the onslaught. Eight, together with Weaver and his two freed Varitai, had been given the role of capturing as many alive as possible; Weaver would loop his thick rope around one and drag him to the ground whilst the others closed in to bind him. Their success was small, only seven more captured alive by the time the Varikum fell, its elegant curving marble hallways liberally streaked with blood from end to end.

Frentis ordered Illian's group to scour the Varikum for survivors then sent Draker and his disguised Realm folk to the battlements with instructions to give every appearance that business here continued as normal. He made his way to the wide sand-covered circle in the centre of the main keep, finding a dense knot of men and women standing in a defensive formation. They had arranged themselves in three tight, disciplined ranks, faces set and grim with defiance, although their weapons consisted of only wooden short swords and spears. The sand around them was littered with the bodies of their overseers, cut down by the archers who had occupied the balcony overlooking the arena. It seemed their attack had caught the Varikum in the middle of its afternoon practice.

"They think we're bandits on a slaving expedition," Lekran commented as Frentis entered the circle. "Finding it hard to convince them otherwise."

Frentis sheathed his sword and strode towards the group, seeing how they tensed at his approach, his eyes picking out the scars they bore. It appeared none had escaped injury, either from the whip or whatever torments the veterans had suffered in the spectacles. He halted ten paces short, scanning for some semblance of recognition among the faces but seeing only suspicion.

"Are there any here from the Unified Realm?" he asked in Realm Tongue. The response was mostly a series of baffled glares though one did stir at the words, a light-skinned man slightly older and even more scarred than the others. Like all of them his head was shaven and he wore a loose shift that revealed a body honed to the kind of leanness that only came from years of hard training.

"Last of the land-bound died two days ago," he said in a Meldenean accent. He cocked his head at Frentis, mouth twisting in faint contempt. "They rarely last long."

One of the others spoke up, a short but well-muscled young woman holding a wooden spear level with Frentis's eyes. "Tell him if he intends to sell us, he better be prepared to bleed for the privilege," she said in Volarian.

"I speak your language," Frentis told her, raising his hands, palm open. "And we come only to free you."

"For what?" she replied, her glower losing none of its intensity.

"That," he told her, "is surely for you to decide."

◆ ◆ ◆

In all some two dozen of the freed Garisai opted to leave, the Meldenean among the first to depart. "No offence, but a pox on your rebellion, brother," he said in an affable tone at the gate, hefting a sack laden with sundry valuables and provisions. "Done two spectacles and that's enough blood for any life. I'm taking myself to the coast where I'll find anything that floats and sail to the Isles. Expect my wife's probably found another willing prick by now, but still, home is home."

"Your people are allied with us," Frentis pointed out. "The Ship Lords have agreed a formal treaty."

"Really? Then a pox on them too." He gave a brief grin of farewell and started off towards the west at a steady run.

"Coward," Lekran muttered.

Or the wisest man I've met in a long time, Frentis thought, watching him go.

The young woman from the practice ground had been elected to speak for her fellow Garisai and named herself as Ivelda. Frentis divined a certain tribal enmity from the hard looks and similar accent she shared with Lekran. "She is Rotha," he had advised, his gaze darkening. "They cannot be trusted."

"Othra means 'snake' in our tongue," she replied, her hand closing on the short sword she had claimed from the pile of captured weapons. "They drink the piss of goats and lie with their sisters."

"If you intend to kill each other," Frentis said as Lekran bridled, finding himself too weary to intervene, "do it outside."

He turned his gaze to the map Thirty-Four had laid out in the luxurious apartments where the Varikum's chief overseer once made his home. Much to the annoyance of the freed Garisai they had failed to take him alive, though great play had been made of his corpse, his head now adorning a spear thrust into the centre of the practice ground.

"The Volarian garrison will no doubt have word of our activities by now," Thirty-Four said, tapping an icon some fifteen miles north-west of the Varikum. "It won't be hard to follow our trail here."

"Our full strength?" Frentis asked.

"Two hundred and seventeen."

"Not enough," Lekran said.

"Craven sister-fucker," Ivelda said with a scornful laugh. "Each Garisai here is worth ten Varitai."

"He's right," Frentis said. "We need more fighters."

"If they come here, they'll have to assault the walls to take us," Draker pointed out. "Evens the odds a bit."

"We can't linger, much as I'm tempted to. Besides, putting this place to the torch gives a clear signal of our intentions. Perhaps even a rallying call to those in bondage." His finger tracked to a cluster of hills thirty miles northeast, the route liberally marked with plantations. "We'll turn to face them there, hopefully in greater numbers. Be ready to march in an hour."

◆ ◆ ◆

They raided four plantations in as many days, their ranks swelling with every attack. The landholdings were larger farther inland, richer in slaves and ample evidence the overseers indulged in a level of cruelty even greater than they had seen on the coast. The bulk of their new recruits were still Realm folk, those born into bondage proving the least willing to forsake a lifetime of servitude, in some cases even striving to defend their masters. This had been particularly evident at the fourth plantation where the most loyal slaves had formed a protective cordon around the owner, a tall grey-haired woman dressed head to toe in black, standing with straight-backed and flint-eyed defiance as her villa burned around her. The slaves protecting her were unarmed but had linked arms, refusing to budge despite Frentis's entreaties.

"Our mistress is kind and does not deserve this," one of the slaves told Frentis, a woman of matronly appearance garbed in cloth noticeably less threadbare than most slaves they had encountered. Her fellow slaves were also similarly well attired and he saw little evidence of any scars. This plantation was also unusual in being the only one so far where they had failed to find a single overseer and featured only four poorly maintained Varitai, all but one easily captured.

Frentis looked at the woman in the centre of the cordon, seeing how she avoided his gaze, stoic in refusing to acknowledge an inferior. "Your mistress has grown wealthy on your labour," he told the matronly woman. "If she's so kind, why doesn't she free you? Come with us and know freedom."

It did no good, they all stood in place and proved deaf to any further persuasion.

"Kill them, brother," one of the Realm folk said, the former blacksmith from their first raid, snarling as he spat at the cordon of slaves. "They betray us with this disgusting servility."

There was a growl of agreement from the other slaves and, he noticed, not all of them Realm folk. The freed fighters were becoming more fierce with every raid, each overseer or master they tormented to death seeming to stoke a greater bloodlust. "Freedom is a choice," he told them, "gather up these supplies and prepare to march."

The blacksmith grunted in frustration, pointing his sword at the straight-backed mistress. "What about the old bitch? Put an arrow in her and they might see sense."

He staggered as Illian appeared at his side and delivered a swift punch to his jaw. "This enterprise is under the command of the Sixth Order," she told him, "and the Order does not make war on old women." Her hand went to her sword as he rounded on her, spitting blood. "Question Brother Frentis again," she continued, voice flat and unwavering, "and we'll settle this with steel. Now pack up and move."

◆　◆　◆

That evening Frentis watched as Weaver freed the captured Varitai. They had rested for the night on a rise ten miles north of the old woman's villa, the Varitai, now numbering some thirty individuals, establishing their own camp at a short remove from the main body. They remained a mostly silent group, uniform in the expressions of wonder and curiosity with which they regarded the world, and rarely venturing far from Weaver, reminding Frentis of new-born fawns clustering around a parent.

The three captives sat in the centre of their group, stripped to the waist and impassive as Weaver crouched at their side, flask in hand. He dipped a thin reed into the flask and touched the tip to their scars, each time provoking a jerking spasm of instant agony and a shrill scream that never seemed to lose its lacerating chill no matter how many times Frentis heard it. The surrounding Varitai came closer as the screams faded, the captives now huddled at Weaver's feet. He bent to touch each in turn, resting his hand on their heads until they blinked and awoke to their new lives, each face a mask of confusion.

This is a ritual, Frentis realised, watching how the Varitai all turned to raise their hands to Weaver, touching the wrists together then pulling them apart. *A broken chain*, he recalled from his lessons in sign language, wondering where they had learned it. Despite their obeisance, Weaver displayed no sign of enjoying the Varitai's supplication, merely replying with a faint smile, his brow drawn in sadness.

"Is he a priest?"

Frentis turned to find Lemera standing nearby, regarding the Varitai with a bemused expression. "No, a healer," Frentis replied in his halting Alpiran. "Owns . . . great magic-power."

"You butcher my language," she said, slipping into Volarian with a laugh. "Did you learn it in my country?"

He turned back to the Varitai, wincing at best-forgotten memories. "I have travelled far."

"I was only eight when they took me, but memories of home are still bright. A village on the southern shore, the ocean was rich with fish and blue as a sapphire."

"You'll return one day."

She moved to his side, gaze low and sorrowful. "There will be no welcome for me there . . . ruined as I am. No man will make offer for me and the women will shun me for my despoilment."

"Your people have harsh customs it seems."

"My people no longer." She nodded at the Varitai now helping their freed brothers to stand, a few voicing soft words of comfort and reassurance. "These are my people now, and the others. You are the King of a new nation."

"I have one already, and my queen is unlikely to tolerate another crown in her Realm."

"The sister says you are the greatest hero in your land. Do you not deserve lands of your own?"

"Sister Illian tends to exaggerate, and servants of the Faith are denied ownership of property."

"Yes, she tried to teach me your faith. An odd notion to worship the dead with such devotion." Lemera shook her head before turning and walking back to the main camp, her parting words faint and barely heard, "The dead can't love you back."

◆ ◆ ◆

They reached the hill country two days later, their number now swollen to over five hundred though many lacked decent weapons, about half armed with nothing more than clubs or farming tools. An increasing number of recruits were now runaways, fleeing their masters upon hearing of the great rebellion as those who had escaped the raids spread word of their exploits. The runaways brought news of the terror they were provoking amongst the free folk of Eskethia, the northern roads now crowded with black- and grey-clad alike, seeking the safety of more heavily garrisoned lands.

Frentis led them deep into the hills, a mostly bare landscape dotted with small trees and distinguished by the monolithic stones adorning the winding slopes. He chose a rock-strewn plateau for their main camp, offering clear views on all sides and shielded on the northern flank by a fast-flowing river.

He sent Master Rensial and Illian to scout the western approaches, reporting back after a two-day ride that the Volarian garrison was pursuing with an impressive turn of speed, a thousand troops force-marching at a pace of fifty miles a day.

"This lot can't face a thousand, Redbrother," Lekran stated that evening. "The new ones still think it's a game and most have never seen a real fight."

"Then it's time they did," Frentis replied. "We can't run forever. I will take the archers, see if we can thin their ranks a little. Sister Illian, get your people to start piling these rocks up into some semblance of a fortification. You and Draker will have charge of the camp until I return." He turned to Lekran and the Garisai woman. "Can I trust you both to perform a task without spilling each other's blood?"

Ivelda gave Lekran a sour glance but nodded, the former Kuritai issuing a terse grunt of agreement. They watched as Frentis scratched out a map in the dirt, listening intently as he explained their role.

"Much could go wrong in this," Lekran observed.

"Even if it doesn't work, it should at least claim half their number and the people here will have a fighting chance." Frentis stood, hefting his bow. "Master Rensial, if you wouldn't mind joining me?"

◆ ◆ ◆

They found a shadowed overhang to hide in as they watched the Varitai march into the hills, Frentis using his spyglass to pick out the officers. Identifying the commander proved an easy matter, a sturdy man on horseback in the middle of the column, his authority plain in the curt nods he gave to the younger men who occasionally rode to his side. The column was tightly ordered but had a loose skirmish line of Free Sword cavalry at its head, flanks and rear.

"This fellow's a trifle too cautious for my liking, Master," Frentis commented, passing the glass to Rensial.

The master held it to his eye for a brief moment then handed it back with a shrug. "Then kill him."

Frentis beckoned Corporal Vinten and Dallin to his side and pointed to the column's southern flank. "Dallin, you'll come with Master Rensial and me. Vinten, take the others and circle around. When they make camp wait for twilight and pick off as many pickets as you can. Once it's done head back to the camp, don't linger."

The City Guard gave a reluctant nod. "Don't feel right leaving you, brother."

"Do this right and we'll be fine. Now go."

They tracked the column until dusk, watching as it formed itself into a square-shaped encampment with the usual disconcerting speed and precision of Volarian slave-soldiery. Watching the way the entire battalion moved like one living beast made Frentis glad he had never had to face them in open field and wondrous as to how Vaelin had managed to beat so many at Alltor. *Little wonder she thought they could conquer the whole world.*

They left Dallin with the horses a half mile ahead of the Volarian camp and approached on foot, making for the northern picket line. He and Rensial wore their Free Sword mercenary garb, basically identical to the standard kit but slightly less uniform in appearance, the breastplates adorned with various scribblings in Volarian. Frentis couldn't read the words but Thirty-Four had translated enough to indicate it consisted of various cynical and fatalistic slogans common to veteran Free Swords: *free in spirit but a slave to blood,* was a typical example. However, their garb was clearly sufficiently similar to the other Free Swords to allow them to approach the first one they saw without raising any sign of alarm.

"Fucking cold tonight," he greeted them cheerfully, steam rising as he pissed against a rock.

Master Rensial didn't speak a word of Volarian but repeated, "Fucking cold," with uncanny precision before stepping close to cut the man's throat. They hid him in the lee of a large boulder and moved on, making it all the way to the camp's fringes without interruption. Varitai were posted at intervals of twenty feet, silent, barely moving sentinels who also offered no challenge as they made their way to the camp's interior, picking out the large tent positioned in the centre. Frentis was dismayed to find two Kuritai standing outside the tent; the Volarian commander's caution was proving ever more trying. They made their way to a fire a short distance away, hands hovering to catch the warmth and listening to the faint snatches of conversation from the tent's interior.

"... every day we delay earns more criticism, Father," a voice was saying, earnest with youthful impatience. "You can bet those bastards in New Kethia are making great capital of our misfortunes already."

"Let them," came a more placid response, the voice older, gravelled and weary. "Victory always silences criticism."

"You heard the scouts yesterday, at least two hundred slaves have taken to foot in the last week alone. If we can't crush this rebellion soon ..."

"It's not a rebellion!" the older voice snapped, a sudden anger banishing the weariness. "It's an invasion by blood-crazed foreigners and you'll not say any different. There has never been a slave revolt in the history of the empire and our family will not have its name sullied by the mention of one. You hear me?"

A pause before a sullen response, "Yes, Father."

The older voice issued a tired sigh and Frentis pictured its owner sinking into a chair. "Get the map. No, the other one . . ."

They waited until the sun had vanished behind the skyline and a flurry of alarm sounded from the southern perimeter, Vinten following his orders with typical efficiency. Frentis filled his palm with a throwing knife and met Rensial's gaze. "Don't kill the son."

They ran towards the tent, Frentis waving frantically at the south with his empty hand. "Honoured Commander, we are attacked!"

As expected the Kuritai both stepped forward in unison to block their path as a curse sounded from the tent's interior, a broad grizzled face appearing at the flap, demanding, "What's all this babble?" in a gravelled voice.

Not so cautious after all, Frentis decided as the knife flew from his hand, flashing between the two Kuritai to take the commander in the throat. Frentis danced aside as the Kuritai on the right lunged, his sword clashing with the twin blades as he spun, his own blade slicing deep into the slave-elite's arm. It barely seemed to slow him, his good arm whipping around to slash at Frentis's chest, their swords colliding with a flash of sparks before Frentis reversed his hold on the short sword, sinking to one knee, and thrusting up at the Kuritai's head. The sword tip caught him under the chin, punching through into the brain.

Frentis looked up to see Master Rensial finishing the other Kuritai, blocking an overhead swing with his sword as his other hand brought a dagger up to find the gap in the slave-elite's armour between armpit and chest. The master stepped back as another figure erupted from the tent, a tall young man swinging a short sword in a double-handed grip, yelling in anger and grief, his blows frenzied and poorly aimed. Rensial sidestepped an overextended thrust and batted the sword from the young man's grip before felling him with a swift backhand across the face.

The young man scrabbled back as Rensial advanced, hands coming up to protect his face, a barely coherent plea for mercy gibbering from his bloodied lips. Frentis went to stand over him, the young man shrinking back farther, eyes wide with terror. "You dishonour your father with this display," Frentis told him with stern disapproval then inclined his head at Rensial. "Master, I believe it's time to go."

◆ ◆ ◆

As he had hoped, Vinten's attack had drawn attention to the southern perimeter and their progress from the camp was largely free of any interruption, shouting to every guard they met that the camp was facing a heavy assault and the commander slain. It had little effect on the Varitai but the Free Swords were soon hurrying to investigate. Only one attempted to block their way, a burly cavalryman of middling years with the bearing common to sergeants the world over.

"You saw the Honoured Commander fall?" he demanded, a grim fury plain in his craggy features.

"Two assassins," Frentis said, putting a note of panic in his voice. "They killed the Kuritai as if they were children."

"Calm down," the Volarian ordered in his sergeant's voice, frowning a little as he took a closer look at Frentis and Rensial, his eyes lingering on their inscribed armour. "Which company are you? What's your name and rank?"

Frentis glanced around, finding no others within earshot and straightening from his fearful hunch. "Brother Frentis of the Sixth Order," he said, jabbing his fore-knuckles into the sergeant's upper lip. "Here on the queen's business."

He left the man barely conscious but alive. From his reaction to their tidings Frentis surmised he had been a long-serving subordinate to the fallen commander whose son might well benefit from such fiercely loyal counsel.

Dallin waited where they had left him on the eastern side of one of the larger rocks, keeping tight hold of the horses despite their skittishness at the burgeoning uproar from the camp. "Press hard," Frentis told him, climbing into the saddle. "No rest till sunrise."

◆ ◆ ◆

The Volarian pursuit proved more sluggish than expected, the dust raised by their outriders not appearing until well past dawn the following day.

"Back in the Urlish they'd've been nipping our heels by now," Dallin observed.

Frentis raised his spyglass to get a better view of their pursuers; thirty men, all bunched together. "I'm starting to suspect their best troops are all lying dead in the Realm."

He ordered Dallin on ahead with instructions for Ivelda and Lekran whilst he and Rensial lingered to leave some obvious traces for the Volarians; an overturned stone, a strip of torn clothing on a gorse branch. He waited until the riders were no more than a mile distant and the infantry could be seen filing along a narrow track in their wake. They rode on for a time then reined in on the crest of a hill, plainly silhouetted against the sky. He could see the infantry more clearly now, a long column of Varitai all moving at a steady run and somehow still managing to stay in step. The outriders were coming on at a good pace, Frentis's spyglass picking out two figures in front, a tall young man closely followed by a burly figure with a discoloured upper lip. *Grief dispels caution,* he thought in satisfaction, turning his mount towards the east once more.

Lekran came into sight some two hours later, axe raised as he waved from atop one of the monolithic boulders, the Garisai appearing out of the rocks on either side.

"All is ready?" Frentis called to him, dismounting to scramble up the boulder's steep side.

"The Rotha bitch holds the southern flank with half the Garisai." Lekran pointed to the box canyon below, a narrow gouge in the landscape some two hundred paces long and about fifty wide. The canyon was closed at the far end where a group of free fighters had made a suitably obvious camp, smoke rising from cookfires and meagre shelters raised among the rocks. "And the hook is baited."

Frentis knew this was a gamble; he could only hope the Volarians' fury would blind them to questioning why their enemies had chosen such a poor spot for a campsite. However, Lekran saw scant risk in the plan. "Volarians see slaves as less than men," he said. "Incapable of true reason. Trust me, Redbrother. They'll swallow it whole and we'll make them choke."

"The gorse?"

Lekran nodded to where Vinten's archers crouched among the rocks just back from the canyon's northern edge, surrounded by bundles of tight-bound gorse. Frentis began to clamber down from the boulder. "I'd best take my place. Remember to let a few Free Swords escape."

He made his way to the far end of the canyon, finding Illian overseeing preparations. "I told you to make ready the main camp, sister," he said in annoyance.

"Draker has it well in hand," she replied, meeting his gaze with little sign of contrition. "And since I have trained these people, I am unwilling to let them face battle without me."

He fought down the urge to order her gone. She was becoming less deferential by the day, exercising a certain flexibility in interpreting his orders and often more than willing to argue her case. It was not necessarily a bad thing, he knew. There always came a point in the Order when novices stepped from their masters' shadow, but he had hoped it might take longer for her; she still had much to learn and he feared the consequences of her ignorance.

"Stay close to me," he said. "No more than an arm's length away at any time. Understood?"

Her defiance softened a little and she nodded, hefting her crossbow and notching a bolt before clasping a second between her teeth in what was now a recognisable pre-battle ritual.

"Brother!" Dallin stood atop a rock pointing to the canyon's west-facing opening where the Volarian cavalry had appeared.

"You know the plan!" Frentis called to the others as they made ready, hefting their assorted weapons and arranging themselves in a loosely ordered line. They were mostly his original fighters from the Urlish mingled with the more able recruits gathered on the march, Weaver and his Varitai among them, laden with ropes and cudgels. All had tied dampened cloths around their mouths, something he hoped the Volarians would interpret as an effort to avoid recognition.

"We have to hold the first charge," Frentis went on. "When their lines break, pair off and cut your way to the centre of the canyon."

The Volarians came to a halt a hundred paces away and began forming up. There was clearly an animated discussion taking place in the centre of their line, Frentis recognising the tall figure of the commander's son as he bickered with the burly sergeant, gesturing impatiently at the waiting rabble of miscreant slaves. *Charging uphill on horseback over broken ground*, Frentis mused, watching the sergeant being shouted down before the commander's son drew his sword, pointing it directly at him. *Your father really would have been ashamed, Honoured Citizen.*

Frentis turned to Illian as the Volarians spurred into a charge, stones scattering as they laboured up the slope. "The big fellow next to the tall man, if you would sister."

The bolt flew free barely a second after she brought the crossbow to her shoulder, rising and falling in a perfectly judged arc to smack into the sergeant's breastplate before the riders had covered half the distance, the burly form falling from the saddle to lie limp on the rocky ground. Illian moved with an unconscious speed to reload the crossbow, grunting as she braced the stock against her midriff, slamming the next bolt into place and biting down on another, all in less than three seconds, a feat Frentis had never seen anyone match. The crossbow string snapped again as the riders came within twenty paces, a Free Sword tumbling to the ground with a bolt protruding from his helmet.

Frentis found himself nurturing a reluctant admiration for the way the commander's son came on, spurs digging into his horse's flanks as he strove to get to grips with his father's murderer, blind hate and rage writ large on his face, seeking to wipe away his shame with courage, a courage that made him oblivious to the fact that the ground had disordered his company and he had outpaced his men to charge alone.

Frentis ran towards a nearby boulder, the hate-filled Volarian now no more than ten feet away, veering to intercept him. He leapt atop the boulder, bringing him level with the son, whirling to deliver a slash that connected with his long-bladed cavalry sword, the Order blade shattering it above the hilt. The Volarian hauled his horse to a halt and tried to wheel it around, fumbling for a spare short sword strapped to his saddle, then arching his back as Illian's crossbow bolt slammed into it.

She ran in as he fell, pinning him to the ground with a boot to his neck and raising her dagger. "Leave him," Frentis said, striding forward to slam his sword pommel into the Volarian's temple, leaving him senseless. "We'll see what he has to tell us later."

He surveyed the fight unfolding around them, feeling an indulgent pride in the way the Volarian charge had been successfully blunted, the fighters leaping from rocks to unhorse the riders, whilst Weaver's Varitai tripped horses with their ropes or dragged the cavalrymen from the saddle before closing in with cudgels flailing. It was done in a few moments, a dozen riderless horses trotting back into the depths of the canyon, every Volarian killed or captured. Their own casualties had been light, four killed and ten wounded. But of course the real battle was yet to begin.

The Varitai came on with a typical indifference, although the slaughter meted out to the Free Sword cavalry had clearly alarmed their officers from the way they spurred their horses to the rear of the column whilst ordering the battalion onward. The Varitai spread out to form an offensive line, four companies deep, each of four close-packed ranks, the first advancing with their unnerving, faultless rhythm, broad-bladed spears held level at waist height.

When the Varitai had covered two-thirds of the canyon's length the archers rose from their hiding places to begin their work. Although few in number their skills were all well honed by now, the arrow storm thin but deadly as it claimed a dozen Varitai with every volley, but, as ever, the slave soldiers barely seemed to notice, coming on with their unfaltering stride, only the slightest ripple of discord in their ranks.

The first bundle of flaming gorse arced down from the canyon wall to land directly in front of the first rank, white smoke billowing, quickly followed by more until it appeared as if the sky were raining great flaming hailstones. A pall of smoke soon covered the canyon floor from end to end, the Varitai concealed by the choking mist.

Frentis fixed the dampened cloth over his mouth and raised his sword, turning to address the surrounding fighters, "Fight well and may the Departed guide your hand!"

They charged forward in a dense knot, running blindly through the smoke to slam into the lead company of Varitai, the momentum of the charge enough to carry them through all four ranks, Frentis and Illian moving in a circular dance, cutting down Varitai left and right. All was soon a confusion of clashing metal and screams of pain or fury. Sometimes they would find themselves in a crush of opponents, shoving and stabbing as they stumbled over the dead, at others all opposition would disappear leaving them isolated in a world of shifting white smoke as the cacophony of battle raged unseen on all sides. Frentis caught glimpses of the freed Varitai at work, dragging their enslaved brothers down and beating them unconscious. But most sights were scenes of slaughter, the Garisai going about their task with all the skill and fury earned in the Varikum. Frentis found himself momentarily distracted by the sight of Ivelda and two other Garisai being lifted by their fellows and thrown over a line of Varitai, twisting in the air like acrobats at the Summertide fair to land and assault their enemy from the rear.

"Brother!"

Illian's warning came a fraction too late, Frentis whirling to confront a Free Sword officer charging out of the smoke on horseback, too close to dodge. He leapt forward instead, grabbing hold of the horse's bridle and wrapping his legs around its neck. The animal reared as its rider hacked at Frentis. The blow was poorly aimed but left a shallow cut on his forearm, forcing him to lose his grip. He landed hard on the rocky ground, the air forced from his lungs by the impact. He rolled, trying to rise, dragging smoke-laden air into his throat and choking. The Free Sword was far more skilled a rider than the commander's son and brought his horse around in a swift display of excellent horsemanship, spurring forward with his sword drawn back for a decapitating swipe at Frentis's neck.

Illian's throwing knife smacked into the rider's face just above the chin guard, forcing him to veer away, though his horse's flank still connected painfully with Frentis as he managed to gain his feet, sending him sprawling once more. He gulped more tainted air and forced himself upright, searching frantically for the rider but finding the saddle now empty. His eyes caught a vague flurry of shadows in the smoke a dozen feet away and he ran towards it, finding Illian confronting the now-unseated rider. Despite the knife embedded in his cheek the Volarian was assailing the sister with a series of expert blows, his long cavalry sword a blur as he advanced, bloodied face snarling. Illian blocked every stroke and leapt to deliver a kick to the side of his face, driving the throwing knife deeper. The Volarian staggered back, blood flowing thick from his mouth as he sank to his knees, staring up at Illian, all fury faded as his eyes held a desperate entreaty.

Frentis paused to catch his breath, the sounds of battle fading around them along with the smoke, revealing the ruin of the Varitai's battalion, their neatly ordered lines shattered into ever-diminishing knots of resistance. Even they couldn't maintain a formation when blind.

He moved to Illian's side as she stood watching the Volarian die. "Killing without need is against the Faith," she explained in answer to Frentis's raised eyebrow.

"Quite so, sister," he said, briefly clasping her shoulder before moving on to seek out Lekran and ensure some survivors were allowed to flee. "Quite so."

◆ ◆ ◆

She feels his return with a rush of joy, untarnished by the fierce enmity with which he colours his mind. The long days of his absence have been hard. Loneliness, once a long-forgotten sensation, has been difficult to master, provoking a despairing ache as she indulges in memories of their glorious time together. Instead of his voice this time he offers a vision, from the clarity she judges he has spent a long time viewing this scene, trying to capture every detail. She deduces that his return is not accidental, whatever contrivance he has used to mask his dreams now removed; he wants her to see.

A thousand or more Varitai and Free Swords lie dead in a canyon, somewhere in the hill country east of New Kethia to judge by the landscape. People in mismatched armour wander among the dead finishing the wounded and gathering weapons. She finds herself smiling in amusement. You win a victory, beloved, *she tells him.* How delightful. I've been searching for some excuse to execute the governor of Eskethia.

The enmity deepens, the thoughts coalescing into words, her heart leaping at the sound of his voice. Come and face me. We will finish this.

She sighs, pushing a hand through her hair and letting her gaze wander over the grey ocean stretching away from the cliff. It is starting to rain, the north-western coastline is ever damp in winter, though the seas are calmer than expected. Her slaves scurry forward bearing an awning, keen to shield the Empress from the elements. She dismisses them with an irritated wave. They are expert slaves, attentive in the extreme, but for a woman accustomed to privation and danger, their devotion to her comfort is an annoyance, leaving scant regret at their imminent fate.

I'm sorry, beloved, *she tells him, eyes now fixed on the horizon and her heart beating faster with the joy of anticipation.* But I have business here. You'll have to amuse yourself with my slaves for a while longer.

The enmity subsides, transforming into a reluctant curiosity. She laughs, exulting as the first masts appear on the horizon, raising her gaze to the sky and finding it rich in clouds. She beckons the captain of her escort to her side, an Arisai like the others, promoted due to his slightly more controlled viciousness. "Kill the slaves," *she tells him.* "Also, we passed a village a mile back. There can be no witnesses to my presence here. See to it."

"Empress." *He bows, his expression one of near adoration, though, like the others, cruelty is rarely absent from his eyes. He turns away, moving towards the slaves and drawing his sword.*

Her limbs tremble as she turns back to the sea, deaf to the screams as she summons the gift. She is slightly regretful at the necessity, having grown fond of this shell. But another awaits her in Volar, this one a little taller though not quite so athletic.

Formalities must be observed, my love, *she tells him, raising her arms and focusing on the clouds, watching them dance in response to the gift.* It is time for an empress to greet a queen.

CHAPTER ELEVEN

Vaelin

The next storm lasted longer than the first, two full days of labouring along behind Cara's gift-crafted shield. The constant exertion had forced her to reduce its reach, obliging them to move in a dense clutch, Orven's guardsmen walking shoulder to shoulder with Alturk's Sentar. For all the jostling and unwelcome proximity there was no trouble; the ferocity of the storm raging on all sides left little room for other preoccupations. Cara began to falter on the second day, stumbling to her knees several times and only managing to maintain the shield by sharing with both Kiral and Marken at once. By the time night fell the other Gifted had all shared to the point of collapse and Cara was barely conscious, mumbling in delirium as blood flowed from her nose and eyes.

"We have to end this!" Lorkan railed at Vaelin, barely able to stand himself. "Any more and she'll die."

Vaelin turned to Wise Bear with a questioning glance. The old shaman frowned and pushed his way to the edge of the company, poking his staff beyond the shield wall into the howling white fury beyond. "Wind dies, but slowly," he reported. He hesitated, glancing back at Cara then straightened with decision. "Make circle, horses on outside. Cover all flesh, keep tight together."

It took some awkward manoeuvring to arrange the horses and ponies in a circle, by which time Cara had weakened yet further. "Stop now, Little Bird," Wise Bear said, maintaining his habit of ignoring their own names for those he chose.

"Can't," she breathed, eyes closed and leaking blood. "The storm . . . the price."

"Storm fades," he said, putting a hand to her forehead. "Stop now."

She groaned, her eyes fluttering for a moment . . . and the shield fell.

The cold was like a hammerblow, raising a pained groan from every throat as the travelers shrank beneath its weight, pressing together in instinctive need. Vaelin held tight to Scar's reins as Dahrena wrapped her arms around his waist and Kiral huddled against his back, chanting softly in Lonak, the words unknown but the lilting tone familiar: *death song*. The horses and ponies screamed as the wind lashed them, some bucking and rearing in terror, tearing free of their tethers to flee into the storm. Scar snorted and stamped, the reins pulling taut in Vaelin's grip as the warhorse gave a great whinny of protest, threatening to pull him free of the company. Vaelin gritted his teeth and pulled hard on the reins, dragging the horse closer and pressing himself and Dahrena against his side in the hope the faint warmth might reassure him. Scar whinnied again but calmed, probably more from the weakening effects of the cold than any instinctive loyalty.

Time seemed to elongate as they endured the storm's assault, every second a test of endurance. The horses started to die after the first hour, slumping down in silent exhaustion, their riders huddling behind the soon-frozen corpses. Vaelin could hear other Lonak voices raised in the same lilting cadence, more death songs gifted to the wind, fading as the endless minutes dragged by.

He had begun to sag when he felt the storm weaken, a sudden removal of the blade-like chill. He released Scar's reins, stifling a shout of pain at the sensation of life returning to part-frozen fingers. Dahrena stirred next to him, a weary smile visible through the swaddle of furs. To his amazement Scar was still alive, though slumped to his knees with snow piled on his flanks, blinking dolorous eyes at Vaelin as he scratched his ears.

Taking stock, they found half the Lonak ponies dead along with a third of the guardsmen's horses. Four of the Sentar had also perished, all veteran warriors a decade or so older than their comrades. In what appeared to be a Lonak custom, Alturk gathered the belongings and shared them out among the other Sentar as they gathered around the bodies. No words were spoken; their only outward regard for the dead was a brief glance at the corpses before moving away.

Vaelin went to Wise Bear's side, watching as the shaman's gaze roamed the ice on all sides, a worried frown on his brow. "Which direction?" Vaelin asked.

Wise Bear continued his survey for another moment then lowered his gaze. "None."

"But the price . . ."

"Ice breaks all around." The shaman made a circular motion with his bone-staff. "Nowhere to walk. This time we all pay price."

◆ ◆ ◆

They made camp and waited, the Realm folk huddling around their fires, the Lonak occupying themselves by butchering the fallen ponies and horses. Meat should not be wasted on the ice after all. The now-familiar booming crack came soon after sunrise. The sound lasted much longer than before, the ice giving full vent to its torment as walls of white mist rose on all sides. Abruptly the ice shifted beneath their feet, the sky seeming to sway above as the entire field shattered for miles around with a thunderclap crescendo. The subsequent silence seemed vast, all members of the company fallen to their knees and staring about in expectation of some climactic calamity. But nothing came. The ice swayed gently beneath them, the surrounding ice-scape moving in a slow but constant drift to the east.

Vaelin joined Wise Bear at the edge of the fragment where they were now marooned, looking down at the cavernous gap between them and the nearest berg, so deep the ocean water below was lost to sight. "The ice is kind," the shaman said in a surprisingly calm voice.

"Kind?" Vaelin asked.

"Islands to the east." A faint smile played over Wise Bear's aged face. "Home."

◆ ◆ ◆

The weather remained calm for the following week as they accustomed themselves to life on their new home. The berg was a good three hundred paces from end to end allowing for a sprawling camp, and, thanks to the storm, they were well supplied with horse-meat. Occasionally the berg would collide with one of its neighbours, the ice shuddering from the impact but so far failing to crack. For Vaelin the ever-shortening days were more worrying than their immobility, the Long Night was coming and he had no illusions as to their chances when it came.

"You had no choice," Kiral told him one morning. He had gone to the edge of the berg in what had become something of a daily ritual. They were so far north now that Avenshura could be glimpsed for a brief time between dusk and sunrise, shining brighter than he had seen before. *No war can be fought in the light that it brings.* Just an ancient delusion, he knew. Life, death, love, war. It would all be played out on this earth until the end of time and Avenshura didn't care. It was just a star.

"These people followed me," he said. "To their doom it seems."

"The song called and you answered. And our journey is not yet done."

She spoke with a calm authority but Vaelin could not suppress his skepticism, gesturing at the slowly moving ice surrounding them. "It holds no warning about this?"

"It has sounded a warning note since we began this journey. But it also holds certainty. We are on the right course, the endless man awaits our coming. I know it."

◆ ◆ ◆

The first island came into view four days later, a small snow-covered rise some miles to the south, several larger cousins appearing a day later. The berg's collisions increased as the floe became constricted by the channels through the islands. After many hours constant shuddering, and an ominous crack that shook the ice beneath their feet, it came to a grinding halt.

Wise Bear led them across the now-fractured ice-scape to the nearest island, taller than the others with bare rock jutting from its snow-covered slopes. His mood became sombre as they tracked around its southern shore, coming eventually to a collection of huts beneath a tall cliff. They were conical in shape, the walls constructed from seal hides over a framework of bone and wood, long out of use from their evident state of disrepair. Many were missing hides and others half-ruined by the constant assault of the elements.

"You know this place?" Vaelin asked the shaman.

"Bear People hunting camp," he said, standing still and expressionless.

"We could press on," Vaelin suggested, sensing his reluctance. "Find another island."

"Nearest two days away." Wise Bear started forward, moving with deliberate purpose and pointing his staff towards the north. "More storm coming. We rest here until it passes."

They repaired the huts as best they could, using horse-hide to cover the gaps, the night coming on fast and bringing a bitter wind. By now they were all well attuned to the moods of the ice, the speed with which a storm could descend, birthing a new level of cooperation between the Sentar and Orven's guardsmen. They worked together with wordless efficiency, seemingly unhampered by any language barrier.

"Once the ice made all men brothers," Wise Bear said that night. They had repaired five huts, enough to shelter the whole company from the storm already howling outside, the surviving horses herded into a single hut with what scant fodder remained. The shaman sat beside the fire in the centre of the hut, the smoke rising to a small hole in the roof as he carved a new symbol into his bone-staff.

"The Long Night longer then, years not months," he went on, eyes fixed on the knifepoint etching into the bone. "No tribes, just one people, made so by the Long Night. When gone, one people became three, brothers no more."

He paused to blow powdered bone from the staff, revealing an irregular pattern of dots, each connected with a line. "What does it mean?" Cara asked, leaning forward. She was still alarmingly thin but had regained a great deal of strength during their time on the berg, though Vaelin doubted she could have endured long enough to shield them from the latest storm.

Wise Bear frowned, seeking the right words. "A story now told," he said finally, his gaze roaming over the Gifted. "Story of journey and joining. When storm passes we make new story, of learning and fighting."

♦   ♦   ♦

Wise Bear led them on a south-easterly course three days later, the islands growing in size and number with every passing mile, some even featuring a few trees or bushes the farther south they went. However, there was little for the horses to feed on and, with the fodder now exhausted, soon only Scar was left, plodding in Vaelin's wake with his head sagging ever lower.

When darkness fell Wise Bear would gather the Gifted, trying to impart some of his knowledge, though his agitation, their ignorance, and his still-rudimentary grasp of Realm Tongue, made it a frustrating task. "Speak!" he commanded Dahrena, raising her hand and placing the palm on his forehead.

"Speak what?" she asked in bemusement.

"Not with mouth," he snapped, jabbing a finger to her temple. "Speak one word, here."

Dahrena closed her eyes in concentration, pressing her hand harder against the old man's forehead but he only grunted in consternation. "Call power," he said. "Not all. Just small power."

Dahrena sighed and tried again, stiffening a little, her face losing expression and taking on a familiar, pale cast.

"Tower!" Wise Bear said with a satisfied cackle, adding, "Stop now. Not use too much."

Dahrena removed her hand from his forehead, flexing her fingers, a look of confused awe on her face. "I didn't know . . . Can all Gifted do this?"

"All with power, yes. Gifts change, power not change. All one thing. Come." He gathered the other Gifted and led them to his war-cats, all waiting placidly nearby. He pointed at the largest of the cats, like the others still fairly ragged of fur but noticeably better fed than when they had first been captured by his gift. "Speak," he told Dahrena. "Give order."

Dahrena approached the beast with obvious trepidation, for all the cat's apparent calm she had seen the carnage meted out by Snowdance who usually appeared no more threatening than an overgrown kitten. She stopped a pace or two from the cat and tentatively reached out to touch her hand to its great head, closing her eyes to summon her gift once more. The cat blinked then lowered itself to the ice and rolled on its back, paws raised. Dahrena gave a delighted laugh and knelt to run her hands over the cat's furry belly.

"All try." Wise Bear jabbed his staff at the other Gifted and waved it at the cats. "Choose, give names. Yours now."

Cara moved forward with obvious enthusiasm, as did Kiral, whilst Lorkan and Marken were much more cautious. "What if they bite?" Lorkan asked the shaman, taking a short step towards one of the two remaining cats.

"You die," Wise Bear replied. "Don't let them."

Vaelin's gaze abruptly shifted to Kiral as she rose from the side of the cat she had chosen, the smallest of the group with a mangled left ear. Her smile faded as she stood and stared towards the east with a sudden and fierce intensity.

"Danger?" Vaelin asked, going to her side.

"A new song." She winced a little, shaking her head in confusion. "Very old, very strange."

Wise Bear said something in his own language as he came to join them, his expression wary rather than fearful as he added, "Wolf People."

◆ ◆ ◆

He led them to another island at first light, the largest they had yet seen, with wide patches of bare rock and a small cluster of trees and bushes on its eastern flank. Vaelin set Scar to feed on what sparse leaves the bushes could offer, the warhorse snorting in appreciation as he began his first meal in days. "Should've named you 'strength,' shouldn't I?" Vaelin asked, brushing the frost from his coat. "Sorry for all you've suffered, old fellow."

Scar gave another snort and kept chewing.

He found Wise Bear waiting where the island's shore met the ice. Nearby Iron Claw sat gnawing on a horse's thigh-bone. "We go, others stay," the shaman said. "Wolf People not hate like Cat People, but won't like too many on their ice."

"Where do we find them?"

Wise Bear's laugh was soft as he turned and started walking, Iron Claw rising to lumber alongside with the bone still clamped between his jaws. "They find us."

They trekked east until the sky had darkened to black and the green fire once again danced in the sky. Wise Bear rested on a stunted plinth-shaped mound of ice, regarding the sky and singing his song to his ancestors.

"What do you tell them?" Vaelin asked when he fell silent.

"Bear People still live. I still live, but not long to wait now."

"Are you so eager to join them? To be with your wife once more?"

"She with me now, watching." Wise Bear gave him a sidelong glance. "You think this . . . a story. Your word . . . the word for not real story."

"A lie."

"Yes. Lie. No word for lie in Bear People tongue."

"A lie is still a lie, even if you don't have a word for it. But no, I don't think it a lie. I believe your people, and mine, crafted legends to better understand a world that often makes little sense. And a legend becomes its own truth in time."

"Legend is what?"

"An old story, told many times and changed with the telling. A story so old none can say if it ever truly happened."

"You had power, when we met. Song like Fox Girl, but stronger. That a legend?"

"No, all very true. But like a legend, it had an ending."

"No." Wise Bear lifted his staff to point at the swirling lights in the sky. "Nothing truly ends. There stories live forever."

He looked over his shoulder as Iron Claw gave a low growl, rising to sniff the air.

"Many come." The shaman sighed, getting to his feet. "War party. Keep hands empty."

The spear-hawks came first, seven of the great birds descending from the clouds to circle them, occasionally swooping low enough to make Vaelin duck. He had heard enough stories from Dahrena to appreciate the birds' deadly power but was still surprised by their size, judging each to have a wingspan of at least seven feet, their beaks as long as spear-points and, he noticed, steel barbs glittering on their talons.

"One shaman controls all these?" he asked Wise Bear.

"If strong enough. They see and he sees." The shaman's gaze settled on the eastern horizon, a disconcerting note of foreboding colouring his tone. "Few strong enough to bind so many."

The black dots appeared on the horizon moments later, at first only a dozen or so but soon growing in number until Vaelin counted over fifty. The dots resolved into loping figures as they came closer, moving with effortless speed and grace over the ice. On nearing, their tight group split apart and formed a near-perfect circle with Wise Bear and Vaelin at the centre. They sat regarding them both with placid indifference, all uniformly white of fur and larger than any wolf Vaelin had seen, save one.

More dots soon appeared on the horizon, moving with less grace but almost equal speed. The sight was so unfamiliar Vaelin was initially unsure what he was seeing, teams of wolves all tethered in a line dragging something behind. As they came closer he realised the wolves were towing sleds, each carrying three men, all armed with spears and flat bows similar to those carried by the Seordah. The wolves towing the sleds were smaller in stature than those surrounding them, and markedly less placid, snarling and nipping at each other as the sleds came to a halt. Vaelin quickly counted heads as the men on the sleds dismounted; over a hundred, less than their own company, but this was their ice and they had wolves and hawks.

The sled-borne warriors spread out to form a second circle outside that fashioned by the wolves, two figures striding forward to approach Vaelin and Wise Bear. One was of similar proportions to the other ice people Vaelin had met, little over five feet tall and stocky of build. But the second figure stood at least as tall as Vaelin, broad at the shoulder but with a rangy, athletic look.

"You know them?" Vaelin asked Wise Bear.

The shaman shook his head, his expression now more tense even than when they had confronted No Eyes. "Trade with Wolf People sometimes," he said. "Not live with them."

The two figures halted a short distance away, reaching up to pull away the fur that covered their faces. The shorter of the two was revealed as a woman of middling years with the high cheekbones and broad features common to the ice people. She regarded Wise Bear with an expression of obvious recognition, even respect, though her bearing was no less tense. Vaelin noted she carried a bone of her own, shorter than Wise Bear's but similarly adorned with etchings. The tall figure at her side removed his fur mask to uncover the face of a young man a few years shy of Vaelin's age, the features holding no vestige of any ice-folk heritage. Vaelin's unease deepened as he took note of the man's colouring: pale skin, eyes and hair dark to the point of blackness, like many Volarians he had seen.

The woman said something in her own language, addressing Wise Bear who replied with a nod and a few words of his own. "Shaman greets shaman," he explained. "It is . . . custom."

The woman's gaze turned to Vaelin, her eyes tracking him from head to foot before she nodded at the young man. He greeted Vaelin with a cautious smile, conveying a sense of youthful discomfort at an important gathering. "My mother asks your name," he said in Realm Tongue, the vowels clipped and heavily accented but still easily understood.

"Your mother?" Vaelin's gaze switched between the two of them as he raised an eyebrow.

"Yes," the young man replied. "Many Wings, shamaness to the Wolf People of the Tree Isles. I am her son, named Long Knife by consent of the people."

"Really?" Vaelin stared at him and let the silence string out, noting how the young man held his arms loose at his sides. He wore no weapon but Vaelin was certain he had at least one knife under his furs and knew well how to use it. He also noted a sudden alertness in the surrounding wolves, their heads rising as if in answer to an unheard call.

"Your . . . mother is not the only shaman here," Vaelin said. "She commands the hawks and you the wolves."

The young man gritted his teeth and forced a smile. "Yes. And we ask your name."

"I'll hear yours first, Volarian. Your true name. I've been obliged to kill far too many of your countrymen to give trust so easily."

The wolves rose from their haunches as one, a snarl sounding from every throat as the young man bridled, stating in implacable tones, "I am not Volarian."

Many Wings spoke again, a terse few words but evidently enough to make the young man suppress his anger, the wolves relaxing once more as he took a calming breath. "My birth name is Astorek Anvir," he said. "And I ask your name."

"Vaelin Al Sorna, Tower Lord of the Northern Reaches by the Queen's Word."

Many Wings waved her bone at him, uttering a guttural exclamation, her face suddenly drawn in irritation. "Mother says you have another name," Astorek Anvir related.

"I am called Avenshura by the Eorhil," Vaelin said. "And Beral Shak Ur by the Seordah."

"We do not know these words," Astorek said. "Explain their meaning."

"Avenshura is the bright star that appears in the morning sky. Beral Shak Ur is the Shadow of the Raven."

Astorek and Many Wings exchanged a glance, faces suddenly grave. They said nothing but from the way Wise Bear straightened Vaelin divined they were communicating by other means.

"Gather your people," Astorek said after a moment. "You will follow us."

"To what purpose?" Vaelin asked.

"Follow and find out." The Volarian turned and started back to his sled, the wolves rising as one to fall in on either side as their master cast a final word over his shoulder, "Or stay here and perish when the Long Night falls."

◆　◆　◆

The island stretched away on either side for several miles, liberally covered with trees, a steep-sided mountain of snow-speckled granite rising from its centre. "Wolf Home," Wise Bear called it in rough translation of its unpronounceable true name. "I not see this for many year."

The journey had taken four days hard trekking across the ice, which became noticeably thinner the farther south they travelled. It was unnerving to see through it when the sun rose high, light playing on the bubbles visible beneath a barrier no more than a few feet thick. "It melts in summer," Astorek explained. "And the islands become isolated, reachable only by boat. Though we have plenty of those."

He had been an affable guide so far, unwilling to take offence at the instinctive suspicion of the Sentar or the open hostility of the Realm folk. "Offering trust to such as him does not seem wise, my lord," Orven advised, his dark expression a mirror of his soldiers as he regarded the Volarian. Like all the men from the Realm he had been forced to abandon a daily grooming regimen and was now of somewhat wild appearance, the unkempt beard and long hair rendering him nearly unrecognisable. "We know to our cost how well they use their spies."

"He's no spy," Kiral said, the only one in their company besides Wise Bear to display no enmity towards the young shaman. "My song tells of no deceit."

"These people trust him," Vaelin pointed out as Orven plainly found scant reassurance in the huntress's words. "And Wise Bear trusts them. Besides, we have little choice."

A large gathering of Wolf People waited on a spit of land on the island's west-facing coast, several hundred men, women and children staring in open curiosity at the newcomers. Clustered among them were several wolf packs each numbering ten or more with a single shaman at their centre, whilst a great flock of spear-hawks circled above. Many Wings raised her bone-staff to order a halt as a man came forward to greet them, a little taller than her with a broader build than most ice people. From the closeness of the embrace he shared with Many Wings and Astorek, Vaelin deduced he was witnessing a family reunion.

"My father bids you welcome," Astorek related. "He leads here. In your tongue his name means Whale Killer."

"I thank him for his hospitality," Vaelin replied, noting that, in contrast to Many Wings, the shaman was required to translate his words aloud to the Wolf People chieftain.

Whale Killer favoured Vaelin with much the same scrutiny shown by his wife, though with a more friendly countenance. "He says it is strange when an old tale takes form," Astorek translated.

Vaelin began to ask for clarification but Whale Killer had already moved on, approaching Wise Bear with arms wide. They embraced, exchanging greetings in the tongue of the ice people from which, despite all the weeks hearing it, Vaelin still failed to discern any meaning.

"We thought the Bear People wiped out," Astorek explained. "My father is glad to see we were wrong."

"They warred with the Volarians," Vaelin said. "Driven across the ice to find refuge in our lands. Not so with your people, I see."

Astorek's face grew sombre and Vaelin noted Kiral's sympathetic wince, making him wonder what tune she heard from her song. "We had war," the Volarian said. "It was ugly, but short."

◆ ◆ ◆

The settlement lay a mile along the coast. Instead of clearing the forest the Wolf People made their home amongst the trees. They were mostly pine mixed with birch, tall and strong enough to support the walkways constructed between them, their branches liberally adorned with ropes and ladders. The larger dwellings were all at ground level, wooden conical structures, part covered in moss and seeming to flow around the trees as if they had grown in their shade like great mushrooms. They were led to the largest structure, an impressive circular building constructed around the tallest tree, its trunk sprouting from the centre of the wooden floor and ascending through the multi-beamed roof. The interior featured numerous low tables but no chairs, the Wolf People habitually sitting on piles of fur they carried from dwelling to dwelling as the need arose. Many had already begun to fill the space by the time Vaelin and the others were led in, Astorek ushering them to a set of tables arranged around the central tree.

"This is your council chamber?" Vaelin asked, sitting on one of the fur bundles with Dahrena at his side. "The place where decisions are made," he elaborated in response to the young Volarian's baffled look.

"Decisions." Astorek sighed a faint laugh, glancing over to where the man he called father was taking his seat, gesturing for Wise Bear to join him. "All decisions were taken long ago. And not by us."

Alturk slumped down opposite before Vaelin could ask anything further, muttering, "My people would have fed us by now. Or killed us." The Sentar war chief had lost weight on the march, as had they all, but whilst the others had mostly recovered in recent days, the depredations of the ice seemed to linger in him. Lonak men did not grow beards and his face had a skull-like leanness, his once-bald head now sprouting a disordered jumble of black hair and his arms lacking the same thickness of muscle. The depth of sorrow Vaelin had seen in him back in the mountains also hadn't lifted and he wondered if Alturk was deliberately holding to it, allowing the sadness to reduce him, perhaps even hoping the ice could do what battle could not.

"You should rejoice," Dahrena told the Lonak. "Now you have the greatest story to tell when you go home."

"Alturk never shares at the fire," Kiral said. "Though my sister once told me he has a story to shame all others. For Alturk, as confirmed by the Mahlessa herself, once heard the voice of a god."

Alturk slammed his hand on the table, grating something in his own language and glowering fiercely at Kiral. Vaelin made ready to rise in her defence but the huntress just smiled, meeting his gaze with a complete absence of fear and saying something in Lonak which she quickly translated for Vaelin and Dahrena: "A story not shared is a waste of riches."

Food was brought in shortly after, wooden platters piled with roasted meat, also bowls of nuts and berries. "Tastes like seal," Alturk observed, taking a large bite of meat. "Though not so tough."

"Walrus," Astorek explained, coming to sit down at their table. "Winter meat. We eat mostly elk in the summer." He gave Alturk and Kiral a curious glance, his gaze switching between them and Vaelin. "You are not from the same tribe."

"No," Alturk confirmed in an emphatic growl, chewing and swallowing. "We are Lonakhim. They"—he jerked his head at Dahrena and Vaelin—"are Merim Her."

"We were enemies for a long time," Vaelin said. "Now we are allies, made so by your people."

Astorek gave a sigh of annoyance but this time refused to display any offence. "These are my people."

"How do you come to speak our language?" Dahrena asked.

Astorek glanced at Whale Killer, now engaged in animated conversation with Wise Bear. "A tale to be told soon enough."

The meal lasted into the night, the copious meat supplemented by a heady brew that smelt strongly of pine. Vaelin took only a sip before setting it aside although Alturk seemed to appreciate it. "Like drinking a tree," he said, voicing a rare laugh as he drained his bowl.

"We ferment wild berries and pine-cones," Astorek said. "Let it sit long enough and you can use it to light fires."

"Lights a fire in my belly, true enough." Alturk lifted another bowl to his lips, drinking it down in a few gulps. As the evening wore on Vaelin was relieved to find the hulking Lonak a morose drunk rather than a fighting one, watching him slump forward, head rested on his hand as he continued to down the pine ale, muttering to himself in his own language, much to Kiral's evident disgust.

"You shame the Mahlessa Sentar with this display," she sniffed.

Alturk curled his lip and said a few short words in Lonak. From Kiral's furious reaction Vaelin judged they were not complimentary. She snarled a curse in Lonak, getting to her feet, her knife half-drawn.

"Enough!" Vaelin told her, voice heavy with command and loud enough to herald a sudden silence in the hall. "This is not your home and you insult our hosts," he went on in a quieter tone, his gaze shifting to Alturk. "And you, Tahlessa, should go and sleep it off."

"Merim Her," Alturk slurred, half rising, fumbling for his war club and promptly dropping it. "Son killer!" He braced his arms on the table and tried to lever himself up. However, the task seemed to be beyond his diminished limbs and he collapsed, his face connecting with the table with a painful thump. He remained in the same position and soon began to snore.

"Varnish," Kiral sneered, sitting down again and glaring at Vaelin. "You should have let me kill him. My song finds little of worth in him."

"A troubled mind deserves healing, not death," Astorek told her, casting a sympathetic gaze over the slumbering Lonak. "And those of the same tribe should not kill each other."

Kiral laughed, popping a berry into her mouth. "Then, since we're no longer allowed to kill the Merim Her, the Lonak would have little else to do."

Astorek gave a sorrowful shake of his head. "All so strange, but so familiar."

♦ ♦ ♦

The feast came to an end some hours later, the Sentar carrying the still-unconscious Alturk to the far end of the hall where Astorek told them they were welcome to make their beds, the settlement lacking any empty dwellings to house so many newcomers. "The tribe grows larger by the year," he said. "We are required to build constantly."

Whale Killer and Many Wings appeared at his side along with Wise Bear, the shamaness pointing her staff towards the hall's broad doorway. "It is time for our tale," Astorek said.

After the warmth of the hall the cold outside felt crushing, stealing the air from Vaelin's lungs and provoking an instant thumping in his temples. Dahrena and Kiral accompanied him as they followed the ice folk into the forest, Astorek leading the way with a flaming torch. The path was steep and thick with snow, the way ever more difficult the higher they climbed though the Wolf People moved with the unconscious speed born of having walked this trail many times.

Finally they came to a flat expanse at the base of a rugged cliff, Astorek lifting his torch so the light played over a narrow opening in the rock face. Vaelin saw how Kiral and Dahrena stiffened at the sight of the cave, and how Wise Bear took a firmer hold on his bone-staff. "Power?" he asked him.

"Much power," the shaman confirmed, peering into the cave with obvious unease. "Maybe too much."

"There is no danger for you here," Astorek said, moving into the cave and beckoning Vaelin to follow. "This place is as much yours as ours."

The cave entrance was narrow but opened out into a broad cavern, the walls dry and the air musty with age. Numerous bowl-like indentations had been carved into the cavern floor, each stained with dried pigment of different hues, but it was the walls that captured Vaelin's attention. The cavern curved around them in a long semicircle, two-thirds of its length richly adorned in paintings, the colours so vibrant they seemed to shimmer in the light from Astorek's torch.

Many Wings spoke, ushering Vaelin towards the stretch of wall nearest the cave mouth. "Mother bids you welcome to the memory of the Wolf People," Astorek said.

Vaelin peered at the images painted onto the stone and was surprised to find the paint fresh, the images clear and easily discerned, a large patch of black paint adorned with small pinpricks of yellow he took to symbolise the night sky. A little farther along he found an image of crude stick figures, all arranged into a single large group, and next to them the same group divided by three black lines.

"The end of the first Long Night," Astorek said, "and the birth of the three tribes, dividing the islands between them. There were no shamans then, and life was hard. But still we prospered." He moved along, the torch flickering over various scenes, the images becoming less crude as they progressed, so that soon there were no more stick figures, but clear depictions of people and beasts. Hunters speared walrus on the ice or cast harpoons at whales from the prow of boats, others raised dwellings among the trees. Vaelin paused at the next image, taking a moment to fully understand the scene; an island, Wolf Home judging by the shape of the mountain, and alongside it a vessel of some kind, but of completely unfamiliar design. It was long and low in the water with only a single mast and far more oars than any modern ship.

"They came from the west in the summer months," Astorek said. "So many years ago the stars have changed their course since. A tall people speaking in meaningless babble but bringing gifts of great value, blades of iron stronger and sharper than any we could smelt, and wondrous devices of glass to cast sight over great distances. We called them the Great Boat People."

He pointed to three figures depicted next to the ship, two men and a woman. The woman was of arresting beauty, dark-haired with green eyes, wearing a long white robe and a golden amulet around her neck: a half-moon adorned with a red stone. The man on her left wore a blue robe and was slight of build, his face handsome but narrow and seemed to be wearing a half smile on his lips. But it was the man on the woman's right who captured Vaelin's attention, an impressive figure, bearded, tall and broad across the shoulders, his brow furrowed as if lost in the depth of thought, the face near identical to one Vaelin had seen before.

"It's him!" he said, turning to Wise Bear, his heart thumping in excitement. "The statue from the Fallen City! You see it?"

Wise Bear nodded, his expression markedly less enthusiastic. "Story known to Bear People," he said. "Great Boat People brought death to the ice."

"Yes." Astorek moved on, his torch revealing a scene of devastation, a settlement like the one they had just left, but littered with corpses. "They came peacefully, seeking to trade treasures for knowledge. They had no warriors, offered no violence, but still they brought death. A great sickness that laid waste to every settlement they visited until the three tribes were but a remnant."

The torchlight revealed the woman again, standing alone this time, her face shown in profile, lowered and drawn in great sadness. Her hands were held to her face, red with blood from finger to wrist. "It was the woman who saved us," Astorek said. "How is not fully understood, but she gave her blood and it saved us, the sickness faded. But . . ." He illuminated the next image, the two men standing over the woman's body. The handsome man's smile had gone, his face now hard with anger, whilst the bearded man wore an expression of stoic forbearance, though whatever ancient hand had captured his face had clearly seen the grief he was trying to hide.

"The tall man took his great boat and sailed away," Astorek said. "But the other man stayed, unwilling to stray far from the body of the woman, refusing to give it to the ice as was custom. Then . . ." He revealed a shadowy image in silhouette, a man pulling a sled through a snowstorm. "He took her body north when winter came and was not seen again by the eyes of the ice people. But . . . he did leave a gift."

Astorek paused, regarding Vaelin with an expression that was part reluctance, part awe. "They knew many things, these Great Boat People, the working of metal and the reckoning of the stars, even the course of the future."

The painting revealed by Astorek's torch was the largest yet, covering the wall from floor to ceiling and executed with an artistry and clarity that would even have outshone Alornis. It was the face of a man, perhaps thirty years in age, his features angular rather than handsome, his eyes dark, a faint smile playing over his lips. It was a hard face, not unused to privation from its slightly gaunt aspect, or violence if Vaelin was any judge. He had looked into the eyes of enough killers to know . . .

All thought fled as the realisation dawned. He felt Dahrena move to his side, taking his hand which, he realised, had begun to shake.

"The one who will save us from a peril yet unseen," Astorek said. "He called him the Raven's Shadow."

PART III

Anyone who claims they have a genius for war should be regarded as the greatest of fools. For the successful conduct of war is an exercise in the management of folly.

—QUEEN LYRNA AL NIEREN, *COLLECTED SAYINGS,*
GREAT LIBRARY OF THE UNIFIED REALM

VERNIERS' ACCOUNT

We put in at Marbellis on the thirty-fifth day of our voyage where the captain took ten crewmen ashore, each laden with an impressive pile of loot and weapons harvested from various unfortunate Volarians at the Teeth and Alltor. "A ship feeds on cargo," he grunted at me before departing. He was slightly more inclined towards conversation these days, but still refused to share any words with Fornella. "Should fetch half a hold's worth of spice with this lot. Stay on board and keep an eye on that witch of yours."

She joined me at the rail as I surveyed the docks and the city beyond. "I had heard this place described as the treasure of the northern empire," she said. "I must say it seems somewhat tarnished."

Marbellis had been in a continual state of reconstruction since the war, the various burnt and wasted districts slowly disappearing as the great port healed itself. But whilst a city could be repaired the hearts of its citizens were a different matter. The years since the war had seen many appeals to the Emperor for more direct and lasting retribution against the Northmen, the loudest and most numerous originating in Marbellis.

"'We found a jewel in the desert,'" I quoted. "'And from it fashioned a charred cinder.'"

"Pretty," she said. "One of yours, I assume."

"Actually, it was penned by a young poet I met in Varinshold. The son, in fact, of the general who commanded the army that nearly destroyed this city."

"Couldn't get to the father, I assume?"

"No. He refused all requests for an interview. His son, however, was happy to talk as long as I paid his nightly wine bill."

"Did he have any excuse for this? Any particular reason?"

I shook my head. "Just regret, and guilt though he took no part in the slaughter. He was keen to point out that his father had been quick to quell the *excesses of his army, executing over a hundred men for various dreadful deeds in the process."*

"Tokrev would have executed them too. Dead slaves are of no value."

I turned back from the rail and started for the cabin we shared. "We have work to do."

◆ ◆ ◆

Over the preceding weeks our researches had done much to expand my knowledge of ancient myth but as yet revealed scant evidence as to the Ally's origins or the whereabouts of the endless man he sought. There were a few references to the machinations of dark gods or malign spirits in the oldest, mostly fragmentary tales left by the denizens of what later became the Volarian Empire, but sorting fact from superstitious delusion was simply impossible. The endless man proved a more fruitful line of inquiry, unearthing no less than seven different versions of his story, mostly from Asrael and revolving around the unfortunate subject's rejection of the Faith. However, there were other tales, one from Cumbrael which cast the fellow as a godless heretic who committed the ultimate crime of burning the Ten Books, finding himself cursed by the World Father to contemplate his sin for all eternity. Today, however, my research uncovered a Meldenean legend telling of a man washed up on the Isles after a shipwreck, a man who should have drowned but lived when all his crew-mates perished. He named himself Urlan, come in search of the Old Gods.

I looked up from the scroll as the tramp of many feet on the deck told of the captain's success in securing cargo. Fornella had fallen to slumber already, lying naked on the bunk as was her perennial wont. She seemed to sleep more as the days went by and ever more grey appeared in her hair. You grow old, mistress, I thought, surveying her nakedness and finding, for all the wrinkles that now etched her face, she was still beautiful. I tossed a blanket over her and went outside.

Night had fallen and the deck was brightly lit with torches, most clustered at the bow where a persistent chopping sound could be heard. I went forward to find the captain standing with crossed arms, stern visage fixed on the sight of a man suspended by ropes to hang over the bow. The man was old but spry, clearly Alpiran from his colouring, working a hammer and chisel over the jawless figurehead, wood chips flying as he erased the scars from its snout. I noted a fresh but as yet unshaped block of wood had been nailed into place to fashion a new jaw for the serpent.

"Crew don't like to sail without a god to calm the waves," the captain grunted, watching the carpenter work. "Paid him triple to have it done by morning."

"Which is he?" I asked, gesturing at the serpent. "An old god or a new one?"

The captain favoured me with a squint, faint amusement in his eyes. "Finding my people worthy of study now, scribbler?"

"It might help, with my mission."

He shrugged, nodding at the figurehead. "Not a he, a she. Levansis, sister to the great serpent god Moesis. Though she despised her brother for his vicious ways, she wept when Margentis destroyed his body and her tears calmed the sea for ten full years. When the storms rise, she's the one we pray to."

My knowledge of Meldenean history was scant but I knew their pantheon dated back to their colonisation of the Isles some six hundred years ago, and from my survey of the ruins found there, they had clearly been occupied long before that. "A new god then," I said. "What can you tell me of the old ones?"

He looked away and I noted how his crossed arms tightened further. "Them we do not pray to."

"But what are they?"

The captain cast a wary eye at the nearest of his crew, two sailors, young but both bearing scars from the Battle of the Teeth, and glaring at me in naked outrage. "Ill luck to talk of the old gods on a ship's deck," the captain said, moving to the gangplank. "Come, I'll let you buy me a drink, scribbler. Besides I have news to impart."

◆ ◆ ◆

He led me to a quiet tavern near the warehouse district, the patrons mostly stevedores indulging in a cup or two of wine at the end of the day's labour. Even in light of the fatigue evident in the other customers, the mood was sombre to the point of oppression, most sitting in silent contemplation of their wine. We sat beside a window, the captain lighting his pipe, the bowl filled with the sweet-smelling five-leafed weed popular in the northern empire but frowned upon elsewhere for its soporific effect.

"Ah, that's the stuff," the captain said, exhaling a cloud of smoke. "Once took some seeds home for the wife to grow. Never did, soil's not right. Pity, could've made a fortune."

"The old gods," I said, pen poised above my scroll. "What do you know of them?"

"Well, they're old for a start." He gave an uncharacteristic laugh, something I attributed to the contents of his pipe. The merriment also raised some heads at the surrounding tables, a few scowling in disapproval, making me wonder what grim tidings had heralded such a mood.

"They were there when we landed on the Isles," the captain went on, recapturing my attention. "The old gods, standing in stone, so lifelike it seems as if they'll stir if you touch them at all."

"You've seen them?"

He took a puff on his pipe and nodded. "Captain's privilege, once you get your own ship, you go to the caves to pay homage to the old gods. Since they were there first, seems only polite. And there are stories aplenty about the ill fates of captains who failed to make the pilgrimage."

"So, they're statues found centuries ago."

"More than statues, scribbler." The captain's gaze darkened at the memory. "Statue doesn't make you sweat the moment you lay eyes on it, doesn't make your head ache when you get near, nor put images in your head when you bow to touch its foot."

My quill stopped its track across the parchment and I concealed a sigh. I had seen enough by now to fully appreciate that what I once thought of as superstition was all too real, but still the inherent skepticism lingered. "Images in your head?" I asked in a passive tone.

"Just for a second. I touched her foot and . . . I saw the Isles, but not our Isles. There was a city, standing where our capital now stands. But so beautiful, gleaming marble from end to end, the harbour filled with ships, longer than ours and mostly driven by oarsmen. And they were not pirates, I could see that. Not a single sailor carried a weapon. Whatever time it was, it was a time of peace."

He fell silent, face now clouded with memory as he took the pipe from his lips, barely stirring when I prompted, "Her foot? The old gods are female?"

"One is. The other two are men, one a great bearded fellow, the other younger and handsome of face. I didn't touch either of them, for the visions they impart are only for the bravest eyes. They say the Shield touched all three though, the only man ever to do so."

"There's a story, about a man who couldn't die. It says he came to the Isles in search of the old gods."

The captain huffed a laugh and returned to his pipe. "Urlan. My old gran used to tell me that one."

"The version I have says he offended them by asking for an impossible gift, so they cursed him to walk the ocean floor for all time."

He frowned, smoke billowing and a faint dullness creeping into his eyes. "Gran's tale was different, but the old stories often change depending on who tells them. She said Urlan was driven from the Isles, set adrift in a boat and warned never to return. And not because he had offended the old gods, but *because having heard his words, the people feared one so young who knew so much."*

He watched me writing down the tale, extinguishing his pipe and tapping the remaining weed into a pouch. "Time I imparted my tidings, scribbler," he said.

"More grave news from the war, I take it?" I replied, glancing around at the grim-faced patrons.

"No, from Alpira." I saw that the dullness had faded from his eyes and he regarded me with a steady, regretful gaze. "Emperor Aluran died a week ago. Before passing he named his successor as Lady Emeren Nasur Ailers, to be known forever more as Empress Emeren I."

CHAPTER ONE

Vaelin

Dahrena called her war-cat Mishara, the Seordah word for lightning, and took great delight in training her. Every morning she would spend an hour or more in the forest, smiling as the beast leapt, ran or climbed trees at her command. "I had a kitten when I was little," she told Vaelin, throwing a ball fashioned from walrus-hide for Mishara to catch, leaping high to snatch it from the air with a fast snap of her impressive jaws. "I named her Stripes. One day she went missing and my father told me she must have run away. I found out later he didn't have the heart to tell me she'd been crushed by a cart-wheel."

She frowned at Vaelin's vague nod, sending Mishara off into the trees with a flick of her wrist before coming to sit next to him, taking his hand. She asked no question, as ever much of their communication was unspoken. "In the Order," he said, "they told us prophecy was a lie, like a god. The province of deluded Deniers mistaking madness for insight. Yet all the while the Seventh Order laboured in secret pursuit of its own prophecies."

"You recall what Brother Harlick told us," she said. "All prophecies are false."

"You saw their wall."

"Pictures painted countless years ago and only visible now because these people maintain them with such devotion." She squeezed his hand tighter. "The visions of Nersus Sil Nin gave the Seordah centuries to prepare for the coming of the Marelim Sil, but still they were driven into the forest. The future is not pigment daubed onto stone, we make the future with every breath and every step. Our mission is vital, you know it. We cannot allow ourselves distraction."

"Kiral tells me her song swells with warning whenever I talk of moving on. For now, it seems this place is our mission."

She sighed, resting her head on his shoulder. "Well, at least it's started to thaw."

◆ ◆ ◆

He inspected Orven's guardsmen in the afternoon, mainly to assure the Lord Marshal of his appreciation for returning them to martial readiness with such alacrity. Throughout the Long Night he had maintained the stern discipline and rigid adherence to routine that characterised the Mounted Guard, the beards grown on the ice soon sheared off and every breastplate scraped clean of rust.

"How goes the training?" Vaelin asked Orven after surveying the ranks and exchanging ritual pleasantries with the men. They spoke up readily enough, all veterans of the march from the Reaches and Alltor, regarding him with an implacable respect he knew might never fade. Even so, despite the generous fare offered by their hosts, many retained the gaunt aspect of those exposed to the worst extremes of climate.

"Fighting on foot is hard for those accustomed to the saddle, my lord," Orven replied. "But it can't be helped. The Lonak sometimes join in with practice. I think they find it amusing, or have little else to do."

Vaelin glanced over to where a cluster of Sentar stood watching one of the Wolf People skin a recently caught walrus, taking note of the fact that Alturk was not among them, nor had he been for much of the Long Night.

"Concentrate on close-order drill," he told Orven. "You've seen how the Volarians fight, whole battalions moving as one. I'm sure it's a feat the guards can match."

Orven straightened, his fist going to his breastplate in a customarily perfect salute. "Indeed we can, my lord."

◆ ◆ ◆

Astorek found him grooming Scar in the small stable the Wolf People had allowed him to construct near the shore. As usual a gaggle of children had gathered to watch as he led the warhorse from his makeshift home, apparently fascinated by the strange four-legged beast, bigger than a moose but without antlers. They seemed to have no inclination to shyness, or awareness that Vaelin might not understand their babble of questions as they clustered around, small hands playing over Scar's coat, occasionally retreating with delighted giggles at the horse's irritated stamps and snorts. One little boy was more insistent than the others, tugging at Vaelin's furs and repeating the same question with a puzzled frown.

"He wants to know why you don't eat him."

Vaelin turned to find Astorek standing nearby, watching the scene with faint amusement. Two of his wolves sat a short distance away, a male and a female of disconcerting size, their scent provoking Scar to a fearful shudder.

"They're too close," he told the Volarian, nodding at the wolves.

Astorek inclined his head and the wolves rose in unison to trot towards the ice, their usual placidity evaporating as they began to leap and nip at one another in a playful dance.

"He's for riding," Vaelin said, turning back to the boy as Astorek translated. "Not eating."

This seemed to puzzle the child even more, his small features creasing into a scrunch of bafflement, so Vaelin lifted him onto Scar's back, taking the reins and leading him on a slow walk towards the shoreline. The boy laughed and clapped his hands as he bounced along, the other children following in a clamour that didn't need much translation; they all wanted a turn. After an hour or so of entertainment Astorek finally shooed the children away with a few short words. Although the Wolf People's discipline of their young folk seemed lax, the instant silence that descended on the children told of an underlying authority that brooked no dissent and they had soon scampered off to find other amusements.

"His description of you was not wholly accurate," Astorek said when the children had gone. "He said you would be fierce."

"Your prophet's words? You talk as if you knew him."

"Sometimes I feel as if I did, I've heard his words so many times. Our people write nothing down but all shaman are taught to recite his message without fault."

Vaelin led Scar back to the stable, fixing a feed-bag over his snout. The islands were poor in grain but rich in root vegetables and berries, harvested in the summer months and preserved through the winter. From his contented snorts and noticeably less denuded frame, it seemed Scar found the mix just as appetising as any bag of corn.

"My mother and father," Astorek said, "bade me ask as to your intentions."

"Intentions?"

"The Wolf People have awaited your arrival for as long as they can remember, knowing it would herald a time of great danger. And yet you spend every day tending your horse, whilst your companions play and the big man drinks his way through our stocks of pine ale."

"Alturk is a . . . troubled man. And we have lingered here because Wise Bear advised venturing forth during the Long Night meant death. We are, of course, grateful for your hospitality."

"You talk as if you intend to leave us."

"We came in search of a particular man. Kiral's song will guide us to him. When she hears a clear tune we will move on."

"Leaving us to our fate, whatever it may be?"

"You put great stock in ancient paintings and long-told stories, especially since you cannot have been born to this life."

Astorek gave a bitter laugh. "Is that it? You deny my people aid because you still distrust me?"

"Your people require no aid, as far as I can tell. As for you." Vaelin took the bag from Scar's snout, scratching his nose. "I've yet to learn how you came to be here, at this time, speaking our language without fault."

"If I were an enemy, would not the huntress's song warn you?"

Barkus, that night on the beach, the mask slipping away in an instant. All those years and the song had told him nothing. "It should, but I know to my cost how well the servants of our enemy can evade detection."

He put the feed-bag aside and hefted a seal fur over Scar's back, the war-horse voicing a rumbling snort of welcome at the increased warmth, then turned to Astorek, eyebrows raised in expectation. The Volarian's gaze became downcast, his response a reluctant murmur, "I was guided here . . . by a wolf."

◆ ◆ ◆

"My father was a wealthy man." Astorek's face was bathed yellow in the fire-light, his gaze fixed on the flames. Vaelin had called the others to the great dwelling they shared to hear his story, the Lonak sitting with their customary attentiveness when promised an interesting tale. The Gifted sat on either side of Vaelin, Orven and his guardsmen arrayed in neat rows behind. Only Alturk was absent, something that provoked a sharp exchange between Kiral and one of the Sentar, a veteran warrior who shifted uncomfortably at her terse enquiry. From her disgusted expression Vaelin divined she found his answer less than satisfactory.

"A merchant to trade," Astorek went on. "Like his father before him. The great port city of Varral was our home, where I grew up in my grandfather's fine house surrounded by fine slaves and fine toys. Most of grandfather's trade came from the Unified Realm and we often played host to merchants and captains from across the sea. Keen to ensure his legacy, my grandfather insisted I be taught all the principal languages of commerce, so by the age of twelve I was fluent in Realm Tongue and Alpiran, and could even converse adequately in the two main dialects of the Far West. I remember being a happy child, and why not? As long as I remained attentive at lessons for a few hours a day, every whim would be indulged, and my grandfather did like to spoil me so."

Astorek's smile of fond remembrance faded as he continued, "It all changed when Grandfather died. My father, it seemed, had once nurtured youthful aspirations to be a soldier, quickly discounted by Grandfather of course, who had little interest in things military beyond trade in weapons. All Volarian males are supposed to serve a minimum of two years in the Free Swords but Grandfather knew whom to bribe to deny his son a chance at military glory. And so, as the years passed, my father nursed his grievance and fed his secret ambition, an ambition given free rein with Grandfather's passing.

"Volaria tends to frown on amateur soldiers, the sons of the wealthy can purchase commission to junior officer status but thereafter promotion is granted strictly on merit. However, my father also knew whom to bribe and soon after securing his commission, and providing funds to equip and recruit a full battalion of Free Sword cavalry, found himself quickly elevated to the rank of commander. But rank wasn't enough, his thirst for glory hadn't abated. Varral, like all Volarian cities, is rich in statues, long rows of bronzes commemorating heroes, ancient and new, and Father badly wanted a plinth for himself. A sudden upsurge in campaigning against the northern savages provided him his opportunity, and, as is custom for the wealthy in Volaria, sons of sufficient age are required to follow their fathers to war. I was thirteen years old."

"Your mother raised no objection?" Vaelin asked.

"Perhaps she would have, had I ever known her. Grandfather told me she had been cast out after revealing herself a faithless whore and Father never said a single word about her. But there was a slave, an old woman who worked in the kitchens, so old she was losing her mind. She caught sight of me once, stealing cakes as I often did, and started screaming, 'Elverah's spawn. Elverah's spawn.' The other slaves quickly dragged her away and I never saw her again. That was the only time my grandfather ever punished me, thirty strokes of the cane, and after every stroke he made me promise never to speak of my mother again."

"She was Gifted," Dahrena said. "Like you."

"I expect so. It's the same among the Wolf People, only mothers with power pass it on to their children. As I journeyed north with my father's battalion the soldiers would sometimes exchange stories of strange folk spirited away by Council agents, never to be seen again. Though they always spoke softly of such matters, for Father was zealous in enforcing discipline, flogging several men in the first week of the march. I suppose he was trying to compensate for a complete absence of any military talent.

"Poor old father. He was a terrible soldier, quick to tire in the saddle, prone to sickness, lax in ensuring sufficient supplies for his men. By the time we joined with the rest of the army his dreams of glory had faded amidst the truth of a soldier's life, which, from what I could tell, consisted mainly of discomfort, bad food and the constant threat of flogging, enlivened only by an occasional wine ration or game of dice. I suspect he had resolved to extricate himself from his new-found career, and might well have done so with a judicious bribe, but for General Tokrev."

The Realm folk all straightened at the mention of the name, causing Astorek to blink in surprise. "You know this name?"

"He committed many crimes in our homeland," Vaelin said. "He's dead now."

"Ah. News I had long hoped to hear. I always suspected he was not destined for a long life, though, like some of red-clads, it was rumoured that he was already far older than he appeared. We knew his reputation, a commander of tactical brilliance, it was said, but also stern discipline. When we first joined with the army he was in the process of hanging three officers for cowardice, one a battalion commander guilty of voicing defeatist sentiments. Tokrev's orders were to concentrate his efforts on the mountain tribes, the slave quota for the year being only half-filled, but he nursed ambitions to go farther, into the frozen north where legend spoke of wild tribes who lived on the ice, said to be far richer in Gifted blood than any people on earth.

"Many of his officers, my father included, were less than happy with this plan. However, Tokrev's demonstration was enough to silence any dissent and north we marched, being obliged to fight our way through the tribesfolk on the way. They are a fierce people, born to a warrior's life, and make a formidable enemy. Luckily, they also take as much delight in warring among themselves as in fighting the hated southron invaders, so never possessed sufficient numbers to pose a serious obstacle.

"Our battalion was given the task of patrolling the flanks, a tricky business for the most experienced commander, and one far beyond my father's abilities. Suffice to say our first engagement was a predictable disaster, Father leading us into a narrow ravine to be assailed from above by archers and slingers. His chief sergeant had enough wit to order a charge that carried us into open ground but they were waiting on the other side, a thousand or more screaming tribesmen charging down from the surrounding hills. I saw my father unhorsed in short order and charged towards him, for all his faults he was my father after all. I managed to get to his side but a tribesman's axe cut through my horse's foreleg, leaving us both on foot and surrounded. Father was wounded, a deep gash to the forehead, barely aware of what was happening, screaming horror all around as his battalion was torn to pieces. The mountain folk were laughing as they came closer, laughing at the boy trying to ward them off with a shaking sword whilst his father staggered about and shouted orders to corpses. That was the first time it happened.

"I saw a group of horses being gathered a short way off, the tribesmen have few of their own so they are a great prize. I knew if I could just get us to a horse we could ride free, knew it with all certainty. I stared at them, willing them to hear my desperation . . . And they came, all of them at once, breaking free of the tribesmen and stampeding through those surrounding us, stamping and kicking. Two halted at our side, both standing still as if frozen. I managed to get Father into the saddle and we rode away, every surviving horse following at our backs. We rode blindly for an age, until I too began to slump, realising I was also bleeding, from my nose, my eyes, my mouth. I remember falling from the horse then all was blackness.

"We were found by a Varitai scouting party the next morning, lying senseless amidst a herd of riderless horses. They took us back to camp where the slave-healer was able to wake Father with some kind of herbal mixture, but he was not the same, looking at me with eyes that saw a stranger, his lips spouting gibberish only he could understand. Loon though he now was, General Tokrev still deemed him an incompetent and a coward. As sole heir I was obliged to watch as he was beheaded, the general decreeing his line unworthy of freedom and condemning me to slavery. Naturally, as the wronged party, all my family's wealth was now his.

"A slave's life is rarely an easy one, but to be a slave in army service is a particular form of torment. My comrades were mostly cowards and deserters, subjected to routine beatings to crush any defiance, the slightest sign of disobedience punishable by prolonged torture and death, a fate suffered by three of my companions during the march north. We were employed as beasts of burden, laden with packs that would have tried the strongest man, fed barely enough to sustain life, our numbers dwindled from two hundred to less than fifty by the time we reached the ice.

"The general's glorious campaign began with the destruction of a small settlement on the shore of the frozen ocean. Perhaps five hundred people, small in stature and clad in furs. It should have been an easy victory but these people were far from defenceless, for they somehow had command of bears. Great white bears unlike any seen before, bears that seemed to feel nothing as arrows or spears pierced their hides, bears that tore whole companies to pieces before being hacked down. The general was compelled to commit a full brigade to the fight, and what was expected to be an easy victory turned into a prolonged slaughter. The settlement was his, though many of its inhabitants had fled onto the ice. The few captives, mostly wounded men and women who had fought a rear-guard action to buy time for their people to flee, sat down and refused to move regardless of what torments were visited upon them by the overseers. They were dragged into cages but refused to eat, perishing shortly after, none speaking a single word.

"Although Tokrev was quick to send an inflated account of his victory to Volar, his troops didn't share his exultation. The cold was already claiming lives and winter had not yet fully fallen, and the Free Swords looked upon the vast expanse of ice before them with great unease. However, none had the courage to gainsay the general when he ordered the advance and I soon found myself hauling a sled across the ice alongside a dozen other unfortunates. Every morning we would wake to find our numbers diminished until soon only I and three others were left. The overseers cursed and beat us but had little option but to lighten the load, vital provisions being left behind because there were insufficient slaves to haul them. Bellies began to rumble and tempers shorten, the Free Swords' fear growing with every step on the ice, fears that proved well justified.

"The Bear People bided their time, letting us spend lives and food with each passing mile, until the days grew so short the army could cover no more than a few miles at a time. Strangely I found myself better fed than before, the chief overseer had contrived to plunge to his death at the bottom of a hidden crevasse and his surviving subordinates were too wearied by the cold to prevent me helping myself to my fellow slaves' rations. They had all perished by now, some due to the beatings, but most taken by the cold.

"I remember the day I last saw the general, standing alone at the head of the column. He paced about on the ice, stamping with impatience and it seemed to me he was waiting for something. Thanks to my increased strength I had begun to harbour insane notions of revenge. The ever-more-neglectful overseers, themselves reduced in number to only two, had failed to notice when I procured a key from one of their fallen comrades, a drunkard who had foolishly passed out after forgetting to properly secure his furs. It would be a simple matter to unfasten my shackles from the sled, sprint towards the general, and hook the chains over his head, strangling him before his Kuritai could respond. It was a hopeless scheme, of course. The man was twice my size and his Kuritai would have been on me before I covered half the distance. But I was young, and hope is ever bright in the young. And the sight of my father's headless corpse had never faded, fool though he was.

"So, as the general paced back and forth I slipped the key into the lock and made ready to execute my plan. I often wonder what would have transpired then had not the eyeless man appeared, most likely there would have been one more dead slave littering the course of this madman's army across the ice. But still, in my less reflective moments, I often think how it would have felt to have that man at my mercy, just for an instant, to know his fear as the chain tightened around his throat.

"But the arrival of the eyeless man forced all such thoughts from my head. He seemed little different from the people slaughtered on the shore, clad in furs, small and broad of face, but instead of bears, he brought cats, very large cats that appeared out of the mist on either side of him, making the few surviving horses rear in alarm, along with more than a few Free Swords. Many began to draw swords but stopped at a command from the general. To my great surprise he then began to converse with the eyeless man, not in some alien tribal tongue, but in Volarian. Even more shocking was his demeanour, his shoulders hunched and head slightly bowed, the posture of a subservient man. Their words were faint but I heard a few snatches of conversation above the constant wind, 'You were told to wait,' the eyeless man told the general. Tokrev appeared to bluster, speaking the kind of military jargon my father rejoiced in but barely understood, talk of seized initiative and bold thrusts. The eyeless man told him he was a fool. 'Come back next summer,' he said before turning away. 'If they leave you anything to return with.' Then he was gone, and his cats with him.

"We remained encamped as night came on, every soul no doubt now silently beseeching Tokrev to order a retreat come the morning. In the event, the Bear People left him no decision in the matter. The spear-hawks attacked first, streaking out of the night sky by the hundred to rip eyes from sockets, tear away faces and fingers so that it seemed a red rain was falling all around. Panic seized the Free Swords and only the Varitai and Kuritai responded to the bugle blasts, forming a defensive cordon around the camp. For a moment all was quiet, the night beyond the torchlight nothing but a silent void, but then the sound came, filling the night, the roar of a thousand bears stirred to fury.

"They came at us from two sides, a solid wedge of charging muscle and claw, smashing through the Varitai as if they were made of straw, then rampaging through the camp. Everywhere men fell shrieking, slashed open or decapitated by sweeping claws, the bears rising and falling as they pounded men to bloody ruin. My last view of the general was the sight of him amidst a cluster of Kuritai, fighting with all their expertise to keep the bears at bay as he fled, a dense knot of fear-maddened Free Swords following close behind.

"As for me, I still crouched next to the sled, now liberally adorned with the remnants of my overseers. Everything had happened with such speed I could scarcely believe it. The bears seemed content to continue dismembering corpses, but then I saw men running from the shadows, many men with spears, more bears running alongside them and the air above alive with the thunder of wings. I knew in an instant to linger here another moment meant death.

"I unlocked myself and fled into the darkness, not thinking to seize some supplies, my only thought of escape. I ran until my lungs burned with the frozen air, collapsing only when my legs gave way. I lay still for a time, trying to recover some strength, but I was so tired, and it was so cold. I thought it might be best to sleep for a while, and might have fallen to an endless slumber had I not heard the steady crunch of a bear's claws on the ice behind me. I forced myself to my feet, staggering on, fuelled only by terror, but even that was not enough to maintain my flight and I fell again.

"Knowing my cause to be hopeless I forced myself to turn and confront my pursuer, a lumbering shape looming ever closer through the darkness, eyes bright, claws and snout red from recent feeding. Volarians have no death songs, believing there are no gods or ascended souls to hear them, but in those final moments I found myself thinking once again of my father's foolish dreams and how I wished I had found the courage to ask him about my mother."

Astorek fell silent, his gaze distant now, a puzzled frown on his brow as if he recalled something not fully understood. Vaelin knew the expression well, having worn it many times himself. "The wolf," he said.

"Yes." Astorek gave a slight smile. "The bear stopped a few feet from me, growling, eyes bright with a malice that I had only ever seen in the eyes of men before. It seemed to be savouring the moment, creeping closer until its bloody snout was only inches away, its breath, hot and stinking on my face . . . Then it stopped.

"I had closed my eyes, refusing to look into its hate-filled gaze, but when I felt its breath recede I opened them again. The bear had shrunk to its haunches, head lowered, eyes now lit with another human trait—fear. Not, of course, of me, but something beyond me. So I turned and saw a wolf.

"Two things struck me at once. First, it was large, larger in fact than the bear that now cringed from it. Secondly, its eyes. They looked into mine and I knew . . . It *saw* me, all of me, skin, bone, heart and soul. It saw me, and felt no malice at all.

"I heard a scraping sound and turned to see the bear fleeing into the night with all haste, the white shape soon swallowed by darkness. The wolf circled me for a short while, its gaze still fixed on me. For all the strangeness and the terror I still felt the great cold enfolding me, the sweat on my skin now frozen, leeching away what strength I had left. My vision began to dim and I knew death would soon claim me . . . Then the wolf growled.

"It was not a voice that came to my head then, more a certainty, an implacable conviction that I couldn't die here. From somewhere I found the strength to stand and the wolf trotted away towards the north, stopping after a time to ensure I was following. I shuffled along in its wake for uncounted hours, or possibly days, for all sense of time seemed to fade. If I faltered, or felt the welling surge of despair that would tempt me to sink onto the ice where at least I could rest, the wolf would growl, and I would keep moving.

"We stopped when a green fire began to flicker in the sky. Not knowing what it was, I finally fell to my knees, thinking this a vision of death, or madness. Perhaps I had already died and my tutors had all been wrong; there is something awaiting us beyond the arc of life. All fear had left me by then, along with all but the most faint sensation, numbed as I was. Now there was only acceptance, a sense of a journey complete.

"And the wolf howled."

Astorek closed his eyes and Vaelin felt Dahrena's hand slide into his, knowing she too was recalling the wolf's howl, that night in the forest when the Seordah heeded its call to war. He knew Astorek couldn't describe how it felt, the sound that seemed to strip away everything but the core of those privileged, or cursed to hear it.

"I would have wept," the young shaman said, reopening his eyes to regard his audience with a sombre smile. "Had not my tears been frozen in my eyes. The wolf's howl faded and it looked at me, one last time, then was gone, bounding across the ice. I stared up at the fire in the sky for a time then lay down to sleep. Whale Killer must have found me only minutes later, for I was still alive to greet the next dawn."

"And you have remained here ever since?" Vaelin asked. "Never tempted to return home?"

"What home would I return to? Everything I had is gone. Besides, when they returned the next summer, I learned full well the vileness of my former people. We knew of the Bear People's great battle with the Cat People, that they had fled to the west in search of easier prey. The Wolf People were not sorry to see them gone from the ice, for they had fallen to unwise ways. But, though the Bear People had won a victory, their losses meant they couldn't withstand another Volarian expedition, especially since the Volarians had learned their lessons well and came better equipped and in much greater numbers. When they were done with the Bear People they came for us.

"Many Wings had taught me much, and I was a very keen student. She had hoped to shield me from the struggle but I wanted to repay their kindness. We killed many Volarians together, my wolves and her hawks, striking where they were weakest, fleeing before they could strike back. For months we harried them until their line of march became a red smear across the ice. But there were always more, and, though I searched for him, I never caught Tokrev's scent again. Two winters ago they stopped coming. We thought we had finally convinced them to leave us be, but it seems they went across the great water to torment your people instead, for which we are sorry."

Vaelin's gaze went to Kiral who gave a short nod. *She hears no lie . . . as I heard no lie from Barkus.*

"They will come again," Astorek went on, eyes intent on Vaelin. "In greater numbers still. But now we have you, Raven's Shadow."

◆ ◆ ◆

The hut where Alturk had chosen to seclude himself was a mean thing, little more than a slanting shack in a small clearing away from the main settlement. The door gave way easily under Vaelin's boot, releasing the fetid odour of an unwashed man mired in overindulgence. Alturk's substantial form lay on a bed of furs, snoring loudly, surrounded by the walrus-tooth flasks their hosts used to store pine ale, all empty. The slumbering Alturk gave no indication of having noticed the intrusion, something that changed abruptly when Vaelin emptied a bowlful of ice water over his shaggy head.

The explosion of rage was instantaneous, the Lonak surging upright, war club in hand, teeth bared in a snarl. He paused at the sight of Vaelin in the doorway, confusion flickering across his dripping face. "Do you choose death now, Merim Her?" he demanded in a hiss.

"*Sorbeh Khin*," Vaelin stated, the Lonak for a formal challenge. "You are no longer fit to lead the Sentar. They are mine now. If you wish to keep them, fight me." He turned and walked into the clearing where the Sentar waited, looking on with shared expressions of grim understanding. Kiral had explained Vaelin's reasoning and, to his surprise, none had raised an objection.

"Faithless dogs," Alturk growled at them as he emerged from the shack, going on to harangue them in Lonak in a short but vehement diatribe that appeared to leave all singularly unmoved.

"You no longer hear the word from the Mountain," Kiral told him. "You make yourself, varnish. This man gives you a chance to prove otherwise."

Alturk gave no reply, consenting only to sneer at her before fixing his unsteady gaze on Vaelin, grip tightening on his war club. "Where is your weapon?"

Vaelin spread his hands, showing the absence of a dagger at his belt, his sword also gone from his back. "Why would I require a weapon? You offer no threat."

Alturk stared at him in fury for a moment longer, then began to laugh, throwing his head back and casting hearty peals of mirth into the trees as he tossed his war club aside. "I should thank you," he said when his laughter finally subsided. "Not every man gets to make his dreams real."

He came at Vaelin in a crouching sprint. Their time among the Wolf People had done much to restore his frame and, for all the pine ale in his belly, his speed was impressive, leaving only the barest time for Vaelin to sidestep the charge and deliver a punch to his jaw. Alturk grunted in pain but didn't falter, replying with a swift round-house blow. Vaelin blocked it with both forearms and drove his elbow into the Lonak's exposed face, following up with a rapid series of punches to the face and belly, dodging Alturk's counterblows as he drove him back, every punch landing with unerring precision . . . Until the Lonak caught one in his fist and hammered a blow into Vaelin's temple.

He reeled from the impact, the world suddenly a blur as he struggled to resume a fighting stance. Alturk didn't afford him the opportunity, however, sweeping his legs away with a kick and driving another punch into his face. For a moment the world went away and Vaelin could see only a vague shadow, surrounded by glittering stars . . .

"You," Alturk grated, looming closer, meaty fist drawn back for another blow. "You made my son varnish. I see him every night, I watch him die every night, because of you, Merim Her."

"I spared a boy," Vaelin replied, spitting blood, feeling his left eye swelling shut. "You killed a man . . . A man who made his own choices." He saw it then, a flicker of something in the Lonak's eyes, a spasm of expression on his craggy face. "You knew," Vaelin said in realisation. "You knew he had betrayed you long before you killed him."

Alturk snarled again, drawing his fist back farther. Vaelin hawked and spat blood into the Lonak's eyes, buying enough time to twist and deliver a kick to the side of his head. He surged upright as Alturk staggered away, charging forward to drive his head into the Lonak's midriff then jerking it up to connect with his jaw. He followed with more punches to the face, Alturk sagging more with each blow, arms flailing as he tried to ward off the assault. Finally Vaelin sent him to his knees with a right hook to the jaw.

Vaelin paused, chest heaving, his fists leaking blood onto the forest floor. "Nishak told me," Alturk said in a dull, weary voice, gazing up at him, blood streaming from numerous cuts. "I . . . didn't listen." He lowered his head, slumping in resignation, muttering, "I make no request for the knife."

Kiral appeared at Vaelin's side with Alturk's war club in hand. "Strike true, Tahlessa," she said, offering the weapon to Vaelin. "He deserves a quick end at least . . ."

She trailed off abruptly and straightened, her gaze going to the south. From the pained expression on her face he knew her song must be sounding a powerful note. However, this time he didn't need to ask the meaning, for he could hear another warning, pealing across ice and forest, undeniable and implacable. The Sentar stirred in discomfort, exchanging fearful glances, for no wolf's howl was ever so loud.

Vaelin turned to Alturk as the howl faded, finding him now on his feet, the defeated slump vanished from his shoulders, his gaze fierce with certainty. "I'll need that," he said, gesturing to the war club.

Vaelin glanced at Kiral, expecting her to voice an objection, but her expression was one of grim, if reluctant assent. "Wise Bear has some healing skill," he told Alturk. "He can stitch your cuts."

Alturk merely grunted. "Had I been sober, you would be dead now."

Vaelin sighed the smallest laugh and tossed the war club into his hands. "I know."

CHAPTER TWO

Reva

Thehe Volarian was dying, she could see it; his skin hanging from the
bones of his face like a desiccated mask, eyes dull with defeat and
recent suffering. Nevertheless, he had told his tale in an unwavering
voice, the tones clear and strong, a man of centuries-long experience in ora-
tory. "The Empress will confront you with only a third of the fleet," he said to
the assembled captains of the Queen's Host, called to council on her flagship.
"After you have defeated them she expects you to sail into the Cut of Lokar.
The full fleet will move from the south to cut you off. That is all I know."

Reva watched as the Shield examined the detailed chart on the table.
They had convened on the main deck of the *Queen Lyrna*, no cabin being
large enough to accommodate so many. The sea was calmer today, though
still fractious enough to make the boat that had carried her here pitch alarmingly, shipping water with every passing minute. Reva found life at sea not
much to her liking, even after she overcame the initial bout of sea-sickness
the confines of ship life were trying in the extreme, as was the recurrent ache
whenever her thoughts strayed to Veliss and Ellese.

"The Cut of Lokar." Ell-Nestra's voice brought her back to the present as
he tapped an inlet on the Volarian coast. "The only direct sea-route to Volar.
Once we sail in there they could bottle us up with comparatively few ships.
Numbers won't matter for much in such close confines. Plus it'll be an easy
matter for them to garrison the north and south banks against a landing."

"This new Empress of theirs sets an elegant trap," Count Marven said
with a note of reluctant admiration. "Sadly, it seems she's no Tokrev."

"An overcomplicated ruse," the queen responded, her voice uncoloured by any respect. "I doubt she's ever played keschet." She turned to the Shield. "Your advice, Fleet Lord Ell-Nestra?"

"Fighting a needless battle is never a good option," he replied, his gaze still roaming the map. "Especially at sea where so much is dependent on chance. And manoeuvring a fleet so heavily laden with troops will prove arduous to say the least. I suggest we simply avoid the enemy, taking a north-eastern course to land here." He tapped a shallow bay a hundred miles north of the Cut of Lokar. "Some of my captains have done a little smuggling on these shores and tell me the beach here is large enough to accommodate at least a fifth of the army at one landing. With the bulk of Volarian forces securing the banks of the Cut, they shouldn't have more than a handful to oppose us. Once the army is landed the fleet will be free to deal with any threat to our supply lines."

The queen turned to her Battle Lord. "Count Marven?"

"It will take three days at least to land the entire army, Highness. Whilst most Volarian forces will be concentrated to the south, we must still expect an attack of some kind from the local garrisons before being fully ready to march."

"We could land farther north," the Shield conceded with a sigh. "But the coast offers few other landing sites for at least another two hundred miles."

"The greater the distance to Volar the lesser our chances of success," the queen said, raising her eyes from the map to scan her captains, her gaze eventually coming to rest on Reva. "And we have one in our ranks who can be considered expert in fending off Volarian attacks."

◆ ◆ ◆

"In addition to your archers and guardsmen," the queen said, "I will give you three regiments of Realm Guard, all veterans, including the Wolf Runners."

"They will be very welcome, Highness," Reva replied.

She had been called to the queen's cabin for a private audience, the first time they had been truly alone. Even the hulking Lord Protector had been ordered to wait outside. Reva found herself once again struck by the queen's beauty, even the faint white lines tracing back from her brow into the now-lustrous red-gold hair seemed to enhance rather than mar her perfection. More than that was the innate, effortless confidence, the peerless authority that ensured she commanded the attention of every set of eyes in any gathering. Despite this, or perhaps in part because of it, Reva had yet to feel the slightest flicker of attraction for her queen. *She was easier to like when burnt,* she decided. *Now the mask is too perfect.*

"Please know you are free to refuse this command," the queen went on. "Without any disfavour."

"We came here to finish this," Reva said. "Besides, I think I'd rather fight on land than sea."

"It's certainly an acquired taste." The queen smiled, though it wasn't one of her dazzling wonders; a trifle wary in fact. "Before he left on his northern expedition, Lord Vaelin asked that I not allow you to expose yourself to inordinate risk. In fact, he implored me to leave you in the Realm, as regent."

Reva suppressed a laugh. *Always so keen to act the elder brother.* "A task I'm hardly suited to, Highness. Although I have been meaning to ask for a clearer explanation of the intent behind Lord Vaelin's current mission."

"If secrets are kept, it is for a good reason. Suffice to say, the opportunities offered by his mission were too great to be ignored." The queen paused, her smile slowly fading. "I have had occasion recently to read more detailed reports of events at Alltor. I hadn't appreciated before how truly difficult the situation became, the extremes to which you were compelled."

The Volarian's face as he knelt at the block . . . No better than us . . . "Survival compels us to extremes, Highness."

"Indeed. Words I should like you to remember when performing your task. This war is not yet won and the survival of our peoples requires victory, at any cost." Her gaze was intent now, the flawless mask devoid of all humour. "You understand?"

At any cost. Looking into the queen's unwavering gaze, Reva felt a sudden rush of recognition, her mind filling with another face she knew so well, one that had also often spoken in similar terms, usually in the moments before he beat her. "Perhaps if you could elaborate, Highness," she said. "My task will be made easier with clear instruction."

The queen's gaze barely flickered. "The Varitai are to be captured only if opportunity arises. All Free Swords are to be killed."

"And if they surrender?"

"Then killing them will be a simpler task." The queen came forward, clasping her hands, her face now a picture of sisterly affection. "As you said, my lady, we came here to finish this."

◆ ◆ ◆

The Shield accompanied Reva back to the *Marshal Smolen*, one of the newly built monsters laden with her House Guard and a fifth of her archers. Ostensibly Ell-Nestra had come to oversee the landings though she sensed a sudden desire to remove himself from the queen's company, perhaps due to the fate of the Volarian. Reva had been making ready to climb into her boat when she saw the man recoil from the queen, his sagging features suddenly white with shock. The queen stood regarding him with an expression of serene satisfaction as he launched himself at her, snarling, hands like claws as he reached for her throat. With practised swiftness the queen drew a dagger from her sleeve and drove it into the Volarian's chest, a smooth unhesitant act performed before her guards could react.

"Throw this over the side," she told Lord Iltis, accepting a cloth from Lady Murel and wiping the dagger clean as she turned away. However, the Volarian had somehow contrived to cling to life and continued to rage at her as the Lord Protector carried him to the rail, voicing shrill curses in his own language. The queen didn't turn as he was cast into the ocean, striding towards Reva with the warmest farewell and good wishes for her venture.

"The man deserved his end, by all accounts," she said to the Shield as they clambered from the boat, scaling the ropes to the ship's deck. "Owner of countless slaves and a member of the Council that sent their army to invade the Realm."

"She killed his son," Ell-Nestra responded, his voice dull with grim understanding. "She wanted him to know before he died."

"Our queen is fair, but her justice can be harsh."

"She is *your* queen, my lady. My allegiance will end when this war is finally done."

He strode off to find the ship's captain whilst she briefed Lords Antesh and Arentes on the plan. "We are to be the vanguard of the army," the guard commander said, stroking his moustache. "A singular honour."

"And a singular risk," Antesh pointed out, ever keen to advise caution in dealing with their monarch. During the march to Warnsclave Vaelin had related the full story of his previous association with her Lord of Archers, leaving her well aware of his once-fierce antipathy towards the entire notion of a Unified Realm. Although his fanaticism had clearly dissipated over the years he still retained a lingering suspicion of all things Asraelin, Queen Lyrna chief among them.

"We are a thousand miles from home facing a vile enemy," Reva pointed out. "Every soul in this army shares the risk, my lord. Please relate the plan to your captains, we land in five days." She was about to add the queen's instruction regarding prisoners but found the words stalled in her breast. Her people needed little such instruction and were like to slaughter any Volarian in arms, but voicing an order condoning their bloodlust still felt wrong, reminding her once again that the Father had never related a single word on the subject of vengeance.

◆ ◆ ◆

Gulls appeared in the sky the next day and the first vague glimpses of land a day later. They sailed at a ten-mile remove from the rest of the fleet, thirty ships carrying the assembled soldiery of Cumbrael and the elite of the Realm Guard. The queen had also seen fit to provide four of Alornis's wondrous new ballistae along with a Nilsaelin woman of slight build who seemed to have an expert knowledge of their workings.

"Lady Alornis said to give you her warm regards, m'lady," she said to Reva with an awkward bow. "Wanted to come herself but Queen Lyrna threatened to tie her to the mainmast."

Reva let her choose the most able hands to crew the ballistae from among the Scarred Daughters, a fierce but appropriate title given to the company formed from those Cumbraelin women keen to volunteer for service with Blessed Lady Reva. They numbered little over two hundred and, like her male conscripts, at least half were below the age of twenty, grim-faced girls for the most part with various awful tales of mistreatment and orphanhood at Volarian hands. Arentes had initially kept them apart from the men, intending that they act as porters or cooks, but a stern look from Reva told him that would not be acceptable. She had taken to training them herself, though their evident awe and unquestioning belief in her continued lie made it something of a trial.

"If I may, Blessed Lady," one of them said the day before the landing, a lissome girl of no more than eighteen, sinking to one knee on the deck before Reva.

"I told you, Lehra," Reva said, "stop doing that."

"My apologies, Blessed Lady." The girl stared up at her with a face that would have been the epitome of youthful innocence but for the scar that ran from her ruined left eye to her upper lip, punishment for a minor infraction during her enslavement. "But we were wondering." Lehra paused to glance at the rest of the Daughters, clustered nearby with heads bowed. "What verse should we recite in the morning? To be sure the Father blesses our endeavour."

The Father has no blessing for war. You think he looks down on this business and smiles? Reva bit down on the words. The lie had carried thousands across the ocean and could hardly be abandoned now. "You must all choose your own verse," she said, pulling Lehra to her feet, less gently than she intended for the girl shrank back in a contrite bow. "'No multitude can think with one mind, for the Father made us all to be different, each and every soul another facet of his love. Find the path to the Father's love with your own eyes and let no other force you from your true course.'" The Book of Reason, she rarely quoted another these days.

"Will we be at your side, my lady?" one of the other girls asked, her eagerness reflected in the faces of the others.

Reva's gaze was drawn to the sight of the Shield leaning on the foremast and regarding the scene with evident amusement. "I would have you nowhere else," she told them. "Now return to your practice."

She moved to the water barrel next to the mast, meeting Ell-Nestra's gaze as she took a drink. "Something to say, my lord?"

"You had a god-gifted vision," he said with a shrug. "I did too, once. Didn't like it much. Made my head hurt."

"Your gods are figments of dreams woven into a tapestry of legend."

"Whilst yours lives in the sky, grants wishes and, when you die, lets you live in a field forever."

"For a man who has travelled so far, I find your ignorance quite astonishing."

His face darkened and he nodded at the Scarred Daughters, now going through the most recent sword scale she had taught them. "You know what awaits them when we land. How many will die believing this fiction of yours?"

Reva found she had no anger for him, the truth was inescapable and she had long accustomed herself to its sting. She watched the Daughters for a moment, finding months of practice had done much to improve their skills; they moved well, the strokes and parries performed with speed and precision. Also, they were fierce, many already fashioned into killers by the Volarians. But still, all so young. *As I used to be.*

"Did you have a choice?" she asked him. "When they came to take the Isles? How many of your pirates died at the Teeth or Alltor? And if this war is so hateful, and the queen so vile, why are you here?"

She had expected anger, but his response was subdued, all amusement gone from his face as he said, "I thought I had a stain to wash away. But it seems all I have done is befoul myself beyond any cleansing."

He looked up as a shout came from the crow's nest. "The bay is in sight," he said, offering her a bow and striding away. "Time to marshal your forces, my lady."

◆ ◆ ◆

They dropped anchor a mile offshore, the sailors hauling the boats over the side as Reva waited on deck with the Scarred Daughters. Lord Arentes and the full complement of House Guards were arranged at the rail as they would be the first ashore, their numbers swelled by a contingent of archers. Antesh waited on the neighbouring ship with the bulk of his men whilst the vessels carrying the Realm Guard bobbed on the waves a half mile west. Watching the activity with growing impatience, Reva reflected on the tendency of time to slow to a crawl during events she wished would pass in a blur.

Seeking distraction, her gaze wandered the ship, finding the Shield at the bows, taking an eyeglass from the ship's captain as he pointed to something on shore.

"The enemy?" she asked, moving to his side.

"A small number only," he replied, training the glass on the beach. "Perhaps thirty cavalry. Nothing you can't handle, I'm sure . . ." He frowned, a bemused smile coming to his lips. "One of them just fell over."

"My lord Shield!" They both raised their gaze to the crow's nest where a sailor could be seen waving frantically to the north. "Storm front!"

She followed the Shield to the stern, drawing up in surprise at the bank of cloud now shrouding the horizon. It was dark to the point of blackness, shimmering with lightning and casting a faint rumble across the sea as it swelled, coming closer with every heartbeat.

"Impossible," Ell-Nestra breathed.

"What do we do?" Reva asked but he stood staring at the fast-approaching storm with blank-eyed amazement.

"My lord!" She took hold of his chain-mail shirt and shook him, hard. "What do we do?"

He gaped at her, blinking as reason returned to his eyes. "Haul anchor!" he shouted, tearing free of her. "Raise every sail! Helm, set your course due south! Captain, signal the other ships to follow! My lady, take your people below."

The crew scrambled to obey as Reva barked orders, sending the Cumbraelins to the lower decks. She lingered however, staying at the stern and watching the storm sweep ever closer. *How can it move so fast?* she wondered, a suspicion building in her mind as she recalled another unexpected storm, at Alltor when the rain fell in sheets by day and snow by night. *The party on the shore . . . What have we sailed into?*

Thanks to the crew's frantic efforts, the great ship soon heaved into a southward course, sails filling the moment they were unfurled as the northerly wind built into a gale. The other ships had followed the Shield's signal, though those crewed by Realm-born sailors were notably slower in responding than the Meldeneans. Reva watched the vessel carrying one of the Realm Guard regiments wallowing in the rising swell as they drew away, only half her sails raised and pitching at an alarming angle as her helmsman tried to steer a southerly course. Soon the rain grew too thick to make out more than a vague shape though Reva was certain she had heard a great moan rise from the huge vessel before it was lost from sight. In minutes the storm came to claim them too, Reva finding herself enveloped in blackness as the world became a howling fury.

The gale was strong enough to pitch her from her feet, the rigging above resounding with the sound of snapping rope and wood, sailors tumbling to the deck or snatched by the wind to be cast into the sea. Reva found herself sliding across the deck, now awash with water. She was carried past the entrance to the hold, close enough to hear the frightened cries of the Scarred Daughters rising from below as water cascaded down the steps. She managed to grab onto the rail before the pitching deck sent her over the side, both arms wrapped tight about the balustrade as wind and rain tore at her. A dark shape tumbled past, a hand scraping over her mail shirt for a brief instant, a sudden despairing wail soon swallowed by the storm.

The deck suddenly descended, the angle of its pitch reversing, swinging her around so that she lay on the deck, gasping in the sudden lull. "My lady!" It was Arentes, running towards her across the deck, arms outstretched. She was reaching for him when the crash came.

The impact jarred her grip from the rail, the pitch of the deck too steep to allow any purchase as she and Arentes were carried towards the starboard side. She saw the guard commander hit the rail, shattering the wood with a bone-snapping crunch, and leaving a gap through which she descended into the roiling sea.

The storm's fury disappeared in an instant, replaced by the silence of the world beneath the waves. She could see only varying swirls of grey as she descended, borne down by the weight of mail and weapons. She let go of her bow, knowing this time Master Arren's wonder would be lost forever, then unclasped her sword belt, letting the blade fall away. She tore at the straps to her mail shirt, writhing in the cloying chill, bubbles spouting from her mouth in a torrent.

No! She forced calm into her thoughts as the straps resisted every desperate tug. *Panic will kill you.*

She formed herself into as still and straight a pose as possible, facing towards the surface to slow her descent, then drew her dagger and cut each of the straps in turn. The mail shirt came loose in an instant and she felt herself rise, but too slowly judging by the now-agonised burn in her chest. She kicked for the surface, forcing every ounce of strength into her lungs and sternly refusing the compulsion to draw breath.

She broke into the air with a shout, dragging in rain-clogged air and coughing, carried high and low by tall waves. There was no sign of Arentes, or anyone else. Then a sudden cacophony, loud enough to reach her through the storm, a great cracking sound, like a thousand trees splintered at one blow. The swirl of the storm shifted for a moment, lessening the darkness to afford a view of the *Marshal Smolen*, the great vessel's hull shuddering as it scraped along some unseen barrier, her sails torn from her rigging and what seemed to be dark droplets cascading from her sides, droplets Reva soon realised were people, her people, casting themselves into the sea as the ship was torn apart beneath them.

The storm shifted again, taking the spectacle with it, but Reva continued to stare, as the cold rose to numb her limbs and she shuddered, knowing death was coming soon and she had no desire to fight it.

I killed them all, she thought as the waves covered her head. *With a lie.*

CHAPTER THREE

Frentis

T he villa was the largest they had yet encountered, more a fortress than a home, its walls thick and tall, the gardens extending for several acres all around. It had clearly been home to a master of considerable wealth, enough in fact to maintain a garrison of two hundred Varitai. Despite the strength of the villa's defences, however, the master had felt little compunction in abandoning it at the first sign of their approach. His Varitai were easily counted, lying in four neat rows in the inner courtyard, each bearing an identical ear-to-ear cut across the throat.

"All valuables gone," Draker reported, "along with the horses. Found most of the slaves inside. Unlike this lot, looks like some put up a fight. Didn't save them though."

"Two hundred of their own men," Illian said, shaking her head in bafflement. "I can make no sense of it."

"They know what we're about now." Frentis nodded at a silent cluster of their own freed Varitai nearby. "Didn't want us to have them." He caught Master Rensial's eye. "From the state of the bodies they can't be more than a day's ride north. See to it, please Master."

Rensial nodded and moved to his horse, his mounted company following as he galloped through the villa's gate. Frentis briefly pondered going with them, given the master's erratic nature, but resisted the impulse. Recent days had seen a change in Rensial, his gaze not quite so blank, even occasionally given to unbidden speech requiring less deciphering than usual. *Only in war does the madman become sane.*

Not all the villa's slaves had been slain before their master's flight, some having been at work in the fields when the slaughter began. Many were seen fleeing in all directions, though a sizeable minority made their way to the villa, cautious and bemused by the welcome they received, some collapsing in grief at the sight of their murdered fellows, mostly men weeping over fallen women. Marriage was forbidden between slaves but everywhere they went there was evidence that people were capable of forging their own bonds regardless of whatever barriers or threats constrained their lives. It was to these bereaved souls that Frentis gave the villa's owner when Rensial returned the following day, dragging the unfortunate black-clad along behind his horse, hands bound and mouth firmly gagged.

"He had a wife and children," Rensial reported as the slaves closed in around their former master, knives and whips raised. "I let them go."

"Of course, Master." *They always beg.* Frentis watched the black-clad collapse to his knees, bound hands raised in appeal. He was a tall man, impressively built with the look of a soldier, attested to by the various military souvenirs found in the villa. *An officer of renown? The villa, the family, the slaves. All fruits of an illustrious career. A hero's reward.* He was far from heroic now, just a terrified, piss-stained man begging for his life. *They always beg.*

He turned away as the torment began, going to where Illian was engaged in training the latest batch of recruits. There were fewer Realm folk now but their numbers had begun to swell since the victory over the Eskethian garrison, the Free Swords they had allowed to flee carrying word of the calamity with impressive speed. Within days a hundred more runaways had arrived in the mountains, the army's numbers swelling to over four thousand in the space of a month. Feeding so many had forced Frentis to order a move to the north-west, into the rich farmlands that stretched towards New Kethia, this villa being the first to fall.

He watched the training for a short time, taking satisfaction from the accustomed ease with which Illian marshalled the recruits, displaying all the authority of a master on the Order House practice ground. She had them learning the staff, the basis for eventual use of the pole-axe or the spear, but also a sign that they still lacked sufficient weapons. He had set the former blacksmith to work in the villa's forge with orders to remake the copious stocks of farming tools into as many axe blades as possible. It meant they would have to linger here for a time, weeks probably, and he chafed at the delay. Keen to maintain the impetus of their rebellion, he had sent Lekran and Ivelda in opposite directions with two hundred fighters each and orders to free as many slaves as possible.

Frentis turned as Thirty-Four approached. The former slave had taken to wearing kit stripped from the bodies of Free Sword officers and gave an impression of impeccable military neatness, every inch of armour scrupulously cleaned and all buckles polished to a gleaming shine.

"He's ready then?" Frentis asked him.

"Healed and fully able to ride, brother. Still refusing to talk though."

"Unusual. They normally can't shut up when they realise what you are."

"Who I am," Thirty-Four corrected, an uncharacteristic hardness in his voice. "What I used to be."

"Yes." Frentis offered an apologetic smile. "Let's set him on his way, shall we?"

The Volarian had refused to offer a name but they had gleaned it from the correspondence found among his battalion's baggage train. "Honoured Citizen Varek," Frentis greeted him brightly, crouching at his side in the shade of the acacia tree to which he had been shackled. "Feeling better I trust?"

Varek remained slumped against the tree-trunk, his face betraying no emotion beyond the simmering rage that had dominated his demeanour upon waking to find himself chained and his battalion destroyed.

"I have good news," Frentis went on, gesturing for Thirty-Four to unlock the chain. "Freedom awaits."

Varek's expression became guarded, Frentis noting how he suppressed the faint glimmer of hope that rose in his eyes. "No trick, I assure you." Frentis took hold of the chain and gave an insistent tug, the Volarian slowly getting to his feet, wary eyes constantly moving in expectation of an attack. Frentis led him through the courtyard, knowing he would take full notice of the many former slaves at training. Draker waited at the villa's arched entrance with a horse, saddled and laden with provisions for several days' ride.

"This was your horse, wasn't it?" Frentis asked, removing the shackles from Varek's wrists.

The Volarian was marginally less wary now, rubbing at his reddened flesh as his gaze tracked from Frentis to the horse. "I will not betray my people," he stated, the first words he had spoken since waking. "Whatever the reward."

"This could hardly be called a reward," Frentis said. "I imagine you know the kind of welcome you'll receive in New Kethia, the defeated, disgraced son to an honoured father. The shame of it will be unbearable, but before you kill yourself please inform your tormentors that what happened to you will soon happen to them. Before the year is out their city will fall and every soul they keep in bondage will be free. But my queen is rich in compassion and willing to offer terms."

The Volarian sighed, shaking his head. "You are mad."

"The city gates to be opened and the walls cleared of defenders. All Free Swords to lay down their arms and all slaves, including Varitai and Kuritai, to be freed. The city will become the property of Queen Lyrna Al Nieren, who will decree a fair redistribution of lands and riches in due course." He stepped closer to Varek, speaking softly, feeling his rage building anew. "Failure to agree to these most generous terms will result in the utter destruction of your city and the execution of every Volarian found in arms."

Varek jerked his head towards the host of recruits. "You truly believe this rabble capable of taking New Kethia? You think the Ruling Council will sit idly by whilst you march? You will be crushed before you even catch sight of the city and every one of these dogs still alive will be flayed and left to rot in the sun, if they are lucky."

Frentis merely smiled. "News travels slowly, it seems." He leaned closer still. "There is no Ruling Council now. You are ruled by an empress and, trust my word on this, she will look on and laugh when I raze your city to the ground."

"Whatever awaits me, I'll bear it," Varek said in a tone of complete certainty. "I'll suffer every torment for a thousand years just for the slightest chance of getting this close to you again."

"Then you had best invest in some sword lessons first." Frentis turned to Draker. "Escort the honoured citizen until nightfall. If he takes one backward glance, kill him."

◆ ◆ ◆

Her new body is stronger than the one she left on the beach, leaping and whirling with all the speed and precision she could ask for, and yet . . .

"Feel it, don't you?" the Messenger asks, lounging in a chair on the balcony. He wears the body of an Arisai, one of the few with Gifted blood, tall and lean. Behind him stand six more, also Gifted, and, although their faces are different, their expressions are identical. She has never met so much of him before and finds it trying, one was always more than sufficient.

She lowers the short sword and straightens from the fighting crouch, naked and sheened in sweat from the practice. If the Messenger finds the sight arousing, there is no sign of it on any of his faces. She is discomforted by the sight of the darkened sky that frames them, realising it was noon when she returned to the Council Tower. Since awakening in this new shell her ability to keep track of time has diminished yet further.

"Feel what?" she asks.

"The numbness. Cold isn't so cold, heat isn't so hot. Gets worse with every one you take. These days I can barely feel a thing." He angles his head, studying her, a small predatory smile on his lips. "Can you hear it this time? You can, can't you?"

She suppresses a flash of anger, resenting his effortless intuition. The shell's owner had been older than the first, and not born to slavery, leaving a deep pool of memory that flares into aggravating clarity all too often: . . . playing with her brother on the shore of some mountain lake . . . laughing when her father showed her his tricks . . .

She initially thought the woman's gift so small it couldn't be discerned but has come to understand that memory was her gift. Every thought, action and word residing in her head, unchanging and always so bright.

"You said to prepare eight," she says, pushing the images away. "Yet I only count seven."

She takes some satisfaction from the sight of them clenching jaws in unison, knowing the Messenger was suppressing his own anger. "Al Sorna has a facility for acquiring useful friends," he says after a short pause.

She sees it then. Although the shells are all youthful and athletic his evident wounding still marks them, colours their eyes with pain, weariness . . . and fear. "You're certain you know where to find him?" she asks.

"He seeks the endless man. I need only journey north and I'll find his trail. You'll have to make me a general, and some sort of grandiose title seems appropriate. Overlord of the North, or something."

"The Northern Armies are commanded by the General Governor of Latethia. I'll give you an execution order. When he's dead call yourself what you like."

"You don't seem to like these governors much, I must say. Does this leave any alive?"

"Only the Governor of Eskethia. I was going to execute him too but I'm becoming more inclined to leave him to his fate."

The faces shift again, all vestige of humour fading and she knows his next words are not his. "You cannot afford indulgence now. This distraction of yours had its uses, but now obstructs our purpose. He requires that you see to the matter without delay."

"The Council is dead and the bitch's fleet wrecked. All at my hand. I have earned indulgence."

"The previous three centuries have been your indulgence. Decades of murder and malice, his gift to you. And now he requires payment."

Her hand flexes on the sword, the true depth of the antipathy she has always felt for this creature becoming apparent for the first time. She sees them tense, the seated speaker rising. *"He knows what you planned," he says. "Your cherished scheme, the dream of ruling with that boy at your side, eternal and terrible with the whole world as your playground. Did you really think it would work?"*

"If he has no more use for me," she says, smiling, "kill me. If you can."

As one their hands reach for the swords at their side. She knows the odds are hopeless, she knows she is choosing death. Watch me, my love, *she thinks, knowing he sees her.* Watch me make you proud.

But the Messenger stops, all seven releasing their swords and filing towards the door in silence. The speaker lingers a moment, his face now that of a weary soldier called to inescapable duty. *"He will always find more use for us. You can keep the boy, if you take him alive. But the matter must be settled."*

Alone once more she closes her eyes, seeking his presence, embracing the steely resolve she finds, joy threatening to burst her new heart. She sees something, a swirl of mist in the darkness, coalescing into a form she knows so well. His words mean nothing, beloved, *she says, reaching out to caress his face.* The world can still be ours.

◆ ◆ ◆

He snatched the hand from his face, snarling in fury, his knife coming up to press into her throat. "Never!" he hissed into her face, pressing the blade deeper.

Lemera whimpered, eyes wide with horror, her face quivering with terror, her head drawn back by the fist that grasped her hair, the smooth flesh of her throat exposed and vulnerable.

The air rushed from his lungs as he dropped the knife, twisting away from her to slump on the edge of the bed, his head in his hands. "What . . . what is it?" he said when the shaking had faded from his limbs.

Her reply was barely more than a whisper. "I heard shouting . . . You were dreaming . . ."

He glanced over his shoulder, taking note of the thin cotton shift that barely covered her, and the depth of fear lingering in her gaze. He turned away, blinking as his eyes adjusted to the dark. He had taken over the master's bedchamber, a spacious display of wealth and luxury, the walls liberally adorned with various paintings, most depicting battles of implausible orderliness. The master himself featured in several, a more youthful version standing tall and proud, sword in hand as he commanded his men with stern-eyed courage, a singular contrast to the bloodied, begging ruin that had been left to expire in the courtyard when the slaves tired of him.

"I . . . have nightmares sometimes," he told Lemera. "I'm sorry if I hurt you."

"I've been hurt worse." He felt her weight shift on the bed then a hesitant touch to his back, her fingers spreading to explore the flesh. "You have fought so much, and yet no scars."

"I had scars, they healed."

"Weaver?"

"No." *The seed will grow.* "No, it was something else. Something I doubt I'll ever understand." He turned again, her hand shifting to rest on his shoulder until he gently removed it. "You should go."

She drew back a little but made no effort to leave. Her face was shadowed but he had a sense she was smiling. "The sister said you were forbidden the touch of a woman. I thought she must be joking."

"The Faith requires all we have."

She shifted again, drawing her legs up to rest her chin on her knees, her head angled as she studied him, now more curious than amused. "And you are so willing to give it?"

"The Order is all I've ever wanted."

"So the world beyond your Order offers no enticements?"

"I've seen the world, with all its enticements. I find myself content with the Order."

"After training yesterday, Draker punched a man for telling a story. A strange tale of how you were taken to the palace, along with a woman possessed of vile magics. And together you killed your king. Was he lying?"

"No. He wasn't lying and Draker shouldn't have done that."

"Yet your queen let you live and sent you here."

"My actions were not my own. The woman's magics bound me, compelled me to do terrible things."

She straightened and he felt her eyes roaming his face. Although he couldn't see her expression the intensity of her scrutiny was unnerving. He was about to tell her to leave again when she said, "So we are not so different, you and I."

She uncoiled, lying down on the bed. "May I sleep here? Just tonight. I have dreams too." She breathed a soft laugh at his evident hesitation. "I promise I'll offer no . . . enticements."

I should make her go, he knew. *There can be no good outcome to this.* But he didn't, finding the cruelty beyond him. So he lay next to her, trying to force the tenseness from his limbs, knowing sleep would be a stranger tonight. After a few moments she shuffled closer, resting her head against his shoulder, her hand finding his, their fingers entwining.

"There will be no victory for us, will there?" she asked in a whisper.

"Don't say that. My queen sails to these shores with a great army. If we hold to our cause . . ."

"I was a slave, but never a fool. This empire is vast beyond imagining and we have killed but a fraction of the force they will bring against us. They will kill us, all of us, for we are slaves and we cannot be allowed even the barest hope of freedom. Without us, they have no empire."

The matter must be settled. "If you believe our cause so hopeless, why join us?"

She came closer still, wrapping her free arm around his, clasping his hand tighter, her breath warm on his skin. "Because you offered something I had forgotten could be offered, a choice. And I choose to die free."

◆ ◆ ◆

Their numbers doubled over the next few weeks as Ivelda and Lekran continued to bring in recruits by the dozen and ever more runaways arrived at the villa. Soon there were so many that feeding them all became a problem, Frentis finding himself compelled to order some into the fields to harvest more crops. A few were resentful of the order though he managed to ameliorate any discontent by promising that all would take a turn at the same chore, himself included. Conahl, the Realm-born blacksmith, had performed prodigious feats in producing large numbers of weapons but still it wasn't enough; only a third of the army could be described as adequately armed and at least as many were still equipped with various farm implements.

"Plenty of weapons in New Kethia," Lekran pointed out at the evening council.

"We still lack the strength to take it," Frentis replied. Thirty-Four was well acquainted with New Kethia and had ample intelligence on the strength of its walls. Plus they had to assume the Empress had sent them some reinforcement by now, or perhaps even come herself. He resisted the urge to allow himself to dream again, resuming the nightly dose of Brother Kehlan's sleeping draught, despite the headaches. The campaign was moving towards its crucial phase and he was unwilling to risk any chance she might divine his plans when their minds touched. He was also aware she would be raging at the sudden absence of contact, and perhaps even prone to misjudgement as a consequence.

"If we wait much longer, this region will be denuded of slaves," Thirty-Four said. "Those that haven't joined us will have been killed or marched off by their owners. If we were to go south, I've little doubt this army could be made mighty within a few months."

"We do not have a few months," Frentis said. "The queen's fleet will already have sailed and marching south will not provide the diversion she needs."

"Over half of our people are not from the Realm and know nothing of the queen. They came because we promised freedom, not to exchange one master for another."

"If we can secure the queen's victory, then every slave in this empire will be free. Her cause is their cause. Make sure they know that."

He returned his gaze to the map. *We have to strike somewhere.* "What is this place?" he asked, pointing to a town on the northern coast, about fifty miles east of New Kethia.

"Viratesk," Thirty-Four said. "A minor port serving the trade routes north."

"Defences?"

"A wall, of sorts. It's a poor place, home to only a few black-clads with scant funds to waste on a wall that hasn't been needed for centuries." Thirty-Four paused, lips pursed in consideration. "They do have a lively slave market as I recall. The market in New Kethia is often full to overflowing so many slavers look to alternatives to shift their stock."

A town so close to the provincial capital put to the torch and they'll be forced to come out from behind their walls. Frentis straightened from the map. "We wait one more week to gather numbers and train, then we march to Viratesk."

◆　◆　◆

He had Thirty-Four draw a map of the town and sent Master Rensial to scout the approaches, cautioning him against being seen. The remaining days were spent training the recruits, making an effort to exchange a few words with as many as possible, gratified that most seemed to be enlivened by the prospect of action. However, he didn't have to look too deeply to see the fear that lingered in many, mostly those born into bondage or veterans of prolonged enslavement; they had risked all to join this rebellion and had no illusions as to the consequences should they fail.

"I nearly ran once before," Tekrav told Frentis one morning as they went over the inventory of supplies. The former bookkeeper had proved himself enthusiastic but unskilled in training, but his facility for numbers remained as sharp as ever. "Not long after my creditors' petition saw me chained. Myself and another newly enslaved hatched a plan during the caravan ride to the master's villa. My co-conspirator was a great, strong fellow, but over-fond of drink and poppy essence as I was overfond of dice. Our intention was for him to strangle the guard when he came close to our cage and take his keys."

"Did it work?"

"He managed to get a hand around the guard's throat all right, but then one of the slave-hounds bit it off at the wrist. They had little use for him after that, except as an example. It took them all day to impart the lesson, by which time he was begging for death. After that I found myself all too grateful for a slave's lot."

"Then why did you join us?"

Tekrav gave a small shrug. "Even now I'm not entirely sure. The master was good to me, only two floggings in all the years I served him. But he was not so kind to the others, and as One, they looked to me for protection. I had subtle ways of diverting his temper, business matters or a new wine vintage to distract him from whatever torment his mean little mind could conceive. But when the war started and the new slaves came . . ." Tekrav trailed off and forced a smile. "Well, he had so many new toys to play with. And I couldn't protect them all."

"Lemera and the others. You joined us because they did."

"A man should stay with his family, don't you think?"

"Yes, he should." Frentis gave his inventory a final glance before handing it back. "This is all well in order. My thanks for your diligence. I would be grateful if you would oversee the baggage-train during the march."

"I will, brother. I was wondering, perhaps I could have a title."

Frentis paused, raising an eyebrow. "I assume you have something in mind."

"Nothing too extravagant. But perhaps . . . Lord Quartermaster?"

"Chief Quartermaster. Any ennoblements will be for Queen Lyrna to decide."

"Of course. I trust you'll assure her of my worth in due course?"

Free for a few months and already he plots his rise. He'll probably end his days as Minister of Works, should he live so long. "It will be my pleasure, sir."

♦ ♦ ♦

Master Rensial returned the next day to report the way to Viratesk clear of Volarian patrols. In fact, he had failed to glimpse another soul during the entire mission.

"Not like them to be incautious," Lekran observed. "Usually a day on the road won't pass without seeing at least one troop of cavalry."

"The empire is always keen to police its people," Thirty-Four agreed.

"So we scared them off," Ivelda said. "Just like my people did to the Othra when they came to take the bronze hills."

"We did take them," Lekran replied with a surprisingly polite grin. "But found them worthless so gave them back."

She laughed, shaking her head. "Your father told you many lies, sister-fucker."

"I made Redbrother a promise, so I'll wait till this is over before I claim your head."

"I look forward to being amused by your attempt . . ."

"Shut up!" Frentis stated, very precisely. He stared at them both in turn until they lowered their gaze. "All of you, prepare your companies to march at dawn."

They left the villa intact this time. Some of the older slaves had petitioned him to be allowed to stay, hoping to make the place their own. Frentis saw little point in attempting to compel their participation, especially since Illian advised they would be little use in a battle. He scouted ahead with Master Rensial's troop, confirming the country as empty for miles around. The fields grew increasingly unkempt as they marched north, devoid of slaves, save a few corpses they took to be runaways from the villas they passed, all also uniformly free of occupation and some already burned by their owners.

"Told you," Ivelda taunted Lekran with a laugh. "Pissed themselves and ran off. When we get to the town they'll do the same."

Viratesk came into sight after a five-day march, a square mile of brick buildings nestled in the bowl of a natural harbour. Frentis's spyglass revealed the walls as poorly maintained, featuring several gaps and the surrounding ditch long since filled in. Also, he could find no sign of any guards on the walls or smoke rising from a single chimney.

"There's nothing here." He sighed, lowering the spyglass.

They found the town gates open and unguarded, the streets beyond vacant and littered with detritus that told of a hasty flight. "Some of them might have had the decency to stay and fight," Lekran grumbled. "Just for a little while."

"Take your company and sweep right, make for the harbour," Frentis told him. "Draker, go left. Myself and Master Rensial will take the centre."

It took only a short time to reach the harbour, passing by rows of vacant houses, the town's only living occupants a few dogs busily feasting on the carcasses of slaughtered horses and goats left to rot in the streets. They found the wharf free of vessels save a single scuttled fishing boat, its mast jutting from the water at what Frentis felt to be an insulting angle.

"No bugger home, brother," Draker reported, expression grim as he strode along the wharf. "Did find a pile of bodies in a warehouse though. All slaves, mostly older folk."

"Culled the less valuable stock before they left." Frentis cast a glance around the town, fighting a sense that the empty windows were all staring back in accusation. *They would have lived if you had not come here.* "Search every building," he said. "Gather anything of value, especially weapons. We need anything with a sharp edge, even the smallest butcher's knife. Lekran, your people will man the walls. You'll be relieved at nightfall."

◆ ◆ ◆

He had their Chief Quartermaster oversee the disposal of the bodies, though he made a point of helping to carry them to the carts. There were about fifty in all, men and women of middling years, stripped naked as their clothes were deemed of greater value than their lives, old whip-strokes visible on most of the rapidly greying flesh. They were carted outside the walls where Tekrav had organised the construction of a huge pyre from the furniture left behind by the fleeing townsfolk. Once the bodies had all been laid upon the oil-soaked wood Frentis turned to address the gathered fighters.

"Amongst my people," he said, "it is customary, regardless of belief, to say words over the dead. Many, if not most of these people lived knowing only a slave's life, destined for a slave's death. To be cast away like a lamed horse, unmarked, unnoticed, unworthy of thought or word. But now we are here to mark their passing, with words and with steel. Hard days lie ahead of us, days when our cause will seem hopeless and your heart tempted by despair. When those days come I ask that you remember what you saw here today, for if we fail, this will be our fate and no voice will be raised to bear witness that we were ever alive."

He went to the walls to watch the pyre burn, the flames rising high in the gathering dark. "Quite the signal fire, Redbrother," Lekran observed.

"They knew we were coming," he replied. "And they know we're here now. With any luck, they'll send their forces against us."

"And if they don't?"

"Then we'll see what they'll make of a march towards New Kethia itself. The time for stealth has gone, it's time we brought our enemies to battle."

◆ ◆ ◆

She has always found it odd that the spectacles never held any attraction for her. If anything, she finds them repugnant, thousands of voices aroused to bloodlust by the sight of combat that few, if any, would have the stomach to experience firsthand. For her, the joy of the fight, and the kill, has only ever come from direct participation.

But they do love this so, beloved, *she tells him, feeling his disapproval.* We took away their gods, but kept the rituals, for the gods were always so fond of blood.

It is the Festival of Winter's End, though once it had been named for a long-forgotten god who demanded the sacrifice of brave souls to bless the fields and bring forth a good harvest. The arena had originally been built in honour of the old gods but all divine trappings were long since stripped away, marble statues replaced with bronze effigies of generals and Council-men, divine motifs substituted for the Imperial crest. But, however much the stage changed, the spectacles remained the same.

Revealing herself to the multitudes is a necessary chore; she couldn't remain hidden forever, and today there are many eyes to see the Empress Elverah in all her glory. She chose the name herself. Of the many titles she has earned over the centuries, only this one gives her any satisfaction, and not a little amusement. Let them bow before a witch.

There has been trouble, of course. The sudden switch from Council rule was bound to disrupt a society wedded to the notion of stability achieved through unchanging order. Her spies, a long-established network crafted over decades, unknown to the Council's own intelligence machinery, bring word of discontent and rebellious conspiracy from all corners of the empire. Most are quickly crushed, the plotters subjected to a protracted method of public execution, immediate and secondary family condemned to slavery and all property seized by the Empress. But, though several thousand have now suffered this fate, each day brings reports of more plots and, were she susceptible to such things, the constant threat of assassination would provoke a lesser soul to paranoia. The previous week a slave girl had contrived to poison the Empress's breakfast of gruel, revenge for a well-loved master subjected to the Three Deaths the week before. It was a brave but clumsy attempt, easily discerned even without the song's warning. The poison had been mixed in too great a concentration, giving off a familiar odour, and the girl must have known she was earning herself a painful end.

"Were you One in his stable?" she had asked the girl, forced to her knees with an Arisai's blade poised to strike the nape of her neck. "He must have fucked you very sweetly to arouse such loyalty."

The girl wept, hard convulsive sobs, but still found enough voice to answer. "He . . . never . . . touched me."

"Then why?"

"He . . . raised me . . . taught me to read . . . gave me a name."

"Really? What is it?"

"L-Lieza."

"Naming a slave is a capital offence in itself, and your former owner was guilty of much more besides." She waved the Arisai away and gestured for the girl to remove the breakfast. "Bring me fresh gruel, Lieza. Then you can read me the morning's correspondence."

Lieza stands at her side now, ready to pour wine into the Imperial cup. She is pale of face but manages not to tremble. Every morning since her failed assassination she brings breakfast and reads the Imperial correspondence whilst the Empress eats. Afterwards she sits and writes as the Empress dictates a list of names for execution. Her calligraphy is quite excellent.

I don't know why I spared her, she replies, feeling bafflement mixing amongst his disgust. I think she reminds me of someone, but can't quite recall who. Perhaps I'll kill her tomorrow. Give her to the spectacles, the dagger-teeth are always hungry.

But today there are no dagger-teeth. Today it is the Sword Races. She recalls her father once telling her the origins of this, the most popular event in any spectacle. In primitive times one of the more enlightened gods, or one of his more enlightened priests, decreed that there should be no more warfare between the tribes that paid him homage. Instead, every year they would send their best warriors to compete in the Sword Races where all disputes would be settled. The rules have been refined over the succeeding centuries but the essence of the contest remains the same: a single sword is thrust into the centre of the arena and the two contesting teams stand at opposite ends, an equal distance away. At a given signal they race for the sword, combat beginning when one team member takes hold of the hilt, the winner being the team with the most men standing at the turn of a ten-minute glass. Logic would suppose that the team to claim the sword would enjoy an advantage, but expert players *are still capable of turning the tide, usually by sacrificing a less-skilled team member in order to seize the sword from their opponents.*

Today it is the Greens and the Blues, two of the six teams representing the six provinces of the empire. The Blues tend to attract the most favourable odds but the Greens have the most experienced players, evidenced by their tactic of forming a tight defensive bunch around their sword-bearer, forcing the Blues to mount a series of costly assaults. Within minutes ten men, four Blues and six Greens, lie dead or crippled on the sands. Sword Racers rarely have long careers though the substantial rewards afforded those who survive to retirement ensure there is never a lack of willing recruits, for these are not slaves but free men. Poor and desperate enough to risk death in front of a baying mob, but still free.

You wonder at finding me here? *she asks him, bored with the contest.* Why am I not in New Kethia raising an army? *She notices how Lieza flinches and realises she has spoken aloud. Judging by the rigidity of the slave girl's posture this is not the first time she has heard her Empress address a question to thin air.*

His answer is faint, though more controlled than before; he has grown accustomed to taking command of his dreams. There is still time. I will wait for you.

Touching, beloved, but unnecessary. That bitch you bow to was clever, sending you in advance of her mighty fleet. Not so mighty now, I'm afraid. Just driftwood and corpses.

His thoughts shift, from uncertainty to denial, though she knows he senses the truth in her thoughts.

How do you find Viratesk? *she continues, taking satisfaction from the resultant surge of alarm.* Your scouts were careful but we saw them. The townspeople didn't want to leave so I let them stay. You did think to check the sewers didn't you?

◆ ◆ ◆

He came awake with a shout, his hand reaching for the sword propped against the bed, finding nothing. His eyes scanned the darkness, seeing only shadows. He felt Lemera's weight in the bed next to him, her visits a nightly ritual now, though they never did more than lie together. He nudged her gently, ready to clamp a hand over her mouth as she woke, pausing at the familiar chill to her skin. Her eyes were half-open, the lips drawn back from bared teeth in an agonised grimace. A single, neat cut stretched the width of her throat.

"You are a disappointment."

Frentis tumbled free of the bed as a figure stepped from the shadows, a young man with the build common to the Kuritai, though he wore red armour and a mocking grin. Behind him two more resolved out of the darkness, one holding his sword. The grinning man's hands blurred and something looped around Frentis's neck, drawing tight to steal his breath before dragging him to the floor. Something fast and hard slammed into his stomach, doubling him over, the coil around his neck tightening ever further as his vision dimmed, the grinning man's words following him into the blackness. "She promised us a challenge in you."

CHAPTER FOUR

Lyrna

"The Thief's Snare," Lyrna said, surprised at the reflective calm she heard in her voice.

"Highness?" Murel looked at her from where she was attempting to keep the shutter on the porthole in place despite the gale hammering at it like an unseen monster seeking entry.

"A rare feature of the long game," Lyrna said. "Any piece taken by the Thief can be used by the opposing player. The snare involves sacrificing both pieces only a few moves later, giving the illusion of weakness in the centre of the board. A stratagem to be employed by only the most skilled players." *And I am an arrogant fool,* she added silently.

It had begun a full two hours ago, descending in a shrieking black tide as she stood watching Lady Reva's thirty ships approach the dim shoreline. Within minutes the world beyond the Queen Lyrna had disappeared and Iltis was dragging her towards the cabin as sailors frantically sought to secure the rigging. She caught sight of Brother Verin, standing in frozen panic on the bustling deck and gestured for Benten to pull him along.

"This storm is not natural," she said, turning to the brother as Iltis slammed the door on the fury outside. "Is it?"

"Highness, I . . ." The young brother shook his head, bafflement and shock dominating his features. "Some are known to have the power to turn the wind, but this . . ." He blanched at her obvious consternation, stammering as he forced himself to continue. "There was . . . something, as the ships neared the shore."

"What something?"

"It was faint but I felt it. A . . . burning you might say. It's commonly felt when another Gifted dies, as if all their power has blossomed at once."

She moved away from him, sitting on her bunk, lost in the enormity of her blunder. *I killed Arklev too soon. Though I doubt he knew his true role.* She gave herself over to contemplation as the ship pitched and groaned around her, there being little else to do. *The Thief's Snare leads to victory in no more than ten additional moves provided the player exploits the opportunity with a swift attack on the opposing Emperor.*

"Lerhnah?"

She looked up to find Davoka standing over her, features softened in concern. Beyond her Murel stood back from the porthole, now open to reveal a sunlit sky. From the height of the sun she judged she had been sitting in silent meditation for some hours. "I need to speak to the captain."

The day-to-day command of the *Queen Lyrna* had been given over to a Nilsaelin named Devish Larhten, a lanky veteran of the trade routes to the Northern Reaches who had also commanded a warship in her father's fleet during the Alpiran war. She found him at the mainmast overseeing repairs to a patch of deck shattered by a falling block. Fortunately it seemed to be the only major damage they had suffered.

"Highness," he greeted her, glancing up as she strode towards him, clearly preoccupied with his task.

"Captain, turn this ship south and make ready for battle." She cast her gaze at the surrounding ocean, finding only four other ships within view and the shoreline no longer in sight. *Scattered and ripe for harvest,* she thought, suppressing a wave of self-reproach. *Indulge your guilt later.* "And signal those ships to close with us."

"All in good time, Highness. We have much to . . ."

"Do it now!" she snapped. "The Volarian fleet is currently north of us and I have little doubt we'll see them within the hour."

Larhten's gaze flicked momentarily to Iltis, who had taken a purposeful step forward. "At once, Highness," he said before moving away and voicing a torrent of orders.

"Find Lady Alornis," Lyrna told Murel. "She is to ensure her engines are in working order. Lord Benten, please tell Lord Marshal Nortah to ready his regiment for battle."

◆ ◆ ◆

Captain Larhten advised that they tack to the west for a time, bargaining they would find more Realm vessels farther from the coast. By midafternoon they had gathered another forty ships, a few missing masts and rigging but all able to make headway. Predictably, the Meldenean ships displayed the least damage and she was heartened to find the *Red Falcon* among them, Ship Lord Ell-Nurin waving from her bow as she came alongside. Only she and the *Queen Lyrna* had so far been equipped with Alornis's fire-spewing engine, upon which she now rested a great deal of expectation.

"We could head back to shore, Highness," the captain suggested as Lyrna stood at the rail, her eyes fixed on the northern horizon. "Pick up a few more strays on the way."

She surveyed her fleet, finding two of the great troop-ships present as well as a good number of Meldeneans. "No," she said. "Drop anchor and pile one of the boats with all the rags and wood you can spare, douse it with pitch to make sure it smokes, and set it ablaze. Signal the other ships to do the same."

This time he knew better than to linger and the boat was swiftly set adrift, casting a tall, twisting pillar of black smoke into the sky, soon joined by dozens more as the other ships followed suit. "Quite the beacon, Highness," Larhten complimented her with a bow.

"Thank you." She returned her gaze to the north. *Though it's like to draw as many enemies as friends.*

The Volarians appeared as the sun began to fade, at least a hundred masts cresting the northern horizon with more appearing by the second. Lyrna's beacon had gathered over thirty more strays as they waited at anchor but she knew any further delay would prove fatal.

"Raise all sails, Captain," she told Larhten. "And signal the *Red Falcon* to remain at our starboard side. The other ships are to follow us."

Larhten gave a sombre nod, eyeing the Volarian fleet with well-justified but controlled trepidation. "The course, Highness?"

She gave a laugh as she moved away, making for the bow, "Towards the enemy, good sir. With all possible haste."

She found Alornis busily checking her engine, her hands moving with a speed and deftness that seemed almost unnatural. "Any damage, my lady?"

"Had to drain water from the pipes. And the fittings require a slight realignment." Alornis hefted a mallet and began hammering at a copper tube on the engine's underside. "But she'll work, Highness."

"Good. Take yourself below. Lords Iltis and Benten will see to the engine."

Alornis didn't even glance up, continuing to hammer away as the Volarians drew ever nearer. Lyrna sighed and turned to Murel. "There's another mail shirt in my cabin. Please fetch it for Lady Alornis." She drew Davoka aside, speaking softly in Lonak, "No harm is to come to her, sister. Promise me."

"My place is by you."

"Not today." She gripped the Lonak woman's arm. "She is your sister today. Promise me."

"You fear her brother's wrath so?"

Lyrna lowered her gaze. "You know it's not his wrath I fear."

Davoka gave a reluctant nod, taking the mail shirt from Murel and striding towards Alornis. "Put this on, little one."

Lyrna joined Lord Nortah arranging a fighting party on the deck, fifty of his best fighters equipped with broad wooden panels for shielding against arrows. "My lord, I should like to address your troops."

He bowed and issued a curt order, the company snapping to attention with a uniform stamp of boots. She scanned their faces, gratified by their lack of fear and the devotion that continued to colour every gaze. "I said once I wouldn't lie to you," she told them. "And I won't. We face a hard fight because I have made a grievous error. But I also tell you no lie when I say that this battle can be won, if you will stand with me."

The instant shout of acclaim was enough to convince her further words were unnecessary. "Spare no enemy," she told Nortah. "Every Volarian that sets foot on this deck must be killed before he can take another step."

Unlike his soldiers, Lord Nortah's agreement was softly spoken, his expression the same cautious frown he always wore in her presence. "I'll see to it, Highness."

She returned to the bow, taking a position on the raised platform just behind Alornis and the engine. Benten and Iltis were close on both sides of her whilst Murel stood behind, dagger in hand. Davoka crouched at the side of the engine, spear held low in readiness.

"I should fetch some shielding, Highness," Iltis said. "Their arrows were many at the Teeth if you recall."

"I recall very well, my lord. But that won't be necessary."

Lyrna watched the Volarian ships come ever closer, the leading vessel closing to a range of about five hundred yards. She glanced towards starboard, taking satisfaction from the sight of the *Red Falcon* alongside, a man standing ready at their own engine. She could only hope he had been properly taught how to use it. A glance towards the stern confirmed the other ships in their small fleet were following in an orderly narrow line, every deck crowded with soldiers and pirates.

The port-side ballista began to clatter as the Volarian ships closed, casting its bolts at the rigging of a small but swift warship tacking into their path. At first the arcing fountain of projectiles seemed to have no effect but they were soon rewarded by the sight of a figure tumbling from the warship's mast to land heavily on the deck, raising an instant cheer from the ballista crew. Soon, however, the Volarian archers were able to bring their own weapons into play, a shower of arrows thumping into the *Queen Lyrna* from end to end. Lyrna watched a shaft smack into the planking an arm's length away but managed to control an instinctive flinch. *Fear is a luxury today. They need to see a queen.*

The port ballista continued to clatter, the crewman winding the mechanism whooping with excitement at the effect on the Volarian vessel, his first bolt striking with sufficient force to pin a man to the deck. A dozen or more close-packed Free Swords fell as the archers in the *Queen Lyrna's* rigging soon joined in, wreaking havoc on the warship as it veered away, littered with corpses.

A whooshing roar dragged Lyrna's attention back to the bow where she was greeted with the sight of Alornis raising the engine to its full elevation, a stream of fire arcing towards the oncoming Volarian ship. It was one of their troop-ships, only slightly smaller than the *Queen Lyrna*, the archers in her rigging assailing them with a cloud of arrows as they closed at ramming speed. At first Alornis's fire-stream fell into the sea, raising enough steam to momentarily obscure the oncoming ship. However, when it cleared, they were rewarded with the sight of a blaze covering her bow from sea to rail. The Volarian ship seemed to shudder, her course altering abruptly like a wounded boar shying from a spear-point.

Alornis turned a fierce glower on the two soldiers working the bellows. "Pump harder! I need more pressure!"

She realigned the engine as the Volarian vessel wallowed in their path, unleashing another torrent of flame that licked along her side before ascending to sweep the deck, igniting men and rigging alike without distinction. Flaming bodies began to leap from the ship, a chorus of screams reaching them through the thickening smoke along with the stench of burning flesh. Alornis faltered then, her hand falling from the spigot, the flames dying, a pale stillness seizing her features.

Lyrna moved quickly to her side, placing a hand on her shoulder and turning her. "A burden not to be shirked, my lady," she said, taking her hand and placing it firmly back on the spigot. "To your duty, if you would."

An arrow came arcing down to smack into the engine, its steel head shattering on the iron fittings as it spun away. Alornis barely seemed to notice, her pale face still frozen as she nodded and returned to her task, altering the angle of the engine to cast flame at the Volarian's sails. Lyrna could see men running around the ship, buckets in hand as they fought flames that wouldn't die. Soon her rigging was ablaze and her crew began to abandon ship with a frenzied alacrity, men trailing flames as they tumbled into the sea by the dozen.

Lyrna cast about for another victim, spying a fast-moving warship some two hundred paces off the port bow. "Tell the captain to make for that one," she said to Murel before turning back to Alornis. "My lady, I believe your engine requires more fuel."

◆ ◆ ◆

By evening they had burned their way through the centre of the Volarian line, dividing their fleet in two and sowing chaos and panic in every sailor and Free Sword to witness the spectacle of a dozen warships blazing in the gathering dark. But the battle didn't end. Although their cohesion had been lost, the Volarians fought on, ships mounting lone, often suicidal attacks, soon left burning in their wake or stormed by the Meldeneans. Only one came close enough to mount an assault on the *Queen Lyrna*. Her helmsman displayed considerable skill by swinging her around just beyond the range of Alornis's device, then hauling the tiller to slam into the *Queen Lyrna*'s starboard side, her complement of Varitai heaving ladders into place and storming across despite appalling losses inflicted by the ballista and the archers above.

Lord Nortah's company met them head-on before they had seized more than a few feet of the deck, attacking with a disciplined ferocity that did great credit to their months of training. The Lord Marshal himself hacked his way through the Varitai's ranks, breaking their formation apart, fighting with an unconscious skill and precision Lyrna hadn't seen since her days with Brother Sollis. His war-cat fought at his side, reaping death with every swipe of its claws. With the Varitai all hacked down or forced over the side, Nortah rallied his soldiers into a tight wedge and led them onto the Volarian ship, overcoming the remaining crew as they mounted a desperate stand around the mainmast. A few had evidently attempted to surrender judging by the number of unarmed men Lyrna saw cast into the sea.

"Highness!" A sailor came running from the helm, pointing to port. "Captain Larhten begs to report more ships to the west."

Lyrna peered into the gathering dusk, making out the faint lines of tall masts. *The dark brings scant relief, it seems.* She looked to the east where the *Red Falcon* could be seen, fire spouting from her prow to engulf a Volarian troop-ship. Beyond her more Meldenean vessels were assaulting the remaining enemy line, the sky alight with a continual cascade of flaming balls as the mangonels did their deadly work.

"Tell the captain to turn west," she told the sailor. "And signal the Realm vessels to follow us. Our allies have this matter in hand."

Unfortunately, it was clear an unseen hand still exercised some form of command over the Volarian fleet, and felt no desire to allow her to confront the latest threat. A squadron of ten vessels separated from the central cluster of ships to plough towards them at full sail. The wind was in their favour and they managed to place themselves directly in the *Queen Lyrna*'s path, heaving about to face them, arrows and ballista bolts filling the air between them as they closed. Lyrna clasped her hands together and stood still as the air buzzed about her, a bolt flicking through her hair just below the ear. Iltis moved his bulky frame in front of her, holding his arm in front of his face as if shielding himself from a rain shower, grunting as an arrow grazed his forearm.

Lyrna turned a questioning gaze to Alornis as she finished refuelling the engine. "The last of the oil, Highness," she reported, her voice as devoid of expression as her face.

"Don't spare it, my lady," Lyrna advised. "A blazing ship makes a bigger impression than a scorched one."

The first Volarian ship to come into range was of considerably smaller draught than the *Queen Lyrna* and Alornis was obliged to depress the spout of her engine as she swept by, liberally dousing her in flame from bow to stern, heralding the now-familiar chorus of screams. Alornis managed another fulsome blast at the next ship, a considerably larger troop-ship well supplied with ballistae and archers. The stream of fire managed to sweep many from the rigging but not before they had killed a dozen or more Realm Guard and the crew manning the port ballista.

Lyrna turned to see the last dregs of fire dripping from the engine's spout, Alornis meeting her gaze and giving an apologetic bow. Lyrna pointed her towards the now-silent ballista.

Despite the flames still licking at its ropes and sails the Volarian troop-ship maintained its course, a full Free Sword battalion assembled on deck. Lyrna was about to order Nortah to bring up the rest of his regiment but saw that the Lord Marshal had anticipated the need, the soldiers running to form ranks with remarkable precision despite the confusion all around.

The port ballista clattered into life once more, Alornis aiming whilst Davoka worked the handle. Lyrna followed the flight of one bolt as it streaked across the gap to claim the life of a Volarian Free Sword officer who had unwisely chosen to stand tall at the rail, no doubt as an example to his men. She hoped they learned the lesson well.

"Highness!" It was Larhten, calling from the helm and pointing to something beyond the Volarian ship. Lyrna blinked away the smoke-born sting in her eyes and sought to discern something through the haze. The King Malcius, she saw as the view cleared. *Fitting that my brother should come to save me.*

The *King Malcius* came on at full sail, her archers casting a shower of fire arrows at the Volarian troop-ship before she ploughed into her starboard hull with a splintering crunch. The fires now littering the sea painted the subsequent spectacle with flickering shadows, the sight of a host of steel-clad men rushing from the *King Malcius* to assail the Free Swords seeming unreal somehow, like something from a dream, or a nightmare.

Lyrna's gaze was soon drawn to the sight of a burly man throwing himself into the densest knot of Volarians, his mace rising and falling with deadly effect. At his side was a taller and more slender figure wielding a longsword. She watched as together they hacked their way the length of the ship, their knights following in a thrashing mass of steel, driving the Free Swords back with such murderous zeal most chose the scarce safety of the sea rather than stay to fight on. By the time the *Queen Lyrna* had drawn up alongside the troop-ship the two figures were standing at her port rail, removing their helms to greet her with a bow.

"Good evening, my lords," she called to Fief Lord Arendil and his grandfather.

"Forgive me, Highness," Banders called back, his broad features slick with sweat. "But are we to land soon? One more week at sea and my knights are like to hang me."

Lyrna turned to survey the scene, the sky now black and the only illumination coming from the many blazing ships. The tumult of combat had faded though she could still hear men screaming somewhere, voices calling for help in Volarian mingled with the odd gurgling sound that accompanied a sinking ship.

"Indeed, my lord," she called to Banders. "A landing is overdue."

◆ ◆ ◆

The ship sat on the beach like some great wounded beast, her masts sheared away and much of her sides stripped of timber, exposing the complex web of beams that somehow contrived to hold her together. It was Benten who recognised her as the *Fief Lord Sentes*; his sea-trained eyes had a knack for discerning the slight differences that distinguished one ship from another. "Seems she's been driven too far up the beach to be taken off by the tide," he said. "It's a marvel she's still in one piece."

The short voyage to the bay had yielded only five ships from the thirty that had sailed with Lady Reva, all severely damaged and barely afloat, though their precious cargo of troops and supplies were mostly intact. The *Sentes* brought the total to six, but she could hardly be described as seaworthy. In all just over two-thirds of the Queen's Fleet had survived the storm, though casualties had been heavy and the battle with the Volarians had claimed at least another thousand lives. Although Lyrna saw the flush of victory of many faces, she knew the battle had in fact been indecisive, Ship Lord Ell-Nurin estimating they had captured or sunk no more than half the Volarian fleet.

"Whoever commanded them was wise enough to withdraw under cover of night," he surmised. "One of our scout ships reported seeing sails on the southern horizon."

She took the first boat to the shore, overriding all objections with a silent glare. The time for caution had died in the storm. For all the acclaim shouted at her from the surrounding ships as the boat wended its way towards the beach, she knew their morale would still plummet like a stone when the reality of their situation became apparent. *They need to see a queen.*

She was accompanied by Lord Marshal Nortah and a full company of Queen's Daggers. Off to the north Brother Sollis led another cluster of boats filled with all that remained of the Sixth Order whilst Count Marven took his best Nilsaelins to secure the southern approaches. They were obliged to row their way through several corpses en route, Lyrna surprised to find most were Volarian, bobbing in the swell with arrows protruding from their armour.

The tide was low and the beach free of breakers as they scraped to a halt, Lyrna leaping free of the boat before Iltis could raise an objection. She heard him smother a curse as he splashed into the waist-deep water behind. She laboured through the surf towards the hulk, eyes scanning the part-ruined hull and finding numerous faces staring down at her, though there were no voices raised in awed acclaim now, most just seemed pale with exhaustion. She noticed a dark cluster of more Volarian bodies on the beach, perhaps two hundred men and horses liberally seeded with arrows.

"Thought we were easy meat," a voice called down from the *Sentes*, Lyrna's gaze finding a stocky man standing in one of the rents in the ship's hull, holding a longbow and looking down at her with a stern regard that contrasted with the usual cautious respect shown to her by Cumbraelin soldiery. "Proved them wrong."

Lyrna stared up at him, holding his gaze until he added, "Highness," in a clipped voice.

"Lord Antesh," she said. "Where is Lady Reva?"

He sagged at her words, head lowered and eyes tight closed. "I take it, Highness, you have no news of her either?"

Lyrna turned to watch the first wave of troops coming ashore, the Queen's Daggers spreading out to sweep the dunes whilst a Realm Guard regiment grounded their boats, more following in a seemingly unending tide. "Lord Antesh," she turned back to him, finding a man now visibly shrinking in grief. "Lord Antesh!"

He straightened at her shout, a spasm of anger flashing across his face before he forced himself to a neutral expression. "Highness."

"I hereby name you Lord Commander of the Queen's Cumbraelin Host. Please remove your soldiers from this ship and proceed inland. There will be a council of captains this evening where I shall require a full accounting of your numbers."

She moved on without waiting for an acknowledgment. *They followed the Blessed Lady,* she knew. *I can leave no doubt that they must now follow me.*

◆　◆　◆

The woman must have been quite beautiful in life, possessed of a dancer's litheness and features of porcelain delicacy. But, as Lyrna had witnessed many times now, death always seemed to rob the body of beauty, bleaching the skin and leaving the features a slack echo of the soul that had once made those rose-bud lips smile. Brother Sollis had discovered more bodies in the dunes a short distance away, slaves judging by their clothing, each with their throat cut. The once-beautiful woman, however, showed no sign of any injury despite the dried blood that discoloured the flesh around her eyes and nose.

Brother Lucin was the oldest member of the Seventh Order she had met so far, stick thin and almost totally bald save for a tuft of white hair that sprouted from the top of his head like a forgotten weed. He wandered around the woman's body for a time, frowning in concentration, occasionally muttering to himself. During her fruitless search for evidence Lyrna had interviewed a number of people arrested on suspicion of Dark practices, finding them all charlatans or victims of malicious accusation. One, a charming but terrified young man, had been all too happy to explain how he would gull rich widows into parting with coin or jewels by claiming to commune with long-dead relatives, providing a demonstration not entirely dissimilar to that now performed by Brother Lucin. In recognition of his honesty, Lyrna had persuaded her father to commute the charlatan's sentence to ten years in the Realm Guard.

"How long will this take?" she asked Aspect Caenis, failing to keep the dubious note from her voice.

"All places have history, Highness," he replied. "Brother Lucin is obliged to sort through a haze of images to find the right event."

"Ack!" the elderly brother exclaimed, his face drawn in a grimace of equal parts disgust and fear.

"Brother?" Caenis said, stepping closer.

Brother Lucin waved him away with an irritated flap of his bony arms. "I felt it," he said, casting an accusatory glare at Lyrna, as if she had led him into some kind of trap. "The thing inside her. Are you trying to kill me?"

"Watch your mouth, brother," Iltis growled, his face dark with warning.

Brother Lucin barely glanced at him. "The past is real," he said to Lyrna. "Not some mishmash of shadows. It has power."

"My apologies if I have placed you in danger, brother," Lyrna replied, realising an insistence of propriety would avail her little with this one. "But our current circumstance requires that we all take risks." She nodded at the corpse. "Was that her?"

The brother looked down at the dead woman with palpable reluctance, edging away as if in expectation she might suddenly spring to life. "There were soldiers with her. They called her Empress. She had a mighty gift, I could feel it, rushing out of her all at once to bend the wind to her will."

"Then she's dead," Count Marven said. "She gave up her life to destroy us. The enemy are leaderless now."

Brother Lucin gave the Battle Lord a withering glance. "This was just a shell, chosen for its gift. You can bet she'll already have woken in another."

"Why kill the slaves?" Marven asked.

"Witnesses," Lyrna replied, looking again at the dead woman's face. *Where did she find you? Did you ever have a name of your own?* "Few if any Volarians will know the true nature of their new Empress. Have the bodies taken to the pyres, I doubt they have anything more to tell us."

◆　◆　◆

"Pretence will avail us nothing now," she told the surviving captains of her army and fleet, gathered together on the high ground beyond the beach where the troops still laboured ashore, the sands dotted with blazing pyres for the dead. "We have suffered a grievous blow. Lady Reva is missing and most likely dead as is Fleet Lord Ell-Nestra. A full fifth of our army has been lost due to my misjudgement. Accordingly, I am bound to ask if there are any here no longer willing to follow my commands."

She scanned their faces, finding most patently baffled by the question. The Meldeneans regarded her with the same surety that had marked their attitude since the Teeth where, she knew, many believed their gods had invested her with some form of divine insight. Far from undermining their faith the events of the previous evening seemed to have cemented it; who but the gods could have snatched victory from such assured defeat?

Similarly, Fief Lord Arendil and Baron Banders exhibited no sign of distrust as did Wisdom, who had come to speak for the small Eorhil and Seordah contingent. The only clear expressions of unease came from Lord Marshal Nortah, which was typical, and Lord Antesh, still evidently in the grip of his grief. But, like the others, he remained silent.

"Very well," she said, nodding to Count Marven. "Battle Lord, our tactical position, if you would."

"We have a secure perimeter extending one mile inland, Highness. Brother Sollis has the Order scouting farther afield, so far there are no reports of significant enemy forces nearby although we have encountered a few cavalry patrols. We'll gain a clearer picture when the remaining horses are brought ashore."

"Those that are left," Baron Banders put in. "A third of our mounts sickened and died on the ships. Horses don't take well to life at sea."

"This region is rich in farmland," Lyrna said. "No doubt we'll find replacements soon enough. Until then I'm afraid any unhorsed knight will have to fight on foot, my lord."

"That'll give 'em something else to gripe about," Banders muttered, soft enough for Lyrna to safely ignore.

"The Volarian fleet?" she asked Ship Lord Ell-Nurin.

"Still no sign, Highness. But I doubt they've gone far. Probably licking their wounds and awaiting reinforcements."

"Then let's not allow them the leisure to do so. I hereby name you Fleet Lord Ell-Nurin. The freighters and troop-ships will sail back to the Realm with all dispatch to gather supplies and reinforcements. You will take every warship we have and harry the enemy without respite."

"I shall, Highness. It would assist our efforts if Lady Alornis were to accompany us. We require more fuel for her engines and my fellows can't quite get the mix right."

"The Lady Artificer is indisposed. Make do as best you can." She paused, making a point of meeting the gaze of everyone present, ensuring they saw no uncertainty in her eyes. "The army must be fully mustered by tomorrow. When it is, we march for Volar. Their Empress will no doubt be revelling in her imagined victory. I intend to disabuse her of this notion in short order."

◆ ◆ ◆

"Reva's dead, isn't she?"

Alornis wouldn't meet her gaze, sitting listlessly on the bunk in Brother Kehlan's tent. If the moans and occasional cries from the wounded troubled her, she gave no sign, her expression as unmoved as it had been during the battle.

"Her ship was wrecked in the storm," Lyrna told her. "We found some survivors, but none have any word of her. I know you were close to the Lady Governess, and I too grieve for her loss. Her spirit, and her sword, will be greatly missed."

"I always wanted to ask her about the siege, what she did. But I couldn't, I saw how it pained her. I used to wonder how a soul so kind could do what they say she did at Alltor, for that was not the Reva I knew. Now . . ." She looked down at her hands, the thin, dexterous fingers moving like pale spiders. "Now I doubt she would know me."

Lyrna reached out to smooth a wayward lock of hair from Alornis's forehead, finding herself perturbed by the chill of her skin. "My lady, there are thousands of people now alive because of you."

"And thousands dead."

Brother Kehlan came to Alornis's side, holding out a cup of something hot and sweet-smelling. "A sleeping draught, my lady."

"I don't want to sleep," she told him. "I might dream."

"There will be no dreams." He smiled, placing the cup in her hands. "I promise."

Lyrna joined the healer as he moved away. Despite many hours' ceaseless work he remained alert, seemingly indifferent to the foul stenches that clouded the tent, and the blood that stained his robe. "Can you help her?" she asked.

"I can help her sleep, Highness. I can give her various remedies to calm a troubled mind. It may return her to some kind of normalcy, for a time. But I have seen this before, the malady of the spirit that arises in those pushed beyond their limits. Once it takes hold, it never really fades. I advise she be returned to the Realm as soon as possible."

"No!" Alornis had risen from her bunk, advancing towards them, formerly placid features now rigid with determined refusal. "No. I am staying here." Her words were a little slurred and she stumbled, Lyrna rushing forward to catch her.

"We have more fires to light together, Highness," she whispered to Lyrna as the queen laid her on the bunk, watching as she slid into slumber, still murmuring, "so many beautiful fires."

CHAPTER FIVE

Vaelin

The Wolf People unveiled their canoes when the solid plane of white surrounding the island thinned then fragmented under the weight of the new sun. Within days all that remained were a few stubborn ice-blocks drifting in the fast-flowing current separating the isles. Like the boats fashioned by the Bear People at the Mirror Sound, the canoes of the Wolf People were all constructed from hollowed-out tree-trunks, varying widely in size. Most were capable of carrying no more than four people at once, others were of sufficient size to accommodate up to ten, but there were three of such dimensions it seemed incredible they could float at all.

"Hewn from the great red trees that grow to the south," Astorek explained as one of the huge craft was manhandled towards a slipway in preparation for launching. "Trees that grow tall as mountains over the life-span of twenty men. Only once in a generation do the Wolf People permit themselves to take a red tree. It's a cause for great celebration when a new big boat is made."

The purpose of the huge craft soon became clear as Astorek led his wolves on board along with the other packs. There was a definite tension in each of the shaman as they stood amidst their wolves, faces set in concentration. The wolves all sat in placid obedience, though every once in a while one would turn towards a different pack, a low growl building in its throat before snapping back to instant placidity at an insistent gesture from its shaman. *Without the shaman's command they become wolves again,* Vaelin realised, once again wondering at the fortitude of the Gifted found among these people. *They use their gifts for hours yet never tire.*

"It's not strength," Kiral said, appearing at his side with her cat in tow. In accordance with Lonak custom she hadn't named the beast, though the other

Gifted had predictably dubbed it One Ear. It was the least well behaved of the cats, prone to voicing a nightly chorus of forlorn wails and a hissing disinclination towards any human company save Kiral's. It greeted Vaelin now with a brief snarl and kept close to Kiral's side with a low-backed wariness.

"It's skill," the huntress went on, nodding at Astorek. "Born of centuries-old necessity. Our gifts are useful, but we can still survive without them. These people *need* their power or the ice will kill them. So they learned to control it, share it, use only as much as they need." She smiled faintly, eyes still lingering on the Volarian. "We must seem like clumsy children to them."

Vaelin and the Gifted were given places on one of the huge boats, whilst Orven's guardsmen and the Sentar were obliged to crowd into the smaller craft, some newly constructed to accommodate the increased number taking part in this yearly migration. Scar trembled a little as he was led onto the canoe, pacified only slightly by a handful of berries. The warhorse had grown partly accustomed to the presence of the wolves but the proximity of so many in a confined space was clearly trying his patience.

"Calm now, old fellow," Vaelin said, trying to soothe him with a scratch to the nose. Today, however, Scar was in little mood for reassurance, eyes wide and fixed on the silent mass of wolves as he tossed his head, teeth bared in alarm.

"Let me try," Dahrena said, moving closer to press a hand to the warhorse's neck. She closed her eyes, a small line appearing in her forehead as she concentrated. Scar calmed almost immediately, his head lowering, eyes blinking in placid contentment.

"I showed him the stables back home," Dahrena said. "He thinks he's there now."

"Your skills grow, my lady," Vaelin said, inclining his head.

"A little." She turned to the nearest shaman, a lean-faced veteran standing with five wolves arranged in an unmoving circle. "Though I doubt any of us will ever match them. Some skills require a lifetime's teaching."

◆ ◆ ◆

All hands save the shaman were expected to take a turn at rowing, two hours or more spent ploughing at the water with a broad-headed oar. As ever, the constant exertion gave Lorkan much to complain about, though Vaelin noted he displayed little actual strain when rowing. He seemed to be taller now, his back straighter and shoulders broader. For all his grumbling, Vaelin knew the boy he had met in the Reaches had been lost somewhere in the tide of war and the privations of the ice. Though, from his constant glances at Cara, it seemed one thing hadn't faded during the journey.

The surrounding islands grew larger and taller the farther south they went, great mounds of snow-topped granite and thick forest from which more canoes would emerge as they neared. There was little celebration in the greetings exchanged between the Wolf People, some waves or nods of respect between shaman, a few calls from old friends, but for the most part they formed their ever-growing convoy with quiet efficiency. Vaelin also found it strange none seemed particularly surprised or perturbed by the presence of so many outsiders, most just eyeing his motley company with grim acceptance.

"They knew we would be travelling with you," he said to Astorek during his twice-daily rowing shift. The shaman spoke little on the water, his face set in a mask of constant concentration as he worked to keep his wolves in check.

"Hawks can do more than kill," he replied, jerking his head at the sky where a great swirling flock of spear-hawks kept track of the convoy. At night they would descend to the forest of perches that sprouted from the canoes, gobbling down the slivers of meat provided by their shaman, most of whom seemed to be women.

"They carry messages?" Vaelin asked. "But your people have no writing."

"No, we have no books." Astorek pulled something from a pocket in his furs and tossed it to Vaelin; a length of elk bone, etched from end to end in straight cuts along a single line. "Each mark represents a sound," Astorek explained. "Put them together and you have a word."

"What does it say?"

"'Long Knife is shaman of thirty wolves.' Many Wings carved it when I reached manhood and sent copies to all the settlements. It's the only time I've seen any of my people indulge in boasting."

Vaelin glanced around at the other packs on the canoe, noting how small they were in comparison, none numbering more than a dozen. "It must be a trial to command so many."

"Command is not really the right word. They . . . accept me."

Vaelin looked closer at Astorek's pack, seeing how their gaze was uniformly fixed on him, enthralled and barely blinking. "They can hear it," he realised. "The echo of the wolf's call. It's still in you."

Astorek's expression flickered in momentary discomfort, one of the wolves turning towards Vaelin with a snarl burgeoning on its lips. It calmed as Astorek reached down to play a hand along its head, gazing up at him in wide-mouthed adoration. "They can hear it in you, also, Raven's Shadow. Some things never fade from a man's soul."

◆ ◆ ◆

They rowed south for three days, gathering ever more Wolf People on the way. By the time the broad coast of the mainland came into view Vaelin estimated their total number at well over a hundred thousand. More were waiting on the shoreline where settlements could be seen amidst the trees, the dwellings larger and covering more ground than those on Wolf Home.

"Why not live here all the time?" Cara asked Astorek as they neared the shore. "It seems a more comfortable place."

"The elk roam south in the winter," he replied. "Too far for us to follow, leaving a frozen wilderness in their wake. But in the isles walrus and whales appear when the ice forms."

The evening saw a celebratory feast where the last of the winter stocks were consumed. The Wolf People clustered around several huge fires to roast their meat on skewers and share horns of pine ale, clicking away in their indecipherable tongue as they exchanged tales of winter hardship. Despite the generally convivial air Vaelin knew this to be a muted affair, noting the many faces regarding him with tense expectation. As they had no word for lie these people also had no word for secret. They had been making pilgrimage to the painted cave for centuries and knew his face, and his name.

He sat with Dahrena away from the main throng, building a smaller fire so they could share a supper of walrus stew. He did the cooking, slicing the meat into strips and seasoning it with herbs and the last of the salt he had carried from the Realm. "I knew brothers who would rather abandon their sword than their salt," he told her, with only slight exaggeration. Life in the Order made most brothers skilled in the art of campfire cookery, and appreciative of the precious comfort offered by a small amount of seasoning.

"Do you ever miss it?" she asked, accepting a bowl of stew. "You were raised to a life in the Order. It must have been hard to leave it behind."

"I had already lost my brothers by the war's end, along with much else. There was nothing to return to." He settled beside her and they ate in silence for a time. As ever the sensation of shared understanding banished his worries with comforting ease. When he was with her it was almost as if his song had returned, her moods being so easily read. He could see it now, the faint tension in her face as she ate, the way her eyes strayed constantly to his face.

"You worry for the future," he said.

"The world is in chaos," she replied. "Worry seems appropriate."

"Were I still a man of the Faith, I might quote a pertinent catechism about the virtues of hope."

"You believe the queen's invasion will succeed?"

"I believe in her. She is . . . more than she was."

"And if we do succeed, what then?"

"We return to the Reaches, where I suspect we'll spend much of our time protecting them from gold-hungry idiots."

"That is your ambition? Just the tower and the Reaches?"

"The tower, the Reaches"—he reached out to take her hand—"and you. Also, the peace to enjoy them."

She smiled, but he saw it was forced. "Father wanted peace too, and hoped to find it in the Reaches."

"Caenis told me he had been exiled for questioning the King's Word. I always assumed it was because he had refused to do what my father did in the Meldenean Isles."

"A climax to a long argument. Father began his career as a guardsman in the Al Nieren House Guard, when the Asraelin noble families feuded endlessly over the Lord's Chair. He told me once Janus had promised him peace, in the days when the Red Hand had finally faded. They were both little more than boys then, facing an onslaught of a dozen houses allied against them, the Al Nieren line having been weakened by the plague and seemingly ripe for plucking. 'We'll kill all these fools together, Vanos,' Janus had said. 'Then we'll make a Realm.'

"And they did, year after year of war, the other houses shattered and brought low, the fiefs hammered into submission, all on the promise of peace. A peace that failed to appear with the birth of the Realm as Janus turned his gaze to foreign lands. So, unable to face another war, Father begged for release, imagining he might find an untroubled retirement in the Reaches, far away from the Realm's troubles and Janus's ambition. But war still found him when the Ice Horde came."

Vaelin squeezed her hand tighter. "With this war won there will be no one left to fight."

"I see the queen, as you do. I met her once before, all those years ago when Father took me to the Realm. And you are right, she is greatly changed. But I still see in her what Father did, that day as she took us on a tour of the palace gardens, all laughter and charm. Father smiled at her witticisms, accepted her flattery, and made a gracious farewell. As we rode away his smile faded, however, and I heard him say, 'And I imagined Janus to be ambitious.' It may have changed but it hasn't gone, Vaelin. When she's done with this war, what then? What will sate her when she's conquered an empire? What more will she ask of you?"

You'll kill for your faith, for your king, and for the Queen of Fire when she arises . . . Words from a long-remembered dream. *Perhaps not all prophecy is false.* "I think she is wise enough not to ask for what I won't give."

◆　◆　◆

Astorek came to fetch them to council in the morning, tracing a path into the forest until they arrived at a tree so large Vaelin at first wondered if it wasn't some shaman-conjured illusion. The trunk was covered in reddish brown bark and stood near thirty paces wide at the base, ascending to well over two hundred feet in height, the top lost somewhere above the forest canopy.

"The name loses much in your tongue," Astorek said. "Wolf Lance is the closest translation. The oldest great tree known to us. Even the grandfathers of our grandfathers couldn't remember it a sapling."

The base of the trunk featured a large, cave-like hollow where a number of Wolf People waited, standing in silent regard as Astorek led Vaelin inside. He made no introduction, simply standing to one side as they stared at his face, recognition and disquiet evident in every gaze. The silence stretched as he stood there, wondering if there was some ritual observance he had failed to make, until Wise Bear came to his side, speaking softly, "They want your words."

"Words?"

Wise Bear gave the assembled Wolf People a tight smile, resembling a parent apologising for an ill-mannered child. "Words of war. They expect you to lead them."

His gaze roamed the assembled council, finding Whale Killer among them, the others also marked as elders from their various accoutrements: necklaces of bone or beads, a knife with an ornately carved handle. Only those ice folk of sufficient age and influence had the time or opportunity to accumulate trinkets. "There are no shaman here," he observed to Astorek.

"Shaman are forbidden leadership," he said. "Too much power sickens the soul. A lesson the Cat People never learned."

Vaelin nodded. "How many warriors do they command?"

Astorek conversed briefly with the council, receiving clipped but swift responses. "We do not reckon numbers as you do," he reported. "But perhaps a quarter of every island's people are of age to fight."

Little over twenty thousand. Hardly the Queen's Host, but they do have their wolves and their hawks. "Have they seen any sign of the Volarians?"

"Scouts were sent south with the first thaw," Astorek related. "As they are every year. They will return when the Volarians cross from the hill country into the plains. They usually come when the sun rises higher, some two months from now."

Vaelin recalled No Eyes's words on the ice; *I am patient and I suspect you still have far to go.* "They will come sooner this year, and we cannot afford to wait. Your people must gather their warriors, and all their wolves and hawks, and come south with me."

The unease of the elders deepened visibly as Astorek translated, though no words were spoken as they exchanged wary glances. *Even after a lifetime's belief,* Vaelin surmised, *still hard to trust your fate to paint daubed on a wall centuries before.*

Finally, one of the elders spoke, a stooped old man leaning heavily on a staff, his voice thin and strained, but still capable of commanding deep respect from the way Astorek related his words with precise solemnity. "Far Walker, oldest and wisest of the Wolf People, asks what promise the Raven's Shadow can offer. Are the words of the Great Boat People made true?"

"I can offer no words regarding your beliefs," Vaelin replied. "And any man who leads others to war on a certain promise of victory is either a fool or a liar. I offer a chance to defeat your enemy and prevent their coming again. Nothing more."

The old man spoke again when Astorek finished his translation, moving closer to stare up at Vaelin, his ancient features alternating between confusion and wonder. "As a child I would ask the elders, 'When will the Raven's Shadow come?' Over and over I would ask them, for I knew he had not come in the time of my parents, or grandparents, or throughout the many Long Nights before then. 'Not as long as you live, little one,' they would tell me, and so I would sleep well, knowing your time would bring great torment and trial for the Wolf People, but I would be spared the sight of it."

He continued to stare at Vaelin for some time, finally speaking a short question in a soft rasp. "How will you defeat our enemy?"

"With your warriors, your shaman, your wolves and your hawks. With the steel of the soldiers I command, and the fierce skill of the allies who followed us here." He paused to glance at Dahrena and the Gifted who lingered at the edge of the hollow. "And the courage of bright and powerful souls."

Far Walker lowered his gaze and turned away, stalking back into the depths of the tree with a weary stride. He spoke again before the shadows swallowed him, the words causing an instant gasp of shock from the other Wolf People. Some called after him, urgent questions cast into the dark, but there was no answer.

"What did he say?" Vaelin asked Astorek, who stood gaping in the old man's wake.

"His will," the Volarian replied in a tone that discouraged further questioning. He turned his gaze to the other elders, asking a question to which they all responded with a series of nods, some more reluctant than others. "We will come with you," Astorek said.

◆　◆　◆

Dahrena sat amidst a circle of fires, eyes closed and face growing paler by the minute as Marken, Lorkan and Cara worked to keep the flames high. Vaelin remained at her side, keeping a seal fur wrapped tight around her slender form until she gave the shudder that signified a return. She sagged against him, groaning as he rubbed her shoulders. "You might think this would get easier with practice."

Cara handed Dahrena a cup of warmed pine ale, which made her cough a little but also restored a pinkness to her cheeks. "They've yet to reach the hills," she told Vaelin. "But they're coming, a great host led by seven generals. I could see them riding out ahead, their souls so dark it seemed as if they swallowed the light, and they were all the same. I've only seen one like it before. On the ice."

"No Eyes," Vaelin said and she nodded. *Seven souls, all the same,* he thought. *The Ally sends the Witch's Bastard with an army. How much does he fear what we seek?*

◆　◆　◆

The Wolf People insisted on a full week of hunting before setting out. Despite the thaw, life on the northern tundra remained precarious throughout the year and stores were needed for the people who would be left behind when the warriors started south. Astorek invited Vaelin and Kiral on his expedition, each shaman being required to lead a hunting party, though he forbade him from bringing Scar. "We hunt on foot, the elk will feel his hooves through the earth."

They trekked east for a day with twenty hunters, Astorek's wolves ranging ahead in a wide arc, pausing constantly to raise their snouts and sniff the air. The wolves would often spur into a run, disappearing over the horizon for an hour or more, but were always found waiting for them a short while later. Their direction changed frequently, veering north then south without warning.

"How far can they travel before you lose them?" Kiral asked the shaman, who seemed puzzled by the question.

"The bond goes deep, so deep distance means nothing. They could be on the other side of the world and I would still feel them."

He stopped, straightening as the wolves came to a halt, all crouched low, noses pointed to the south west. The Wolf People all dropped to the ground as one, Vaelin and Kiral sinking down at Astorek's side as he raised a hand to the air, turning it to gauge the wind. He gave a brief jerk of his head and the wolves immediately streaked off towards the south, moving in a tight bunch. "They will bring them to us."

The hunters crawled forward until they formed a line parallel to the shaman, lying prone with spears in hand. The grass that grew on the tundra was stunted, providing little cover but also a clear view of the horizon. Each hunter carried three spears, all with barbed iron heads, Vaelin noting the scratchlike script with which they had decorated the hafts. Every spear had its own story, it seemed.

"Ever hunt the great elk?" Kiral asked, notching an arrow to her bow.

Vaelin shook his head, readying his own bow. His arrows were all suited for war rather than hunting, narrow and pointed to pierce mail or armour, so Kiral passed him three of her own, barbed like the hunters' spear-heads but fashioned from the same unbreakable black glass used by the Seordah. "One won't suffice," she told him. "Ignore the flanks and aim for the neck."

He heard them before he saw them, a thunderous tremor reverberating through the ground accompanied by the faint yelping of wolves. When the leading elk came into view it seemed at first as if a tree had suddenly sprouted on the skyline, a broad-branching silhouette bobbing as it grew in size, a small forest springing up around it. He had seen the Eorhil sporting fragments of elk antler and gained an appreciation of their size from the Wolf People's cave painting, but the sight of a living beast was truly impressive. The first stag to appear had antlers fully ten feet across, the animal itself standing almost as high as two men, raising a thick cloud of dust as it sped towards them, head low, the tips of the antlers as long as sword blades.

When the elk were within thirty paces the hunters rose as one, their spears flying free in quick succession, the lead stag and two others tumbling to the ground in a mass of flailing hooves and shattered antlers. The rest of the herd veered away from the danger, streaking off to the north with the wolves in pursuit. One of the wounded stags managed to rise, snorting and swaying its part-broken antlers about, before charging directly at the nearest hunter. Kiral sent an arrow into its neck, Vaelin following with two more, but the animal barely slowed, antlers scraping the ground as it bore down on the hunter. However, it transpired he had little need of their help, sprinting forward at the last second to leap over the stag's head, revolving in the air to plant both hands on its neck and vault himself over it in a somersault that would have impressed any acrobat.

The stag snorted and wheeled about, trailing blood and bellowing in frustration before Kiral finished it with a carefully aimed shaft through its eye, a feat of archery Vaelin doubted even Reva could have matched. Vaelin moved to Astorek as the hunters fell to butchering their prey, long knives flashing as they gutted and dismembered the carcasses with automatic speed. He could see the wolves a hundred paces off, clustered around another carcass, their usual placidity vanished as they squabbled and snapped at each other, white fur besmirched with gore from snout to tail.

"Their reward," Astorek said. "Isn't good to bind them too tight. Sometimes they need to remember what they are."

In the distance a dust cloud told of the remaining elk continuing their flight. "You don't take them all," Vaelin observed.

"If we do, there'll be none to take next year."

"When we come to fight the Volarians it will not be a hunt, but a battle. None can be allowed to flee. We will take them all."

"You imagine I have some scruple about killing my former people? It's nothing I haven't done before."

"This will be different. This time they are led by something far worse than an overambitious general."

Kiral approached, wiping gore from her arrows and casting a cautious glance at the shaman. "Lord Vaelin speaks true," she told him. "I feel your compassion. But it will kill you when we face the Ally's favoured dog."

Astorek frowned, shaking his head in bafflement. "Ally?"

◆ ◆ ◆

"And it lives in this . . . beyond place? A place beyond death?"

Vaelin struggled to formulate a precise answer. Explaining the concept of the Beyond to someone raised without any form of faith was proving difficult. Also, unlike the people who had adopted him, Astorek felt no worshipful tendencies towards the green fire that continued to flicker in the night sky, though its light was now just a dim glow on the northern horizon. "One of nature's many mysteries," was his only opinion.

They had begun the march the day before, the Wolf People's warriors gathering together in loose affiliation and moving south without particular order or ceremony save brief, intimate farewells to family. However, there were some who would neither be travelling south nor staying on the tundra. Vaelin watched as a group of people gathered on the shoreline, men and women of advanced age each with his or her own canoe carrying only a small stock of provisions. He saw Far Walker among them, handing out various items to a group of younger folk he took to be the elder's children or grand-children: a knife, a necklace, a spear. They all accepted the gifts in silent respect, the youngest sniffling as the old man climbed alone into his canoe and pushed away from the shore, paddling off towards the north without a backward glance. *His will,* Vaelin thought.

Later he joined Astorek at the head of the army, leading Scar at a walk as the shaman sent his wolves ahead to scout their line of march.

"I realise it may be hard to credit," Vaelin said. "But I have been there, and heard his voice. Much as I would like to dismiss him as a figment of leg-end or delusion, his hunger for our destruction is all too real."

"I thought you had to die to gain entry to the Beyond."

Vaelin turned his gaze to the horizon. Talking of what had happened at Alltor was never easy, perhaps because so much of it still escaped his under-standing. "You do."

"Then how do you come to be here?"

Vaelin glanced back at Dahrena, laughing with Cara as their cats rolled together in a play fight a short way off. "I have always been greatly fortunate in my friends."

Another week's march brought them in sight of the mountains, a range of steep-sided ridges and peaks stretching away south for as far as they could see. The valleys seemed rich in pine but the peaks were mostly bare granite, painted a pale blue in the haze. Off to the east a dim orange glow could be seen beneath a low bank of dark cloud. "Fire mountains," Astorek said. "Even the tribesfolk don't go there."

"Do your people trade with them?" Vaelin asked. "Speak their language?"

"They speak Volarian, of a sort. Difficult to make out for the less-attuned ear. And no, there is no trade between us. They keep to their hills fighting their endless feuds, or the Volarians when they come to fill their slave quotas, rarely venturing across the tundra." Astorek glanced up at the ever-present swirl of spear-hawks as a group separated from the main flock to fly towards the hills. "Mother will warn of any who come to greet us."

But there was no one waiting as they crested the foothills, the heights ahead free of any sign their way might be barred. "My people would do the same," Alturk said, eyes narrowed as he scanned the silent hills. "Allow us to enter, march on until we imagine ourselves safe then attack in the night."

"There are no eyes on us," Kiral said with a note of certainty. She turned to Vaelin, her expression grave, "But someone comes. My song is clear: we should wait."

They camped on a series of hills affording good views of the surrounding country, the spear-hawks providing constant vigilance and the wolves kept in tight packs on the perimeter. But still the hills remained silent. As night fell the glow of the eastern fire mountains grew bright, occasional flashes of lightning threading through the smoke they cast into the sky.

"So Nishak's arm reaches around the world," Alturk observed in a rare fireside comment, his gaze lingering on the distant fires. He had recently abandoned his usual practice of eating and sleeping away from the main body of the company, his head once again shaven to stubble. The contempt still felt by some of the Sentar was evident in their faces, but others showed a grudging resumption of respect.

Looking around the company, Vaelin noted how they were mingled now, guardsmen and Lonak sitting alongside each other with a natural ease, the Gifted among them, their cats snapping at the scraps tossed to them by the warriors. *The ice was a forge,* he decided, recalling distant days spent watching Master Jestin at the anvil, the three rods of an unborn sword gradually melding under his ceaseless hammer. *It beat us into something new.*

"Did you really hear his voice?" Dahrena asked.

Alturk's gaze lowered in discomfort, though there seemed to be no anger in him, just regretted memory. "I heard it, a sound that could only have come from the mouth of a god."

"The Cave of Mists," Kiral said. "The Mahlessa told me only one other besides her has ever seen it."

"It was the Mahlessa who guided me to it. Though my club and my knife had made me Tahlessa of the Grey Hawks, husband to six wives and father to a fine son, I was still a youth dreaming of greatness, a greatness I thought I would find in the Cave of Mists where the voices of the gods are said to still echo. So I went to the Mountain and asked for guidance from the Mahlessa. I was not permitted in her presence, for no man is worthy, but she gave me a guide and sent us forth with words I thought a blessing but later knew as a warning—'There is only truth to be heard from the gods.'"

Alturk paused to regard Kiral with a faint grin. "My guide was a woman of grim aspect who spoke rarely except to voice insult, calling me a fool, and a braggart, and son to a mother who had clearly spread her legs for an ape. Were she not a Servant of the Mountain I would have pitched her from the highest cliff, as she well knew."

"You would have tried," Kiral said in a hard voice.

"Your blood-mother was the harshest-tongued woman I ever met," Alturk returned. "And I married the worst six bitches in the mountains."

"And wanted her for the seventh." Kiral returned his grin. "Only she had more sense."

Alturk grunted and waved a dismissive hand. "In any case she guided me to a cave, a small gap in the side of an unremarkable mountain. 'You'll die in there, ape-spawn,' she told me, then walked off with no other word spoken. I could feel the heat flowing from the cave, knowing that what lay beneath would prove the greatest trial. But I wanted so much to hear Nishak's voice, I *knew* he had great things to tell me.

"At first all was blackness, my torch the only light as I climbed ever lower. Sometimes the walls of the cave would fall away, leaving me crouched on a narrow ledge with the void all around, not knowing if a single stumble would send me tumbling to my death. Then I came to the bridge, in truth a narrow arch of rock spanning a great chasm, with a fierce torrent of water falling like a curtain halfway across. On the far side there was only blackness. The test was clear, if I went on my torch would die in the torrent and I might never find my way again. The gods are wise in their tests, choosing only those worthy of their voice, for a coward would have turned back." Alturk paused, the softest laugh escaping his lips. "And only a fool would have gone on. And I did.

"The bridge was slippery, the water chill as ice, and all became dark when it claimed my torch. I dropped to my belly and crawled, feeling my way forward until the narrow bridge became broad rock and ahead, the faintest glimmer of light, drawing me ever onward. The light grew as I neared, the walls of the great cavern I had entered giving off a green glow and in the centre a pool of roiling water, constantly bubbling and birthing a fine mist. At first I found the smell of it harsh and like to turn my stomach but the scent faded as I drew close to the pool, as close as I dared for its heat was vast . . . And I heard it, low at first, like a tremor in the earth, but building, becoming clearer and stronger until I felt my ears might burst from it.

"I knew then I was a fool, a bug crawling across the feet of a giant, for what would such a voice have to say to a speck such as I? But . . . he did. 'Do you know who speaks to you?' he asked me and through my fear I babbled his name. 'Yes,' he said. 'I who gave the gift of fire to all mankind. I who saved you from the all-dark. I who has succoured you with warmth for all the ages. For I am the most generous of gods, and yet you always ask for more.'

"I would have fled if my legs had not failed me, left me crawling on the cave floor like the bug I knew myself to be. I begged him, like a captured Merim Her facing the just knife, I begged and wailed and soiled myself in fear. But Nishak knows neither pity nor anger, he is generous but his gift can burn as well as succour, for truth is a flame that burns deep. 'I know what you came for, Tahlessa of the Grey Hawks,' he told me. 'Your mind is so easily picked apart. So much anger, so much ambition, and what's this? A child you imagine worthy of a great future, a child you believe will lead the Lonak against the Merim Her. Look closer, see more.'

"And through the fog of memory I saw it; the boy's cruelty to all around him, the time I had found him with a strangled pup, the older boy who had fallen to his death when they climbed together, the lies I deafened myself to as he told of an accident, a missed handhold that led to a broken neck. I saw it all."

Alturk's head slumped in shame, his craggy features so steeped in sorrow even Kiral seemed discomforted by it, wincing and averting her gaze. "Instead of accepting this gift," Alturk went on, "I raged at Nishak, finding the strength to stand. 'My son has greatness in him!' I cried. 'He will sweep the Merim Her into the sea.' And Nishak laughed, long and hard. 'Think on that when you kill him,' he said. 'Now go.'

"All became silent save the roiling of the water. I lingered a while longer, calling for Nishak to return and take back his lies, but he had no more words for such an ungrateful bug. I found another passage from the cavern, narrow and winding, but also lit with the same green glow. After hours uncounted it brought me back to the world above, which now seemed so very cold."

Alturk fell silent, looking towards the distant fires with the eyes of a tired man soon to confront the twilight of his life. He didn't turn when he spoke again, though it was obvious to whom he addressed his question, "That thing the Mahlessa freed you from. Did it find him or did he find it?"

"The Sentar had already been reborn before I was . . . taken," Kiral said. "Your son had been one of those who remade it, finding others of similar mind, hungry for blood and seeking to justify their cruelty. He hated the Mahlessa for his disgrace, claiming he could have killed the greatest of the Merim Her but for her weakness, for she was old, and corrupted by the ages. But they were few in number and their plans chaotic, being possessed of a shared madness. To fulfil their mission the Sentar needed leadership, and found it in me." She grimaced, her voice taking on a note of apology, "You would always have had to kill him, Tahlessa. Only truth can be heard from the gods."

◆ ◆ ◆

He was roused by one of the wolves, a huge male with an insistent tongue and foul-smelling breath. It jumped back a little as Vaelin jerked awake, dagger in hand, angling its head at him in curiosity before voicing an impatient yelp.

"What is it?" Dahrena groaned at his side, her pale and bleary-eyed face appearing above the furs.

"I think someone has finally come to welcome us," he said, reaching for his boots.

Astorek, Kiral and Wise Bear waited at the foot of the south-facing slope, a line of wolves spread out before them and a cluster of spear-hawks overhead. "How many?" Vaelin asked, coming to Kiral's side.

"Just one."

Vaelin peered into the distance, picking out a single figure, hooded and cloaked, striding towards them without any apparent alarm at the cloud of spear-hawks descending to circle him at head height. Vaelin went forward to welcome him as he came to a halt before the line of wolves, a man of average height, broad but not overly muscular, drawing his hood back to reveal lean but deeply lined features, and eyes that spoke of a depth of experience Vaelin now knew to be vast.

"Ah," said Erlin. "I thought it might be you."

Chapter Six

Reva

S he awoke to pain, a fierce, piercing ache in her right hand, banishing the blackness with a persistent, pulsing agony. She groaned, shaking her hand, but the pain flared rather than faded. She winced as her eyes opened, sunlight sending a bolt of white fire into her brain. For a time all she could see was a faint yellow blur, her ears constantly assaulted by a roaring hiss. Forcing herself to blink, she managed to focus, the yellow blur resolving into a beach, the roar the rushing waves that jostled her, and the pain in her hand the result of a small red crab attempting to eat her thumb.

She pinched its claw and tugged it free, tossing it into the surf, gritting her teeth against the sting of salt in the wound but finding herself oddly grateful for the sensation; it confirmed she was, much to her surprise, alive. Barely able to move and lying prostrate on a beach whilst waves pounded her, but still undeniably alive.

Why? she asked the Father, more curious than angry. *You cannot think I deserve to live. You cannot reward one whose lie has killed so many.*

The voice was so unexpected, and shocking in its volume, she thought for an instant the Father had actually deigned to respond. Her heart calmed when she realised the voice called out words she couldn't understand, her still-cloudy vision finding the owner, a hulking shape in black labouring through the surf towards her. The details of his garb became clear as he neared, a black leather jerkin, a silver medallion worn around the neck, and a whip on his belt. *Overseer.*

She let him take hold of her hair and haul her free of the water, keeping her features slack and uncomprehending as his brutish face came closer, eyes moving over her in expert appraisal. He called over his shoulder to an unseen companion, confirming he wasn't alone. She kept her eyes half-open as he dragged her from the sea, counting six more shapes standing on the beach, and many more lying prostrate and unmoving.

The overseer dumped her on the sand where she forced herself to remain limp and immobile, breathing deep but soft, gathering strength. They made the mistake of waiting several minutes before returning to examine their catch, the overseer who had found her pulling her onto her back as his companions gathered round. She counted two with spears as her head lolled to one side, the others with short swords. The overseer pulled up her blouse, revealing her breasts as he voiced a question to his companions. There were a few murmurs of agreement, one of them adding something with an appreciative cackle.

"My friend . . . like you," the overseer said in broken Realm Tongue, taking hold of her face and turning it so she could see his leer. "Want to . . . fuck you. Might lower the price . . . But I owe him. You . . . want fucked, pretty thing?"

It was really the smile that killed him, not so much the blow, making him frown in puzzlement at her welcoming, lustful grin, drawing back in surprise just enough to expose his throat. Vaelin had taught her the blow; the priest's lessons in unarmed combat had never been so thorough, nor so effective in practice. Her stiff fingers drove into the overseer's neck with enough force to crush his larynx, leaving him writhing on the sand, bloody froth gouting from his mouth. Reva rolled on the sand, dodging a plunging spear-point then grabbing the haft before its owner could withdraw for another try. She flicked a kick into his face, sending him reeling, then surged to her feet with his spear in her hands.

She whirled as they closed, the spear-point slashing the disarmed spearman across the eyes, another the face. The second spearman came at her with an overextended thrust, indicating a level of expertise best confined to abusing helpless captives. She parried the thrust without difficulty, deflecting the spear with the haft of her own and spinning to slam the blunt end into the back of his neck which snapped with a gratifying crack.

She stood watching the others as they dithered, casting wary glances at the man she had blinded, screaming as blood seeped through the hands he held to his face. "Come on!" she whispered as they exchanged uncertain glances. "You cannot think I deserve to live."

A horn sounded somewhere close by and Reva's eyes found a group of horsemen cresting the dunes a few hundred paces distant. She turned to see more riders approaching from the north end of the beach. Any thought she might soon be rescued faded at the sight of the slavers' evident relief.

The lead rider pulled up next to the body of the overseer with the crushed larynx. The riders differed from other Volarians Reva had seen, clad in red breastplates and greaves. She would have taken them for Kuritai but for the patent amusement on the leader's face as he regarded the overseer's corpse, an amusement shared by the thirty or so riders at his back.

The slavers greeted the red-armoured man with a babble of outrage, suddenly less cowed now there were other eyes to witness the scene. The rider ignored them, shifting his gaze to Reva, his grin growing wider. He held up a hand to silence the slavers then asked a question, raising his eyebrows at the response, the slaver with the slashed face seeking to staunch the blood with a rag as he gesticulated at her, voice shrill with fury.

The man in red armour, however, seemed unmoved by their entreaties, reclining in his saddle and nodding at Reva as he voiced a short command. The slavers' confidence visibly waned on hearing his words, casting wary glances in her direction, fidgeting in uncertainty. The rider spoke again, voicing a single word, the other riders all drawing swords with identical speed and fluency. The leader pointed his own sword at the slavers then at Reva, repeating his first command with slow deliberation.

The slavers, now pale of face and shrinking from the many blades surrounding them, began to advance towards Reva in a slow crouch. She saw little point in prolonging the encounter, choosing the tallest and sending the spear into the centre of his chest, then sprinting forward, rolling under the wild slashes of the remaining slavers to claim his sword. After that, the others offered no more challenge than a light practice.

◆ ◆ ◆

Crouched in her chains in the back of a caged wagon, two of the red-armoured Volarians standing close by, she forced herself to watch as the other captives were inspected. She had managed to scar one of them back on the beach, throwing her sword at the first to come close. He dodged with an uncanny swiftness, but not before the spinning blade had left a long cut on his jaw. She had expected death to follow quickly but the scarred man seemed to find the event as amusing as his companions. They were already greatly entertained by her treatment of the slavers, slapping their hands to their breastplates in appreciation when she killed the last one, a gangly man who had tried to flee only to be kicked back to face her. He hadn't lasted long.

She had started to run, intending to leap at one of them, pitch him from the saddle and ride clear, but soon found herself flat on her face with a mouthful of sand, a cord tightening about her leg. She thrashed, trying to tear free but another cord wrapped itself around her wrist. The rider who had spoken to the slavers dismounted to crouch at her side as she struggled, smiling in warm appreciation as he smoothed a hand across her face, speaking a single word in Volarian, "Garisai."

They bound her from foot to shoulder, banishing all thought of escape, heaving her onto the back of a horse to be carried a few miles to this camp. They had been greeted by more slavers under the command of an overseer who displayed a strangely cowed demeanour in the presence of the red-armoured men, his head bowed as the leader gave curt instruction and Reva was placed at their mercy. She had steeled herself for further suffering, seeing the hatred in the faces of the slavers as they chained her, one holding a knife to her throat, two more standing with spears no more than an inch from her chest as the shackles were snapped into place. But whatever vengeful thoughts they harboured, it seemed their orders forbade any mistreatment beyond some rough handling as she was hauled into the caged wagon. But, as she surveyed her new surroundings, it became clear she was not to be spared all forms of torment.

She had to strain against her chains and crane her neck to see it, but with sufficient effort could view the spectacle of other captives being brought in and subjected to the slavers' attentions. Their injunction against harming her clearly didn't extend to the other prizes claimed from the shoreline. The first was an archer judging by the breadth of his frame, stumbling to his knees before the overseer who bent to view a deep wound in the man's chest before standing back with a dismissive wave. Another slaver came forward, curved dagger in hand, and slit the archer's throat before Reva formed sufficient thought to cry out in protest.

She refused to look away as more were brought in, though her body ached from the strain. They were mostly Cumbraelins, with a few Realm Guard, slaughtered or spared depending on their injuries. The storm had evidently wrought considerable damage for it seemed more were discarded than spared. She resisted the faint seed of hope nurtured by the fact that neither Antesh nor Arentes were among the prisoners. *Lost to the sea or slaughtered on the shore, what difference does it make? I killed them all regardless.*

The last captive provided the hardest trial, a slender figure with cropped hair, moving with a straight back despite her shackles, refusing to be cowed by the men who towered over her. "Lehra!" Reva called out, slashing her chains against the bars of the cage. A slaver thrust his spear-butt through the bars to push her back, then stepped away at a harsh glower from one of the red men. Reva strained to see Lehra again, finding the Scarred Daughter standing with a smile as she beheld the Blessed Lady, eyes shining with undimmed awe. "I knew the Father would spare you, my lady!" she called, voice bright and joyous.

The overseer grunted a curse, raising a hand to deliver a cuff to the girl's face. Lehra didn't shrink from it, instead angling her head and opening her mouth wide as the slaver's hand connected with her face, biting down hard. A girlish shriek erupted from the overseer's mouth as he tried to tear himself free, but Lehra held on, even as the other slavers assailed her with whips and cudgels, shaking her head like a terrier as she worried at the flesh, stopping only when a spear was thrust through her back, pinning her to the sand.

Reva heard a woman screaming somewhere, feeling a hard thumping in her forehead and a warm trickle of blood cascading down her face. A Volarian voice barked at her and she felt rough hands pulling her back from the bars, now bloody from where she had pounded her head against them. She heard the woman's screams fade and choked over the sudden catch in her throat. She found herself staring up into the face of the red-armoured man from the beach, the one who seemed to command the others. His grin was gone now and he regarded her with an expression of faint puzzlement, head tilted like a cat regarding a shiny novelty.

His face dimmed and she knew that fatigue, pain and despair were conspiring to drag her into unconsciousness. She found enough hate to keep it at bay a moment longer. "I am the elverah," she told the red man in a hoarse rasp. "I have killed more of you than I can count, and I am far from done."

◆ ◆ ◆

She awoke to find herself no longer alone in the cage. The face of the man slumped opposite her was concealed by a lank cascade of blond hair, swaying with the motion of the wagon. Reva could tell he was tall, and no stranger to work or war judging by the strength evident in the scarred and powerful hands resting on his knees, the shackles tight on his well-muscled wrists. Reva sighed, not for the first time wondering at the Father's inexhaustible supply of trials for a sinful soul.

"Wake up, my lord," she said, kicking out to nudge his bare foot. Like her, his boots had been taken.

The blond man stirred but failed to wake, voicing only a faint grunt. Reva kicked him again, harder. "My lord Shield!"

His head jerked up with a shout, blue eyes wide with alarm and, she noted to her dismay, not a little fear. His panic faded at the sight of her, though his survey of their surroundings provoked a barely concealed moan of despair. "I dreamed I died," he muttered, head slumping. "It was a good dream."

"They took you on the beach?" she asked.

His head jerked in affirmation. "A dozen or so of us. I managed to cling to some wreckage in the storm with a few others. We swam to shore at first light. We were heading north, making for the landing site, then they came."

"The slavers?"

"No, the others." The Shield's hands tightened into fists, his chains giving off a faint rattle.

"The men in red armour?"

"We had no weapons. Nothing to fight with." A strange guttural sound escaped him and she realised he was laughing. "So they gave us swords. Each of us, given a sword by our enemies. I fought so hard . . . But I couldn't save them. When it was over they killed the wounded and took me, the only one left, too spent to even stand. They seemed to find me . . . entertaining."

"Garisai," Reva murmured.

The Shield's head came up again, his gaze suddenly bright. "What?"

"One of them called me that when they took me. You know what it means?"

He leaned back, some vestige of his old humour showing in the sardonic twitch of his brows. "Yes, it means we would have been fortunate if they'd killed us."

◆ ◆ ◆

The succeeding days in the wagon took on a dreadful monotony. They were never allowed release from the cage; their food, consisting of two bowls of gruel a day and two cups of water, was shoved through a slat in the wagon's iron-braced sides. No utensils were provided so they were obliged to eat with their fingers. They had been provided a bucket for bodily waste, emptied whenever they stopped by means of a collaborative effort to tip the contents out through the bars. They had learned to wait until the slaver driving their wagon had stepped down from the board as he took great delight in spurring the oxen on a step or two in order to douse them in their own filth.

"Redflower," the Shield observed on the morning of the tenth day, gazing at the passing fields of crimson blooms. "Puts us perhaps forty miles from Volar."

"You know this country?" Reva asked.

"Came here as a boy sailor many years ago. Merchant vessel, before I saw the wisdom, and profit, of a pirate's life. The Volarians grow the best red-flower, and it always brings in decent coin, if you can stomach their ways long enough to strike a deal."

"Your hatred was birthed before the war, then?"

"Hatred? No, merely vague disgust in those days. My people are rich in faults, I know, but slavery has never been amongst them. Any Meldenean captain found to have carried slaves would soon find himself shunned and shipless."

Reva looked up, feeling the wagon begin to slow, her gaze drawn to the driver staring at something ahead. It took a moment for the object of his interest to come into view, a tall pole set alongside the road, topped with a protruding beam in the manner of a gallows. Suspended from the beam was something so mangled it took a moment for Reva to recognise it as a corpse. The legs were blackened and charred to stumps, the stomach cavity open and empty, and the head . . . The face was probably male, rendered into an ageless cracked leather mask by decomposition, but the teeth bared in a wide, frozen scream, testifying to the agony with which this man had met his end.

The driver murmured something to himself, looking away from the sight and snapping the reins to urge the oxen to a faster pace.

"The three deaths," the Shield translated. "An agonising poison first, then burning, then disembowelment. Traditional Volarian punishment for treason, though it hasn't been used for many years."

Reva glanced up as another pole came into view, the corpse that dangled from it similarly abused, though this one's eyes had been put out. She asked Ell-Nestra if this held any significance but he shrugged. "Only that someone enjoys his work, I suspect."

By the time night fell they had counted over a hundred poles, ten for every mile they covered.

◆ ◆ ◆

Volar came into view the following morning. Reva raised herself into a back-straining crouch to get a better view as they crested a hill a mile or so west of the Imperial capital. The road, flanked on both sides with more corpse-bearing poles, became an unerring straight line at the foot of the hill, drawing the eye to the western suburbs, consisting of tree-lined rows of one- or two-storey houses. Volar appeared to have no walls or defensive fortifications, the Shield explaining they had been swallowed up by the city's growth centuries before.

"The largest city in the world, or so it's said," he told her. "Though I've heard there are a few in the Far West that might also claim the title."

The height of the buildings grew as they moved deeper into Volar, plush individual dwellings giving way to close-packed streets and tenements. Maze-like avenues stretched away from the road, reminding her of Varinshold's less salubrious districts, now of course razed to the ground.

"She wanted to burn all of this," the Shield said softly, frowning as he gazed at the passing streets. "And we would have helped her wield the torch."

Reva's thoughts flashed to Lehra, as they often had during this dreadful journey. She had been one of the free fighters to emerge from the forest country south of Alltor, leading a group of a dozen other girls, all freed from the slavers' clutches by their own agency, steeped in blood and hungry for more. Reva recalled how they had gathered around her, sinking to their knees in unbidden respect; the tale of the Blessed Lady had already flown far and seeing her in the flesh seemed a confirmation of a cherished legend, a sign that their sufferings had not been in vain. The awe in Lehra's eyes that day had been no less bright than the moment she died. *Her voice was so full of joy . . . She died believing my lie.*

"The barest chance is all I need," she muttered to the Shield. "Just one chance at freedom and I'll burn this place to the ground."

He slumped back down, voice faint and bitter, "It was all a madwoman's dream, my lady. And she made us mad with the sharing of it. Look at this place. How could we have thought to bring down an empire capable of crafting a city like this?"

"We crushed an army that should have crushed us," Reva pointed out. "Their cities may be strong but they are weak, their souls blackened and sickened by ages of cruelty."

He lifted his wrists, jangling the chains. "And yet, here we are. Brought here to die for their amusement."

"'Despair is a sin against the Father's love, for it is but indulgence, whilst hope is a virtue of the stronger soul.'"

"Which one is that?"

"The Third Book, The Book of Struggle, Verse three, Trials of the Prophets." She realised the Book of Reason had been absent from her thoughts since her capture. *And why not? Reason will not avail me here.*

◆ ◆ ◆

The Volarians seemed highly fond of statuary, bronze warriors for the most part, standing amidst the cascading fountains and neatly kept parks that greeted them once they cleared the cramped outskirts. However, the most salient feature of the city's inner region was the towers, great marble structures of hard-edged symmetry rising on all sides. Strangely this district seemed mostly empty but for the huddled forms of slaves tending the parks or scrubbing bird droppings from the statues. Reva supposed the absence of citizenry might be explained by the sight of the bodies that hung from the towers by the dozen. Some had clearly been strung up whilst still alive judging by the red-brown streaks that adorned the high walls.

"Their Empress seems keen to make an impression," the Shield observed.

The wagon train drew up to the largest structure they had yet seen, a tall oval-shaped wonder of red and gold marble. It stood fully seventy feet high, constructed in five tiers, and differed markedly from the other architecture she had seen. There was little evidence of the Volarian liking for straight edges here, the tiers constructed from elegant arches and gently curved columns resembling the stem of a wineglass.

"The great arena of Volar, my lady," Ell-Nestra said. "Enjoy the view, it's unlikely either of us will see another."

A tight circle of red-armoured men surrounded the wagon whilst the driver unlocked the cage, standing well back and ordering them out with near-frantic impatience. From his guarded expression and the sweat sheening his face Reva surmised he was keen to be away from their guards. She climbed out with difficulty, legs and back aching with every movement. She had tried to flex her muscles during the journey but such prolonged constraint was bound to weaken even the strongest body. The Shield groaned as he stepped down, sinking to his knees with teeth clenched.

"Stand up." The voice was uncoloured by any anger or threat, the words spoken in unaccented Realm Tongue. Reva looked up at a man perhaps forty years in age, dressed in a plain black robe, his dark hair, greying at the temples, drawn back from a smooth forehead and lean, inexpressive features.

The Shield glanced up at the black-clad, squinting in the sun. "Can't see a whip on you," he said.

"I do not require a whip," the man replied. "You obey me or you die."

Ell-Nestra jerked his head at the arena behind them. "Here or there, what difference does it make?"

"In there you have a chance of life, at least for a time." The black-clad's eyes went to Reva, narrowing in careful appraisal. His gaze was intense but she saw no lust in it, also, she noted with surprise, no hint of cruelty. "My name is Varulek Tovrin," he told her. "Master of the Great Volarian Arena and Overseer of Garisai, by the gracious consent of the Empress Elverah."

He turned and beckoned to a pair of red-armoured guards, Reva noting the mass of tattoos that covered his hands from fingertip to wrist. They were unfamiliar in design, much more dense and intricate than those worn by the queen's Lonak woman, and she could only wonder at the hours, and pain, endured to craft such a complex web into his flesh. He caught her scrutiny and his expression transformed into something shockingly unexpected: sympathy. "She wishes to see you."

◆ ◆ ◆

The chilled stiffness of the wind grew with every rhythmic heave on the gondola's ropes, the hundred slaves below moving with well-drilled uniformity as they hauled her towards the tower's summit. She was flanked by two of the red-armoured men but they seemed content to allow her to turn about and take in the view, the majesty of the city revealed in full, a true wonder that made Alltor and Varinshold seem like no more than a mean clutch of stunted hovels.

Viewing the pristine orderliness of the vast conurbation laid out before her, she was forced to concede it was the most impressive example of human creativity she would ever witness, every street, park, avenue, and tower arranged according to precise rules of form and function, with hardly a curve to be seen. But the small, dark specks that covered the smooth flanks of every tower in sight told a different story. Volar was a lie, a facade of precision and beauty covering a vile truth.

The gondola halted at a balcony perhaps twenty feet short of the tower's pinnacle. A female slave of distracting beauty greeted Reva with a formal bow, turning to lead her inside, the guards following close behind. The interior was dimly lit with a scattering of oil lamps, silk drapes of various hues covering the windows and painting the decor a colourful melange that swayed as the wind swirled around the tower. Despite the gloom and the confusion of colour, it took Reva only a second to find the Empress, her eyes long attuned to seeking out the greatest threat in any room.

She sat on a stool before a small table, wearing a plain gown of white, her bare feet poised on the marble floor, toes flat and heels elevated, like a dancer. In one hand she held a length of fabric constrained in a circular frame of some kind, her other hand wielding a needle and thread. Her face was shadowed, the elegant profile drawn in intense concentration as her hands worked the thread through the fabric. Reva's gaze took in the sight of a dozen or more frames scattered about the floor, each adorned with a mass of irregular, clumsy stitches. Some were ripped and the frames that held them shattered. Reva wondered why the slave girl hadn't cleared them away.

"You have been using my name," the sewing woman said, not glancing up from her task.

Reva said nothing. Hearing the slave girl's suppressed whimper, she turned to find her face tense with warning and barely suppressed tears. She gave an almost imperceptible shake of her head, eyes bright with a silent plea. *I'll find no mercy here, in any case,* Reva wanted to tell her. *But thank you for your concern.*

"So, Lieza likes you."

Reva turned to see the woman now addressing her directly. Her hands were enfolded in the fabric, a bright spot of blood spreading out from the needle embedded in the woman's finger. If she felt it, she gave no sign, offering Reva a smile of apparently genuine warmth as she rose and came closer.

"I can sense her *very* deep regard," she said, halting just beyond the reach allowed by Reva's chains. She was taller than Reva by a few inches, her form toned and athletic. She appeared little more than twenty years in age but one glance at her eyes and Reva knew she was in the presence of something far older. Something, she knew with grim certainty, that possessed a gift Vaelin had lost at Alltor.

"But is it returned, I wonder?" The woman angled her head, eyes closed as if listening to something, her smile becoming faint, wistful. "Ah. So sorry Lieza dear, but her heart is taken by another. She does feel a flicker of lust for you though, if it's any consolation. Love may claim our hearts but lust will always claim our bodies. It is the traitor that lurks in every soul." She opened her eyes again, smile gone as she frowned in sudden confusion. "Did I say that? Or did I read it somewhere?"

She stood in apparent bafflement for some time, unmoving but for a spasming tension to her face, eyes shifting from side to side in rapid jerks, mouth moving in an unheard dialogue until, as abruptly as it had begun, the confusion faded.

"Embroidery," she said, holding up the frame with its inexpert needle-work, Reva noting the multiple brownish stains on the material and the dried blood on the Empress's fingertips. "The wealthy women of Mirtesk were renowned for it. My father thought it the most productive use of time for a young lady of good birth." The Empress looked at the fabric, sighing in frustration. "But not in my case. It was the first of Father's many disappointments. Still I am improving, don't you think?"

She held out the frame for Reva's inspection. Amongst the bloodstains Reva made out some green and red thread tightly bunched into what might have been a rough approximation of a flower.

She said, "A blind ape could do better."

The slave girl, Lieza, gave another involuntary gasp, eyelids blinking rapidly as she lowered her gaze, unwilling to witness what came next. "Oh stop mewling," the Empress told her, rolling her eyes. "Don't worry, the object of your fascination has many lively days ahead of her, I'm sure. Just how many is up to her of course."

Her gaze swivelled back to Reva, a new focus lighting her eyes. "A few of my soldiers survived Alltor, did you know that? Suffering great travails and privation to make it to Varinshold before it fell. General Mirvek, always a punctilious fellow, was assiduous in compiling their accounts before having them executed. Such wild talk would only unnerve his men after all. You see, these men spoke of a witch at Alltor, a witch made invincible by the power of her god, wielding a sword that could cut through steel and a charmed bow that never missed. One even claimed to have met her and, half-mad though he was, he did provide a fulsome description."

Reva recalled the prisoner they had hauled from the riverbank the morning after the first major assault was driven back, a twitching, wide-eyed wreck of a man. It was strange, but she found herself regretting his death. The Volarians had been monstrous, but that scared, wasted soul had no more threat to offer than a starved dog.

"Elverah," the Empress went on. "They stole my name and gave it to you. I should be angry. You know its meaning?"

"Witch," Reva said. "Or sorceress."

"'Sorceress' is a silly word, meaningless really since sorcery is just fable. Incantations scribbled in ancient books, foul-smelling concoctions that do nothing but churn the stomach. No, I always preferred 'witch,' though the meaning changes a little in the dialect of the people who named me Elverah. You see, they afforded authority to those with the greatest power, regardless of its source. Be it skill in arms or what your people call the Dark. Power is power, so the name Elverah could also be translated as 'queen.'" She gave a soft laugh. "When my soldiers called you a witch, they were also calling you a queen."

"I have a queen."

"No, dearest little sister, you *had* a queen. I expect to receive her head shortly, should my admiral recover her body from the sea."

Reva fought to contain the upsurge of rage and uncertainty. *Everything you feel tells her more,* she admonished herself. *Feel nothing.* But it proved a hopeless cause, for thoughts of Queen Lyrna's demise inevitably led to images of one who had not been with her.

"Ah." The Empress said with a weary sigh. "And so *he* comes to plague us yet again." She regarded Reva with a raised eyebrow, her mouth slightly twisted in faint annoyance. "I hear he marched an army the length of your Realm in less than a month just to save you. What will he do now, I wonder?"

Feel nothing! Reva filled her mind with calming images, joyfully coiling in the dark with Veliss . . . Ellese stumbling about the gardens with her wooden sword . . . But it all faded in the light cast by a single thought, bright with certainty: *He will come here, free me and kill you.*

The Empress's face twitched again, all humour faded, and when she spoke her voice was flat, emotion vanished by the coldest logic. "He has a singer with him, doesn't he? I can hear her. Her song is strong, but dark. Stained by too much innocent blood. But I expect you know how that feels."

She stepped closer, the framed fabric dropping from her hand, raising blood-smeared fingers to caress Reva's face. "It has been over a century since I enjoyed a woman," she continued in the same empty voice. "A sweet girl from some northern town, the family newly risen to the red. Raised in indulgence, she found fascination in extremity, taking wicked delight in my many tales of murder. I doubt she found her own so delightful, though I made it quick."

Feel nothing! Reva's cheek bunched under the Empress's touch, provoking a treacherous tremble in her flesh, the shackles taut between her wrists.

"But," the Empress said, tracing a fingertip along Reva's chin, "since my return I find there is scant allure in any flesh, and all that once gave me joy is now but a dim remembrance. I didn't understand it before, the Ally's need. But now it becomes clear, endless years of awareness uncoloured by feeling, save the hunger for it to end. Worse than any death."

Unable to bear it any longer, Reva jerked her face away from the Empress's touch, her cheek stinging as if she had been slapped. "You should kill me," she grated. "Here and now. If you are wise, you will not allow the slightest chance I might loose these chains."

She heard Lieza take an involuntary step backwards, her breath now coming in ragged, panicky gasps.

"And where would be the entertainment in that?" the Empress asked, her voice regaining some expression. "My people do love their spectacles so, and they'll find plenty to bay at in you, I'm sure . . ."

Abruptly, the Empress fell silent, all expression fading from her face as she raised it, turning towards the western wall. Just for a second a spasm of naked anger crossed her face, the elegant features drawn in frustrated rage, but then softening as she hissed a soft breath. "It appears, little sister," she said to Reva, "I have an admiral to execute. Your queen clings stubbornly to her head after all. Still, I've no doubt she'll provide as much entertainment as you, in time."

She turned to the guards, "Return my little sister to Varulek, and give him this one too." She flicked a hand at Lieza. "They are to be confined together, I'm keen to provide my new sister with all comforts, in between spectacles. Tell him I think the tale of Jarvek and Livella would make for a fine introduction. The crowd always do appreciate the classics."

She moved away, casting a final command over her shoulder, softly spoken but dark with intent, "And tell the overseers in the vaults to finish preparing my new general."

CHAPTER SEVEN

Frentis

He clawed at the cord, fingers digging into his flesh as he sought to gain enough purchase to snap it. The red-armoured man laughed and drove another kick into his belly, forcing the air from his body, the cord stifling an involuntary shout. "No more now," the man cautioned with a grin, looming closer. "She doesn't want you damaged."

He placed a booted foot on Frentis's chest and forced him to the floor, his two companions coming forward with shackles. "She said to tell you," the man with the cord went on, pressing harder with his boot, "you can choose which one of your friends gets to live. Just one though."

Frentis tried to kick out at the man crouching at his feet, but he dodged the flailing foot, catching his ankles and bearing down with a crushing weight. The other one had already taken hold of his arms, pulling them over his head and snapping a manacle over his right wrist.

"Can't think why she wants you so badly," the grinning man said, eyes tracking over Frentis's prostrate form with calm disinterest. "When she could have any one of u—"

A sudden crash of breaking glass and the grinning man appeared to have grown a crossbow bolt from his temple, head swivelling as his lips slackened to mumble gibberish before he collapsed facedown on the floor. The window opposite exploded as Illian propelled herself through it feet-first, landing astride Lemera's corpse with sword drawn. She flicked a cut at the man holding Frentis's arms, leaving a deep wound on his forehead as he dodged away with a remarkable swiftness. His companion avoided her next blow altogether, rolling and coming to his feet with sword drawn in a perfect backward somersault. However, they had both been obliged to release their hold on Frentis.

He came to his knees in a whirl, the chain manacled to his wrist blurring like a whip as it caught the man nearest him about the legs. He jerked it tight, bearing his enemy to the floor, then leapt, bringing both feet down on his head, the neck snapping with a crack. Frentis claimed the man's sword and turned to find Illian engaged in a desperate struggle with the other, her sword moving in frantic swipes as he drove her back, her face a picture of frustration whilst the red-armoured man wore the same maddening grin as his fallen comrade. Frentis whipped his chain at him, causing him to dance aside with a speed that would have shamed even a Kuritai, but leaving enough room for Illian to thrust at his neck. He parried the blow with consummate ease but had no counter for the stroke Frentis delivered to his leg, the blade sinking deep enough to grind on the bone. The man swore, but his face betrayed no anger, just amusement and even admiration, inclining his head at Frentis in appreciation even as Illian's sword point pierced his throat.

"Brother!" she rushed to his side, eyes scanning him for injury.

"I'm unhurt." He moved to the corpse of the man with the broken neck, finding a key for the manacles tucked into his boot. "You were guarding my room?"

"We take turns. There's a comfortable ledge on the roof outside."

His gaze went to Lemera, framed on the bedsheets in a spreading blossom of dark blood. *I choose to die free . . .*

"I know you didn't break your oath, brother," Illian said, following his gaze. "She told me she found comfort sleeping at your side."

Frentis hauled on his shirt and trews and reached for his boots. "What's happening outside?"

"All quiet. I had no notion of any alarm until I heard the struggle." She went to the first man she had killed, crouching to extract her bolt from his skull with a grinding squelch. "What are they?"

"They're called Arisai. And I've little doubt there are more." He retrieved his sword and rushed to the window, eyes tracking across the empty streets below to the walls where the sentries strolled on the parapet. Nothing, no indication of any threat. *You did remember to check the sewers . . .* His eyes went to an iron-covered drain in the cobbled street below. *Waiting. Commanded to ensure they fulfilled their Empress's mission above all else.*

He shuddered at the realisation he would now be shackled and his people facing slaughter but for her warning, a warning he knew had been no mistake. *She wanted them to fail.* He glanced back at the silent room of corpses. *And they don't know they have.*

"Fetch Draker, Lekran and Master Rensial," he told Illian, going back inside. "And Tekrav. Be quiet but quick."

◆　◆　◆

He hung between Lekran and Rensial, head slumped, the chains on his ankles rattling on the cobbles as they bore him towards the iron drain cover in the shadow of the town's main warehouse. Unlike Lekran and Rensial, Draker's red-enamelled breastplate didn't quite cover his frame, obliging him to keep to the shadows as he followed. Frentis was certain the Arisai would be watching carefully, his albeit brief experience convincing him of the dangers of underestimating their abilities whilst also giving a clue to a potential weakness. *The way they smile. They take joy from battle, from killing, and joy can make us overeager.*

A red-armoured shape resolved out of the shadows as they approached the drain, Frentis looking up at him with half-closed eyes, gratified by the welcoming grin. "No trouble then?" he asked in whispered Volarian, unwisely keeping his gaze on Frentis as they came closer.

"None," Lekran agreed, he and Rensial dumping Frentis at the Arisai's feet.

"Thought he might've done for one of you at least," he said, drawing a dagger and crouching to tap the pommel three times on the drain cover.

Lekran glanced down at Frentis, his own grin now genuine. "His legend greatly exceeds his skills, it seems."

The Arisai grunted and moved back as the drain cover was hauled up and to the side by unseen hands, beckoning impatiently at Lekran. "Get him below, we've work to do."

"No," Lekran told the Arisai, drawing his gaze as Master Rensial stepped behind him. "You're done now."

Rensial's dagger flashed across the Arisai's throat, leaving him kneeling on the cobbles, blood seeping through his fingers as he coughed a laugh of appalled surprise. An Arisai's head emerged from the drain, hands clutching the sides to haul himself free, falling back in a cloud of blood as Lekran's axe swept down.

"Come on you lazy buggers!" Draker called, running from the shadows and gesticulating wildly as Tekrav appeared at the far end of the street with a dozen or so of his porters, each rolling a barrel.

Lekran raised a bugle to his lips and sounded a single long pealing note, the town coming to life around them as the rebels answered the call, torches flaming and people running to preallocated stations, weapons in hand.

Frentis risked a glance at the blank opening of the drain, jerking his head back as a knife came spinning out of the blackness, missing him by the width of a hair. He could hear the multiple splashes of many feet running through water, but no voices, no sign in fact of any alarm or panic, provoking him to an uncomfortable notion: *Perhaps they can't feel fear.*

"How much?" Tekrav asked, dragging his barrel to a halt at the drain's edge.

"All of it," Frentis said.

Tekrav turned the barrel about and Lekran brought his axe round to smash the lid, lamp oil gushing forth into the drain. They tipped the barrel up to empty the contents and followed with another, the other porters sweeping by to trundle their own barrels to every drain in the town.

Frentis looked up at the warehouse roof where Illian now stood, waving a torch to confirm all the drains were now surrounded by at least one company of fighters. "No reason to wait," he told Tekrav.

The Chief Quartermaster stepped forward, face grim but determined as he raised a flaming torch. "For Lemera," he said. The torch disappeared into the hole, birthing an instant column of yellow flame at least ten feet high. It subsided to a modest-sized blaze after a few seconds, Frentis straining to gauge the results. *Nothing. Not a single scream.*

He left Draker and his company guarding the flaming drain, running with Lekran and Rensial to the next one where Ivelda and half the Garisai clustered around the opening, watching as the porters poured more lamp oil into the sewers. A strong stench of burning oil rose from the opening along with a thickening pall of smoke, but it remained eerily silent. "If they're down there, brother," Ivelda said, "they know how to die quietly."

Frentis turned as a shout came from the hole, seeing one of the Garisai reeling away with a dagger embedded in his shoulder as a figure erupted from the drain, launched by his comrades to rise five feet in the air amidst a glittering cascade of water and oil. His sword began to flash as he landed, hacking down a Garisai and wounding another before a pole-axe cleaved into his chest. Two more Arisai were propelled from the drain in quick succession, oil flying from their spinning forms as they hacked and slashed, seeking to drive the Garisai back from the hole. One was quickly cut down but the other fought on, blocking thrusts and inflicting wounds with deadly precision. Frentis ran in, sweeping aside the Arisai's blade to deliver a kick to his breastplate, sending him sprawling back towards the drain. The man clung on however, arms and legs spread, his comrades' hands reaching up from below to propel him back to the fight, his grinning face fixed on Frentis in direct challenge.

Frentis snatched a torch from one of the Garisai and tossed it onto the Arisai's chest, stepping forward to stamp down as the flames engulfed him, returning him to the oil-soaked sewers. The column of fire was taller this time, the blast of heat singeing the hairs on Frentis's arms as he reeled away.

A rising tumult drew his attention to the dockside where he could see a dense knot of fighters attempting to contain a group of Arisai emerging from one of the larger drains fringing the wharf. Weight of numbers managed to keep the red men at bay but more and more were clambering free by the second, claiming lives with every sword stroke.

"Your people with me," Frentis told Ivelda. "This will be a long night."

◆ ◆ ◆

By morning Viratesk lay under a cloying pall of grey-black smoke, every brick and tile as besmirched as the dazed rebels who wandered the streets or sat stooped in exhaustion. Frentis passed many huddling together, a few weeping from the strain of the night-long battle, most just leaning against each other, the eyes wide, blank holes in soot-covered faces.

"Seven hundred and eighty-two dead," Thirty-Four reported. "Four hundred wounded."

"How many of them?" Lekran asked, running a cloth over the blade of his axe. Although he was even more blackened than everyone present, the tribesman's axe gleamed with a polished sheen.

"We counted just over a hundred bodies," Thirty-Four replied. "Though, judging by the smell, many more perished in the sewers."

"Seven to one," Draker muttered, casting a wary glance at Frentis. "That's bad odds, brother."

"When were our odds ever good?" Frentis turned as Weaver approached, their only captive at his back, tightly bound by several chains. The Arisai was shaking his head, uttering a soft, wry laugh as the freed Varitai around him looked on with uniformly sorrowful expressions.

"It won't work," Weaver stated. "Not on him."

"The binding is too strong?" Frentis asked.

"His binding is less constricting than the Varitai. He is . . . wrong.

Twisted, in mind and body. Were we to remove his binding, we would be unleashing something terrible upon the world."

"Then let's wring what we can from him and have done," Lekran said, nodding at Thirty-Four.

"He'll tell you nothing," Weaver replied. "Any torment you visit on him will be just another amusement."

"Can you heal him?" Frentis asked. "Mend his twisted soul?"

Weaver glanced back at the Arisai, hands clasped together, his face betraying the first sign of fear Frentis had seen in him. "Perhaps," he said. "But the consequences . . ."

"Something comes back," Frentis said. "Every time you heal someone, they give something back."

Weaver nodded, turning to him with a tight smile. "If you wish me to try . . ."

"No." He moved towards the Arisai, drawing the dagger from his belt. The man's amusement deepened at Frentis's approach, his laugh rich with genuine mirth.

"She did say you would prove interesting," he said.

"Does she give you names?" Frentis asked him.

The Arisai shrugged. "Sometimes, those of us she bothers to recognise. She called me Dog, once. I quite like it."

"You know she sent you here to die?"

"Then I am pleased to have served her purpose." The man met Frentis's gaze with steady eyes, fearless, even proud, but still mostly just amused.

"What did they do to make you this way?" Frentis asked him, surprising himself with a sudden flare of pity. Weaver was right, this man had been born to a life that twisted him into something far from human.

The Arisai's grin turned into a mocking snicker. "Don't you know? Your time in the pits taught them so much. For generations they bred us, trained us, tried different bindings to make us the perfect killers. It never worked, our forebears were either too wild or too much like the Kuritai, deadly but dull, requiring constant supervision. My generation was no different, yet another failure. Ten thousand Arisai destined for execution, after they had bred us with suitable stock of course. Then came you, our saviour, a shining example of the advantages of cruelty, the discipline and cunning inherent in the soul of a true killer. When she sent us here she told us we would be meeting our father, and I must say, I do find it a privilege."

"So," Frentis mused, "there's at least nine thousand more of you?"

For a moment the Arisai lost his smile, frowning in consternation like a child fumbling for an answer to an awkward question. "Not perfected after all," Frentis observed, moving behind him, dagger poised at the base of his skull. "What do you know of the Ally?"

Dog brightened once more as the point of the blade touched his flesh, laughing with a wry shake of his head. "Only the promise she made us on his behalf the day she led us from the vaults; 'All your dreams will be made flesh.' We had been waiting so long, and had many dreams. Should you chance to see her again, father. Please tell her I—"

Frentis thrust the dagger in up to the hilt, Dog the Arisai arching his back and convulsing before slumping lifeless to the ground. "I'll tell her," Frentis assured him.

◆ ◆ ◆

Why?

The question comes to her without warning, causing her finger to slip yet again, another spot of blood spreading across the taut fabric. She regards the needle embedded in her finger with cold understanding; the flesh is like ice, devoid of pain. The needlework is poor, a child's fumbled attempts to mimic adult skill. It is tempting to blame the shell and its numbed digits, but this particular craft has always been beyond her. The memory is dim, as are all her recollections of childhood, but there was a woman once. A kindly woman, with a face of feline beauty, who could sew with amazing skill, her fabrics adorned with a clarity and art that could match the finest paintings. They would sit and sew together, the woman guiding her small hands, pulling her into a kiss when she did something right, merely laughing at her frequent mistakes. She is sure this memory is real, though for some reason her thoughts continually shy away from the woman's name, or her fate. Instead they always shift, becoming darker and she finds herself abed, whimpering as she stares at her bedroom door . . .

A squeal of ropes and gears draws her gaze to the balcony. I have an exalted visitor to greet, my love, *she tells him.* An Empress shouldn't neglect her duties.

Why? *The thought is implacable, irresistible in its demand.*

You know why, beloved, *she tells him.*

Images swirl and coalesce in her mind, another precious gift captured by his sight: flames erupting from the sewers of Viratesk, the Arisai fighting, killing and dying with all the fury she expected. One, ablaze from head to foot, whirls in a welter of flame, still killing and laughing even as the arrows slam home.

I know you have nine thousand more, *he tells her.* Where are they?

Her hands clutch the embroidery as delight surges through her, the wonderful resumption of their lost intimacy. This was how it had been during their journey, the joyful mingling of hate and love, every murder eroding the walls between them. She realises her heart is thumping, faster and faster like a trapped beast raging at its cage. Until now she had thought this shell incapable of all but the most rudimentary feeling, but he, *of course only* he, *can bring it to life.*

The gondola jerks to a halt outside the balcony and she glimpses her guest. She feels his alarm flare at the sight of her, causing her to wonder if jealousy might lead her to pitch this pretty thing from the top of the tower. However, a note from the song as the girl's gaze sweeps over Lieza tells her such suspicions are misplaced.

Leave her be! *he shouts in her mind.* Touch her and you'll never lay eyes on me again. I swear it.

She resists the impulse to wallow in his rage and allows her heart to calm, trying to colour her response with cool detachment. The sooner you come to me the greater the chance of her survival.

She winces a little, feeling the reforged connection between them strain as he masters his anger. When he returns his thoughts are dark with reluctant acceptance. The Arisai, *he presses.* Where are they?

I can tell you where they are not. *She finds she has to stifle a giggle.* New Kethia.

◆ ◆ ◆

"Idiots," Draker said, watching the Volarian column with a practised eye. "They ain't even scouting their flanks."

"Why would they?" Frentis asked. "They're expecting nothing more than a victory march when they reach Viratesk."

"Just over four thousand," Thirty-Four said, returning the spyglass to Frentis. "Only one battalion of Varitai and a scattering of Kuritai. The rest are a mix of Free Sword mercenaries and conscripts from New Kethia. By my calculation, the bulk of the military strength left in this province."

"Idiots," Draker repeated, shaking his head.

The country west of Viratesk was largely devoid of the heights and forests Frentis had always found so useful. However, Master Rensial's scouting along the coastal road to New Kethia had identified a broad depression in the farmland six miles to the west, too shallow to be called a valley but the southern rise sufficiently high to conceal the bulk of their army. The height of the crops was another advantage, tall enough to hide their archers, and dry enough to catch fire at the first lick of flame. The cavalry at the head of the Volarian column had evidently failed to take account of the mile-long strip of barren ground scorched into the rise and running parallel to the road, a hundred yards wide and the product of a morning spent in careful burning. The many farmhands in the army advised that such firebreaks were a common feature of Volarian agriculture and unlikely to draw undue attention from those who had never worked the land.

"Some are bound to make it through," Frentis told Illian and Draker. "If outnumbered, fall back and form a defensive circle." He met Illian's gaze, speaking with grave authority. "The issue will be decided on the flanks, so there is no need for excessive courage."

He saw her suppress a sullen grimace and force a nod. "Of course, brother."

He left them crouched amidst the tall corn-stalks and made his way to the lee of the rise where Master Rensial waited with their mounted contingent. The Volarians found little reason to educate slaves in riding but some knew horses from their previous lives, mostly Realm folk and a few Alpirans, enough to form a company of light cavalry some three hundred strong. Another thousand infantry were crouched a little farther back, mostly those lacking decent weapons, though some bore the swords and daggers taken from the fallen Arisai. The bulk of their infantry were with Lekran and Ivelda on the left flank, ready to charge in the Garisai's wake when the time came.

Frentis mounted a stallion captured in the hill country, well trained like most Volarian cavalry horses, but lacking the speed and aggression of an Order mount. Still, Master Rensial had been diligent in training both riders and horses so he was confident the animal wouldn't shy from the charge. He nudged his heels to the stallion's flanks and trotted to the crest of the rise. The Volarians would be sure to see him outlined on the skyline but it was of little matter now their lead company had drawn level with the end of the firebreak. Frentis drew his sword and raised it above his head, the archers in the cornfield standing at the signal, bows drawn. He could see a rider at the head of the column wheeling his horse about, waving frantically at the bugler, all too late.

Over four hundred arrows rose from the cornfield and arced down into the centre of the Volarian column, raising a tumult of shouted alarm and discordant bugling. Apart from the initial chaos, however, the effect of the volley was minimal, claiming barely a dozen soldiers before their officers managed to whip them into reasonable order. As usual, the Varitai were first to form ranks, three battalions assuming a defensive formation in the space of a single minute. Frentis was pleased to see they had been placed in the centre of the column, meaning the flanks would be held mostly by Free Swords and recently pressed conscripts. *Draker had it right,* he concluded. *These men are commanded by fools.*

The archers kept up their barrage without pause as the Volarian line took shape, continuing to loose as a chorus of bugles pealed out the signal for a general advance. Frentis had no need to issue further commands, the archers having been well drilled in what to do next. Even though the corn was tinder dry, Frentis had taken the precaution of liberally scattering oil-soaked bundles of kindling about the field, providing aiming points for the archers which their fire arrows soon found with creditable precision, birthing an instant conflagration. They had strict instructions to loose five arrows in quick succession then run for the firebreak, though some continued to let fly even as they retreated from the smoke-shrouded field. The inferno took hold almost immediately, a bright wall of flame stretching the length of the advancing line and birthing a thick curtain of black smoke that concealed all from view.

Frentis turned and nodded to Master Rensial then kicked his stallion into a gallop. They had burned a broad avenue through the corn on either side of the main firebreak, wide enough to accommodate a charge by a full company of cavalry quickly followed by a thousand infantry. Even so, the thickness of the smoke made for an unnerving ride, his horse voicing a whinny of protest at the proximity of the flames. Frentis kicked his flanks again, spurring him to a faster gallop and they drew clear of the smoke, finding himself confronted by a pair of startled Volarian cavalrymen. He rode between them, slashing left and right, hearing simultaneous shouts of pain before charging on.

All was confusion now, the smoke descending and lifting according to the whim of the wind. When it cleared he cut down any Volarians within reach, when it thickened he charged on, his only indication of the progress of the battle coming from the screams of pain and fury on all sides. He caught occasional glimpses of Master Rensial, killing with typical artistry, his horse seeming to dance at his slightest touch of the reins, confounding those unwise enough to challenge a man Frentis now knew to be the finest horse-borne warrior in the world.

The Volarians proved to be a mixed bag, some fleeing at the first sight of Frentis, others immediately rushing to confront him. As the smoke thickened once more he found himself assailed by a mounted Kuritai, apparently unconcerned by the diminished view, charging at him on a fine stallion two hands taller than his own. Frentis twisted in the saddle as the Kuritai closed, his sword sweeping down to cleave into the neck of Frentis's stallion. He leapt clear as the animal screamed and reared in a fountain of blood, landing nimbly on both feet and casting a throwing knife at the Kuritai. It struck home, sinking into the slave-elite's face just above the jaw, but failed to divert his charge.

Frentis rolled, trying to slash at the charging stallion's legs as it thundered by. But the Kuritai was too skilled a rider, angling the animal's course at the last moment to avoid the blade. Frentis threw another knife as the Kuritai wheeled for a second charge, the steel dart sinking into his horse's rump and causing it to rear. Frentis sprinted forward, leaping and slashing, the Order blade cleaving through the greave on the Kuritai's wrist. He tumbled from the saddle, rolling to his feet and whirling to face Frentis with sword levelled, blood still jetting from the stump of his severed hand. Frentis heard a familiar snarl behind him and sank to one knee, Slasher and Blacktooth leaping over to attack the Kuritai with well-honed precision, the bitch fixing her jaws on his legs whilst her mate tore at his throat.

He didn't wait to view the spectacle, running through the haze in search of further opponents. His ears were soon assailed by a great roaring followed by the multiple clang of clashing weapons, his ears leading him to the sight of his infantry tearing apart a battalion of Free Swords. They had evidently charged headlong into their line, given the way it had bowed and broken in the centre, hacking and stabbing with their axes and scythes, every face lit with a desperate fury.

The Free Swords tried to stand their ground for a time, bunched together in compliance with the shouted orders of their officers, many freed slaves falling to their short swords, but their line had been broken and, unlike those they fought, they still entertained notions of long lives and families. After another few moments' frenzied resistance they began to break, men turning and sprinting into the smoke, at first singly or in pairs, then a dozen at a time. One ran in Frentis's direction, skidding to a wide-eyed halt and landing on his backside, his sword apparently already dropped. Frentis paused to regard the man, taking in the terror in his quivering face, the unintelligible pleas spouting from his lips, and pointed sternly towards the west. The Free Sword gaped up at him for a second more then scrabbled to his feet, sprinting away, still begging for mercy.

"Form up!" Frentis called to the milling freed folk, some still stabbing away at the Volarian dead. "Gather weapons and form up!"

Through a judicious mix of shouts and jostling he managed to reimpose some order, those appointed as sergeants returning to their senses at the sight of him and forming their companies into an offensive line, many now armed with swords and cavalry lances.

"Keep at it until you clear the smoke," Frentis ordered, turning and striding towards the Volarian centre. The line held until they heard the sound of further combat, unquenched bloodlust raising a cheer from the freed folk as they broke into a spontaneous charge. Knowing they would be deaf to further orders, Frentis charged with them, the smoke parting to reveal a solid wall of Varitai, blank faces regarding them above levelled spears.

He leapt at the last moment, his sword sweeping aside an upraised spear, boots impacting on a Varitai's breastplate, propelling the man backwards. He landed clear of the Volarian line and turned, hacking down two Varitai in quick succession, his sword finding gaps in their armour with deadly accuracy. The freed folk were quick to spot the opportunity, piling into the gap in a dense mass of thrashing men and women. The useful panic that had gripped the Free Swords was absent here, however, the Varitai falling back in response to a strident bugle call to form another defensive formation twenty yards on. Frentis could see two figures in the centre of the shrinking circle of Varitai, a burly man with a bugle raised to his lips, a veteran sergeant judging by his armour, and a slighter figure with the plumed helm of a junior officer.

"Hold!" Frentis held up his sword as the freed folk gathered themselves for another charge. The rage had gripped them all now, every soot-streaked face alive with a desperate thirst for more blood, gore-covered weapons in every hand, trembling with anticipation.

"We can take them, brother!" a woman called out in hoarse Realm Tongue, dagger in one hand and short sword in the other, both red from tip to hilt. It took a moment for Frentis to recognise this panting, black-faced figure as Lissel, the former chandler from Rhansmill.

"You've done enough for today, mistress," he told her. *And we have losses to make good,* he added silently. "You'll find Sister Illian and Weaver on the rise, please fetch them here."

He moved around the near-perfect circle of Varitai, peering through the fading smoke to confirm the defeat of the Volarian left flank. Free Swords were running in all directions and the Garisai advancing in good order towards the Varitai, Ivelda and Lekran at their head. Frentis held up a hand to halt them in place, turning to quickly count the remaining Varitai. *Three hundred.* Double the number already in the army.

"Brother." Illian came to a halt at his side, crossbow in hand. He took in the sight of a bandage on her forehead, the wound just below the hairline and still leaking blood. "Kuritai," she said with a shrug.

He nodded, turning back to the Varitai. "Wait for my order." He strode closer to the circle of slave soldiers, gaze fixed on the two figures in their centre. The burly sergeant stood stock still and back straight, staring at Frentis, grizzled face showing a stern defiance he couldn't help but admire. The officer at his side was at most half the sergeant's age and considerably less defiant, eyes constantly roaming the surrounding freed folk, face pale with terror.

"You're alone," Frentis called to the burly man across the ranks of immobile Varitai. "Your officers are dead or running back to New Kethia. If you want to join them, give the order for these men to lay down their arms."

The sergeant's face twisted into a disgusted grimace and he spat on the ground, speaking but one word, laden with contempt, "Slave!"

Illian's crossbow bolt smacked into the sergeant's breastplate just left of the sternum. At such close range it had little difficulty penetrating armour and bone to find the heart.

"And you, Honoured Citizen?" Frentis called to the young officer, now gaping at the fallen sergeant, the tears streaming from his eyes making him appear no more than a child lost amidst a field of dangerous strangers. After a moment he mastered himself sufficiently to retrieve the bugle from the sergeant's body. The call he sounded was faltering and thin, but evidently sufficiently clear. As one the Varitai laid down their weapons and stood in ranks, every face expressing no more emotion than a stone.

"Can you heal so many?" Frentis asked Weaver as the healer appeared with his freed Varitai.

Weaver gave a soft laugh, surveying the neat ranks of slave soldiers with his now-habitual sad smile. "You talk as if I have a choice, brother."

◆　◆　◆

New Kethia burned. Tall columns of smoke rose from its close-packed streets, most of the fires seemingly concentrated around the docks where a number of ships could be seen drawing away from the harbour. They were all low in the water, one so heavily laden it capsized on reaching the harbour mouth, tiny antlike figures scuttling over its hull as it rolled in the waves. To the south a long line of people were streaming from the city gates, Frentis's spyglass confirming the vast majority as grey-clads, stooped and burdened with various household items, dragging wailing children in their wake, confusion and fear on every face.

"They might've waited till we got here," Draker grumbled.

"One less battle to fight," Frentis said. They had encamped amidst a large collection of ruins on a low plateau just under a mile east of the city, Thirty-Four naming the place as the site of Old Kethia, destroyed centuries before in the Forging Age. The former slave returned from his reconnaissance in late afternoon, he and Master Rensial having been sent ahead in the morning.

"It seems news of our victory had a dramatic effect," Thirty-Four reported. "The governor hatched a plan to execute every slave rather than allow them to fall into our hands. Given that the city's slaves outnumber the free population by a factor of two to one, this proved an unwise course of action. The riots have been raging for three days, thousands have died, more have fled."

"The slaves hold the city?" Frentis asked.

"Only a quarter." Thirty-Four pointed to a district that appeared even more shrouded in smoke than the others. "Lacking arms, their losses were heavy. We picked our way through to contact their leaders." He turned to Frentis with a smile. "It seems they have heard much about the Red Brother, and are eager for his arrival."

"One less battle," Draker muttered, getting to his feet.

◆ ◆ ◆

"Why was this done?"

The body hung from a pole in New Kethia's main square, the feet reduced to blackened stumps, stomach torn out, and the face frozen in an agonised scream. Despite all the mutilation visited upon the corpse Frentis could still recognise the features. *I'll suffer every torment for a thousand years,* Varek had said. From the state of him Frentis doubted he had lasted more than an hour.

New Kethia's Deputy Treasurer, a pinch-faced black-clad who seemed equal parts baffled and terrorised by his continued survival, had to cough several times before finding the voice to speak. "The Empress's orders," he said, the tone wavering despite his efforts to master it. "They arrived before he did."

Didn't like what he said to me, Frentis decided, feeling an odd sense of disappointment. Varek had seemed so determined, it would have been interesting to see how far his quest for vengeance would have taken him. But he was one of just several thousand corpses littering this city, bloating in the sun and birthing clouds of flies that swarmed amidst the burgeoning stench. *Thousands of stories snuffed out before the ending.*

It had taken a day and a night of hard fighting to win the city, Frentis leading the infantry in a slow but inexorable advance towards the docks whilst Lekran and Ivelda took charge of the surviving rebels. They had been obliged to fight from street to street, their opponents a mix of Free Swords and townsmen, capable of furious resistance now their homes faced destruction. But they were too few and too badly organised to prevail, their barricades ramshackle constructions crafted by hands unused to work. Frentis soon evolved a tactic of seizing the surrounding rooftops and assailing the defenders from above, forcing them back whilst the barricades were torn down. They had made a final stand of sorts at the docks, a few hundred sheltered behind stacked barrels and crates, refusing all calls for surrender. It was Weaver's freed Varitai who finished it, simply pushing the barrels over and storming in to club down the defenders.

What was left of the governor had been roped to the base of the pole; unlike Varek his face was truly unrecognisable. The man had been a general before entering politics, choosing to meet his end on the steps of the governor's mansion with a few loyal guards. Unfortunately his heroics hadn't secured him a speedy end, the great mob of slaves sweeping aside all resistance as they stormed the mansion in the final attack, but possessing enough presence of mind to ensure the governor was taken alive. Having witnessed the horrors wrought by the governor's attempts to cull the slave population Frentis felt no inclination to interfere in his protracted, and inventive, punishment.

"The Empress is a monster," the Deputy Treasurer added, a faint, hopeful ingratiation in his tone.

"She is Volarian," Frentis replied. "As the only Imperial official left in this city, I require you to act as liaison to the surviving free populace. You will find them quartered under guard at the docks. Inform them that, as free subjects of the Unified Realm, they are afforded the protection of the Crown and I personally guarantee the safety of all those innocent of any part in the atrocities committed here. However, all property formerly owned is forfeit to the Crown as spoils of war. By the Queen's Word slavery is now outlawed in this province and any found to be engaged in it subject to summary execution."

He walked away as Draker led the black-clad towards the docks. "Don't sniffle now, there's a good fellow. Don't you know how lucky you are to greet a new dawn in the Greater Unified Realm?"

Picking his way through the streets, all strewn with bodies and the myriad wreckage of a shattered city, Frentis found himself recalling a dream, or what he now understood to be the beginning of his connection with a soul the Deputy Treasurer thought monstrous. *I would have been terrible,* she had said as they gazed on a shoreline awash in corpses. *But terrible as fate would make me, I am not him.*

He paused at the sight of a mother and child, crumpled in death outside a baker's shop. The little girl's eyes were open, her head lying close to her mother's, the mouth slightly agape as if frozen in some unheard final question. Seeing the wounds on the mother's arms, earned no doubt as she tried to shield the girl from the frenzy of blades that killed them, he couldn't suppress the notion that he and the Empress were conspiring to make that sea of death a reality.

"Brother?" It was Illian, regarding him with an expression that bordered on amazement. He felt the dampness on his cheeks and quickly wiped the tears away.

"What is it, sister?"

"The Garisai found a few hundred grey-clads hiding in the vaults beneath the merchants' quarter. The city slaves are clamouring to get at them. It could turn ugly." She forced an uncertain smile, eyes still lingering on his. Frentis's gaze went to the cut on her forehead. Thirty-Four had done a typically precise job of stitching it closed but the scar would be deep, and long. "Stopped itching, at least," she said, her fingers going to the wound.

No uncertainty in her, he surmised. *All this death and she remains undaunted. She was right, the Order is the best place for her.*

"I'll be there directly," he said. "Tell Draker to form the free folk into a working party to clear these bodies. They'll be paid in bread, we shouldn't expect them to work for nothing."

CHAPTER EIGHT

Lyrna

They soon began calling it the Mud March, a name Lyrna somehow knew would persist into the history of this campaign, should there be any scholars left to write it. The rain started the day they began the inland march and didn't let up for the following two weeks, turning every track into soft, clinging mud, trapping feet, hooves and cart-wheels until the army ground to a halt having covered less than a hundred miles.

"The price, Highness," Aspect Caenis explained at the council of captains. "The crafting of such a storm created a great imbalance in the elements."

"How long will it last?" Lyrna asked.

"Until the balance is restored. A day, or a month. There is no way to tell."

"Is there none in your Order who can assist us?"

He gave a helpless shrug. "The girl from the Reaches was the only soul I ever met who held such a gift."

Lyrna ignored the pointed implication in his words, knowing he still chafed over her refusal to compel the Gifted from the Reaches to join his Order. In some ways she was finding Aspect Caenis just as unyielding as the unmourned Tendris.

"We need a road, Highness," Count Marven insisted. "Volarian roads are famously well-made, and immune to the elements." His finger tracked across the map to a line twenty miles north. "This one serves the northern ports. It's a four-day diversion from our intended line of march but it should save us weeks of slogging through mud."

Although she disliked the notion of abandoning the direct approach to Volar, Lyrna could see no alternative. She was about to confirm the order when a rarely heard voice spoke up.

"That would be a mistake, Highness."

Lord Al Hestian stood near the rear of the tent, a gap on either side of him as none of her captains seemed to relish proximity to the man now referred to as the Traitor Rose. She had tended to exclude him from these meetings but the impressive performance of his men during what had quickly been dubbed the Battle of the Beacon, and the recent loss of so many captains, provoked her to a change of heart. She had spared him for a reason, after all.

"How so, my lord?" she asked, seeing Count Marven stiffen. Of all her captains, he seemed to harbour the greatest enmity towards Al Hestian, something she assumed had been born of their time in the desert war.

"The obvious line of march should always be avoided," Al Hestian said. "The road will be patrolled, policed. Word of our position will be conveyed to Volar within days. If we are to send forces north, they should only be diversionary."

"Whilst we continue to wallow in mud," Count Marven said.

"No rain can last forever, Dark-born or no. And if we can't march through it, neither can the enemy."

"Time is the true enemy," Lyrna said. "Every day of inactivity allows the Empress leisure to gather forces at Volar." She straightened and nodded at Count Marven. "Battle Lord, issue orders to change the army's line of march come the morning. My lords, to your duties."

◆ ◆ ◆

Alornis was drawing again when she returned to her tent, the charcoal stub moving with feverish industry across the parchment as she hunched over her easel. During the day she would tinker with the cart-mounted ballista, all the time barely saying a word, but at night she would draw. It was only when she worked that her face took on some animation, tense with concentration and eyes lit with memory, though, judging by the nature of her drawings, Lyrna divined they were memories best left alone. Burning ships, burning men, sailors screaming as they flailed in a storm-tossed sea. Page after page of expertly rendered horror produced in a nightly ritual of self-flagellation.

"Did she eat something, at least?" Lyrna asked Murel, shrugging off her rain-soaked cloak.

"A little porridge only, Highness. Though Davoka had to practically force it on her."

She went and sat by Alornis for a time, the Lady Artificer acknowledging her presence with a barely perceptible nod, her charcoal continuing to move without interruption. Lyrna took some heart from the fact that this sketch differed from the usual finely crafted carnage, a portrait of some kind. Alornis set out the basic shape of the face with a few expertly placed lines then began to detail the eyes, dark eyes, narrowed in judgement and reproach, eyes she knew well.

"Your brother loves you," she told Alornis, reaching out to still her hand, feeling it tremble.

Alornis didn't look at her, eyes still fixed on the picture. "It's my father," she whispered. "They had the same eyes. He loved me too. Perhaps, if the Faith has it right, he still sees me. It could be that he loves me more now, for we are the same are we not? He too once killed thousands by fire. Sometimes he would dream of it, when he got older and the sickness came, thrashing in his bed and calling out for forgiveness."

Lyrna resisted the impulse to shake her, slap her, try to force a return of the bright, sweet girl she had met in Alltor. But looking into her confused eyes she knew that girl had gone, consumed by fire along with so many others. "Take your sleeping draught, my lady," she said instead, gently but firmly tugging the charcoal from her fingers. "Hard marching tomorrow, you need your sleep."

◆　◆　◆

They made the road in three days, the rain slackening a little by the third day, though the going was scarcely any better to the north. Brother Kehlan reported numerous cases of men falling out on the march due to a condition known as "guardsman's foot," an affliction brought on by constant immersion in water whereby the skin became like a sponge. Soon almost every wagon was laden with grey-faced soldiers, their feet bound in bandages wrapped in canvas to keep the rain off. So it was with considerable relief that they first set foot on the road, a truly remarkable example of human construction that shamed the dirt tracks typical in the Realm. *Malcius, if you had seen this,* Lyrna thought, noting the gentle curve to the road's surface that allowed the rain to flow off to the sides. *You would have scraped the treasury clean to cover the Realm in such wonders.*

"Should do thirty miles or more a day on this," Count Marven said with a satisfied grin, stamping a boot to the brick surface. "More when the rain lifts."

"Be sure to scout all approaches," Lyrna said. She was reluctant to tell her Battle Lord his business but Al Hestian's counsel had instilled a lingering caution. They were certain to meet the enemy somewhere along this road; the only question was in what strength.

"Of course, Highness."

The rain finally began to abate three days later, revealing a pleasing landscape of rolling hills and broad valleys, lush with grass and little sign of habitation save the occasional small villa, all of which proved empty of occupants.

"All livestock slaughtered and crops burnt," Brother Sollis reported two days later. He had led his brothers on a wide-ranging reconnaissance in force, finding no sign of the enemy but ample evidence their approach had been detected. "All wells spoiled with carcasses. A few bodies here and there, mostly old people, slaves by the look of them."

"Was there ever a more vile race than this?" Lord Adal said, shaking his head. He had taken the North Guard south on a similar mission, returning with equally grim tidings.

"So," Lyrna said, "we have no forage."

"Our existing supplies should last us to Volar, Highness," Brother Hollun advised. "Where no doubt we will find more, once our . . . business is concluded."

"If I might enquire, Highness," Lord Nortah said, "as to the exact nature of our business in Volar."

Lyrna met his gaze, finding his usual willingness to return the scrutiny in full measure. "We will exact justice for the wrongs visited upon the Realm," she said. "And ensure they will not be repeated."

"Yes, as you have stated before. However, I should like to know how this justice will be administered. Do you intend to hold trials, perhaps?"

"I don't recall any trials at Alltor," Lord Antesh said, regarding the Lord Marshal with a harsh glower. "And I know there were none at Varinshold." He rarely spoke at council and kept to his own troops when on the march. The Cumbraelins had taken on a uniformly grim demeanour since the loss of Lady Reva, along with her aged guard commander and so many of their countrymen. Whenever she toured their ranks Lyrna found herself greeted with curt nods or barely concealed resentment; she had sent their Blessed Lady to her death, and they knew it. However, any anger they might have felt towards their queen was greatly outshone by their burning hatred for the Volarians, birthed at Alltor and a thousand other nameless atrocities, now stoked to greater heights by a feral hunger for retribution. Lady Reva had been their link to the Father's love and guidance, surely He would bless all efforts to avenge her passing.

"There were no trials at Alltor," Lord Nortah returned, "because the Volarians are a disgusting, pestilent race raised in cruelty and murder. We, on the other hand, imagine ourselves a people of reason and compassion, or are our virtues to be cast aside now?"

"Courage and fortitude are equal virtues," Baron Banders pointed out. "Our people look to us to secure their future. It won't be done with a soft heart."

"I have journeyed the length of the Reaches and the Realm," Nortah said. "Taking more lives in the space of a few months than I did in all my years in the Order. I have led my regiment through battle, fire and hardship because I thought it just and right . . . and my wife told me it was necessary. But I do not wish to look into her eyes when she beholds a man who took part in wholesale murder."

He turned to Aspect Caenis, whose eyes remained fixed on the map, unwilling to meet his brother's gaze. "And you, brother? Are you content for the Faith to be stained with innocent blood?"

The Aspect didn't reply immediately, lowering his head for a moment's silent contemplation. When he finally opened his eyes and spoke, his tone was regretful but also certain. "The Empress and her empire are merely tools for a greater enemy. We all know this, though often we dare not speak of it. Knowing the nature of this enemy, I see the only path to his defeat in employing all measures at our disposal. If that makes us murderers, then I accept the name and the guilt. For if we fail, brother, there will be no wife for you to return to."

"I cannot believe the path to victory lies in staining our souls so black we become indistinguishable from those we fight." Nortah looked to Brother Sollis, voice strained now. "Master? Surely you see the Faith compels us to a more reasoned course. The Order has always sought to defend the defenceless."

"And to preserve the Faithful," Sollis replied, his tone no less certain than the Aspect's. "Should we fail here, the whole world may fall to ruin. The Faith gave its support to the queen's course in full knowledge of the import of this mission. We cannot afford virtue now, brother."

"And I," Antesh grated, face flushing red, "did not come to these shores to leave the greatest soul in Cumbraelin history unavenged."

"Vengeance is not justice!" Nortah's fists thumped the table as he leaned forward. "And if Lord Vaelin were here . . ."

"He is not," Lyrna stated, her voice soft but implacable. "I am here. And I am your queen, my lord."

She watched the Lord Marshal master himself, knowing he was fighting to keep unwise words from his lips. *Of all of us,* she thought, *he stands immune from the lure of vengeance.* The realisation stirred a flare of envy, a yearning for a part of her lost somewhere amongst the flames.

"You are a good man, Lord Nortah," she told him. "The Realm is enriched by your service. And so I give you my word as your queen that this army will do all it can to spare innocent blood. But, be assured that when we reach Volar I will see it destroyed down to the last fragment of stone and the earth salted so that nothing grows amidst the ruins. If you have no stomach for this course, you are free to resign your command and depart without disfavour."

Lord Nortah lowered his head, teeth gritted as he hissed a sigh. "No innocent blood," he said, head still lowered. "You promise me?"

Lord Iltis bridled with a growl, "The Queen's Word is given, and not for you to question, my lord."

Nortah's head came up, his eyes blazing at the Lord Protector for a second before casting his gaze around the other captains. Lyrna wondered if he thought himself the only sane man in an army of maddened souls. As his gaze settled on her, he spoke again, his voice the flat, precise promise of a very dangerous man, "Your word may not be for me to question, Highness, but I will hold you to it nonetheless."

◆　◆　◆

Another week of marching took them from the pleasing hill country and into a broad dusty plain, its only feature of interest a long river stretching away east in a winding course roughly parallel to the road. "At least we won't be taken unawares," Count Marven commented, peering at the barren vista. "You couldn't hide a single horse out here."

The following day saw a dim, jagged shape appear on the haze-covered horizon, resolving into a strange sprawling building adorned with multiple tall spires. It sat in a wide bend in the river, the size of a small town, but absent any dwellings. Instead it consisted of a series of pyramidal structures arranged in a spiral, all topped with towers of ascending height, the tallest rising to at least two hundred feet.

"A fortress?" Benten wondered as they closed to within a half mile of the building.

"No defensive walls," Iltis said. "And no one to hold them if there were."

There was no sign of any response to their approach, the varied structures devoid of light and movement. Lyrna turned at the sound of a galloping horse, finding Wisdom reining in at her side. Lyrna had left Arrow back in the Realm, unwilling to subject her to the possibly deadly discomforts of the ocean crossing, and discovered her new mount wandering near the dunes when they landed. It was a handsome stallion with a coat of pure black, so finely bred Lyrna wondered if it hadn't carried the Empress to the shore the day she crafted her storm. She named him Jet in honour of his colouring.

"Great Queen," Wisdom said, a habitual greeting that always left Lyrna wondering if she wasn't being mocked. "Impressive isn't it?" the Eorhil elder went on, gesturing at the building.

"Indeed," Lyrna agreed. "I would be more impressed if I knew what it was."

"Navarek Av Devos, which means Portal of the Gods in your tongue. The last great temple of the Volarian gods. The only one to survive the Great Cleansing, I suspect because of its size and remoteness."

Lord Adal's North Guard rode ahead to inspect the temple, finding it deserted but for a colony of nesting vultures. At Marven's suggestion Lyrna agreed the army would camp there for the night; the temple lacked fortifications but still had roofs aplenty and she knew many of her soldiers would appreciate a night under cover of stone rather than flimsy canvas. There was room enough for about half the army, Marven posting the remainder in a wide defensive arc anchored on the river. The temple extended up to and beyond the riverbank where a long row of monstrous statues lowered their heads to the waters. They were mostly impossible combinations of various beasts, a tiger with the head of a lizard, a great eagle with a long scaly tail. There were also two human figures amongst them, improbably muscled warriors kneeling to lower a hand to the swift-flowing current.

"Gods of some kind?" Lyrna asked Wisdom as they toured the city. She couldn't help a certain fascination in the sheer eccentricity of the place; to construct such a vast building with no practical purpose whatsoever was both baffling and delightful, as well as providing an appreciation of the long history of the people she had come to fight. *They were not always as they are now.*

"The fifty guardians of the gods," Wisdom replied. "Crafted from all the beasts of the earth to fight an eternal battle against the Dermos, denizens of the great fire pit beneath the earth, the eternal enemies of all humanity."

Lyrna's gaze was drawn to the largest of the statues, a broad-backed ape of some kind, with a long serrated tail and arms as thick as tree-trunks.

Murel's mouth twitched in suppressed laughter as she switched her gaze between Iltis and the statue. "How did they manage to capture your image long before you were born, my lord?"

She smiled sweetly at his baleful glower, pressing a fond kiss to his cheek before dancing away.

"That's Jarvek," Wisdom said. "Long held to be the greatest of the guardians, until the shadow folk tempted him into all-consuming lust for a human queen. He bore her away to his lair far beneath the earth but, before he could inflict his vile desires upon her, she was rescued by her sister, Livella, the warrior maiden who carried a spear blessed by the gods." Wisdom pointed to another statue nearby, a tall female figure on a plinth, standing straight and proud with spear in hand. The sight of her provoked a fresh burst of laughter from Murel.

"First his lordship, now you, my lady," she said, pointing at Davoka. "This place is truly uncanny."

Davoka merely gave a faint grin, casting a critical eye over the statue's improbably generous proportions. "A woman made like her would spend her days falling over."

"Statues of guardians, statues of heroes from myth," Lyrna said. "Where are the gods?"

"You will not find them here," Wisdom replied. "The gods were considered so divine that for a human to attempt to capture their image was considered blasphemy. Even their names were known only to a small, select priesthood. Those wishing to seek the aid of the gods would petition the priests who would in turn petition the requisite god. For a price, naturally."

Iltis and Benten drew their swords at a sudden shout from the centre of the temple, soon transforming into a scream that echoed from the granite walls. Lyrna shrugged off Iltis's objections and went to investigate, making her way to the circular space in the centre of the temple where she found Aspect Caenis crouched over Brother Lucin. The elderly Gifted lay on his back, face contorted in a grimace of pain and horror, foam frothing on his lips.

"He had a yen to see this place before its abandonment," the Aspect explained, holding the brother down as he convulsed.

"An unfortunate decision," Wisdom commented, pointing at a squat stone plinth nearby. "The gods were generous, but also thirsty."

The plinth was three feet tall, narrow and rectangular with a semicircle carved into its upper edge. Positioned at its base was a bowl-shaped indentation in the stone floor from which numerous channels led off towards the surrounding pyramidal structures.

Brother Lucin's convulsions subsided, the old man's eyes fluttering open, wide with shock at whatever they had witnessed.

Blood, Lyrna thought, eyeing the plinth. It had been scrubbed clean by centuries of wind and rain, but she knew it had once been red. *Always blood with these people. Once spilled to sate the conjurings of their own imagination. Now drunk to banish the spectre of death. Killing their gods didn't change them.*

◆ ◆ ◆

She hadn't dreamt since the Battle of the Teeth, spending every night in a deep, untroubled slumber. She would have liked to imagine it the sleep of a just and contented soul, but knew it had more to do with simple exhaustion, each day being so full. So it took some time to realise that her bare feet were not really treading on the temple's stone floor, taking her towards the plinth with a slow but steady stride. It was red now, as it had been when this place commanded the faith of so many deluded souls, slick with blood from top to bottom, the bowl-shaped indentation brimming with it, the channels taking the offering to the silent houses of the gods.

A woman of dreadful appearance stood next to the plinth, knife in hand. She wore a besmirched blue dress, the bodice and skirt stained to blackness, though Lyrna could see it had once been a fine garment, worthy of a princess in fact. But it was the woman's face that commanded her attention, raw and freshly burnt, faint tendrils of smoke still rising from the charred flesh.

"I have been waiting," the burnt woman said, fixing Lyrna with a fierce gaze, her tone full of admonishment.

"For what?" Lyrna asked in mystification.

"You of course." The woman beckoned impatiently at something in the shadows and a young man stepped into the light, short of stature but possessed of delicate good looks. "Your worshippers are keen to make offering."

Lyrna watched the young man kneel at the plinth, his gaze locked on hers, face expressionless. "I kept my promise," Lyrna told him, unable to keep the tremble from her voice. "I found your mother. She travels with my army, a sister of the Seventh Order, come to win justice for her son."

Fermin smiled, his lips widening to an impossible extreme, revealing long rows of triangular teeth, the teeth of a shark.

The burnt woman's knife flashed and Fermin's throat gaped open, blood gushing forth in a torrent, cascading down the sides of the plinth to fill the bowl. The burnt woman shoved the body aside and beckoned again, another figure coming forward. He was taller, well-built, his scarred face telling of a hard life, though his smile was the same one that came to his lips when the ballista bolt speared him through the back. It was still there, the steel head protruding from his chest, scraping over stone as he knelt.

"You had a choice." Lyrna knew the words a lie even as they spilled from her lips. Harvin, however, seemed to find her dishonesty amusing, for he laughed as the knife flashed again.

"I didn't do this," she insisted as the burnt woman pushed the body away and beckoned again. "They served me willingly."

"As they should," the burnt woman said. "Mortals live only to serve their gods."

Furelah came next, bowing to Lyrna with a dagger in each hand, her face and hair slick with seawater, eye sockets empty, the surrounding flesh partly eaten. Just before the knife opened her throat a small crab crawled from the black circle of her eye, its pincers snipping at Lyrna as if in accusation.

She tore her gaze away from the spectacle, but found no relief. The temple was crowded now, a long line of people, a few she knew, most she didn't. The Meldenean archer who had tumbled from the rigging at the Teeth, a Seordah woman who had fallen at Varinshold, and so many others. Eorhil, Nilsaelins, Cumbraelins, like Furelah, all dripping brine, their flesh partly claimed by the sea . . .

"I HAD NO CHOICE!" she railed at the burnt woman, falling silent at the sight of the figure now kneeling at the plinth.

"Choice?" Malcius asked. His head was cocked at an obscene angle, though his face was kind, his smile rich in affection and sympathy. "Choice is not the province of those who presume to rule," he told her. "The world is yours to make, my sister. As I always knew it would be. Don't you think it would have been kinder to kill me sooner, before I took the throne? Didn't it ever occur to you? A small drip of poison in my wine cup? It would have been such an easy thing."

"No," she said in a whisper. "You were my brother . . . I once did a terrible thing for you."

"You set me free to preside over the destruction of my Realm, the murder of my wife and children." He raised his arms as the burnt woman stepped closer. The knife didn't flash this time, instead she pressed it to his flesh with delicate, even loving tenderness, her other hand cradling his head to her breast.

"Do not turn away now, Lyrna," Malcius said as the blade traced across his throat. "For the gods are always thirsty . . ."

◆　◆　◆

She came awake at Murel's gentle prodding, the lady starting visibly at Lyrna's wide-eyed stare. "The Battle Lord sends word, Highness," she said. "A Volarian host approaches from the east."

She found Count Marven at the temple steps, the plain beyond him busy with soldiers forming ranks and riders galloping to their companies, a thick pall of dust rising to shroud the morning sun. "Brother Sollis estimates their number at sixty thousand, Highness," the Battle Lord reported. "Almost all Free Swords, which is unusual. They approach in good order though."

Sixty thousand. Little over half our number. The Empress makes a desperate gamble to stem our advance, perhaps? "Take no risks, my lord," she told Marven. "We cannot afford significant loss."

"Battle is always a risk, Highness. But I'm confident this matter will be settled come noon." He bowed and went to his horse, galloping off and soon lost in the morass of men and dust.

Lyrna looked up at the tallest tower in the temple. She was tempted to spare herself the sight of the battle, the dream having dispelled any desire to witness more bloodshed, but it seemed cowardly to turn her sight from the army now. "My lady, see if you can find a spyglass," she told Murel, making for the tower.

Ascending the tower proved a trying business, her legs aching with the effort as she forced herself up the narrow steps without slacking the pace, Iltis and Benten huffing along in her wake. It was hard not to be distracted by the tower's internal decoration. Every surface, including the steps beneath her feet, was adorned with some ancient Volarian script, the symbols at the lower levels carved with a delicate precision and elegance that faded the higher she climbed, so that by the time she reached the top the symbols were a confusion of haphazard etchings, seemingly carved by some random feverish hand. She made a note to ask Wisdom as to the meaning of it all when time allowed.

The top of the tower consisted of a crenellated spike ascending from a flat granite platform a dozen feet in diameter. Like the steps the surface of the platform was adorned with more writing, so wildly confused she knew she looked upon the work of a maddened soul. The platform held no balustrade or shelter of any kind, a hard, cutting wind whipping Lyrna's hair about as she stepped free of the staircase. Benten ventured forward to peer over the unguarded edge before making a hasty, slightly pale-faced retreat. "Best stay close to the centre, Highness," he advised.

Lyrna looked to the east, seeing two great walls of dust edging towards each other across the plain. The pall lifted sometimes to reveal the marching regiments and provide some clue as to Marven's dispositions. He had placed a solid line of Realm Guard on his left, close to the river, which would prevent any flanking move in that direction. The centre was held by a mix of Nilsaelin and Realm Guard infantry whilst the bulk of the cavalry moved in parallel to their line on the right flank. Behind the main body were four more regiments of infantry and the Renfaelin knights, though only two-thirds were horsed, the remainder obliged to suffer the indignity of walking to battle.

"Quite a sight, Highness," Iltis said with a rare grin.

She had seen her fill of battle, but as only a participant, and seeing one unfold at such remove provoked a strange sense of guilt, as if she were a spectator at some bloody entertainment. "Indeed, my lord," she replied, forcing a smile. "Quite a sight."

Murel appeared at Lyrna's side, sagging and out of breath. "With Brother Hollun's compliments, Highness," she gasped, holding out a spyglass. Lyrna took it, extending it to full length to train the lens on the Volarian host. It took several moments before the dust faded sufficiently for her to make them out, finding their ranks were arranged in neat order, the Free Sword battalions marching in a steady rhythm. Like Marven, their commander had seen the wisdom of anchoring the left flank on the river, with most of the cavalry on the right. However, she could tell their line was stretched thin, the infantry moving in ranks only two men deep so as to form a front wide enough to match that of her army. She raised the spyglass, the dust shifting enough to allow a view of their rear.

"No reserve," she murmured. *Does she seek to bleed us? Spend the lives of an entire army to reduce our numbers?* Even for a deranged mind it seemed a facile strategy. *Why not gather enough force to meet us in equal numbers farther down the road?*

Marven halted the army three hundred yards short of the Volarians, Cumbraelin archers moving forward to form three dense ranks in front of the line. The storm had left her with only a third of the number that had sailed at the Blessed Lady's behest. However, the arrow-riddled corpses she had seen at Alltor had provided ample evidence of what even a small number of skilled longbowmen could do, and she had over three thousand. Added to the archers were the twelve cart-borne ballistae now being wheeled forward. Lyrna checked each one with the spyglass to ensure Alornis had not somehow contrived to escape Davoka's care, breathing a soft sigh of relief at her absence. She had given the Lonak woman stern instructions to bind the Lady Artificer hand and foot should she try to join the battle and hoped it hadn't proved necessary.

A ripple went through the loose ranks of the archers as the Volarian line came to within two hundred paces, the spyglass picking out men standing with bows drawn and raised high, each with a thicket of arrows thrust into the earth around his feet. They loosed as one, the arrow storm thick enough for her to discern the flight of the shafts, a dark arching cloud forming between the archers and the Volarians. Their line seeming to shimmer under the weight of the assault, the centre taking the brunt of the punishment.

The ballistae were soon adding to the barrage, at least twenty men falling to the first volley, the ranks of the central battalions thinning with every step. Lyrna watched as a battalion was decimated, trailing a dozen or more dead and wounded every ten yards, until it inevitably began to slow, marching men faltering as their comrades died around them. She watched an officer wheeling his horse about at their rear, waving his sword and shouting unheard exhortations until a ballista bolt punched through his breastplate with enough force to carry him clear of the saddle. The battalion slowed further, halted, then broke, men dropping weapons and turning to flee, bowed low under the unending deadly rain.

Lyrna couldn't hear the shout that must have erupted from the Cumbraelins then, but knew it would be a savage expression of vengeance barely satisfied. They surged forward in an unbidden charge, discarding bows to draw swords and axes, pelting towards the gap in the Volarian line. Not a man to miss an opportunity, Marven gave the signal for an immediate advance, the entire Realm Guard moving forward at the run, the cavalry on the right spurring to an immediate charge. Lyrna saw the Cumbraelin assault strike home before the dust grew too thick to see more. She had a glimpse of the Volarian centre fragmenting under the fury of their onslaught but soon the entire field became a mass of roiling dust and the vague, flickering shadows of men in combat.

"Well," Iltis commented. "That was a piss-poor show."

"Highness." Lyrna turned at Murel's soft but insistent call, seeing her point to something to the north, another dust cloud on the far bank of the river. Lyrna trained the spyglass on the base of the cloud, discerning a mass of horsemen moving at the gallop.

"Cavalry," she murmured, watching the horsemen come closer, noting their armour was red instead of the usual Volarian black. Also it was a sizeable force, over five thousand by her reckoning. *The Empress sends her Arisai,* she mused, recalling Brother Frentis's description from one of his dream visions. *Why not send them with her army?*

"The river's too deep to ford for miles around," Benten said. "Even if they have boats, the battle will be over before they can make a crossing. The archers will cut them to pieces."

Lyrna felt a certain unease build in her breast as the red-armoured horsemen came closer, their course becoming more clear as they neared. She had expected an attempt on the army's flank, presuming they had some means to cross the river, but instead the horsemen were riding directly towards the temple, towards her.

"How many guards did Count Marven leave us?" she asked Iltis.

"Two regiments, Highness. The Twelfth and the Queen's Daggers."

Lyrna moved closer to the platform's edging, looking down at the temple below. Lord Nortah had clearly spotted the horsemen and was arranging his own company of archers at the riverbank. As if sensing her scrutiny he looked up, gesturing at the onrushing cavalry with a baffled shrug. *Why would they charge just to mill about on the other side of the river? The river . . .*

She trained the spyglass on the fast-rushing current, seeing only churning water, grey with silt. It was when she lowered the spyglass that she noticed something odd about the waters, how the current seemed marginally faster as it neared the temple, the waters slightly paler in colour. "There's something under the water," she whispered, knowing it was far too late.

The lead company of horsemen galloped towards the far bank and plunged into the river without pause, their horses sinking no more than two feet into the water, churning it an instant white as they continued their charge. Before Iltis grabbed her hand to drag her to the stairwell she had a glimpse of one of the red-armoured men, a blazing smile on his face as he neared the southern bank, laughing at the meagre volley from Lord Nortah's archers.

◆ ◆ ◆

Davoka waited at the bottom of the steps, face grim and spear already bloodied. Alornis was at her side, staring in white-faced immobility at the carnage unfolding in the temple. The noise was near deafening, colliding metal mixed with the screams of the dying, the roaring challenge of those still fighting and the laughter of the men who had come to kill her.

On emerging from the stairwell, Lyrna glimpsed one of the Queen's Daggers, a hulking fellow heaving an axe, shouting in rage with every blow as his red-armoured opponent danced aside and slashed repeated and precise cuts into his face. Beyond them the temple was a tumult of whirling combat and steel, Lord Nortah just visible amidst the fury, hacking down an Arisai and dragging one of the Daggers to his feet, voice raised as he attempted to assemble a defensive formation. Despite his skill, Lyrna could see his survival owed much to Snowdance, the war-cat a blur of claws and teeth as she took down one enemy after another, apparently numb to the wounds they slashed into her sides.

"We must . . ." she began, starting forward.

"NO!" The Lord Protector's considerable fist closed over her arm, tearing Lord Nortah from sight as she was dragged away.

"Lord Nortah!" she protested, trying to wrestle free.

"Will die here defending you, Highness." Iltis pushed her against a wall as an Arisai appeared from around a corner, voicing a delighted laugh as he thrust at the Lord Protector with a narrow-bladed sword. Iltis twisted aside, the Arisai's blade tip shattering on the stone, though he still retained enough steel to parry Iltis's overhead counterblow, but insufficient speed to dodge Davoka's spear thrust to the groin. Iltis shoved the corpse aside and took hold of Lyrna's arm once again.

"The horses are tethered on the western edge of the camp," he said. "Should I fall, Highness, do not linger."

Two more Arisai appeared to block their path, Davoka and Iltis instantly charging forward to meet them. This part of the temple was mostly narrow walkways threading a complex course between the various pyramidal structures, constricting the movements of the combatants, though it seemed to favour Iltis. The hulking lord locked the hilt of his sword onto an opponent's, bearing him down with his bulk, slamming a knee into his chest to wind him before smashing his unarmoured head against the wall, again and again until the skull cracked like an egg.

Davoka's assailant managed to fend off her precise jabs with apparent ease, voicing a laugh that died as Lyrna sent her dagger spinning into his neck. A clash of steel at her back made her turn, seeing Benten, backed against a wall, sword moving with frantic speed as he tried to fend off two Arisai.

Murel, crouched at Lyrna's side, uttered a screech of rage and launched herself at the nearest foe, her dagger sinking into his arm. The Arisai tore his arm away before she could retrieve the blade for another blow, slamming a punch into her face that sent her reeling, advancing towards her with a broad grin, then collapsing as Benten's sword cleaved into his neck. The other Arisai lay dead at his feet but the young lord's hand was clamped over a wound in his side, the blood flowing thick through his fingers.

"My lord!" Lyrna rushed towards him, finding herself restrained by Murel. The girl's eye was swelling shut and she seemed a little unsteady on her feet, but still had enough strength to prevent Lyrna from going to Benten's side as three more Arisai appeared, one sparing a brief glance for the wounded lord before laying his throat open with a swift, efficient slash.

"Lerhnah!" Davoka's hand gripped her shoulder, pulling her along, the world becoming a blur of frenzied combat. Iltis led the way, attempting to find a course through the maze of stone, now littered with corpses at every turn. Davoka guarded the rear, pausing to spear any pursuing Arisai who came within reach. At Lyrna's side Murel had hold of Alornis's hand, the Lady Artificer's face betraying scant notice of the surrounding horror.

Iltis gave a shout of frustration at finding their way blocked again, ducking under a sword swing and delivering a counter that left his assailant giggling as he regarded his severed fingers. The Lord Protector cast around, his features betraying a panic Lyrna had thought beyond him. It was his fear that restored her, banishing the sight of Benten, the blood flowing from his gaping neck to soak the temple floor. *The gods are always thirsty . . .*

"To the centre, my lord," she told Iltis. "At least there are allies there."

He hesitated a moment then gave a shallow bow. "I crave forgiveness for my failure . . ."

"Time is against us, my lord." One of the Queen's Daggers lay nearby, a lean, dark-haired woman, her hatchet cradled in her arms as if clutching a beloved infant. Lyrna bent to retrieve the weapon and nodded at Iltis to proceed.

They were obliged to fight their way through to Lord Nortah's surviving defenders, perhaps fifty of them in a tight circle in the centre of the temple, ringed by a growing wall of dead. Iltis hacked down an Arisai from behind, laying about on either side with great two-handed blows of his sword, carving sufficient passage for Lyrna and Murel to force their way through with Alornis between them. Iltis tried to follow but fell as an Arisai delivered a kick to his legs, others closing to finish him but reeling back as Davoka landed in their midst, spear whirling to claim eyes and outstretched hands. She paused to haul Iltis to his feet, the Lord Protector barrelling through the throng of red-armoured men as she followed close behind, spear still whirling.

Lyrna was quickly conveyed to the middle of the formation where she found Snowdance slumped on her side, ragged flesh dangling from her claws, fur matted with gore and the stone beneath slick with blood. Despite her injuries the cat's great yellow eyes stared up at Lyrna as bright as ever. She even uttered a soft purr as Alornis knelt to run a hand over her head.

Lyrna looked up as the cacophony suddenly abated, the clash of weapons fading to leave only the groans of the wounded. The Arisai were thick on all sides but seemed to have retreated somewhat. Many were wounded, some grievously so, missing eyes or standing with gaping wounds to the face or blood flowing freely from rents in their armour, but they were all smiling, not in mockery, or cruelty, but joy.

This is what they were made for, Lyrna thought, her eyes playing over the sea of happy faces. *A new race born to delight in slaughter. The Volarian bred to perfection.*

Around her the Queen's Daggers all stood, drawing breath in ragged gasps, tensed for the next assault. Most had bloody scars, some wide-eyed in shock or grief. *But still no fear,* she saw, seeing how their ranks tightened around her, many casting furtive glances as if fearing her disapproval. *The Empress made something vile,* she decided. *I made something great.*

"We make them happy it seems," she said, rising from the war-cat's side. She raised her hatchet above her head, the gore-covered blade evidence its owner had died hard, as she intended to do. "Stand with me and we'll make them weep!"

As one the Queen's Daggers roared, a savage blast of defiance and bloodlust, waving their weapons at the Arisai and voicing taunts rich in obscenities. "I'll feed you your balls, you grinning fucker!" a stocky man with a halberd spat at the nearest Arisai, who seemed to find this even more cause for amusement.

Lyrna met Lord Nortah's gaze, reading a grim certainty in his expression. He glanced down at Snowdance, her eyes closed now, and his face spasmed in mingled rage and grief before he straightened. "We are taking our queen out of here!" he told his soldiers. "Assault formation!"

The response was immediate, the Queen's Daggers moving with the unconscious precision born of months of training, ordering themselves into a wedge shape in the space of a few seconds. Nortah raised his sword, preparing to give the order to advance, then paused at the sight of some commotion in the ranks of Arisai. The throng parted to reveal a tall figure, armoured in red as they were, but his face that of a much older man, the features long and lean, thin lips and pale blue eyes. Also, unlike the Arisai, he wore no smile.

Lyrna saw Nortah's sword arm sag as he gaped at the tall man, face drawn in mystification. "Aspect?"

CHAPTER NINE

Reva

"Why you not . . . afraid?"

Lieza's Realm Tongue was adequate but not accomplished, though considerably better than Reva's Volarian. She sat on the only bed, knees drawn up and clasped in her arms, eyes bright as she watched Reva go through her scales. On the first day of their confinement Varulek had provided her with a wooden short sword and some intently spoken advice, "Ready yourself with all vigour. The arena cares not who you were, only what you might be."

Their quarters consisted of a windowless cavern-like chamber providing more than ample room for practice. Reva danced across mosaic-tiled floors, dodging between elegant pillars of black marble veined in white. The walls were decorated in faded paintings depicting various beasts and men in combat and she noted how Lieza did her best not to look at them. At the far end of the chamber a large bath was inset in the floor, supplied with hot water via some hidden contrivance of pipes. Besides the bed, however, there was little in the way of furniture, or anything of sufficient weight to make a decent weapon. Even her wooden sword was made from sandalwood and like to shatter at the first contact with anything substantial.

"Fear kills," Reva told the slave girl, spinning through a final combination of parries and thrusts. "You'd fear less if you trained with me."

The scale was her own invention, a much modified variant of one of Vaelin's Order standards, designed for confronting the Kuritai. Although from what Lieza told her of the spectacles Reva concluded a contest with the slave-elite might be preferable. She had quizzed the girl closely for several hours, leaving off only when she began to cry, tears flowing as she stumbled over a description of some kind of cat with teeth like daggers.

"I not a . . . fighter, like you." Lieza hugged herself closer, resting her head on her knees.

"Then what are you?" Reva asked.

"Slave." The girl spoke in a murmur, not raising her head. "Always just slave."

"You must have skills, abilities."

"Numbers, letters, language." Lieza's shoulders moved in a shrug. "My master taught me much. Won't help here. I am Avielle, you Livella."

"And they are?"

"Sisters. One weak, one strong."

Reva grunted in annoyance, going to the bed and grabbing the girl by the wrists, hauling her to her feet. "Look at me!" She took hold of her chin and raised it, shaking her until her eyes opened, wet and bright with alarm. "Enough of this. Whatever waits for us here will need all our strength, yours and mine, if we are to survive it."

The girl sagged, tears flowing once again. "I not like you . . ."

Reva drew a hand back to slap her. *Beat some spine into her, make her practice and beat her every time she falters. She'll learn quick enough if I put some bruises on those perfect legs, the miserable, fatherless sinner . . .*

Her hands gave an involuntary spasm, allowing Lieza to sink back onto the bed, head slumped in misery. "I'm sorry," Reva said, retreating from the weeping girl, her heart thumping.

A jangle of keys came from outside the thick iron door. It swung open on squealing hinges to reveal Varulek with two Kuritai at his back. His eyes tracked from Reva to the still-weeping Lieza. "I have been instructed to punish this one if she fails to please you," he said.

"She pleases me well enough," Reva told him. "What do you want?"

He stood back from the door, inclining his head in a surprisingly polite gesture of respectful invitation. "The blond man fights today. The Empress thought you would like to see it."

Her initial thought was to refuse, having little desire to witness the Shield's murder. But she would find no opportunity for escape here, and perhaps the pirate deserved his end to be witnessed by at least one ally. She tossed the wooden sword onto the bed next to Lieza. "At least try," she said quietly, placing a hand on her shoulder. "Copy what you saw me do."

The girl's head bobbed in what might have been agreement and Reva went to the door, noting how the Kuritai maintained no more than a six-inch gap between themselves and Varulek. *He fears me,* she decided, depressed by continual evidence the Master of the Arena was no fool. He remained unmoved by the insults she cast at him, was always just out of reach and ensured her wrists were shackled on the rare occasions she was permitted out of the chamber.

She kept still as one of the Kuritai held a knife to her throat, the other snapping the manacles to her wrists. She calculated dispatching one would be relatively simple, hook the chains over his throat and snap his neck, but had yet to formulate a manoeuvre that would prevent the other killing her a heartbeat later. Also, she considered it unlikely Varulek would simply stand idle and watch her escape. Although he was of average proportions, she could tell from his bearing and the evident strength in his tattooed hands, he was no stranger to combat. *Once a soldier, perhaps?*

"Your quarters are acceptable?" he asked, leading her along the passage. They were deep in the bowels of the arena, the passage leading to a long flight of stairs ascending in a curving arc in line with the giant oval of the arena.

"A table and chair would be nice," she said as they began the climb.

"Also easily broken and the legs used for clubs," he replied. "So, sadly, I must refuse."

She concealed a sigh of frustration, wondering again at the Father's liking for placing obstacles in her path. *Why not allow me a stupid gaoler?* she asked him. *If it is your object to punish me, attempting to escape this place will certainly achieve such an end in short order.* There was no answer, of course, the Father as deaf to her entreaties as he had always been, though now at least she discerned a reason. *I lied in your name. I cannot think I deserve to live.*

"Some books for the girl, then," she said. "I think she would appreciate a distraction."

"I'll see to it."

They climbed in silence for a time, passing by several sentry platforms, each home to a pair of Kuritai standing with their typical blank-eyed immobility. The higher they went the more ornate the surrounding structure became, bare, unplastered brick giving way to smooth walls decorated with mosaics and the occasional relief sculpture. She was surprised to note that most of the decoration showed signs of unrepaired vandalism: unfamiliar script chiselled away or motifs subjected to shattering hammerblows. From the colour of the stone she deduced this to be ancient damage.

"This is a very old building," she observed as they neared the arena's ground level, the narrow passage echoing with a low-pitched hum, growing with every step. It was a sound she knew well enough, similar to the collective shouts of the archers on the walls of Alltor when they called for the Volarians to march into yet another arrow storm, the baying of many souls hungry for blood.

"Indeed," Varulek replied. "The oldest building in the city, in fact. Product of a less enlightened age." She detected a new inflection to his normally uncoloured voice, a faint but clearly discernible note of contempt.

"Less enlightened?" she pressed.

"So the Imperial historians have it." She saw how his eyes lingered on a statue as they crested the final step and emerged onto the broad arched walkway leading to the arena proper. It was a bronze figure typical of the many she had seen on her journey here, a man, as they usually were, holding a short sword aloft in a gesture of heroic defiance. She could tell from the lustre of the bronze the statue was relatively recent, but the plinth on which it stood was far older, a finely carved cylinder of red-gold marble, an iron plaque hammered onto its side with little regard for the stone, which was cracked and chipped in several places.

"Someone else stood there once," she said. "Who was it?"

Varulek turned his gaze away from the plinth, lengthening his stride. "Savorek," he said in a flat voice. "Greatest of the guardians."

"Guardians of what?"

He led her to another staircase, this one leading to the upper tier. He remained silent until they had climbed the stairs, and the hum of the crowd became a ceaseless cacophony, almost drowning his reply, but she caught it, "All that was taken from us."

He led her through a series of hallways, their path lined with guards every ten paces. They were mostly Free Swords here, though their armour and weapons were of a less uniform appearance than the conscripts she had fought in the Realm. Despite their lack of uniformity, however, she noted they all shared the same expression: eyes wider than normal, faces pale and jaws bunching intermittently. *They're all terrified*, she realised, her gaze going to the balcony ahead where a slender figure sat in silhouette on a cushioned bench.

The Empress rose to greet her as she was led out onto the balcony, her smile disconcerting in its genuine warmth. She came close, leaning to press a fond kiss to her cheek. "Little sister, how nice of you to come."

Reva clenched her fists at the closeness, disliking the fact that the Empress's perfume was a subtle delight to the senses. But any violent impulse was checked by the sight of the five Arisai on the balcony, each greeting Reva with a welcoming grin, infuriating in its familiarity. *They think they see one of their own,* she thought, sickened by the realisation.

The Empress moved back, turning to Varulek and waving an impatient hand at the crowd. "Shut them up."

The black-clad moved to the balcony's edge, raising a hand to unseen eyes below. Almost without pause there came the sound of many trumpets, the notes forming a strident tune rich in implacable authority. The crowd instantly fell to an absolute silence, unbroken by even the faintest cough or wayward call, as if every soul present had taken a breath in unison and feared letting it out.

"Honoured Citizens and sundry scum!" the Empress called to them, moving forward until her bare toes protruded over the edge of the balcony, her voice carrying with almost unnatural ease to the farthest reaches of the arena. "Before I delight your pestilent hearts with yet more blood, I should like to introduce a distinguished guest from across the ocean." She gestured to Reva, her lips formed in the encouraging smile of an elder sibling. Reva remained still until one of the Arisai gave a pointed cough, stroking his chin with an apologetic grimace, his other hand resting on a dagger at his belt. She moved slowly to the Empress's side, flinching as she took hold of her manacled wrist and raised it high.

"I give you Lady Governess Reva Mustor of Cumbrael!" the Empress called again. "Many of your sons and husbands no doubt met their end at her hands, deservedly so I might add. Still, even though none of you are worthy to kiss this woman's feet, I have still ordained that she will entertain you here in due course. Is not your Empress generous?"

Her grip on Reva's wrists tightened as she stood there, face set in a mask of profound malice. She stood regarding the crowd for what seemed an age, eyes scanning every silent row, darting about as if in search of the slightest expression of disloyalty. Finally she grunted and released Reva, moving back to her bench and gesturing irritably at Varulek. "Get on with it. Little sister, come sit by me."

The trumpets pealed forth once more, a less strident tune this time, almost joyful. The crowd's murmur rose again as Reva slumped next to the Empress, hearing no cheers amongst the tense babble of thousands exchanging fearful whispers.

A slave brought tea in small glass cups, along with a selection of finely crafted cakes, each a perfect cube of variously coloured icing topped with a tiny gold-leaf motif of some kind. "My crest," the Empress said, holding up one of the cakes for Reva's inspection, the crest revealed as a tiny dagger within a chain circle. "Death and servitude, my two gifts." She laughed and popped the cake in her mouth, frowning in consternation as she chewed, her face betraying no more enjoyment than if she were eating plain bread.

Reva turned her attention to the arena, finding the balcony offered a near-complete view of a great sand oval. She judged it perhaps two hundred and fifty paces wide and near four hundred long. The sand was tended by a number of slaves, busily raking over numerous dark patches, no doubt evidence of some earlier slaughter. Her gaze tracked over the crowd, noting how the pitch of their mingled voices had changed, the fear giving way to a collective buzz of anticipation. *They fear her but can't resist what she offers here,* she decided with a surge of contempt.

"Yes, horrible aren't they?" the Empress commented, sipping tea.

Reva swallowed a sigh. *Feel nothing. Think nothing.*

"Do you hate your people as I hate this lot?" the Empress went on. "Their gullibility must be trying at times."

Reva knew she was being baited, this thing attempting to stoke an anger that might reveal some new insight. But she found her thoughts free of rage as they turned to her people, her trusting, believing people. "They fought off your finest army for months," she said. "Starved and shorn of hope, they gave blood and life to save each other. Your people rejoice in cruelty and make murder an entertainment. I'll reserve my hate for them."

"And your guilt for yourself." The Empress took a bite from another cake, raising her eyebrows in faint disappointment. "All tastes like ash," she muttered, tossing the cake aside.

Reva tried to ignore the weight of the Empress's gaze as she concentrated on a new commotion in the arena. Two groups of men were emerging from doors at opposite ends of the oval, the initial upsurge in cheers from the crowd soon fading as their condition became clear. They were all naked, most of middle or advanced years, pale and trembling under the scrutiny of the crowd, some with hands clasped protectively over their genitals, others standing in apparent bafflement or shock.

"Pardon me a moment, little sister," the Empress said, getting to her feet once more. She moved to the balcony's edge where an Arisai waited, bowed to one knee as he proffered a short sword. "As yet more proof of your Empress's boundless largess!" she called, her arm sweeping in a grandiloquent gesture from one end of the arena to the other. "I add another two teams to the venerable Sword Races. To my right the Honourable Company of Traitors, to my left the Exalted Order of Corrupt Officials. Both have earned my displeasure with their disloyalty and greed, but my compassionate, womanly soul compels me to mercy. There will be only one victor of today's contest, permitted to live out his days in slavery and his family spared the three deaths."

She took the sword from the kneeling Arisai and threw it into the centre of the arena. Reva couldn't help but be impressed by the skill of the throw, the sword sinking into the sand up to the hilt. The Empress turned away as the trumpets blasted a short note, the crowd's murmur now a mingling of dismay and confusion.

The two groups of naked men stood immobile as the note faded, exchanging wary glances or looking up at the crowd with tear-stained faces, bereft of all but the faintest hope. For a time it seemed as if they would just continue to stand there, anchored by terror, until a group of Varitai archers positioned on the upper tiers sank a volley of arrows into the sand around their feet. One of the naked men immediately broke from the group, sprinting towards the sword in a surprising turn of speed for a fellow with such an extensive belly. Several men began running in his wake, provoking their opponents into belated motion. Soon both groups were pelting towards each other in a stampede of flabby, sweat-soaked flesh, voices raised in desperate challenge. The plump man was first to the sword, scooping it up and flailing at the onrushing team as they closed, a bright plume of blood appearing in the mass of colliding flesh. The plump man was soon lost to sight, sinking under a forest of flailing limbs as the combatants thrashed at each other with inexpert ferocity. The sword appeared again, held aloft in the hand of a stick-thin old man with straggly grey hair. He stabbed down at the surrounding throng again and again, eyes wide with madness, before he was dragged from view.

"Don't waste your pity," the Empress cautioned Reva, taking her seat once more. "Black-clads all, and not a man among them without blood on his hands." She moved closer, voice dropping to a conspiratorial whisper, as if they were two girls exchanging gossip. "So, are you enjoying Lieza? Don't you find her the sweetest thing?"

Reva determined not to answer, keeping her gaze on the now-diminished throng of battling unfortunates. Many were lying on the sands, too injured or exhausted to fight on, but a dense knot of them were still struggling in the centre of the arena, a tight revolving scrum of reddened flesh with the sword at the centre.

"I can provide a replacement," the Empress went on. "If she's proving not to your . . . taste."

Think nothing. Feel nothing. "She . . . is acceptable to me."

"I am glad. You are the Most Honoured Garisai after all. The quarters you were given have traditionally been reserved for the most exalted of champions. In ages past the Garisai were not slaves you see, but free men and women, come to honour the gods with blood and courage. The undefeated would be raised to great status, lavished with all comfort and pleasures, for the gods favoured those who could slake their endless thirst."

"What happened to them?" Reva asked, watching as a group of five survivors surrounded the man who now held the sword, edging closer as he attempted to ward them off with clumsy jabs, face grey with exhaustion. "Your gods."

"We killed them," the Empress replied, returning her attention to the arena as the contest neared its conclusion. The man with the sword hacked down a tall but aged opponent before the others closed in and bore him to the ground, fists rising and falling in a frenzy until one broke free with the sword, immediately turning to hack at his former allies, voicing a feral scream with every blow. The crowd had fallen silent once again and the man's rhythmic fury reverberated across the ascending tiers, coming to a ragged stop as he finished his last victim and slumped to the sands, weeping, his sagging, barely muscled torso red from neck to waist.

The Empress squinted at the slumped figure for a moment. "One of the corrupt," she mused, before turning to Varulek. "Make sure he finishes the wounded, then send him to the mint. Hauling sacks of gold and silver for the rest of his days might educate him in the true value of money."

She reclined, reaching out to trace her fingers through the tresses of Reva's hair that had escaped her long braid. "The gods," she said in a reflective tone, "were of no more use to a people willing to embrace a great future, a destiny that could only be fulfilled by unity and unclouded reason. Or so my father once told me."

"They weren't real," Reva said. "Your gods died whilst the World Father endured." She watched as a pair of Arisai dragged the lone survivor to his feet, pushing him towards the prostrate form of a man with a gaping stomach wound, one hand clutched to his spilling guts whilst he raised the other in a vain plea for mercy. "You built a nation of horrors."

"And what is your nation, little sister? A perfection of civilisation? I've seen it, and I think not. You grovel to a dream scribbled down centuries ago, pursuing your endless quarrel with those who in turn grovel to the imagined souls of the dead."

"A quarrel now ended, thanks to you."

"And to you, Blessed Lady. She who speaks with the Father's voice." She issued a soft laugh as Reva's unease deepened. "Oh yes, I can see it. You *lied*. Thousands followed you here to their deaths, all because of the words you spoke on behalf of a deaf-mute god. And though you have never truly heard his voice, still you fear his judgement."

She leaned closer, Reva keeping her gaze fixed on the arena and the final man, tottering like an infant as he went from one maimed figure to another. "Let it go, little sister," the Empress whispered, her tone urgent with honest entreaty. "I can show you so much."

Reva watched the last of the wounded meet his untidy end before the Arisai dragged the survivor from the arena, suspended between them, head thrown back as he gabbled in a madman's voice. "I've already seen enough," she said.

The Empress's breath ghosted across her cheek as she gave a small sigh, pressing a kiss to her skin before leaning back. "I find I must disagree, my lady."

It took the better part of a half hour for the slaves to clear the bodies from the arena and rake the pooled blood from the sand. The Empress remained silent throughout, her face taking on an oddly vacant cast as she sat with dimmed eyes. Occasionally her lips would move in a silent murmur, her brow creasing in confusion at some inner puzzlement, at times her features tensing into a mask of such sorrowful bafflement Reva found herself suppressing a pang of pity. *This thing is mad*, she realised. *A mad Empress for an empire built on unclouded reason.*

The trumpets sounded again and the Empress blinked, straightening to view the figures emerging from a door in the arena wall. There were two of them, both tall, one blond, the other dark-haired. The blond man carried a short sword whilst his companion bore a spear. They wore trews of leather but no armour, standing bare-chested as they stared up at the surrounding tiers. Unlike the unfortunate black-clads who preceded them their faces were void of any entreaty, tense certainly, but unwilling to beg.

The crowd regained some animation at the prospect of more familiar entertainment, numerous voices raised in scorn or appreciation, the horror of the Sword Race seemingly forgotten. Reva's wrists chafed on her manacles as her fists clenched, her gaze going to the Shield's face. His beard had been sheared away, revealing the fine-chiselled features she knew had captured the attention of many a Realm-born lady. She saw his recognition as his gaze went to the balcony, lowering his head in a momentary greeting. Reva shifted her gaze to the dark-haired man, finding him a youth of no more than twenty years, face rigid with controlled fear, fear that vanished as he caught sight of her. The rush of recognition was almost sickening, Reva finding herself on her feet as the tall young man sank to his knees, his spear held aloft in both hands. He shouted something, lost amidst the crowd's feral baying, but she knew the meaning well enough. *I rejoice at the sight of you, Blessed Lady.*

"You know the younger one too?" the Empress asked, her gift reading Reva's feelings with execrable ease.

Reva didn't know why she bothered to answer. Perhaps because she wanted him to have some form of memorial, someone to speak his name before he died. "Allern Varesh," she said, the words grating from a dry throat. "Late of the Riverlands and Guardsman to House Mustor."

"So much guilt." The Empress laid a sympathetic hand on her shoulder, drawing her close. "You need to accept who and what you are." She flicked a hand at the kneeling Allern. "He and his kind will never reach our heights. Nature has ordained them our servants. A truth I believe your queen realised long ago."

She gave Reva a final hug and moved to the balcony's edge once more, the crowd falling to instant silence at the trumpets' blast. "In days long past!" she called. "When this empire was fractured by superstition and delusion, this day was known as the Feast of the Fallen Brothers. A celebration of the final battle fought by the only mortals ever to be raised to the holy state of Guardianhood. I give you Morivek and Korsev!" She extended an arm to the Shield and Allern, the youth now raised to his feet, gaze still fixed on Reva, smiling now and seemingly deaf to the Empress's words or the burst of cheering from the crowd.

"Rejoice as they battle the most deadly of the Dermos," the Empress intoned, raising a hand to a gate at the western end of the arena. "The Harbingers of the Fall!"

The gate swung open as the trumpets pealed once more, the crowd erupting into cheers at the sight of the creatures entering the arena. Reva initially took them for relatives of Lord Nortah's war-cat but quickly realised they were another breed entirely, leaner of body and not so tall. Also their colouring was different, the fur striped in yellow and black from neck to tail. But the main difference was their teeth, each possessed of a pair of daggerlike fangs which they bared continually as they strained against their chains. There were nine of them, chained in groups of three under the control of a handler, large men in leather armour clutching the cats' chains in one hand and a long whip in the other.

"Dagger Teeth," the Empress said, returning to Reva's side. "Said to have been spawned in the fire pit by the Dermos and sent forth to herald the impending fall of mankind. The old priests were always foreseeing the end of everything, great calamities and plagues that could only be averted by yet more obeisance to the gods, and tribute to the temples naturally."

Reva tried to calm her heart as the handlers allowed their eager charges to prowl closer to the two men in the centre of the arena, the cats hissing and writhing against their bonds, seemingly maddened by a desire for blood.

"They're bred from the most vicious kittens," the Empress went on. "Kept in a perpetual state of near starvation. The arena is the only place with which they associate a glut of meat. Hence their eagerness."

Allern and the Shield moved closer together, the young guardsman favouring Reva with a final bow before taking on a fighting stance, crouched low with the spear held level with his chest. *Arentes taught him well,* she thought, losing the battle to control her heart, sweat beading her skin as it thumped against her chest.

"Don't," she said in a whisper, forgetting all pride and defiance, knowing this to be something she couldn't witness. "Please."

"You ask a favour, little sister?" The Empress put her hands on Reva's shoulders, turning her so they were face-to-face. "What will you give me in return?"

"I'll fight," Reva breathed. "In their place."

"You'll fight here in any case. And I promised my dreadful people a spectacle. What else can you offer?" She drew Reva into an embrace, her breath soft against her ear. "When my beloved comes to me, we will bring down the Ally and all the world will be ours. Come with me, little sister. I will give you the Realm to rule in my name. Keep your World Father if you like, I don't care what lies you tell. Take these two as your servants, with the right conditioning they will be fierce indeed. You could destroy all other creeds, banish forever the heretic faith, bring the love of the Father to all corners of the Realm."

She stepped back, smiling fondly as she stroked Reva's cheek, thumbing away the single tear that escaped her eye. "Isn't that what you always wanted?"

Reva looked at the arena, seeing how the handlers had manoeuvred the cats into a circle around Allern and the Shield, edging ever closer.

"You have a gift," Reva said to the Empress. "A song that tells you the feelings of others."

"It tells me many things."

Reva turned back, meeting her gaze. "What's it telling you now?"

There was a flicker of alarm in the Empress's face, her mouth twitching in a mingling of amusement and frustration as she began to draw back, a fraction too late.

Reva's head snapped forward, slamming her forehead into the Empress's mouth, sending her reeling back. The Arisai responded immediately, swords hissing from scabbards as they closed on all sides, save one. Reva sprinted for the balcony's edge and leapt.

CHAPTER TEN

Vaelín

Dahrena returned to her body with a shout, doubling over as her face tensed in distress. Vaelin pulled her close, holding her until the shudders subsided. She had flown for only a short time, at her own insistence since the mountain folk continued to make no appearance, so he deduced her anguish was not due to the depredations of her gift.

"They're in the mountains now," she said, looking up at him with pale intensity. "Killing all they can find. He knew, Vaelin. He knew I saw, and he laughed."

He gathered the Wolf People elders to hear her full report, watching the last vestige of hope fade from each face; the Raven's Shadow had truly fallen and the long-promised tribulation had arrived.

"There are many Varitai among them," Dahrena said, "Kuritai too. The Free Swords are not so numerous, mostly cavalry, and their souls are troubled, flaring red with suspicion and fear. They entered the mountains two days ago, I saw evidence of a battle and the remnants of a settlement. All were slain, young folk and old, no captives were taken. They do not come for slaves." She paused, eyes closed as she forced herself to recall the memory. "Things were done to those they took alive, their torments were many and prolonged." Her gaze met Vaelin's. "He wanted me to see."

"Where are they now?" he asked her.

"Moving to the north-east. They're maintaining a close formation, mounting few patrols. I saw many souls gathering to oppose them, but in small groups, none with the strength to halt their advance."

"Then they will need our aid," Vaelin said.

"No." The hooded man was the only one present to be seated, perched close to a campfire that he prodded with a sturdy walking stick.

"You have advice to offer, Master Erlin?" Vaelin asked him.

"Just obvious fact, brother." Erlin sighed and drew back his hood, offering Dahrena a smile rich in sympathy. "They have more than twice our number, do they not, my lady?"

She shot a guarded look at Vaelin and nodded.

"The tribes would have to unite to have a chance against them," Erlin said, turning to Vaelin. "And they won't. I tried to warn the chieftains but they wouldn't listen, thinking this just another slaving campaign. Every few years the Volarians come, sometimes they can be bought off with ore and captives taken from the other tribes, sometimes they fight them so the young warriors can earn their first scars. It's been going on for over two hundred years now and is almost ritual. They do not understand what they face. By the time you join battle they'll be defeated and scattered."

Erlin turned back to the fire, Vaelin noting the whiteness of his knuckles on his stick as he prodded the embers. *He's afraid,* he realised. *What could scare a man who cannot die?*

"You are known to the tribes," he said. "You can guide us to them? Speak for us?"

"They do not speak as one. When the tribes are not fighting each other they fight amongst themselves. By the time we had negotiated with all it will be too late. In any case, they will see you and these people as just more enemies to fight."

"You expect me to sit here and ignore a slaughter?"

"The Ally's creature is trying to draw you out, surely you see that. And you did not come here for war, you came for the knowledge you imagine I hold. The key to defeating the Ally."

Vaelin frowned at the sardonic note in Erlin's voice, the tone of a man facing an all-too-predictable outcome. "This has happened before?"

"There have been a few over the centuries. Scholars, kings"—he gave Vaelin a brief, regretful grin—"warriors. All facing the unhappy truth of the Ally's existence, guided to me by ancient lore or gifted power. Though none found me in times quite so troubled as these."

"The Ally means to make an end. This time it will be different."

Erlin sighed and got to his feet. "Then I had best show you what I showed them, brother." He pointed his stick towards the east where the black clouds hung low over the peaks. "Though I doubt these folk will find the climate to their liking."

◆ ◆ ◆

The hills remained stubbornly empty as they marched east, tracking through valleys devoid of life save a few elk that scattered at the first tinge of their scent on the wind. "The mountain folk are miners," Erlin explained. "Digging copper and tin from the mountains which they trade to the Volarians, despite their perpetual difficulties. There are few seams this far north and any scouts will be preoccupied with this latest incursion."

"You have lived here a long time?" Vaelin asked.

"Six years this time, though I once lingered for nearly three decades. That was two centuries ago, when the people here were not so fierce."

"What kept you here?"

"A widow with several children. She had a harsh tongue but a kind heart and didn't seem to mind if I stayed and played the husband. When she passed the children had grown and the Volarians were mounting their first slaving operations. I thought it best to move on. Though I am always drawn back."

"By what?"

Erlin's expression clouded as he paused to regard the fire mountains in the distance, their fiery glow brighter now, and the sky above ever more dark. "In good time, brother."

In the evening Lorkan, Cara and Marken gathered around Erlin, keen for stories of his travels. Cara's memory of him was the dimmest of the three but she still recalled his tales from her childhood sojourn to the Fallen City. "Did you return to the Far West?" she asked. "To the temple above the clouds?"

"Indeed I did." He glanced up at the Sentar who had also gathered round. They seemed to be amongst the few people with whom he had little experience and found their endless hunger for a story a surprising contrast to their fierce reputation. "Though I stayed only one night."

"Was she there?" Cara pressed. "The Jade Princess?"

"She was, and as lovely as ever. Unmarked by age and still singing her beautiful song. I was glad I made the effort to hear it again, though the journey was harder than before. Even the land of the Merchant Kings is not immune to strife."

"Jade Princess?" Vaelin asked.

"The only soul I have met who has lived longer than I. Consigned to the temple above the clouds five hundred years ago by the Merchant Kings, who still make pilgrimage to seek her counsel, imagining she has the ear of Heaven. I think she finds them greatly amusing, though it's difficult to tell. Her moods are often as inscrutable as her words. But her song . . ." He closed his eyes in remembrance of something blissful. "Uncounted years spent in practice of voice and harp. I alone have been blessed to hear it more than once in a lifetime."

Vaelin saw Kiral shift in discomfort and knew what her song told her; this was a man fully expecting never to hear the Jade Princess again. *We bring his doom, that's what he fears.*

"I heard a story once," he said to Erlin. "A tale about a Renfaelin knight saved from death by a boy with the power to heal, travelling in company with a man who couldn't die. The knight related how this man sought to preserve the Gifted in the hope that one would be born to the Realm with the power to kill him, for he was tired of his endless life."

"Tired?" Erlin reclined a little, pursing his lips in contemplation. "Life is endless sensation, ceaseless change and boundless variety. We are not made to tire of it, and I haven't. But I have always known it would end, as many years as I have had, I cannot endure forever, nor should I. The Jade Princess knew that, the first time I sought her out, hoping for an answer, a reason why I stayed young whilst others aged, why those around me perished from plague or sickness and I did not. She gave no answer, as is her wont. Many who climb the treacherous path to the temple are often sent away disappointed, and even those to whom she chooses to speak find her words opaque, often beyond their ability to decipher. But though she gave no answer, she did allow me to hear her song, and that was answer enough. There is a flaw in it, you see. Small, barely perceptible to the untutored ear, but to one as long-lived as I, as jarring as an apprentice minstrel stumbling over his first chords. It's but a brief sequence of notes, so complex as to be beyond the skill of perhaps all who ever held a harp, even her. Her song is not perfected, she hasn't finished, perhaps she never will."

◆ ◆ ◆

A three-day march brought them in sight of the only settlement they had seen, a small cluster of stone houses at the foot of a flat-topped mountain. The air had a faint sulphurous tint and the sky above continually shrouded in roiling grey cloud, darkening to black in the east where the fire mountains raged ever brighter. Erlin had them halt a mile short of the settlement where a number of figures could be seen running from the dwellings, perhaps a hundred, all armed.

"The Laretha don't have many visitors," Erlin said. "They're small in number and living so close to the fire mountains provides a certain security." He turned to Vaelin, gesturing towards the settlement. "They'll expect to parley with the chieftain of this new tribe."

Vaelin asked Astorek to join him as they followed Erlin towards the settlement where the warriors stood in a thin but steady line. They were mostly men, all armed with either an axe or a long, narrow-bladed spear. They all wore calf-length kilts of leather, decorated with various painted symbols, and breastplates of bronze that gleamed dully in the muted daylight. A stocky man of middling years stood in the centre of their line, an axe clutched in either hand, long greying hair tied back from his face in thick braids. His rigid posture seemed to relax a little at the sight of Erlin, but his countenance remained fierce with suspicion as he scanned Vaelin then darkened into rage at the sight of Astorek. He raised both axes as they neared, his people immediately adopting a fighting stance on either side.

"Pertak!" Erlin called to the stocky man, smiling in welcome then gesturing to Vaelin and Astorek as he spoke on.

"He says he brings many allies to the Laretha," Astorek reported. Vaelin noted the deep unease on the shaman's brow. "This is foolishness, Raven's Shadow. These people offer only death to outsiders."

Vaelin nodded at Erlin, now approaching the chieftain with arms spread. "But not to him."

Erlin halted a few feet short of the chieftain, his words soft and lost to them, though the tribesman's countenance lost some of its fierceness, if none of its suspicion. After a few moments Erlin turned and beckoned them forth. "Pertak, Chieftain of the Laretha, demands tribute if you are to besmirch his lands with your presence," he said, though Vaelin had yet to see the stocky man speak.

"Tribute?" he asked.

"A symbolic offering only," Erlin explained. "If he allows you to stay without it he appears weak and one of the younger men will challenge him."

The chieftain spoke, pointing one of his axes at the assembled ranks of ice folk and voicing a guttural demand. Vaelin followed its course to find the axe pointed to where Dahrena stood holding Scar's reins. "He wants my horse?"

"Ah, no." Erlin gave a tight smile. "He wants your woman."

"That is not acceptable." Vaelin's hand went to a pouch on his belt, loosing the ties to extract a stone, a finely cut ruby of medium weight given to him by

Governor Aruan at the Linesh dockside barely two years ago, though it seemed like many more now. There had been times when he had been tempted to sell it, especially when on the road, Reva being so constantly hungry, but the blood-song had flared in warning whenever he considered it. He hoped this was why.

The chieftain dropped one of his axes to catch the gem as Vaelin tossed it to him, eyes wide with instant fascination. The warriors on either side of him forgot their discipline to crowd round, every face lit with an enthralled greed. Pertak snarled something, raising his remaining axe in warning, and they shrank back, though their gaze returned continually to the ruby.

Pertak spoke again, directing his question to Vaelin as he held the ruby up to the light. "He wants to know what power it holds," Astorek translated, a faint note of contempt colouring his voice.

"The mountains are rich in ore," Erlin said, "but not gems. They have a certain irrational regard for them."

"Tell him it has the power to capture men's souls," Vaelin said. "He really shouldn't stare at it for too long."

A brief gleam of fear shone in the chieftain's eyes as Erlin related the warning, his fist closing over the stone in a fierce grip before he raised his gaze to Vaelin, squinting in contemplation. He grunted a short clipped sentence and, with considerable deliberation, turned his back and walked towards the settlement, his small host following close, all concern at the arrival of such a large body of intruders now apparently vanished.

"You may stay one day and one night," Erlin said. "A most generous concession, I must say."

"Is that enough?" Vaelin asked him. "For our purposes?"

Erlin looked up at the mountain towering above the settlement, the flattened summit part obscured by a thin mist. "You'll find time loses its meaning here, brother."

◆ ◆ ◆

He forbade anyone but Vaelin from accompanying him, though Dahrena and the other Gifted protested loudly. "We have come so far," Cara said. "To be denied knowledge now . . ."

"I seek to preserve," Erlin broke in, "not to deny. Trust me, you would not thank me for this knowledge."

He led Vaelin to a track that curved around the Laretha settlement to the base of the mountain, halting amidst a cluster of ruins. Vaelin scanned the granite blocks and part-tumbled walls, finding a familiarity in the way they had been shaped, the elegance of their line and the wind-blasted motifs carved into the stone. "The Fallen City," he said. "This place was built by the same hands."

"Not quite," Erlin replied. "Though they shared the same language." He gestured to a stairwell rising from the ruins to join with the flank of the mountain, Vaelin's eyes picking out more steps carved into the stone, ascending in a winding track all the way to the top. "And the same gods."

"So," Erlin said as they climbed, the steps damp from the perennial mist and the air growing chill around them, "you no longer hold to the Faith."

"A man can't hold to a lie."

"The Faith was never a lie. Confused in some regards, overly wedded to dogma in others. But having seen what the rest of the world has to offer in regards to the divine, I find it suits me well enough."

"When we first met you said you had no choice but to follow the Faith. When I came to understand who you were I thought you meant the legend was true, the Departed had cursed you for denying the Faith."

"Cursed? I thought so for a long time, when I was driven from the village of my birth, still seemingly a man in his thirties whilst those I had grown up with became ever more stooped and wrinkled. My wife was chief among my persecutors, grown bitter with envy at my continued youth, hating me for the grey in her hair and the absence of lust in my gaze. I had never been particularly observant of the Faith, mouthing the catechisms without real thought as to their meaning, occasionally muttering caustic words at the brothers and their tedious moralising. 'Denier!' my hating wife called me, desperate to find reason in this mystery. 'The Departed have cursed you.' I suppose that's where it all began, a bitter old woman's insult birthing a legend."

"So you never heard their voice? You were not denied the Beyond?"

Erlin paused, breath misting as his face became sombre. "Oh I heard them, but not until many years later. Despite appearances, brother, I am not in fact immune to death. I do not age and I do not sicken. But without food I starve, and if cut, I bleed the same as any man. I can die, and once, long ago, I did. Or at least came so close it makes scant difference.

"I travelled far after the villagers drove me away, the length and breadth of the four fiefs, for there was no Realm in those days. I suppose I was searching for something, an answer to the enigma of my unending life, but had little notion of how to find it. Mystics and charlatans were not hard to find, all promising wisdom in return for gold, and all proving themselves mad or dishonest in time. One day I paused in a Nilsaelin tavern and heard a minstrel sing of the strange ways of the Seordah, how they preserved their forest home with Dark enchantments. It seemed a good place to seek answers, I was just one man after all, and certainly no warrior. What threat would they see in me? I think I walked for half a day beneath the trees before a Seordah put an arrow in my belly.

"He came to watch me bleed, a tall fellow with a hawk face that betrayed little reaction as I begged for aid. In time his face faded and the chill blackness of death came for me. It was then I heard them, the voices, whispering, shouting, pleading . . . There were so many. 'This is the Beyond?' I thought. 'Just a void echoing with the voices of the dead?' No endless serenity and wisdom. No eternity of calm. I must say, it was quite the disappointment.

"I realised the voices had faded, taking a collective breath as if suddenly muted in fearful expectation. Then one spoke, it was not like the others. They were thin, like the last echoes of a whispered song. This was the full, strong voice of a complete soul, but old, so very old."

"The Ally," Vaelin said, recalling the ancient chill in the voice he had heard as Dahrena dragged him from the Beyond.

"A name I didn't hear until much later. But yes, it was he. And he had an offer to make. 'I will return you,' he said, 'if you will be my vessel.' I was awash in terror, not only of him but also of the prospect of eternity in this terrible void. The fear was such I might have agreed in an instant, but for something I heard in his voice: a boundless, desperate hunger, a *need* for what he sensed in me. It was overpowering, sickening, and I knew then there were worse fates than death.

"He felt my refusal, my repulsion, and I felt his will. The Beyond is a place that is not a place, a place of souls, but a place also of pain, if you know how to inflict it, and he did. I could feel him tearing at me, stripping away shreds of my being as his will lashed at me, not in hate but in precise, agonising flares. 'Serve me,' he said again, 'Whilst you still have a soul capable of service.' There was no hate in that voice, for I think he was beyond hate by then, formed by the ages into a being of purest purpose.

"I thrashed, I screamed, I wept . . . I begged. But still, I refused. It was then I felt another surge of will, but not his. This was something else, something not so old, but in its own way just as powerful, powerful enough to rend me from his grip. I could feel my soul re-forming then, though still much had been stripped away, memories of childhood and friendship lost forever. Even today I cannot recall my mother's face, or the name of the wife who grew to hate me.

"My rescuer spoke to me, a woman's voice, her will so different from his. Soothing where he hurt, banishing the terror he sought to instill. 'You are not done,' she told me. 'I have seen your end, man of many lives, and this is not it. Seek out those like you, preserve all you can, for when you return, it is their strength that will sustain you, and bring the end you will come to crave.' Then she said just three more words before casting me from the void and back into my body. The Seordah was still there, starting in surprise as my eyes flew open. From the blood seeping through my fingers I judged I had been gone for only a few seconds. The Seordah said something, sounding faintly annoyed, and drew a knife from his belt . . . then dropped it when I spoke the three words I had last heard in the Beyond, 'Nersus Sil Nin.'"

"The blind woman sent you back," Vaelin murmured. "She's there, in the Beyond. She fights him."

"She fought him then, but now . . ." Erlin shook his head. "Now it seems his power grows unchecked."

Vaelin pushed the myriad questions aside, long accustomed to the realisation that any answers would be slow in coming. "The Seordah healed you," he said.

"Yes. He brought others and they took me to their camp. My wound was grievous and it took many months before I could travel again. I learned their language, their legends, the truth of how our people had taken their land from them. I also learned there are no Dark enchantments protecting their forest, just great skill and fierce courage birthing enough fear to keep us at bay. In time, I said my farewells and went forth to fulfil the mission she gave me. I have not always been assiduous in my duties, given to distraction and sometimes wearied by the often-repeated mistakes and cruelties that beset humanity. But, I think I did what I could"—he glanced up at the misted steps above—"in the end."

◆ ◆ ◆

The mountain top lay under a vast silence as thick as the mist that covered it, only vague shapes visible in the swirling haze as they crested the final step. Erlin sagged a little from the effort of the climb, leaning hard on his walking stick and eyeing the shadowy forms ahead with naked trepidation. "I hate this place," he breathed, voice soft as he straightened and started forward. "But then, so did those who built it, I imagine."

They started forward into the mist, the shadows resolving into a cluster of buildings, all showing signs of having been crafted by the same hands that had built the ruins at the base of the mountain. They were mostly one-storey dwellings and smaller structures Vaelin took to be storehouses, forming a miniature echo of the Fallen City. But these were not ruined. The silence became ever more oppressive as they moved through the buildings, each empty doorway and window an uncaring witness to their passage. Despite the lack of damage Vaelin knew this to be an ancient place, the corners of the buildings smoothed and rounded by the elements. Also, in contrast to the Fallen City there were no statues here, the only decoration the faded motifs carved above doorways or windows, robbed of meaning by centuries of wind and rain. Whoever had built this place seemingly had scant time or inclination towards art.

It took only moments to clear the buildings, leaving them standing at the edge of a wide flat circle, in the centre of which stood a single flat-topped plinth. "Memory stone," Vaelin said.

Erlin nodded and Vaelin heard the faint tremor in his voice as he replied, "The last to be carved, by the hand of a god no less."

Vaelin's mouth twitched in unwanted amusement and he turned to Erlin with a grin. "A god is a lie."

They shared a laugh, only for a moment, the sound of their mirth soon lost amidst the mist and ancient stone. "Well." Erlin took a firmer grip on his walking stick and started forward. "Shall we?"

Like the surrounding buildings the plinth's edges had been softened by ages of exposure, though the flat top was smooth and unmarked, the indentation in the centre a perfect circle. "You've touched this before?" Vaelin asked Erlin.

"Four times now. I often seek out the ancient places, guided by the myths and legends I hear in my travels. One told of a forgotten city of towering majesty hidden in the mountains and guarded by savage tribes. I wasn't overly surprised to find the reality didn't match the legend, it rarely does."

He extended his hand so it hovered over the stone, meeting Vaelin's gaze. "Ready, brother?"

"I have touched these stones twice before," Vaelin said, seeing the tremble in Erlin's fingers. "They hold knowledge but no threat."

Erlin gave another laugh, harsher this time. "All knowledge is a threat to someone."

Vaelin extended his hand and Erlin took it, entwining the fingers. Closing his eyes, he took a breath and lowered their hands to the stone.

PART IV

By Alpiran reckoning King Janus Al Nieren was born in the tenth year of the New Sun, under a configuration of stars known to Alpiran astrologers as "The Rearing Lion," a fact that would provide portents aplenty for admirers and detractors alike over the succeeding decades. His daughter, by contrast, was born under the comparatively mundane constellation of "The Hay Bale," named for its resemblance to recently harvested wheat. The fact that the Loyal Guild of Imperial Astrologers recently voted to rename this constellation "The Vengeful Flame" says much for the subsequent course of Realm history, not to mention the essential vacuity of the astrologer's art.

—VERNIERS ALISHE SOMEREN,
A HISTORY OF THE UNIFIED REALM: INTRODUCTION,
GREAT LIBRARY OF THE UNIFIED REALM

Verniers' Account

"Did she know?"

I watched the harbour as we drew near, its vastness testimony to Alpira's origins as the greatest trading hub of the lower Boraelin. It stretched in a broad curve some three miles long, piers and moorings beyond counting, and many ships, more than was usual in fact. As we drew closer I noted most were warships, an army of labourers at work on every vessel, steel plating hammered onto hulls and mangonels hauled into place.

Empress Emeren calls her fleet to the capital, *I deduced.* For what purpose?

"My lord?" Fornella prompted. Her rapidly greying hair was tied up today, drawn back from her features, which remained handsome despite the growing number of lines. With her plain dress and tightly wrapped shawl she conveyed the appearance of a comely matron, those ashore perhaps mistaking her for the captain's wife. The thought provoked me to a short laugh.

Fornella frowned in annoyance but refused to be diverted. "She did, didn't she? She knew about you and the Hope."

I shrugged, giving a slight nod. She glanced at the captain and edged closer. "Pay the pirate to take us away from here."

"We have a mission to perform, Honoured Citizen."

"Not at the expense of your life."

"I gave my life to the Emperor. The law decrees I now offer it to his successor, along with my wise counsel."

"You really imagine she'll listen?"

"I know she will. What she does afterwards is more of a mystery."

We docked at one of the minor berths near the northern edge of the harbour, the captain being obliged to pay double the normal mooring fee to a harassed junior port official.

"I'm on official business from the Unified Realm and the Meldenean Isles," the captain growled. "That's got to be worth a discount at least."

"You've also got a hold full of spice," the young official replied. "And space is at a premium." He handed the captain a chit for the berth then held up his hand in expectation.

"Is there a problem?" I asked, moving to the captain's side.

The young man stared at me for a long moment, retreating a step with rapidly paling features. "You are Lord Verniers," he breathed.

I was accustomed to a certain notoriety in the better-educated corners of the empire, but it was usually confined to politely spoken compliments or requests for attendance at various learned functions. So the sight of the pale-faced bureaucrat stumbling backwards along the gangplank before turning and running along the wharf was somewhat unnerving, his return a short time later even more so, since he was accompanied by a squad of soldiers. They proceeded towards the ship at a run, the young official trotting in their wake and gesticulating wildly as he called to the surrounding stevedores. "The traitor! The traitor returns!"

"I think, Captain," I said, hefting my bag of books and making for the gangplank. "You had best be on your way."

"Ship Lords told me to keep you safe," he said, though his shrewd eyes betrayed a deep concern at the commotion unfolding on the wharf.

"And I am grateful for your efforts." I extended a hand, expecting him to ignore it. Instead he gripped it tight, grimacing in regret.

"Luck to you, honoured sir," he said in surprisingly good Alpiran.

"And you, honoured sir." I glanced at Fornella, seeing how fearfully she eyed the approaching soldiers. "I should be grateful if you would take her back to the Realm."

"No." Fornella took a deep breath and moved to my side, forcing a smile. "We have a mission, after all."

We waited on the wharf, watching the captain hound his crew into frantic motion as they hauled oars to push them back from the quay. The sailors soon set to work rowing themselves towards open water in accordance with the bosun's urgent drumbeat.

"What was its name?" Fornella asked. "The ship."

"I never thought to ask." I turned as the soldiers came to a halt a short distance away. They were conscript infantry judging by their armour, half a dozen youths under the command of a less-than-youthful sergeant.

"Your name?" he demanded, striding forward, hard eyes intent on my face.

"Lord Verniers Alishe Someren," I replied. "Imperial Chronicler . . ."

"No," he growled, moving closer with his hand on his sword. "Not now you aren't."

◆ ◆ ◆

They took us to the harbour-master's station, a sturdy building equipped with a few cells for sundry smugglers or excessively boisterous sailors. Thanks to the excitable port official a crowd had begun to form on the wharf by the time the soldiers closed in around us. "If I am liable to arrest," I said to the sergeant, "I have a right to hear the charge."

"Quiet!" he snapped, face flushing as he eyed the gathering throng on the quayside. "It'll be all I can do to get you clear of here without this lot stringing you from the nearest mast."

I could hear them now, despite the thickness of the walls that surrounded us, a classic baying mob. The words "Hang the traitor!" and "Avenge the Hope!" seemed to be the most salient amongst their chants.

"'It is only in the Alpiran Empire that the rule of law is truly respected,'" Fornella quoted in a faintly bitter voice. As ever her memory for my writing was aggravatingly accurate. "'Justice being applied equally regardless of station. All, from the meanest, most beggared subject to the Emperor himself, can expect equal treatment before the law.'"

She paced back and forth, prowling the cell and wincing at the occasional upsurge in the mob's fury. "What can you have done to arouse such ire, my lord?" she asked, her tone more than a trifle sarcastic. "Perhaps offended the Empress in some way?"

"You didn't have to stay," I pointed out.

She sighed and sat down next to me on the mean wooden bench, tracing a hand through her hair and issuing a groan of annoyance at the grey tresses coming away in her fingers. "Where else is there for me to go?"

I watched her hold the hair up to the light from the small window, thinking they resembled tarnished threads of copper and making a mental note to write the observation down later, should I be afforded the opportunity. "Is this what happens?" I asked. "When you are denied the blood of the Gifted?"

"To the best of my knowledge no other recipient of the Ally's blessing has undergone this particular trial. Some have been killed of course, assassinated or fallen in war, such is the nature of Volarian politics. But, once blessed, none have tried to exist without feeding."

She opened her hand and let the hair fall to the floor, pausing a moment to flex her fingers in the shaft of sunlight, a faint smile on her lips. "Strangely, I find I don't miss it at all. Mortality, as it transpires, has its compensations."

A clattering of locks and the tramp of boots told of a visitor. I rose to regard the tall figure coming to a halt on the other side of the bars, an imposing fellow with handsome if somewhat weathered features and close-cropped hair that now had more white in it than grey. "Hevren," I said, taking note of his uniform and the star embossed onto the centre of his breastplate, the crest of a Cohort Commander. "Promoted at last, I see."

"Lord Verniers." His tone was neutral, though his eyes betrayed a deep caution as they tracked from me to Fornella. "Who is she?"

"Fornella Av Entril Av Tokrev," she said, getting to her feet. "Late of the Volarian Empire and now ambassadress on behalf of Queen Lyrna of the Unified Realm."

Hevren returned his gaze to me. "Named a traitor and now you appear in company with a Volarian. I must say, my lord, I do begin to question your vaunted wisdom."

Named a traitor . . . *For all its falsehood the accusation still stung.* All I have given, all the years of service, and this is my reward. *"Might I know who has slandered me so?"*

A spasm of anger flashed across his face and he stepped closer. "You are named traitor by Empress Emeren herself," he grated. "And I therefore advise you to exercise great care over every word you speak."

There was a time I would have retreated from such a man; these brutes always did make me excessively nervous. But it seemed constant exposure to their kind had dispelled much of my former timidity. They were just men after all, men who could kill, as could I. "The particulars of the charge?" I asked, meeting his gaze.

My absence of fear seemed to give him pause, his anger fading as he moved back. "All in due course, as dictated by law." He paused, regarding me with grim reluctance. We had never harboured any affection for one another but there had always been a mutual respect of sorts, however grudgingly offered. "All you had to do was watch him die, Verniers," he said. "Would it have been so hard?"

◆ ◆ ◆

It's said the Merchant Kings of the Far West possess palaces so vast they resemble cities, sprawling over many acres and housing innumerable servants. However, greatness is not measured only by size but also wealth, and I have never been able to conceive of any building that could outshine the Alpiran Imperial Palace in sheer architectural opulence. It stood atop a tall hill, its steep slopes rising from the broad waters of the Tamerin River, crowned with a building born of a time when modesty and restraint were not chief among Alpiran virtues. It was essentially a great six-pointed star of a building, the wings extend-

ing from a circular centre topped with a dome, and it was the dome, of course, that captured Fornella's immediate attention.

"Do your Emperors like to blind their people?" she enquired, shielding her eyes. The midday sun was high overhead and the dome blazed bright enough to conceal its shape. I had always thought it best viewed at sunset, when the orange glow would play over the silver surface like a candle-flame, flickering towards extinction as night fell. Sometimes Seliesen and I would ride out beyond the walls, watching the spectacle from a hilltop. He said he had a poem in mind which might do justice to the sight, but if he wrote it, I never knew.

Hevren had brought two full companies of cavalry to escort us from the docks, though they proved only just adequate to prevent the gathering mob from making good their screaming threats. It was not the threats that pained me though, it was the faces I saw as we rode along the narrow channel Hevren's men forced through the throng. Face after face contorted in hate, men, women, children. Whatever lies had been voiced against me had clearly gained near-universal acceptance. I knew then that, regardless of what transpired here, my home was now lost to me. It wasn't just that these people would never accept me, more that I would never forgive their gullibility. A phrase Al Sorna had once spoken came back to me as we cleared the crowd and made for the palace at the trot. He had been quoting Janus at the time, relating the tale of his king's machinations in the prelude to invasion: Give them the right lie and they'll believe it.

Hevren veered from the road to the main gate as we neared the palace, leading us to the north-facing wall and a much-less-ornate entrance: the Soldier's Gate, reserved for guards, servants and the occasional Imperial prisoner. I had rarely ventured to this end of the palace and was struck by the absence of formality, or the clean orderliness that ensured a life of untroubled ease for the honoured members of court. This was all bustling workshops and stables shrouded by a haze rich in the mingled odour of food and dung. Before my journeyings I might have wrinkled my nose at such a place, but now it stirred no more than a vague unpleasantness; my senses had been assailed by far worse in the course of the preceding year.

We were greeted by a man I recalled from Al Sorna's trial, a beefy fellow in plain black clothing, bearing a set of chains in his meaty fists. Seeing little point in protest I climbed down from the saddle and proffered my wrists, expecting some growled threats from the gaoler as he snapped the manacles in place. Instead he greeted me with a deep bow and an expression of grave respect.

"My lord, long have I wanted to speak to you in person . . ." He trailed off, raising the chains with an embarrassed wince. "But not like this."

"Leave it, Raulen," Hevren told the gaoler.

"But he's to be taken directly to the Empress, Honoured Commander."

"The security of the Empress is my concern. I'll convey Lord Verniers to the cells in due course."

The interior of the palace is easily navigable thanks to its straightforward construction; all corridors lead to the centre where the Emperor, or rather Empress, holds court. However, the inordinate length of those corridors does leave ample time for contemplation or awkward conversation. "I was wondering," I ventured to Hevren. "Regarding Emperor Aluran's passing . . ."

"He was near eighty years old and grew more frail every day," Hevren stated in a clipped tone. "There is no mystery or suspicion to be probed, my lord."

"And his final testament?" It was tradition for the incumbent Emperor, once the impending end of his reign had become apparent, to compose a testament, praising those who had served him in life and offering guidance to their successor.

"Your legacy was generous," Hevren said. "Lands on the northern coast, an annual pension, plus several rare volumes from the Imperial library. Whether you'll be permitted to keep it . . ."

"I have no interest in my legacy," I said. "Only in his guidance for the Empress."

Hevren walked in silence for a time, his visage becoming notably more grim as we neared the entrance to the Imperial courtroom, great mahogany doors near twenty feet high. "It consisted of just one sentence," he said. "'Forsake all luxury.'"

"Hevren." I stopped, forcing him to a halt, the surrounding guards part drawing their swords. I ignored them and stepped closer to the commander, speaking in low earnest tones. "She has to hear me. Whether I am condemned or not. She has to hear my words and the words of this woman."

"I am a soldier," he stated, turning as the doors were hauled wide. "Not a counsellor."

He stood, gesturing for me to continue, his stance respectful rather than threatening. I glanced at Fornella, who stood eyeing the revealed throne room with naked trepidation. "It's my head she wants," I told her. "When she takes it try to make sure she listens."

The Imperial throne room takes the form of a circle, ringed on all sides by thick marble pillars to support the great dome above. There are no seats save the throne, positioned atop a raised dais in the centre, the dais itself formed from solid cylindrical blocks of diminishing diameter, creating six steps where the Imperial counsellors stand. The status of each counsellor is denoted by the position on the dais; senior military officers typically occupy the lowest step whilst lawmakers and scholars could expect to stand on the second or third tier. I had been unique in being the only Imperial historian ever to ascend to the fourth step. Only the Hope or those whose advice was most cherished by the Emperor could expect a place on the fifth tier. The sixth step was always left vacant, a reminder that the ruler of the Alpiran Empire must ultimately bear the weight of power alone.

My eyes briefly tracked over the counsellors, finding some faces I knew, all either unwilling to meet my gaze or staring in unconcealed, if somewhat forced, fury. I was surprised to find two counsellors on the fifth step, and one a soldier. Horon Nester Everen, High Commander of Imperial Forces, had always been a difficult man to read. Partly because of the habitual scowl he wore, but more so in recent years due to the extensive burns he had suffered in the final assault on Marbellis, scarring the left side of his face from brow to neck. The attitude of the other man on the fifth step, however, was much more easily discerned. Merulin Nester Velsus, the Imperial Prosecutor, had never regarded me with much affection, or I him. He had always struck me as a man engaged in a perpetual quest for the weaknesses of others, as if in confirmation of his boundless capacity for judgement. Seeing the new depth of his enmity, I deduced my current predicament fulfilled long-held suspicions.

However, my attention was soon fully captured by the figure seated at the top of the dais. My last glimpse of her had been in Linesh on returning from the Isles. She had descended the gangplank to the wharf and strode off alone without a backward glance. We hadn't exchanged a single word during the voyage and watching her pace the deck, face set in constant, unyielding spite, had convinced me there would never be any scope for accommodation between us. I had lost my hate but she clung to hers. It was then the decision came to me. My scholarly curiosity, rekindled by Al Sorna's tale, yearned for answers to the many tantalising questions left in his wake. I would return to court, deliver my account of events in the Isles to the Emperor, and take ship to the Unified Realm. In time, of course, I came to regret making such a rash decision. Though, as I looked upon Empress Emeren I, I suspected it would have made little difference to my current circumstance.

Her face was set, the fine features impassive, composed and free of animosity.

But she couldn't keep it from her eyes, the way they bored into me, seeming to gleam with anticipation, told me that, whatever pretence to impartiality she might make, my fate had already been decided.

"Uncle Verniers!" I started at the joyous shout, my gaze snapping to the boy scampering from behind one of the pillars. Iveles had grown in the months since I had last seen him, taking on a lankiness that told of early-arrived adolescence, though he still retained a boyish spirit. He ran towards me, uncaring of the surrounding guards, a toy soldier in each hand, wrapping his arms around my waist, gazing up at me with eyes so like his father's I found myself momentarily robbed of words.

"Did you bring me something from the northlands?" he demanded before speaking on with only the barest pause. "Bad people came to kill me and Mother but one turned into a good person and let us go and Hevren fought them and the villa burned . . ."

"Iveles!"

The Empress had risen to her feet, face still composed, though only barely. The guards had all drawn swords, save Hevren, who crouched to gently disentangle the boy's arms from my waist. His face tensed in stubborn refusal and his arms tightened, attempting to hold on.

"It's all right, Iveles," I told him, placing my hands on his shoulders to gently push him away. "I'm sorry, but I forgot your present. I did bring a story though, one I hope to tell you soon. Now go to your mother."

The boy shot Hevren a resentful glare then turned and ran to the dais, scampering up the steps to his mother's side. Watching how she drew him into a protective embrace, her eyes still fixed on me, I realised her detestation was at least partly inspired by the closeness I had always enjoyed with her son. Appointed the boy's tutor in Imperial history by the Emperor, we had spent many hours together, and, though I tried to dissuade him from it, he had come to call me uncle. "You and father were like brothers," he said. "So you will be my uncle. I don't have any others."

The Empress smoothed a hand through the boy's hair, speaking softly. "But I want to stay!" he protested. The Empress's tone became harder and Iveles gave a sullen pout before stomping off to the rear of the dais, his rapid footfalls echoing through the chamber as he sought other amusements.

The Empress sat in silence for a time, regarding me with practised detachment before turning her gaze to Fornella, her mouth twitching in momentary disgust. "Lord Velsus," she said to the Imperial Prosecutor. "The prisoner has the right to hear the charges levelled against him."

Velsus bowed to her before turning to me, producing a scroll from the folds of his robe. "Lord Verniers Alishe Someren, Imperial Chronicler and First of the Learned, is hereby charged with treason," he read. "Be it known, as established by credible testimony, Lord Verniers conspired with the Imperial Prisoner Vaelin Al Sorna to effect his release and evade just punishment for his crimes. Be it also known that Lord Verniers did conspire with agents of a foreign power, to wit the Volarian Empire, to injure the person of the Empress and her son Iveles."

So there it was, not one lie but two. I cannot truly account for the icy calm that possessed me then, much as I remain unable to explain the presence of mind that allowed me to sink a knife into the base of General Tokrev's skull. It could be that there are occasions when fear becomes redundant. "Credible testimony?" I enquired.

Lord Velsus blinked and I deduced he had been expecting some outraged protestation of innocence, no doubt to be shouted down by a well-prepared, and suitably theatrical rebuttal. He recovered his composure quickly, however, and gestured to the guards at the door. "Bring in the witness."

I was expected here, *I realised as we waited in silence.* The trap is too well laid.

The witness was duly led in, a young woman in a plain dress, her colouring typical of the northern empire, dark hair and skin of an olive hue save for a cluster of livid red stripes on her neck. She was clearly overawed by her surroundings, hands clasped together and head held low, her eyes alighting on me for only a second before she snatched them away.

"State your name," Lord Velsus ordered.

The young woman had to cough twice before she got the words out, her voice coloured by a barely suppressed quaver. "Jervia Mesieles."

"That is your married name, is it not?" Velsus enquired.

"Yes, my lord."

"State your birth name."

"Jervia Nester Aruan."

"Quite so. Your father was formerly Governor of Linesh, was he not?"

"Yes, my lord."

"In fact, he held stewardship of the city at the time of the Hope Killer's occupation. An occupation many believe led to an outbreak of the red plague, during which you yourself almost perished. Is this not so?"

Jervia's hands twitched and I surmised she was fighting an impulse to touch the marks on her neck. "It is so, my lord."

"However, you were saved by the intervention of the Hope Killer, who called for a healer from his homeland. So, it would be fair to say your father considered himself in the Hope Killer's debt, would it not?"

Jervia closed her eyes, raising her head and drawing a breath. When she opened them and looked at me I saw the unmistakable apology they held. "It would, my lord," she said in a laboured tone, the voice of a reluctant actress.

"It is said," Velsus went on, "your father was given a gift by the Hope Killer shortly before his arrest. What was it?"

"A sword, my lord."

The Imperial Prosecutor's gaze swept the assembled advisors, brows raised in surprise. "He accepted a gift of the Hope Killer's sword, the very blade that had been stained with the divine blood of the Hope himself. A man of more noble spirit might have found such a gift an intolerable burden on his honour, but given your father's ineptitude in defending his city and failure to take the honourable course in the aftermath of defeat, hardly surprising. Tell me, was there anything unusual about this sword?"

Jervia took another ragged breath. "Yes, my lord. The blade had strange markings upon it, and sometimes . . . sometimes Father would take it out, at night when he thought no one could see. He would draw the sword and the blade would glow with a strange, white fire. It . . . did things to Father, changed him, somehow . . ."

She faltered as I laughed, her face suddenly bleached white and eyes moistening.

"Forgive me, honoured lady," I said. "Please continue."

Velsus rounded on me, face twisted in anger, finger pointed in accusation "Mark well this man's humour, my lords! See how he delights in his own evil!"

He turned back to Jervia, calming himself with an effort that made me suspect this was not all theatre. "You have seen this man before, have you not?"

"I . . ." She looked down at her clasped hands, white now and shaking. "Yes . . . Yes he came to see Father, the night before the Hope Killer was brought to the city."

"You witnessed their meeting?"

"I did, my lord. I wasn't supposed to, but I knew a hidden place in Father's study where I could hear his meetings. I was worried, you see. The sword had changed him so much, and with the Hope Killer's return I wondered what he might do. Father told Lord Verniers he intended to return the sword to the Hope Killer. Lord Verniers became very angry, calling Father a traitor, saying he would have the Emperor send guards to arrest him . . . But Father showed

him the sword, and he became quiet. Father said with this sword the Hope
Killer was sure to prevail in his duel in the Isles, if Lord Verniers voiced no
objection to its use he would receive a great reward."

"I see. And the nature of this reward?"

"Knowledge. The Hope Killer would relate the story of his life and the reasoning of mad King Janus in starting the war."

"A rich reward indeed, to be cherished by any historian."

Velsus levelled his gaze on me, his aspect the unwavering focus of a leopard
eyeing cornered prey. "You did travel with the Imperial prisoner to the Meldenean Isles, did you not?"

"At the Emperor's order," I said.

"Quite so, but also, I recall, at your own request. And during the voyage
did the savage keep his end of the bargain? Did he tell you his sorry tale?"

"He related what I believe to be a partially accurate account of his role in
the invasion."

"And you gave him the sword."

"Governor Aruan gave him the sword. A plain weapon of little distinction,
I might add."

Velsus gave a dismissive wave. "The Northmen were renowned for their
ability to conceal their magics. And on arrival at the Meldenean capital, having received your reward, did you feel no obligation to warn the Hope Killer's
opponent that he now faced a foe rendered invincible by unnatural means?
And in doing so did you not ensure the Hope Killer would prevail in the duel,
a contest that by all accounts lasted barely a second, thereby robbing our murdered Hope of all justice?"

"There was no warning to be given." I glanced at Jervia, her head now lowered, face drawn in abject misery. "I do not know what threats have forced lies
from this unfortunate woman. And it grieves me to see her distressed on my
account. But if Al Sorna was made invincible that day, it was not by such a
mundane thing as his sword."

Velsus descended the steps, moving with measured deliberation as he
advanced towards me. "See how he wriggles on the hook, my lords. See how
he squirms and gives voice to yet more falsehood. This vile man, picked out
and ascended to high station by the Emperor's grace, and yet willing to sell
himself like the cheapest whore for the words of a savage. Were that his only
crime, it would be perhaps forgivable, upon receipt of due punishment naturally, for all men are weak and liable to seduction. However, my lords, it transpires this creature has an even greater crime to account for."

He turned back to the dais, pausing to address Jervia with a few curt words of dismissal. She raised her gaze to me as the guards led her out, tears flowing freely as she mouthed, "My father," eyes rich in appeal for understanding. I replied with the barest nod, even managing a small smile before she was led from the throne room.

"I humbly call upon the Empress Emeren I," Velsus intoned, bowing low before the dais. "To graciously consent to bear witness in this matter."

The Empress waited a moment before standing, an action that required all others present to kneel. I duly sank to one knee, gesturing for Fornella to follow suit. This was one piece of etiquette we could not afford to ignore, disrespect of the Imperial person being punishable by instant death.

I noted how Emeren's eyes lingered again on Fornella, seeing the brief moment of calculation before she turned away. A wrinkle in her scheme, I decided. An unwanted complication.

"As all here will know," the Empress began, "shortly before my Choosing, an attempt was made on my life and the life of my son. Many trusted and beloved servants died in this attack and my son and I escaped death by only the narrowest of margins. My attackers were a Volarian woman and a servant of the same fanatical heretic sect as the Hope Killer himself. It became clear to me in the course of my ordeal that these assassins had received intimate intelligence regarding my home, for how else could they gain access with such ease? Before I was rescued by the brave intervention of Commander Hevren, the woman spoke to me." She raised an arm, the finger pointed at me, straight and unwavering. "Naming this man as the source of her intelligence. Apparently, he wanted me to know of his involvement, as befits a man mired in jealousy and hatred."

I met her gaze, seeing only triumph. Beloved Emperor, I thought. What have you done to us?

I sighed and rose, keeping my gaze locked on hers, refusing to look away even as Hevren's sword blade pressed against my neck. It stopped as the Empress raised a hand. "I will not spare this traitor a trial," she said. "Our people deserve truth and the observance of law."

"If you intend to kill me," I said, "then do so, and spare me your farce of a trial. I only ask you first listen to my account of the conflict in the Unified Realm, to be verified by this woman, for it is of grave import to this empire."

It was barely a smile, just a slight curl to her flawless lips, but I saw then a woman experience perhaps the sweetest moment of her life. "Lord Verniers, I have already heard far too much from you."

CHAPTER ONE

Vaelin

As before, the first thing he noticed was the change in the air, the sulphuric taint of the mountain top replaced by something altogether sweeter. The damp chill was also gone, transformed into the warm caress of sunlight, leavened by the gentle brush of a summer breeze. But this time the sounds were different, no creak of forest branches or birdsong, but the clamour of many hands at work. The ground beneath the memory stone had also changed, carved rock replaced by smooth tiles of freshly hewn marble. Vaelin raised his gaze, finding that they in fact no longer stood atop the mountain but on a raised platform in the centre of a newly risen city.

Everywhere men worked amongst scaffolding, hauling ropes or carving stone, teams of tall shaggy-footed draught horses hauled huge wagons laden with blocks of granite and marble. The air was filled with calls and songs as the men worked, the absence of any whip-cracks or chains a clear sign these were not slaves. If anything they all seemed cheerful in their labour. His eyes alighted on the tallest structure, a narrow, rectangular tower near fifty feet high, its walls covered in scaffolding, but he could see the red marble and grey granite beneath. His gaze shifted to another building closer by, the walls in place but the roof not yet complete. It was a sizeable structure, larger than those surrounding it. A mason sat in a sling suspended over the lintel, his chisel leaving a line of symbols in the stone, symbols once ascribed meaning by Brother Harlick: library.

"The Fallen City," he said aloud, a glance at the southern landscape confirming it. The ages might erode a city but not the mountains.

"Quite so." Erlin stood nearby, hands enfolded in his cloak as he regarded a tall figure standing a short way off, head lowered as he read an unfurled scroll. "And the man who built it."

The man lifted his gaze from the scroll, Vaelin moving to view his face, somehow knowing what he would see. He was bearded with a heavy brow, though not so aged and lined as his statue would later depict him, younger even than the painting on the Wolf People's cave wall. But still there was a gravity to his expression as he surveyed his newborn city, eyes narrowed, occasionally flickering in suppressed frustration.

What could he find to dislike in such an achievement? Vaelin wondered, glancing around at the burgeoning elegance on all sides. "He is king of this place?" he asked Erlin.

"I doubt such a word had any meaning here."

Vaelin gestured at the toiling workers. "But these men do his bidding."

"And seem happy doing so, don't you think? I see only what the stone shows me, brother. But I've seen nothing that would indicate this man commanded through fear or force of arms. Search the entire city, you won't find a single sword."

A raised voice caused the bearded man to turn, his teeth suddenly bared in a bright smile as a young woman ran to his side. Once again, Vaelin was unsurprised to note her resemblance to the woman from the cave paintings: green-eyed and dark of hair. She shared a warm embrace with the bearded man, fingers entwining in automatic intimacy as they kissed. She drew back with a laugh, turning and extending her hand, speaking words Vaelin couldn't fathom, though her tone was rich, joyous even. A narrow-faced young man moved into view, approaching to within a few feet of the couple, smiling a tight, reluctant smile. He was subtly different from the figure depicted in the cave, younger and without the sardonic twist to his mouth, but still recognisable. The woman laughed and reached out to draw him closer, presenting him to the bearded man, who ignored the young man's hand to enfold him in an embrace.

"Brother and sister," Vaelin realised, his gaze switching between the woman and the young man.

"I think so," Erlin said. "The first time all three were together. But far from the last."

Abruptly the memory shifted, the buildings and the people gone to swirling mist around them, as if they stood at the centre of a vortex though there was no sensation of wind. Soon it slowed, the mist coalescing into the city once more, though now the buildings were all complete. Spring had come to the mountains and the air was fresh, the city lively with people; parents with children, lovers walking hand in hand. Music seemed to rise from every quarter, a man with a harp of some kind singing from a rooftop nearby, a cluster of singers a few streets away adding their own voices. There were also knots of people engaged in animated discussion, gesticulating at each other with scrolls and odd devices Vaelin took to be some form of sextant.

"Put more than one philosopher together and you'll birth an argument," Erlin commented. "A truism I've observed the world over. In fact, I once saw one argue with himself, it got quite violent in the end." He moved to the edge of the elevated platform, extending his arm in a broad sweep. "I think that's why he built this place. A haven for thinkers, artists, scholars. In all my travels, I've never seen a city like it."

An angry voice drew Vaelin's attention to the approach of the dark-haired woman, striding ahead of the bearded man, hands moving in emphatic, negative slashes. Her brother followed behind at a distance. They were all older than before, though perhaps by only a few years. The younger man's timidity seemed to have vanished, the weary amusement on his face an echo of what he would later depict on the cave wall.

The woman went to the memory stone and Vaelin saw it now had a twin, identical in shape but not in colour, for this stone was black, its surface free of any flaw or vein. *Something black,* Vaelin recalled Wise Bear's deep unease as he touched the space where this thing now stood.

The woman paused to regard the black stone, her face briefly transformed into a mask of confusion before turning back to the bearded man, pointing at the stone, voice raised in emphatic tones. He sighed, moving to stand opposite her with the stone between them. He spoke softly but his words were no less certain than hers, and also carried an unmistakable note of refusal. The woman began to rail at him, handsome features marred by a deep anger. She calmed a little as her brother came forward, moving close to the stone, though Vaelin noted how he put his hands behind his back. He spoke for a short time, shrugging often, his sister evidently annoyed by his apparent lack of concern. Eventually she threw up her hands in an exclamation of angry defeat and strode away.

Her brother and the bearded man exchanged rueful glances but no more words. After a short pause the bearded man extended a hand to the stone, letting it hover over the smooth surface, Vaelin seeing the involuntary shudder in his fingertips. The younger man spoke, just a few short words, but all humour had vanished from his face and the tone was sharp, almost commanding.

The bearded man hesitated, a brief spasm of anger twitching across his features. Then he laughed, withdrawing his hand and moving back, patting the young man on the shoulder before walking away at a sedate pace. He descended the steps to the street below, exchanging good-natured greetings as he moved through the throng, every face around him rich in respect and affection.

The young man watched him go then turned back to the stone, fingers tracing over his chin with brow furrowed in thought. After a moment he brightened and began to walk away, but paused on reaching the steps. His back straightened as if in response to some unheard alarm and he turned, eyes tracking across the platform until they came to rest on Vaelin.

"He sees me," Vaelin said.

"Yes," Erlin said. "I always wondered what made him pause at this point. Hopefully, now his next words will make some sense."

The young man walked forward slowly, his expression one of cautious amazement. He came to within a few feet of Vaelin and stopped, reaching out as if to touch his cloak, though the fingers slipped through the material like mist. He drew back a little, his lips fumbling over a question in a language not his own. "You . . . have . . . name?" he asked in heavily accented but discernible Realm Tongue.

"I have many," Vaelin replied. "Though I suspect you will know me by only one."

The young man's brow furrowed in bafflement. "I . . . Lionen," the young man said. "I seee you . . . before." He tapped a finger to his temple. "In dreams . . . In waking . . . Hear your tongue . . . Learn it."

"You have the gift of scrying," Vaelin said, elaborating in response to another baffled frown, "You . . . see what is to come."

"Sometimes . . . Sometimes it . . . changes. You, always same." His gaze went to the black stone. "So too this."

"What is it?"

Lionen's face tensed in consternation and Vaelin realised he was fumbling for words to describe something even he didn't fully understand. "A box," he said finally. "Box full . . . of everything, and nothing."

"Your sister fears it."

Lionen nodded. "Essara sees great danger in this. Her husband great . . . use."

"And you?"

"I see you, and it." His gaze tracked to Erlin. "And him . . . But he is not him when he touches it."

His face clouded and he turned towards the city, now bathed in a faint orange glow as the sun began to descend below the western mountains. "In your time . . . this place is gone, yes?"

"Yes. Brought to ruin many ages before."

Lionen lowered his gaze, features dark with sorrow. "I . . . hope I see it wrong." He took a breath and straightened. "If . . . I see you again. Bring . . . happy words."

"Wait." Vaelin reached for Lionen as he began to walk away, though of course his hand made no purchase. "You have knowledge I need. We face a great danger . . ."

"I know," Lionen replied with a shrug. "I . . . face danger too."

Vaelin caught a glimpse of his face before the memory broke apart once more, his half grin returned for an instant, then sublimed into mist as the vortex swirled.

"What did he mean?" he demanded of Erlin.

"I wish I knew, brother," the ancient man replied. "But I suspect we have now ventured far beyond the limits of my knowledge."

This time the vortex coalesced into a scene of chaos, the city burnt and tumbled around them, accompanied by the screams of thousands in torment. Vaelin ducked instinctively as a thunderous tremor shook the stone beneath his feet, his gaze immediately drawn to the tower, standing tall and glorious in the night sky, but only for a moment. The ground shook again and the tower fell, its stone flanks bent like a bow as it tumbled to earth, shattering the houses beneath in an explosion of stone and flame.

Vaelin went to the edge of the platform, drawing up in shock at the horrors unfolding below. A woman staggered through the streets with a headless child in her arms, face blank with madness. A portly man in a long robe ran past her, screaming in fear, chased down and dismembered in seconds by a group of men in red armour, laughing gleefully as their swords rose and fell in a joyous frenzy.

Vaelin's eyes roved the dying city, finding scenes of slaughter and torment everywhere, Sella's words from years before coming back to him, *They had lived in peace for generations and had no warriors, so when the storm came they were naked before it.*

It raged on for an hour or more, the city tumbling down around them as its people died. The men in the red armour were inventive in their cruelties, delighting in the screams of those they raped or flayed, though apart from their laughter they were mute killers, going about their bloody work with no words exchanged.

"What are they?" Vaelin asked in a whisper.

"In time the people who will build the Volarian Empire will call them the Dermos," Erlin said. "Imagining them the product of some fiery pit beneath the earth. When they're done here they will cross the ocean to assail every place they can find where humanity resides, birthing legends and gods in the process." Erlin pointed to something in the smoke-shrouded streets below. "Their onslaught will continue until the one who commands them falls."

The figure moved through the carnage without seeming to notice it, stepping over corpses and striding through pooled blood in a steady, untroubled stride. The red-armoured men moved aside at his approach, not in respect, for they made no bows or other show of obeisance, but as if in answer to an unspoken command. Once he had passed they would return to their ghastly amusements without a glance in his direction. His face became clear as he neared the platform steps, pausing to gaze upwards, brow so deeply lined now it appeared scarred, the glow of a thousand fires flickering on the grey of his beard.

He grimaced as he began to climb, his legs stiff and back stooped from the effort. On reaching the platform he paused, issuing a loud, weary groan, then glanced back at the chaos below. The expression on his aged face was one Vaelin knew all too well. *The one who commands them*, he thought, seeing the hungry malice that twisted the bearded man's features.

"He did this," Vaelin realised aloud. "He destroyed his own city."

"And a great deal more besides," Erlin said as the bearded man moved to the centre of the platform, halting before the black stone plinth, looking down into the void of its surface. He stood there for some time, until the screams and the last thunderous rumble of destruction faded, leaving only the continuing roar of the flames.

The bearded man raised his visage to the night sky, eyes closed as he extended a hand to the stone. His malice seemed to have vanished now, leaving a depth of weariness Vaelin found almost pitiable. Where before his hand had trembled, now it shook as if afflicted with palsy, the bearded man's mouth opening in a silent scream . . .

Abruptly he whirled away from the stone with a shout, chest heaving and features livid with rage and another expression Vaelin knew well; the twitching, bright-eyed mask of a prideful man unwilling to acknowledge his own defeat.

A large troop of red-armoured men ascended the steps at a run, bearing several long wooden beams. The bearded man moved away from the black stone as his servants moved in. They placed the beams under the plinth's wide, mushroom-like top and lifted it up, bearing it away quickly, seemingly uncaring of the weight as they proceeded down the steps and through the corpse-choked streets below.

The bearded man lingered for a moment, eyes narrow as they scanned the platform. There was also a slight smile to his lips, a faint glimmer of humour in his eyes. *He knows I see this,* Vaelin decided, the freezing chill of realisation coursing through him as he saw the malice return to the bearded man's face, his smile lingering as he turned and descended the steps without a backward glance. *No more than a great stone head waiting for the ages to turn him to dust . . . The Ally.*

◆ ◆ ◆

"Did you know?"

"I had suspicions." Erlin raised a hand to the memory stone. "But these memories are so ancient. So many lives have been lived since, a thousand kingdoms risen and fallen, spawning countless mysteries."

"Lionen said you would touch the black stone," Vaelin pressed. "But not be you when you did. What did he mean?"

"I think he meant we have much to think on." Erlin extended his other hand to Vaelin. "Nothing else will occur here, though I once waited the best part of a month to confirm it. Wait long enough and perhaps you'll see the Lonak arrive."

Vaelin sighed, casting a final look at the still-smouldering ruins before moving to take Erlin's hand, then drawing back in alarm as it turned to dust before he could grasp it. The vortex returned in a heartbeat, taking Erlin with it. There seemed to be a new ferocity to the swirling dust now, the colours changing, a more complex dance to the spiral of chaos. It faded as quickly as it had come, revealing the mountain top above the Lathera village. Except now he was alone and it was night, the clouds above turned into a roiling orange roof by the glow from the fire mountains. Their fury seemed brighter now, his eyes picking out a gout of molten rock amidst the flame and smoke, a small tremor pulsing through the rock beneath his feet.

"So," a voice said. "Do you have happier tidings for me?"

Lionen walked towards him from the cluster of dwellings. He was older, his long hair mostly grey, his face still lean but also lined. He paused a few feet away, frowning as he took in Vaelin's appearance. "Ah. It has only been moments for you, has it not?"

Vaelin nodded. "My friend . . ."

"This memory is not for him." Lionen turned, extending a hand towards the dwellings. "I was about to have supper. Would you care to join me?"

"Your knowledge of my language has improved," Vaelin observed, following Lionen to one of the larger dwellings. He noted the others were all silent, the windows absent any light.

"I have had many years to study it. And several others, though I find it my favourite. Less flowing than Seordah but more poetic and functional than Volarian." Lionen stood aside at the door to his house, gesturing for Vaelin to precede him. Inside the air was warm, the chamber sparsely furnished with a low wooden bunk and some scrolls stacked in the corner. A small iron pot steamed over a fire, the smoke escaping into a narrow channel in the roof.

"I would offer you some stew," Lionen said, taking a seat beside the fire. "But it would be a redundant gesture."

"I can feel," Vaelin said. "But not touch. Why?"

"The stone captures place and the time, but they are unchanging. As is our conversation. It has already happened, even though for both of us it appears to be happening now. What has happened cannot be changed, and so you cannot touch it. Change is the province of the future."

He lifted the lid on the stewpot, tasting a sample with a small spoon. "Quail with wild thyme and mushrooms," he said. "Pity you can't have any. I've had a great deal of time to perfect the recipe."

"How long have you been here?"

"Fifteen years since I built this miniature city. I had companions then."

"What happened to them?"

"Some left, bored with my inactivity. Others disappointed by my lessons and seeking wisdom elsewhere. The remainder I sent away. I find youth tedious these days, they're always so terribly earnest."

"The stone outside, you carved it, filled it with your memories."

"And more besides. The stones were not simply repositories for memory. They were also a means of communication, each one connected to the other. A useful innovation for a civilisation that spanned half the world."

"All brought down by your sister's husband?"

"Yes. Whilst I roamed the ice searching for the impossible, he had other work in mind."

Vaelin recalled the cave paintings, the three visitors who became two. "Your sister died saving the ice people. You brought sickness and she healed them, though it cost her life."

"She was a healer. She saw it as an obligation, though we begged her to stop."

"Is that what changed him? Made him hate what he built?"

"Essara's death may have darkened his soul, but I suspect his first steps along the path to what he is now were taken long before. It was the disappointment, you see, the constant dissatisfaction. He tried so hard to build his perfect world, a civilisation that would see humanity ascend to something greater. But people are still people, however comfortable their surroundings. They lie, they feud, they betray and however much you give them, they always want more. Without my sister's influence it grew harder and harder for him to keep giving, keep guiding in the hope they would one day fulfil his great vision. And so, having proved themselves unworthy of the world he had crafted for them, he resolved to bring it all down."

Lionen took a bowl and began filling it with stew, from the aroma Vaelin judged his liking for the recipe to be well-founded. "Tell me," he said, settling back, bowl in hand, "did the Eorhil woman find the stone I left for her?"

Vaelin recalled Wisdom's tale of her journey to the fallen city, the meeting with the shade of Nersus Sil Nin. "She did, with help from a blind woman who shared your gift."

"Ah, the blind woman." Lionen smiled fondly as he ate. "Often seen in my visions, but never spoken to. Such a comely thing in her youth, I should greatly have liked to meet her."

"You crafted the stone that gave Wisdom her name," Vaelin said. "Knowing she would find it one day."

"The vision changes, sometimes she finds it, sometimes she doesn't. I suspect the blind woman saw the need to give destiny a small nudge. I journeyed back to the city after my time on the ice, finding long-rotted corpses and destruction, a scene my gift had never revealed to me for it has always cast my sight far into the future. The black stone had gone and the memory stone lay shattered, though I was able to pull enough knowledge from the fragments to divine who had done this thing. I spent years amidst the ruins, lost in grief, diverting myself with learning the language and lore revealed by my gift. One day it brought a vision of the Eorhil woman holding a perfectly square stone fashioned from the same material as the memory stone, except such an artifact did not exist in this fallen city, so I made it. I recrafted the memory stone, chiselling away for the better part of a year until it was just a small cube, and into it I poured all the knowledge revealed by my gift. I hope it made her happy."

"It made her . . . of great use to her people, and mine. For which I thank you."

Lionen gave an affable shrug and returned to his meal. "What were you looking for?" Vaelin asked him as the silence grew long. "Out on the ice where you took your sister's body."

"A legend. I know to you my people are little more than myth, but in this time we have our own tales, old songs from the days when the earth was young. I've seen much that would suggest this world is far more ancient than we could ever comprehend, a mother to countless wonders. I went in search of one, a being the people of your time would term a god, said to have the power to return the dead."

His gaze grew distant and he resumed his meal, eating in silence. Vaelin wondered if this meeting was so familiar to Lionen he had become wearied with the repetition. It occurred to him that his gift was truly a curse, filling his mind with visions of a future so distant and removed from this time but holding a terrible truth, robbing his own age of meaning.

Another tremor shook the ground, stronger this time, causing the shutters on the windows to rattle and shaking Lionen from his silence. He scraped the last of his stew from the bowl and rose, taking it outside. Vaelin followed, finding him tying it to a length of rope strung between two dwellings. "It's a long climb down to the river," he said. "The wind will scour it clean. An empty gesture, but I've always found habits hard to break."

"Did you find it?" Vaelin prompted. "This god of legend?"

Lionen's gaze shifted to something beyond Vaelin's shoulder. "I think you know what I found, oh Shadow of Ravens."

He knew what he would see, even though it had made no growl this time, and its approach had been silent. It was not so large as before, its shoulders level with Vaelin's waist, though he had long suspected it could assume whatever size it chose.

The wolf trotted closer, nose close the ground as it sniffed the stone around Vaelin's feet, reminding him of how Scratch would search for a scent. "He can smell you, though you are but an echo cast back from times to come," Lionen said. "It would seem he wants to be able to find you again."

The wolf sat back on its haunches, long pink tongue sliding over its lips as it yawned, green eyes regarding Vaelin with placid affection. "He followed you from the ice?" he asked Lionen.

"Yes. I found him so far north I suspect I stood atop the entire world. He was bigger then, every inch the god I expected to find. He came close, sniffed at Essara's body, used his teeth to pull away the shroud covering her face. For one mad second I thought he was going to eat her, but instead he licked her face, just once . . . And I heard her voice."

Lionen's face clouded and he started back to the memory stone, Vaelin following with the wolf padding alongside. "You have more questions for me," Lionen said. "Please make them quick. Time grows short."

"The black stone," Vaelin said. "What is it? Why did he take it?"

"I told you, it's a box. One we opened together, and this world is the result."

"You said Erlin would touch it, but not be him when he did. What did you mean?"

"The ancient man told you he was nearly taken before, when he came close to death and touched the Beyond. You know the Ally uses others to wreak his havoc in the world, souls captured and twisted to his purpose. Why do you suppose he didn't send one of them to steal Erlin's body?"

Lionen halted before the stone, smiling faintly. "The last one ever to be carved, by my own hand. The stone itself comes from but one mine, deep in the mountains found in the place you call the Northern Reaches. We also found the black stone there, just one huge nugget of it with very singular properties. It was his idea to carve it, of course, though my sister argued against it. 'Such power should not be placed in human hands,' she said. He laughed and held her close, saying, 'All power should be in human hands, my love. For how else can we transcend humanity?'"

"Power," Vaelin said. "He is drawn to it."

"As a vulture to a corpse. And what greater power is there than the ability to defeat death itself?" There was a weight to Lionen's words now, a grave intent in his eyes, the meaning all too clear.

"I will not do that," Vaelin stated.

"Then watch your world die as I watched mine. The land that surrounds us is barren, and so it is for mile after mile in all directions. Small villages survive here and there, a few towns that somehow weathered the storm, the attentions of what they called the Dermos. In time they'll grow, build kingdoms and then an empire, forgetting their legends and making themselves ripe for his purpose with their endless greed. For now, he waits. I can feel him, coiling in the Beyond, plotting, planning. Not yet strong enough to capture me when I pass, though I've little doubt he'll try."

"You killed him," Vaelin said. "You're the reason he is in the Beyond."

"How else would I have gathered followers in such a barren land? With the wolf's help I sought out those that could help me, a band of brave warriors and those possessed of gifts they barely understood, all grieving over family or lovers lost to his onslaught. The Volarians will call them the Guardians in time. Together we killed him."

Lionen gestured to the stone, casting an urgent look to the east as the ground shook again. "It's time."

"Something is about to happen," Vaelin said.

"A long-promised ending." Lionen turned to face the fire mountains, Vaelin seeing their fiery glow grown even brighter, the blanket of cloud above now a deeper shade of red. "An eruption fifty miles from here is about to cast forth a cloud of hot ash that will descend upon this mountain faster than any man could hope to run. It will settle, concealing this place from human eyes for centuries, though eventually the elements will strip it away, and my bones with it. The only vision of my own time I was ever permitted, my own death."

"You have seen my future?" Vaelin asked. "You have seen what happens to my people?"

Lionen glanced over his shoulder and smiled. It was a smile of genuine regret, rich in sympathy and absent any irony. "I have seen enough to pity you, Shadow of Ravens." He turned back to the fire mountains as the ground shook once more, the force of it making him stagger.

"You need to kill his creatures," he said. "Trap them in their stolen bodies and kill them. Without tools in this world his need to act will be even greater, the lure of power impossible to resist. The black stone resides in the arena in Volar. When it's done, take him there. One touch and it gives. A second and it takes."

A booming roar came from the east, accompanied by a huge gout of lava, ascending in a fountain of fire before streaming down the flanks of the mountain that had birthed it. The mountain top shook, sending Lionen to his knees, the sky above turning black as the fire mountain's glow diminished, a thick fog vomiting forth from its sundered summit and sweeping down its slopes with impossible speed.

Next to Vaelin the wolf gave a soft but urgent whine, nuzzling his hand and pressing him closer to the stone. He reached out to it, though found he couldn't look away from Lionen, now kneeling with his arms spread wide, the burning ash sweeping towards him in an unstoppable black tide.

"My sister spoke my name!" he cried out as the ash crested the mountain top and swallowed him. The heat was unbearable, the ash choking as Vaelin pressed his hand to the stone . . .

. . . he blinked, the instant change in the air making him gasp. His eyes went to the spot where Lionen had been kneeling a second before, embracing his death. The stone was bare, without the faintest sign of his passing.

"What did you see?" Erlin asked, his brow creased in an uncertain frown. "It kept you. It must have shown you something more."

What greater power is there? Vaelin looked away, finding the confusion in Erlin's eyes hard to bear. *I will not do that.* He moved back from the stone and started towards the steps. "As you said, we have much to think on."

◆ ◆ ◆

Lorkan blinked into existence and slumped down beside Vaelin, ignoring the agitated murmur from the Sentar. Astorek's wolves also began a distressed chorus of whines until he calmed them with a look. "I'd guess about five thousand people," Lorkan said. "All crammed into the guts of that mountain." He pointed to a steep-sided peak little over a mile away, a jagged scar visible in the rock a third of the way up its flank. "I didn't go too far in, but saw enough to know they're in a grim state, plenty recently wounded, some dying. Perhaps half are children. The older ones don't seem to be getting on, sitting in different groups and glowering at each other."

Vaelin had been angered to discover Dahrena had flown once more in his absence, returning to the camp to find her slumped next to the fire with Cara and Kiral pressed close on either side. "No more of this," he said, sinking to his haunches before her, smoothing a hand over her ice-chilled brow. "Even if I have to drug you unconscious."

"Oh don't grumble," she murmured with a smile, lips pale and eyes dim with fatigue. "I think I may have found some allies."

"Did any see you?" Vaelin asked Lorkan.

"A little boy started pointing and screaming when I tried to go farther in. Assuming he was gifted, he was the only one amongst them."

"We should go alone," Erlin said. "A large party will arouse too much fear."

"Fear can be useful." Vaelin turned to Astorek. "Tell your father to bring the full host to this valley."

He waited until midday then guided Scar towards the mountain at a walk, coming to a halt at its base. He gazed up at the jagged scar in its side, now revealed as a cave mouth, dark and silent, not even a tendril of smoke emerging to betray its occupants, though he had little doubt they had seen his approach.

He relaxed his grip on Scar's reins, allowing him to nibble on the sparse grass of the valley floor, eyes fixed on the cave mouth. He had no real certainty of achieving his aim. Pertak had laughed when Erlin related Vaelin's request for an alliance. The Lathera chieftain had a fresh scar on his jawline and a newly dug grave had appeared outside the walls of his settlement. He kept one hand close to the pouch on his belt and moved with the hunched, narrowed-eyed pose of a man in constant fear of attack. His laughter though, was entirely genuine.

"Let the southern goat-fuckers die," Erlin translated as Pertak stomped back to the settlement, still chuckling. "Then their seams will be ours to mine."

The first of them appeared after a wait of several moments, a single kilted figure standing at the cave mouth, staring down at Vaelin with axe in hand. Vaelin raised both arms, showing his hands to be empty. Several more figures resolved out of the blackness of the cave, growing in number until perhaps six hundred people stood regarding him in silence. Vaelin lowered his arms and waited, hearing the growing tumult raised by the approach of the Wolf People. The spear-hawks came first, calling out their pealing cries as they glided into the valley and wheeled above, then the wolves, several packs numbering well over a hundred individuals. They loped forward to surround Vaelin, drawing an involuntary shudder from Scar.

Vaelin peered at the face of the first figure to appear as the Wolf People marched into the valley. He was too distant to fully make out his features, but Vaelin judged him to be the oldest tribesman present, possibly a chieftain. However, judging from the mismatched symbols and colours adorning the clothing of his companions, he doubted this man would be able to speak for all those who had taken refuge here. Nevertheless, he clearly commanded some form of regard, exchanging a few short words with the others before starting down the slope. Some of his companions followed immediately, all wearing similar colours and symbols to his own. The others lingered for a short time, exhibiting a fractious disunity as they exchanged shouts and threatened each other with raised weapons. Their disagreement proved short-lived, however, and soon all were following the older man to the valley floor.

Vaelin kept his eyes on the leading figure, not turning to witness the Wolf People coming to a halt at his back. The man walked towards him without undue haste, though there was a definite purpose to his gait. He halted twenty paces away, the other tribesfolk lining up on either side. Vaelin took hold of Scar's reins and trotted him forward, stirring a ripple of unease throughout the small throng, though they made no move to oppose him.

He halted Scar a few yards short of the possible chieftain, looking into his face and seeing the besmirched, near-maddened gaze of a man who had lost much of his world in the space of a few days. Kiral had advised her song told of rage and confusion among these people, but sounded no note confirming they were on the right course. "My song grows darker and less tuneful every day," she said. "Ever since we found the endless man. I doubt I have any more certainty to offer."

But looking into the pain behind this man's eyes, Vaelin saw all the certainty he needed. He had seen this face many times during the march towards Alltor. The face of the tortured, the raped, the widowed . . . and the vengeful.

His Volarian was poor, but Erlin had coached him on the correct pronunciation. "We go south," he said, patting his chest and pointing to the southern end of the valley. "Kill Volarians. Come with us."

CHAPTER TWO

Lyrna

Aspect Arlyn's face betrayed no recognition as he regarded Nortah, nor any emotion at all as his gaze shifted to Lyrna, though his eyes narrowed slightly. *Bound,* Lyrna realised. *Like Brother Frentis or the Kuritai.* The Aspect reached over his shoulder to draw a sword of the Asraelin pattern, the steel bearing the signature flame-like markings of an Order blade.

"Aspect!" Nortah said again, taking a forward step, sword arm now limp at his side. "Do you know me?"

The Aspect's gaze switched back to Nortah, the long features giving a faint tic of remembrance. "I know you, brother," he said in a soft, reflective tone. "You died."

He raised his free hand, paused a moment in expressionless consideration, then gave a barely perceptible flick of his wrist and the Arisai surged forward, manic joy on every face, swords moving in a blur of expertly wrought carnage. At first the Queen's Daggers recoiled from the assault, Lyrna finding herself crushed between Davoka and Iltis as the surrounding ranks compressed, but the pressure slackened as they voiced another savage roar, rallied and fought back.

She struggled to turn, catching a glimpse of Nortah in combat with the Aspect, face drawn in reluctance as he fended off Arlyn's blows. "Sister!" Lyrna called to Davoka, holding her spear above the thrashing ranks, eyes watching hawk-like for an opportunity to use it.

"The flasks!" Lyrna forced her way to the Lonak's side, grabbing her arm. "Do you have the flasks?"

Davoka blinked at her in momentary bafflement then nodded, patting the small satchel at her side. "Only two."

"Stay by me."

She slapped Iltis's shoulder to get his attention and pointed to Nortah, now backing away under a furious assault from the Aspect, dodging thrusts from the surrounding Arisai as he did so. Iltis nodded and began to push through the ranks of soldiers. As they neared the edge of the formation the Lord Protector was obliged to sidestep a thrust from an Arisai, the red-gauntleted hand holding the sword flashing into the space between him and Lyrna. She hacked down with the hatchet, the blade biting through the grieve to part sever the wrist. The Arisai collapsed at her feet, looking up with a grin, rich in lust and admiration. Lyrna's hatchet came down again, shattering his skull above the eyes.

Iltis cleared the outer ring of soldiers and forced the Arisai back with wide sweeps of his sword. Lyrna held out a hand to Davoka who instantly filled it with a flask, the stopper already removed. Another Arisai slipped past Iltis, sword raised level with his head for a short, expert stab at Lyrna's throat. Her hand jerked reflexively, casting a stream of dark liquid from the flask directly into his eyes. The reaction was instantaneous, the Arisai's sword falling from his grip as he arched his back and howled, hands scrabbling at his face, fingers digging into the flesh. Watching him collapse to writhe on the temple floor, Lyrna had the satisfaction of seeing that all vestige of a smile had vanished from his face.

Nortah was only a few feet away now, forced to a crouch by the weight of Aspect Arlyn's blows, all delivered with a blurring fury whilst his face remained a pale mask. A trio of Arisai charged into Iltis's path, the combined assault forcing him to a halt, cuts appearing on his sword arm and forehead. Lyrna stepped to his side and swept the flask from left to right in a wide arc, the Mahlessa's compound spraying forth to spatter onto the Arisai, most of the liquid falling onto their armour but enough finding exposed flesh to send them screaming to the stone floor.

Beyond them Nortah was now on his back, scrabbling away as the Aspect loomed closer, blade flashing. The Lord Marshal fended off the blows with typical efficiency, but Lyrna noted how he still restrained himself, failing to thrust at the openings left by the Aspect's relentless assault.

"Aspect Arlyn!" He paused at her call, sword drawn back and sparing her only a short, incurious glance, but it was enough. The flask was empty save for a few droplets on the nozzle. She put all her strength into the throw, the flask turning end over end to collide with the Aspect's face. For a moment she thought it hadn't worked, that all the compound had been exhausted, but then saw a single glistening bead on his cheek, his face transformed into a wide-eyed, frozen scream. He sank to all fours, his sword clattering to the stones, shuddering as he fought to control the convulsions.

One of the Arisai gave a regretful chuckle and rushed forward, blade poised to strike at the Aspect's back, then doubled over as Nortah's sword stabbed up to pierce his breastplate. The Lord Marshal surged to his feet, sword moving in a silver blur as more Arisai closed in.

"Rally to Lord Nortah!" Lyrna called to the surviving Daggers. There were no more than thirty now, but all still fighting and willing to follow their queen's commands. She held out her hand to Davoka, taking the second flask and casting the contents at the Arisai as they surged anew, felling a dozen or more and causing the others to reel back. The sight of their comrades' screaming convulsions seemed to denude their humour, many smiles faltering, and their laughter fading. *Pain makes them human,* Lyrna decided, moving to stand with the Daggers, now formed into a greatly diminished circle, only one rank thick. Nortah stood in the centre, crouched at the Aspect's side, face livid with concern.

"My lord!" Lyrna snapped. "To your duties if you would!"

Nortah shot her a glance of barely concealed resentment then rose, moving to her side. "If Your Highness has any brilliant stratagem for this circumstance, I am keen to hear it."

"Kill the enemy," she said, tossing the empty flask aside and hefting her hatchet.

The spectre of a grin played over his lips for a second and he nodded. "What it lacks in subtlety it gains in directness, Highness."

The Arisai edged closer, eyes fixed on Lyrna, wary for any sign of another flask. Their fallen comrades had stopped writhing and lay in rigid stillness, each face a rictus mask of agony, frozen in death. *At least I taught them how to fear.*

Her gaze was abruptly drawn to the temple's southern quadrant by a rising blossom of orange flame, accompanied by the faint tumult of combat and curiously, the yapping of enraged dogs. Any elation she felt at the sight, however, was negated by the sheer number of Arisai standing in her way; the Empress had been wise in sending an ample supply.

Another gout of flame erupted beyond the Arisai followed by some kind of commotion, too distant to make out but she discerned a certain discord in the rear of their ranks. She saw one of the Arisai who had been edging closer come to a sudden halt, standing with his sword held up before his face, turning the blade in apparent bafflement. He blinked, brow furrowed in deep confusion, then, without pause, turned to the Arisai on his left and slashed the blade across his throat. One of his companions immediately cut him down, only to draw up short himself a second later, his face also taking on the same baffled expression. This newly confused Arisai abruptly launched himself into the midst of his comrades, slashing wildly with his sword, killing three before he too was hacked down.

"What is this?" Nortah breathed. "Your Lonak elixir, Highness?"

"No." Lyrna's gaze returned to the rear of the Arisai host, seeing the enemy ranks parting as if sliced by an invisible blade, allowing a trim figure to stride through, ignored by the surrounding Arisai, who all seemed to be wearing the same identical expression of utter bemusement. Aspect Caenis strode clear of the Arisai, offering Lyrna a stiff bow, blood streaming from his nose, eyes, ears and mouth, before turning his full attention to their enemies.

Off to the right another Arisai drove his sword into the belly of the man next to him, then another and another. The discord rippled through the red ranks like a wave spreading out from a pebble tossed into a pond, but birthing a storm instead of a ripple. Soon it seemed every Arisai in sight was fighting his neighbour, hacking at each other with a ferocity that belied their baffled expressions.

Caenis stood aside, gesturing at the path he had carved through the enemy ranks. "Go!" Lyrna ordered the surviving Daggers. "Escape this place."

But they stayed, unwilling to leave without her. She went to Caenis's side, seeing how he shuddered, the blood flowing in thick streams and his skin bleached white as snow. "Come, Aspect," she said, taking hold of his hands.

"I . . . regret I must . . . abide here a while . . . Highness," he replied, a red torrent escaping his mouth to cover his chin.

"Brother!" Nortah rushed forward, reaching out to grab at Caenis's arms but the Aspect staggered away, reeling into the whirling mass of maddened Arisai, lost to sight amidst their fury, now rising to an even greater pitch of self-destruction. Nortah started after him, restrained only by Iltis and Davoka at Lyrna's shouted instruction. She ordered the Daggers to gather up the still-unconscious Aspect Arlyn and led them through the battle to the temple steps, Nortah screaming in fury as Iltis and Davoka dragged him along in her wake.

Outside there were more bodies littering the steps and the ground beyond, Arisai and Realm Guard, plus a few in the unarmoured garb of the Seventh Order. A young woman with honey blond hair knelt at the side of a plump sister, tears streaming down her face, a brace of bloodied darts clutched between her knuckles. The plump woman was plainly dead, the steps beneath her covered in blood though her body showed no sign of injury. A dozen hunting dogs surrounded them, all sunk low to the ground and uttering piteous whines. Nearby Trella Al Oren stood amidst a dozen blackened bodies, her face streaked in blood and soot. A burgeoning dust cloud rose to the east, the dark shapes of many horsemen visible at its base, blue cloaks and green— the Sixth Order and the North Guard racing to the queen's rescue.

Nortah was still straining against Iltis and Davoka, spouting rage-filled curses at them as he fought to return to the temple. Lyrna turned back, seeing how the Arisai's fury continued unabated for several minutes then abruptly stopped, retreating from one another as if in answer to some silent command, gazing at the carpet of corpses covering the temple from end to end.

"Enough!" Lyrna said, striding to Nortah and delivering a hard slap to his jaw. His struggles ceased and he gaped at her, eyes momentarily so devoid of reason she wondered if he had been rendered mad. "He's gone," she told him, trying to gentle her tone. "See to your regiment, my lord."

The Lord Marshal slumped, moving back from Davoka and Iltis, his eyes tracking over the remnants of the Queen's Daggers now numbering barely two dozen souls. "Of course, Highness," he muttered in a tone both caustic and weary. "My mighty force is yours to command."

He pulled away and began to organise his survivors into some semblance of order. Lyrna turned as Brother Sollis reined in nearby, leaping from the saddle to hurry to where Aspect Arlyn lay between Murel and Alornis, his face betraying both shock and relief.

"Highness!" Brother Ivern drew up close by, staring down at her with an appalled concern that made her consider her appearance, liberally spattered with blood from head to toe and holding a reddened hatchet. "Do you require a healer?"

"No, thank you, brother." Her eyes went to the North Guard, galloping to form a cordon between her and the temple. To the east more dust rose above a dense mass of running infantry, the banner of Al Hestian's Dead Company visible through the haze.

"Where is the Battle Lord?" she asked Ivern.

The young brother's expression became grim. "Wounded, Highness. It's bad. There were Kuritai hidden among the Free Swords, at least a thousand of the bastards." Lyrna noted the bloody bandage covering Ivern's hand. "They took some killing, I must say."

She nodded and turned to the temple, watching the remaining Arisai forming themselves into well-ordered ranks once more. She couldn't see their faces but the sound of their laughter was clear enough. *One-half compelled to kill the other and it's all just a fine jape.*

"Find Lord Al Hestian," she told Ivern. "He is to ring the temple to prevent the enemy's escape. Have your brothers convey word to the other regiments to follow suit. Then bring me Lord Antesh."

◆ ◆ ◆

They tried to break out before the Realm Guard were fully in place, a tight wedge of five hundred Arisai launching themselves at Al Hestian's regiment whilst the remainder split into smaller groups and attempted to escape to the south. Al Hestian's dead men stood firm however, their line buckling under the impact of the charge but failing to break, their Lord Marshal taking position in the centre of the first rank. Lyrna heard later how he had used his spike to impale one of his men who turned his back on the enemy. After a quarter hour's savage fighting, with the Realm Guard moving to outflank them, the Arisai retreated in good order, having lost about half their number. The smaller groups were continually assailed by the North Guard and the Sixth Order, cut down by the dozen until they too began to fall back. The Arisai formed a dense defensive square as they retreated, moving like a single laughing beast as it ascended the steps to dissolve into the confines of the temple.

"Give the word, Highness," Lord Adal said, his usually handsome features rendered ugly by a lust for retribution. The Arisai seemingly had no notion of surrender and he had lost many North Guard in containing their escape. "We'll scour the place clean for you."

"If I may, Highness." Lyrna turned to find Al Hestian pointing his bloody spike at the river. "Our cavalry should cover the hidden causeway and the northern bank. It's their only remaining line of retreat."

She nodded. "Lord Adal, join with the Nilsaelin horse. You will guard the causeway whilst the lancers shield the northern bank."

The North Guard commander gave a reluctant nod. "And the assault, Highness? I would still beg the honour of leading it."

Lyrna scanned the army, the Realm Guard and Nilsaelin infantry drawn up in good order, Antesh's archers forming up at their rear. The cavalry patrolled the flanks in a wide arc sweeping around as far as the river to block all avenues of escape. All done with but a few orders and no formal plan. *What a deadly instrument we built,* she thought. *Scarred and dented enough for one day.*

"That won't be necessary, my lord," she told Adal before turning to Al Hestian. "The army will hold in place. Send word to bring up the ballistae."

The Arisai continued to make small-scale sorties as the ballistae were hauled into place, a few having retained enough horses to mount a charge to the west, attempting to break through the cavalry screen only to be met by Renfaelin knights and cut down to a man. Lyrna also received reports of others attempting to swim the river, the few making it to the far bank providing welcome sport for the waiting Nilsaelin lancers.

Alornis reported the ballistae ready by late afternoon. As ever, working with her devices seemed to bring some animation to her features and she stood by, watching with a faintly prideful expression as the last engine was trundled into place alongside its fellows. The small corps of artisans who served the ballistae worked their various levers and windlasses until every one was armed and ready, the crossed bowstaves all drawn back, waiting.

"At your discretion, my lord," Lyrna said to Antesh. The Lord of Archers nodded and lifted his bow above his head. The archers, arrayed immediately behind the line of ballistae, all raised their bows to a high elevation, strings drawn back behind the ear for maximum range. Antesh lowered his arm and the arrow storm began. The sky was still light enough to follow the dark mass of arrows as they rose and fell onto the temple, a black rain continuing unabated as Lyrna had ordered every possible shaft scavenged from the battlefield. She could see the blood still glistening on many of the arrowheads launched by the longbows. The archers seemed tireless, many grunting with the effort of drawing and loosing at such a rate, but their faces all set in determined hatred. Apparently slaughtering so many Free Swords hadn't been enough to sate their vengeance.

Lyrna used her spyglass to scan the temple, seeing an Arisai fall as he attempted to run for one of the pyramidal god-houses, pierced by three arrows a foot short of shelter, two of his comrades falling onto his body a heartbeat later. *They are already mad,* she thought, the spyglass settling on an Arisai who shook his head in amused resignation as he regarded the two shafts protruding from his breastplate. *Can they be maddened further?*

The answer was not long in coming, a great shout of joyous abandon rising from the temple before they came streaming forth. All cohesion had been forgotten now and they simply charged at the line of ballistae in a disordered

red tide. Lyrna waited until the leaders had cleared the steps before giving the order for the ballistae to loose, the range having been narrowed to less than fifty paces. The effect was remarkable, the leading Arisai cut down by an invisible scythe, those following tumbling over the bodies or spinning from the impact of the second volley. In some cases a bolt would pierce an Arisai with enough force to continue on through to claim one of his comrades. Despite the losses however, the Arisai's charge retained sufficient momentum to come within twenty paces of the ballistae, at which point Antesh's archers moved forward, lowering their aim and unleashing another arrow storm that halted the red host completely.

"Highness," Al Hestian said, "I believe the time is right."

She nodded and he gestured to the cluster of buglers nearby, sending them running towards the opposite flanks of the army, the call for a charge of cavalry pealing forth. Antesh walked the line of archers barking orders to cease, though some continued to loose with frenzied disregard for orders and had to be forcibly restrained. Fortunately, both archers and ballistae had stopped by the time Fief Lord Arendil led his knights from the left flank and Brother Sollis the Sixth Order and the Realm Guard cavalry from the right. The surviving Arisai met them with what could only be described as matchless valour, leaping to bring riders down, cutting the legs from under the horses, fighting to the last, voicing their joyous mirth to the end.

◆ ◆ ◆

Count Marven drifted in and out of wakefulness as she sat with him, holding a damp cloth to his burning brow when his distress blossomed into weeping panic. Brother Kehlan had been free with redflower in treating the Battle Lord, his face grim when Lyrna questioned the wisdom of giving him so much.

"His spine is shattered below the neck, Highness," the healer replied. "If he were to live, he wouldn't walk again. And he won't live."

"I . . ." Marven coughed, eyes suddenly wide as they found her face, "I killed a Kuritai, Kerisha. Did they tell you?"

Kerisha, she knew, was the name of Countess Marven. "Yes, my love," she said, working the cloth over his brow and along his cheek. "They told me."

"What's wrong?" he demanded, suddenly wary. "Why are you angry?"

"I'm not angry," she said. "I am proud. Very proud."

"You're . . . only kind when you're angry," he muttered, easing a little. "A tongue that could cut silk, the Fief Lord always said . . . The queen, though." He paused to smile in fond reflection. "You might have met your match in her. However, I think she'll be amenable now . . . That castle you always wanted . . ."

"Yes," Lyrna assured him. "I'm sure she will."

"The boys . . ." His voice grew softer, eyes dimming as his head sank farther into the pillow. "You were right . . . No soldiering for them . . . There's gold in the Reaches, lots of it . . . We'll send them there . . ."

He slept for a time, untroubled by the whimpers and cries of the wounded crowding the tent. Messengers and captains came to her throughout the night, all turned away by Murel and Iltis. She stayed and watched Count Marven until the swell of his chest had stopped and all colour faded from his face.

"Murel," she said, the lady moving to crouch at her side. The flesh around her left eye was a deep shade of purple and she bore a three-inch row of stitches across her cheek. "Make a note. A grant of land for Countess Kerisha Marven of Nilsael and sufficient funds for the construction of a castle."

"Yes, Highness." Murel hesitated, gaze intent on Lyrna's face. "You must sleep, my queen."

She shook her head. Sleep meant dreams, and she knew what they would show her. "Ask Brother Kehlan for something to keep me awake. And tell Brother Hollun I require a full account of our losses."

◆ ◆ ◆

The blond sister named herself as Cresia, standing with head lowered as the body of her Aspect burned behind her. Lyrna had watched them say their words, these few survivors of a greatly diminished Order, each stepping forward with a story of kindness, wisdom or courage. Lord Nortah was also there, along with Brother Sollis and many of the Sixth Order. The Lord Marshal had faltered during his words, a tale of their time in the Martishe Forest, left unfinished as he fell silent, staring at the body on the pyre as if in incomprehension. "He never got to meet his nieces and nephews," he said finally, voice faint and empty of feeling. "For he was my brother, and I know they would have loved him."

"By any measure Aspect Caenis was a great man," Lyrna had said. "A greatness revealed only recently, but bright enough to outshine us all. It will be known forever more that this man never faltered in his course, never shied from the hardest duty and gave everything in service to Realm and Faith."

There were other fires to light of course, more words to say. Murel, Iltis and Davoka waited at Benten's pyre and the plain was liberally dotted with more. In accordance with tradition soldiers from the same regiment were being committed to the flames together, meaning there were dozens of fires, rather than thousands.

"Your Order has made its choice then?" she asked Sister Cresia.

The young woman hugged herself tight, hair covering her lowered face like a veil. "Yes, Highness. Though I begged them to choose another." Her hair parted as she lifted her face to regard the pyre, Aspect Caenis now just a dark shape amidst the flames. "I can never be him. He was . . . great, as you said."

"War has a tendency to rob us of choices, Aspect. Get some rest. Tomorrow I shall require an accounting of your numbers."

"There are twenty-three of us left, Highness," Cresia told her. "The Seventh Order was never overly numerous, perhaps four hundred souls at its strongest."

"You will rebuild, in time."

Cresia lowered her gaze once more and Lyrna had little difficulty discerning her thoughts. *Another battle like this and there will be nothing left to rebuild.*

◆　◆　◆

The early-morning sun played over the river's churning current, raising a fine mist from the waters. Aspect Arlyn stood alone on the bank, his red armour gone now, a tall figure in a blue cloak no doubt taken from the body of a fallen brother. Brother Ivern stood nearby, bowing with a weary smile as she approached. Lyrna wondered if he was there as guard or gaoler.

"Has he spoken?" she asked.

"A little, Highness. He asked after Aspect Grealin, and Lord Vaelin."

"What did you tell him?"

Ivern seemed puzzled by the question. "Everything. He is our Aspect."

She nodded and moved to the Aspect's side, Brother Verin keeping within ten feet of her as ordered. Arlyn turned to her, dipping his head in the shallow bow he had always offered to her father and brother. His expression was sorrowful, as might be expected, but she also discerned a judgemental cast to his gaze, one she knew he had never been shy in showing to Janus.

"Highness," he said. "Please accept my condolences on the loss of King Malcius."

"Thank you, Aspect. Though we have all suffered losses."

His eyes flicked to Brother Verin. The young Gifted had seen much since taking ship with her and was less inclined towards displays of nerves, though he still squirmed a little under the Aspect's gaze.

"I have learned caution in dealing with those who have met the Empress," Lyrna said.

The Aspect nodded in placid acceptance and turned back to the river. They were parallel with the point where the Arisai had made their crossing, the current more disturbed here than elsewhere, churning white where it met the bank. "How was it made?" Lyrna asked. "The causeway. Lady Alornis considers it quite the feat of engineering."

"With brick, bone and blood," he replied. "Three thousand slaves labouring for ten days at my command. The river is swift, as you see, and the Arisai found much amusement in the whip. By the end there were barely five hundred slaves left."

"The Empress's stratagems are clever, but costly, it seems."

He gave a faint shake of his head. "This was my stratagem, Highness. Conceived at her command, naturally. But the whole notion of attacking you here was mine."

"I know you were not responsible for your actions. Our enemy employs many vile devices."

"Indeed. A compulsion towards unreasoning vengeance being chief among them."

"I make no apology for securing the future of the Realm."

"Is that your intent, Highness? If so, the Empress would be greatly surprised."

Lyrna folded her hands into her gown, unwilling to let him see how they clenched in suppressed anger. "If you have intelligence on the enemy's designs, I would hear it."

"She would come to me sometimes, down in that cavern of horrors where they carved their binding into my flesh. She asked questions mostly, testing my knowledge of history, my experience of command. I expected her to force from me every secret I held regarding the Faith and the Realm, but it soon became apparent she knew more than I did. It also became apparent that she is quite mad, an inevitable consequence of centuries spent in service to the Ally." He lowered his head for a moment, eyes closed and breathing suddenly shallow. "Even a brief exposure is the harshest trial."

"What will she do next?"

"Formulate another plan to kill you, I expect. She seems to find you greatly irksome. 'I have birthed a thousand vengeful souls, but none so troublesome as this fire-breathing bitch.'"

"How many more Arisai does she have?"

"Perhaps seven thousand. Plus another eighty thousand Varitai and Free Swords."

Lyrna glanced at Verin's hands, confirming he gave the sign for truth. *Though she has hidden lies in truth before, and I failed to see it.* She said, "I had assumed there would be more."

"The war in the Realm swallowed the bulk of their best troops and discord grows in every corner of the empire. New Kethia has fallen to a slave rebellion, inspiring revolts across the provinces. She also seemed preoccupied with some mission to the north. She had me execute a senior general for questioning the wisdom of sending more troops there."

A mission to the north . . . Vaelin. He made it across the ice. A small smile played over her lips. *Of course he did.*

"Tell me more," she said, "of this discord."

Chapter Three

Vaelin

The tribesman's name was either Hirkran or Red Axe; they seemed to be interchangeable given the frequency with which Erlin used them. "He's lost three sons to the Volarians," he reported. "One taken as a slave years ago, the other two in the last week."

"He's chieftain of these . . . Othra?" Vaelin asked.

Erlin shook his head. "Red Axe is an honorific, a title given to the tribe's principal warrior. 'Champion' would be a better translation. And the Othra are but one of six tribes sheltering here. Every chieftain died in the fighting. He doesn't speak for all."

"Does he know if the others will fight with us?"

Erlin related the question to Hirkran, who cast a stern glance back at the cave where the gathered tribesfolk lurked in the shadows, all eyes apparently intent on this meeting.

"He isn't sure," Erlin translated. "Some won't simply because the Othra will. Some will stay here and piss themselves forever."

"Can he guide us to the Volarians?"

Hirkran gave a long pause before answering, his gaze fixed on Vaelin. "He will but first he insists on being named leader of the army."

Lorkan, who stood nearby with his cat, gave a derisive snort provoking the tribesman to a snarl, starting forward with an upraised axe. Vaelin stepped deliberately between them as the cat crouched, teeth bared in a hiss. He had noticed Lorkan's courage had increased considerably since acquiring the beast.

"He has a reason for asking this, I assume?" he asked Erlin as Hirkran continued to glower.

"These people respect only strength. If he is not named leader, they will see him as merely vassal to a foreigner, meaning he'll face an instant challenge from a younger rival. You could call it a ceremonial title if you like. These are their lands, Vaelin. Diminished as they are, they still deserve your respect."

Vaelin looked at the ragged figures shifting in the gloom of the cave, younger folk clutching weapons whilst the children gathered around the elderly. Each half-shadowed face bore the dirt and grime of days spent fighting for life; many were plainly exhausted and slumped by the pain of recent wounds. But he saw there was still a defiance in their eyes, even the youngsters. They might have been beaten, but were hardly defeated.

"Tell me what to say," he told Erlin.

◆ ◆ ◆

Hirkran tracked a winding course southward along a tall ridge, six of his warriors scouting ahead. Vaelin followed with Erlin, Kiral and Astorek. The scouting mission could have been avoided if he had agreed to let Dahrena fly once again but one look at her still-wan features caused him to voice a stern refusal.

"I would remind you, my lord," she grated, "I hold no formal rank in this army and am, in fact, free to do as I wish."

"And I am free to employ any one of the several methods at my disposal to render you unconscious without injury," Vaelin replied. "You will stay here and rest, my lady."

She had scowled and walked away, Mishara providing clear illustration of her feelings with a brief hiss before bounding off to pad alongside.

They had covered perhaps eight miles when Hirkran called a halt, Vaelin noting how Astorek's wolves had taken on a more cautious gait, keeping low among the craggy spine of the ridge and pausing frequently to sniff the air. They were clearly a disconcerting presence for Hirkran and his people, though from their carefully observed indifference, he discerned outward displays of fear were seen as a great disgrace.

Hirkran lowered himself to a crouch and made for the edge of the ridge, Vaelin crawling alongside. Below them the ridge fell away in a steep cliff, affording a fine view of the valley ahead. It was broad with a flat plain in the centre perhaps a half mile wide, divided by a shallow river. The Volarian host was encamped in a circular perimeter of dense pickets and neatly arranged tents. It seemed the Witch's Bastard was an efficient general.

Hirkran said something in a terse murmur which Erlin translated as an obscene curse involving the invocation of various ethereal entities as well as an inventive and cannibalistic form of genital mutilation.

"Why would they eat those?" Kiral asked with a distasteful grimace.

"To absorb the strength of an enemy," Erlin said. "And symbolise the end of his line. The tribes put great stock in having children. An infertile man or woman is seen as a curse and subject to exile, or worse if they're unwise enough to linger."

The huntress cast a disgusted glance at the surrounding warriors, muttering, "Savages."

Hirkran spoke again, gesturing at the Volarian encampment.

"Our leader demands the army be brought here for an immediate attack," Erlin said. "One he will lead personally. This must be done quickly or the spirits will judge us weak and refuse to help."

"They expect their gods to help?" Vaelin asked.

"They don't have gods, as such. They believe these mountains are possessed of souls of their own, either kindly or vindictive according to whim. When the storms come they are angry, when the winter is kind they are pleased. But they always take a dim view of cowardice."

"And we will be happy to honour them with our courage. But first I must ask what he has seen of these invaders. Particularly those that lead them."

Hirkran's face darkened and he looked away before voicing a series of short, grunted answers. "When they came we thought it would be as before," Erlin related. "They come, we fight them, they steal children, they leave. Sometimes the children can be bought back for copper or fire metal. Mostly not. This time they took children and killed them. They killed everything, even the wild goats and elk. We fought . . ." Hirkran's face took on a mask-like quality, as if the horrors he had witnessed were beyond expression. "We fought so hard . . . But they were so many, much more than had come before. We did not see who leads them, though the Rotha spoke of seven red men with powers that rivalled the spirits, but they are notorious liars."

Powers that rivalled the spirits. "Are there any Rotha here?" Vaelin asked, gesturing to the other warriors.

Hirkran spat and made a disgusted noise. "Back at the cave. Their stench dishonours us."

Vaelin nodded and moved back from the edge, causing Hirkran to bark a question at Erlin. "Where are you going?"

"To muster the army for our mighty leader's attack. Where else?"

◆ ◆ ◆

The Rotha were led by a stocky woman of middling years with a deep matrix of decorative scars carved into the flesh around her eyes. "Mirvald," she stated when Erlin asked her name, going on to add a few other titles which apparently indicated her status. "She's a mix of counsellor and shaman, said to have the ability to hear the word of the spirits."

"She saw the seven red men?" Vaelin asked.

Mirvald eyed Vaelin closely for a second before replying. "The Rotha were the first to feel their wrath. The Seven came to their settlement alone. Because they were strangers the warriors tried to kill them, but were themselves killed. The Seven are not like other men. They move and fight as one, as if each hears the thoughts of the others. Even so the Rotha would have prevailed had they not had other powers. One could kill with a single touch, another had the power to freeze a man's heart with fear. They killed many Rotha, and then their army came and killed many more."

"Thank her for her knowledge," Vaelin said.

The woman inclined her head at Erlin's words then asked a question of her own. "How do you intend to defeat the Seven when others could not?"

Vaelin glanced over to where Wise Bear held counsel with the other Gifted, all gathered round as he imparted another lesson from his bottomless well of knowledge. "Tell her we have powers of our own. If she would see them, she should come with us."

Erlin listened to her reply and forced a placid smile. "She will, but only if you name her leader of the army. Her people won't come otherwise."

"We already have a leader."

"I suspect it won't matter if you name two. The tribes rarely speak to each other except to exchange insults. I profess myself amazed they've managed to spend more than a day here without finishing what the Volarians started."

"Very well." Vaelin gave a weary nod and bowed to Mirvald before turning back to Wise Bear. "I await her wise commands and, with her permission, will now consult with my captains."

◆ ◆ ◆

"How do we find them?" Marken asked. "Hidden in such a host?"

"The Rotha woman said they move as one," Vaelin said. "I suspect if we find one, we find them all. Even so it will be no easy task in the midst of battle."

"My song may guide us," Kiral said. "But the tune is so uneven now . . ."

"No." Vaelin shook his head to clear red-tinged memories of Alltor.

"Singing during battle is best avoided." He turned to Astorek. "Could your mother's spear-hawks find them?"

"Commanding a beast becomes difficult when the killing begins," he said. "The sound, the scent of blood, makes them either fearful or hungry. It requires great concentration to ensure they attack the enemy and not our own people. To maintain enough focus to seek out a particular prey would prove difficult, perhaps impossible."

"I can find them," Dahrena said, her tone soft but certain. "Their souls are like black pearls in a sea of red."

"You have flown enough during this enterprise," Vaelin stated.

"There is no other way, as I suspect you know, my lord. Besides"—she reached for Cara's hand—"I have friends to share the burden."

"More than one," Marken added, moving to her side. "Doubt my old bones are fit for fighting in any case."

"So you see, my lord." Dahrena met his gaze with a bright smile. "Our course is set."

◆ ◆ ◆

"Remember, they need to be taken alive," Vaelin told Astorek. "Until Wise Bear touches them, they must not be killed."

The Volarian nodded as his wolves moved to take up position alongside Vaelin and Scar. The army had mustered to the north of the ridge, marching through the night to arrive before the onset of dawn. Dahrena would remain atop the ridge with Cara and Marken, their cats prowling the cliff-top with twenty of the Wolf People's most trusted warriors.

Vaelin went to Dahrena, the others retreating to a respectful distance. Her anger seemed to have dissipated and she clasped his proffered hands without demur, returning his kiss and letting it linger.

After a moment he drew back, speaking softly, "I have asked too much of you . . ."

She put a hand to his lips. "No more than you ask of yourself. We came to make an end, and I hunger for it. I want to go home, Vaelin. I want to go home with you and that can't happen until this ends."

He touched his forehead to hers and clasped her hands once more before moving back and striding towards Scar and the wolves.

◆ ◆ ◆

The Witch's Bastard had chosen his campsite well; the only cover was provided by the shallow river running through the valley floor. He led Scar at a walk through the waters, the banks just high enough to conceal his tall frame.

The wolves moved ahead, keeping to the sides. The predawn gloom was fading fast by the time he paused a mile short of the camp and requested Alturk take his Sentar in a wide sweep around the Volarians.

"Lorkan will go with you," he told the Tahlessa. "Carve a hole in their picket line."

"Can't wait," Lorkan said, forcing a smile, his new-found courage now plainly faltering despite the presence of his cat.

"The first break of dawn," Vaelin told Alturk, extending a hand. "Not before."

Alturk stared at his hand for a moment before briefly clasping his forearm. "My son's name was Oskith," he said. "It means Black Knife, he was aptly named." He glanced over at Kiral, crouched in the current and playing a hand through her cat's damp fur. "As was my daughter. I would have her know this."

"Then live and tell her yourself."

"That would make me a liar. Last night I sang my death song to the gods."

Alturk rose from the water and crept up the riverbank at a crouch before disappearing from view followed by the hunched, shadowy forms of the Sentar. Vaelin saw Kiral watch them go, seeing the knowledge in her eyes and realised he would have nothing to tell her if Alturk fell. *Few secrets can be hidden from the song.*

A short way on he bade the tribes folk to halt, and, like Alturk, make their attack at the first break of dawn, striking at the camp's northern edge. They were clumped together in their tribal groupings, obliging him to visit each one with Erlin. The six newly risen chieftains were all now under the impression they held ultimate command of this army and Vaelin thanked them all for the honour of allowing him to make the first attack.

He led the Wolf People on through the chill current, stopping when parallel with the main body of the camp. Whale Killer paused at his side with an affable smile before proceeding at the head of the warriors. They would circle around to the camp's south-facing perimeter, like Alturk making their attack at the first sign of the sun ascending above the eastern mountains.

Vaelin's gaze tracked the length of the river, now crowded with wolves, Astorek and the other shamans crouched among them, each strained face telling of the effort required to prevent a betraying explosion of snarls to the proximity of so many disparate packs. The wolves fidgeted but were mostly still, Astorek's most of all. They had remained close to Vaelin for the entire journey, their gazes rarely leaving him.

He turned to Erlin and Wise Bear crouched nearby. "You will take no part in this," he told Erlin, noting the hatchet gripped in his fist.

"I've fought on many occasion, brother," Erlin replied. "It could be I've seen more battles than you."

"Even so, remain in the rear. If the day goes against us, take yourself off, perhaps circle the world one more time."

"And watch it fall to ruin as I do?" Erlin shook his head. "I think not."

"You will be needed." Vaelin met his gaze, feeling the guilt surge anew. *I will not do that . . .* "Stay in the rear."

He turned to Wise Bear before Erlin could speak further. "Are you prepared?"

The shaman glanced to the east where the peaks were starting to take on the golden hue that heralded a new day. The sky was clear today, the air possessed of a pleasing freshness, coloured by a faint floral tint from the heather that covered the valley floor. "The green fire not seen here," the shaman reflected with a faint note of regret then sloshed through the river to where Iron Claw waited. The great bear issued a low rumbling growl as Wise Bear climbed onto his back and turned him towards the bank.

Vaelin beckoned to Lord Orven and hauled himself onto Scar's saddle. "If all goes well, there should be a decent gap in their ranks," he told the guardsman. "Concentrate on the Varitai if you can."

"I shall, my lord." Orven gave a salute, standing straight as the current flowed about him. "At this moment I'd trade everything I own for a horse."

Vaelin grinned and reached over his shoulder to draw his sword. "I expect there'll be plenty to choose from when we're done."

He kicked Scar into motion, splashing free of the river and waiting as Astorek's wolves took up position in front, the other packs swarming from the banks to close in on either side. Mishara padded through the throng and sank to her haunches at his side. Vaelin looked down to meet her gaze, wondering if Dahrena saw him through her eyes. Mishara merely blinked and licked her fangs before turning her attention to the Volarians.

The camp sat about three hundred paces distant, silent beneath the pall birthed by the dead fires of the previous night. Vaelin could see the pickets moving through the morning haze, their gait leisurely and free of any alarm. He waited as the sun grew warm on the back of his neck and his shadow faded into view on the ground ahead, a long dark arrow pointed at the Volarian host.

Nortah's words came back to him as he took a firmer grip on Scar's reins, *You're not going to do anything foolish, are you?*

He gave a soft laugh and kicked at Scar's flanks, the warhorse issuing a shrill, joyous whinny as he spurred to the gallop. The wolves surged forward with them, keeping pace with ease and voicing a collective growl no doubt birthed by the excitement of their shamans. Vaelin saw the pickets start to react, running to form a ragged line as discordant bugles sounded throughout the camp, men stumbling from the tents and scrambling to gather weapons and armour.

Naturally it was the Varitai who reacted first, two full battalions, probably kept awake to guard against a surprise attack, forming up to bar his path with their customary efficiency. They stood in two ranks, the first kneeling and presenting a hedgerow of spears. However, for all their unconscious discipline, even they were not immune to the sun. Vaelin saw many lowering their heads as the sun rose free of the mountains. It caused a certain ripple in their ranks but was not enough to disrupt them; for that he required something more.

The first spear-hawk streaked past his ear, close enough to feel the wingtip brush his skin, dozens more following on either side an instant later. They struck the centre of the Varitai line in a tight black swarm, streaking out of the blinding sun too fast to dodge or duck. The centre of the Varitai's line became a roiling mass of thrashing birds and men, the hawks rising from the melee trailing blood and flesh from their steel talons, hovering for a brief second then diving back down. By the time the wolves joined the struggle the Volarian ranks had already been broken.

Vaelin took Scar directly through the chaos, seeing a Volarian officer dragged down by a trio of wolves, his throat torn out in short order. The Volarians had formed more battalions beyond the Varitai, Free Swords standing in much-less-well-ordered ranks. They seemed younger than the Volarian soldiery he had fought before, many youthful faces betraying shock and outright terror at the sight of the horde of beasts wreaking havoc before their eyes. The bulk of the wolves tore into them without pause, the closest battalion falling to pieces under the onslaught in the space of a few seconds. The neighbouring formation fared better, forming itself into a tight defensive circle and managing to cut down many of the wolves that assailed it. They had no answer to the spear-hawks, however. Having dealt with the Varitai, their shamans re-formed their flocks and sent them against the Free Swords, streaking down in a black rain as the wolves continued to attack, running forward in pairs to fasten their jaws on the legs of the Volarians and drag them from the ranks.

Vaelin caught sight of a battalion commander on horseback nearby, sword raised high as he rallied his men, veteran sergeants running to his side and barking orders. He angled Scar towards the commander, Astorek's wolves loping ahead to bring down his horse. The man leapt clear as the horse screamed amidst a welter of blood, coming to his feet in time to turn and take Vaelin's sword full in the face. He galloped on to scatter the partly rallied men, cutting down a sergeant who unwisely chose to stand his ground.

Vaelin reined Scar to halt, glancing around to find Iron Claw pounding an unfortunate Volarian to death with his massive paws, Wise Bear appearing almost comical as he bounced on his back. Beyond him Vaelin caught glimpses of a vicious fight as the tribesfolk tore furiously at the northern perimeter. The tumult arising from the south and west indicated the plan had worked, at least initially. The Volarians were now assaulted on all sides and their ranks broken in the east. But the camp was not overrun and they were still fighting, too many regiments were formed and moving with the automaton rhythm typical of Varitai. This battle was far from won.

He looked to Mishara, finding her standing stock still, low to the ground and nose pointed at the centre of the camp where the densest mass of Varitai could be seen. He wheeled Scar about and spurred him to a charge, hearing Iron Claw's eager growl as he followed, the wolves soon striking out ahead, ignoring the wounded or dazed Free Swords wandering about.

The spear-hawks re-formed once more, circling the Volarian centre in a dense mass. They were fewer in number now, but their ferocity seemed undimmed as they rose and fell in a ceaseless, deadly spiral, raining blood as eyeless men staggered from the ranks, Free Swords screaming and Varitai lashing out at thin air in dumb obedience to their conditioning.

Vaelin saw them then, a knot of men at the heart of the Volarian ranks, flickering glimpses of red amidst the roiling black. He angled Scar towards them, the wolves massing around him to tear a hole in the wall of Varitai. He struggled through it, parrying spear-blades and hacking down any who strayed too close.

The first two red men appeared before him as he slashed his way clear of the throng, both mounted on tall warhorses and wheeling in a tight circle, their swords blurring as they cut spear-hawks from the air. Vaelin charged straight for them, the closest whirling towards him, face livid with hate-filled recognition. He spurred his horse to the left whilst his companion went right in a coordinated attack. Vaelin leaned low, half-hanging out of the saddle as they closed, parrying the stroke from the left as the other missed by inches. He regained the saddle and wheeled, hauling Scar to a halt as the two red men turned for another charge. They paused, seemingly puzzled by his immobility, staring back as he waited, meeting their gaze in turn, fixing them.

Iron Claw reared up with a bellow, both claws raised high. The red men tried to spur their horses aside but too late as the claws came down, digging deep into the spine of both animals. They screamed and thrashed as blood fountained, the red men rolling clear of the carnage, coming swiftly to their feet before being brought down by Astorek's wolves. They struggled in silence, each held fast by four wolves, their jaws clamped on each limb. They stared up at Vaelin with all the malice he remembered, malice that turned to outright terror as Wise Bear climbed down from Iron Claw's back.

They begged and screamed in unison, both uttering the same pleas and guttural exhalations as the shaman knelt and pressed his hands to their foreheads. The shuddering ceased in an instant, both red men falling silent, then blinking in confusion as Wise Bear removed his hands and retreated. They gaped at each other then at Vaelin . . . then the wolves.

"Brother . . ." one said, looking up at him in white-faced entreaty.

Vaelin turned Scar about as the wolves did their work, deaf to the brief screams rising above the chorus of snarls. Mishara was at his side once more, nose pointed to a dense mass of battling figures near the western edge of what remained of the camp. A brief survey confirmed most of the field was now in their hands. The southern flank had been completely shattered under the weight of the Wolf People's numbers. He could see the warriors moving through the mist, long spears held low, bunching occasionally to deal with small clusters of resistance. To the north the tribesfolk had surrounded what appeared to be the remnants of the Volarian cavalry, a few hundred mounted men hemmed in and trying vainly to break free. He watched rider after rider falling to the mountain people's flailing axes, their ingrained disunity seemingly forgotten now.

"My lord!"

Vaelin ducked instinctively at Orven's shouted warning, something flickering past his head too fast to see. He dragged Scar about to face three men running towards him through the haze, each lightly armoured and bearing a sword in each hand. *Kuritai.*

Orven blocked the charge of the leader, crouching low to sweep his sword at the slave-elite's legs. The Kuritai leapt the blade easily and whirled in mid-air, his blade aimed at Orven's neck. The captain, however, was no novice and parried the blow, jabbing his own sword into the Kuritai's face, then bringing the sword up and around in a swift and near-perfect riposte that left the man staggering with a gaping throat wound.

He turned to engage another as the third dodged past them and made for Vaelin, leaping with twin swords raised high. Mishara met him in midair, fastening her fangs on his head and bearing him to the ground, shaking him until his neck gave an audible crack.

Vaelin spurred Scar forward, seeing Orven being hard-pressed by the remaining Kuritai, the twin swords delivering a swift and complex pattern of blows that forced the guardsman to his knees. Vaelin was still ten feet short of them when the Kuritai sent Orven's sword spinning from his grasp and raised his blades for the final blow, then abruptly stiffened, head snapping up as Lorkan blinked into view, arm extended to thrust a dagger into the base of the slave-elite's skull.

The Gifted withdrew the blade with a distasteful grimace and looked up at Vaelin as he trotted closer. His face was streaked with blood from a cut somewhere in the dark mane of his hair, obliging him to continually wipe it from his eyes.

"You have to come," he said, swaying a little as he pointed his bloody dagger to the raging struggle nearby. "It's Alturk."

The wolves went ahead of him, tearing apart the ragged Volarian line of wounded and part-blinded Varitai, allowing him to charge through with Wise Bear and Iron Claw close behind. He saw Alturk twenty yards ahead, war club whirling as he spun and dodged amidst a circle of red men. The Sentar were attempting to come to his side but were being held back by a company of Kuritai, Lonak and slave-elite locked in a vicious struggle as the Tahlessa fought hopeless odds. But still he lived, cuts on his arms, face and legs, but he remained standing as the red men danced.

Vaelin urged more speed from Scar but the warhorse was tiring now, foam covering his flanks and mouth, his stride laboured and shuddering with effort. Vaelin watched as Alturk dodged a sword and brought his club around to slam into his assailant's side, deliberately avoiding the killing blow to the head as Vaelin had instructed. The red men, however, had clearly allowed the blow to land to draw Alturk forward, two of them dancing closer to slash at his legs. He sidestepped the first stroke but not the second, the blade biting deep into his thigh and sending him to one knee, teeth bared in a grimace.

Another red man leapt and delivered a kick to Alturk's jaw, sending him sprawling. The red man landed nimbly astride the Tahlessa's prostrate form, a wide smile on his lips as he raised his sword. Alturk spat blood into his face and the red man stepped back, smile vanished into a snarling mask of malice.

Scar collided with a Kuritai, sending him spinning, Vaelin rising high in the saddle as the red man lunged at Alturk, then collapsed as an arrow sank into his leg. Another red-armoured figure darted towards the Lonak but drew up as Vaelin closed, sword raised too late to counter Scar's flailing hooves, taking a kick to the chest and flying backwards.

The remaining red men closed on Vaelin, moving with uncanny speed. Another arrow streaked from the surrounding turmoil to take the leader in the leg. The others paused, crouched low and eyes scanning for enemies. Kiral came into view, walking forward at an almost leisurely pace as she loosed arrows from her stout flat bow, each of the red men falling as the shafts found their legs.

The wolves moved in as Vaelin dismounted, running to Alturk's side where Kiral was already crouched. The red men screamed and railed as the wolves took hold of their limbs and Wise Bear slid from Iron Claw's back. He walked from one to the other, crouching to touch his palm to their heads, their cries falling silent one by one. He paused at the last one, drawing back with his squat features tensed in confusion.

"Can't . . ." Alturk grunted and clutched at the wound in his leg. "Can't you even allow me a decent death?"

Kiral slapped him, a hard smack to the cheek, berating him in her own language. Vaelin's knowledge of Lonak was poor but he did catch the word "father" amidst the angry torrent. Alturk's anger faded as she continued to rail at him, tearing a strip from his buckskins and moving to bind his wound.

Vaelin rose and went to where Wise Bear stood over the remaining red man, the wolves' teeth having silenced the others. The shaman frowned, shaking his head in confusion as the red man stared up at him, spread-eagled in the wolves' grip, sweat covering his face, blood flowing freely from his nose and the corners of his eyes. Vaelin felt it then, a sudden doubling of his heartbeat, a tremble seizing his limbs.

The power to freeze a man's heart with fear, he recalled and found himself laughing. "Fear," he said, crouching next to the red man and capturing his gaze. "In truth it's a small thing, and an old friend." He drove the pommel of his sword hard into the man's temple, leaving him sagging and barely conscious. Wise Bear shook his head, muttering a curse in his own tongue then crouching to press a hand to the red man's brow. He stiffened for a moment, a chilled gasp escaping his chest, then lay still.

Vaelin turned away as the wolves finished the task, watching the last of the Kuritai fall to the Sentar. Somewhere behind him the tribesfolk were singing some kind of victory song, the tune was discordant but they all seemed to know the words.

"My lord," Lorkan said, appearing as his side, a bloody rag pressed to his head. "I feel this an opportune moment to resign from your service. For this is an experience I should not like to repeat, regardless of Cara's opinions."

"Accepted, good sir," Vaelin told him. "And with thanks for your service."

He turned as Mishara gave a sudden hiss, her hackles rising as she turned and began sprinting towards the ridge where they had left her mistress.

Vaelin's gaze tracked over the corpses of the red men. *Four, and the other two. Six. But Mirvald said seven . . .*

He ran to Scar and leapt into the saddle, heels thumping hard into his flanks as he spurred to the gallop.

◆ ◆ ◆

The ridge was wreathed in cloud and rain as he halted a near-spent Scar at its base. He had seen the clouds descend as they rode towards the ridge, far too fast to be anything other than Cara's work. Mishara was several yards ahead and quickly disappeared into the curtain of rain as lightning flashed somewhere up ahead.

Vaelin hurled himself up the ridge, seeing bodies lying amidst the rocks, the Wolf People's warriors, all seemingly cut down in seconds. He found Marken's cat next, slumped and lifeless, the hulking Gifted himself lay a few yards on, bearded features slack and unmoving in the lashing rain.

Vaelin tore his gaze away and forced himself on. The smell reached him first, burnt, acrid, cloying. The stench of recently seared flesh. Cara came into view as he crested the ridge, a small, still form sitting in the rain, pale features staring with wide eyes at something nearby, something blackened and charred but somehow still moving, the part-melted remnants of red armour sticking to the roasted flesh as it twitched.

"Didn't see it," Cara said in a whisper. "We shared . . . I couldn't see . . . It happened so fast . . ."

Vaelin crouched next to her, seeing the blood streaming from her nose, turning pink and dissolving in the torrent. He touched his hands to hers. "Enough," he said. "It's done."

She blinked at him, then sagged, the rain dwindling to drizzle as he caught her. "Lightning," she murmured. "Didn't know I could."

"Cara." He lifted her chin. "Where is Lady Dahrena?"

Somewhere up ahead he heard Mishara voice a plaintive, forlorn call.

"I'm sorry," Cara said, voice small and choked. "It happened so fast . . ."

He rested her back against a rock and rose from her side, moving away and following the sound as Mishara continued to voice her mournful cry.

She was slumped on her side next to the rain-wasted remnants of the fire he had built for her the night before, still wrapped in furs. There was no blood, no sign of any injury at all. *One who could kill with a single touch* . . .

He sat next to her, drawing her small, limp form into his arms, teasing the silken hair back from her ice-chilled forehead. "I want to go home," he said. "I want to go home with you."

CHAPTER FOUR

Reva

She landed hard, rolling with the impact to absorb the shock, but still it left an aching burn in her legs as she surged to her feet, sprinting towards the nearest beast-handler. She was grateful for the crowd's bloodlust, their roaring excitement at her appearance robbing the handler of any warning until she was nearly on him. He turned just before she whipped her manacles across his face, teeth shattering and lips shredded by the impact, his scream a shrill gurgle as he collapsed to his knees, the chains slipping from his hands.

The three dagger-teeth he had been guiding towards their prey immediately whirled at the sudden loss of restraint, hissing at Reva and crouching to spring. She dived towards the handler, snatching the whip from the strap on his wrist, snapping it at the nearest cat, forcing it back. She raised her gaze, finding the Shield and Allern standing unmolested in the centre of the arena, the two other handlers staring at her in wide-eyed shock. The Shield reacted first, sprinting forward to hack down the nearest beast, the short sword cutting through its neck as its companions howled and lashed their claws at him. He danced back on nimble feet, though not without suffering a trio of parallel scars on his chest.

The fallen handler's cats lunged at Reva, dragging her attention away. She struck with the whip again, then ran forward, leaping over a slashing claw. She whirled as they pursued, the whip cutting the air with a vicious crack. The dagger-teeth recoiled once more, then paused as one, as if in answer to some unspoken but shared understanding, turning to regard the wounded handler, now attempting to stumble towards a door in the arena wall, hands held to his face as he trailed blood across the sand. The cats gave an identical hiss and bounded after him, one leaping onto his back and bearing him to the sand, whilst the others savaged his legs, their long fangs piercing flesh and bone with appalling ease. His screams were short and the cats soon fell to contented feeding, ignoring Reva completely.

She turned to see Allern attempting to keep the three cats facing him at bay with short jabs of his spear. Their handler, however, was considerably distracted by Reva's charge, blanching and dropping his chains before sprinting away. He made it to within ten feet of a door before a volley of arrows from the Varitai archers on the upper tiers streaked down to pin him to the sand.

Free of restraint, his cats began to circle Allern, moving in a whirling dance of slashing claws and teeth-baring lunges, seeking an opening as he spun, his spear moving in a blur. Reva sprinted towards the nearest cat, the whip snaking out to wrap around its leg, pulling it back as it thrashed and howled. Allern saw his chance and speared the beast in the shoulder, though the force of the thrust sent the spear-blade through the animal, stuck fast amidst bone and sinew. Allern cursed, trying to draw the weapon free, the two other cats closing in for the kill.

Reva's whip cracked once more, forcing them back. "Leave it!" she told Allern, pushing him back from the corpse. "Take this." She handed him the whip then placed her foot on the haft of the spear, stamping down to snap it in two. She rolled the dead cat over and took hold of the spear-blade, drawing it clear of the carcass in a gout of blood.

"Keep them back!" she ordered Allern, turning to see the Shield now on his back, legs raised to hold off the cat snarling atop him, jaws snapping, its terrible fangs within a whisker of his face. The surviving handler loosed his remaining cat and retreated, gazing wildly about, knowing to flee meant death but clearly wanting no part of this suddenly equal struggle. The freed cat circled the struggling pair in a rapid scrabble, sliding to a halt near Ell-Nestra's head, tensing for a strike, jaws widening as it leapt . . . Reva's broken spear-blade took the cat in the side in midair, its limp form colliding with the dagger-tooth atop the Shield, forcing it to rear back, leaving just enough room for Ell-Nestra to thrust his sword up into its neck.

He rolled free as the corpse came down, dragging the blade from the body, then crouching as the handler's whip left a long red stripe on his upper arm. He turned to regard the plainly terrified beast-master with a raised eyebrow. "Are you sure?"

The handler stared at him in terrorised indecision; fighting or fleeing meant the same fate. Reva spared him further consideration, leaping to plant both feet in the centre of his face, sending him senseless to the sand. She knelt to retrieve his whip and a small dagger protruding from his boot.

"May I say, my lady," the Shield greeted her with a bow, "how very fetching you look today. Red is truly your colour."

She grunted and ran towards Allern. "You'd have a better chance with these beasts."

Allern had driven the two surviving cats to the edge of the arena, chest heaving as he swung the whip, containing every rush and lunge they tried to make. Reva used her own whip to snag one around the foreleg, dragging it down so the Shield could finish it with his sword. She killed the last one herself, taunting it into a charge, dodging to the side, then leaping onto its back, the dagger stabbing down beneath its shoulder blades, again and again until its struggles ceased and a final piteous hiss escaped its snout.

As she rose from the corpse the exultation of the crowd descended like a deluge, the tiers above a sea of joyous faces, screaming in admiration and, she saw with disgust, naked lust. Men leered at her, women bared their breasts, and a torrent of flowers cascaded onto the sand. One landed near her feet, an orchid, the petals a pale shade of pink that darkened to deep red at the edges.

"Pick it up!" the Shield hissed at her and she noted he had a clutch of flowers in his hands. "You too, lad!" he called to Allern. "Pick them up, quickly!"

Reva knelt and retrieved the orchid, noting how the crowd's feverish adulation rose to an even greater pitch.

"A sign of their favour!" the Shield shouted to her above the tumult before casting a cautious glance at the Empress's balcony. "Hard to ignore for those who orchestrate these spectacles."

Reva looked to the balcony, seeing the Empress's slender form still seated on her bench, face veiled in shadow. She seemed utterly still and Reva wondered if she had slipped into another vacant episode. She also doubted that the Empress held any regard for the traditions formerly observed here. *She hates them,* she remembered, glancing at the crowd. *What does she care for their favour?*

She saw the Empress raise a hand to cast a casual flick at Varulek, the black-clad striding forward to order the trumpets sounded once more. This time the crowd's obedience was not so instant, the exultation and lust taking longer to fade, leaving a simmering murmur that continued even after the Empress rose and moved to the edge of the balcony. Reva's spirits sank at the expression she saw on her face. No fury or frustration, just warm, and sincere, affection. Her lips moved in a silent endearment, easily read, "You truly are my sister."

◆ ◆ ◆

She found Lieza pacing when they returned her to the chamber, the girl starting in surprise and relief as Reva stepped inside and the door slammed shut. Lieza came forward with a tremulous laugh, drawing up short at the sight of the blood that spattered Reva from head to toe, though she seemed more shocked by what she held in her hands.

"Where you get that?" she asked.

Reva glanced down at the orchid. She had kept hold of it as the Empress decreed the spectacles had concluded for the day and a dozen Kuritai trooped into the arena. Allern and the Shield were shackled and led off to another door, though not before the young guardsman sank to one knee before her, gazing up with near-frantic devotion. "The Father has blessed me, my lady!" he called as they dragged him away. "In allowing me to fight with you this day!"

The Shield was notably less enthused. "We won no victory here," he said over his shoulder. "You know that, I assume?"

"We're alive," she replied. "And you're welcome, my lord."

Reva wondered why Varulek hadn't taken the flower from her. The Master of the Arena had been silent on their journey back to the cell, his expression more tense than before and his eyes continually straying to the flower in her grasp. "Did I spoil the story?" she asked him as they came to the chamber door. "The legend had a different ending, I suppose."

"Morivek and Korsev stood at the entrance to the fire pits and held back the harbingers for a day and a night." The black-clad stood back as the Kuritai removed her shackles with their customary caution. "Morivek, the eldest, fell mortally wounded and beseeched his brother to flee. But Korsev stayed, possessed of such a rage that he killed every harbinger to emerge from the pit and, seeing his brother now dead, cast himself into the bowels of the earth, seeking yet more vengeance, never to be seen again. Though, as with any legend," he added as the door swung open, "the tale changes depending on the author."

"In the arena," she told Lieza, holding out the orchid. "Take it if you want."

The girl shrank back, shaking her head. "Not for me." She glanced again at Reva's bloodied form and moved towards the far end of the chamber. "I make you bath."

Reva sat on the marble steps as the water gushed from the ornate bronze spigot in the wall, massaging her wrists as the steam rose. "I wash that for you," Lieza said, pointing to Reva's bloodied clothing.

"You are not my slave," she said.

"Not free either." Lieza shrugged. "Nothing else to do."

Reva stood, staring at Lieza in expectation. The girl seemed puzzled for a moment then laughed and turned her back. Reva kicked off her shoes then removed her blouse and trews, leaving them piled on the floor as she stepped down into the water, sighing at the soothing warmth.

"Who you fight?" Lieza asked, grinning a little as she knelt to retrieve the clothes, gaze still averted.

"Cats with big teeth."

"You kill them all?"

"All but three." Reva recalled the sight of the three surviving cats, busily gorging themselves on the body of their fallen master, fangs and faces red from frenzied feeding. Despite the horror of the spectacle she couldn't help but feel a pang of pity. For all their fury these were wretched creatures, continually starved, brutalised and denied the role the Father had ordained for them. *This is what they do*, she decided. *Twist the world out of shape according to cruel whim.*

She spent a few moments unpicking her braid and sank under the water, working her fingers through the tresses to dislodge the matted blood. The bath was deep, allowing her to fully submerge herself, sinking down until her feet touched the tiled bottom. The feel of hair on her fingers stirred memories of Veliss, how she loved to comb her hair, shape it into one of the thousand designs she knew. *Veliss, Ellese . . .* So far away and most likely lost for good.

A disturbance in the water caused her to resurface where she started at the sight of Licza sinking naked into the bath. "What are you doing?" she demanded, looking away.

"Clothes need washing." The girl reached for Reva's piled garments and dumped them into the water, a faint smile on her lips.

"Do it later."

"Not your slave." Lieza's smile broadened as she reached for a cake of soap and began to scrub at the clothes. Reva turned away, moving to the edge of the bath, wanting to climb out but knowing the girl's gaze would follow her if she did.

"Your people have no respect for each other," she muttered. "No regard for life, or privacy either it seems."

"Privacy?" Lieza asked.

"Being . . ." Reva struggled to translate the concept, finding it harder than expected. "Being alone, keeping secrets. Protecting modesty."

"Modesty?"

"Never mind." She heard Lieza stifle a giggle as she returned to scrubbing her clothes. "Not so afraid now, I see."

"No, still afraid. Comes like a . . ." Reva heard her splash at the water.

"A wave?"

"Yes. Wave. Big wave when I try to kill the Empress. Smaller wave now."

Reva found herself turning in involuntary surprise, then averting her gaze again at the sight of Lieza's breasts protruding just above the water. "You tried to kill her?"

"With poison. Didn't work. Kept me with her." Lieza's tone darkened. "Found me . . . funny."

"Why did you do it?"

"My master . . . not just my master. Father also. My mother a slave. She die when I'm little. He raised me, loved me. Couldn't free me, the law. Didn't like the Empress and said so. She gave him the three deaths, took all his slaves as her own."

"I regret your failure. Though, on behalf of my queen and people, I thank you for the effort."

"Queen is also word for Empress, yes?"

"I suppose, though they are very different."

"Your queen not cruel?"

Reva recalled the sight of the queen sinking her dagger into the Volarian's chest back on the ship, her instant and complete change of demeanour as his body was thrown over the side. "She is fierce in her dedication to our cause, it being just."

"You think she win this war?" Lieza's tone held a distinctly dubious note.

"With help." Reva felt her eyelids grow heavy, the heat of the water and the strain of her recent exertions combining to overwhelm her. She turned back to the edge of the bath, resting her head on her arms. "There is a man, a friend of mine." She found herself smiling. "My elder brother, in any way that matters. If I can survive here long enough for word to reach him, he will come for me." She closed her eyes, voice fading to a whisper. "Though I would not have him risk any more on my account . . ."

She let it fade away, the arena, the Empress's fond smile, losing herself in the water's warm embrace, letting it seep into her, soothing, caressing . . .

She jerked awake, Lieza's hands vanishing from her shoulders as she reared back in alarm. "You . . . tense," she said. "I know how to make it go away." She raised her hands, flexing the fingers, then slowly reached out to trace her nails through Reva's hair.

"Don't." Reva took hold of her hand, hating the electric thrill provoked by the feel of her skin, gently pushing it away. "Please."

"I not your slave," Lieza said. "I willing . . ."

"I can't." Reva fought down a wave of self-reproach at the regret in her voice. "There is someone, someone who waits for me."

She pushed herself to the steps and climbed out of the bath, moving to the bed and covering herself with a sheet. She slumped against a pillar, keeping her gaze from Lieza, who she knew would be staring after her, sinking to the marble floor with a whisper, "Loyalty is all I have left to give her."

◆ ◆ ◆

She awoke in darkness, Lieza slumbering next to her, still naked and absent any coverings. She had washed her own clothes after finishing with Reva's and left them to dry. "No other place to sleep," she said, hovering by the bed after dimming the lamps.

Reva turned onto her side, facing away. "Then sleep."

Lieza groaned as Reva rose, eyes tracking to the near-invisible door, realising she had been woken by the sound of the lock turning. She rose from the bed, tossing a sheet over Lieza's distracting form and retrieving her still-damp clothes. She managed to drag them on by the time the door opened to reveal Varulek, standing with oil lamp in hand. Reva blinked in surprise as she realised he was alone and the tunnel behind him free of Kuritai.

Careful, she cautioned herself against the instinctive impulse to rush the black-clad. *He would not come here defenceless.*

So she stood in silence as he entered, his gaze sweeping across the chamber, pausing only slightly at the sight of Lieza's partial nakedness. His face was tense with well-controlled but palpable fear, the face of a man forcing himself to unavoidable duty, an expression she knew well.

"I have something to show you," he said, voice kept to a whisper.

Reva said nothing but gave a pointed glance at the empty tunnel beyond the door.

"If you find no interest in what I offer," he said, following her gaze, "killing me would be the greatest favour."

A blow to the temple to put him down, another to crush his larynx and prevent him screaming. Cover his nose and mouth as he chokes to death. Wake the girl and find a route out of this place of horrors. All so easy. But there was something in his gaze that gave her pause, another expression she also knew well, having seen it so many times at Alltor. *Hope. He sees hope in me.*

"The Father takes a dim view of betrayal," she said, reaching for her shoes. "And so do I."

◆ ◆ ◆

The lamplight was meagre, forcing her to keep close to him as he led her along the tunnel to a small door, working a heavy iron key in the lock and hauling it aside. The stairwell beyond was narrow, the steps and walls roughly hewn and lacking the precision evident in every line of the arena.

"This father you speak of," he said as they descended the stairs, "he is your god?"

"The only god, who made us so we might know his love." She stifled a cough at the mustiness of the air, growing thicker by the step. The air smelt of little save dust, but had the close, cloying feel unique to places rarely visited.

"Ah," Varulek said in recognition. "The Alltorian heresy, expunged in the Cleansing. So the followers of the Six Books found a new home in your Realm."

"Ten Books," she corrected. *Though I promised them an eleventh.* "Are you saying my people came from this land?"

"The Cleansing forced thousands to flee across the ocean. Questers, Ascendants, Acolytes of Sun and Moon. Though your people were among the most numerous, along with the Servants of the Dead."

Servants of the Dead. "The Faith. The Faith originated here too?"

"It blossomed just before the Cleansing. Some say it caused it. In the space of barely twenty years thousands had forsaken the gods, preferring to grovel to the dead, begging a place in their imagined paradise beyond life. Such devotion was anathema to a Ruling Council intent on fostering absolute loyalty to the empire. The Servants of the Dead were the first to feel their wrath, though they resisted well, led by a man named Varin. In time though, they were forced into exile, taking ship to a damp land across the sea, where more followed in time as the Council sought to wipe away all vestige of what they termed irrational belief."

"You killed your gods," Reva said, recalling the Empress's words.

"No." They came to the bottom of the stairwell, Varulek crouching to unlock another door, pushing it open on squealing hinges. "We hid them."

The space beyond the door gave a long echo as he stepped inside, though the absolute blackness prevented any estimation of its size. He paused next to the door, holding the lamp to a torch set into the wall, moving away as the flames blossomed. Reva followed him in, the chamber gradually revealed as he moved from torch to torch. Her gaze went immediately to the statues, three figures, two men and a woman. They were life-sized, and posed as if frozen in a moment of discussion. The woman leaned forward, hands raised and seemingly addressing both men at once. The taller of the two men stood stroking a bearded face, his brow deeply furrowed as if in sombre reflection. The other man was clean-shaven with narrow handsome features and appeared to be in mid-shrug, regarding the woman with a half smile, his expression one of affable disagreement.

The three figures stood around a plinth of some kind, flat-topped with a circular indentation in the centre. It seemed completely unweathered by age, its lines clean and free of chips or scars. It also contrasted with the three statues, being carved from some form of black stone, whilst they had been hewn from a kind of grey granite.

"The gods?" she asked Varulek.

"The gods are too divine to be captured by a mortal hand, in word or in stone."

She frowned at his tone, hearing a faint echo of the priest's rantings in the terse note it held. "These are the Tyrants," he went on, gesturing at the three figures. "Progenitors of the Dermos. Once they ruled all the world with vile magics, casting down any who dared speak against them, a triumvirate of tyranny. In time the gods brought them down, banishing them to the fire pits beneath the earth where they spawned the Dermos. No, these are not the gods." He moved away, going to a wall to play the lamplight over the stone. "This is where you'll find them."

Reva moved to the wall, finding the stone to be rough, shaped by unskilled hands into a vaguely flat surface, and marked with tiny indentations from end to end. Peering closer she saw the indentations were symbols of some kind, arranged into clusters, neat at first but becoming more irregular as they progressed along the wall.

"Scripture?" she asked Varulek.

"Only a few in every generation are chosen," he said. "Those with the strength and will to contain the essence of the gods, their hands guided to impart their wisdom and guidance, chipped into stone whilst life and strength remain. Though, inevitably, a blessing of such power has a price."

He moved along the wall, the light revealing yet more scripture, every cluster and symbol becoming less uniform until they were nothing more than vague scratches on the stone. *The work of a madman scrawling in the dark,* Reva concluded, deciding it best left unsaid for the moment. As he moved past her she noted again the tattoos covering Varulek's hands, finding an unmistakable similarity to the wall markings.

"What does it say?" she asked. "You can read it can't you?"

He nodded, eyes still fixed on the wall. "Though I doubt there is another soul in all the world who could." He moved to the far end of the wall, where the markings were most coherent. "'The Tyrants return,'" he read, finger tracking over the first cluster. "'Hidden behind the face of a hero, unseen Dermos, set free upon the earth. Even this refuge will be lost to the gods.'"

This refuge. "The arena," she said, "it remained a shrine, even after they banished the gods." Her gaze returned to his hands. "You are a priest."

He inclined his head, acknowledging her insight. "Perhaps the last. The secret charge of my family for generations, as is this arena. My ancestors had charge of this temple long before the Council rose with its pestilent notions of rationality. We were wise enough to make a show of throwing off our piety, amongst the first to swear loyalty to Council and empire, the first to accuse others. Building trust that lasted all the ages. So complete was the destruction of the gods we were able to reclaim the symbol of our true allegiance." He held up his hand, splaying the fingers to display the tattoos. "The Council thinking it no more than a tradition of those charged with maintaining the arena. *She* knew differently of course."

"The Empress knows what you are?"

"She knew long before her ascension. She came here years ago, when she wore a different body. 'You have a secret,' she told me, commanding that I bring her here or face denunciation. Knowing one word from her would be enough to secure my execution, I complied. And she laughed." His mouth twisted in rage and shame. "She *mocked* this divine place." He calmed himself with an effort, pointing to the plinth between the three statues. "But she stopped when she saw that."

Reva angled her head to study the plinth once more, finding little remarkable in it save for the precision of its construction. It was free of any markings, anything that might indicate its purpose. She moved towards it, stepping between the woman and the bearded man. *A font, perhaps?* She leaned closer, extending a hand towards the indentation in the centre.

"Do not touch it!" His voice was barely more than a whisper but held such a depth of warning her hand instantly froze.

"What is it?" she asked.

"I do not know. Nor did any who came before me. But it is the most implacable commandment instilled in every member of my family since we undertook our divine duty: do not touch the stone."

"Did *she* touch it? When she came here?"

He shook his head. "I had hoped she might, but no. She knows too much. But she was not alone when she came here. There was a young man, red-clad, barely older than you. Also, plainly besotted with her. 'If you love me,' she told him, 'touch the stone.' And he did."

Varulek moved closer, playing the torchlight over the surface of the plinth; the black surface gleamed. *Centuries down here and not a speck of dust,* Reva saw. "What happened to him?"

"She didn't want me to see, commanding me to stand at the door. But I saw the boy shudder, crying out as if in both pain and pleasure. She leaned close to him, whispering some question I couldn't hear. The boy's reply was faint but filled with awe, holding his hands up, hands that glowed with some strange light, flickering like lightning. She told him to touch it again, 'see what other gifts it brings,' she said. And he touched it once more. This time, he gave no cry, becoming very still the instant his hand touched the stone, as still as these statues, giving no answer to any whispered question. I saw her smile, a smile of great satisfaction . . . then she killed him, stepping closer to break his neck. 'Give that to your beasts,' she told me, pointing to the corpse. 'I shall come back one day, some years from now I expect. Or much sooner if I learn your tongue has been loose.'"

"No other has seen it?" Reva asked. "None of her . . . fellow creatures."

Varulek shook his head. "Only her."

Keeping secrets of her own. Reva remembered the Empress's whispered offer, *When my beloved comes to me, we will bring down the Ally and all the world will be ours . . . What is she plotting?* Reva sighed in frustration, wishing she could ask for Veliss's counsel, she would reckon this in an instant. As would the queen.

"I can offer no insight here," she told Varulek. "But if you can somehow convey a message to my queen . . ."

"An impossibility. I am bound to this place by more than duty. To stray outside the precincts of the arena by a single step would mean the three deaths."

"Then why show me this?"

"This is not what I want to show you." He returned to the wall, holding the torch close to a barely discernible cluster of symbols near the end, just before they dwindled into utter obscurity. "Here," he said, beckoning her closer, his finger tracking over the marks. "'Livella will be made flesh when the Fire Queen rises.'"

"Livella?" She remembered Lieza saying the name that morning, in a voice laden with fear. She found herself drawing back from the sudden intensity of Varulek's gaze.

"A great warrior of legend," he murmured. "Favoured by the gods with skill and strength beyond that of any woman. She journeyed into the pits and fought the Dermos themselves, killing three. One with a sword, one with a spear, and one . . ." He handed her the torch and moved away, going to a shadowed corner of the cavern and returning with something wrapped in a threadbare cloak. She saw how his hands trembled with excitement as he drew back the cloth, revealing a stave little under five feet in length, the wood pale and shiny from use, decorated on either side of the central span, one side showing crossed swords, the other crossed axes.

"And one," Varulek went on, breathless now with mingled awe and fear, eyes shining in the torchlight. "One she killed with a bow fashioned from wych elm."

CHAPTER FIVE

Frentis

"Your vengeance is hard indeed, brother."

Fleet Lord Ell-Nurin's expression betrayed a mingling of disgust and judgement as his gaze swept over New Kethia, taking in the ruined houses evident in every quarter and the smoke rising beyond the south-facing walls. Corpses were still being consigned to the pyre, a task that had occupied fifty freed folk for six days now. "Your people certainly have a talent for destruction."

"Justice, as ordained by the queen." Frentis could hear the hollow note in his voice. The sight of the grey-clad girl lying dead in her mother's arms was yet to fade. So many years of battle and death, so many faces forgotten, but he knew this image would never dim.

"And the city is not destroyed," he added. "Any damage will be restored according to the queen's design, in time."

"A task dependent upon a successful outcome to this war." The Fleet Lord's gaze went to the harbour, crowded with Meldenean ships and captured Volarian prizes, many more vessels anchored in the estuary beyond. They had arrived the day before, the sight of so many masts on the northern horizon provoking the newly freed populace to panic. Frentis had managed to calm them, though not before several hundred had fled the city with their bundled spoils. He arrayed his own people at the dockside in a thick defensive formation with archers on the surrounding rooftops, then ordered Draker to begin a cheer at the sight of the *Red Falcon* sailing into the harbour.

"I believe we have sufficient space to carry your entire command," Ell-Nurin said, gesturing at the fleet. "I have to say there wasn't much heart in the enemy when we caught up to them. Seems their admiral committed suicide rather than face the Empress's wrath. Most gave up without a fight."

"Carry my command where, my lord?"

"Volar of course. The queen will expect reinforcement."

"Most people now bearing arms in this city were slaves up until two weeks ago. The others joined me to win freedom, not acceptance to the Realm. The Realm folk we freed will come, I've little doubt of that. The Garisai too, though many will expect payment. Perhaps two thousand swords in all. The others have suffered much, more than I would ever have asked them to."

"They may have seized a city and slaughtered their masters, but lasting freedom will only come through victory. As I'm sure you'll explain to them." There was a hardness to Ell-Nurin's voice, a reminder that he held rank here.

Frentis sighed and gave a slow nod of assent.

"Very good. This"—the Fleet Lord turned to a young woman standing amidst his entourage of captains—"is Sister Merial. You will give her a full report of your operations, and any useful intelligence gathered, for onward conveyance to the queen."

Frentis frowned at the woman, finding her perhaps a year or two shy of his own age, dressed in clothing he assumed had been chosen for its plainness. She was also palpably uncomfortable in the presence of so many Meldeneans, though they seemed inclined to provide her with ample space. "Seventh Order?"

"Quite so, brother." Ell-Nurin leaned closer. "And, however tempting it might be, you really don't want to touch her."

◆ ◆ ◆

"Nine thousand more, y'say?" Sister Merial spoke with a strong Renfaelin accent, largely devoid of honorifics and rich in dubious inflection. "Of these terrible red men."

"They're real enough," Draker growled. "Plenty of us with the scars and burns to prove it. Got one on my arse if you want to see it."

"I think I've seen sufficient horrors recently." Merial gave Draker a broad but empty smile and accepted a bowl of goat stew from Thirty-Four.

They had occupied the unfortunate governor's mansion, though much of it was rendered uninhabitable due to the mob's attentions. Frentis camped in the main courtyard, the rest of the army that had followed him from Viratesk taking up residence in the extensive gardens. He had been surprised and gratified by their discipline, keeping to their companies and taking a comparatively small part in the looting that continued to preoccupy the newly liberated populace. Perhaps a dozen fighters had disappeared in the aftermath of the city's fall, and a few more had asked his permission to leave, either to return to distant homes or in frank admission they had seen their fill of war. He told them all the same thing, "You freed yourselves the moment you joined me. Queen Lyrna thanks you for your service."

"So the queen marches on Volar?" Illian asked Merial. "Despite losing so many at sea?"

"Not a woman to be easily dissuaded, the queen." Merial took a bite of stew and favoured Thirty-Four with an appreciative grin. "Better 'n that slop the pirates dish out, when they're not bein' overly free with their hands."

"When do we sail?" Illian asked Frentis, a keen eagerness shining in her eyes.

Will she ever grow tired of it? he wondered. "At the discretion of the Fleet Lord. He holds rank here."

"Fuck his rank," Lekran muttered around a mouthful of stew, speaking in his laboured Realm Tongue. "Don't know him."

Frentis turned back to Merial. "You say the queen believes Lady Reva dead?"

She nodded. "Gone to the bottom along with half her heretic followers."

"No, she lives. In Volar." He shuddered at the memory of the previous night's dream, the surging joy as she drank in the sight of Lady Reva battling the dagger-toothed cats. "Though for how much longer I can't say."

Merial frowned at him, a line of suspicion appearing on her brow. "You know this, brother?"

"I do. Beyond doubt."

Her frown deepened as she angled her head, eyes tracking over his face. "I sense no gift in you . . ."

"I know it," he said, an edge colouring his voice. "And the queen should know it too."

She gave a cautious nod and returned to her meal. "Allow a girl to fill her belly first, then I'll have a word with my darlin' husband."

"What husband?" Draker asked with a bemused frown but Merial just grinned and kept eating.

Later she sat apart from them, taking on a concentrated stillness, eyes close and face devoid of expression. "Don't like this, brother," Draker murmured, moving to Frentis's side and eyeing the sister with obvious distrust. "Dark ain't s'posed to be seen."

"The world changed when Varinshold fell," Frentis told him. "Now none of us have anywhere to hide."

Sister Merial gave a sudden jerk, her back arching and eyes flying open, a small but distinct gasp of shock escaping her lips. She slumped forward with a groan, hands covering her face, slim shoulders moving in jerking sobs.

"Don't like this," Draker muttered again, moving back to the fire.

Frentis went to Merial, now hugging herself, face set in forlorn misery. "Sister?" he prompted.

She glanced up at him then looked away, hands tracing over her tear-streaked face as she rose, walking from the courtyard without a word. He waited a while before following, finding her perched atop a podium in the gardens. The statue it once held had been torn down and hauled off during the riots, no doubt destined for the smelter, bronze being a valuable metal. Sister Merial suddenly seemed very young, legs dangling over the edge of the podium as she raised her still-damp face to the sky. She spared him a brief glance before returning her gaze to the stars.

"They're different," she said. "Not all, just some."

"The Maiden's arm points home," he said.

She nodded, lowering her gaze. "Aspect Caenis is dead."

He winced as the pain hit home, a slashing stroke of instant grief. Sagging a little, he went to the podium, resting his hands on its heavily chipped edge. "Your husband told you this?"

"Brother Lernial, whom you've met I believe."

"I didn't know the Seventh Order were permitted to marry."

"'Course we are. Where d'you think all the little brothers and sisters come from? We've always been more a family than an Order, ever on the hunt for new blood though."

He sighed a weary laugh. "How did it happen?"

"A battle. The details are vague, my husband's gift is a tad erratic, 'specially when coloured by so much grief. A rather terrible encounter, from what I can gather. Your red men are a ghastly lot indeed. It seems the queen secured victory in the end, so I doubt they number nine thousand any longer."

Caenis . . . He had seen him only once at Varinshold, a brief exchange at the gates of the Blackhold. "Many trials await us, brother," he had said. "I can only wish you well."

Caenis, who had laboured to tutor him on the Order's history, with only marginal success in the end but still he cherished the lessons. During his ordeal in the pits he had occupied the time between combats by delving into memory, attempting to recall Caenis's many stories, knowing they somehow kept him anchored in the Order, kept him a brother and not a slave.

"The Aspect and I were brothers once," he told Merial. "I learned much from him."

"As did I. He was my master, y'see. We'd meet in secret, whenever the Order could spare him. He taught me so much, the Faith, the mysteries . . ." She raised her gaze once more. "The stars."

He touched his hand to hers for a second. "I grieve for your loss, sister."

"I told my husband," she said as he turned away, "about Lady Reva, and everything else."

"Did you divine anything regarding the queen's intentions?"

"Only that they are unchanged." She turned to the city spread out before them, fires flickering amidst the many ruined buildings, the pyres still burning beyond the walls. "On to Volar," she murmured.

◆　◆　◆

"Who were they?"

He stands in the street outside the baker's shop, looking down at the girl and her mother once more.

"How can you be here?" he asks.

She moves into view, wearing the face he remembers, the face she wore when they killed together. "You dream, I dream." She nods at the mother and child. "Did you know them?"

He sees then that the face is not truly the same, the cruelty, the madness not quite gone, but diminished, as if this shared dream somehow strips away much of her waking self.

"No. They died when the city fell."

"Always so intent on drowning in guilt, beloved." She moves closer, stepping over the corpses that carpet the street to cast an incurious glance over the lifeless mother and daughter. "It's always the way with wars. Battles rage and the small people die."

An old, long-stoked anger builds in his breast. "Small people?"

"Yes my love, the small people." Her voice carries a note of weary impatience, like a tutor lecturing a child on an oft-forgotten lesson. "The weak, the petty, the narrow of mind and purpose. Those, in fact, who are not like us."

His rage builds, stirring words he had longed to utter during their journey of murder, unchecked now by any binding. "You are a pestilence," he tells her. "A blight upon the world, soon to be wiped away."

Her face betrays no anger as she looks up, only a faint smile, her gaze sad but also rich in knowledge, reminding him of just how old she is, how many corpses she has seen. "No, I am the only woman you will ever love."

He finds himself drawing away, though also unable to take his eyes from her face. "I know you feel it," she says, following as he retreats. "However deep you bury it, however much rage you stir to drown it. You saw the future we could have shared, we were meant to share."

"A vile illusion," he says in a whisper.

"Our child will never be born," she says, implacable now. "But we will make another, heir to a dynasty so great . . ."

"Enough!" His rage is enough to give her pause, the heat of it sending a ripple through the ground, threatening to tear this dreamscape apart. "I never wanted any part of your insane plots. How could you imagine I would ever surrender myself to your ambition? What madness drives you? What twisted you into this? What happened on the other side of that door?"

Her face becomes utterly still, eyes locked on his, not in anger but naked terror.

"You dream, I dream," he tells her. "A girl, lying in bed, weeping as she stares at her bedroom door. Do you even remember it when awake? Do you even know?"

She blinks and takes a slow, backward step. "There were times I thought of killing you. When we travelled, sometimes I would take my knife and lay it against your neck as you slept. I feared you, although I told myself it was only anger at your many cruelties, your practised hatred. Somehow I knew my love for you would kill me, and so it proved. But I have not a single regret."

She reaches for him, and he doesn't know why he lets her touch him, why he allows her hands to trace over his own, why he opens his arms and welcomes her into an embrace. She crushes herself against him, and he hears the restrained sob in her voice as she whispers in his ear, "It's time you came to Volar, beloved. Bring your army if you like. It doesn't matter. Just make sure the healer is among them. If I do not see both of you in the arena within thirty days, Reva Mustor dies."

◆ ◆ ◆

The leader of New Kethia's former slaves named himself as Karavek, apparently the name of the master he had beaten to death during the first night of riots. "He stole freedom from me, I stole his name," he said with a thin smile. "Seemed a fair exchange."

He was a large man, somewhere in his fifties, with grey-black hair sprouting in an unkempt mass from his once-shaven head. However, despite his size and fierce appearance his voice told of an educated past and a mind keen enough to fully appreciate the reality of their circumstance, unalloyed by the glow of recent triumphs.

"Volar is not New Kethia," Karavek said when the Meldenean made his formal request for alliance on behalf of Queen Lyrna. He had arrived at the governor's mansion in company with a dozen fighters, all bristling with weaponry and regarding Fleet Lord Ell-Nurin with a naked suspicion that bordered on hostility. "This city is a village in comparison."

"There are many still in bondage there," Frentis said. "As you were."

"True enough, but I don't know them and neither do my people."

"The queen has granted all in this province a place in the Unified Realm," Ell-Nurin said. "You are now free subjects under her protection. But freedom carries a price . . ."

"Don't lecture me on freedom, pirate," Karavek growled. "Half the slaves in this city died paying that price." He turned to Frentis, lowering his voice. "Brother, you know as well as I how precarious our position is. Any day now the southern garrisons will march to reclaim this city for the empire. We can't fight them if our strength is off dying in Volar."

Victory at Volar will end this empire, Frentis wanted to say but felt the words die on his tongue, knowing how hollow they would sound. "I know," he said. "But myself and my people must sail to Volar, with any willing to join us."

"We rose because of you," Karavek said. "The Red Brother's rebellion, the great crusade birthing hope in the hearts of those condemned to a life in chains. Now it seems just a diversion so your queen faces fewer enemies on the road to Volar. And if it falls, what then? Sail away leaving us to face the chaos of a fractured empire?"

"You have my word," Frentis said. "Regardless of my queen's intentions, when our business in Volar is complete I will return here to help in any way I can." He glanced at Ell-Nurin. "And the queen has given assurance that, should your position here prove untenable, her fleet will carry your people across the ocean where you will be granted land and full rights in the Unified Realm."

Karavek straightened at this, narrowing his gaze at the Fleet Lord. "He speaks true?"

Ell-Nurin maintained an admirably placid expression as he said, "Only a fool with no regard for his life would dare to speak falsely in the queen's name."

The rebel leader grunted, running a hand through the shaggy mess of his hair, brow knotted in consideration. "I'll speak to my people," he said eventually. "Should be able to muster a thousand swords to go with you. I trust your queen will appreciate the gesture."

"She is your queen now," Frentis reminded him. "And she never forgets a debt."

◆ ◆ ◆

The freed Varitai were encamped in the ruins of Old Kethia, along with a large number of grey-clads who found the former slave soldiers more welcoming company than the newly freed denizens of the city itself. A few dozen had been chased into the ruins by a mob in the immediate aftermath of the city's fall. Their pursuers' bloodlust abated somewhat at the sight of seven hundred Varitai drawn up in full battle order, Weaver standing at their head with his arms crossed and face set in stern disapproval. Even so the mob had lingered for a time, their fury still unquenched, and the matter might have degenerated further but for the arrival of Master Rensial's mounted company. Since then a steady stream of beggared Volarians had made their way to the ruins, more trickling in from the south every day, having found life in the wilderness too great a trial.

"Will the Varitai come?" Frentis asked Weaver as they sat together in what he assumed had been the old city's council chamber. It was a rectangular structure comprising six rows of ascending marble benches around a large flat space. The roof had vanished but the massive pillars that once supported it remained, though standing at perhaps half their former height. The floor was covered in a vast mosaic, the tiles faded in the sun and pounded to fragments in many places, but still complete enough to convey a sense of accomplished artistry, a greatness brought low in the fury of war.

"They have a new name now," Weaver said. "Politai, which means unchained in old Volarian. And yes they'll come, there being so many more of their brothers to free in Volar. I shall ask them to leave enough men here to guard these people though."

"I've obtained assurance from Karavek they'll be left in peace, provided they don't venture into New Kethia."

Weaver gave a slight nod, his eyes roving the ruin. "Did you know, the people of this city would choose their own king? Every man who owned house or livestock was given a single black stone every four years. A vase would be placed before each of the candidates who would stand there," he pointed to the head of the chamber, "and each man would reach his hand into every vase, keeping his fist closed whenever he drew it out, so none would know into which vase he had dropped his stone."

"What if you dropped two stones?" Frentis asked.

"A great blasphemy punishable by death, for this was a rite as well as a custom, ordained by the gods. All shattered and lost when the Volarians came of course, but Queen Lyrna found it interesting. From a historical perspective."

"Do you truly hold her memories?"

Weaver gave a small laugh and shook his head. "Her knowledge, her insight you might say. They are not always the same as memory." He turned to Frentis, his humour fading quickly. "You dreamt again."

"More than a dream. We spoke. She wants me to bring you to the arena in Volar. For what purpose I can't imagine. But I doubt she means you well."

"And if you don't?"

"She holds Lady Reva, makes her fight in the arena. I'm certain she'll face worse if we do not come."

"You care for her?"

"I barely know her. But my brother sees her as his sister, which makes her my sister. I do not wish to tell him I turned my back on a chance to save her. But I can't command you in this, nor would I wish to."

For a time Weaver said nothing, his face gradually clouding into an expression so troubled it seemed his youth had vanished. "When I was a child," he said, "I didn't understand the nature of my gift. If I saw a wounded creature, a bird with a broken wing or a dog hobbling on a twisted leg, it seemed such a wondrous and simple thing to restore them with a touch. But for a long time everything I healed became a shadow of what it had been, an empty-eyed husk plodding through life and often shunned by its own kind. I didn't know why until I came to understand that my gift doesn't just give, it takes. Those I heal are opened to me by the touch, everything they have is laid bare and there for the taking. Their memories, their compassion, their malice . . . And their gifts. Although I try to stop it, something always comes back, bringing with it the temptation to take more, to take it all.

"I first met your brother years ago, when my mind was . . . less clear than it is today. I had occasion to heal him, Snowdance being so hard to restrain." Weaver looked down at his hands, spreading the nimble fingers. "His gift was great, brother, and the temptation stronger than ever. So I took, just a little. If I had taken it all . . ." Weaver shook his head, shame and fear mingling on his face. "The song is faint," he continued, "but if I listen hard enough, I can hear it, and it guides me, tells me where I need to be. It led me to follow him to Alltor, guided me to the queen when she needed healing, and to the ship that brought us to this land. And now, brother, it tells me to go to Volar, and its tune is far from faint."

He patted Frentis's knee and got to his feet, casting a final glance around the council chamber. "They also killed children here," he said. "To seal the people's choice with a blood offering to the gods. The sacrifice would be chosen by lot, their parents considering it a great honour."

He turned and started up the steps. "I should speak to the Politai, they're becoming ever more insistent on explanations."

Chapter Six

Vaelin

The red man's lips had been part seared away, exposing teeth and gums in an obscene grin. Vaelin couldn't escape the sense of being laughed at, the Witch's Bastard enjoying his final triumph.

A series of gurgles came from the ruined face, spittle and blood spraying as the red man's lidless eyes stared up at him. Was he begging? Taunting? Vaelin crouched, leaning close to try to discern some meaning amongst the choking babble. The red man jerked and convulsed, tongue sliding over his teeth as he attempted to shape the words. "O-one . . . left. Stiiillll . . . one . . . moooore . . . leeeeft."

"Where?"

"K-kuhhhh . . . killlll . . . meeee . . ."

Vaelin stared into the thing's bloodshot eyes, unable to read any expression as the surrounding flesh had been seared to the bone. "I will."

The thing choked, tongue twisting behind the teeth as it fought to shape an answer. "Alpiraaah . . ."

Vaelin rose and went to Wise Bear and Erlin. "He says there's another," he told the shaman. "Far from here. Will it matter?"

"Matter to what?" Erlin asked.

Vaelin gave no response, keeping his gaze on Wise Bear, who glanced uncertainly at the ancient man before replying. "Other one stay in body it stole, won't matter."

Vaelin glanced back at the wasted, blackened thing lying amongst the rocks, various tempting notions flickering through his head. *Let it linger until the last second. Have Astorek set the wolves on it. Take a hot blade to its eyes . . .*

Cara's sobs drew his attention to the far end of the ridge where Orven's guardsmen were constructing the pyre. She sagged in Lorkan's arms, face buried in his chest. The Sentar stood nearby in respectful silence, their numbers halved in the struggle with the Kuritai, Kiral standing beside Alturk. The Tahlessa leaned heavily on a spear, sweating with the effort.

"Finish it," Vaelin told Wise Bear, jerking his head at the blackened thing and moving towards the pyre. "I leave the manner of its passing to you."

◆　◆　◆

He sat on the cliff edge as the fire dwindled behind him and the sun dipped below the mountains. Out on the valley floor the tribesfolk were still picking over the Volarian dead. The aftermath of victory had seen them instantly revert to prior allegiances and the different groups squabbled over the spoils, threats and curses echoing across the valley, each chieftain no doubt stating a claim to the collected loot as leader of the army and architect of victory.

He hadn't said any words as the fire blossomed, watching Dahrena and Marken's fur-wrapped bodies wreathed in flame and smoke as the others said their peace. Even Alturk managed a few terse words of respect for those fallen in a common cause. They drifted away as evening fell, Cara still crying and making him wonder if she would ever stop.

"Why won't it matter?"

He looked up at Erlin, seeing the cautious but determined set of his features. Vaelin returned his gaze to the valley and the dead, stripped and pale in the gathering gloom. They were spread out in a vague teardrop shape, bulging at the river and narrowing to the west where the survivors had attempted to flee. As far as he knew none had escaped, the victors having no tradition of offering quarter to the vanquished. The dead hadn't been counted either, the Wolf People were content in the knowledge of a secure future and he doubted the tribesfolk could count past ten. *Sixty thousand?* he wondered. *Seventy?*

"What else did you see in the stone?" Erlin persisted.

"You have had centuries on this earth," Vaelin said. "Gaining many lifetimes' worth of knowledge. And yet you have never before made any effort to bring an end to the Ally. There must have been chances before now. You said others sought you out. Why take a stand now?"

"Before I always knew it would be hopeless, probably fatal."

"Well now it is certainly fatal. That's what the stone showed me."

Erlin sank down at his side, turning to the valley, the tribesfolk's squabbles still audible in the gathering dark. "My gift, it will draw him."

"Yes."

"How will you do it?"

"The choice is not mine to make." He got to his feet, turning his back on the valley and moving to the pyre. The flames had died away, leaving only a fading pall of smoke rising from the ashes. He knew if he peered close enough, he would see her bones and closed his eyes against the temptation. *She would never want you to torture yourself.*

"You're saying I can leave?" Erlin asked. "You will simply allow me to walk away from here?"

"In the morning I set out for Volar, where I believe we will find the ending we seek. I hope you will join me. If you do not, I will understand."

"What awaits us in Volar?"

He watched the thinning tendrils of smoke rise into the night, twisting in the air until lost amongst the stars. *Is she snared?* he wondered. *Did he catch her as he caught me? Does he torment her now, twisting her into the same thing that killed her?*

"A box," he told Erlin. "Full of everything, and nothing."

◆ ◆ ◆

There were more than enough horses for all, though the Sentar would have greatly preferred their stout ponies to the taller and more placid Volarian cavalry mounts. "At least they'll make good eating when the snows come," Alturk commented as he severed the stirrups from his horse's saddle, casting them aside with a contemptuous grimace.

Vaelin had spent much of the morning dealing with the tribal chieftains who seemed to be labouring under the collective delusion they would now be obliged to fight the Wolf People for possession of lost territory.

"We don't want your lands," an exasperated Astorek told them, repeating the words in Realm Tongue for Vaelin's benefit. "My people are already returning to the tundra."

Hirkran said something, maintaining a rigid pose in an ornate Volarian breastplate, axe in one hand and looted short sword in another. "He wants to know what tribute we demand," the shaman explained to Vaelin.

Vaelin found himself fast wearying of these folk; their endless feuds and unalloyed suspicion now seemed so unutterably petty. "Stay away from your people as they march north, and mine as we march south."

Hirkran narrowed his gaze and spoke again. "He says they garnered much in the way of gold and jewels from this field," Astorek said. "And doesn't believe you would simply ride away without trying to take it."

"Then"—Vaelin's hand went to his sword as his weariness turned to sudden anger—"he can fight me and I'll prove it by piling all the gold on his corpse before I leave."

Astorek's translation was clearly unnecessary judging by the way Hirkran bridled, uncrossing his arms and adopting a crouched stance with a challenging growl.

"Enough!" Kiral stepped between them, surprising Vaelin by addressing the tribesman in a fluent but harsh torrent of Volarian. Hirkran's aggression lessened in the face of her tirade though his eyes narrowed further, his face taking on an expression of grim understanding. He voiced a brief snarl as Kiral fell silent, his eyes flicking momentarily to Alturk before he backed away, still crouching, as if expecting an attack at any second. He uttered a soft, intent sentence at Kiral then abruptly turned and walked away, calling to his warriors.

"What did you tell him?" Vaelin asked her.

"That their weakness and disunity has been noted by my father." She gestured at an oblivious Alturk. "A great warlord who will return with all our tribe to claim these mountains, for they are unworthy of the riches offered by the spirits."

Astorek gave an appreciative chuckle. "If anything will unite them, it's that."

Kiral inclined her head with a smile, her humour fading as she looked at Vaelin. "My song indicated you would have killed him."

"Your song was right." Vaelin turned away and started towards Scar. "We ride within the hour. Astorek, please convey my thanks to your people and assure them of the continued friendship of the Unified Realm. I've little doubt my queen will send ambassadors to formalise our alliance in due course."

"From what Wise Bear tells me," Astorek called after him, "if your mission fails, our victory here will prove no more than a respite from greater dangers."

Vaelin paused, turning to offer the shaman an impatient nod. "Hence my keenness to depart."

Astorek glanced first at Kiral, then at the burgeoning dust cloud beyond the ridge where his people were breaking camp. "Then I will go with you. I . . . feel the wolf would want me to."

Vaelin felt the faintest flutter of humour as he saw Kiral carefully avoid his gaze. *Is he answering a wolf's call? Or a cat's?*

"You will be welcome," he told him, resuming his stride. "Please be brief in your farewells."

◆ ◆ ◆

The journey through the mountains was rich in grim sights testifying to the destruction wrought by the Witch's Bastard. Murdered tribespeople littered the heather, burnt settlements became a common sight as did the bodies of Volarian soldiers lashed to wooden frames, the flesh of their backs flogged down to the spine. From the frequency of such sights it was clear the red men had led a reluctant army, displaying little imagination in maintaining discipline.

"Even Tokrev wasn't so cruel," Astorek said as they neared a row of a dozen flogged men, a cloud of crows rising from the frames as they approached.

"I found his cruelty more than sufficient," Vaelin replied. He spied a settlement ahead, charred and mostly ruined but still possessing some intact roofs. "We'll shelter there tonight. Lord Orven, scout the hills in a five-mile radius. Victory or no, this remains enemy territory."

Erlin came to his fire when the night had grown fully dark. Vaelin had sat apart from the others since the march began. The Sentar were rich in new stories and, though he barely understood a word, their evident relish in recounting the battle roused him to unwise anger. *This is what they came for,* he chided himself. *Another story, the Mahlessa's gift to her bravest warriors is the chance for a richer tale.*

"Astorek and Kiral are missing," Erlin said, sinking down opposite him, hands spread to the warmth. "Haven't seen either since nightfall."

Vaelin glanced at the blackness beyond the part-tumbled walls of the dwelling he had chosen, a place he would have shared with Dahrena, as Kiral and Astorek now shared another. "I suspect they're safe enough."

"She told me of a compound she carries," Erlin said, face tense as he stared into the fire. "Some ancient Lonak concoction that can instill pain, enough to bring a man to the point of death if used in sufficient quantity, or purge him of an unwanted soul."

Vaelin nodded. Lyrna and Frentis had left him in no doubt of the power contained in the Mahlessa's compound, though he had yet to see it for himself.

"The Ally had a gift," Erlin went on. "The nature of which we do not understand, but it was powerful enough to bring down an entire civilisation. A gift he may well bring with him should he be drawn back from the Beyond."

"I know," Vaelin said. "But we have come to a point where I believe we have little option but to trust the words of the seer. You will touch the black stone in Volar, but it will not be you."

"How do we know it will end this? How do we know it won't simply make him stronger? You saw him in the memory stone, he wanted to touch it."

"But he also feared it, enough to have it secreted away for centuries."

Erlin's hands trembled as he held them to the fire, Vaelin frowning at the grin that played over his lips. "I'm afraid, brother. All these years, so much seen and heard and tasted. And yet I still want more. My nameless wife was often heard to call me selfish, usually before she threw something."

"You have saved many," Vaelin reminded him. "Two of them children who grew into the brave people who ride with us now."

"Just more selfishness, I'm afraid. If I saved enough, I imagined they would eventually fight the war for me, bring down the Ally, and spare me the trials of battle." He gave Vaelin a sidelong glance. "What would your queen do, if she were presented with this particular dilemma?"

"She would act for the good of the Realm."

Erlin grunted a laugh. "You mean she would have had me tied in a trice and force-fed the Mahlessa's compound until the Ally was safely caged in my flesh. Should you prevail in this struggle, don't you worry what she might become? I've seen many a monarch, brother, but none like her."

"She is not the Ally. Nor will she ever be."

"Are you so certain? You saw him in the city he built, the way his people loved him. And yet somehow his power grew to a point where it became absolute, and there was no one to stop him."

"Lionen stopped him. He killed the Ally and sent him to the Beyond."

Erlin lowered his hands, drawing them back to cross his arms. "We could wait, delay until we reach Volar . . ."

"His creature still has possession of a body in Alpira. If we delay, it might die, and the Ally could send it for you."

Vaelin watched Erlin's face for a moment, seeing the faint tic below his eye, the bulge of his jaw as he clenched his teeth. *No notion of how many years he's lived, witness to every wonder this world can offer, subject of myth and legend, now just a scared man shivering in a ruined hut.*

"If it should come to pass that you can't get him to the stone," Erlin said, "I require your promise you will not kill this body. You will use the compound to return him to the Beyond."

"You have it. I will preserve you."

"Me?" Erlin bared his teeth in what might have been a smile. "I doubt there will be any me left when he's done, brother." He rose, still hugging himself tight and moving away with a stiff gait, his parting words little more than a whisper. "Give me tonight. We'll see it done in the morning."

◆ ◆ ◆

He had Alturk see to the binding, the Lonak made strong rope and the Tahlessa's knots were unlikely to loosen. "Room enough to breathe only," Vaelin told him as he drew the rope tight around Erlin's chest.

Kiral came forward as Alturk finished the final knot, Erlin wincing with the strain as he knelt, chest roped from shoulders to waist and his arms secured behind his back. Kiral took a deep breath as she undid the stopper on the flask. "I . . ." she began, crouched next to Erlin, her voice faltering. "This will . . . hurt. I'm sorry."

He gave an impatient bob of his head. "So I'm told, my dear. Best get it done quickly then."

She rose, placing a thin reed into the flask. "One drop to cast them out," she said in a murmur, presumably reciting a lesson from the Mahlessa. "Two to draw them in."

Erlin's eyes flashed at Vaelin as she stepped closer. Words were irrelevant, the meaning clear in his moist gaze. *Do not forget your promise.*

Kiral drew the reed from the flask, the tip gleaming with something dark and viscous, then lowered it so two drops fell free to land on Erlin's exposed skin. Vaelin had expected screams, but instead Erlin stiffened, teeth clenched together and neck bulging, his face transformed into a red mask of purest agony. After a second he collapsed, writhing on the ground as foam bubbled from his mouth, legs drumming the earth. The convulsions continued for a full minute until Erlin finally lay still, all animation seeming to seep from his limbs, his head lolling slack on his shoulders.

For a moment Vaelin was certain he had killed him, that this great design had been revealed as the desperate ploy of a grieving fool . . . But then, Erlin blinked.

He rolled upright, remaining on his knees, sparing a brief glance at the ropes that bound him before raising his gaze. His expression was curious, inquisitive, lacking malice or anger as his eyes tracked across them, lingering on Vaelin, whereupon he smiled. It was a genuine smile, warm, even appreciative, as was his voice when he spoke, Erlin's polyglot accent moulded into something stronger, the tone deeper, "Thank you."

He closed his eyes and raised his face to the sky, smiling yet wider as the air played over his skin.

"Kill it!" It was Kiral, standing well back from the bound man, face bleached to near whiteness as her cat crouched at her side, fangs bared. "This is wrong!"

"The decision is mine," Vaelin told her. "Regardless of your song."

"We should never have done this." Her hand moved unconsciously to the knife in her belt. "My song screams it." She started forward, drawing her knife.

"He needs to be taken to Volar," Vaelin said, stepping into her path. "And I will take him there."

"You don't understand," she hissed at him. "This entire journey, every life taken and lost, every battle fought. We have done everything it wants, taking it closer to its goal with every step."

Vaelin turned to the bound man, now regarding him with placid features, free of fear or protestation. "We will make an ending, you and I," he said, and began to laugh.

◆ ◆ ◆

"What was your name?"

The bound man didn't turn at Vaelin's question. He sat at ease on the saddle he had been tied to, continually preoccupied with the passing landscape as Vaelin rode ahead leading his mount, eyes bright and wide as if trying to capture every detail. "My wife called me husband, my children called me father," he said. "The only names I ever truly needed."

Vaelin frowned in consternation. The idea of this thing fathering offspring was both absurd and appalling. "You had children?"

"Yes. Two boys and a girl."

"What became of them?"

"I killed them." The Ally looked up at the sky, a faint expression of wonder on his face as he spied a lone bird wheeling above, one of the broad-winged vultures common to the mountains.

"Why?" Vaelin asked.

The Ally's face darkened a little as he turned to him, puzzlement and anger mingling on his brow. "A father's duty is often a hard one, but cannot be shirked. A truth you will never discover, for which you should thank me."

"So you intend to kill me?"

"You killed yourself the second you opened this body to me. The girl is right, this particular circumstance suits my purpose very well."

"How? How does it suit your purpose?"

"You know I won't tell you that, regardless of what tortures you might inflict on this flesh. Fear not though, the answers will not be long in coming."

They rode in silence for much of the day, Orven's guardsmen scouting ahead whilst the Sentar guarded the flanks and rear. Kiral kept close to Astorek, both staying far back along the line of march with his wolves close on all sides. From the continued paleness of her complexion Vaelin deduced her song hadn't abated. Lorkan and Cara were less afraid, regarding the Ally with a wary curiosity, though so far only Vaelin had spoken to him.

"Why don't you ask me?" the Ally said eventually, his eyes lingering on clouds gathering to shroud the late afternoon sun. "Surely you want to know if I caught her."

Vaelin gripped the reins tighter, Scar issuing a faint snort as he sensed his rising anger. "Did you?" he demanded in a hoarse whisper.

"Oh yes. And greatly diverting she was too, if tiresomely stubborn. I could see why you loved her, such a bright soul is rare. Had I the time, no doubt I could have shaped her, crafted a dream rich in all the necessary temptations. I did the same for your brother, Caenis was it?"

Vaelin came to a halt, the Ally's mount bringing him closer until he was no more than a sword length away. He stared into the Ally's blank, uncaring gaze, his hands trembling.

"He had a suitably heroic death," the Ally said after a moment. "Saving your queen from one of my servant's delightful traps. He would have been of great use, his gift being so strong, but thanks to you, all lost. Along with that woman you loved so dearly. Had you left me there, you might one day have heard their voices again, but now they are gone, vanished to nothing like any other soul. You did that when you brought me here, for without me there is nothing to hold them."

"You're lying," Vaelin said, finding he had to force the words out. "Something held you in the Beyond. It could hold them too."

"The Beyond," the Ally repeated with a caustic sigh. "What a ridiculous name. Still, I suppose you had to call it something. My people never thought to name it, as if in denying it a title, they could wipe away the crime of creating it."

More lies. The Beyond is surely eternal. Caenis and Dahrena will be bound there forever . . . The notion stirred a fresh welling of grief, and yet more unwise anger. The sword felt heavier on his back now, a constant temptation.

Vaelin turned Scar about and kicked him into a walk.

"We didn't know, you see," the Ally continued, his tone reflective but also cheerful, an avuncular uncle relating past mischief to a curious nephew. "We imagined ourselves so wise. And why would we not? The marvels we crafted on this earth would have left your primitive mind reeling. But that is the eternal dilemma of curiosity, its boundlessness. Having conquered much of one world, a conquest won without battles or blood I might add, why not seek out others? The stones were the key of course, as they were the key to everything in our world of wonders. Dug from the earth and shaped, and only with the shaping was their power revealed. The power to store memory and knowledge, preserving our wisdom for all the ages, and, it transpired, the power to reach between worlds."

"The black stone," Vaelin said, refusing to turn.

"Yes." The Ally laughed in surprise. "I clearly don't give you enough credit. Yes the black stone was to be our greatest achievement. I imagine you must be burning to know what it is."

"I know you made it, and feared what you had made."

"What did Lionen tell you? That it was a box to lock me in, perhaps?"

Vaelin glanced over his shoulder, finding the Ally's gaze more intent now, his cheerfulness displaced by calculation. *So he doesn't know everything.* "He told me your wife's death had driven you to destroy the world you built, and he killed you to prevent that."

"True enough, though I suspect it was more a matter of primal hatred. He didn't give me a quick death, you know."

"I saw what you did to your people. You had much to atone for then, and yet more now."

"Atonement? I have spent countless years without pain, pleasure or the knowledge of anything that might be called human sensation." He reclined in the saddle, shrugging in his bonds. "Please, feel at liberty to inflict whatever torment you like upon this flesh. I'll take it all and ask for more."

"What is the black stone?" Vaelin demanded, the sword shifting on his back as he rounded on the Ally. "If it is not a prison, what is it?"

The Ally glanced over at Lorkan and Cara, riding just within earshot. "In my time there were none like them. None who were born with a gift, with the power burned into their souls and passed through the bloodline for generations. Our gifts came only from the black stone."

Touch it once and it gives . . . "There was no Dark in the world," Vaelin said in realisation. "You unleashed it."

The Ally's face betrayed a mix of scorn and amusement. "How little you know. There has always been power here, in the water and the earth, ancient and capricious, but beyond the reach of human knowledge. The stones brought something new, something different, a gift of power from across the chasm that divides the worlds. We took it and built wonders . . ."

The Ally trailed off, glancing around at the Lonak and the Gifted, his expression darkening into contemptuous disdain. "And this world is our legacy," he went on. "Did Lionen tell you when he first received his visions he thought he was seeing the past? Some long-forgotten age of barbarism where people killed each other over mere superstition. Then he saw the ruins of my city and knew he looked upon the future. A future we built together."

♦ ♦ ♦

The Ally didn't speak again, remaining apparently content in his bonds, riding without protest and accepting the food spooned into his mouth with a grateful smile. Vaelin asked many questions during the first two days of silence but gave up when it became plain this thing had nothing more to share.

They left the mountains behind ten days later, proceeding into the plains beyond. It was pleasant country, dotted with small, forested gullies and, the farther south they travelled, plantations and villas of varying size and luxury. Some showed signs of recent abandonment, others were littered with bodies and part destroyed by fire or deliberate vandalism. Vaelin initially suspected the Witch's Bastard of having vented his malice when he led his army north, but it soon became clear this destruction arose not from oppression, but revolt. Time and again they found black-clad bodies hanging from the archways of partially destroyed villas, often families who had met an identical fate, the corpses showing signs of torture.

"The red men conscripted their Varitai on the way north," Astorek surmised after surveying a particularly large villa that had been reduced to its foundations by fire. "The slaves rose and they were defenceless."

"Why kill the children?" Cara asked. The villa had burned but its owner had not, his body lay spread-eagled and eviscerated in the forecourt alongside a woman and a small boy, both recipients of the same treatment.

"A lifetime of rage is not easily tempered," Astorek said. "Children born into slavery are taken from their parents and sold, those permitted to live that is."

"Doesn't make it right," Cara murmured. "Nothing about this dreadful journey has been right."

Vaelin saw the Ally regarding the burnt remnants of the villa with an incurious eye. His demeanour over recent days had been one of boredom, reminding Vaelin of the privileged nobles he had seen suffering through the banal entertainments of the Summertide Fair. *He grows impatient for his end. As do I.*

◆ ◆ ◆

Another week's travel brought them to the first town they had encountered, a walled collection of somewhat mean houses rising from the green fields like an ugly growth. Astorek struggled to place its name but did remember being garrisoned there with his father's regiment before they proceeded north to their fateful encounter in the mountains.

"The men got drunk and started a brawl with the townsfolk," he recalled. "Knives were drawn, it got very ugly. The next day Father had one hanged and ten flogged. Oddly the men didn't seem to mind that much, I think that was the only time he might have won some respect."

"Stinks worse than the Merim Her hovels," Alturk commented. "Our numbers are small. We should go around."

"The Northern Road begins here," Astorek said. "It'll take us to Volar. We can pick it up to the south."

The townsfolk, however, proved unwilling to let them pass. As they neared the road a motley group of about three hundred people emerged from the town gates to place themselves astride it. As Vaelin drew near he saw they wore a variety of clothing, black and grey with the occasional flash of red, and all were armed, though not particularly well and their line was distinctly ragged.

A large man stood at the head of the mismatched host, bare muscular arms crossed and staring at Vaelin with stern defiance. He wore a red tunic and black trews, his meaty wrists liberally festooned with bracelets of gold and silver.

"Tell him he's in our way," Vaelin said to Astorek as they closed to within fifty paces of the townsfolk.

Astorek called out to the large man, receiving a loud, and prolonged tirade in response, the man waving his braceleted arms about and pointing in various directions.

"He says he is king of this land for as far as the eye can see," Astorek related. "He has killed many men to win this city and will kill many more to keep it."

"What does he want?"

"Tribute and obeisance, if you want to use his road."

"He's a slave?"

"A Garisai if I'm any judge. It appears this province has undergone a political transformation recently and, amidst chaos, the strongest are likely to gain authority."

"Tell him we have seen many murdered children in these lands. I would know if he is responsible for that."

The large man spat contemptuously on the ground as Astorek related the question, gesticulating with even more fury and pointing at Vaelin in obvious challenge. "He has wiped the cursed blood of the masters from these lands, their seed will never again rise to trouble them. He is master here now, and demands his due."

"And he'll have it." Vaelin climbed down from Scar's back, approaching the large man with a swift stride. The new-made King's heavy features tensed in puzzlement then outright alarm as Vaelin drew his sword. He dropped into a fighting stance, short swords appearing in both hands from sheaths hidden beneath his tunic, displaying considerable poise in his stance, one sword held low, the other high.

Vaelin sent a throwing knife between the twin blades, the steel dart sinking into the large man's eye socket up to the hilt. He staggered, his blades moving in an automatic counter that rebounded from Vaelin's parry with a clang before Vaelin brought the Order blade up and round in a blurring arc. The blade made it perhaps two-thirds of the way through the Garisai's thick neck, obliging Vaelin to withdraw it and deliver another blow to sever the head from his twitching corpse.

He raised his gaze to the ragged host of risen slaves. Instead of surging forward to avenge their fallen king, they had retreated several paces, each face displaying a gratifying level of shock and dismay. Vaelin turned and beckoned Astorek to his side.

"Translate every word as I say it," he told him before addressing the crowd, "I hereby claim this province in the name of Queen Lyrna Al Nieren of the Unified Realm. Until such time as she makes provision for fair and just governance, you will conduct yourselves as free citizens of the Realm, refraining from murder and thievery. If you do not, the queen will be swift in making judgement, and"—he paused to nudge the large man's head with the toe of his boot—"she is not so forgiving as I."

He flicked the blood from his sword and returned it to the scabbard, walking back to Scar. "Now get out of the way."

◆ ◆ ◆

The land grew more populous farther south, but no less troubled. They would often catch sight of people on the road ahead, weighed down with goods, either their own or the product of looting. Most would flee at the sight of a large group of mounted warriors, scattering to the surrounding fields where, incredibly, some slaves continued to labour. Not all would flee however, some, mainly the old or those burdened with children, would shuffle to the side of the road and stare in dumb fascination as they rode by, the young ones shushed to silence as they pointed at the strange men. Nor were all so cowed, they endured many insults from the dispossessed, those who had lost everything to marauding slaves seemingly had little left to fear. One old man in a torn black robe assailed them with missiles drawn from a pile of horse dung, his face a mask of unreasoning fury as he spat unintelligible insults. Alturk rode forward to stare down at him, war club resting on his shoulder until the old man finally collapsed, sinking onto his odorous munitions as he wept.

"These people are very strange," Alturk said, trotting back to the column. "Seeking out a good death then falling to tears when it's offered."

They covered two hundred miles over the next week, at no point encountering a single Volarian soldier, though they did find evidence of battle. They lay strewn across the road, perhaps over a hundred bodies, mostly men but women too, Astorek judging them as a mingling of slaves and free folk from their garb. Many had died in mid-struggle, hands still clutching throats or knives, one young woman lying with her teeth clamped onto the forearm of the black-clad who had killed her.

"If this continues for much longer," Astorek said, "your queen will have nothing left to conquer."

"Except land," said the Ally, the entire company starting at the sound of his voice. He cast a dispassionate eye over the carnage before adding, "Land is the only true wealth in a world like this. Your queen will do rather well out of it all, I expect. Pity I can't let her keep it."

"You might speak differently," Vaelin told him, "if you had met her."

◆ ◆ ◆

He couldn't dream. Every night he lay down and slept, falling into slumber with barely a pause, and each time his sleep remained free of dreams. He had dreamt every night in the Emperor's dungeon, of Dentos, Sherin, even Barkus. At the time he had thought it a torment, well-earned torture fulfilling a desire the Emperor resisted. Now he knew it as a blessing. Dahrena was gone, truly and completely, and he was denied even the delusion of a dream, the brief, precious lie that she still lived, even though the waking would be hard, when the knowledge descended like an axe blade as he reached for the cold, empty place beside him. Still, he yearned for it.

"She spoke of you."

Vaelin rose from his bedroll, avoiding the Ally's gaze. The hour was early and the sky not yet bright enough to see well, rendering the Ally a slumped, shadowed form on the other side of the still-smoking ashes of last night's fire. "Don't you want to know what she said?" he asked.

"Why choose now to speak again?" Vaelin countered. "Is it because we draw nearer to Volar?"

"No, just honest boredom. Also, you primitives are proving more diverting by the day. I may have bequeathed you an age of ignorance but you do make it interesting. Tell me, why didn't you keep that man's head? Presumably there was some ritual significance in taking it."

"Can you really be so ignorant of us? You have orchestrated havoc in this world for centuries. How can you know so little?"

"I see only through the eyes of those snared in the Beyond, and even then the visions are often dim. Death does things to a soul, stripping away much that gives it substance. There was a philosopher in my time who argued that the sum of a soul is merely memory, the soul itself no more than metaphor."

"Evidently he was wrong."

"Was he? Haven't you ever wondered why it is only the Gifted who reside in the Beyond? Can it be only they are worthy of soulhood and all these other unblessed condemned to slip into nothing when death claims them?"

"Life has taught me to be tolerant of mysteries, especially those with no answer."

The Ally laughed, soft and sincere, then shuffled closer. His features became clear as he leaned forward, his gaze intent and questing, seeking understanding. "I am the answer. The Beyond is not the eternal domain of the dead, it is the result of folly and pride, it is a scab covering a seeping wound, eternally corrupted and corrupting. To exist there is to know the chill of death for all eternity, to feel yourself slowly ebb away until you are nothing but formless consciousness, shorn of memory but aware, knowing nothing but that endless cold."

"And yet, somehow, you retain enough reason to plague us." Vaelin rose, moving to the Ally's side, crouching and leaning close to voice his demands in a harsh whisper. "What is your gift? What awaits us in Volar?"

The Ally said nothing for a moment, Vaelin seeing the calculation return to his gaze. "She spoke of how much she loved you, how you mended a heart torn by grief. Though she worried over the woman you loved before her, fearing when this war was done you would seek her out. But mostly she worried for the child you made together. She hoped for a girl but knew it would be a boy, a boy who might one day be tempted by his father's martial ways . . ."

The Ally reeled from the blow, blood and teeth erupting from his mouth. Vaelin was only dimly aware of the feel of his fist pounding Erlin's features into bloody ruin, or the torrent of hate that spilled from his mouth, and he never felt Alturk's war club clip the base of his skull, sending him into the deepest sleep.

And this time the dreams came.

Chapter Seven

Lyrna

"**L**ord Lakrhil Al Hestian is hereby appointed Battle Lord of the Queen's Host."

She had called them to the temple's tallest tower, far above the smouldering pyres that littered the plain. The dark red mass of slain Arisai could be seen, stripped of weapons then piled near the riverbank and left to rot. "These men had no souls," she said when Brother Kehlan made a tentative suggestion some form of observance might be appropriate. "One cannot honour what does not exist."

She scanned the faces of the captains, seeking sign of dissent, but whatever feelings they might have harboured towards the elevation of a man named a traitor were kept well hidden. *They know me too well now,* she surmised, oddly dismayed by their timidity. Only Lords Nortah and Antesh exhibited any clear reaction. The Lord Marshal gave a silent and weary shake of his head. He and Al Hestian had a tendency to ignore one another with the kind of rigid indifference that told of deep mutual enmity, the spike protruding from Al Hestian's stunted right arm a constant and inescapable reminder of a long-unresolved grievance. The reaction of her Lord of Archers was more pronounced, his face tensed in suppressed anger.

No desire to follow the butcher of Greenwater Ford, Lyrna surmised. *How fortunate I have another card to play.*

"Lord Marshal Nortah will assume command of the Dead Company in his stead," she went on. "The Queen's Daggers are hereby enrolled in the Mounted Guard under command of Lord Iltis."

She turned to Al Hestian, "Battle Lord, your report on the state of the Queen's Host, if you please."

"Our full losses amount to little over fifteen hundred men, Highness," he replied. "Plus three hundred wounded and unable to fight. Three regiments besides the Queen's Daggers were so badly mauled I must advise they be merged into one. However, our losses may be considered slight in comparison to the enemy. More than thirty thousand slain and a thousand captured, the remainder fled and in no state to fight again. Count Marven deserves great credit for such a victory."

One of the Nilsaelin twins spoke up, the one with the red-enamelled breastplate though Lyrna still found it of little help in distinguishing between the two. "Our noble grandfather will ensure his memory is honoured the length and breadth of Nilsael. My brother and I will personally fund the construction of a statue in Meanshall."

Lyrna pushed away the image of Marven's bleached, panicked face, weeping as she pressed the cloth to his burning brow. *He would rather have just gone home to suffer his wife's cutting tongue.*

"A thousand prisoners?" she asked Al Hestian.

"Indeed, Highness. I intended to ask what you wanted done with them."

"The river's deep and fast-flowing," Baron Banders pointed out. "Spare us the effort of cutting so many throats."

The other captains exchanged nods and murmurs of agreement, though she noted Nortah's grimace of disgust. "No," she said. "They are to be preserved. Wounded are to be cared for and food provided. I understand from Brother Hollun most hail from this province."

"They do, Highness," Al Hestian confirmed. "They're an uncommonly poor lot for Volarian soldiery, I must say. Few veterans among them, most little more than boys conscripted barely two months ago."

"I believe there is a town several days' march along our road, I assume many will hail from there."

"Urvesk, Highness. A sizeable place from all reports. I was going to advise we bypass it, the garrison is unlikely to be numerous enough to threaten us and a siege would cost time and lives we can't afford."

She shook her head. "No. We will march there with all dispatch. Please make the army ready to move by dawn tomorrow. We've lingered here too long."

She dismissed them and stood regarding the view as they trooped down the winding stairwell, though, as expected, one decided to linger. "You have words for me, Lord Antesh?" she asked without turning.

He moved to stand at a respectful distance, though his darkened visage told of a simmering anger. "I cannot command my people to follow that man, Highness," he stated. "When they hear of this . . ."

"Lady Reva would have followed him," Lyrna said. "Wouldn't you agree?"

"Lady Reva had a soul blessed by the Father himself. I do not, neither do my archers. When we lost her . . . we lost our heart."

"Then you will no doubt rejoice to hear you have a chance to regain it." She turned, meeting his gaze squarely. "I have sound intelligence from the Seventh Order that Lady Reva lives and is captive in Volar."

She watched his face transform from dark anger to pale shock, soon followed by hope. "This . . . this has been confirmed?"

"Speak to Brother Lernial, he will provide assurance. Then I assume you will wish to share this joyous news with your people."

"I . . . yes." His head jerked in a bow and he backed away. "My thanks, Highness."

She turned back to the view as his rapid footfalls echoed up the stairwell, stumbling occasionally in his haste. "They really think their god talks to her?" Murel wondered allowed.

"Who's to say they are wrong." Lyrna's gaze tracked to the markings on the flat surface that topped this tower, the mass of meaningless symbols carved centuries before.

"Wisdom tells me," she said, "that each tower in the temple was allocated a priest upon construction, one said to have been touched by the gods. It was their lifelong mission to carve whatever insight the gods had imparted to them into the tower, from the lowest step to the very top. A lifetime spent etching their visions into stone, forbidden any other task, never allowed to venture from their towers. Little wonder they were insane by the time they finished, their messages no more than the scrawl of gnarled and maddened hands. And when they were done . . ." She went to the edge of the platform, her slippered toes protruding into space as she raised her arms, the wind whipping her gown and hair. "They would fly and the gods would reach down and snatch them from the air."

"Highness?"

She turned to see Iltis moving closer, reaching out a tentative hand to draw her back from the edge. She lowered her arms and waved him away with a small laugh. "Worry not, my lord. It's not my time to fly, I still have so much to do."

◆　◆　◆

She had Al Hestian send the North Guard ahead to Urvesk with orders to make themselves as conspicuous as possible. The Nilsaelin cavalry were divided into companies and dispatched north and south with the mission of freeing all the slaves they could find, though Lyrna fully expected their talent for looting to be given free rein. They had been cautioned to spare the free populace where possible and send them east with a full appreciation of their queen's intent. Accordingly, as they marched away from the temple and the dusty plain into the verdant hill country beyond, the horizon on either side was marked by tall columns of smoke rising from villas burned in the Nilsaelins' wake. From their reports it seemed many in this region had been told not to flee since the invaders would soon be crushed by the Empress's invincible forces.

By the fifth day many companies had returned, somewhat burdened by sundry valuables, but also trailing a collection of freed slaves, soon growing to more than a thousand over succeeding days. Lyrna made a point of personally greeting as many as possible, finding most to be young and prone to addressing her as "Honoured Mistress." Their older brethren were apparently too steeped in lifelong fear to accept this new queen's offer of freedom.

"Some of them wept when we burned their master's house, Highness," a baffled Nilsaelin captain told her. "A few even tried to fight us."

She had Nortah take charge of their new recruits, with Wisdom's assistance since the Lord Marshal spoke no Volarian. "It'll take months to turn this lot into soldiers," he told her as she toured his makeshift training camp. They had paused in a broad valley ten miles short of Urvesk, taking up residence in a plush villa the Nilsaelins had been thoughtful enough to spare for her comfort.

"You turned former slaves into fighters before, my lord," she pointed out.

"They had only been in chains for a few days, weeks at most. And their hatred burned bright enough to overcome a lack of skill and discipline." He gestured at the recruits labouring under the tutelage of sergeants from the Dead Company, who seemed intent on compensating for a lack of shared language with volume. "Most of these have known nothing but bondage."

"I'm willing to wager their hatred will burn bright too," Lyrna said. "When sufficiently roused. Keep at it my lord. We move on in three days."

◆ ◆ ◆

The city of Urvesk lay close to a fork in the river that ran alongside the road, birthing a smaller tributary snaking off to the north. It reminding her vaguely of Alltor with its high walls; however, the similarity faded at the sight of the many gaps, and the sprawl of mean housing that spread beyond them to the edge of the river. *The price of stability is unpreparedness,* she decided as Lord Adal galloped towards her.

"The place grows less populous by the day, Highness," the North Guard commander reported. "They've been fleeing north or east in a steady stream since they first caught a glimpse of us. No sign of any soldiery beyond some sentries on the walls, perhaps two hundred at most."

"Thank you, my lord. Please rest your men."

"Highness, I . . ." He hesitated, a keen entreaty in his eyes. "I had hoped to lead the assault."

What is this man's hunger for glory? she wondered. She greatly valued him as a captain, being one of the few true professionals in the army, but grew ever more concerned over his desire to place himself in peril. Accounts from the battle of the temple were rich in reports of his reckless valour, though he contrived to emerge from it all without a scratch. "There will be no assault, my lord," she told him. "Conserve your courage for Volar."

She turned Jet and cantered to where the prisoners had been arrayed, just over a thousand grey-faced men and boys standing shackled in four loosely ordered ranks. "Are there any officers here native to this city?" she called in Volarian.

They shuffled in fearful silence, many not daring to raise their heads, one boy near the front weeping openly.

"Speak up, you filth!" Iltis barked in Realm Tongue, making his meaning clear with a vicious crack of the overseer's whip he had secured from somewhere.

A man with a bandaged face in the third rank slowly raised a hand and was soon dragged from the throng by Iltis.

"You are an officer?" Lyrna asked the prisoner as Iltis forced him to his knees before her.

"A captain," he said in a wheezy voice. The bandage on his face covered his right eye, dark with dried blood, his complexion telling of a man moving closer to death with every step. "Called from the reserve to fight the Empress's glorious war of defence." He gave a bitter laugh and Lyrna divined he fully expected to die in the next few moments.

"Get up," she told him. "My lord, remove his chains."

She guided Jet closer as the one-eyed captain stared up at her in bafflement, seemingly uncaring of the blood that seeped from his chafed wrists as Iltis removed the manacles. "You will go home, Captain," she told him, pointing to Urvesk. "And tell whoever holds charge of this city that your comrades here will be freed, for I do not come to this land for slaughter, but justice. In return the city will release every slave in bondage and open its gates to me.

If they do not, I will kill ten prisoners every hour until they do. If reason still does not prevail, they will find themselves drowning in ash and blood when I send my army through their ragged walls."

She nudged Jet closer still, leaning down to stare into his one good eye. "Ask them if they really want to die for the Empress."

◆　◆　◆

By nightfall over three thousand slaves had emerged from the gates. Lyrna watched the last of them troop out and waited, concealing a sigh of relief as the gates remained open. *Did you ever manage this, Father?* she asked the old schemer's ghost. *To take a city by words alone.*

"I should go ahead with the Realm Guard, Highness," Al Hestian suggested. "Ensure a proper reception for your entry."

It would be so easy, she thought, eyes still fixed on the open gates. *So many wooden houses, so much fuel, the flames would light the sky for a hundred miles.*

"I shan't be entering the city," she told Al Hestian. "Send as many men as you think fit to ensure they haven't contrived to retain any slaves and secure additional supplies for my new subjects. No looting on pain of execution. Leave them sufficient stocks to guard against starvation, and their horses. I'm keen for word of our actions here to spread. Be sure the army is ready to march by dawn."

She glanced at the prisoners huddling together in the gloom, shivering as much in fear as from the oncoming chill. *Like all those souls I left to drown in the bowels of the slave ship,* she thought, hands clutching her reins until they ached. *It would be so easy . . .*

"Release this lot an hour before we march," she ordered, wheeling Jet about and galloping back towards the villa.

◆　◆　◆

They covered a hundred miles in three days, the Battle Lord insisting on a pace that saw many soldiers collapsing at the end of a day spent on what many now referred to as the "blood road." The march had made Lyrna intimate with the varying moods of her army. The Nilsaelins were the most vociferous grumblers, issuing a collective groan of relief and exhaustion at the conclusion of the second day. The Realm Guard were the most disciplined on the march though also the most fractious in the evenings; fistfights over card-games or petty disputes were still annoyingly common. The Renfaelins were by far the most cheery, their encampment rich in song and laughter most evenings, providing a stark contrast to the muted efficiency of the Cumbraelins, though their relative quietude had assumed a grim determination since the temple. They marched at a faster pace than all the other contingents, Lyrna having acceded to Lord Antesh's request to lead the column, and would often be two or three miles ahead by nightfall. Also, judging from the way they would cluster around the few priests among them come evening, news of Lady Reva's survival seemed to have birthed a resurgence of piety.

"I find myself ashamed, Highness," Antesh said on the evening of the third day. She had sought him out during her nightly tour of the camp, finding the Cumbraelins more respectful than usual, their bows deeper though their ever-cautious gaze still lingered.

"Ashamed, my lord?"

"After the storm, when we thought Lady Reva lost, I doubted the Father's purpose in bringing us here. At Alltor everything had been so clear, she seemed to shine with His love. But if He could take her from us, how could He bless this endeavour? I thought perhaps it might be punishment, a judgement on our willingness to ally with you. Now I see how foolish that was. *She* would never have guided us along a false path."

Hearing the certainty with which he coloured every word Lyrna resisted the impulse to ask if, in fact, her Lord of Archers worshipped a goddess rather than a god. "She is a truly great soul," she said. "I long to see her again."

She inclined her head and moved away but Antesh reached out, his hand stopping just short of her sleeve. "Highness, if I may. I know you have no belief in the Father, in truth I doubt you have much truck with your own Faith either. But know, although you may not feel his love, he gives it nonetheless."

Lyrna found herself beset by the unfamiliar sensation of not knowing what to say. She had never been comfortable around displays of devotion; her infrequent meetings with the late Aspect Tendris had been a considerable trial, as had her exchanges with Aspect Caenis, though he had provoked as much pity as discomfort. *Lives dominated by the spectres of ancient dreams,* she thought. *But it never seems to make them happy.*

"Be sure to thank him for me," she told Antesh, putting an edge of finality into her tone and turning away.

"There was one other thing, Highness," he said, moving to her side, then drawing back as Iltis gave a huff of warning. "Lady Reva," Antesh went on, "I worry she might become hostage to our intentions. By all accounts this vile Empress of theirs will not baulk at putting her to death should we attack Volar."

Won't your World Father reach down and save her? Lyrna smiled to cover her annoyance. "I will not allow that to happen."

"So you have a stratagem? Some means of securing her release?"

"Indeed I do." *Take the city and trust in the girl's deadly abilities to ensure her own survival.* She extended her hand to forestall his next words. "Please assure your archers there is no greater purpose for me than securing the Blessed Lady's life, even at the risk of my own."

Antesh hesitated before sinking to one knee and pressing his lips to her hand. "I shall, Highness."

◆　◆　◆

The following days saw the rolling hills flatten into undulating farmland, much of it dominated by fields of redflower, stretching away like an endless crimson carpet broken by the occasional villa or small town, most showing signs of hasty abandonment. This region also held another singular distinction in the poles with which the Empress had chosen to adorn the road.

"Little wonder they won't fight for her," Baron Banders commented, squinting up at one of the rotting corpses dangling above. "Could be we'll have a clear road all the way to Volar."

Lyrna gazed ahead at the long procession of poles disappearing into the distance, discerning a faint pall of dust rising above the horizon. "I doubt the Empress intends our passage to be an easy one."

Al Hestian had sent the Sixth Order ahead that morning and Brother Sollis soon returned to report the approach of a host some seventy thousand strong. "About half Varitai, by my estimation," he said. "They're a more ragged lot than we're used to. I suspect the Empress has commandeered every privately owned slave soldier in the region. The Free Swords don't seem much better, old men and boys mostly. However, their cavalry is another matter, keeping in good order and patrolling the flanks with keen eyes. We were lucky to return without being seen."

"No Kuritai or Arisai?" Lyrna asked.

"None that I could see, Highness."

"The temple taught us a hard lesson," Al Hestian said. "We can expect them to have hidden their elite among the fodder."

"In any case it's suicide," Nortah commented, shaking his head. "There are well over a hundred thousand souls in this army now, and growing by the day."

"If our enemy is intent on their own destruction," Lyrna said, "I am more than happy to oblige. Battle Lord, you will wish to make your dispositions."

◆　◆　◆

Al Hestian sent the Nilsaelin horse and North Guard galloping off before his main battle line was fully in place, ordering them to engage as many Volarian cavalry as they could. The Realm Guard cavalry were kept back to secure the flanks of the infantry, which he arranged in a surprisingly compact formation. The lead grouping consisted of just three regiments, standing in close ranks with the rest of the Realm Guard arranged behind and Lord Nortah's Dead Company, flanked by the loosely ordered mass of barely trained slaves, forming a rear-guard with the Nilsaelin foot. Out in front he placed the Renfaelin knights and Cumbraelin archers.

"I assumed Your Highness wished this matter concluded quickly," the Battle Lord stated in response to her cautious observation that this order of battle was beyond her experience.

"Quite so, my lord," she said, watching him ride off with his flag-men and signallers, wondering if she shouldn't ask Davoka to stay at his side throughout the battle, ready to kill him should this stratagem reveal itself a great, and perhaps deliberate folly. She pushed her misgivings away at the sight of Al Hestian riding along the flank of the army she had given him, seeing the total absorption on his face as he cast his expert eye over their ranks. *War is his art,* she realised. *His one remaining passion. Like Master Benril's statues or Alornis's sketches.*

Her gaze went to the Lady Artificer, moving among the line of ballistae arranged on a low rise on the left of the army's line of march. She had voiced a strident objection when Al Hestian advised the engines would not be required for his assault, calmed only slightly at Lyrna's suggestion they be employed to guard against a counterattack. *Enlivened only by the prospect of blood,* Lyrna thought, her gaze tracking Alornis's slim form as she moved from engine to engine.

Lyrna had placed herself at a short remove from the ballistae, under close escort by the remnants of the Queen's Daggers and the Seventh Order's most gifted members. The rise offered a fine view of the unfolding drama. The Volarians were approaching in reasonably good order, their front line composed almost exclusively of Varitai, with the Free Swords behind. A large plume of dust rising from the redflower fields beyond their left flank told of a fierce battle already raging between the North Guard and the Free Sword Cavalry, the Nilsaelin lancers streaming towards the struggle at full pelt. A three-battalion contingent of Volarian cavalry could be seen arcing round on the right, presumably with the intention of threatening their rear, but a series of flag signals from the Battle Lord's attendants soon sent the Realm Guard horse in pursuit, the opposing mass of riders meeting in a headlong charge some three hundred yards short of the rise. Lyrna saw Alornis pacing about amongst the ballistae, face set and fists clenched in frustration as not a single Volarian horseman emerged from the melee to provide a welcome target.

A familiar hissing sound drew Lyrna's attention back to the main body of the army, allowing her a brief glimpse of the first Cumbraelin volley descending on the centre of the Volarian line. It seemed to shudder from the impact, its pace slowing but still keeping on despite the continuing arrow storm, Lyrna's spyglass revealing the blank faces of Varitai marching blithely forward as their comrades died around them. She had expected Al Hestian to halt the army and let the Cumbraelins do their work for a time, but the sounding of multiple bugles told of a different intent.

She lowered the spyglass as the Renfaelin knights spurred into a charge, thunder rising from the earth as they accelerated, a cloud of shredded red-flower ascending in their wake, rendered oddly beautiful in the sunlight. The Cumbraelins immediately ceased their arrow storm and began to form ranks for their own charge. Discarding bows and drawing swords and hatchets, moving in a more coordinated fashion than their maddened charge at the temple to fall in alongside the leading Realm Guard regiments.

Lyrna lifted her gaze to watch the Renfaelin charge strike home, a spectacle she hadn't witnessed before though her father had often spoken of it. *Imagine an arrowhead of unbreakable iron, but fashioned by a giant.* She heard Murel issue a curse of amazement as the great wedge of steel and horseflesh struck home, the impact birthing an instant tumult of screaming men and horses mingling with the harsh, discordant notes of colliding flesh and metal. She saw several knights fall, tumbling with their horses in a tangle of armour and flailing hooves, but for the most part the knightly host retained its cohesion to skewer the Volarian line, tearing all the way through to the Free Swords and the open country beyond.

More bugles sounded and the entire mass of Al Hestian's infantry increased its pace to a run. The comparative cohesion of the Cumbraelin contingent evaporated as they ran, covering the remaining distance to the Volarian line in a frenzied sprint of flailing swords and hatchets, tearing into the already disordered mass of Varitai. The leading Realm Guard regiments struck home seconds later, halberds rising and falling in a practised display of disciplined slaughter, stripping away any remnant of order in the Volarian ranks, which buckled, fell back and disintegrated.

Ever more petals rose from the field as the battle became a rout, obscuring much of the unfolding carnage in a haze of drifting scarlet. The cavalry battles on either flank raged on for a time but soon the Volarian horse could be seen fleeing east as they discerned the fate of their infantry. The spyglass revealed the sight of Lord Adal leading the North Guard in pursuit of the escaping riders, despite the foam covering the flanks of his horse, green cloak streaming behind as he spurred it on, reddened sword extended straight as an arrow.

As her gaze returned to the centre of the battlefield she found a dense cluster of Free Swords had formed amidst the onrushing mass of Realm Guard. The spyglass revealed mostly fearful men, fighting with the kind of ferocity that was only born of survival.

"Send a rider to Lord Al Hestian," she told Iltis. "I am keen to secure more prisoners . . ."

"Ah, Highness . . ."

She turned at Murel's half-whispered words, the sight that greeted her making her wonder if some new enemy hadn't appeared in their midst, so disordered were the ranks of the Realm Guard, thousands of mostly unar-moured figures struggling through their lines. *The slaves,* she realised, catching sight of Nortah on horseback, vainly attempting to hold back his recruits as they charged towards the surviving Free Swords. The first hun-dred or so were cut down in seconds, but the others came on as if maddened, uncaring of the swords that slashed and hacked their unprotected flesh. She saw a man claw his way through the Volarian ranks with his bare hands, tearing at faces and necks, seeming not to feel the blade that sank into his chest as he bore its owner to the ground, prizing his helmet away to fix his teeth on the flesh beneath. His fellows piled into the shallow gap he had rent in the Volarian line, the Free Swords' desperate courage turned to panic by the savagery of the onslaught. Some ran to the Realm Guard, empty hands raised high and sinking to their knees. Most were not so fortunate.

Justice, Lyrna thought as the last speck of Volarian black disappeared in the seething mass of former slaves. Many were now waving captured weap-ons, or even severed limbs and heads in celebration as the petals continued to fall. *We are not the only hungry souls here.*

◆　◆　◆

"Do you think I'm pretty?"

The young woman elected to speak for the freed slaves was in truth pos-sessed of a certain delicate beauty, her features smooth with skin a pleasing olive hue, marred somewhat by the bandage that covered her partly severed left ear. She wore a mismatched variety of captured armour and weapons, standing with arms crossed, glowering at Lyrna in open defiance, the lack of any bow or honorific rousing Iltis to issue a threatening rumble as he started forward. Lyrna calmed him with a touch to the arm and gestured for the woman to continue.

"My back is not so pretty," she went on. "My first night in the pleasure house I cried, greatly displeasing the red-clad who had paid a handsome sum to take my virginity. My master had me flogged every day for a week then sold me to a pig farmer. The pigs ate better than I did and the farmer didn't care if I cried when he pawed me. Would you like to see my back, Great Queen?"

"I grieve for all you've suffered," Lyrna told her. "My wrists were once bound by chains so do not imagine your pain is unknown to me. Nor should you imagine that I care for the enemies we kill. However, if your people are to march with us, they must regard themselves as soldiers, bound by the orders of those who command them."

"We have no intention of trading one master for another," the woman returned, though her tone was more cautious. "And we are grateful for your coming. But there is much to account for, and we have only just begun."

"You'll have your accounting. When this war is won give me the name of the master who flogged you and I'll see the same done to him, and the pig farmer. Have your people make lists of the wrongs done to them and I'll ensure every soul receives justice. But until then I must ask that your people conduct themselves as soldiers and not a mob. You will be paid the same as any soldier in my Realm Guard, but service requires discipline. Lord Nortah is a fine commander who will not waste your lives, you would do well to heed him."

"And if we do not want to serve you?"

Lyrna spread her hands. "You are free people and may go where you wish, taking with you payment for service already rendered plus my thanks and friendship."

The woman thought for a moment, her stance marginally less closed. "Some will leave, some will stay," she said. "Many, like me, were stolen from their homelands years ago and will wish to return."

"I will make no effort to prevent them, even provide ships to carry them home when our task is complete."

"You'll make an oath to this, in front of all of them?"

"I will."

The woman nodded. "Come to us this night, I will ensure they listen." She gave an awkward half bow and went to the tent flap.

"You didn't give me your name," Lyrna said.

"Sixty-Three," the woman replied, a faint grin playing over her lips. "I'll resume my own when I go home. And don't worry about the pig farmer, his hogs ate better than ever the day I left."

◆ ◆ ◆

It's beautiful. She had reined Jet to halt beside Aspect Arlyn and Brother Sollis, waiting with the Sixth Order atop a low hill, all sitting in silent regard of the sprawling city in the distance. The sky was clear today and the unconstrained sun played over the panoply of marble, making it gleam before painting a glittering shine on the waters of the Cut of Lokar to the south. The absurdity of her mission became clear as she took in the myriad towers and countless streets; the destruction of such a city would be the work of years and she doubted even Alornis could conceive of a device capable of birthing a conflagration great enough to bring it down.

"No enemies to report, Highness," Brother Sollis said. "No sign of any defensive works in the suburbs either. There are some fires raging farther in, large numbers of free folk seen fleeing to the north. The slaves flee in our direction."

Lyrna nodded. She had ordered the release of the few hundred prisoners captured two days before, having been provided with fulsome descriptions of the dread queen's intentions. It seems sufficient numbers had fled back to Volar to bring about the desired effect.

"Highness!" It was Brother Ivern, raised up in his saddle and pointing to the south. It took a moment for her to recognise the dark shapes dotting the waters of the Cut. She used the spyglass to pick out the Meldenean battle flags flying from the thicket of masts, all clustered in an arc around the harbour, dozens more visible farther downriver, the unmistakable sleek shape of the *Red Falcon* among them.

She beckoned to one of the Queen's Daggers. "Ride to the Battle Lord. He is to proceed to the centre of the city forthwith, destroying any opposing forces he should encounter. Tell him I believe our newly freed subjects would be best kept in reserve." She turned to Aspect Arlyn. "Aspect. I trust you recall the route to the arena."

"I do, Highness."

"So then." She spurred Jet into a gallop, descending the eastern slope amidst a flurry of crimson petals. "Courtesy requires I greet the Empress, and I should not like to keep her waiting."

CHAPTER EIGHT

Reva

"**W**here did you get that?"

Reva found herself reaching involuntarily for the bow. The design was unfamiliar, axes and swords in place of the stag and the wolf, but the craftsmanship was unmistakable. *A bow of Arren.*

"You know this weapon?" Varulek asked her, his eyes shining with the same intensity.

"I once owned its twin, which now rests at the bottom of the ocean. They are heirlooms of my family. Fashioned for my grandfather by the finest bow-smith in Cumbraelin history, lost in the wars that built the Realm." She met Varulek's gaze, tightening her grip on the bow. "Where did you get it?"

"It is my family's charge to serve the gods, and the scripture they left us. As masters of the arena our reach has always been long, and our pockets deep. Volaria is rich in merchants and traders who appreciate the virtues of discretion. Twenty years ago one of them brought this bow to my father. He was well paid for his trouble."

Reva's fingers traced over the carvings, recalling the feel of her own bow, the way it had always seemed to fit her so well. Antesh had told her each one had been decorated to reflect the varied interests of her great grandfather. The one she had carried through Alltor had provided evidence of his passion for hunting. This one, it appeared, showed a keen interest in war.

"What would you have me do with this?" she asked Varulek.

"Your spectacle will be a great trial. Jarvek and Livella. I will not lie to you, the chances you might survive it are slender, but should you do so, I can hide this bow in the arena at a place within range of the Empress's balcony."

"There are archers on the upper tiers. I'll be dead before I draw the string."

"The arena has its own Kuritai, they answer to me. Plus there are some Free Sword mercenaries with grudges to settle, the Empress's purges have left few families in this city untouched."

"If I kill her, I will only be loosing what's inside, and it will surely find a new shell."

"Your queen approaches. The Empress's latest scheme to defeat her failed. I was witness to her reaction to the news, and it was a bloody sight. She's now scraping together what strength she can, but the best troops are off in the north, facing a new threat, and the empire seethes with rebellion. No help will come from the provinces. Your spectacle will take place three weeks from now, and your queen marches closer every day. Should you kill the Empress in front of thousands, she could find a new body but it will not matter. Who would follow her? Your queen may well find a city in chaos, ripe for the taking."

"And you will no doubt expect a reward when she does."

"You worship a god, but she does not, and yet she permits your worship. When Volar falls she will be Empress, an empress willing to tolerate a return of the old gods."

She's more likely to tear this charnel-house down around you. Reva's gaze tracked over the bow once more. *Uncle Sentes would have seen the Father's hand in you, as he saw it in me.* It occurred to her that this event, should it ever become known, would form the key verse in the Eleventh Book. The Blessed Lady and the Bow of Arren, a gift from the Father. The storm couldn't kill her, the arena held no terrors for her and, with the Father's love to guide her aim, she sent an arrow into the black heart of the Empress herself.

"I will do this," she told Varulek, handing back the bow. "But if I do not live, you will ensure this thing is burned and no mention of it ever made to my people." *I've told them enough lies.*

◆ ◆ ◆

"Owwwww!" Lieza squealed, rolling on the floor and rubbing her knee. For such a finely made person she remained aggravatingly clumsy and mostly devoid of coordination, despite two weeks of constant training.

"Get up," Reva sighed. "Let's try again."

"You too quick," Lieza grumbled, getting to her feet. She pouted at Reva's insistent frown and assumed the crouch she had been taught, bent almost double, one hand touching the floor. The information Varulek had provided about her upcoming spectacle had left Reva in little doubt that attempting to train the girl in combat would be unlikely to aid her chances of survival, but the ability to dodge a charging opponent might.

Reva met her gaze, forcing a smile. This time Lieza wasn't fooled, springing to her right, rolling and coming to her feet, just beyond the reach of Reva's flailing arm as she flashed past.

"Better," she said. "But the thing we face will have a longer reach."

"You really think you can kill it?"

If I get my hands on the bow quick enough. "We have a chance. Remember what I told you. There will be chaos, when it happens you run for the western exit. Do not wait for me, do not look back."

Lieza blanched, hugging herself as the fear returned. It was less frequent now, but still had occasion to leave her shivering and tearful. Reva had grown accustomed to waking with the girl's slender form pressed against her, tear-stained face nestling into her shoulder. She hadn't yet found the will to push her away.

Lieza started as the locks on the door rattled for the first time in days. Their food was provided via a slot in the base of the door, the only means of gauging the passage of time as they had been left alone since Varulek's surreptitious visit. When it swung open she was dismayed to find the black-clad absent. Instead two Arisai stood there, grinning as they bowed, unconcealed lust in the gazes they directed at her and Lieza.

One of them spoke, deepening his bow and gesturing at the corridor. Lieza swallowed before providing a translation. "She wants to see you."

◆ ◆ ◆

Think nothing. Feel nothing.

She knew she was asking the impossible of herself; how could any living mind think nothing? But still she found the constant refrain a comfort, placing her faith in the Empress's patent madness, the hope her mind was too clouded to allow her gift free rein.

To her surprise the Arisai led her from the arena and out into the broad parkland that surrounded it. The Empress was overseeing some form of modification to a life-sized bronze statue standing on a plinth opposite the main entrance, a team of slaves moving quickly at her shouted instruction. Most of their work seemed to be focused on the statue's head, working feverishly to hammer iron pegs into its bronze neck. Nearby a dozen Arisai stood guard, a kneeling man in their midst, naked, slumped and chained.

"Ah, little sister," the Empress greeted her, pulling her into a warm embrace. "And how does the morning find you?"

Think nothing. Feel nothing. "What do you want?"

"We haven't had occasion to speak since your delightful demonstration. I wouldn't wish you to think I harboured some anger towards you. Sisters shouldn't fight."

"We're not sisters."

"Oh but we are. I'm quite convinced of it. I was meant to have a sister, you see. But she died before she could be born." The Empress's gaze snapped back to the slaves and the statue. "Hurry up!"

Their efforts instantly became frantic, hammers moving in a blur as the last of the iron pegs were pounded into place. "Handsome fellow, isn't he?" the Empress asked as the slaves secured ropes around the statue's head. "Not to your taste, I know. But still, I assume you can still appreciate the aesthetic qualities of male beauty."

Reva glanced at the bronze face, now partly obscured by a net of ropes. He had certainly been a handsome man, strong-jawed with a narrow nose, though his expression was even more stern and commanding than the plethora of heroes the Volarians erected in every spare corner of their city. He wore the armour of a senior officer, though it seemed more elaborate and ornate than others she had seen.

"Savarek Avantir," the Empress said. "The greatest military commander in Volarian history. And my father."

The slaves hurriedly hitched their ropes to a team of horses and began flailing at their flanks with whips. The iron pegs in the statue's neck fell free as the rents they had forced in the metal widened, the bronze giving a whining groan of protest until the head finally came loose, falling onto the plinth with a loud clang.

"Conqueror of the southern provinces," the Empress went on, moving to the plinth and laying a hand on the metal head. "Victor of sixty-three separate engagements. One of only two citizens to gain the red by virtue of martial merit rather than property, creator of the Varitai and Kuritai and the first to receive the Ally's blessing. A fellow of singular achievement, wouldn't you say?"

"Did he kill as many people as you?"

The Empress's mouth twitched in a smile as she caressed the head. "More than both of us combined, little sister. And we have killed so many, have we not?"

Think nothing. Feel nothing. "If he took your Ally's blessing, where is he? I thought your kind lived forever."

"Even the Ally's gift is no defence against a skillful blade." She turned to regard the man kneeling amidst the Arisai. "Nor it seems, sufficient reward to ensure good service."

She waved a hand and the Arisai hauled the kneeling man upright, dragging him forward. He seemed to be absent any injury but sagged as if wounded, head lolling and limbs slack. He made no sound though the stench arising from the dark stains that covered his thighs spoke of bowels loosened by fear.

"Allow me to introduce General Lotarev," the Empress said as the Arisai allowed the stinking man to slump to his knees before her. "Commander of the Third Volarian Army, whom I elevated to the red and promised the Ally's blessing should he fulfil his boast of bringing that golden-haired bitch before me, preferably in chains though a corpse would have done. In the event his heroic troops fled the field with such alacrity I've little doubt some have reached the eastern shore by now."

She crouched down, taking hold of the unfortunate general's hair and jerking his head back, revealing a face twitching in unalloyed terror, bleached bone white and the eyes betraying a near complete loss of reason. "Why did you come back, Lotarev?" she asked him, her tone not unkind, though since she spoke in Realm Tongue, Reva doubted the man could comprehend a word. "What did you imagine your reward would be? Was it duty? All those years of service don't fade easily, I suppose. The capital in peril, you racing to bring me warning regardless of the risk to your own neck. Hoping for a statue of your own, eh?"

She leaned closer, speaking softly, her hand cupping his unshaven chin. "Don't you understand? The blond bitch can slaughter every soul in this city and rend it to dust, and I suspect I'll laugh at the spectacle. No, I just wanted her." Her other hand tightened in his hair, jerking the head again and drawing a fearful whimper. "She once took something from me, you see. I owe her a considerable debt."

She released him, rising and turning to the headless statue with a contemplative air. "Still, your dutiful service shouldn't go unrewarded. I'm minded to spare you the three deaths and give you the statue you hunger for. Fashioned by the expert hand of my own little sister."

One of the Arisai came to Reva's side, proffering a broad-bladed axe, the others dragging the general around until he knelt before her, head bowed.

Reva ignored the axe, fixing her gaze on the Empress. "No."

"Really?" She raised an eyebrow. "How terribly uncharacteristic. The reports from Alltor were fairly lurid in their description of your willingness to do this very thing."

The heroic Free Sword's head spiralling blood as she cast it over the wall . . . The prisoners being led to the block . . . No better than us . . . Think nothing! Feel nothing! "Do your own killing," she said.

"But I need for us to understand each other better." The Empress reached out to clasp her shackled wrists, meeting Reva's gaze with intent sincerity. "Blood will bring us closer. A lesson I learned from my beloved. In time we will be a family . . ."

Reva wrenched her hands away, burgeoning rage sending unwise images through her mind; Varulek's secret chamber, the bow of Arren, how it would feel in her hands when the time came . . . *Think nothing!*

"What is this, little sister?" The Empress frowned, tilting her head in a now-familiar gesture. "Do you scheme? Do you plot? With whom, I wonder?"

Reva closed her eyes and drew breath, calming herself with an image of Veliss, that day in the gardens as they watched Ellese stumble through her scales. *I have never asked you for a promise . . . Stay alive and come back to me.* "I already have a family," she said. "And you could never be part of it."

"And Lieza?" the Empress asked. "Does she deserve a place in your family? What will you tell that woman you pine for if you return? Why don't I spare you the complication? I can have her brought up, and my father's statue can have a girl's head instead of a coward's."

Reva lunged for the axe, tearing it from the Arisai's grip and whirling towards the Empress, though she had danced out of reach, a delighted laugh escaping her lips. "Enough play," she said, her mirth fading as she pointed to the kneeling general. "Time to craft your art."

◆ ◆ ◆

"She make you fight again?" Lieza stared at the blood discolouring Reva's blouse, coming forward, eyes wide in concern. "You hurt?"

"No." Reva moved away, tearing the blouse off, suddenly uncaring of what she saw. *Lotarev gaped up at her in vague comprehension, drool beading on his lower lip . . .*

She stripped, filled the bath and scrubbed herself clean. *So much death wrought by these,* she thought, staring at her hands as the blood turned to mist in the water. *Why do I feel it so now?*

After a while Lieza came to wash her blouse. This time she made no effort to enter the water, avoiding Reva's gaze and crouching at the edge as she worked the soap into the material.

"Have you ever killed anyone?" Reva asked her. "I know you tried with the Empress, but have you ever actually succeeded?"

The girl shot her a guarded look and shook her head.

"Well, to escape this place you may have to. I won't be able to protect you when it starts."

Lieza spoke in a soft voice, her hands still busy, "Won't leave without you."

"This is no game!" Reva thrashed at her, scattering reddened bath water. "This is no story! You will die here and I can't save you!"

Lieza was on her back, pinned beneath her, the concern in her eyes now turned to fear. Reva couldn't recall leaping from the bath. *Lotarev didn't speak as she raised the axe. It made a crunching sound as it bit into his spine, just like the prisoners and the Free Sword, Fatherless sinners all . . .*

She shuddered and scurried away from Lieza until her back met the wall, drawing her legs up and burying her head in her knees. She felt Lieza come to sit beside her, soft fingers gently tracing through her damp hair until Reva raised her head. Her kiss was tentative, so unlike Veliss in its lack of experience . . .

Reva moved back. "I can't . . ."

"Not for you," Lieza murmured, kissing her again, more insistent now, Reva finding her heart pounding, knowing she should push her away and yet her arms opened to enfold her, drawing her close. Lieza drew back a fraction, their breath mingling as she stared into Reva's eyes. "For me."

◆ ◆ ◆

Varulek arrived after the morning meal with a dozen female slaves, some bearing clothing, others combs and various concoctions used for dressing hair or painting faces. They dressed her in armour, of a sort, specially tailored to her size judging from the closeness of the fit. The breastplate was tight around her torso, fashioned from stiff leather but too thin to ward off anything but a glancing blow. Similarly the kilt of leather strips, each weighted at the lower end with a brass stud, was too flimsy to afford more than basic protection. She soon realised this was not truly armour; she was required to play a role and this was her costume. However, she took some comfort from the fact it was light enough to allow her to move quickly.

Lieza was dressed in a long gown of flowing silk, dyed a pale shade of violet that complemented her eyes. Her hair, grown longer than any slave was usually permitted over the weeks of seclusion, was moulded into a lustrous ebony cascade, adorned with a small silver diadem.

"Avielle was a queen," Varulek explained. "Granted the throne by her elder sister who eschewed power for service, preferring to fight rather than rule. When the Dermos fired Jarvek's lust to carry Avielle off to the dark places, they baited a trap Livella could never resist."

Reva met Lieza's gaze and the girl smiled, seemingly immune to fear now. Reva had woken awash in memories that alternated between Veliss and the previous night, guilt and delight stirring to a fugue of confusion. She disentangled herself from Lieza's embrace and roamed the chamber, vainly searching the Ten Books for some words to comfort a betraying soul. Lieza was markedly less confused, waking and coming to her with more kisses.

"No." Reva turned away, softening the rejection with a clasp to her hand. "No. Today we fight. One last practice before they come for us."

Varulek dismissed the slaves when Reva grew fractious at their constant fussing, snarling at a matronly woman attempting to brush some reddish powder onto her cheeks.

"I doubt the Empress will notice any imperfections," he said when they had gone. He glanced at the two Kuritai at the door, presumably to confirm no Arisai had joined them in the interval. "Rumour has it your queen is fifty miles from the city. Panic spreads but the Empress has her spies everywhere. A hundred free men received the three deaths yesterday and she has decreed all citizens of age attend the arena."

"The bow," Reva said.

"There's a motif carved into the centre of the lintel under the Empress's balcony, an eagle with wings spread. The bow is beneath the sand fifty paces directly in front of it. You will have six arrows."

With luck, five more than I'll need. "I have another condition," she said, turning to Lieza once more. "Should I fall, you will secure her escape from this place and take her to the queen. She will be my assurance your words are true."

"The task we face is perilous. I can make no promises . . ." He trailed off in the face of her glare, eventually giving a reluctant nod. "I will do what I can."

◆　◆　◆

The trumpets blared as they were led into the arena, the tiered terraces so filled with people it seemed they might overflow the walls and spill onto the sand. Apart from the trumpets, however, there was barely any sound save the continual faint groan of thousands drawing breath. Reva picked out numerous specks of red and black amidst the throng; Kuritai and Arisai strategically placed to ensure their continued attendance. She shifted her gaze to the lowest tier, scanning the faces within sight. There was none of the bloodlust she had seen before, just a parade of scared people, tense with dreadful expectation.

Was this her intention? she wondered. *To make them hate the spectacles they loved?*

A pair of Kuritai led Lieza to a new structure rising from the centre of the arena—three circular platforms of descending size placed one atop the other to form a dais, constructed of wood but painted to resemble marble. The Kuritai secured Lieza's manacles to a sturdy wooden pole that arose from the topmost platform whilst those guarding Reva placed a long, broad-bladed spear and a short sword on the sand in front of her before removing her shackles and quickly trooping off to the nearest exit.

The trumpets faded, leaving a tense hush as the slender form of the Empress appeared from the shadowed recess of her balcony. "Honoured Citizens!" she called out, her voice absent the mockery evident before. Now it was rich in joyous celebration, a benevolent ruler greeting loyal subjects with a grand reward. "Not for a generation has this spectacle been gifted to the Volarian people. The Council was ever mean in its responsibilities, grubbing to fill their own pockets and begrudging you the smallest entertainments. Now behold your Empress's generosity, rejoice as I give you the legend of Jarvek and Livella!"

She spread her arms wide and the crowd cheered, though it sounded to Reva like the hoarse baying of some tormented monster. The people in the lowest tier screamed themselves red in the face in their desire to display loyalty as an Arisai looked on, teeth bared in mocking laughter.

The Empress lowered her arms, heralding an instant silence. "Be it known to the ages," she said in tones of grave recitation, "that the Dermos did conspire to steal away good queen Avielle to the darkest pit beneath the earth." She assumed a theatrical pose as she pointed at Lieza standing shackled atop the dais. "And there they did chain her under threat of vile torment, knowing her loving sister would brave any danger to bring her into the light once more. All will acclaim Livella, bravest of the Guardians!" Her finger swept towards Reva, drawing another chorus of hoarse cheering from the crowd.

"But the Dermos were ever cunning in their evil," the Empress continued when the tumult subsided. "For having tempted the mightiest of the Guardians into lust and treachery, they filled his heart with malice and spite, moulding him into their most vile and savage servant. Behold Jarvek!"

The door at the opposite end of the arena swung open with an audible boom, the crowd screaming on cue, then gradually falling silent as nothing happened. For a moment Reva suspected some trickery on the part of the Empress, a great prank to stoke her fears before revealing yet another novel cruelty. However, a glance at the balcony showed her to be staring at the empty arch with palpable annoyance.

Then the roar came.

It seemed to fill the arena from top to bottom, cutting through Reva like a blade, not with its fury, but its pain. The anguish she heard in this cry was searing, the torment it spoke of unimaginable.

Varulek had told her what manner of beast she faced this day, but mere words could not have captured the sight of it. When she and Vaelin had travelled with the minstrel's players she had seen some monkeys, small mischievous creatures prone to hissing and scratching at fingers unwisely poked into their cage. Come the evening show, their owner would play a flute as they danced, or rather capered about with some vague relation to the tune. The idea that what she saw now could in any way be related to those chittering imps seemed absurd, making her wonder if Varulek's garish legends might have some substance after all.

It entered the arena at the run, or rather gallop, moving on all fours and raising a sizeable cloud of dust. Its full size was revealed as the dust settled, and a spontaneous gasp rose from the terraces. Even though it was crouched, this monkey, or great southern ape as Varulek called it, stood close to eight feet tall. Its fur hung in shaggy tendrils from its arms and shoulders, brownish red in colour except on its densely muscled back where the fur was shorter and steely grey.

It roared again, a vast howl of pain and fury, baring teeth like blunted ivory nails. As it reared Reva saw the scars that covered its torso, deep and barely healed. It raised both hands and she saw a gleam of steel, noting the leather straps over its wrists.

"They are peaceable beasts, in truth," Varulek had said. "Keeping to their forests and valleys, eating only leaves, shy of man and not without good reason. Finding one with sufficient innate aggression to play the desired role is difficult, but when they do . . . Well, after a suitably harsh training period, they always seem to know what's expected of them, and the steel claws we give them."

Reva saw the truth in his words as the ape's gaze swept the arena, fixing first on Lieza and then her. There was a definite knowledge in its eyes, an all-too-recognisable understanding of its circumstances. It growled, scratched at the sand with its steel-augmented claws, and charged.

Reva sprinted forward, scooping up the spear and short sword. The ape made straight for Lieza, covering the distance in a few loping strides. Reva saw Lieza standing stock still, as if frozen, all the training perhaps driven from her head by terror. But then, as the beast closed, she dived to the right, rolling away as the steel claws tore at the pole to which she was shackled, shattering her chain. She scrambled to her feet, gathering up the chain as Reva had told her.

The ape skidded to a halt, snarling and readying itself for another charge.

Lieza issued a shrill scream as she lashed at the ape with her chains, raising dust but giving it only a second's pause before it charged again.

Not yet! Reva implored as she ran towards them. *Don't dodge too soon.*

Lieza, however, timed it perfectly, springing to the right and ducking under another slash from the claws, then rising and running back towards the dais. She sprinted up the steps and crouched behind the pole, the ape pounding after her. It thrashed at the pole, the claws shattering the timber above Lieza's head, showering her crouching form in splinters, then drawing back, both claws raised high for a killing blow.

Reva's short sword spun through the air to sink into the ape's leg just below the knee. It roared, reeling away from the dais, rolling onto its back, thrashing the sand into a yellow fog.

"Are you hurt?" Reva crouched at Lieza's side.

The girl gaped at her for a second then amazed her with a grin. "Today, maybe I am Livella too."

Reva felt a flicker of prideful amusement, vanished in an instant as she saw the ape emerge from the dust, plucking the sword from its leg with a howl of rage. "Stay behind me."

It circled the dais, trailing blood and dragging its maimed leg. The injury had slowed it but also done much to focus its attention. Its gaze was now fixed on Reva, the eyes gleaming with a disconcerting sense of understanding. *It knows,* Reva thought. *It knows one of us has to die.*

Without warning the ape charged again, ascending the dais in a frenzy of slashing claws. The faux-marble steps were rent to splinters, Reva and Lieza diving clear as the beast tore away any vestige of protection then rounded on them anew, repeatedly lunging forward and swiping at them with its claws. Reva danced aside as each slash came close, Lieza following her example though she was visibly tiring.

It's too clever, Reva decided, seeing the tense concentration in the ape's eyes. *Trying to wear us down.*

"We need a distraction," she told Lieza, ducking under another swipe. She managed to ward off another with a jab of the spear but the ape retreated barely a few feet before edging closer. "Dive to the left when it attacks next. Use your chains, only once mind. Then run."

The ape issued a determined grunt and made another limping charge, both arms extended to the sides like poised scissor blades. Reva dived to the right as the arms closed, the claws slashing close enough to snip off the end of her trailing braid. She snatched a glance at Lieza, sighing in relief at the sight of her scrambling to her feet as the ape wheeled for another attack. Lieza took hold of her chain in both hands and swung it, shouting with the effort. The steel whip snaked upwards to score a hit on the ape's face, Reva catching sight of a ruined eye as its head jerked to the side.

It rounded on Lieza with its loudest roar yet as the girl turned and ran, making it only a few steps before stumbling into the sand. The ape bellowed in triumph, crouching for an attack, its back now fully turned to Reva. She surged to her feet, sprinting forward and planting the spear's blunt end in the sand, vaulting into the air and landing astride the ape's shoulders. She grabbed ahold of the shaggy fur on its neck with her free hand as it thrashed, trying to throw her off. Her legs flailed as the beast wheeled and heaved, swiping at her as if she were a bothersome fly, forcing her to duck as the steel barbs missed her by inches.

Abruptly the ape staggered, ceasing its swipes at her and sinking to one knee. Reva caught sight of Lieza, back arched and arms taut as she hauled on her chains. Reva's gaze tracked the chain to where it was wrapped around the ape's injured leg, blood pulsing from the wound as it tried vainly to loosen the steel links pressing into the flesh.

She released her hold on its fur, standing upright and hefting the spear in both hands, whirling it about and sinking the broad blade into the ape's shoulder. She put all her weight on the haft, teeth gritted as she forced it deeper, feeling it grinding on bone and slicing through sinew until it protruded from the ape's chest.

It convulsed as she dived clear, a gasping bellow of pain and confusion issuing from its mouth. It stood fully erect for a moment, eyes tracking from the spear-blade to Reva, now crouched in the sand, ready to dodge another charge. Seeing its eyes, however, dulled with pain and the knowledge of defeat, she saw it was done even before it sank to its knees with a gurgling whine.

Reva glanced about, finding herself less than a hundred yards from the Empress's balcony. She was standing close to the edge, smiling with sisterly pride as the crowd's unbidden exultation filled the arena. A brief look at the upper tiers confirmed the absence of archers; Varulek had kept his word.

She rose and walked towards the balcony, her eyes picking out the eagle motif in the centre. Flowers cascaded down from the terraces as she walked, liberally covering the sand around her in a multi-coloured floral carpet. She lowered her gaze, concealing a grunt of frustration at the growing blanket of flowers. *How to find it amidst all this . . .*

Then she saw it, a faint irregular line in the sand, only partially obscured by a cluster of roses. She raised her eyes to the Empress, seeing her incline her head in acknowledgment. *Think nothing. Feel nothing.* Reva went to one knee, keeping her gaze on the Empress, her fingers sinking into the sand and inching towards the line until they felt the rough weave of coarse fabric. Her fingers bunched on it, ripping it away, sand erupting in a large plume to reveal the bow, strung and ready . . . and a single arrow alongside it.

The crowd fell to instant silence as something landed in the sand with a soft thud. Reva closed her eyes, air escaping her in a hiss. *Just one arrow.*

She opened her eyes, finding herself staring at Varulek's slack, lifeless face. From the fresh blood still seeping from the stump of his severed neck it was clear he had died only moments before.

Reva raised her gaze, expecting to find the Empress now shielded by a wall of Arisai, but instead she stood as she had before, precariously close to the edge, arms open with no protection at all.

"You displayed great skill in concealing yourself from my song, little sister," she said. "The Honoured Master of the Arena did not."

The doors in the arena walls slammed open in unison, Arisai emerging from the tunnels in a run, perhaps fifty of them, all forming a circle around Reva, Lieza and the dying ape. Lieza tried to run to Reva's side but was quickly brought down by a trio of Arisai, laughing as she spat and thrashed in their grip.

"I am pleased to have made such a valued gift to my sister," the Empress said as Lieza was forced to her knees. Reva dragged her attention back to the balcony where the Empress still stood, maddeningly close, such an easy target.

"But, if we are to share power," the Empress continued, "I am forced to conclude that you require a lesson in its cost. Power was never won without blood, ambition never fulfilled without sacrifice. So before dear Lieza receives the three deaths, the Arisai have orders to rape her in front of you for a day and a night. But, of course, you can spare her such a fate." She pointed at the bow and the single arrow a few inches from Reva's hand. "It seems you have a choice to make, little sister."

CHAPTER NINE

Frentis

"Volar features the most heavily fortified harbour in the world," the Fleet Lord said, his gloved hand sweeping across the map. It was an old chart, the edges frayed and the waxed parchment yellow with age, but also highly detailed. "Towers on either side of the harbour mouth and high walls on the moles that enclose it. The dockside itself has six different strongholds, each holding a battalion of Varitai."

The map fluttered a little in the wind, obliging him to weight it down with a dagger. The day had dawned with an ominous sky and an unseasonal chill to the air. Frentis could see the trepidation on the faces of many Meldeneans working the *Red Falcon*'s rigging, knowing they feared the onset of another Dark-born storm though Ell-Nurin himself scoffed at such notions. "Sailed the Cut half a hundred times. She's ever prone to summer squalls, nothing Dark about it."

"How do you propose we attack such a place?" Karavek asked the Fleet Lord. "Unless you intend to commit my people to some suicidal enterprise."

"I certainly don't." Ell-Nurin's finger tracked to a shallow inlet five miles east of the city. "This is Brokev's Notch, favoured haunt of smugglers for as long as there's been an empire."

One of the other captains, an Asraelin from his garb, stepped forward to peer at the map with a dubious eye. "The channel's barely wide enough for three ships abreast that far in." Ell-Nurin said nothing, staring at him in silence until the captain gritted his teeth, and added, "My lord."

"We land in relays," Ell-Nurin said. "Form up on the beach and march on Volar from the east, the least expected direction."

"The Empress is mad but not foolish," Frentis said. "She may well have anticipated the move. We could find ourselves facing a fortified shore."

"Which is why a third of our ships, those not laden with troops, will linger outside the harbour come the dawn, giving every appearance of being about to make an assault. With luck the Empress will concentrate her forces there."

"They could sally out," the Asraelin captain pointed out. "Seek to break the fleet in two before we land."

"Thanks to Lady Alornis's marvellous devices," Ell-Nurin replied, "and our considerable advantage in numbers, I'm certain we can contain any sallies they might attempt." He turned to Frentis. "Brother, I leave it to you to decide the order of landing."

Frentis nodded. "My own people first. The Politai next. Master Karavek's people last."

"Want the glory all to yourself, eh, brother?" Karavek asked, though not without a note of relief.

Ell-Nurin straightened, lifting his chin and gazing off to the east. "My lords, Captains of the Fleet and honoured allies, come the new day we will have struck a deathblow to this most vile of empires. For we come with justice in our hearts and freedom in our souls. Let all who sail with us know, destiny awaits and will not be denied."

Ell-Nurin held his pose, seemingly expectant of some response, a hearty cheer perhaps. After a moment, as the silence stretched and thickened, he coughed. "To your duties, lords and sirs."

"What an arse," Draker muttered as he and Frentis made their way below. "We truly have to take orders from him, brother?"

"Arse he may be, fool he isn't. The plan is sound. Make sure the others know that."

Draker nodded and began to move away, then paused. "Always wondered, brother. What's my rank?"

"Rank?"

"Yeh. You're a Brother, Illian's a Sister, the arse is a Fleet Lord. What am I?"

"You can be a sergeant, if you like."

Draker's bushy brows bunched in disappointment. "Got more folk answering to me than any sergeant I ever saw. Over two hundred of the buggers at last count."

"Captain then. Captain Draker of the Queen's Free Company. How's that sound?"

"Sounds like it'd earn a pension."

Frentis sighed a laugh. "I expect it will."

Draker smiled, though his voice held a sombre note as he said, "Sorry for the beatings, brother. If I never said before. I was drunk the whole time, see? Don't think I had a sober day till Varinshold fell."

"It was a long time ago, Captain. See to your company, if you would."

He sought out Sister Merial, finding her in company with a pipe near the stern, the sweet-smelling smoke escaping through an arrow-slit in the hull. "Meldeneans can always be counted on for some prime Alpiran five-leaf," she said, offering him the pipe. "Been over a year since I had a toke on anything this fine."

He declined with a raised hand. "Any word from your husband?"

"Indeed." She took a deep draw, blinking with watery eyes, her gaze losing focus. "Think I might've been a bit too generous with meself, brother."

"Any word?" he repeated as she patted her chest and coughed a little.

"The queen won another victory," she said, voice a little hoarse. "Becoming a bit of a habit with her. Battle of the Flowers they're callin' it, don't know why. In any case the road to Volar was open as of this morning. They should get there within two days."

He nodded, thoughts clouded with visions of Lady Reva in the arena, and more besides. *Bring the healer . . .*

He had resumed taking Brother Kehlan's sleeping draught in New Kethia, keen to avoid any more shared dreams, wary of what they might reveal to her, though it also robbed him of any clues as to her intentions. *Doesn't care if I bring my army. Seems indifferent to the queen's approach. What does she plot now?*

"We're landin' first, I take it," Sister Merial said.

"My company is. You will remain on the ship."

"A dog's fart I will. Sailed half the world for this, and Aspect Caenis deserves a reckoning."

"You are skilled in arms?"

She gave a short laugh and returned to her pipe, twiddling her fingers at him with a grin. "You'll see what I'm skilled at, brother. Just don't stand too close when you do."

◆ ◆ ◆

Brokev's Notch was formed of a small bay flanked by craggy bluffs. Beyond the beach the ground rose in a steep incline to the redflower fields beyond.

The sun was only just beginning to glimmer on the horizon and the promise of poor weather had manifested as a light morning drizzle.

"Even a handful of enemies on those heights, Redbrother," Lekran said with a grimace. "And this bay will become a slaughter-house."

Frentis said nothing, keeping his gaze on the cliff-tops as the boat neared the shore. It was low tide and the surf was negligible, the oarsmen heaving away at a high tempo regardless of noise; speed was more important than stealth now. He could see no sign of any movement on the bluffs, nor the ground beyond the beach.

"Remember," he told Lekran. "Do not linger for a second, regardless of loss."

He had placed the Garisai in the leading boats along with all their archers, Draker and Illian's people following behind with orders to secure the bluffs. Master Rensial had opted to accompany him, probably in hopes of finding a horse as quickly as possible.

Frentis leapt clear at the sound of the boat's hull scraping on the sand, sinking into the water up to his knees and immediately labouring towards the beach. In accordance with their orders the archers spread out with arrows already notched and bows raised, constantly scanning the bluffs for any sign of an enemy. The Garisai churned the tide-water into a white froth as they charged with Frentis, all making it onto the sand untroubled by the telltale hiss of an arrow storm or shouts of alarm.

Frentis permitted no pause on the beach, running across to the grassy slope and halting only on reaching the top. The Garisai immediately assumed a defensive formation though there was no sign of any opposition. The fields, rendered a dull shade of crimson by the morning gloom, stretched away silent and unmarred by a single living soul. Off to the west he could see the rising sun playing on towers ascending from the redflower like silver pins in a vast red blanket.

"Volar," Lekran said in an oddly reverent tone. "All those years a slave to this empire, and this is the first time I've ever laid eyes on it."

And perhaps the last, Frentis mused. *There may be nothing left when the queen gets done.* The thought stirred memories of the grey-clad girl and her mother and he shifted his gaze to the beach in search of a distraction. Draker and Illian's people were already ashore and in the process of splitting up to make for the bluffs. The Politai were fast approaching the beach, Weaver's curly-haired form visible in the lead boat. *Bring the healer . . .*

"This smells wrong," Ivelda said, scanning the poppy fields with a suspicious squint. "Not even a scout to greet us. Where are they?"

Frentis watched as Volar's sprawling suburbs were revealed by the burgeoning sun. *No walls to fight our way over, but a house can be made a fortress easily enough.* "I suspect we'll have an answer within the hour."

They found the first body two miles on from the bay, a boy of about fifteen lying amidst the flowers, grey-clad and barely two hours gone by Frentis's reckoning. He had been killed with a single thrust to the back, probably from horseback judging by the angle.

"Three more here," Ivelda said from nearby. "Man, woman and child. Someone killed a family."

They kept on towards the suburbs in a tight formation, Garisai skirmishing in front, Draker's company on the right and Illian's on the left. Karavek's people followed in a dense mass with the Politai acting as rear-guard. Frentis set a punishing pace; moving across open ground with no cavalry to secure the flanks instilled a keen sense of vulnerability. More bodies were discovered on the march, grey-clads and a few slaves with the occasional black-clad. Most had wounds to the back, indicating they had been cut down whilst running. Frentis counted over a hundred by the time they reached the first houses whereupon he stopped counting.

What is she doing?

They lay in every doorway, every street corner, the gutters running red as evidence of the freshness of the slaughter. There was no sign of torture on the bodies, few with more than two wounds, most with one. This had been an efficient massacre, performed without regard to age, sex or station. Children lay alongside the elderly, slaves were entwined with overseers. Black, grey and enslaved all united in death.

"The queen?" Draker asked Frentis, skin pale beneath his beard. "I know she wanted justice, but this . . ."

"This was not the queen," Frentis told him. "The Empress has set her Arisai to work."

"Those red bastards? Thought we killed them all."

Nine thousand more . . . He sighed at his own stupidity. *They must have all been given the same lie to tell if captured.*

"Varitai and Free Swords are one thing, brother," Karavek said. "Even Kuritai. But my people can't stand against the red men . . ."

"Then go back to the beach and beg Lord Ell-Nurin to take you home." Frentis turned back to Draker. "Choose your fastest runner, send them to the

Notch with a request the Fleet Lord come ashore with every sailor who can hold a blade." He turned to view the death-choked streets ahead. "He'll find us at the arena."

They were drawn by the screams, a shrill chorus of terror and pain echoing across the bloodied streets. Frentis led the Garisai towards it, ordering Illian and Draker to work their way around on both flanks and sending the archers onto the rooftops. A hundred paces on the streets opened out into a square, displaying typical Volarian orderliness with its neatly arranged lawns, spotted with statuary and bisected with stone pathways, and, in the centre, a dense crowd of Volarians being systematically slaughtered by some two hundred Arisai. The people had been hemmed in on all sides, clustering together in instinctive terror as the red men methodically hacked their way through the throng, visibly shrinking by the second amidst a growing circle of corpses.

"I don't expect you to fight for them," Frentis told Lekran, raising his sword to the archers on the rooftops.

"I fight with you, Redbrother," the tribesman told him, briefly twirling his axe. "Until this is done. You know that."

Frentis nodded and lowered his sword. The archers unleashed their volley, the arrows streaking forth to claim at least a dozen Arisai as he sprinted forward, the Garisai following with a collective shout. *Until this is done. For good or ill, it'll be done today.*

◆ ◆ ◆

The Arisai rebounded from Sister Merial's outstretched hand to collide with a wall, tendrils of grey smoke rising from the blackened handprint burned into his breastplate as he sank to the ground, all sign of life vanished from his frozen features. The sister turned to Frentis with a tired grin and flexed her fingers. "Handy in a tight spot, aren't I, brother?"

"Down!" He grabbed her shoulder and forced her aside as an Arisai charged from a shadowed doorway, short sword outstretched and a joyful smile on his lips. Frentis turned the blade with his own and spun, bringing the sword around to slash across the Arisai's eyes, finishing him with a thrust to the throat as he staggered, laughing in gleeful surprise.

Frentis paused to drag air into his lungs, surveying the street, littered with corpses from end to end. He spotted Ivelda among them, lying dead atop the Arisai she had killed, her dagger still embedded in his neck. They had fought from street to street for close to an hour now, forcing the Arisai to leave off their slaughter and face them. The fighting descended into chaos the farther in they went, as the streets grew more narrow and the Arisai revealed a fiendish talent for ambush. They would attack alone or in pairs, launching themselves without warning from alleys, doorways and windows to assault his fighters in a frenzy of delighted carnage before being brought down by weight of numbers or a well-placed arrow from one of the archers above. They had learned their lessons well in New Kethia, their advance made possible by the archers, who continued to leap from rooftop to rooftop, killing any Arisai seen in the streets below.

Frentis spied Lekran with half a dozen Garisai at the north end of the street and ran to his side, Merial following with an unsteady gait. He had seen her kill three Arisai already and knew she was risking collapse with every use of her gift.

"The last of the cowards from New Kethia pissed themselves and ran," Lekran reported with a grimace of disgust. "I will kill Karavek with my own hands."

"You'd have a difficult task," Merial groaned, leaning against a doorway, ashen features sagging. "I saw him die two streets back."

Frentis's gaze rose at the sound of someone calling his name, finding Illian's slim silhouette standing atop a two-storey building twenty yards away, waving her crossbow above her head. "Weaver!" she called down to him as he ran closer, indicating a point where the dense streets opened into what appeared to be a market square. "And Master Rensial!"

Frentis gestured for the Garisai to follow and sprinted for the square, finding it in shambles, carts and trestles overturned amidst the slumped forms of murdered slaves and free folk. At the north end of the square some fifty Politai were formed into a dense wedge, moving steadily forward against a seething wall of Arisai perhaps twice their number. The Politai moved with all the precision born of their years of ingrained discipline, their broad-bladed spears jutting out like the spines of a porcupine as they edged forward, Weaver's blond head visible in their centre. Curiously the Arisai seemed to have lost much of their maddening humour when confronted with the former slave soldiers. Frentis saw naked fury on many faces as they launched themselves at the well-ordered ranks, most dying on the unyielding hedge of spears but some managing to hack their way into the formation, claiming one or two Politai in the process.

At first Frentis was puzzled by the determined nature of the Politai's advance; there appeared to be no one left in this square to save, then he saw him, a lone rider amidst the Arisai, wheeling his mount with matchless grace, sword moving in elegant arcs as the red men fell around him. But he was just one, and they were many.

Frentis forgot all caution and hurled himself into the Arisai, sword gripped in two hands as he hacked his way through, whirling and killing as the Garisai charged in his wake. He dimly heard a shout from the Politai, not in exultation, for such emotions still seemed to be beyond them, more an acknowledgment of an order. Their formation doubled its pace as the Arisai's ranks thinned about them, forcing their way closer to the lone rider.

Frentis ducked under the sweep of a sword and drove his blade through the breastplate of the Arisai who held it. The man refused to die however, latching onto his sword arm and holding Frentis in place, red teeth bared in a broad, affectionate smile. "Hello, Father," he rasped, hands like a vise on Frentis's arm.

One of his compatriots lunged forward, sword levelled at Frentis's neck, then drawing up short as something streaked down to skewer him through the forehead. For a second his eyes rolled up to regard the crossbow bolt as he stood, drooling, before Lekran's axe cut his legs away. The tribesman spun, the axe sweeping up to sever the arm of the Arisai still latched onto Frentis. He tore his sword arm free of the Arisai's remaining hand as Lekran's axe came down to finish him, turning to see Illian standing on a nearby rooftop. He raised a hand to acknowledge her assistance but her attention was elsewhere, a bolt clamped between her teeth as she sprinted and leapt to the next rooftop, gaze fixed on the lone rider up ahead. *Master Rensial!*

Arrows fell with increasing rapidity as he fought his way through, Lekran at his side and the Garisai behind, more and more archers appearing on the surrounding rooftops. The Arisai's ranks thinned ahead of Frentis as he saw three fall to the archers in quick succession, charging clear of the struggle and making for Master Rensial, a shout of fury and frustration escaping his throat as he saw an Arisai dart forward to plunge his sword into the flank of the master's horse. It reared, mouth gaping as it screamed and collapsed, legs thrashing. The surrounding Arisai closed in, swords raised and laughing. The Politai's formation issued another shout and broke into a charge, pushing aside the remaining Arisai and sweeping towards the cluster surrounding the fallen rider. Frentis lost sight of the horse as the Politai struck home, cutting down the Arisai then forming a defensive ring with their typical, unconscious swiftness. He forced his way through, drawing up short at the sight of the still-twitching horse, noticing for the first time that it was a fine grey stallion. He could only wonder where the master had found it. He leapt the dying animal, issuing an explosive sigh of relief at the sight of Master Rensial pinned beneath it, frowning in annoyance as he attempted to tug his sword from the body of an Arisai lying dead at his side.

"We need to find another stable," he told Frentis, grunting as the blade slid free of the corpse.

"Of course, Master." He knelt and put his shoulder to the horse's body, heaving until the master was able to draw his leg clear. From the twisted, mangled state of the limb he could see Rensial would not be riding, or walking again for some time.

"Redbrother!"

Frentis rose at Lekran's shout, finding they were surrounded on all sides by Arisai now, more having materialised out of the surrounding houses, every one of them seemingly staring at him with a mixture of fascination and delight. Arrows continued to fall from the rooftops but they seemed not to care, barely glancing as their brothers fell beside them. *Drawn to me,* he decided, seeing something more in the collective gaze. *Madness. She has set them loose, and they all hunger for the joy of killing their father.*

"This can end here!" he called to them, moving to stand with the encircling Politai. "She has freed you, I see it. Now free yourselves. Let go your madness."

They laughed at him, of course. Great hearty peals of mirth sweeping through their ranks, some still laughing as the arrows took them.

"As you wish," Frentis sighed, raising his sword. "Come, receive your cure!"

A new sound cut through the continued babble of their laughter, a faint, rumble echoing from the surrounding streets, soon rising to a roar, the roar of many angry men.

The Meldeneans came streaming from every street and alleyway, sabres flashing as they tore into the red-armoured throng. The Arisai fought, as they were made to, killing with happy abandon, but for all their skill and ferocity they had no counter to the tide of pirates that swept over them, islands of red soon swamped and drowned in a scant few moments. The Meldeneans shouted their victory to the sky, sabres raised and heads thrown back in feral triumph.

"Took them long enough," Lekran muttered as the carnage subsided.

Frentis turned to find Weaver standing over Master Rensial, head cocked as he cast a critical eye over his leg. "Can you help him?" he asked.

"I'm sorry, brother." The healer shook his head with a grimace, then raised his gaze to a massive curved structure rising above the rooftops to the west. "I have a sense I will soon need all my strength."

◆ ◆ ◆

He left Master Rensial in the care of the Meldeneans, most of whom seemed content to stay and loot the many vacant houses, proving deaf to entreaties to join the advance on the arena. Frentis could find no sign of Fleet Lord Ell-Nurin, or any other Meldenean of appreciable rank beyond that of second mate, so was obliged to leave them to their rewards and move on. They found Thirty-Four stitching a cut on Draker's arm a few streets on, the dozen surviving members of the newly appointed captain's company clustered around them amidst the bodies of some thirty Arisai.

"Can't you get through one battle without a wound?" Illian asked Draker, her caustic tone leavened somewhat by the affectionate hand she ran through his shaggy hair.

"I do like my souvenirs," he replied, teeth gritted as Thirty-Four tied off the thread. He raised an apologetic gaze to Frentis and nodded at something lying nearby. "Sorry, brother."

Slasher lay on his side with Blacktooth whining as she nuzzled his head. A short sword was buried in his chest and an Arisai slumped dead against a nearby wall, his face a ruin of chewed gore.

"We can't linger," Frentis said, tearing his gaze away to survey the drained, pale faces of all present. There were perhaps a third of the number that had followed him from New Kethia. *So many lost saving those that enslaved them,* he wondered, fighting down the mingled grief and admiration that threatened to moisten his eyes.

"Captain," he said to Draker, "form your people up as a rear-guard. Sister, take the archers and scout the approach to the arena."

"Surely there can't be any left after this," Sister Merial said. Her pallor was slightly improved, though the red smudges around her eyes and nose spoke of an attempt to conceal her exhaustion.

"We thought the same back in Eskethia," he told her. "Stay by me and do not use your gift again except in direst need."

The dense maze of streets soon gave way to broad avenues and parks, also littered with corpses. They were mostly black-clad here, plus a few slaves cut down at they tended the grass or polished the bronze statues. Of the Arisai, however, there was no sign. A hundred yards ahead the streets fell away completely to reveal the arena, every fighter and Politai come to a halt at the sight of it, the gently curving, red-gold tiers made vivid in the sun. They could hear a great tumult from within, thousands of voices raised in adulation, no doubt of some dreadful spectacle orchestrated by their Empress.

Baying like sheep as their city dies around them, Frentis thought, unable to suppress the bitter notion that these people were not worth the blood spilled on their account.

"No guards," Illian reported. "As far as we can tell it's completely undefended."

Frentis looked at Weaver, for the first time seeing a troubled wrinkle to his brow as he regarded the arena, even a twitch of fear to his lips. *Bring the healer* . . . "You don't have to," Frentis told him. "Remain here with the Politai. I'll send word when it's safe."

Weaver's brow smoothed as he turned to him, banishing the fear with a faint smile. "I do not believe there is any safe place today, brother."

Frentis nodded, stepping forward and turning to address them all, finding his voice hoarse and having to force the words out. "You have all done more than I could ever ask. Wait here, Weaver and I will proceed alone."

There was no response, nor any change in expression as they all, as one, took a step forward.

"I do not know what awaits us in there," he told them, hearing the note of desperation in his voice. "But I know many of us will not survive it . . ."

"Wasting time, brother," Draker said. Beside him Illian hefted her crossbow, meeting his gaze with expectant eyes.

He turned back to the arena as another roar sounded from inside, from the volume and length it seemed the Empress's spectacle had reached some form of climax. "Our objective is to secure Lady Reva and kill the Empress!" he said, raising his sword and starting forward at a run. "Show her no mercy, for she has none for you!"

CHAPTER TEN

Vaelin

*S*tars. He blinked, trying to clear what he knew must be an illusion, but they were still there, shimmering and bright. And there were so many, more than he could ever count. Some were brighter than others, so bright it seemed they eclipsed those around them. A few were dark, shimmering between red and black. They were all moving like tiny miniature ants on a vast dark blanket of green and blue. *Not stars,* he realised. *People.*

"Vaelin." She was there, floating nearby in the night sky, for he saw now that they were flying far above the earth. He could only stare at her, words choking in his throat, grief and gratitude combining to make him shudder. She smiled and drifted closer, hands reaching for his. "I wanted to show you," she said. "I wanted you to see what I see."

"I . . ." He stammered, clutching her hands. "I should never have . . ."

She moved into his arms, her warmth wondrous, banishing his guilt. "All choices were mine to make." She pressed her forehead to his, then drew back, turning and gesturing to the star-speckled earth below them. "Look," she said, "the world as it was, about to change forever."

He held her hand as they drifted closer to the earth, approaching a landmass with a coastline he recognised as that of the Unified Realm. They paused above a dense cluster of stars in the centre of what would one day be known as the Fallen City, the stars resolving into shimmering forms of people as they flew lower. Two figures stood at the centre of the cluster, next to something so dark it seemed to swallow all light, Vaelin taking a moment to recognise its foreshortened shape. *The Black Stone.*

One of the figures next to the stone differed from the others in the way his light shimmered, flaring bright one second then dark red another. The flicker made it difficult to discern any features, but Vaelin gained the impression of a tall man, a man with a beard. *The Ally.*

The figure at the Ally's side was shorter and, judging by the stoop of his back, considerably older. Unlike the Ally his light was constant and bright, the hue a warm shade of blue. Vaelin watched as the Ally placed his hand on the older man's shoulder in respectful assurance then stood back. The older man stood still for a moment, head lowered as if gathering strength, his light dimming slightly, then he took a step forward and touched his hand to the absolute void of the black stone.

For a second nothing happened, but then a red circle appeared in the centre of the stone. It was small but glowed with a fiery energy, pulsing rhythmically like a heart. The glowing hand of the old man reached for it, fingers extended to grasp it . . . The circle gave off a sudden flare, its pulsing increased to a rapid thrum, and the old man reeled away as something erupted from the stone, cascading up and out in a multi-coloured fountain, rising high into the sky as a circle of pure energy spread out from the stone at ground level, expanding and streaking away to the horizon like a wall of flame. Most of the lights it passed through without apparent effect, but here and there one would flare even brighter as the wall touched them. *The power,* Vaelin recalled. *Burned into the bloodline . . .*

The spectral fountain faded slowly, the fiery circle in the stone diminishing in size until it was no more than a pinprick, whereupon it vanished. The old man rolled on the ground beside the stone, jerking in obvious agony, his light shimmering now, but pulsing brighter than before. His agony subsided slowly, reaching up to take the Ally's hand as he knelt at his side. The Ally, however, made no move to take his hand, staring down at the prostrate old man, his light now more red than white.

Abruptly he reared, raising something dark above his head and bringing it down with all his strength. The old man's light flared then seemed to fracture, dimming into two faint glows, one big, the other smaller. *His head,* Vaelin realised. *He took his head.*

The Ally bent to retrieve the head, raising it up until the stump touched his lips whereupon his light instantly turned a permanent shade of red, a dark crimson glow that pulsed with the same rhythm as the fiery circle in the stone.

The Ally cast the head aside and turned to the crowd of onlookers. They had all retreated from him in evident fear, many turning to flee. Then, as one they came to a halt, all standing frozen and immobile. For a long moment the Ally regarded the crowd in careful scrutiny, then he began to walk among them, pausing next to a frozen man of athletic build and a yellowish glow, touching a hand to his head. The selected man's back instantly formed a rigid arc as he voiced a silent scream, his light turning the same shade of red as the Ally in the space of a heartbeat.

The Ally moved on touching a dozen more men in quick succession, then striding from the crowd and standing to watch as the reddened figures began to murder their white companions. Some were strangled, others clubbed with rocks or branches for these people seemed to possess no weapons. All the while the Ally stood and watched the massacre, head tilted slightly in dispassionate observation. When it was done, every white glow snuffed out, the Ally walked off towards the north and the red men followed him.

Dahrena gripped Vaelin's hand tighter as they flew higher, time accelerating beneath them, the Ally's cluster of red blossoming in the north and spreading, issuing smaller clusters that spread like spores across the length and breadth of the Unified Realm, white lights snuffing out everywhere they went.

"The Ally's gift," Vaelin said.

"No," Dahrena told him, "never a gift. A sickness, a plague. Like the Red Hand."

"This is but a dream. How can I know this?"

"We know it." She floated away from him, spreading her arms as more people appeared out of the surrounding blackness, forming a circle around them. They were mostly strangers but he recognised some. The sister from the Seventh Order who had conspired with Alucius in Varinshold. Marken was there too, smiling grimly behind his beard, and Aspect Grealin, still fat even here . . . And one other.

Caenis wore the garb of a brother of the Sixth Order, even though he had died Aspect of the Seventh. "Brother," Vaelin said, reaching out to him but Caenis only smiled and inclined his head in fond recognition.

"We who lingered when you drew him from the Beyond," Dahrena said. "It is not just his will that can bind us there. We spent our remaining strength in crafting this vision. It was all we had left to give."

He saw the circle of souls fading, drifting into darkness, Caenis the last to go, his hand raised in reluctant farewell before the dark claimed it.

"So you are truly gone now?" he asked Dahrena. "Your souls vanished forever?"

"Soul is memory," she told him, pressing herself to him again, arms enfolding his head. "You are my Beyond now, Vaelin. You and all those I loved, even those I fought. For me to endure, so must you."

She drew back, hands gripping his face. "Remember, a plague like the Red Hand. And none who caught the Red Hand and lived ever caught it again. And now, you really must wake up."

◆ ◆ ◆

He awoke to raised voices. Lonak voices, angry and aggravatingly loud. He groaned as he rolled upright, his fingers instinctively exploring the growing lump on the back of his head. The voices stopped and he looked up to see Kiral and Alturk retreating from one another, the Tahlessa sparing him a reproving glance before moving to stand in front of the Ally's slumped form. He seemed to be unconscious, head lolling forward as a trickle of blood fell from a gash on his forehead.

Orven stood close to Vaelin, his guardsmen all around, glaring at the assembled Sentar on the other side of the clearing. He discerned it had been but moments since Alturk had clubbed him senseless. Vaelin extended a hand to Orven, who obligingly hauled him upright. He walked to Alturk and gave a shallow bow. "My thanks, Tahlessa. Lord Orven, break camp. We still have a long way to go."

◆ ◆ ◆

More towns appeared along the course of the road the farther south they went. They were usually sprawling places, having long outgrown the protective walls of the pre-Imperial age. Most had clearly suffered riot and rebellion, a few were little more than blackened ruins, and fewer still had contrived to remain intact by virtue of newly raised walls and barricades, often held by armed townsfolk happy to launch arrows at strangers who ventured too close. Vaelin avoided them all, having no inclination to embroilment in unnecessary battle, though the Sentar often chafed at the need to suffer an unanswered challenge.

The Ally now rode at the rear of the column, his bruised and partially remoulded features bland and cheerful as ever. Orven's guards had been given stern instructions to gag him if he attempted to speak again, but he had maintained a continual silence since waking from the beating. Kiral stared at him constantly, hands often bunching on her reins and Vaelin knew she was resisting the impulse to reach for her bow. *The song's guidance is rarely mistaken,* he knew, missing his lost gift more keenly than ever. But Dahrena's vision had held no desire for the Ally's immediate death, and no inclination he was on the wrong path.

A line of red appeared on the horizon five days later, growing as they drew closer until they paused amidst a vast array of redflower fields and, in the hazy distance, the tall towers of a marble city.

"Volar," Lorkan breathed at Vaelin's side, shaking his head in unabashed wonder. "I truly never thought to see it."

Vaelin called for Lord Orven and pointed to the west and east. "Send out your scouts, we need word of the queen's whereabouts. We'll make camp here . . ."

"You don't have time!"

Vaelin turned to see the Ally regarding him with cold intent, all vestige of humour vanished from his still misshapen features. The guards on either side moved closer to fulfil their orders but Vaelin waved them back, trotting Scar closer, meeting the Ally's glare. "Why?"

"My servant plays with your sister in the arena as we speak. Or rather, that perverted bitch you call your sister. Delay further, and I suspect she'll be dead before long, after a suitable period of well-deserved punishment. She did always irk me so."

Vaelin looked at Kiral, who gritted her teeth and nodded. *Reva! His creature has Reva.*

"She holds no gift," the Ally went on. "No place in the Beyond for her . . ."

Vaelin wheeled away from him, spurring to the head of the column and barking an order at Orven to follow, making for Volar at the gallop.

CHAPTER ELEVEN

Lyrna

*I*t seems I have come far to visit justice on a people intent on their own destruction. The city seemed to be ruled by the dead; there was not an avenue, doorway or garden free of corpses. They also hung from the many towers like ragged, long-forgotten dolls. It was clear to her this had been a wealthy district, the opulence of the houses and the extensive walled gardens rich in cherry blossoms and statuary told of great privilege and high status, but whatever had swept through here had little regard for rank; copious enslaved dead told her this was not the product of revolt.

"Arisai, Highness," Brother Sollis reported, his horse's iron-shod hooves a jarring intrusion into the silence covering this place. He clattered to a halt nearby, pausing to offer Aspect Arlyn a respectful nod before addressing her. "We found twenty or so in the neighbouring district, killing all they could find. We dealt with them but I've little doubt there are more."

He shifted in his saddle as his fellow brothers reined in a short way off, clearly impatient to be off. "The route to the arena?" she asked him.

"Clear, Highness. There appear to be no other Volarian soldiery in the city. I believe you have sufficient protection to proceed there."

Whilst you ride off to save the people we came to destroy, no doubt. She was about to order him to form up his company in escort when Murel abruptly leapt down from her horse and ran towards a pile of bodies lying near the arched entrance to one of the larger houses. She pulled the topmost corpse away, a slender woman in a red robe with a gaping wound to her neck, and reached into the bloody mess beneath, emerging with a small, half naked figure. She clutched it in a tight embrace as Lyrna trotted Jet closer, dismounting at Murel's side as she wiped fresh blood from the face of a girl perhaps eight years in age, alive but oddly still, staring about with wide, dark eyes. Murel was weeping, the first time Lyrna had seen her do so since the day of her ennoblement at the Wensel Isle.

The girl blinked at the lady then looked up at Lyrna with a curious frown. "I know you," she said in a somewhat prim voice.

"You do?" Lyrna moved closer, going to her haunches and reaching out to tease back a stiff strand of matted hair from the girl's forehead.

"My father told me," the girl went on, pouting a little in defiance. "You've come to burn everything down. You're the queen of fire."

Lyrna closed her eyes. A breeze played over her skin in a gentle caress, carrying the scent of cherry blossoms, the perfume delicate but rich enough to mask the stink of gore and bowels voided at the point of death. She tried to recall another odour, one she knew so well, one that choked the throat and stirred bile from the gut, the stench of her own flesh burning. But she couldn't find it, not today.

"No," she told the girl, reopening her eyes and pausing to cup her cheek with a smile. "I'm just a queen."

She rose, touching a hand to Murel's shoulder. "Take her to Brother Kehlan." She turned and strode back to her horse. "Brother Sollis, take your company and hunt down any remaining Arisai. Volarian citizenry found alive are to be conveyed to safety if possible. I'll send word to the Battle Lord to allocate forces to assist you."

He bowed in the saddle, his face betraying a sense of gratitude she hadn't seen before, nodded again to the Aspect, and wheeled about, his rasping voice calling out orders to his brothers as he galloped off.

"Don't like it, Lerhnah," Davoka said as she climbed into the saddle, casting a critical eye over the surviving Queen's Daggers. "We are too few."

Lyrna turned at the sound of a multitude of voices at their rear, causing Iltis to wheel about with sword drawn. He calmed as the first Cumbraelin came into view. A well-built man, as many archers were, running with his bow across his back and hatchet in hand, pausing to offer her the briefest bow before running on, making for the unmistakable bulk of the arena, now only a half mile distant. He was quickly followed by hundreds more, the surrounding avenues filled with their panting prayers, the words "Blessed Lady" most frequent among them. *Al Hestian couldn't hold them,* she surmised. *I hope he was wise enough not to try.*

"I think we'll have enough, sister," she told Davoka, spurring Jet to a gallop.

◆ ◆ ◆

The head stared down at her with sightless eyes, mouth slack and tongue lolling from between its teeth. It had been fixed on to the stump of the statue's neck with iron nails, hammered through bronze and flesh alike, streaks of dried blood covering the metal down to the plinth where the original head lay.

"These people are never short of horrors, it seems," Iltis observed in a disgusted tone.

Lyrna guided Jet past the statue and on to the arena, the Cumbraelins now streaming through its arches. She had caught a glimpse of Lord Antesh urging them on before disappearing inside, but had no opportunity to impart any orders to him, not that she expected him to follow them now with the Blessed Lady so close.

She dismounted before the tallest arch and proceeded into the gloomy interior, shouts of combat echoing through the vaulted stairs and corridors as the Cumbraelins overcame any opposition. The Queen's Daggers spread out around her in a protective arc, Aspect Arlyn and Iltis both close on either side with swords drawn.

"If I may, Highness," the Aspect said, pointing to a stairway nearby, leading down into the depths of this structure. Lyrna raised a questioning eyebrow and he went on, "The cages where the Garisai are kept. They may be of use."

She nodded and gestured for him to proceed, following as he led the Daggers into the stairwell. The tumult of battle greeted her as she descended, emerging into a long rectangular chamber, lined on each side with cages. The Daggers and the Aspect were engaged in a struggle with a dozen Kuritai. The Aspect moved with the typical fluid grace of the Sixth Order, belying his years as he parried and spun in the melee, cutting down a Kuritai and blocking the blade of another who lunged at one of the Daggers. But the Kuritai were also fearsomely skilled and Lyrna forced down a surge of rage at the sight of yet more of her people falling to the blades of the slave-elite. *I am just a queen.*

She sent Iltis to join the struggle with a flick of her hand and looked around, her eyes alighting on a corpse lying nearby, a man of considerable girth with a stab wound to the chest, a gaoler judging by the keys dangling from his belt. She bent and tugged them free, going to the nearest cage and drawing up short at the sight of the occupant.

There was no smile on his lips now, no mischief in his eyes, his hair hung limp and greasy over a face devoid of all humour, or admiration. "So you see," the Shield said, voice barely above a grunt, "you managed to put me in a cage after all."

She said nothing, turning the key in the lock and hauling the cage open, standing aside with an impatient gesture as he lingered. He emerged slowly, casting a brief glance at the continuing struggle in the corridor, the Kuritai now reduced to three, backed up against the bars of the cages as hands reached from within to claw at them in desperate fury.

"This is the last war I fight for you," the Shield said.

Lyrna tossed him the keys as the last of the Kuritai was brought down, moving to the stairwell and ascending without a backward glance.

CHAPTER TWELVE

Reva

"K ill her!" Lieza shrieked, thrashing in the Arisai's grip. "Kill her and it ends!"

Reva's hand jerked in the sand, inching closer to the bow as if by its own volition, her eyes still fixed on the Empress's smiling face. "She makes a fair point," she called. "With me gone this war is over, but she will still die and you will remember her end for a long time. I've ordered them to spare you, for how could I harm my sister? Wouldn't you rather give her a quick death?"

Reva tore her gaze away, turning to Lieza, now sagging in the Arisai's clutches, eyes imploring, her ragged breaths the only sound in the arena, the silence unbroken by the barest murmur as Reva's hand closed on the bow . . .

Something whined past her head and thudded into the sand next to the bow. An arrow, the fletching shuddering with the impact. Reva's gaze snapped up to the top tiers of the arena, finding a line of figures silhouetted there, each holding a bow. She groaned as her despair deepened. Varulek's Kuritai hadn't done their work after all. One of the archers raised his bow above his head and Reva squinted, finding something familiar in his bearing, the breadth of his shoulders reminding her of someone she knew, someone surely lost to the ocean. Her eyes went to his bow. It was long with a single elegant curve, so unlike the double-curved strongbows favoured by the Volarians.

Slowly she turned and lowered her gaze to the arrow buried in the sand. *Swift-wing feathers,* she saw, eyeing the fletching. *A bird only seen in Cumbrael in the summer.*

She raised her gaze to the Empress, and returned her smile.

She snatched up the bow and Varulek's arrow, pivoting to the left, notching and loosing in a single motion. One of the Arisai holding Lieza staggered back, staring at the arrow jutting from his chest in gasping amusement. The other immediately drew his sword, raising it to plunge into Lieza's back, then falling dead as Reva sent Antesh's arrow into his neck.

The air thrummed as she rose and sprinted towards Lieza, every Arisai in sight falling in unison as the arrow storm swept down. She skidded to a crouch at Lieza's side and pulled her upright. The girl gave a shout of alarm as an Arisai laboured towards them, teeth bared in a fierce smile as he struggled closer with arrows jutting from his shoulders and legs. Reva snatched another arrow from the sand and sent it into his eye from five paces, then grabbed Lieza's arm and pulled her towards the nearest doorway. The heavy iron-shod door was firmly locked but the stone arch at least offered some protection. She could see Varitai archers on the lower tiers, vainly trying to contest the longbowmen above as the crowd convulsed around them, people massing in dense, roiling throngs as they stampeded for the exits.

Then the arrow storm began to abate, slowly at first, but soon dwindling to nothing. Reva stepped out from the archway, scanning the upper tiers and finding them full of thrashing men, red and black amidst the grey-green of the Cumbraelins. Her gaze went to the door where the unfortunate Jarvek had entered the arena, finding it still open. "Come on," she told Lieza, taking her hand and starting forward.

The Empress landed in their path and rolled into a fighting stance, short sword held low and regarding Reva with a stern frown of annoyance. "You spoiled my spectacle."

Reva backed away, ushering Lieza behind her and casting about frantically for another arrow as the battle raged above.

"All my lessons," the Empress said, dancing closer, sword held low. "All my generous tutelage, cast back in my face. I am very disappointed, little sister."

She lunged and Reva rolled to the side, dragging Lieza with her, the blade missing by inches. She came to her feet and swung the bow like a club, aiming for the Empress's head. She ducked it easily, rounding on Reva with a disapproving scowl. "Our mother died with you inside her, as I lay abed and listened to her screams beyond the door. The Ally had told my father of the blessing, you see, and he was thirsty."

She lunged again, Reva pushing Lieza to the left as she dodged to the right. She saw an Arisai's body no more than ten feet away, feathered with arrows and a sword lying under its hand.

"Mother would have loved you more than me," the Empress told Reva, leaping into her path as she started towards the body. "I know this. But I don't mind, you would still have been my sister."

Reva glanced at Lieza, imploring her to run, but the girl stayed, hefting her chains and adopting a clumsy approximation of a fighting stance. The Empress laughed at her, then sobered. "Such devotion," she said, shaking her head. "All I ever received was fear and lust. I would have loved you, sister. But the envy would have been hard to bear."

Reva looked again at the Arisai's body, gauging the distance and calculating her chances of leaping over the Empress's sword . . . Then she saw something else.

"I am not your sister!" she shouted to the Empress, capturing her wide-eyed gaze. "You have known nothing but fear and lust because that is all you are. You are just a madwoman who has lived far too long."

"Mad?" The Empress's humour returned, her sword lowering a little as she laughed. "What do you think the world is if not just an endless parade of madness? To make war is madness. To seek power is madness." She laughed louder, throwing her arms wide. "And madness is glorious!"

Reva assumed the ape was simply attempting to complete the role it had been trained for, trailing a red stain across the arena as it dragged itself towards the Empress with its steel claws, taking her for Livella as she was the only one armed. With a rasping roar it reared up and lunged, claws lashing out as the Empress turned, taking the three steel barbs full in the chest.

The ape gave a final bellow, either of triumph or rage, and sagged onto the arena floor, sand flying high as it breathed its last. Reva moved closer as the Empress struggled, still somehow alive, blood flowing in torrents from her mouth as she laboured to heave herself off the ape's claw, finally succeeding with a shriek of agony. She lay panting, breath coming in hard, convulsive tics as she stared up at Reva with the same wide, unreasoning eyes, smiling with a genuine affection that made Reva's hand itch for a sword.

She became aware of the sound of battle once more, looking up to see that the conflict had spread across the tiers, the Volarian citizenry huddled together as the fighting raged around them. It appeared the Cumbraelins had been reinforced by Realm Guard, Lord Nortah's free fighters judging by the number of women in their ranks. Also she glimpsed the trailing blond hair of the Shield on the lower terraces, fighting alongside several dozen freed Garisai. She sent a prayer to the Father to ensure Allern was amongst them. The knots of red and black were shrinking under the combined assault, though, as ever the Arisai showed no dismay at their own imminent passing, fighting to the last and laughing as they died.

Reva started as the Empress issued a loud, hacking snarl, arms flailing as she sought to rise, gaze fixed on something at the north end of the arena, a single word discernible among her blood-choked babble. "Bitch!"

Queen Lyrna Al Nieren strode across the sand, accompanied by her hulking Lord Protector and a tall, aged brother of the Sixth Order Reva didn't recognise. A dozen or so Realm Guard fanned out on either side as she came towards Reva, waving away her bow and drawing her into a warm embrace. "My lady. Please accept my sincere apologies for not reaching you sooner."

CHAPTER THIRTEEN

Vaelin

They were obliged to force their way through a horde of fleeing Volarians, all too panicked and livid with terror to even recognise a group of foreign invaders. Many pelted through the redflower on either side of the road, shorn of any baggage as they fled, recent horrors etched into bleached features. In contrast the families moved in dense, wary knots, clutching meagre bundles with their children held close, small faces bunched in tears or frozen in fear.

Astorek leaned down to pull a man from the throng, a balding grey-clad of middling years with a little boy clinging to his side. He answered the shaman's questions in clipped tones, habitual servility overcoming his dread.

"The Empress has set her Arisai on the city," Astorek reported, releasing the grey-clad, who stumbled on without pause. "They're killing everyone. He seemed to think it was punishment for not attending the arena, even though the place could never hold all of them."

Vaelin turned to the Ally, regarding the passing refugees with only vague interest. "Is this your doing?" he demanded.

The Ally shrugged and shook his head. "She was mad even before I took her. And these people have always stirred her hatred."

They moved on, breaking free of the fleeing mob after another mile and proceeding into the city. The eastern district seemed to be the merchants' quarter, rich in warehouses and canals, their dark waters thick with floating corpses. Here and there dazed people wandered into their path, wounded or shocked into passivity. Horrors greeted them at every turn, women wept over murdered children and mystified infants prodded fallen parents. Vaelin closed his heart against it all and kicked Scar to a faster trot, his gaze fixed on the arciform mass of the arena rising from the centre of the city. He shot continual inquisitive looks at Kiral, who could only confirm the urgent note of her song.

After a tortuous hour-long ride they broke into the parkland surrounding the arena where he forced Scar to full gallop, hearing a rising cacophony as they neared the great red-gold edifice. Something flickered in the corner of his eye and he turned to see a line of people running towards the arena's south-facing wall, perhaps five hundred, all armed. His gaze went to the figure in the lead, picking out the dark blue cloak and the familiar, precise gait of his run. He angled Scar to the left, leaping corpses and thundering over marble and grass to charge into the path of the onrushing fighters, dragging him to a halt and raising his hand.

The charging line came to a slow stop as Frentis waved his sword. They were an odd bunch, men and women in motley armour bearing the marks of recent battle, some with Volarian colouring, others plainly Alpiran or of Realm origin. He breathed a sigh of relief at finding Weaver among them, standing amidst the only group in this company to present a truly soldierly appearance.

"Brother!" Frentis greeted him, running to his side. Vaelin was struck by his appearance, besmirched with blood and soot from head to toe, his sword blade stained red from end to end. However, he took comfort from his gaze, aged since he had last seen him, but steady and free of the madness that seemed to have gripped this city.

Vaelin nodded at Weaver and the well-ordered Volarians surrounding him. "Are those Varitai?"

"They call themselves Politai now," Frentis said. "It means 'unchained' in old Volarian."

Vaelin glanced over his shoulder as Orven's guards and the Sentar rode into view, the Ally among them, his posture now considerably more alert as he scanned the arena. Vaelin saw the smile playing on his lips. *No need to conceal his anticipation now.*

"Unchained," he repeated, turning back to Frentis. "As were you, brother."

Frentis nodded, frowning a little in puzzlement. "Lady Reva," he said, pointing his sword at the arena. "I have sound intelligence . . ."

"I know." Vaelin climbed down from Scar's back and drew his sword, striding towards the arena and beckoning Frentis to follow, speaking softly. "We do not have much time, so listen well . . ."

◆ ◆ ◆

All sound of battle had faded by the time he entered the arena. They had been delayed by a few Kuritai found in the maze of corridors that led them here, but the Sentar and the guardsmen were numerous and skilled enough to cut them down without difficulty. Vaelin's gaze tracked over the surrounding terraces as he stepped out onto the sand, finding them only a third full, nervous huddles of Volarian citizenry keeping their distance from companies of Realm Guard and Cumbraelin archers. The queen stood in the centre of the arena, smiling as she exchanged words with Reva, alongside what appeared to be a monstrous ape of some kind, lying dead with a spear jutting from its back.

Reva ran to him as he approached, her embrace fierce and warm. "Too late this time," she chided, moving back to deliver a playful slap to his cheek.

He nodded and forced a smile, bowing to the queen as she came to greet him. "Highness. I am glad to see you well."

"And you, my lord." He found her gaze oddly cool, the unaffected smile she had shown him in the past now more considered. *The greatest conquerer in Realm history,* he reminded himself. *More than a queen now.*

"Lady Dahrena?" she asked, her gaze tracking over the company behind him.

He met her gaze and shook his head, seeing the brief spasm of lost composure she betrayed, her face clouding in genuine grief. "A . . . great loss, my lord."

His gaze was drawn by a choking sound behind her, seeing another body slumped next to the monstrous ape, her eyes fixed not on him but on Frentis. Her lips moved in some form of greeting, spitting blood across the sand as her hands twitched.

"May I present Empress Elverah of the Volarian Empire," the queen said.

Vaelin saw how Frentis paled and shifted at his side, seemingly unable to look away from the dying woman as she continued to voice her greeting. He stared at his brother until he turned, meeting his gaze and holding it, hoping he remembered his task. Frentis gave a barely perceptible nod and turned away from the Empress, drawing a plaintive groan from her as she clawed at the sand, desperately trying to pull herself closer to him.

"I have an introduction of my own," Vaelin told the queen, beckoning to Orven's guardsmen to bring the Ally.

"Your ageless Gifted?" the queen asked, casting a critical eye over the Ally's bound form. He returned her gaze with a distracted nod and looked up at the surrounding tiers, eyes narrowed in careful calculation.

"Not exactly," Vaelin said. "I don't know his true name, but we have become accustomed to calling him the Ally."

"I never liked that name," the Ally commented in a faint tone. "Perhaps, in the years to come you can compose a better one. Something more poetic. You see, I have decided to become a god."

Vaelin opened his mouth to command him to silence, and froze. He tried to raise his sword arm and found it immobile. He attempted to turn to Frentis but his neck refused to budge. All sensation had fled his limbs, the only movement in his chest which continued to draw breath, and his eyes which flicked about with panicked speed. He could see the queen, standing frozen with the same frown of critical scrutiny, Lord Iltis close behind her, still like a statue, as was every other living soul in sight, even those in the terraces above. The arena was silent now, save for the Empress's dying gasps and the sound of the Ally's soft steps on the sand as he moved closer to Vaelin, peering into his eyes.

"You asked about my gift," he said. "Here it is, or one of them. So many years since I wielded it in this world without need of a proxy. Not so taxing now, thanks to you and your ageless friend. See?" He angled his head, moving it from side to side. "No blood. This body will sustain me for quite some time I suspect. Perhaps until the death of this world, though I've no desire to see that."

He moved away, pausing to peer closely at Lyrna then Reva, just visible in the edges of Vaelin's vision, as still as everyone else. "So well-made," the Ally said, his gaze lingering on Reva. "Pity to spoil her, but this one will require a reward if she's to continue as my dog."

He moved away, going to the Empress, the only body in sight not frozen, though her movements were now confined to a faint twitching. The Ally went to his knees beside her, leaning back to press the ropes around his torso to the steel claws protruding from the hand of the dead ape. He grimaced with the effort, working himself up and down several times until the bonds gave away.

"Ahh," the Ally breathed, standing upright and tossing Alturk's ropes aside. "That's better." He flexed his arms for a brief moment then crouched to inspect the Empress, pursing his lips at the small glimmer still visible in her eye then grunting in satisfaction.

"I have often been called arrogant," he said, looking up at Vaelin. "And I'll admit to a certain reluctance in admitting failure. But, so many years of awareness have given me a new appreciation for humility. I did fail, of course, and Lionen tortured me to death for it. But it was the method rather than the intent that brought me down. The method was flawed. To attempt the slaughter of every Gifted in the world by myself, even with the ability to twist sufficiently malicious souls to my purpose, was all too great a task. But I had plenty of time to ponder a new approach."

He bent to the sand and retrieved a fallen short sword before placing a foot under the Empress's body and heaving her onto her back. "Why strive for the impossible?" he asked Vaelin. "When the endless greed of humanity can do it for me? It was to be the Volarians' role, once moulded to suit my purpose. It never occurred to them why I always ensured there was never enough, no matter how many they bred in their pits, I simply gave my blessing to more of their nobility so they would always need more, compelled to expand, an empire crafted to conquer the world in search of gifted blood, driven by their hunger for eternal life. All come to nothing thanks to you and these others. The wolf's doing, I suppose. Still, no matter."

He raised the sword above his head and turned to the terraces, calling out in a strident voice, "Take heed of this! The old gods are risen in me! Great power runs in my veins! Behold my blessing!"

He moved closer to the Empress and pressed the blade of the sword to the flesh of his arm, the cut short but deep. He lowered the wound to the Empress's face, letting the blood trickle onto her lips. At first she barely reacted, lips betraying only the slightest twitch, but soon her mouth opened wider, allowing the blood to flow into her throat as her back arched. The Ally moved away as she continued to convulse, tossing the sword aside and tearing a rag from his shirt to bind the wound.

"Since you took my empire away," he said to Vaelin, teeth gritted around the rag as he pulled it tight, "we will make another."

He moved closer, pausing at Lyrna's side once more, her eyes darting about in her perfect face with frantic alarm. "She will be the Saviour Queen, come from across the ocean to deliver the Volarian people from the murderous reign of the Empress Elverah. And you"—he grinned at Vaelin—"her great and noble general. Think of the armies you will build together, the lands you will conquer. And in every land you seize you will seek out the Gifted."

His grin evaporated as he moved to Vaelin, all pretence of humanity falling from his face, the sheer malice of this thing revealed in a tremulous snarl. "And you will sacrifice them to your new god. It may take decades, it may be that I will have you father sons on my puppet queen so they can continue the work. But in time every Gifted on this earth will be gone, and I can finally move on."

He stepped closer still, voice dropped to a whisper. "The grey stones were the foundations of our greatness, receptacles of memory and wisdom, able to carry our thoughts across vast distances. With them we crafted an age of peace and wisdom, then we found the black stone and thought it another blessing. Oh the gifts it gave, my wife the power to heal, her brother the ability to pierce the mists of time. Such wondrous gifts, but not for me. For me it had a curse. Do you know what it is to live in a world of harmony, a world unmarred by greed, and possess true power? The power to command by a single touch, the power to force a man to murder. I didn't want it, I wanted something better, something more. But the black stone only ever holds one gift, permits only one touch. For, as those who dug it from the earth discovered to their cost, touch it once and gain a gift, twice and you lose your soul.

"So, year after year, decade after decade, I resisted my gift. I built cities, I taught, I spread wisdom across the earth, and never once did I use my gift. And my reward? A wife sacrificed to save a race of savages without the wit to even write their own name. This world, this world of flawed beasts who imagine themselves above nature. What loyalty did I owe it now? Why not take what I had been denied?

"His name is lost to me, but he was the first to touch the black stone, the first to receive a gift. A mighty power, like mine one he preferred not to use. Though there were occasions when he would demonstrate it, holding willing volunteers frozen for hours at a time, a harmless amusement you might think. But I saw it for what it was, a barrier, the counter to the power I had been gifted.

"In time we grew to be great friends. As age wearied him and he began to contemplate the trials ahead, it was a small matter to persuade him to a final adventure, a second touch to the stone which would spare him so much pain, leaving his body empty, whilst his gift lingered in his blood.

"I didn't know, of course. I didn't realise what I would be unleashing. We touched something, you see. When we reached into the Black Stone. We touched something beyond this world. Another place, a place where what you call the Dark holds supreme, a place of utter chaos. In having such a powerful soul touch the stone, I pierced the veil between the worlds and let it loose in ours, spreading out through all the world like a plague, latching onto a few souls, seeping into their blood so every generation would birth more, and creating a snare for their souls. For we had made them real, by giving them a place to reside, we had created the soul. We had created life beyond death. It's them that hold me in the Beyond. Their power sustains me, feeds me, keeps me chained in that eternal prison. I tried so hard not to, but even there, in a place without form or any feeling save the endless cold, even there the instinct to feed is irresistible, and if there are none left here, there will be nothing more to sustain me when I choose to slough off this flesh."

He moved back, his alien visage returned to its previous blandness. "In all honesty I wasn't at all sure I could twist you to my design. Some souls are simply too lacking in malice to make suitable tools. But then I saw you hack the head from that animal in the north. Do not think me ungenerous." He raised a hand and reached towards Vaelin's forehead. "I'll make you a god too, if you like."

The hand stopped, barely an inch from Vaelin's skin, the Ally's eyes widening in shock as he regarded the fist clamped to his wrist. "The seed grew," Frentis told him.

CHAPTER FOURTEEN

Frentis

The Ally slammed his free hand onto Frentis's fist, his face contorted, the flesh turned red as he no doubt sought to summon his gift. Frentis slapped the hand away and pushed him back, forcing him to his knees.

"They are forever bound to me," the Ally snarled at him, gesticulating at the frozen figures all around. "Whilst I live in this world they are mine. Only the death of this flesh will free them."

Frentis ignored him, eyes going to the open door at the north end of the arena in expectation.

"So that's why Revek hung on to his shell for so long." The Ally gave a grating cackle. "Taking another would have left him susceptible to my touch once more. So he gave you his blood to free you as he had freed himself." His mirth evaporated and he hissed at Frentis, eyes bright with baleful promise. "You shouldn't have revealed this little secret, boy. All you have done is ensure the death of any formerly bound by my will. Though it may take me years. Do you imagine time is any barrier to me? The centuries I endured in the Beyond . . ."

Frentis cuffed him on the side of the head, the force of the blow enough to leave the Ally stunned and barely conscious. "You seem overly fearful, for a god."

"Beloved."

She stood next to the ape's body, red from head to toe but whole again, the rents torn into her chest sealed and smooth. Her face was a stranger's but the gaze was the same: unselfish affection, naked love. "Did you bring the healer?" she asked.

He looked back at the doorway, seeing the Lonak girl enter, leading Lekran and the Politai into the arena. Vaelin had told her to wait until her song told her it was safe. Weaver walked at the head of the Politai, his gaze fixed on the Ally.

"I see you did," the woman observed. "I don't suppose it matters now. It seems your brother found a better vessel."

He turned back to her, noting she had reclaimed a short sword from the sand and was moving purposefully towards the queen.

"Don't!" he told her, moving to block her path.

She stopped and issued a sigh of frustration. "She took you from me," she explained in her impatient tutor's voice. "There must be a reckoning."

"Yes." He raised his own sword. "Yes there must."

"Don't you see?" she railed at him in sudden anger, pointing at the Ally. "He is broken now. I will drink from him, take his gifts. The world can be ours."

"And what would you do with it? I fought my way through a city of horrors today, all of your design. How can you dream I would allow you to do that to the world?"

"Because you love me!" Her new eyes were beautiful, he saw. Dark, limpid pools in a pale mask, free of any cruelty, but utterly mad.

"You are sick," he told her. "And I brought the healer . . ."

She gave a shout of frustration and attempted to dodge past him, sword reaching for the queen's exposed back. He forced the blade aside with his own and tried to grab her wrist, hoping to disarm her. She was too fast, spinning away and slashing a cut into his shoulder.

"You talk of sickness," she spat. "We live in a world of sickness. You mourn for those I killed today. Did any ever mourn for me? I killed for decades to build this empire of filth and greed. It was mine to bring down."

Frentis felt his left arm growing numb as warm blood coursed down his back. "Please!" he begged her. "If he can heal a body, perhaps he can heal a mind."

She paused for a second, a confused frown appearing on her brow. "The night I killed my father he wasn't afraid. He sneered at me, he spat in contempt. He said, 'I should have drunk your blood the night I drank from your whore mother.' Can he heal that?"

"I don't know." Frentis reached out to her, chilled arm trembling. "But we can . . ."

The arrow took her in the chest, quickly followed by two more. She staggered, her confusion fading as she looked down to regard the fletchings, her expression one of complete and sane understanding.

The Lonak girl stepped to Frentis's side, bow drawn, and sent another arrow into the woman's neck, folding her body onto the sand. Frentis watched the girl move closer and deliver a hard kick to the corpse, eyes narrowed as she scanned her for the slightest sign of life. She glanced at Frentis, frowning at what she saw on his face. "The song was clear," she said.

He heard a faint moan behind him and turned, seeing Weaver gently taking hold of the man lying slumped in the sand and guiding him into a seating position. The Politai stood around them, spears levelled at the Ally. "There is a great sickness in you," Weaver said. "Let me help."

The Ally's senses seemed to return as Weaver drew him into a tight embrace, struggling feebly then throwing his head back to issue a scream.

PART V

*Any found to have promulgated the falsehood that human life may be
extended by the foul practice of drinking the blood of the Gifted are
liable to summary arrest, their punishment to be determined under the
Queen's Word. Any writings containing this falsehood are subject to
immediate seizure and destruction.*

—*THE QUEEN'S TENTH EDICT,*
SIGNED INTO REALM LAW BY HER GRACIOUS CONSENT
IN THE SIXTH YEAR OF HER REIGN

Verniers' Account

Despite the stubbiness of his fingers Raulen had a fine, flowing script the equal of any scribe. Also, his reading voice was similarly accomplished, reciting my recently dictated words in even tones free of any stumbles. "'. . . and so it came to pass that Queen Lyrna Al Nieren walked once more on the soil of her beloved homeland,'" he read. "'And terrible would be her vengeance.'"

"Very good, Raulen," I said. "I think that's enough for today."

"Thank you, my lord." He rose from the stool and went to the cell door. "Same time tomorrow then."

"Tomorrow my trial begins," I reminded him.

"Yes," he sighed, pausing at the door and forcing a smile. "No doubt this great work will be complete when your innocence is proved."

"No doubt." I returned the smile, grateful for his artifice.

"Even your gaolers are scholars," Fornella observed after the heavy door had slammed shut, leaving us alone. She sat on her narrow bunk, surrounded by bundles of parchment. With little else to occupy her during the long months of our shared captivity, she had taken on the translating of my manuscript into Volarian, despite full knowledge it would most likely remain unfinished.

My gaze tracked over her now almost all-white hair, tied back from her face into a tight bun. In recent weeks the skin on her scalp and hands had developed faint red spots and the lines around her eyes grew ever deeper, though she bore it all without complaint. Despite the many messages I asked Raulen to convey to every Imperial official I could recall, she had never once been allowed out of this cell to relate the warning she held. Our journey was indeed an abject failure and it seemed the survival of this empire now depended entirely on Queen Lyrna's vengeful designs. An absurd hope, I knew. For all her wits, and Al Sorna's martial cunning, the Volarian Empire was monstrous. It requires an empire to destroy an empire, I concluded, reaching for pen and parchment to write it down.

"Something to aid your defence, I hope," Fornella said, glancing up from her own work.

"I have no defence, save the truth. And that will avail me nothing now." The Empress, in her wisdom and benevolence, had sent no less than six learned counsel to act on my behalf at trial. All experienced legal scholars of impeccable reputation and, I saw clearly in their faces, absolutely no hope or expectation of securing my acquittal. I had listened to them all politely before releasing them from their duty with an assertion I would be conducting my own defence, much to their evident relief.

"The girl was lying," Fornella went on. "The blindest fool can see that."

"And were I to be judged by a jury of blind fools, I might have a chance. But there will be but one juror, and she is far from blind. However, even she cannot deny my right to speak following conviction. I can only hope there are ears to hear the warning."

◆　◆　◆

Despite my continued calm, a calm that I confess still baffles me, sleep eluded me that night. I had spent the evening arranging my manuscript and penning an outline for Raulen regarding the completion of the final chapters. He had agreed to take copies to a select few scholars of my prior acquaintance, though I harboured suspicions that those who didn't immediately burn it might seek to claim it as their own work. Another copy would be conveyed to Brother Harlick in Varinshold, where at least it would receive a home in the Great Library he hoped to rebuild. As the small, barred window above my bed grew dark I took a quill and scrawled the words "A History of the Unified Realm" on a blank sheet of parchment, a little chagrined that my script wasn't near so elegant as Raulen's, and placed it atop the neatly arranged bundle.

I lay back on my bunk seeking rest I knew would elude me and pondering a particular point of scholarly regret. I never heard Al Sorna's full account.

Somewhere past midnight, my half doze was interrupted by a faint creaking sound. I rose, blinking in the gloom and feeling my heartbeat lurch at the sight of the cell door slowly swinging open.

She decided not to wait for a trial, I concluded as my perennial calm dissolved and I cast about desperately for some kind of weapon. However Raulen was too diligent a gaoler to allow a prisoner any implement beyond the small wooden candlestick I wrote by.

I expected Hevren, or more likely some anonymous Imperial servant suitably skilled in crafting convincing suicide from murder. Instead the door swung open to reveal a slender form in a black dress, her eyes wide and fearful as she beckoned to me with desperate urgency. Jervia.

For a second I could only stare in amazement as she continued to beckon, her movements becoming frantic, then I swung myself off the bunk, dressing quickly and moving to Fornella. Over the weeks she had slept more soundly than I, either through the rapid onset of age or a salved conscience. In either case it took several attempts to wake her and several more to coax her from the bed.

"Why is she here?" she whispered, a deep frown on her wrinkled brow as she regarded Jervia fidgeting in the corridor.

"I don't know," I said, returning to my bunk to pull on my shoes. "However, we are provided with an open door, and I intend to use it."

Jervia put a hand over my mouth as I came to the doorway, forestalling my whispered questions, moving away and gesturing for me to follow. I glanced back at Fornella, now dressed but no less suspicious. "I'm not sure I can run," she murmured, coming to my side and taking my hand.

I led her along the corridor, past the other cells, all empty I noted, to where Jervia waited at the barred gate. I came to a rigid halt at the sight of Raulen, standing aside and holding the gate open.

"It's all right," Jervia whispered. "He doesn't see us."

I stepped closer to the gaoler, taking in the sight of his features, the eyes focused but not on me, a fond smile on his lips; the face of a man viewing a long-cherished sight.

"You did this," I murmured to Jervia, sliding past Raulen's bulk to come to her side.

She gave a nervous smile. "His daughter died at Marbellis. I gave her back to him."

Gifted, I realised, glancing back at the gaoler and gaining a new appreciation for his sense of duty. All those years with the Hopekiller in his grasp and he never sought vengeance.

"It won't last," Jervia said, tugging at my sleeve.

She led me through Raulen's meagre quarters and into the only slightly more ornate north wing of the palace; a series of storerooms and living quarters where the army of Imperial servants slept. We encountered only two guards, all wearing the same expression of focused delusion as Raulen. I saw Jervia wipe her cuff across her face as we moved on, noting the dark smear of blood on her skin and wondering how much strain she endured to facilitate this escape.

We stole through the courtyard in a crouch, though the pair of guards on the northern gate showed no sign of having noticed our passing. "We must hurry," Jervia said, making for the grassland beyond the road. "The illusions will fade soon."

"The road . . ." I began but she shook her head.

"Too well guarded, my lord. I have a rope placed on the cliff, and a boat waiting on the river."

"I . . ." Fornella gasped, coming to halt, features sagging in the scant moonlight. "I can't."

"It's not far . . ."

"Leave me," she groaned, doubling over and sinking to her knees, drawing air into her lungs in ragged heaves.

"My lord!" Jervia implored.

I leaned down, putting a hand around Fornella shoulders, frowning at the sight of her face, eyes alert with warning and free of fatigue. "It's him," she breathed. "The Messenger. I know his stink."

I straightened, meeting Jervia's gaze, seeing only a scared young woman forced to a courageous act. "A moment please," I said. "She grows older by the day."

Jervia gave a reluctant nod, eyes darting about constantly for any sign of pursuit.

"Tell me," I said. "What threats did the Empress make to coerce your testimony?"

Her face showed a pained grimace. "Father was arrested on charges of treason. It happened when word began to reach us of what had transpired in the Unified Realm."

"She knew my return would be imminent, and prepared her trap accordingly."

"I expect so."

"And that ridiculous story about the sword?"

"Invented by Lord Velsus, at the Empress's behest. I had no choice, my lord."

"Of course." I squeezed Fornella's shoulder and moved away, keeping a distance from our rescuer. "I have known Lord Velsus for close to twenty years," I said. "He's an arrogant, self-regarding, judgemental bully. But he's never been a liar, as I expect he lacks the imagination for deceit."

She said nothing, but I saw how her eyes narrowed and her hand reached into the fold of her dress.

"You played your part very well," I said, continuing to move away from Fornella, Jervia pivoting to match my every step, the muscles of her forearm bunching at she gripped something tight. "So reluctant and contrite, bound to win my trust when you came to open my cell door. When did it happen? Was it when the Red Hand took you?"

Her eyes flicked to Fornella, now groaning as her grey head lolled forward, then turning back to me with a different face. It was as if she had contrived some magician's trick, switching the face of a sweet, brave maiden for something altogether older, its malice plain in every coarsened line and the twisted sneer of her lips. "When last we met you were not so courageous," she said, Jervia's well-spoken vowels moulded into something harsher, and familiar.

"Courage?" I gave a very soft laugh. "I find courage is just another of life's illusions. In the end, we all do what we must."

"Very profound. And true. For tonight you must walk off a cliff, having effected an escape by use of foul magics, no doubt learned from your friends in the north. Perhaps it was guilt that made you do it, or it could have been a final act of defiance. A refusal to allow the Empress just recompense for all your dreadful deeds. I'm sure scholars will ponder the question for years to come."

"Don't you ever grow tired of this? All these years spent in murder and cruelty? Don't you want to be more than a slave to a monster?"

"Slave?" The crooked bow of her lips parted in a laugh. "He did not enslave me. These many years in his service have never been a punishment. Every life taken, every seed of chaos sown, my just reward, for this world deserves all the havoc I can wreak upon it. With you gone to your deserved end the Empress's gaze will inevitably turn north, where the Unified Realm lies barren of much of its strength as their queen pursues her mad vendetta across the ocean. Why do you think she gathers her fleet?"

"Spurred to do so by more of your lies, I assume?"

"She finds much wisdom in my counsel, and in time, so will her brat. I've just about convinced her the practice of choosing an heir from among the populace is an archaic, even unwise tradition. Who better to rule than a child born to those who know the burdens of power? A child born to an Empress and a Hope no less."

I took an involuntary step towards her, fists bunching in fury. "That boy is not for you."

Her hand came free of her dress, the knife it held glittering in the moonlight as she dropped to a crouch, forcing me to stop. "That boy will complete the ruin of the Unified Realm and go on to conquer the Volarian Empire," she said. "His children will build a mighty fleet to carry Alpiran civilisation to all corners of the world. Is that not a prospect to rejoice at, my lord? Your lover certainly did."

I took another forward step and she lunged, the blade flashing just close enough to force me back. "You're a liar!" I raged.

She laughed, shrill and delighted. "He was such a clever fellow. So well-read, and fascinated by the opportunities offered by those with singular gifts. We didn't corrupt him, Verniers. We didn't seduce him. He came to us, but, as ever, Al Sorna's blade contrived to complicate our plans."

I charged at her, my rage dispelling all reason, uncaring of the knife. She danced aside, lithe and quick as any dancer. "If you don't believe me," she said, spinning to a stop and gesturing towards the cliff-top. "Why not ask him?"

I was about to lunge for her again but stopped as something shimmered into view in the blackness beyond the cliff, something that flared into blinding white fire for a moment before swirling into a familiar form.

I stood frozen, my eyes playing over his face, all thought fleeing my mind save one. "Seliesen."

He stood there, smiling the smile I knew so well, clad in the simple robes he preferred to wear in private, the robes in fact he had been wearing the last time I saw him. It would be preferable, and dishonest, to record that I had no inkling this was an illusion, that I was completely deluded and my reason undone by the wicked precision of the Messenger's stolen gift. But, I knew this to be a phantom, I knew I was being lured to my death as I rushed towards the cliff-top calling his name. And I simply didn't care.

He vanished as I came to within a foot of the edge, flickering like a candle-flame caught in the wind before being snuffed. I shouted in grief and bitter defeat, sinking to my knees and calling out into the uncaring dark. The only reply was the soft hiss of the wind through the grass.

I turned at a hard, choking sound behind me, seeing Fornella pull a knife free of Jervia's neck, releasing a fine spray of blood as she held her upright. "You should've taken the gaoler's knife," she muttered before casting the body away with a grimace.

She sank to her knees as I approached, fatigue obvious and unfeigned now, her smile forced and small. "I owed you a life, did I not, my lord?"

I went to the body, fighting nausea and heaving it upright, proffering the still-gushing wound to her. "Drink," I said.

She watched the blood flow with detached interest for a second, then looked away. "No."

"It will restore you . . ."

"I am already restored. Please take that thing from my sight."

I let the corpse slip from my arms and moved to her, catching her before she could fall. She lay back against me, her breath coming in slow, shallow gasps. "It will be morning soon," she whispered.

I could see only a faint glimmer on the horizon—dawn would be hours in coming—but still I held her close, and whispered, "Yes," into her ear.

I heard the soft tramping of boots on grass, a full company from the sound of it, but didn't bother to turn as a large, soldierly form came to a halt at my side.

"So," I said, "the Empress never believed her."

Hevren paused before replying, an edge of discomfort in his tone. "She was curious to see what would transpire."

"Well, I trust this satisfies her curiosity."

"Your innocence will be proclaimed in the morning. For now, she demands your presence . . ."

"Later." I held Fornella closer, feeling only the faint, diminishing flutter of her heart as her grey hair played over my face. "My friend and I wish to stay a while and watch the sun rise."

CHAPTER ONE

Vaelin

He became fully human as Reva led them down into the bowels of the arena, like any other man facing his end; begging one moment, bargaining the next, his temper flaring into brief, unreasoning defiance. "You think you visit justice upon me? This is simply vengeance . . . You do not know what I suffered . . . I know many things, I have great wisdom, wisdom any queen would be grateful for . . . Don't you know what I am? What I have done! You are the merest speck on my greatness . . ."

He fell silent on seeing the black stone sitting amidst its silent companions, Reva's torch painting a yellow gleam on its edges. "You . . ." the Ally choked, shaking as he forced the words out, "You think to destroy me with this? You . . . You will be making me a gift of more power . . ." His words were given the lie by the way he shied from the stone, twisting in Frentis's grip.

Lyrna cast her gaze over the statues before stepping between them, providing Vaelin an unwelcome reminder of her father as she surveyed the black stone with owl-like scrutiny. "You say this was dug from the Northern Reaches?" she asked him.

"Yes, Highness. Thousands of years ago."

"So there may be more?"

"The seer made no mention of it. However, it was clear to me he thought it best left buried."

The queen gave a slight nod, her gaze moving across the statues until it rested on the bearded man. "This is truly him?" she asked with a dubious glance at the Ally, who had begun to whimper.

"Yes, Highness."

"How far we can fall," she mused softly, eyes returning to the noble lines of the bearded man's face, "if we surrender to malice." She turned back to the stone, gesturing for Frentis to bring the Ally.

He railed. He screamed. He struggled, collapsing and clawing at the floor with his nails, obliging Vaelin to assist his brother in dragging him to the stone where he thrashed himself to exhaustion, eventually sagging between them, head lowered as he wept piteous sobs. "Just," he gasped, "Just kill me . . . All my gifts are gone, the Beyond will not snare me."

"That would require the death of the body you stole," Vaelin replied. "And I made a promise to its owner."

"You are a fool!" The Ally's head snapped up, spittle flying as he lurched at Vaelin. "You don't know what this thing is!"

"A gateway to another place, somewhere I suspect you will be more at home."

"You don't understand." His eyes widened as they played over the smooth surface of the stone, unblinking, fixed in terror, his voice dropping to a grating whisper. "When I touched it, when I received my gift, I looked into that world . . . and something looked back, something vast, and hungry."

Vaelin looked at the Ally's sweat-covered face, his unblinking eyes, seeing no vestige of a lie. He began to demand clarification but Lyrna reached out to take hold of the Ally's wrist. "Then let's feed it," she said, slamming his hand to the stone.

There was no sound, no glimmer of light from the blank depths of the stone, not even the faintest change to the musty air of the chamber. The Ally gave a short intake of breath then froze, Vaelin seeing the light fade from his eyes, features soon becoming slack, devoid of all animation.

They held him in place a moment longer, Lyrna's gaze searching the empty features of what had been Erlin's face. Vaelin released him and stood back, Frentis and Lyrna also retreating from the still and silent man as his hand slid limp to his side.

"Well," Reva said, tapping her boot against the stone. "What do we do with it?"

◆ ◆ ◆

"The mountain folk will not be so friendly this time."

"Rather them than the big water." Alturk threw a blanket across his horse's back and settled the saddlebags over it. The Tahlessa moved with a noticeable limp these days, alleviated slightly by the salve Brother Kehlan had provided to anoint his wound, the only gift he would accept from the

Merim Her. "And we have him to speak for us." Alturk jerked his head at Lekran, bidding farewell to Frentis a few strides away.

The former Kuritai had caused something of a stir when presented to the queen the day before, failing to bow and instead making a formal declaration of love and proposal of marriage. She had listened patiently to his lengthy list of victories, his apologies for not providing the heads as proof, and confident assurance that, should she agree to the union, he would happily kill the requisite number of enemies in less than five years, his life being forfeit should he fail.

"Only a thousand?" she had asked, breaking the tense silence that followed. "Make it three and I'll deign to consider it. In the interim you can have a captaincy in my guard and I'll make you ambassador to your people. Go back to the mountains and tell them the slaving days are over and we'll pay a fair price for whatever metals they care to sell us."

"You truly intend to brave the ice once more?" Vaelin asked Alturk.

"The shaman says it's easier in summer months. And it will make a fine story." He tightened a strap on the horse's bridle and paused. "She was a good woman," he said. "I will be proud to tell her story and have it placed in the Mahlessa's library. For she was Lonak, and we should not forget our kind, whatever names they choose."

Vaelin stood back as the Tahlessa climbed onto his horse, hefting his war club. "Thank you."

Alturk looked down at him, eyes arch beneath his heavy brows. "One day . . ." he began.

"The Lonak will sweep the Merim Her into the sea," Vaelin finished. "I know."

"No." Alturk shook his head. "One day the Lonak will fade, scattered and slaughtered in war or our blood mixed with the Merim Her until our stories are forgotten. It will be so with the Seordah, the Eorhil, the ice people and the mountain folk. I see it now. The Mahlessa has been trying to shield us from our fate, we have become like stones clinging to a mountainside. But the mountains always shake, and the stones always fall."

Vaelin watched him ride away, the Sentar closing in alongside as they took the Northern Road.

"Come with us." He turned to find Wise Bear sitting astride Iron Claw, bone-staff in hand. "This place is bad, full of stink and heat, and too far from the green fire."

626 · ANTHONY RYAN

"I'll see you at the Mirror Sound before long," Vaelin told him but Wise Bear just smiled, clicking something in his unfathomable tongue as Iron Claw lumbered towards the road.

Mishara came to nuzzle at his hand as Kiral stood close by and Astorek waited amidst his wolves. She offered no embrace, nor even a smile, her scar rendered near invisible in the bright sunlight. Davoka stood nearby, head lowered and arms folded. Their farewell had been lengthy and not without rancour.

"My song is varied when I look at you," Kiral said eventually. "I hear so many different notes now, as if it doesn't know what path you will take. Some are bright, some dark. It was not so when we first met."

Mishara gave a final lick to his hand and bounded off in Iron Claw's tracks, the bear issuing an irritated growl as she nipped playfully at his rump. "When I see you again I hope it will be clearer," Vaelin told Kiral, glancing at Astorek, who gave a cheery wave, his wolves breaking into an instant chorus of howls. "I am glad your song guided you to happiness."

"It will be good to hunt again," she said, pausing to offer a final glance to Davoka before climbing onto her horse. He watched as the dust of their passing faded on the Northern Road, though the wolves could still be heard long after.

◆ ◆ ◆

"I promised I would return," Frentis said, hefting his pack. "Even though it was a promise made to a man now dead. And Aspect Arlyn has directed me to establish a joint mission house with the Fifth Order."

Still they cling to it, Vaelin thought, following Frentis along the wharf. *Despite all the knowledge gained, the Faith remains and seeks to grow.*

"Besides," Frentis continued. "I feel the queen would be more comfortable with me gone."

Vaelin could find no argument to this point; the queen remained icy in his brother's presence and he knew she recalled his final words to the Empress all too well. However, as the principal architect of what was fast becoming known as the Great Liberation, Frentis's status among the freed population had increased to near-mythic proportions. Everywhere, former slaves would pause to bow to him, some running to his side with fervent thanks and offerings. Nor were all his admirers slaves; many free citizens had witnessed him fighting to save them from the Arisai.

"You know there is always a place for you in the Reaches," Vaelin said. "Should you ever tire of the Order."

"That day will never come, brother. I think you know that." Frentis paused a short distance from the gangplank, glancing up at the collection of expectant faces arrayed along the ship's rail. Sister Illian, regarding Vaelin with a somewhat stern visage. The hairy captain exchanging a ribald joke with the former slave. And mad Master Rensial, balancing on crutches and frowning at Vaelin as if seeking to recall his name. *He has his own Order now*, Vaelin decided, a pang of envy mingling with satisfaction in his breast.

"Kiral said you tried to save her," Vaelin said. "The Empress."

"We once murdered our way across an empire and killed a king," Frentis replied. "And yet I was saved. Why not her?"

"She was monstrous. Brother Hollun estimates near half a million people died at her command."

"She was what she was made." His hand went to his shirt, feeling for scars that no longer existed. "As was I. In my heart I know she could have been made . . . better."

He gave a tight smile and they embraced. "My regards to your sister," Frentis said, drawing away and stepping onto the gangplank, pausing once more. "The dreams still come, brother. Not every night, but most. She comes to me and I find she is easier to bear now."

He smiled again and ascended to the ship, the last of the faith-hounds jumping in excitement to lick his face as he stepped onto the deck and disappeared from sight.

◆ ◆ ◆

The queen held court in what had been the house of Council-man Arklev, a sizeable mansion with extensive grounds that benefited from a tall surrounding wall and a large audience chamber. A small army of clerks laboured in the mansion's many rooms to deal with the copious correspondence generated by an empire that now found itself part of a Realm. The issues were many and varied, from famine in the south to declarations of secession in the east where some Volarian military strength had contrived to linger, apparently due to the pragmatic attitude of the provincial governor who had taken his forces on protracted manoeuvres, thereby avoiding Imperial messengers bearing his death-warrant.

Over the weeks since the city's fall the queen had faced a continual stream of petitioners, dozens at first, then hundreds. Various rebel groups sought recognition, representatives from the more quiescent towns and cities demanded protection from less placid neighbours and, most of all, merchants came with generous offers for exclusive trading concessions.

Vaelin was met at the chamber door by Lady Lieza, saved from the arena and now elevated to the queen's side by virtue of her skill with correspondence, not to mention an intimate knowledge of the varied laws and customs of this newly conquered land.

"The queen bids you enter immediately, my lord," the lady said in her rapidly improving Realm Tongue.

"How many today?" he asked as she bade the guards to open the door.

Lieza gave a tense smile. "Just one."

The queen was speaking as he entered, her tone surprising in the anger it held. "And your Empress expects me to simply agree to this without negotiation?"

Lord Verniers seemed to have aged since Vaelin last saw him, though he also appeared to stand a little straighter now and displayed scant reaction to the queen's ire. "She does you the courtesy of informing you of her actions, Highness," he said. "And sees no scope for conflict in this matter."

He fell silent at Vaelin's entry, pausing to offer a shallow bow of welcome.

"Lord Vaelin," the queen greeted him. "Lord Verniers, it seems, has gained stature since leaving us. May I present the Alpiran Ambassador to the Unified Realm."

"Congratulations, my lord," Vaelin told Verniers, returning the bow.

"He comes to tell me one of my own cities is now in the hands of his Empress," the queen continued.

"Verehl was an Alpiran city long before the Volarian Empire even existed, Highness," Verniers responded. "And I should point out its capture occurred whilst your war was still ongoing. The actions of an ally, in truth."

"An ally would have sailed her fleet into the Cut and helped take this city, not steal another." Lyrna rose from her throne, approaching Verniers, face tense with anger. "Does your Empress have any notion of the army I now command? Of the nature of the sword I wield? I took an empire in the space of a few months. Had I a mind to, I could take a world."

"Highness . . ." Vaelin began but she waved him to silence, moving away and sighing in frustration. "I find, Lord Verniers, it would be best if you came back tomorrow, when my temper will be better suited to diplomacy. Lord Vaelin, you will stay. We have military matters to discuss."

Vaelin touched a hand to Verniers' sleeve as he bowed and made for the door. "The Volarian woman?"

Verniers took a deliberate step back from him, face unchanged as he said, "She died."

"I'm sorry. We had intelligence there was an agent of the Ally in Alpira . . ."

"It died too." Verniers bowed again and walked from the chamber.

"What do you think?" Vaelin turned to find the queen greeting him with a smile, her anger abruptly vanished. "A little overdramatic, perhaps?"

"I'm sure Your Highness knows best how to deal with an ambassador."

"Actually, it's a skill I'm having to learn with some rapidity. So, do you think we should retake Verehl?"

"The decision is not mine to make, Highness. And you have a Battle Lord to advise on the practicalities of such an undertaking."

"I don't need Al Hestian to tell me it would be impossible, not for another year at least. Verehl sits on the southern coast, a fairly unpleasant place by all accounts, surrounded by jungle and subject to yearly storms of legendary ferocity. Its only value comes from the spice trade, contributing less than one-half of one-hundredth to the Imperial treasury. I suspect Empress Emeren seeks to test me, baiting a trap to see if I'll bite."

"Given the animosity between our peoples, a city of little value seems a small price to pay to heal the rift."

She gave a small laugh, shaking her head and moving back to her throne. "Always the peacemaker, even now."

"I hoped Your Highness had called me here to discuss my petition."

"Indeed I did, though it suited me to add a little theatre for Lord Verniers." She settled onto the throne, accepting a cup of water from Iltis. "You want to go home."

"With my sister, yes."

Lyrna's face clouded a little as she drank. "Lady Alornis is . . . improving I hear."

"She has nightmares every time she sleeps and, when awake, tinkers constantly with the engines she built on your behalf. They grow more deadly by the day, she tells me. She seems keen to see them at work. I am not."

"We agreed this war had to be won, Vaelin, and we all gave much in the winning. Your sister more than most, for which I'm sorry. But she is a grown woman and I never forced her to any action."

"Nevertheless, my petition stands, and I request your answer."

She turned to Iltis, handing him the cup and requesting he leave them alone. "You will require a new commander for the North Guard," she said when the Lord Protector had withdrawn. "Lord Adal has petitioned to be released from your service."

Vaelin nodded in grim acceptance. Imparting news of Dahrena's death to Adal had been a hard trial, made worse by the man's rigid composure and clipped response to every question. Though the accusation on his face as he bowed and withdrew was plain enough. *She would have lived if she had loved him instead.*

"I trust you will find him suitable employment," he told the queen.

"Indeed. I'm minded to create an East Guard for my new dominions. War has left us with many able hands to fill the ranks and who better to command them?"

"A fine choice, Highness. I would request Lord Orven as his replacement."

"As you wish, subject to his agreement. I believe he has earned the right to choose his commands."

Lyrna rose once again and went to the window. Council-man Arklev's home stood on a hill offering a fine view of the harbour, still crowded with the fleet, though somewhat diminished now. The Shield had sailed away two days after the city's fall, taking with him perhaps a tenth of the Meldeneans. There were rumours of a fractious dispute with the Fleet Lord, of challenges made and sabres drawn, though Lord Ell-Nurin seemed unhurt when Vaelin next saw him, bowing low to the queen as she gave him a sword, and a grant of land on the south Asraelin coast.

"Do you remember the night we met?" she asked.

"You surprised me, I threw a knife at you."

"Yes." She smiled. "I kept it. It saved my life in fact."

"I'm glad."

"There was a question I asked you then, one I won't ask you again, since both question and answer are now redundant. But, I've always been curious, did you ever regret saying no?"

Her hair was fully grown now, he saw, longer than it had ever been, a golden cascade in the light from the window. And her face, the porcelain perfection enhanced by the few small lines of experience and the keen intellect shining from her eyes, no longer subject to any constraint.

"Of course," he lied. "What man wouldn't?"

◆　◆　◆

Weaver stood among the Politai, speaking in low but earnest tones as they clustered around. They were more animated than Vaelin had seen them before, many speaking up to interrupt, faces betraying distinct emotions, ranging from sadness to anger. The more recently freed stood on the fringes, frowning in bafflement but keeping close to their brothers. Frentis said it was always the way with them, an inability to be alone or tolerate the company of those not of their kind.

Did we free something? Vaelin wondered. *Or unleash it?*

After more than an hour of discussion Weaver finally called a halt and the Politai began to disperse back to the surrounding houses they occupied. This district had been thoroughly depopulated by the Arisai, leaving copious empty dwellings, although the former Varitai chose to live a dozen or more to each house.

"They didn't seem happy," Vaelin observed as Weaver came to take a seat on the bench next to him.

"They know there are other Varitai still in bondage in some places," the healer replied. "Freeing all of their brothers has become something of a sacred mission."

"One the queen has given her word to complete."

"Without me."

"Her reasoning is sound . . ."

"And I don't dispute it. The Ally's gift is a terrible thing."

Vaelin's gaze tracked over Weaver's sturdy frame, knowing he now looked upon possibly the most powerful being in the world. He found some comfort from his expression, as open and free of calculation as he had ever been. "Have you used it?" he asked. "Since the arena."

Weaver shook his head. "I feel it though, roiling away inside me like a simmering pool."

"And Erlin's gift?"

"Time alone will tell. What accommodations has the queen arranged for me in the Realm?"

"The war left many estates vacant, you will have a wide selection to choose from."

"An honour indeed, to choose one's own prison."

Vaelin said nothing, unwilling to voice a lie. "The ship leaves with the morning tide," he said, getting to his feet and offering his hand. Weaver blinked in surprise. Since the Arena, few who knew of the events there had been willing to talk to him, and certainly not risk his touch. His expression remained unchanged, but his voice held a new edge of certainty as he took the hand and shook it.

"I won't be there to meet it, my lord. As I suspect you know, since you chose to come here alone with no guards to enforce the Queen's Word."

Vaelin gripped his hand tighter, holding it for a moment longer before letting go. "Where will you go?"

"There are a few corners of the world Erlin never visited. And I've a yen to hear the song of the Jade Princess with my own ears."

"You have Erlin's memories?"

"In a manner of speaking. Much of his knowledge resides in me, but not how he acquired it. So much slips away as the years pass."

"So you also have the Ally's knowledge?"

Weaver's expression became markedly more clouded. "More than I would like."

"He spoke of the wolf. I would know what he meant."

"He meant . . ." Weaver frowned, struggling to find the right words. "He meant there's a reason why you're willing to let me go. He meant that we are all, regardless of what gifts we may possess, very small and brief lights upon this earth. The difference is I am happy to accept it, he never was."

He got to his feet and started back towards the house he shared with the Politai. "Please give my regards to the queen," he said, pausing at the door, "and, when she sends assassins to follow my trail, tell her to be sure to choose well."

◆   ◆   ◆

He watched Reva from the bow of the ship, needing no song to discern what passed between her and Lady Lieza as they embraced on the quay. The girl drew back, head bowed and fighting tears as she moved to the queen's side. Reva made her final bows and ascended to the ship with her tall guardsman at her back, the assembled Realm Guard lifting their weapons in salute and voicing a shout that echoed across the harbour.

"Louder than the one you got, brother," Nortah observed with a grin.

"I think she earned it."

"My lot didn't even come to see me off. Probably still squabbling over their list of rightful demands for the queen."

"Rightful demands?"

"Yes, they want to choose their own officers, an end to land ownership and the right to appoint the queen's councillors. Can you imagine? Faith save us from the newly freed."

Vaelin joined Reva at the stern as the ship made its way through the narrow harbour mouth, the walled moles thick with cheering people, their words meaningless to him but she was able to discern a few. "Livella is reborn," she murmured, watching the torrent of flowers arc into their wake. "Perhaps Varulek will get his gods back after all."

"Varulek?" he asked.

"A dead man, and servant to dead gods." She surveyed the cheering throng as they drew away, the helmsman taking them into the Cut as the captain ordered the sails for a westward tack, towards the distant ocean. "Not long ago many of these would have been screaming for my death in the arena. Now they rejoice at my survival."

"They are not alone." Vaelin glanced at the young guardsman, standing at a respectful distance, his gaze rarely straying from the Blessed Lady. "It seems you have your own Iltis."

"I offered Guardsman Varesh a boon for his service." Reva gave the youth a somewhat strained smile. "All he asked was to stay at my side. I'm minded to find other employment for him when we get home."

Vaelin turned to regard the three hulking troop-ships now pulling away from the quayside, each laden with Cumbraelins. A few had elected to stay, lured by the generous pay the queen offered for experienced archers, but most chose to follow the Blessed Lady home. "Lord Antesh has already begun to quote from the Eleventh Book I hear."

"He has recovered much of his fervour since Alltor," she said. "And more since coming here. I think I preferred him jaded. The world might be a better place were it ruled by disappointed souls."

"Shouldn't you write that down? The Blessed Lady's wisdom should not be wasted on a heretic."

She gave short laugh then lowered her gaze, her voice taking on a sorrowful pitch. "I told Antesh it had all been a great lie. Never once in my life have I heard the Father's voice. Not during the siege and not here. He said, 'You are the Father's voice, my lady.'"

Her eyes went to Alornis, busy tending to the engine on the starboard rail. Apparently it could spit flame, with fearsome results if the accounts Vaelin had heard were true. Alornis seemed incapable of leaving it alone, her deft hands removing the various plates to explore its mysterious insides, her face rapt, uncaring of anything else.

"I'd happily tip that thing into the sea," he said. "But these devices of hers are the only thing that brings any life to her eyes."

"Then let's discover why." Reva went to crouch at Alornis's side, watching her work for a moment before asking a question. Vaelin expected his sister to ignore her, as she often ignored him, but instead she seemed to become enthused, hands moving with passionate animation as she pointed to the machine's innards, explaining each pipe and spigot in detail as Reva nodded encouragement.

He watched them for a time, seeing his sister relax, even voicing a laugh or two, then found his gaze drawn inexorably to the canvas-wrapped bulk lashed to the mainmast. The queen's instructions had been clear, lacking any ambiguity, but still he found the questions plagued him. *What do we do with it?*

◆　◆　◆

"I couldn't save him, brother!"

He had been called from his cabin by the third mate to find Nortah reeling about the deck, wine bottle in hand. The swell had increased as night fell and they drew into what the sailors called "the Boraelin mountains," a region renowned for tall waves and vicious storms. The wind was certainly harsh tonight, though not quite a gale it still managed to lash the deck with hard, driving rain.

"Killed a dozen of those red bastards," Nortah railed, "fought the Aspect himself, and still I couldn't save him!"

He stumbled as the deck lurched anew, staggering towards the port rail and nearly tipping over. "Stop this!" Vaelin caught hold of him, drawing him back and catching hold of the rigging.

"Killing." Nortah laughed, lifting his arms and shouting to the rain-filled sky. "Only thing I was ever good for. Just cos you hate a thing doesn't mean you aren't good at it. Wasn't enough though. He still died."

"He died saving you," Vaelin told him, holding him tight as he sought to break free. "So you could see your wife again. So you could hold your children again."

Nortah subsided at the mention of his family, head slumping as the wine bottle fell from his limp hand and rolled away. "They killed my cat," he mumbled. "Have to go home without my cat."

"I know, brother." Vaelin patted his soaked head and tried to pull him upright. A cloaked figure emerged from belowdecks, coming to his side to assist in lifting the now-passed-out Lord Marshal. Together they took him below, laying him in his cabin.

"My thanks," Vaelin offered to the cloaked figure.

"From what I gather," Erlin said, drawing back his hood, "this man deserves a better end than falling drunk from a ship's deck."

"That he does."

They left Nortah snoring and sat together in a corner of the hold, Vaelin knowing he would gain scant rest tonight with the wind howling at such a pitch. He watched as Erlin rubbed at the small of his back, groaning a little. "This will take quite a bit of getting used to," he said.

"Your first back-ache?"

"No doubt the first of many." Erlin smiled and Vaelin concealed a wince at the changes in his face. The beating had left him with a crooked nose and somewhat misshapen jaw, though his eyes seemed to shine brighter, like a young man in fact.

"Have you decided?" Vaelin asked.

"Cara invited me to live with them when we get to the Reaches," Erlin said. "Though I'm not sure Lorkan appreciated the gesture. Newlyweds need privacy after all. I do hear tell of a hut on the beach in need of an occupant though."

"After all your travelling, you will be content with a hut on the beach?"

"For a time. I find I have a lot to think on."

"Do you remember? When he . . . took you. Were you aware?"

Erlin remained silent for some time, his newly bright eyes dimmed somewhat, and when he spoke Vaelin knew he voiced a lie. "No. It's all just a fog, like a bad dream best forgotten."

"So you have no notion why it spared you? Why the stone didn't take you when it took the Ally?"

"The Ally had touched it once before, I hadn't. Perhaps it knew the difference."

"He spoke of something looking back . . ."

"He spoke of many things, brother." There was an edge to Erlin's voice now, a patent weariness of questions. "And all best forgotten." He brightened, slapping his knees and rising. "I think I shall seek out a sailor with some wine to spare. Care to join me?"

Vaelin smiled and shook his head. He watched Erlin disappear into the shadowed recesses of the hold and wondered if persuading Lyrna not to kill the ancient and now-giftless man would one day prove to be something he regretted.

◆ ◆ ◆

"The future is ever uncertain," she had said at the docks, fighting anger at the non-appearance of Weaver, an anger that was all too genuine today. "Find your deepest mine and bury it there, the location to be known only to you and myself. The Orders are never to learn of this thing's existence."

He waited until the captain advised him they had reached the deepest part of the Boraelin, whereupon he told him to trim his sails. It was only a little past dawn and he was alone on deck save for the night watch. They looked on in bafflement as he set aside the sledgehammer he had borrowed from the ship's carpenter and cut away the rope binding the canvas. It duly fell away to reveal the smooth, unblemished surface of the black stone. He stepped back, hefting the hammer and lifting it above his head.

"Stop!"

It was Alornis, huddled in a blanket near the hold, staring at him, eyes wide and appalled.

"I have to," he told her.

She frowned, puzzled, then shook her head. "Not like that you won't." She pointed an implacable finger at him. "Don't move until I return."

He watched her disappear below, standing uncertainly with hammer in hand as the crew looked on, curiosity or amusement on their faces.

"I'd never be able to face Master Benril again," Alornis said, reemerging from the stairwell with her leather satchel on her shoulder. "Letting you break a stone like that."

She placed her satchel on the deck and undid the straps, choosing a small hammer and a narrow iron chisel from the rows of tools.

"Don't touch it," Vaelin told her as she approached the stone.

"I know." She made a face at him. "Reva told me."

She placed the chisel in the centre of the stone, tapping it until a small crack appeared in the surface then delivering a series of well-placed blows with the hammer until no more than a few inches protruded. She retrieved two more chisels from the satchel and repeated the process, placing them on either side of the central peg and hammering away until the stone featured a crack across its surface about a half inch wide.

"As you will, brother," she said, stepping back.

He stared down at it, seeing the way the surface seemed to swallow the light, suddenly uncertain. *You don't know what this thing is!* he had said. *I looked into that world . . . and something looked back, something vast, and hungry. Touch it once and receive a gift . . .*

He raised a hand, extending it to the stone, letting it hover over the surface, almost touching. *What will it give me? Another song? The Ally's gift?*

"Alucius told me he loved me," Alornis said, drawing his gaze. She held her blanket tight, blinking as the wind drove tears from her eyes, tracing across her pale skin like molten silver. "The freed slave came to me with a message, his last message. He said he loved me and begged forgiveness for not telling me sooner. He said he had done many things he regretted, but that was the worst. And he told me not to hate, Vaelin. He said there was sufficient hate in this world and he wanted to look at me from the Beyond and see at least one soul untouched by it. But I couldn't . . . They killed him, and I hated them, and I burned them."

"You did what we all did, sister," he said. "You, the queen, Reva, Frentis . . . Alucius and Caenis . . . The woman I would have married. We won a war that needed winning."

He looked down at the stone and withdrew his hand. His thoughts were full of many things as he raised the hammer, many faces, some gone, some still living, all changed or damaged. He thought of the battles he had fought and the brothers he had lost, and he thought of Dahrena. *You are my Beyond now. For me to endure, so must you.*

The first blow drove the central peg deep enough to split the stone down to its base. It fell apart, thumping heavily onto the deck. He raised the hammer and brought it down, again and again, heaving with tireless fury as a cloud of black dust rose around him. Some drifted away on the wind but for the most part it settled into a pile on the deck, glittering in the fast rising sun. When the last fragment had been pounded to powder he ordered it all gathered up in the canvas and cast over the side. The stain of it roiled their wake, lingering for only seconds before fading completely as they sailed on, carried home by the westerly winds.

APPENDIX

Dramatis Personae

THE UNIFIED REALM

The Court of Queen Lyrna Al Nieren

Lyrna Al Nieren—Queen of the Unified Realm

Iltis Al Adral—Sword of the Realm, Lord Protector of the Queen's Person

Benten Al Grey Gull—Sword of the Realm, Protector of the Queen's Person

Orena Al Vardrian—lady to the queen

Murel Al Harten—lady to the queen

Hollun—brother of the Fourth Order and Keeper of the Queen's Purse

The Queen's Host

Vaelin Al Sorna—Tower Lord of the Northern Reaches and Battle Lord of the Queen's Host

Alornis Al Sorna—artist and sister to Vaelin, later Lady Artificer to Queen Lyrna

Dahrena Al Myrna—First Counsel to the North Tower

Caenis Al Nysa—brother of the Sixth Order, Sword of the Realm and Lord Marshal of the Thirty-fifth Regiment of Foot; later Aspect of the Seventh Order

Count Marven—commander of the Nilsaelin contingent of the Queen's Host

Adal Zenu—captain of the North Guard, later Lord Marshal and Sword of the Realm

Kehlan—healer and brother of the Fifth Order

Orven Al Melna—captain of the Third Company, King's Mounted Guard; later Lord Marshal and Sword of the Realm, husband to Insha ka Forna

Insha ka Forna (Steel in Moonlight)—Eorhil warrior, wife to Orven

Harlick—brother of the Seventh Order, Archivist of the North Tower; later First Librarian to the Great Library of the Unified Realm

Nortah Al Sendahl—friend to Vaelin, later Lord Marshal of the Queen's Daggers and Sword of the Realm

Snowdance—war-cat

Sanesh Poltar—war chief to the Eorhil Sil

Wisdom—sage elder to the Eorhil Sil

Ultin—mine foreman at Reaver's Gulch, later captain of the First Battalion of the Army of the North

Davern—shipwright and sergeant in the Army of the North, later Master of the Queen's Yard

Furelah—guardswoman in the Queen's Daggers

Atheran Ell-Nestra—Meldenean sea captain and Shield of the Isles, later Fleet Lord to Queen Lyrna

Carval Ell-Nurin—Ship Lord and captain of the *Red Falcon*

Cara—gifted resident of Nehrin's Point

Lorkan—gifted resident of Nehrin's Point

Marken—gifted resident of Nehrin's Point

Weaver—gifted resident of Nehrin's Point

Cumbrael

Reva Mustor—Lady Governess of Cumbrael

Lady Veliss—Honoured Counsel to the Lady Governess

Arentes Varnor—Lord Commander of the City Guard

Bren Antesh—Lord Commander of Archers

The Reader—leader of the Church of the World Father

Ellese Brahdor—orphan and ward of the Lady Governess

Allern Varesh—guardsman to House Mustor

Varinshold

Darnel Linel—Fief Lord of Renfael, Volarian vassal

Alucius Al Hestian—poet, friend to Alornis and Vaelin, son to Lakrhil

Lakrhil Al Hestian—father to Alucius, Battle Lord to Darnel

Elera Al Mendah—Aspect of the Fifth Order

Dendrish Hendrahl—Aspect of the Third Order

Benril Lernial—renowned artist and brother of the Third Order

Mirvek Korvin—commander of the Volarian garrison

Twenty-Seven—Kuritai, guard to Alucius

Cresia—sister of the Seventh Order

Inehla—sister of the Seventh Order

Rhelkin—brother of the Seventh Order

Renfaelin Border

Frentis—brother of the Sixth Order, friend to Vaelin, known as the Red Brother

Davoka—warrior of the Black River Clan, Servant of the Mountain, friend to Lyrna, fighter in the Red Brother's company

Sollis—sword-master and Brother Commander of the Sixth Order

Rensial—horse-master and brother of the Sixth Order

Hughlin Banders—knight and Baron of Renfael

Ulice—illegitimate daughter to Banders

Arendil—son to Ulice and Darnel, heir to Fief Lordship of Renfael, fighter in the Red Brother's company

Ermund Lewen—knight and chief retainer to Banders

Draker—former outlaw, fighter in the Red Brother's company

Illian Al Jervin—escaped slave and fighter in the Red Brother's company

Thirty-Four—former numbered slave and torturer, fighter in the Red Brother's company

Ivern—brother of the Sixth Order, stationed at the Skellan Pass

Slasher—faith-hound and friend to Frentis

Blacktooth—faith-hound and friend to Illian

Others

Wise Bear—shaman to the Bear People

Kiral—Lonak huntress of the Black River Clan and sister to Davoka

Alturk—Lonak Tahlessa of the Grey Hawk Clan

Verniers Alishe Someren—Imperial Chronicler to the court of Emperor Aluran

Fornella Av Entril Av Tokrev—Volarian captive, sister to Arklev Entril

Belorath—Meldenean captain of the *Sea Sabre*

Lekran—warrior of the Rotha, later fighter in the Red Brother's company

THE ALPIRAN EMPIRE

Aluran Maxtor Selsus—Emperor

Emeren Nasur Ailers—former ward to the Emperor

Iveles Maxtor Seliesen—son to Emeren

Neliesen Nester Hevren—captain in the Imperial Guard

Merulin Nester Velsus—Imperial Prosecutor

Horon Nester Everen—High Commander of Imperial Forces

Raulen—gaoler to the palace dungeons

THE VOLARIAN EMPIRE

Arklev Entril—member of the Volarian Ruling Council, holder of the Treasurer's Seat

Lorvek Irlav—member of the Volarian Ruling Council, holder of the Slaver's Seat

Varulek Tovrin—Master of the Great Volarian Arena and Overseer of Garisai

Lieza—slave

Hirkran of the Red Axe—champion to the Othra mountain tribe

THE ICE

Whale Killer—leader of the Wolf People, husband to Many Wings

Many Wings—shamaness to the Wolf People, wife to Whale Killer

Astorek Anvir, also "Long Knife"—shaman to the Wolf People, adopted son of Whale Killer and Many Wings